Pericles went to Aspasia and took her gently in his arms and kissed her brow and her lips. She rested against his breast, but she was still afraid. She clung to Pericles, and for the first time in this day of horrors she wept. He held her tenderly.

"I will have Pheidias design a giant wasp in marble, for your gardens," he said, "with eyes of turquoise. It will be a warning to you, my sweetest one, never to trust a stranger. In truth, never trust anyone absolutely."

"Not even you, lord?" she asked, smiling through her tears.

TAYLOR CALDWELL

Glory
and the
Lightning

FAWCETT CREST • NEW YORK

GLORY AND THE LIGHTNING

THIS BOOK CONTAINS THE COMPLETE TEXT OF THE
ORIGINAL HARDCOVER EDITION.

Published by Fawcett Crest Books, a unit of CBS Publications,
the Consumer Publishing Division of CBS Inc.,
by arrangement with Doubleday and Company, Inc.

ISBN: 0-449-23972-1

Selection of the Doubleday Bargain Book Club, February 1975

Printed in the United States of America

17   16   15   14   13   12   11   10

For My Dear Friends,
WILLIAM EVERETT STANCELL,
and "BOB" CURRAN,
of *The Buffalo Evening News.*

"THE GLORY THAT WAS GREECE—"

"The genius of a nation strikes but once in its history. It is its glory and its immortality in the annals of men. It is aristocratic, discriminating, radiant and selective, and abjures all that is mediocre, plebeian and mundane. It is regnant. It is spiritual. It is the flame emanating from the core of the Universe, which is the generation of life. It is the lightning which sets fire to the small spirits of men, and raises them above the field and the plow, the house and the hayfield, in a sudden revelation of grandeur. It is, above all, masculine, for the aristocracy of the soul is purely masculine and never feminine, which is concerned only with petty matters and insistent trivialities. It transcends the humbleness of daily living and stands even the least important of men upon Olympus for a brief hour. It is never democratic, for democracy is a destructive thing, conspired in the inferior minds of envious men.

"If that nation which would survive in glory would cultivate only the masculine principle its name in history will be written in gold and blaze through the centuries."

ZENO OF ELEA

Foreword

I am refraining in this book from giving a complete bibliography, for all the students of Greece and Pericles know them too well, and have read them as carefully as I have read them.

From childhood I have been fascinated by Greece, and particularly Athens, but not by the endless wars and skirmishes of the period of Pericles. Wars, though sometimes interesting, especially when they are fought for freedom and the dignity of man, tend to repeat themselves throughout history, and not always for virtuous reasons.

The glory that was Greece was not the glory of the people of Athens but of their few sons, who, against the most terrible opposition and persecution, fought to make her the wonder of the world. It was in Greece that the first movement was made to control and limit the power of government, to give the people a voice in that government and to encourage them to vote and express their opinions. That later they were only too happy, for a little security, to surrender their right to free speech and inhibit their government when it became oppressive is the sad lesson of history which has repeated itself over and over since the days of Pericles.

As Aristotle said, "That nation which will not learn from the past is doomed to repeat it." We have seen that over and over in history, and again are about to repeat the doom.

This is the story of men who made Athens glorious and who made her history, rather than the story of tedious wars and oppressive government, though, to make the heroes relevant and in context, it is necessary to show how their own government, conceived under the noble laws of Solon, became despotic, and how the heroes fought that government and sometimes—but rarely—succeeded.

If the story sounds familiar, it is because it is indeed familiar. A little study of present history will also show how ominous and pervasive of tyranny our present world is at this exact moment. If we do not learn from the past we will be doomed to repeat it.

TAYLOR CALDWELL

PART ONE

Aspasia

*"She was not only the most beautiful of women but a
woman of mind and character and charm and tenderness,
and the women of Athens owe much to her."*

SOCRATES

CHAPTER 1

The beautiful young mother came weeping to look upon her child, Aspasia.

"She is like Aphrodite, newly risen in pearl from the sea," she said to the older woman, Thargelia. "Who knows her fate, mysteriously woven by the direful Sisters? Her father desired to expose her. I am glad that I rescued her and brought her to you. Is not her hair like gold, my child, and her eyes like autumn leaves and her flesh like nacre? Who could destroy such? Alas, her father would kill her even now if he knew she lived, for what man is proud of begetting a female?"

"She is extremely intelligent," said Thargelia in a tone of consolation. "She has a mind that scintillates, throwing off myriad lights like a prism. She will become a magnificent courtesan, even more than you were, my little one."

The mother moved restively. "I should prefer her to be married to a distinguished man."

The older woman smiled with an ironic twist of her mouth. "And to be relegated to the women's quarters while her husband amuses himself and converses with exciting women?"

"She would be safe," murmured the mother, Acilia.

"No woman is ever safe with a man," said Thargelia. "Wife, mistress or courtesan—women are never safe with men. Therefore, we must protect ourselves with a thousand wiles and nuances and stratagems."

"But a wife has safety under the law," said the mother, stroking her child's head.

"A law which can be broken at a man's will, dear little one."

The lovely mother smiled and all at once she was a girl again. "Women are more powerful than the law. For we know no law but our natures and nature is above law." She wiped her tears on a silken kerchief which flowed with an exotic perfume. She looked upon her child again. "Yes," she said, "women are superior to the law, though we are not lawless by nature. In truth, we are the law, itself."

"I have always said," Thargelia remarked, "that you should have been a philosopher."

"Alas, I loved," said the mother. "When a woman loves she is not a philosopher."

"Nor is a man," said Thargelia. "Love is the great destroyer of logic and intelligence. The genitals rule us all—until the

13

day our genitals fail us. Then we become wise. But wisdom is a cold fire which enlightens but does not warm."

The mother gazed at the absolute blueness of the Asia Minor sky and then at the gulf which was no deeper in color, so that water and the heavens appeared to be one vast curtain hanging and palpitating adjacent to the earth. Acilia was tumultuous with her distressed thoughts. "If my child's father, Axtochus, my lover, could but see her now and her beauty and hear her converse, young as she is, he might take her into his house with me and his other concubines. But I do not wish her to become a courtesan."

Thargelia pondered. She had assumed her name because it had once belonged to one of the most beautiful and intellectual courtesans of Miletus. But she, herself, was not beautiful, though possessing a fascinating and changeful countenance. However, intelligence was like a glow on her face, and her eyes, though cynical—having known too many men—were brilliant with the liquid she used to enhance them. They were also hard and amused. Kohl blackened her eyelids, and red unguents, which glistened, were smoothly spread on her cheeks and lips. This gave her a debauched appearance which men found tantalizing. She led the fashion among the ladies of Miletus, even among virtuous matrons and maidens, for her taste was exquisite. She talked with the young mother at her side, stroking her peplos of mingled crimson and green; her dyed golden hair, vivid as the sunlight, was entwined with green ribbons. Her figure was the figure of a virgin, fluid and youthfully graceful. Only her hands betrayed her age, and not all the oils of Asia could drown the protruding veins or silken away the wrinkles. But they were eloquent, her hands, and she wore many rings of rich gems which helped to conceal the harsh knuckles. A lover had once said that she created music in the air with her hands, so fluent they were of gesture, with never an abrupt movement or awkward pose. She had trained them in the dance.

"You brought Aspasia to me," she said, "when she was but a few days old, fleeing with her from the house of your lover, at night, after you had concealed her from the sight of her father. It was from my house that Axtochus chose you for his own, and he has been faithful to you, in his fashion, more than he has been faithful to his wives and other concubines. You are happy, Acilia, for I see happiness in the sleekness of your skin, the shimmer of your hair, and in the glitter of your jewels. Would you be so happy as an immured wife, under the law, neglected by your husband, relegated to the women's

14

quarters, sighing alone, while some concubine lay with your husband?"

Acilia thought. "No," she admitted. "But every mother desires safety and honor for her daughters, and where can safety and honor be assured for a woman except in a distinguished marriage?"

"Bah," said Thargelia with a shrug. "It is only fools who yearn for safety. I disagree that marriage is the only haven for women. Property and education and jewelry and power over a man are much more to be desired. Men rarely tire of an engaging concubine, but they inevitably tire of their wives. Concubines know how to amuse a man, and, at the end, that is a woman's true function. We teach our maidens here that a woman's destiny is to amuse, entertain, serve, console and love a man, and for these lovely gifts any man will pay a fortune, and even lay down his life. How many men in history have died for their wives? But our poets sing of men who sacrificed all for a mistress."

"Men are very strange," said Acilia.

"That is the first lesson we teach our maidens," said Thargelia. "It is impossible for a woman to understand a man, who is very primitive, while women are born Sophists. I have argued with many noble philosophers in this house, and they have decared that they worshipped my conversation and my mental endowments, and that I was as subtle as themselves, which I did not consider a great compliment. But inevitably they slipped their hands under my peplos or onto my breasts and we ended our learned dissertations in my bed. Does that make men incomprehensible? Men never forget that they are first of all men, and that they love women—despite their intelligence. That is both flattering and irritating. But, did we make this world?"

They sat in the outdoor portico of the beautiful pillared house of courtesans, overlooking the Gulf of Latmic, near the mouth of the Meander river. The scent of jasmine was rising, and the sweet effluvium of roses. Women were singing joyously in the house and strumming lutes and harps, and for an instant Acilia's fair face was filled with memories and longings. She looked down at her child, Aspasia, and mused. Would it not indeed be better for Aspasia to be trained as an accomplished courtesan, courted and honored and loved and gifted by eminent men, than to be an imprisoned wife in dreary quarters, seeing her husband only at his indifferent command when he needed children, and having for her company only unlettered slaves and looms and kitchen servants and women as ignorant as herself?

Acilia and Thargelia sipped the best of wines imported from Pylos where the delectable wine-grapes grew on dry and sunny slopes, and they ate dainty pastries as they sat in the outdoor portico and listened to the music and the distant rustle of the sea and the laughter of fountains in the gardens which surrounded them. Two female slaves waved feathered fans over their heads, and a breeze was rising from the waters, which had begun to blaze as sunset approached. It was very peaceful and languorous, and Acilia sighed again, remembering her happiness and mirth in this house as a child and a young maiden.

Aspasia was leaning against her mother's knee and contentedly eating a pastry stuffed with poppy seeds and honey and citron peel. Acilia smiled down into her daughter's large light brown eyes, which were filled with mysterious liquid lights and shifting sparkles and shadowed and starred with golden lashes of enormous sweep and length. The child's hair hung far down her back and seemed to be a mass of soft gilt threads. Her features were delicate and hinted of increasing maturity, though she was but six years old. When she smiled, as she did now, dimples raced over her cheeks—softly colored —and flew in and out around her full scarlet lips. There was an endearing charm about her, a certain enthrallment. She is far more beautiful than I was, thought Acilia with pride. Alas, the destiny of woman is very sorrowful, whether mistress or wife or concubine or slave. Should we not have a higher destiny than this?

Thargelia saw the mother's changing and melancholy expression, and she said, "I have trained many children and maidens, but Aspasia is more than them all. Though very young she is already a philosopher. Her appearance is enchanting. Her mind will command the attention and the respect of even the most dissolute men. I predict a marvelous future for her. She has fate in her eyes, profound and immeasurable."

"Women must change this world of men," said Acilia, suddenly, and put her hand in protection on her child's shining head.

Thargelia shrugged. "Would it be to our advantage? Men are now our adorers and our slaves. Let us not long for equality with them! We would lose our privileges and gain nothing but coarseness, anxiety, toil and disrespect."

She laughed. "Let men continue to protect us and we will

continue to rule them from our beds and with our blandishments. He who sits on a throne is never at peace or at rest. But she who is the voice behind the throne, however concealed, has all the advantages of power, and all the prerogatives, and can sleep tranquilly of a night."

"So long as she is young and beautiful," said Acilia, sighing.

Thargelia was vexed. "It was one of your faults, dear little one, that you were always sighing even when most happy. Youth? Clever and noble men may proclaim that they prefer green fruit. But they are ruled by women who are not young but remain dazzling, as any woman can remain if she desires. It is only the dull failed man who seeks his own futile youth in the youth of a woman, and thinks of a woman as merely a thing, like a slave."

The young Aspasia was sipping her own small goblet of wine, but she looked up at her mother over the rim and her eyes were wise and merry and full of understanding. She is six years old, thought Acilia with some uneasiness, but she was never young!

Thargelia, watching with her astute eyes, said, "I have had a soothsayer for Aspasia. He predicts that she will glow like the moon over her country and have great men in her power, and everywhere she will be the inspiration of poets."

"Soothsayers!" said Acilia with indulgence. Nevertheless, she was flattered and pleased. She laid a purse of gold coins on the ivory and lemonwood table. "Nothing must be denied my daughter. I trust you, Thargelia, for I have had reason to trust you. You are wiser than I. Do with Aspasia as you will, for I see you love her."

Thargelia drew the child to her and kissed her milky brow and ran her fingers through the bright cobweb of her golden hair, which was airy and fine. "Aspasia and I understand each other," she said, with affection, "for all we have our moments of rebellion. There are no uncertainties in her mind, no doubts, no hesitations. She will have what she wills, as a woman, and her will is already formidable."

Acilia rose, seeing that her litter with four Nubian male slaves—gleaming blackly and naked to the waist and with crimson turbans on their heads—had arrived at the gates. Their ebony faces were carved and impassive and full of secret dignity. They had drawn aside the crimson embroidered curtains for their mistress, and Acilia entered the litter and reclined on the yellow silk of the cushions. She did not close the curtains as she was borne away. There was a sad premonition in her, as if she knew that never again would she see her daughter, who was on the steps of the portico and waving to her with the easy indifference of a child. Even as Acilia watched, Aspasia turned and ran swiftly into the house, forgetting her mother. Acilia sighed, and a tear fell from her lashes, which had been dusted with gold powder. She found her small silver mirror in her purse and carefully wiped it away. Axtochus, she recalled, detested reddened eyes in a woman, and fled from them impatiently. She arranged a beguiling smile on her face, careful not to wrinkle the skin about her pretty mouth. She opened a little alabaster pot, also from her purse, and smoothed a perfumed attar over her lips. In a moment she was thinking of the gilded cloth from the Orient and her dressmaker.

CHAPTER 2

Thargelia sat with her choicest maidens—all chosen for both their beauty and their intelligence—in the outdoor portico facing the west. It was her favorite hour, before dining, for she did not care for the day during which she slept after a night of festivity. But bathed in scented water, oiled with fragrance, painted delicately and powdered, her hair arranged artistically, her peplos draped to her satisfaction, her pins sparkling and a necklace of jewels about her neck to hide the sallow wrinkles, she felt capable of facing life again. "The night was made for love, reflection, philosophy and laughter," she would say. "But the day is made for wars, peasants, arduous workers, muscles, men of activity, and farmers and goats and sheep. In other words, for those who care little about the delights of living and know nothing of them, being engrossed with labor and sweat. From this, we hetairai have been mercifully delivered; while the laborious wives sleep we rejoice in the company of their eminent husbands. Truly, our lives are enviable, and that is why we are hated by the stupid and lightless matrons of energetic households."

She had aged but little over the fourteen years since Aspasia had been delivered by her mother to this house. "A woman must not frown; it creates wrinkles on the brow and between the eyes, and gentlemen detest wrinkles. Nor must she laugh too much; that induces furrows about her mouth. A merry face, yes, always. But never one which resembles the masks of the theatre, with too much emotion and emphasis. A soft smile, with a regard to curvature, a twinkling of the eyes, as you have been taught, a gentle inclination of the head—these are desirable and do not age a woman. They enhance her charm. Gestures, too, must never be too emphatic. It annoys gentlemen, for they do not like vigorous women, except in their kitchens and in their beds. A woman must always imply; she must never assert. I repeat these admonitions, my treasures, so that you will be successful and rich and endlessly amusing and seductive."

There were eight among her choice maidens, and among them was her favorite, Aspasia, of incredible beauty and incredible intelligence, which she had been taught must never be aggressive among men. "Compliance, always. Entertainment, always. But never without elegance."

She controlled the diet of her maidens sedulously, and as vigilantly as she preserved their virginity, which would be delivered to the richest and most eminent bidder, and for a very high price to Thargelia herself. But the maidens were not virginal in their minds and their hearts. "Even green fruit must prophesy ripeness and deliciousness, my treasures." She wished a sheen on her maidens, so she encouraged love among them—with discretion so that they would later be lovers of men and not lovers of women. In truth, if a maiden became too ardent over a sister neophyte Thargelia would remove her to another building where she could be trained to be a pleasure to some rich widow or dissatisfied wealthy matron.

"A woman's complexion and the softness of her body skin are her greatest assests," she would teach the young girls. "Therefore, they must not be exposed to the sun, but shaded at all times, and carefully covered, for the kiss of Phoebus burns and darkens and turns to fissured leather, and such is repulsive to gentlemen of taste and discrimination." The girls were bathed only in water in which perfumed oils were dissolved, and then sweet lotions were applied. Hair was brushed night and morning for at least an hour, with the help of slaves, and flesh was massaged to the polish and smoothness of marble. "A woman's natural beauty, no matter how great, begins to fade at eighteen and twenty, if wantonly neglected. She must begin to preserve it no later than the age of five years, and guard it always. Many ladies of this school are notable beauties even in their sixties. It is an art which women must cultivate all their lives, for men, alas, no matter their intellectual endowments, never look below a woman's complexion, firm breasts and rounded loins and thighs, to discover any mental attainments. It is the rare man who appreciates a woman's mind; in truth, men are irritated by it unless it is accompanied by a handsome face and body. Then it is an added joy. A full rosy mouth which invents epigrams, and which can discourse on learned things, is delectable. But withered lips uttering wisdom cause a man to flee."

She would say, "Only a girl at puberty can face daylight without fear. After fourteen or fifteen the light of Artemis is infinitely flattering, and the light of soft lamps and candles. There is a new fashion now, of having lamps suspended from the ceiling. Avoid them like a traitor, for they are indeed traitorous to any woman beyond puberty."

All the maidens, and not only the eight of the choicest, found little leisure in the school for courtesans. They attended classes presided over by female and male teachers of the best mentality, where they learned—not the arts of a household, which were the province of illiterate ladies intended for marriage by their parents—but the arts of politics, philosophy, exquisitely perfect language, rhetoric, music, dancing, the arrangement of garments, the nuances of perfumes, seduction, conversation, history, gentle athletics to preserve the figure and enhance it, a smattering of medical lore, mathematics —"One must deal with bankers later"—artistic placing of furniture, selection of fabrics most flattering, graceful movements, hairdressing, charming sophistries, penmanship, the keeping of books, literature, poetry, sculpture, painting, science, but, above all else, how to please and entrance a man and all the arts of love, including perversions.

"Young men are bulls," Thargelia would say with severity, "therefore, unless they are tremendously rich and important, I deliver none of my maidens to them. A slut and one of my delicate courtesans are all the same in bed to them, and, as they have the identical equipment, there is no distinction. So, I am careful not to arrange matters between them and one of my young ladies, except on rare occasions and only by consent of the young lady. There is a greater danger, too: A maiden may fall in love with a young man, alas, and there is no worse fate, for young men are capricious and are soon discontented even with the most desirable of girls and look for novelty and are not interested in conversation. But a middle-aged man needs to be coaxed, and when coaxed to fulfillment he is endlessly grateful, and gratitude leads to pleasant establishment, money and jewels. Also adoration. Be careful, then, about love, which is a deceiver and a liar and men are also all deceivers and liars, and must be dealt with capably, or a woman is lost."

The maidens were taught delicacy. "There is nothing more

20

abhorrent than a coarse lewd woman," said Thargelia and the other teachers. "Never must an indecent word cross your lips or a lascivious jest, not even in passion—which I trust you will never feel. (Passion can destroy a woman.) You must keep in mind that you are great ladies, of taste and discrimination and learning. You must always be in control of your emotions, and never utter a hasty harsh reproach, no matter how provoked. Pleasantness is most desirable."

Once Aspasia said in her lovely soft voice though her eyes flashed with rebellion: "We are, then, only toys for the pleasure of men who may be inferior to us."

Thargelia smiled at her, for it was impossible to be irritable with Aspasia. "Say, better, that we are jewels, precious jewels. How is a jewel preserved? In fine cloth, guarded and cherished, valued above all things, adored, proudly displayed. We are not utensils of the kitchen. They serve their purpose, and are used by wives, whose husbands give us gold and gems and lay their heads on our knees and worship us. Do they worship their wives? They flee from them."

The girls were taught intensively of the nature of men, and how to preserve themselves from entanglements in their own emotions, which could ruin them. Thargelia was vehement in her admonitions that the maidens must cultivate a contempt for men, which, certainly, they must never reveal.

"Once you become contemptuous of men you will always be serene in their company, and even happily affectionate, as one feels affection for a dog. For your contempt will make you impervious to destructive inclinations, and devoid of passion and natural indignation, and will render both your emotions and your countenances bland and unwrinkled and undistorted. Contempt banishes pity. Once you pity a man, you will love him, and that is a detestable and alarming and dangerous condition, and leads ultimately to despair. Certainly, you must assume an attitude of discreet devotion, for men desire all women to be devoted to them. But never must you be truly devoted. It is suicide."

Love, in short, must be for one's self, and never must it be wasted on a man. "Let the poets sing of love," said Thargelia. "But that love is not for their wives; it is only for women who contain their sentiments and are elusive as well as daintily wanton, and are never fully possessed. Had Artemis fallen in love with Acteon, and had married him, he would soon have become wearied of her love and sought a more fugitive joy. Men demand a woman's whole heart. Pretend to give it, and then when he feels secure in its possession give him cause to feel alarm, not overtly, but with a smile, an averted head, a gentle disentanglement from his arms. He will then begin the pursuit once more, and sue for your affections with gold and jewels."

"We must, then, live only for ourselves," said Aspasia with the most demure of countenances.

"Who else is there but ourselves?" Thargelia asked. "Once I listened to the dissertations of a famous philosopher who was dexterous and wise enough to convince anyone that all is delusion, that we are all dreams except to the dreamer, that none exists but one's self. How can we prove the existence of any other? How can we be certain that we are not entirely alone in a dream?"

The school engaged expert men and women who employed all the arts and perversions of love before the fascinated students. "There is more to such joys than mere copulation, which we share with the beasts," Thargelia would admonish, "and has for its purpose gross reproduction. It is a hasty affair, such, and without delicacy or enhancement. While you must restrain your own selves from the utter pleasure, you must learn to give pleasure to the utmost, and if engaged in that pleasure yourselves you cannot be expert with a man, nor make him delirious with exotic sensations. Be voluptuous but never vulgar. Be abandoned daintily, but never with complete abandonment. A veil is more alluring than a naked body. Subtlety is more to be desired than shamelessness. A woman never must give all, not even in pretense, except for a moment or two."

She trained the maidens never to express disgust or aversion, or even to feel either. "However," she would say, "if you cannot control such revulsions completely invent epigrams or a poem while engaging in love with a man, or think of a lovelier way to dress your hair, or your money. So long as you are clever and proficient, and remember your lessons, the man will never guess your true feelings. Again, a woman must never fully surrender herself at any time. She must never listen to pleas, but only smile beckoningly, and promise."

As she sat with her maidens this sunset she rejoiced in their beauty, and especially in Aspasia's, for the promise of the maid's childhood had not been false but in truth it had not fully prophesied. Aspasia was taller than the other girls, which had first made Thargelia apprehensive, and then she remembered the greeting recorded by Homer: "Daughter of the gods, divinely tall and most divinely fair!" Aspasia was certainly divinely fair, and Thargelia could not recall any of her earlier maidens who could compare with her, nor even her present companions. Amidst all that loveliness of black and brown and russet and fair locks, of brilliant eyes and rosy cheeks and white throats and young creamy bosoms, of dimples and curved red lips and alabaster chins and springlike bodies, Aspasia was a girlish Aphrodite among mere mortals. They diminished, for all their loveliness, in her presence, as bronze dims before gold, and they became, despite their choice and unusual grace and sensuous charms, mere milkmaids before a queen. They all wore the plain white peplos which announced their virginity, and with silver girdles of modest design, but the peplos became radiant upon Aspasia's perfect body, hinting of sensuality and incomparable delights. There was a translucence about her flesh, so that strong sunlight seemed to strike through it, rendering it almost transparent in its tint of rose. Her golden hair was, as her mother had said, a web of light, floating in the slightest wind, and falling to her knees when it was unbound, a gilded cloak which she loved to gather about her after her bath. Thargelia, the pragmatic and the shrewd, felt poetic when she gazed at the girl's countenance, the oval of the cheeks ending in a dimpled chin of tender roundness, and the whole head set upon a long slender neck as flexible as a serpent's and as pale as milk. Her nose was of the classic Grecian shape, worshipped by sculptors, and her mouth, deep red and velvety soft, was without flaw, neither too generous nor too small, and when she smiled dimples twinkled about it, enchantingly. Her eyes were unusually large, set in fine pale violet shadows and surrounded by thick golden lashes, and were of an arresting color, like light brown wine and luminous.

All this, at the age of fourteen, and a virgin, was enough to drive men out of their senses, Thargelia would think with pleasure, but beautiful though Aspasia was her intellect surpassed it. Thargelia had sometimes regretfully observed that unusual beauty was sometimes accompanied by lesser intelligence, but this was not so with Aspasia. She was not only accomplished in music, and had a voice of strong sweetness and range and feeling, but she was a superb dancer whose movements were at once carnal and innocent. Her conversation was not by rote or mere memory from her teacher's lessons, and sparkling and witty, but excelled in subtlety and intimations and a naughty impudence which aroused laughter even among the sullen and the most grave. She observed everything and her comments were inventive and full of perception, and often startlingly wise and deeply thoughtful. She outwitted her teachers in an exercise in rhetoric, and could declaim movingly on almost any subject, and she had a gaiety which aroused gaiety where sadness lived before. Thargelia feared that at times that there was a power not of the flesh but of the mind in Aspasia, and that Aspasia's thoughts were not always feminine. Alluring beyond description though she was, and an ecstasy to the eye, her remarks were sometimes too sharp and pungent, too scornful of pretense. For this reason Aspasia's teachers endeavored to teach her self-control more than they taught the other girls, and though she was acquiescent and listened carefully there would appear a shining and shifting glint in her eyes, humorously defiant.

This glint had been particularly present this warm and scented evening in the outdoor portico, as if something had aroused Aspasia's latent bent for rebellion, and so Thargelia's remarks had been pointed as she glanced frequently at the girl. Did not the maiden realize that she had the appearance of an empress and a mind which could command respect even from the most learned men, and that these gifts must never be threatened by overt contempt and hasty repudiations and an air of impatience? Men did not like forward women, and Aspasia, for all her charm and grace and beguiling ways, could be ruthless and forward, and could reveal her disdain for fools. Sometimes her beauteous eyes and wonderful face would glitter or darken with temper or resentment, and passion would leap over her features like lightning, not the passion of a sensual woman but the passion of an angry one or one who found the present conversation distasteful.

"You wished to speak, Aspasia?" asked Thargelia, seeing that the maiden's countenance was changeful with seething thoughts.

"Yes, Lady," said the girl at once, with a promptness more like a youth's than a girl's, and her entrancing voice was clear and forceful. "Am I not a woman, with flesh and blood and mind and emotions and opinions? Yet I am to suppress all these, make all these subservient, in the service of a man, who may be inferior to me despite his wealth and position! Am I to pretend that before him I am only a mere female, though lettered and excelling in learning and have the passions of a human creature who has observed much and thought even more? Yes, Lady, this you have taught me. I find myself in revolt against such a fate."

Thargelia smiled faintly, though she was somewhat frightened. "Did we women make this world? Was it we who ordained that the female be subject to the male, even when he is less intelligent than ourselves, and coarser and more stupid? Nevertheless, we can rule men as no man can rule them, and enslave them at our will. We are a mystery to these grosser creatures and in our mystery lies our power. They both fear and adore us, for we are more subtle and far more clever and have the strength of earth in our flesh and in our spirits. We are unsurpassed at gentle and deliberate deceit, and we laugh in our hearts. The goddesses are swifter than the gods, and more wily, and you will observe that Athene and Aphrodite and Hera are revered by the gods as well as loved, and that they can strike terror even into the soul of Zeus, the king of them all. Let us cherish these thoughts, and think of our resplendent futures."

She added, with a wider smile and an uplifted admonishing finger: "Who really rules gods and men? Aphrodite, the goddess of love and beauty, the unashamed voluptuary. Even Athene, wiser than gods and goddesses, or Hera herself, is not worshipped with such total devotion, nor does she move worlds as does Aphrodite. The loins of the goddess of love are more powerful than the brow of Athene, and Aphrodite is not a virgin, and has breasts."

The girls laughed happily and even the dissenting Aspasia was forced to smile.

Then Thargelia said, and she was suddenly serious, "What is it that you wish from this life, Aspasia?"

The girl shrugged and bent her head. "Something more than my intended fate, but what it is I do not know."

Thargelia stood up and said, "Find it in the arms of a man, for there only will you find it and nowhere else." When rebellion flashed in Aspasia's eyes the older woman added, "For men have what we want, no matter what it is we want, and they give it to us."

Thargelia saw that Aspasia's eyes welled and darkened and increased with thought, and she nodded with satisfaction.

The tutors for the maidens were usually erudite females, some of them former courtesans themselves, and learned, but Thargelia also employed male teachers who were of a respectable age and of no prepossessing appearance, for one must guard virgins.

A year ago the tutors had solemnly approached Thargelia, saying, "The maiden, Aspasia, is of an intricate mind, and excessively talented. She desires to know all things, and not superficially. Discourses on medicine, mathematics, and art engross her, and her questions are incisive and controversial, and she will not be satisfied with idle answers. In short, she will demand to know all that we know, and will not accept cursory instructions. She has the mind of a man, which may be unfortunate."

"I have suspected this," said Thargelia, not without pride. "But what human brain can contain all knowledge? Still, if one is talented one is gifted freely by the gods, who pour down upon the chosen one a full lavishness of mental treasures, just as when a beautiful woman is created she is perfection in all ways. Truly, Aspasia is formidable in talent as well as in loveliness. She wishes to encompass all things. But in what is she most proficient?"

An elderly sage said, stroking his gray beard, "She is fascinated with Solon, the founder of democracy, and all his laws." He hesitated and then continued, "She wishes to know why Greece does not follow the laws of Solon, as laid down over a hundred years ago. We have explained that the Athenians were too capricious and too inconstant a people to demand that their rulers obey an unchangeable Constitution, for they suspected what they considered inflexibility, even in perfect laws."

"Our Aspasia, then, is a politician as well as an artist and a mathematician," said Thargelia, smiling.

"Lady," said a woman tutor, "is it not our custom to discover the talent of each maiden, and train her therein, that she may be the perfect companion of a man of that bent and occupation?"

"True," said Thargelia. "But our Aspasia is protean, and her talents are equally enormous. She has myriad eyes, all developed. Would you say, then, that she is most proficient in politics, mathematics, art, science?"

"She is also engrossed with medicine," said the physician, "and is most dexterous and inventive in potions. She is constantly in the infirmia and often I conjecture if Apollo was not her father."

Thargelia laughed. "I am assured that that is not so. But it is a pretty concept, for does she not shine like the sun? What a maiden this is! Only a mighty Persian satrap would be worthy of her. Do not discourage her. Answer her deeply and with candor, respecting her intelligence. She was born in Miletus, and not in Greece, where women and their intelligence are despised. It is true that we are now under Grecian dominance but she is a daughter of Asia Minor."

She smiled at the uneasy tutors. "The gods must indeed be

her guardians, for had she been born in Greece she would have been confined to the gynaikeia (women's quarters) and would have been forbidden the meanest learning. Give to Aspasia all that is in your power, and do not fear that you will fatigue her. The mind has no boundaries."

She contemplated the price that Aspasia would bring, but still she was as proud as if she, herself, had been Aspasia's mother. The damsel was a prodigious gem, deserving of polishing and of a setting that would reveal all her colors and her glory. A jewel like this, and a virgin in addition, was worthy of even more than a Persian satrap. An emperor was more to be desired. Still, the Persians were very rich and powerful and, it must be admitted, somewhat more subtle than the Greeks, even the antic Athenians with their philosophers. They had an ancient and cynical wisdom, incomprehensible to the westerners. They were less muscular and direct, though they were terrible warriors when aroused. Thargelia was fascinated by mankind in all its manifestations. Man was created by the gods either in a fit of utter madness or they were commanded by something superior even to themselves. That was a subject for philosophers who pretended to understand the nature of man and were as ignorant as the lowest peasant. Thargelia considered one of the superstitions of the Greeks: the Unknown God, Whose altar was still bare, but Whom they reverenced. Did not the Persians hint of Him also? Thargelia shrugged. Men pursued the gods, but women pursued life, and perhaps they were the same. But it was a woman's womb which produced both gods and men, and therein lay women's power and their wisdom. Zeus was the king of gods and men, but Zeus was ruled by his wife, Hera, and he lived in terror of her. Thargelia laughed. It was a great comedy. It was no wonder that men were afraid of women, both gods and men. Women had a mysterious power. They could raise men to Parnassus or deliver them to Hades.

The teacher of science said to Aspasia, "There is no verity except when an experiment can be repeated time after time with the same result, with no deviations. That is reality, and reality is all we can know."

"What is reality?" asked Aspasia.

"Reality," said the teacher, "is what can be proved, can be discerned by our five senses, and can be, as I have said, repeated over and over at all times in the same experiment. All else is metaphysics and conjecture and fable and the dreams of madmen, and drunken poets."

27

"Such as Homer," said Aspasia with that demure expression of hers which her teachers often found exasperating.

The teacher frowned. He lifted a bundle of sticks and wagged them in Aspasia's face, while his other pupils exchanged smiles and shifted on their wooden benches. "Here," he said, "are ten thin sticks. A decade. All mathematics are based on the rule of ten, no matter how esoteric or what symbols are used. So, we can call this reality." He threw the sticks into the air and let them drop on the table. They fell into a disordered pattern. Aspasia leaned forward to study them.

Then she said, "But reality is based on causality—cause and effect?"

"True."

"And the pattern, the experiment, is endlessly repeated in all respects, if it is valid?"

"True." The man stroked his beard and regarded Aspasia with no great pleasure, for her beauty did not entrance him and her remarks often disconcerted him, to the high amusement of the other maidens.

Aspasia lifted the sticks and her sparkling eyes regarded the teacher enigmatically. She let the sticks drop, tinkling, on the table, and did not remove her gaze from the teacher. The sticks fell into another pattern. She studied them. "Causality, reality. The experiment is always the same, and never varies. Behold those sticks. I let them drop as you dropped them, Cipo, but they formed another pattern entirely. I will demonstrate again." She lifted the sticks in a profound silence, which was broken only by the raucous shriek of a peacock in the garden. She let the sticks drop. They formed still another pattern. She studied them as if with surprise. "The selfsame sticks, the selfsame gesture, even to the placement of my fingers on them. Yet, the pattern is so different each time. Ten sticks, ten thousand, perhaps, differing patterns. So, reality then must have ever-changing patterns, and experiments are never the same nor the results of them, though the conditions are identical. Shall we then conclude that reality has millions of faces and never is repeated and that if an experiment can be reproduced exactly it is only a delusion and not a truth?"

The teacher felt a desire to strike her. He said, trying to control his rage, "That is a fool's and a woman's reasoning. A tremor of your fingers, a bounding of your pulse, a slight wind, could destroy the exactitude of the experiment. Were you able to drop the sticks, through all eternity, with the same exactitude, under the same absolute condition, they would form an unchanging pattern."

"That is theory," said Aspasia. "It cannot be proved. And have you not said that that which cannot be proved is not reality?"

When he did not answer she continued: "Nothing remains the same. All things, all conditions, change, including the stars in their passage, and the winds in the air. Reality, then, is ephemeral, and what is real, today, is false tomorrow or even in the next moment. Poor mortals that we are! We must rule our lives in the hope that there is some changelessness in our affairs, and that causality is inevitable and reality a fact. But none of this is true. We are helpless barks floating on waters of mystery and on waves which never repeat themselves, and the very stars betray us. Nothing is fixed or certain, and therein lies our distress. Our concepts of reality are subjective, not objective, for objectivity does not exist."

"You deny objectivity, Aspasia?"

"Of a certainty. Our attempts at objectivity rise from our unique subjectivity, and each man has his own and none is alike."

"You believe in no absolute?"

She lifted her gilded eyebrows as if with astonishment. "There is no absolute." Her expression changed subtly. "Except, perhaps, with God, Whose reality has not as yet been proved, at least to the satisfaction of our scientists. He, too, is subjective. I consider objectivity only a confusion of men's minds, and only private opinion, for on what subject can all men totally agree?"

"Your reasoning is shallow and chaotic!" shouted the teacher, now beside himself with anger. He swept the sticks from the table and they fell, clattering, onto the floor. He wished he could do the same with Aspasia.

"Reveal to me my error," she said.

The other maidens were delighted, but Aspasia frowned on them and said, "It is more than possible that my conclusions are as foolish as those of our teacher or of any other mortal. None of us has the truth about anything at all."

"You disturb and distract my students, to their disadvantage and destroy my authority," said the teacher. "Remove yourself from my room and do not return until tomorrow." He was more enraged than ever at her sudden smile of pleasure as she rose and left the room, her hair drifting behind her like a bright cloud, her lovely face serene and aloof. She resembled a nymph who had wandered here, unseen and unseeing, bent only on her own thoughts and desires and unaware of her surroundings.

29

She went into the gardens where the shadows of sycamores and oaks and myrtle trees were sharp and greenly dark on the grass and the pebbled walks, and where birds in cages hung from branches and chattered with those free in the brilliant air. The flowers in their beds stung the eye with their intense vividness and the sky and the large fishpool resounded with passionate blue. To Aspasia color had sound for the ear, and the frail resonances of the warm fountains appeared to her to have a secret color of their own. In her all the senses were one and interchangeable, so that taste, smell, hearing, seeing and touching met in a single emotion, often too acute and ardent to be borne without an overwhelming turbulence of the spirit. She could hear the deep murmur of the sea beyond the gardens. The statues in grottos and in the fountains were clothed in light. A slight breeze lifted her hair and stirred her white long tunic and the sun heated her cheek and her feet and hands. A cluster of palm trees clattered their fronds, and a parrot in a cage screamed and then laughed. There were no other sounds but these.

She could give herself wholly to joy and to the vehemence of the moment. She had already forgotten her unfortunate teacher. She had some time before she entered another classroom as a pupil. She lifted her delicate hands and let the sunlight stream through them, marveling at their sudden translucence and the rosy blood at their margins. What a wondrous thing was this world and all in it! A blade of grass, a stone, a leaf, held glories and mysteries beyond the words of any poet or philosopher. There was no common thing; nothing was gray or dull or lifeless or without beauty, but all shone with an inner splendor and astonishment at their own being. Nothing could be adequately explained or understood; nothing could be fully known. Therein lay the most profound of excitements, and amazements. She examined a lock of her hair, feeling its silken texture, its living presence. But, what was it in truth besides its seeming? What deeper reality was there behind what could be felt, tasted, heard, seen or touched?

Her thoughts were still childish and full of wonder, but her intensity was not childlike, nor the passion that rose in her nubile breast when contemplating all that existed. She was seized with restlessness, and she suddenly clenched her hands together to restrain her fervor. She wished to fly, to rush into the sea, to fling her body upon the ground, to hold all things in her arms and make them one with herself. There was an enormous hunger in her which had no name, no lineaments, no shape, no form, but which devoured her and moved her, at times, to weeping. She longed for embraces from all that she saw and heard. A butterfly, as red as blood, blew like a rose petal onto her knee and while she gazed at it her eyes filled with tears. It was not only the beauty of the insect which caused her heart to beat wildly. It was its very existence, and the enigma of its existence. She was overcome with adoration, but for what she did not know.

Behind her the pillared house with its painted frescoes seemed formed of white fire and appeared to float rather than to rest on the ground. Then there was the sound of lutes and singing, and she rose, trembling, and tried to compose herself, for now she must go to the room of the physician, who taught the maidens what they must know of the arts of healing.

She looked at the sky and whispered impetuously, "O gods, permit me a little wisdom, a little knowledge, a little comprehension, that I may be more than a beast of the field who chews his cud and lays down his offal! Let me be fully human, and preserve in me the divine fever of amazement, the divine questing for an answer!"

CHAPTER 3

The physician, a lively man of middle age and with an agile expression, was, like Aspasia and Thargelia, an Ionian of Miletus. His name was Echion. He had never been a slave, but had been born free and of a prosperous family who manufactured silver and gold ornaments, and he had attended an Egyptian school of medicine. He was broad and fat and muscular, with a round red face and eyes like glittering blue stones, yet mirthful, and he was bald and had a rosy dome rising above his thick black eyebrows, and several fatty chins which testified to a good digestion and an excellent appetite. He affected short tunics in many hearty colors, none of them subdued, and they revealed legs of an admirable shape for all their bulk. He was one of Thargelia's lovers, and she paid him well and did not underestimate his talents in bed or in the schoolroom. She loved his full and red and lustful mouth which was almost always smiling, for he had perfect teeth of which he was proud. He was not so proud of his nose, which Thargelia fondly called a turnip, and his nostrils were filled with virile black hairs.

He was quite content to instruct the maidens of the school for the hetairai, and if he yearned after any of them he was prudent enough to confine himself to an apparently paternal touch on the shoulder or arm or cheek. He was also very lazy in spite of his vigorous appearance, and preferred the luxurious life in this house to any medical practice in the city, for such practice could be arduous and held few rewards in money or esteem. He had his own small marble house on the grounds of the school, from which Thargelia summoned him when she was in the mood to be amused and treated roughly in bed. He was amiable and shrewd and a fine physician, and had much wit and, to the respect of many, his knowledge of medicine was astounding and his potions magical. A cynic, he had little pity for suffering, and illness to him was a challenge to his ego. Disease was an affront to him, and did not arouse any compassion, for he despised all that was sickly and struggled to abolish it. The Egyptians said that a physician could cure only if his heart was moved and his emotions engaged in behalf of a patient, but Echion had proved that to be false and sentimental. It needed but skill, and disease was an enemy which must be understood and defeated, for it was ugly and he hated ugliness. He also had a deep suspicion, with which the Egyptians did not concur, that a man was his own malady and induced much of his own torment. He bullied the sick and reproached them even as he ministered to them, and he felt his triumph over illness was also a triumph over the weak and recalcitrant, who obstinately preferred disease to health. Above all, he detested weakness, for at heart he was a warrior. There was, in him, that cruelty which is the endowment of an expert surgeon, and never did his hand tremble as it wielded the scalpel nor did anxious sweat ever moisten his face.

He loved all that was healthy and blooming and admired it openly, and so he had a reputation as a discerning man of much sensibility, which was entirely untrue. Unknown even to himself, disease terrified him and he felt it a threat to his own life, and a portent for the future.

He had an eye which could sight the enemy even when it was hidden behind a rose-lipped young face or concealed behind bright eyes, and many were the maidens whom he had induced Thargelia to dispose of hastily to the first bidder. She never disputed him. She had seen the results too often when she had not followed his advice. The girls soon sickened and died, to the surprise and bewilderment of their patrons, but not to Echion. "Did I not tell you that the maiden had diseased kidneys or sluggish blood or a feeble heart, though these were not evident to you or to others?" he would say to

Thargelia when she would read a mournful letter from some wealthy man who had taken the girl in good faith. "You did well to rid yourself of her. The purchaser?" Echion laughed. "A man who buys a horse or a woman should be knowledgeable in the matter, or he is a fool and deserves no sympathy." He well knew that no maiden was actually purchased, for she was not a slave, and could leave her protector at her own will at any time, but he liked to consider the potentially ill, and therefore the weak, less than dogs or cattle.

Above all the other beautiful maidens Aspasia enchanted him, though she was less than a docile pupil and provoked him into controversy. He preferred her disagreeable dissents, sharp remarks and questions, and disputations to the meek acceptances of the other girls. He saw little slavish respect in her great brown eyes, and knew that she listened avidly not only to learn but to pounce upon him if he showed doubt. But when she honestly admired him and leaned forward so as not to waste a single word his gratification was immense. He felt, to his own amusement, that he had received an accolade from a colleague and not a mere chit.

"She is, in all truth, possessed of the soul of a physician," he would say to Thargelia. "I marvel at her prodigious talents. It has been said that the beauteous woman has the soul of an ape, but it has been my experience that those endowed by the gods with intelligence are also agreeable to the eye."

"She is worthy of an emperor," Thargelia would repeat.

"Or of Apollo, himself," he would reply. "But let us hope that Zeus, in whom I do not believe, does not discover her and bear her off in a shower of gold. Or impregnate her as he did Leda, though a woman who lays an egg might be an interesting spectacle to a physician."

"You are no Zeus," Thargelia said on one occasion, with an affectionate but warning smile. "Let us remember that."

"But you are a veritable Hera, my adored one," he replied with gallantry, and Thargelia laughed and shook her finger at him. "It is said, in the city, that you are tireless," she remarked.

"But, my divinity, that is only rumor. Am I not faithful to you?"

"No," said Thargelia. "But you amuse and satisfy me and I enjoy your conversation, and that is my contentment." She looked momentarily troubled. "There are times when I fear that Aspasia will not be the happiest of companions to a man, for men do not cherish a dagger tongue in a woman. She is rebellious and not too supple of character. I advise and rebuke her often."

"There are men who prefer a woman of fire to a complaisant woman in their arms. Who would not prefer to subdue a spirited horse rather than a donkey, or a listless mare? You have a treasure in your house, Thargelia."

"Whom I guard," she replied.

So Echion, though he lusted after Aspasia, who was healthy and wondrous in appearance and intellectual, was ever decorous with his pupil. He luxuriated in his pleasant life, and not even an Aspasia would ever threaten it however much he desired her. But he had his fantasies, which had to satisfy him.

The maidens streamed into his classroom this day like rose petals blown by the wind, and Echion licked his lips. He saw Aspasia and noticed, with his physician's eyes, that she appeared perturbed and preoccupied. That was an omen that she would be more contentious than usual. She sat down on one of the chairs and looked at him with distant eyes. It did not occur to him that she was hardly aware of his presence. He thought, in his egotism, that she was thinking of him and the lesson to come. He gave her a wary smile, to which she did not respond. She looked down at her clasped hands.

"We will discuss, today," he said, thinking that his classroom resembled a garden of flowers, and rejoicing in the vision, "the truth that a sound body is the result of a sound mind. We have discussed this before, but I wish to enlarge on it."

Aspasia came to herself and raised an imperative hand. Echion frowned, but he inclined his head. "It is your argument, Echion, that a man is his own malady and that health is only a matter of judicious thought and a serene philosophy."

"True, Aspasia."

"Then all ills, apart from an accident, are created in the mind of the sufferer?"

"True."

Aspasia smiled contemptuously. "Then an infant or a young child, afflicted with the White Sickness, is responsible for his deathly ailment?"

The physician stared at her, nonplussed. Aspasia smiled again. "An infant is born with a deformity or an illness which will kill him. Tell me, sire, if he is to be accused of wrong thinking."

Echion felt less than affection for the maiden and became

34

insensible to her charms. He coughed slightly. "There is a theory among the Egyptians that men carry with them, into their present lives, mental corruptions of previous lives, and the corruption appears in their extant bodies."

"Do you believe that, my teacher?"

It was not accepted by the Ecclesia that men had lived prior lives to their current one. Echion felt himself in danger from this disputatious chit. He said, with caution, "There are many mysterious things, my child."

"But you have advanced the theory that man is his own malady! Tell me, then, how an infant, just born, can be diseased, and die of that disease."

The physician lifted his hands and beamed like the sun and resorted to an aphorism. "Who knows what is in the mind of a child?"

Aspasia said, "Infanthood is not far behind me, nor childhood, and I am, at fourteen, still young. I recall my infant and childish thoughts. They were not mysterious. They were concerned with appetite and little pleasures, as are all the thoughts of all children. Why, then, am I in health and others sicken?"

"You had parents of health," said Echion.

Aspasia said, "I never knew my father nor did I ever hear his voice. My mother died three years ago. My mother was not of the best of constitutions, otherwise she would not have died of the plague of the lungs." She paused. "You have remarked that I had parents of health. Is it possible, then, that a healthy child will be the offspring of healthy parents? Yet I have seen slaves in this house who were not of a sturdy body, who gave birth to children who were neither sick nor deformed. I have also seen a young and vigorous mother delivered of a child who could not survive, so ridden with illness was he. Considering these things, should we be careful not to say that every ill is self-wrought, and therefore we should not despise the sufferer?"

"Medicine," said the physician, his face a deep and swollen red, "is an exact science. But every man is an individual and what will kill one man will not disturb another or cause him any inconvenience."

"It is, you will admit, a mysterious and occult and subjective art? It is unique that it is not applicable to every man?"

This was against all Echion's convictions and theories. He bit his lip.

Aspasia smoothed her hair with both hands and her smile was derisive. "Medicine, it would appear, is an art and not a

35

science, and only artists should engage in it, men of subjective reasoning and occult prescience."

Echion wondered why he had ever considered the maiden beauteous. He saw the discreet smiles of the others. He said, "I have cut for the stone, and the stones were identical! There was no art in it!"

"But," said Aspasia, "some lived after the operation and some did not. Therefore, the sufferers were not identical, nor could their lives or their deaths have been anticipated."

Echion said with triumph, "Those who survived were healthful of thought, and those who did not were diseased of mind!"

"How can that be proved—if medicine is an exact science —sire?"

When he did not reply Aspasia said, "It is all subjective. There is no way to prove it with exactitude, and so it is not a science but an art, and art is unpredictable."

"I have said, Aspasia, that though medicine is an exact science no man is like another."

"You have never admitted that before," said the maiden, and nodded with approval. "So men are not always their own malady, but are driven by mysterious courses which we do not as yet discern and may never discern. Tell me: Is a disease in one man exactly as it is in another?"

"No. But again it is the matter of the individual response of the mind."

"The mind, then, is subjective. Who has seen a mind? Can you cut for it, or change it with a scalpel? It can be subdued with opium, as you have once told us, but it will not remain subdued. True it is that a man can kill himself by his own thoughts, and as the mind is subjective then it follows that the body is also. But is it not true that a diseased body can affect the mind, that pain can turn a philosopher, however much of a Stoic he is, into a screaming animal without shame or dignity?"

"He induced it first in his mind," said the physician, who was beginning to hate the damsel.

"How can that be proved, sire?"

"It cannot be proved, of a certainty!" he shouted.

"Then that which cannot be proved of a certainty is not objective, and not a science. It is only a hypothesis. Does it not follow then that medicine is hypothetical?"

There had been Egyptian teachers who had spoken of this, and Echion had despised them as arcane dreamers, unacquainted with reality. "Is it your contention, Aspasia, that we should regard medicine as mere thaumaturgy?" His voice had become softly vicious.

"We should not discard thaumaturgy as part of subjective medicine," replied Aspasia with the utmost seriousness. "Do we not have Delphi and the priests and our religion, which is based on magic, contemplation, reflection and belief in what is not discernible by the open eye? To deny that is blasphemy and heresy."

"You are a Sophist," said Echion, suddenly turning deadly pale. "You also twist the truth and muddy crystal waters with your vaporings. Your reasoning is fallacious. What do you consider you are, you mere maiden?"

"I am a subjective realist," said Aspasia, with another of her lovely and apparently innocent smiles.

"A contradiction in terms!"

"As is all our philosophy, and even our lives, themselves."

Echion thought of Thargelia, who had often teased him with similar dissents. Yet he knew that Aspasia also disagreed with Thargelia on many matters. "You are disputatious," he said, with severity. "You argue only for your own pleasure, and I doubt you believe in those arguments yourself."

"I seek only knowledge," said Aspasia, with unbearable demureness.

"And what has your limited knowledge taught you?"

"That nothing exists but the mind, and as the mind is subjective all else is subjective also."

"My child," said Echion, recovering himself and achieving a superb smile, "if ever you are cut for the stone, or deliver a child, you will of a surety know that the pain is objective and not subjective."

"If I suffer, then, the pain which all suffers under the same circumstances, it will be my guilt, the guilt of my deformed mind?"

"We will go to the infirmia," said Echion, exasperated almost beyond control. The girl's arguments, he told himself, were jejune and not worthy of the response of a man of science, and she sought glorification and attention for herself, as all inferior womanhood did—recognizing its own inferiority. She made but noises, like a heifer, and considered them philosophy. She needed a flogging and not indulgence. The girls tittered discreetly about him and he felt a swollen pressure in the sides of his throat. He hated Aspasia now, and his hatred made him feel voluptuous and he longed to get her into his bed where he would teach her true objectivity! To his horror he had a sudden physical manifestation which, the girls

37

discerning, provoked them to more titters, and they pretended to be embarrassed, they covering their fresh faces with widespread fingers through which they peeked. He tightened his girdle in mortification.

He must talk with Thargelia with the utmost severity. He had heard from the master of science that Aspasia also contended with him on the same subject of objectivity and subjectivity. It was well to train a hetaira so she could converse with the eminent man whose mistress she would become, but it was another matter to deliver a maiden who preferred argument to all else to such a man.

They walked through a narrow white hall of marble. On the left were simple Doric pillars between which the gardens flashed with changeful light and color. The fountains glittered and sparkled in the sun and as a portion of the water fell on blossom and shrub a seductive fragrance seeped on the warm breeze. Aspasia thought. If there was any reality at all it was beauty, and if there was any truth it existed in harmony. As men were not in the least harmonious there was no truth in them, and as their thoughts were dark and intricate and insidious they were blind to beauty for all their ecstasies about it. We are a perfidious race, thought the damsel, ugly and incongruent in this world, and why the gods endure us is a great mystery—if the gods exist.

They entered the infirmia, a clean bright long room with open windows. Here there were only single narrow beds and not the usual crowded beds of sanitoria. This was the infirmia of the slaves, both men and women, and children. The room beyond, prettily decorated, was for the young hetairai, private cubicles, and filled with flowers, and with skilled attendants. Only two or three of the hetairai were interested in the infirmia, and among them was Aspasia. Immediately on entering the rooms Echion forgot the maidens, for here was his authority and his skill and his subjects. He walked from bed to bed, examining, frowning, questioning the patients and their attendants in a sharp concise voice, and Aspasia followed and listened with admiration and deep attention. Now her respect for the physician returned. He might not be kind or thoughtful, and he might be rough in examinations, immune to the cries of the sick, but his judgment was faultless and he betrayed here his cynical understanding of the vagaries of the human mind and was quick to discover the whimperers who preferred illness to work and duty, and to denounce them. Aspasia pondered. In numerous ways both Echion and herself were right; they both had part of the truth. There were ill-

38

nesses which indeed were self-induced voluntarily or involuntarily, but there were illnesses which came of themselves. But it was almost impossible to decide the category.

Echion's rosy bald head gleamed in the shifting sunlight. His eyes were attentive if without pity. He was more interested in the disease than he was in the sufferer. In this he was the scientist and not the physician. He carried with him a tablet and a stylus for his own information. He paused by the bed of a fat male slave of about thirty and looked upon him with disgust. "Here is one who not only devours to the full the excellent and abundant food given him in this house but pilfers tidbits from the kitchen, especially those redundant in oils and spices and rich flavorings. He has been seen to snatch, slyly, the very food from the plates of his fellow diners at the table, thus depriving them of their necessities, which they have dutifully earned. He sips, unseen, from their glasses and not even the threats of the overseer are heeded, nor is he restrained by punishment. What is left on the plates of the mistress of this house, and her teachers and pupils, is devoured by him before they reach the kitchen. Look upon his belly! Observe the saffron of his thief's countenance, the yellow in his sullen greedy eyes! Consider his many chins! Hunger does not drive him. He is a slave to his stomach, which is his god. Is there wonder that he has stones in his liver and gall bladder? No! He has been in this infirmia many times, suffering agony as the stones moved. Has that halted him? No!"

He glared at the sick man, then flicked his strong fingers painfully on the slave's cheek. The man winced, then groaned. Echion nodded fiercely and smiled a most unamused smile. "When first he would appear here I would give him a draught of opium to relieve his anguish, for indeed the anguish is even more painful than a difficult birth. But, no more! He writhes upon his bed and calls upon the gods to give him death, when he is in torture. But he shall have no opium until he has learned that judicious eating is the only answer to his affliction. Then, of a certainty, he will suffer no more nor need opium."

Aspasia said in a subdued voice: "What is it that compels him to eat so disastrously, to steal food?"

"Greed," replied the physician. He glanced at the girl formidably and then was pleased to see her face devoid of mockery, and respectful. He said, "He was born in this house and was never deprived of plenteous food since his birth. He was given enough to satisfy the hunger of any man, and more."

"Then why," asked Aspasia, "is he not content, but must force food upon himself to his disaster?"

"Ask him yourself," replied the physician with contempt.

Aspasia bent over the sick man whose oily and icteriod face swam with sweat and whose eyes and mouth were twisted with the pity of self. His expression implored Aspasia's compassion, and he whimpered. She frowned.

"You are fat," she said, "and you have heard the physician's condemnation of your greed and your enormous appetite. You have known that such indulgence leads to suffering, and may cause your death, but you do not refrain. Why is this?"

The slave muttered, "I am hungry."

"For what do you hunger?"

The man was silent. He looked up at Aspasia's smooth and impassive face and thought he saw reflected there a tender and youthful pity. He licked his thick and greasy lips, dropped his eyes and murmured, "For freedom."

Aspasia considered. Her wonderful hair fell about her cheeks as she bent over him. A great disgust filled her, but she revealed none of this. Then she said in a grave tone, "That is easily remedied. The Lady Thargelia is of a merciful and kindly character, and I am her favorite. I will persuade her to give you your freedom so that you may depart at once from this house and live and die as freemen do, working for what stipends you can gather and feeding and clothing yourself and finding your own shelter. As the stipends will be small and the labor arduous you will be forced to refran from lusting for luxurious food, sleeping when you will in a soft bed, and amusing yourself with the slave girls. The wine of the country will be your portion. Then shall your fat disappear and your pain be abolished. That is freedom and I congratulate you that you should prefer poverty to richness of living, and a random shelter instead of a sound roof above you."

The slave's eyes widened with sudden fear and they lost their sly and injured expression. He suddenly sat up, moistening lips that appeared to have shrunk. "How shall I live?" he cried.

Aspasia smiled. "As other free men live—by your labor and your wits and your unending industry. What is it you do in this house? You assist in the kitchen and preside over the table of the Lady Thargelia and clean the copper and the silver. But you will have to find different employment, for such gentle duties are performed by pampered slaves in other houses. But rejoice! Hard labor will reduce your fat and your hunger, and a rigorous life will lengthen your days."

She winked at the physician, who had become extremely interested. "Echion," she said, "you will join me in my plea to the Lady Thargelia to release this injured and pining man who desires freedom above all things?"

"Of a certainty," he replied at once. He looked at the slave who had paled excessively and he patted him upon his shoulder. "Tomorrow, you shall be free, for the Lady Thargelia will take you before the officer. Then you will gather up your possessions and will depart at once from this house."

The slave glanced desperately about him, shrinking from the wide smiles of the girl and the physician. "Wine, in the name of the gods!" he cried in a trembling voice, and he extended a shaking hand as if he were dying of thirst in a desert.

The physician shook his head. "No. As you are now a free man there will be no more free wine in this house; and since you will receive many gifts from your generous mistress you will have money in your pouch. I will order wine for you— but only if you pay for it. Twenty drachmas for a small jug. You may request it at will from the attendant."

He made as if to turn away but the slave suddenly grasped the physician's green robe in a frantic grip. He almost fell from his bed as the weight of his belly pulled him to the edge. "Master!" he groaned. "That is cruelty!"

The physician raised his eyebrows as if in astonishment. "Cruelty, do you say? For granting you your heart's desire for freedom so that you will no longer suffer and will walk in dignity as a free man? Is that not what you wish?"

The slave continued to grasp him. He began to pant. His yellowish flesh quivered in his extremity. His jaundiced eyes rolled in terror. Then he said in a bursting cry, "I do not wish to be free!"

The physician, who had assumed a benevolent expression during the conversation, let his features and his eyes show his revulsion and contempt, and the slave quailed. He said, "You do not wish to be free. Your only wish is to continue a parasite's existence and to indulge your loathsome appetites. I will tell you. I will not press the Lady Thargelia for your freedom, seeing that you truly despise and fear it as the majority of men do in this craven world. They prefer to be slaves, so long as they can escape responsibility!" He looked at Aspasia. "That is the history of mankind. Liberty is not desired if it entails hard labor and want and the risks of danger and hunger and if one fails by one's own weakness."

41

Aspasia inclined her head. "Mercy!" wailed the slave, intent only on his own dilemma. "I do not wish to be free."

The physician let a long pause follow, as if considering, and his face was stern. He said at last, "I have said I will not press the Lady Thargelia for your freedom, but on one condition only, that you control your pig's appetite. I am weary of seeing you in this infirmia. However, should you continue to indulge yourself and steal food beyond your needs, you shall have your freedom promptly and be sent away from this house. You understand me?"

The slave gave him a tremulous smile. Relief poured from him in sweat. He nodded like a chided child who has been forgiven. "I will obey your directions, Master," he said, almost sobbing. "But opium, Master, for this pain which I vow to you will occur no more."

The physician shook his head. "There will be no opium. You will endure this pain with thankfulness that it is the price of your past indulgence, which you will permit no more. That pain is nothing to the pangs of freedom, which upright men prefer to soft slavery. But you are not an upright man."

He struck the slave's grasping hand from his garments and left him. Aspasia followed, with a thoughtful expression. He said to her, "You will have observed that the man is his own malady, as I have insisted before. Are there sufferers who are born with painful defects? Of a surety. But their parents were feeble and should never have been permitted to beget and conceive."

"But the sufferer is not responsible for his agony," said Aspasia, following him.

He stopped and wagged his finger in her face. "All crimes against health must be paid for, either by parents or their offspring. That is the law of life, and who am I to dispute it?"

"Not in the name of mercy?"

"Mercy! Do the weak extend that to the strong they have exploited or ruined? No! They leave the body of the host as parasites leave it, when they have brought death to the host. It is the strong and the brave and the free which I admire, and which I will help." He continued shaking his finger at her. "I am almost alone in this. We have philosophers who maintain that a man is entitled to be preserved for the simple reason that he was born—though none asked for his birth! Is that not a contemptible fallacy?"

"Truly, in many ways," said Aspasia, as the bored maidens joined them. "Indiscriminate mercy, I have seen, is a destroyer on occasion. But are there not some to whom we should extend mercy?"

"I have not seen them, except for those who have been the victims of other men's weakness," said the physician with growing impatience.

"If they had been strong, would they have permitted themselves to become the victims of such weaklings?"

The physician stopped. Then he laughed loudly. "You have an argument!" he cried, and touched her fondly on her shoulder and then let his ringed hand slide down the length of her bare round arm. He felt its silken texture and its warmth, and his hand lingered. He looked into those clear brown eyes and smiled. "I congratulate you, my pupil. You should be in government, for all you are a woman."

They visited the beds of others. Aspasia's inner eye had sharpened. She saw what she had not seen before, though in many cases she was dubious. They came on the bed of a young female slave who was groaning, unable to deliver her child immediately. Aspasia said, "Has she sinned against health that she suffers so?"

The physician said, "If I had my will I should let this slave die. For inability to deliver normally is a physical defect, which can be passed on to daughters. Why should she be permitted to inflict such suffering on her offspring?"

"It is a hard decision," said Aspasia.

"This is a world of hard reality," said the physician, "as I have told you before. Ruthlessness in the name of health and sanity and justice is not to be despised. Many would die before their time? Ah. But think of the misery such deaths would curtail!"

Aspasia thought. It was, of a certainty, a law of nature that the weak and the defective must die. Human mercy often abrogated that law. Was that virtuous or evil? She must consider this when alone. Nevertheless, she did not believe that the physician was entirely correct. She said, "What of soldiers who are wounded, and those who have been afflicted, by no fault of their own, by other men?"

"Those I will help," said the physician, and Aspasia smiled.

The physician laughed at her with affection. "My child," he said, "you have maintained that nothing but the mind truly exists, and that all is subjective. Is pain subjective? Your argument would maintain this. If subjective, it can be controlled by an effort of will."

Aspasia laughed aloud. "I am defeated by my own argument," she answered. But still she was not entirely convinced that mercy was unrealistic and a weakness that must be detested. What of men who were imprisoned or done to death by the powerful Ecclesia, who endlessly sought for heresy and impiety? Were these men not deserving of mercy and justice? Were not mercy and justice sometimes one and the same? The world was full of riddles. Of one thing she was sure: There was no broad law which could be extended to cover the vast intricacy of human conduct and being. Nature had broad laws only, but men had intellect and should be discriminating. The defeat of nature had created civilizations and beauty and order and philosophy and art and had released the great imponderables of the human mind. Nature, herself, was chaotic and must be restrained if life were not to regress again to the jungle and savagery.

The maidens entered the classroom presided over by a severe female teacher, who looked at Aspasia with no affection. The girl's beauty inspired her envy; her controversies annoyed her. The teacher, Maia, regarded the Apollonian art of mathematics as true law and order, inflexible and objective, and endlessly valid. Mathematics ruled the universes, and the teacher reverenced it as the manifestation of the wisdom of the gods. Without the rule of mathematics there would be no life at all, and no planets or stars guided in their passage by eternal and precise edict.

"But we have minds," said Aspasia today, when the teacher again expounded on the subject. "Our minds are not precise, nor are they ruled by mathematics. If we were so ruled then every man's conduct would be the same as every other man's and every man would be reduced to a mere set of numbers and his thinking predicted. What of the mind, which is no slave to apparent validity and the rule of precision and mathematics?"

"If governments would insist that the rule of mathematics be applied to human affairs then we should have no disorders, no revolutions, no unprecise thinking, and no destructive emotions," said the teacher.

"We should not, then, be men," said Aspasia.

Goaded, the teacher exclaimed angrily, "What is a man?"

"Ah," said Aspasia, "that is the question, which cannot be explained by mathematics."

"Would you prefer chaos to law and order," demanded the teacher, outraged.

"The majority of men prefer law and order, but deny that

44

mathematics have aught to do with it," said the girl. "They are the result of intelligence and reflection and an observance that men cannot exist in chaos and disorder."

"It is an observance that is based on the truism that two and two make four," said the teacher, more and more exasperated.

Aspasia shook her head gently. "It is true that in this world two and two equal four. But, how can it be proved that such a law prevails on other worlds which wheel about the suns? In those worlds it may be that two and two equal five. Could it be that mathematics itself is subjective and does not prevail everywhere at all times?"

"It is not subjective, Aspasia! There is but one law throughout the universes."

"How can you prove that, Maia?"

"By induction and deduction, you young dissenter."

"But these are also subjective, Maia. They originate in the mind."

"There is a Mind greater than yours, my girl, Which has set the laws that govern the universes with precision and unshakable quantrums."

"It, Itself, is subjective, Maia."

The teacher looked at her cunningly. She mimicked, "How can you prove that, Aspasia?"

Aspasia laughed and the girls joined her. "It is all a tremendous mystery, which is very exciting. And conjecture is exciting in itself. A man without constant questions is only a beast."

Nevertheless mathematics deeply interested her, even if, as she believed, or considered, the precise laws of it may pertain only to this world. She sharpened her mind on the minds of others and dialogue could reveal interesting vistas. But her teachers resented dialogues not in accord with their opinions. They did not know that it was their didactic convictions which vexed the maiden, for she did not believe in any absolute. The minds of men should be free to roam as they willed, and should be restrained only when they impinged on the minds of others and caused destruction and oppression. In short, liberty was the law of flourishing life and when it was abdicated by evil men it induced death.

She did not tell Maia that mathematics was, to her, the greatest mystery of them all and endlessly interesting. Maia would be aghast, the girl would think, to encounter one who believed that mathematics was in any way mysterious, as mysterious as the One who had ordained it. She was already discerning, if somewhat dimly, that those who dispensed with mysteries, and denied their existence, were dull no matter their learning. Aspasia was beginning to despise the dogmatic. She feared those who believed they had all the answers.

She pondered, forgetting the classroom. All the sciences were based on the "law" of causality. Aspasia doubted that causality governed everything. The mind of man leaped to conclusions without an objective cause on many occasions. As men were often too emotional, and too little ruled by wisdom, it should be considered that concrete causes did not always lead to inevitable results, and were seldom predictable.

The other maidens yawned through the lesson, though some, thinking of their future wealth, were interested in mathematics. But riches were not precise and immutable, Aspasia thought. When governments degraded coin, such as reducing the quantity of gold in coins, or cutting the coins, wealth—the god of merchants—frequently vanished or was worthless. Of one thing man could be truly certain: There was nothing certain in this world. It amused and saddened her that the majority of men stubbornly denied this. One should flow with events, interested in them all but refraining from drawing iron conclusions, the last refuge of fools. Why was it that learning inevitably was the enemy of mystery? Yet none could adequately explain what was a man, or irrefutably prove his origin. Without wonder, learning was dead.

I will never be the mistress of a man devoid of wonder, she vowed. But where was such a man? Thargelia had never spoken of such.

There was one subject which engrossed her whole mind and her joy, and that was art. Following that were history and government. It distracted her that Thargelia did not emphasize these things in the teaching of her maidens, considering them as relevant only when they could teach the hetairai to chatter, with seeming intelligence, on these matters, if the hetairai became the mistresses of men engaged in them. "Even so," she would remark, "men resent a woman too conversant on the subjects."

Nevertheless, her teachers were competent. Thargelia despised incompetence.

To Aspasia art was the supreme jeweled crown on the mind of man, and had the only real validity, even though it was subjective. She entered her class with that joyous anticipation which is the attribute of a true scholar. The other girls, with few exceptions, considered art to be truly art only when it enhanced a woman's charm and made her delectable to men. They preferred the art of cosmetics, and liked dancing and music because they made them desirable and because they had the exuberance of youth.

CHAPTER 4

The artist-teacher, Tmolus—named after a mountain—rejoiced in Aspasia, his best pupil and a docile and eager one. Unlike most Greeks, he did not denigrate the minds of women. Without women, could art exist? No, he would tell himself. Women were the supreme art of the gods. (Even if they also destroyed both gods and men. But, was not beauty in itself the immortal exquisite terror and was it not therefore destructive?) Without art, the gift and the adornment of the gods, there could be no civilization, no justification of life. All else was mundane and prosaic and deadening. Nothing else so engrossed the intellect and joy and wonder of the mind, so exhilarated it and raised it above the flesh. It made man truly man. Tmolus had seen that Aspasia agreed with him. Once she had said to him, "Tmolus, you are truly a philosopher," and he understood. He had received her comment as an accolade, even though she was only a maiden and he an old man.

He was small and slight of body, and bent and gray, but his eyes were vividly alive and filled with unquenched youth and joy in living, for he found, as did Aspasia, all things beautiful, even a warted toad or a lichened stone or a weed. Ugliness did not revolt him, for he believed all things intrinsically lovely. "A withered crone with no teeth, with whitened hair, with crippled hands, has an innate glory," he would say. "Does she not live and have being? So, she is beautiful. Her life and her thoughts have molded her. Have they been hideous? But— they too have mystery, and therefore their own charm. When we learn that nothing is boring, nothing too mean or despicable, we can have serenity, for serenity is the soul of art."

"Even if it depicts violence?" Aspasia had once asked.

"Violence is part of living, and often it is a quickening and a drama, child. We can contemplate it for what it is, an aspect of life, and living is an art in itself." He found only men who would not see as disastrous, and unworthy of being called human. Moreover, they were a threat to other men.

"Not everything that walks in the form of a man is human," he would explain. "Many there are who do not have full humanity, or any humanity at all. Aspect is not all. There is the soul. I have heard that some birds create charming and delicate bowers for their females, choosing between colors and texture of flowers, and completing a haven of symmetry and fragrance. Are they not more human, in the full sense of the word, than a man who considers mere stone and wood and brick an adequate shelter? The gift of humanness is not confined to mankind. I have heard that many animals display the virtues of compassion and justice and law and tenderness and love. They are more human than the men who do not possess these."

He loved the gods, though reputed that they were often debauched and capricious and often too human. For, were they not beautiful, even the lame Vulcan? Zeus had violated Leda, and out of her eggs had come the Gemini and Helen of Troy and Clytemnestra. "But the story of Leda and the swan is immortally beautiful," he would say. "Consider the delightful young maiden in all her wondrous loveliness and the white-winged swan beating against her breast."

The girls had giggled at this, archly. But Aspasia had dubiously understood. Out of tumultuous violence had come beauteous Helen and the Gemini; out of lustful love had come the forms of gods and the unforgettable face and lure of Helen of Troy. But one did not condone senseless violence, which was despicable, but only that violence which produced beauty, Aspasia thought.

Tmolus excused everything which resulted in loveliness. But sometimes the recalcitrant Aspasia wondered. However, she loved Tmolus and forgave him.

Beautiful male and female slaves posed for the hetairai for their lessons in painting and sculpture and mosaics. The bodies were carefully chosen for their grace and youth. Though Thargelia instructed the teacher that he should emphasize the attribute of alluring sexual differences, and expose the male slaves to the utmost scrutiny of her virgins, and discourse on their attributes and endowments, Tmolus preferred that these matters be discussed in the frame of artistry. "There is no coyness or libidinous aspects to Art," he would say. "That which is exquisite is above tittering and filthiness. The evil is not in the object but in the viewer. We bring to art all our falsities and degradation, but in themselves the objects are neither lewd nor meretricious. In short, what we view can be interpreted innocently and with admiration, or debauched. It is in ourselves."

The majority of the maidens preferred to peek and giggle,

which outraged Tmolus. "You are fools!" he would cry. "Did not the gods create man and woman? Did they find either licentious, in their bodies, or obscene? These things are in your own minds, and that is sad. But I have discerned that youth is innately gross and is born impure. That is the curse of mankind."

Once Aspasia had said to him, "But does not the belief that certain things are evil and disgusting enhance their value in human minds?"

Tmolus considered this. Then he said, "Alas, it is true."

But still he struggled with the young girls assigned to him. • Art, he would tell them, is above good and evil. He knew that in this he defied the purse-lipped Ecclesia who found evil in everything, and even denounced naked athletes, and, of a certainty, beauty itself. "No doubt they would destroy bees, who fertilize the flowers, if they dared," Tmolus complained bitterly.

Aspasia put this into her mind and pondered on it, and knew it was true. Like Tmolus she deplored the fact that sculptors painted the noble white majesty of marble statues. "Let there be innocence," Tmolus endlessly repeated. "Why must mankind inflict its meanness and mediocrity on that which is natively simple and complete? If there is any evil at all it is in the complicated intricacy of the deformed human soul, which must daub and smear its offal on that which is pure."

From Tmolus she learned more of true glory and reverence than she did from her teachers of theology.

She had known since childhood that she was not capable of creating great sculpture nor was she adept at painting, for all her efforts. Tmolus consoled her. "It is not necessary to create beauty to appreciate it, my child. For what do sculptors and painters labor? For the joy of those who view. We cannot all be artists. But is the viewer who loves and reverences less than he who also loves and creates and reverences? Do the gods demand that we be gods also? No. It is enough for us to rejoice in them and in those they have gifted."

Aspasia would hold cool marble in her hands and often she became ecstatic over it. Her heart lifted when she touched mosaics and gazed on pictures. This reproduction of nature exalted her. Her taste was immaculate and sure. She, like her teacher, hated mediocrity. "Excellence," said Tmolus, "is the utter goal of a true artist. It is not relevant that all who love excellence in art be artists themselves. It is enough to appreciate it. That appreciation is the accolade and the contentment of all artists. Without an understanding of excellence a man is an animal."

He would add, "Alas, no artist ever attains, in his work, the perfection for which he strives. Perfection is beyond humanity, but that does not mean we should abandon it as a goal."

To Aspasia, who desired to be excellent in all things, this was a consolation. So she cultivated her adoration of beauty and her understanding of it. She fervently hoped that some day she would be able to influence a powerful man to become a patron of the arts. It would not be possible to endure a man who would revel in her own loveliness and not be aware of its greater meaning. Sensuality was not enough. Physical beauty was transient. That which was graven in stone and was painted in luminous colors and written eloquently in books endured. Helen of Troy was dead, but the memory of her beauteousness remained to inspire poets and artists. Legend was eternal, and never grew old and ugly. That was why the gods continued to be magnificent, beyond human pollution.

Today, Tmolus had a new model for his maidens.

The young girl, nude and gleaming like amber, was of some twelve years, innocently unaware of her nakedness. Her long black hair touched breasts still budlike and she had little pubic hair. She looked with curiosity at the maidens who trooped in, but it was a childlike curiosity, vacant and only vaguely aware. She stood with one elbow leaning on a half pedestal of marble and moved restlessly. Her name was Cleo. Slender and delicate, she was being considered by Thargelia as a candidate for the hetairai, for she was quick of thought and beguiling, when it concerned herself. Thargelia had recently received her as a handmaiden, and she was reputed not only to be the child of a beautiful courtesan but of a man of some importance in Miletus.

Cleo looked more closely at the maidens who assembled at their stations for clay molding and painting and mosaics, considering them somewhat elderly. Then her eyes fixed themselves on Aspasia, who seemed to bring a lambent light into the room. Immediately, she was filled with childish adoration, as one is transfixed at the sight of a nymph. Drawn by the girl's intent gaze, Aspasia looked intently at her and she was touched with admiration. She was like a statue of the young Eros, and resembled spring. As always, Aspasia felt sadness and frustration that she was unable to mold in an exceptional manner and that never could she re-create in perfection what she saw. One of the maidens was adept at painting, and Aspasia went to the girl's easel and saw, again with a lurch of envy, that the maiden was already delineating Cleo's head with swift strokes of a piece of charcoal and had even sketched in that perfect young body. Aspasia went to one of the other maidens who was patiently matching small stones for her mosaic. I do not have the patience, she thought. My mind leaps too much. However, she found a small blue stone for which the maiden was searching. When it fitted exactly she was almost overcome with gratification. My eye is good, she thought, though, alas, my hands will not obey me.

She looked at Cleo again. Sunlight touched the form of the child and seemed to glimmer through it, as through honey. Aspasia sighed. She understood now what Tmolus meant when he had said that no one could reproduce nature in her living radiance, no matter how he dreamt and worked and sighed, and why he was never satisfied with what he had created.

Tmolus, who loved Aspasia, saw her longing face and he thought: Why cannot she understand that one cannot be excellent in all things? But he understood that it is the nature of genius to desire nothing but perfection, so he did not rebuke Aspasia for her air of desperation when she attempted to mold in clay or chisel in marble, or when she dashed a brush to the floor when working at her easel. She despised herself in this room. Yet she could not have enough of being in it.

The next class was in rhetoric, in which Aspasia excelled. Here she could forget her humiliation in Tmolus' room. Her voice, resonant and firm and exceedingly musical, moved her teacher to wonder and tears. It was a voice without the coyness of a woman's. The other maidens would listen, enthralled, even if they barely understood the subject. Aspasia's eyes would take on an unusual brilliance and her gestures had more than grace. When she quoted a passage from Homer the room seemed filled with the glory of the Gemini and Achilles and Apollo and Hercules and Odysseus. She has a Syren's voice, the teacher would think. She will be able to lure men to good and evil. Helen of Troy must have possessed such, for beauty is not enough to enthrall men.

After this class came dancing and music and instructions on the lyre and flute. Here, too, Aspasia excelled, though she considered dancing of no particular importance. But music enchanted her. She could, even now, manipulate the musical instruments so that they appeared to have an extra dimension and depth, and struck the heart with emotion.

Her lessons in theology were no felicitous occasions. But

51

she held her tongue, knowing the punishments inflicted by the Ecclesia on anyone suspected of heresy or dissent against the prevailing religion. Her face would flash, however, and her eyes become scornful at some pious pedantry. The teacher would reduce the grandeur of the gods to mere mortality, he believing that degrading the inexplicable and the majesty to low human understanding and status and familiarity made them more comprehensible.

He made Olympus, the abode of the gods, a suburb of Athens, or even of Miletus.

Aspasia always felt embattled when she went to her class in politics and history, and her teacher detested her for her arguments and controversies. "Who writes history?" she had asked him once. "Mere mortals, who make their own interpretations, according to their whims and subjective opinions, of what has transpired. History is easily distorted. As for politics, it is an exercise in hysteria." But the subjects engrossed her as well as angered her. It was said that if Helen of Troy's nose had been longer or her eyes less luminous Troy would never have been burned, nor would her husband have desired her to the death, nor would Paris have abducted her. On such trivialities did the affairs of men founder! She found both politics and history endlessly amusing, for the light they shone on the vagaries of human nature. "They should be the province of comedians," she once remarked, "but certainly should not be regarded as objective and immutable truth." At one time she had even said that history was made by madmen, and wars were the ultimate madness, a remark that did not endear her to her teacher.

"Is not everything made by man and the result of man?" he had asked her, to which Aspasia said, "No. There are imponderables beyond the knowledge and the understanding of man." The teacher complained she was a mere chit, and a woman, and so therefore of no importance, and her opinions of no consequence. The maidens, who did not love Aspasia for her beauty and superiority to them, would titter. At least Aspasia dispensed with the ennui of teaching with her arguments, and for that they were grateful.

The teacher, Aeneas, was a Greek. Therefore he expounded frequently on the defeat of the Persians at Thermopylae. "I am not superstitious," he would say, "but I believe in the Fates. Athens, and all of Greece, was preserved by some mysterious intervention. It seemed impossible that Xerxes could be defeated by us, we contentious Greeks, who suspected and even hated each other and were constantly quarreling and envious—men from the sallow mountains, the hot cliffs and passes, the fishing villages, the small towns even smaller than Athens, which is itself small and insignificant. Outnumbered by at least a score or more to one—and the immediate invaders but the first wave of a sea of soldiers and sailors—the Greeks had met the foe on their sacred land and waters and had driven him ignominiously away. This little land, all burning silver dust and mountains, all furious green torrents and crags and small green valleys and brilliant purple seas and miserable villages and stony roads and powdery fields and ardent blue skies, had stubbornly refused to be conquered and held slave to the mightly Xerxes and preferred, in all truth, liberty or death."

Aspasia admired the poetry of his words, but she had said, "Solon declared that all men should be free. But we have slaves. Is not a slave a man?"

The teacher had glared at her. "We believe a slave to be a thing, not a man. The gods ordained his fate. The gods ordained freedom for men. If a man is not born free, then he is not truly human."

"There is something wrong with your syllogism," Aspasia said.

"Enlighten me!" said the teacher with wrath.

"Solon was a great and wise man," said Aspasia. "He desired to establish a republic, but Athens has declined into a democracy. Therein is a great tragedy in government. But no matter. When Solon declared that all men should be free, and free from inquisitive and interfering government, he did not divide mankind into those born free and those who were born slave. Again, he demanded that slavery be abolished, so he did not consider a slave a mere thing, but a man."

The teacher had then ignored this chit, had drawn another breath and continued with his history lesson.

"Certainly the Spartans—whom I usually deplore for their austerity—were the most disciplined and were a community of soldiers and lived only for war, but they were nothing to the armies and navies of Xerxes. As for us Athenians," and he smiled fondly, "we are volatile and pride ourselves on our wit and our energy and our love for beauty, and we practice roguery in the market place, and it is alleged we cannot be trusted by our fellow Greeks. But less can be said of the men of Thebes, whom everyone agrees are uncivilized.

"The towns and the villages were in panic, and sent as few as possible of fighting men to confront the enemy in various places, keeping most of their warriors at home to defend their wives and children and the gritty walls of their habitations, and their scabrous domestic animals. But the armies of Xerxes were as locusts, Arabs, Cabalians and Milyans, Tibareni, Colchians with carved wooden helmets, Medes with their thin dark faces and their reputation as valorous soldiers, Negroes in the skins of animals, Pisidians, Moschians, Saspires, Thracians—and rivers of horses and oxen and glittering war chariots. Ninety thousand archers and spearsmen alone, not to mention swordsmen with leather shields and Persians, themselves, who are famous for ferocity, and mercenary Cissians, Assyrians, Scythians in felt trousers and barbaric Caspians in high-heeled boots and vari-colored clothing —all these poured onto the burning plains of Greece and the scintillating dust rolled over them in clouds that caught the igniting sun. They also engaged the Greeks in the incandescent waters.

"At Thermopylae the Persian forces confronted but seven thousand Greeks, poorly armed except with courage even in the face of their own cynicism and fear, and prepared to die to defend the pass. It was said that Xerxes, himself, pitied them and admired them.

"His spies had told him that that wretched and quarrelsome army of Spartans, Thebans and some Athenians was being led by Leonidas of Sparta, a fierce captain and a man of fiercer independence. I may note here, as an Athenian, that the Spartans are as mindless as a hill of ants, as well as great warriors—"

"It would follow," Aspasia interrupted.

The teacher's face swelled with angry blood. He raised his voice and went on: "How such a society, alien to us free Greeks, could have bred a man like Leonidas is a mystery, and was a mystery to Xerxes also. He was a surly man, but intelligent, unlike his fellow Spartans who are only cruel and valiant. However. The earth at Thermopylae rumbled like a drum and the thunder of the gods under the feet of Xerxes' armored men of many nations, including his Company of the Immortals, his personal and finest troops. And the Greeks met them in the narrow pass and held them immobile until they were betrayed by one of their own, who had led the Persians behind the pass. Xerxes killed the heroic Spartans to a man and advanced on Athens and burned her to the ground."

"A man is always betrayed by his own kindred and by those he loves the most," said Aspasia.

"Hah!" cried the teacher, moved to fresh anger. "You, who

54

are of such a great and venerable age, how do you know this?"

Aspasia answered with her exasperating demureness, "You have taught us history, Aeneas."

"Hah," he said, but in a milder voice. "We will continue. The Spartans and the barefoot Thebans, with a number of Athenians, men of no importance, defeated the irresistible Xerxes at Mycale, and, greatest of all, at Salamis and later at Platea. How was it possible? At the last they had, these brave men, only their naked hands and bleeding feet and teeth and nails, when their thin spears and iron swords and weak little ships had splintered and disintegrated. What great secret heart had moved them to fight thus, and made them larger than the average man, if only for a few hours? What had inspired envious little souls and quarrelsome little minds and had given them divinity and incredible courage?"

"They were fighting for their lives," said Aspasia. "They had nothing to lose but their lives."

"You deny heroism, and the ability of men to fight for something greater than themselves?" cried the teacher, goaded beyond endurance.

"I do deny that men will fight for something greater than their own selves," said Aspasia. "It is against human nature."

"You do not believe in personal nobility?"

"I have not observed it."

"You are a cynic, my child, and I pity you."

"I am a student of mankind. A man fights to protect himself and his own cherished rights, and if he fights for anything else he is either a madman or a god."

The teacher let a portentous silence fall while he regarded Aspasia with hooded eyes. "You equate madness with the gods?" he asked in an ominously soft voice, he who had often hinted he did not believe in the gods.

Aspasia saw the dangerous trap. "Madness, it is often said, is akin to divinity. You have told us that yourself, Aeneas. 'The divine madness.' "

"I was referring to poetry, and to the divine madness of a man who will fight for something nobler than himself, and the divine madness of artists. War is an art, also, as we Greeks have always said, though you Ionians are slow to discern it."

"We once allied ourselves with Sparta," said Aspasia, "which, I agree, was a madness to itself."

Today, to the maidens' fatigue, Aeneas continued his quarrel with Aspasia over the difference between a republic and a

democracy. He asserted they were the same, as he had asserted before. But Aspasia said, "Solon desired a free republic.
But though the Greeks honor that desire they are only a democracy, and so dangerous. Unfortunately, though Solon
conceived the permanent base for a republic he did not frame
the establishment of such. So, the rule of Athens fell into the
hands of the Tyrants, who introduced democracy. The Athenians are too volatile and too active in insignificant affairs and
too full of laughter and change, and too excitable, to extend
Solon's dream of a republic."

Aeneas said, "As you are so wise, my pupil, define the difference between a democracy, which is Athens, and a republic."

Aspasia said with patience, "I have done so before, my
teacher. But I will do it again. A republic, as Solon has said
over a century ago, is government by written and permanent
law, instead of government by incalculable and changeable
decrees, which is democracy. A republic, he has said, is
when the people obey the rulers and the rulers obey the laws.
But in a democracy the rulers obey the mass, which is whimsi-
cal, violent and greedy. Hence chaos and finally the tyrant."

The wrangle continued. In Aeneas' opinion the voice of the
people was the voice of the gods, hence democracy. He now
fell into the trap. A republic did indeed represent the people,
but it believed too firmly in law, and did not take into thought
the changing desires of those it governed. To which Aspasia
replied, "Is law then—established just law which assures the
people of a stable government and the respect of government
for law—to become the light plaything, like a ball, in the
name of Demos? Is it to be interpreted by whim by the self-
serving and the naturally lawless and exigent, and by those
who are ruled by their bellies and not by their minds, and
have no respect for orderly government?"

"You have but contempt for the people, Aspasia."

"I only observe, Aeneas."

Few of the maidens understood the controversy, but all
were pleased by Aspasia's composure and Aeneas' wild anger.
It relieved the monotony of dull lectures.

It was now sunset and the class was dismissed. The western
sky was a vivid and burning gold, seething with light, and the
sea and the land below it lay in mute purple and shifting shadows. The leaves of the myrtle were plated with gilt, and the
cypresses stood pointing in blackness against the sky and the
palms were tremulous in the soft evening wind. From the
earth there rose a passionate scent of jasmine and roses and

cooling stone and water, and the fountains threw up frail arms touched with gold and lilac.

Wandering in the garden before the evening meal Aspasia came on Cleo, who was sitting by a pool trembling with golden reflections. The young girl wore a short tunic the color of silver and her black hair was rolled on her nape. She looked at Aspasia shyly, and rose. Aspasia gazed at the pool in which iridescent fish swam idly, and then at Cleo.

"Tell me," she said, "what is your heart's desire, Cleo?"

The girl looked at her with wide eyes. Then she tittered. "I should like to be a hetaira like you, Lady."

"I have heard that you will be. Will that satisfy you?"

The girl was bewildered. "But it is the most desirable of all things, Lady."

Aspasia sighed. She, herself, was a fool to expect anything but this reply, for Cleo knew nothing. Why am I always looking for intelligence in mankind, in which it rarely exists? she said to herself.

She was conscious, as she increasingly was, these days, of a restlessness of spirit and a strong rising of something she could not as yet name. There was a loneliness in her, she who had never been lonely before, a longing without a form, an itch, a heat which was both profoundly physical and as profoundly spiritual.

She stood watching the sunset and the wind lifted her hair and when it fell upon her shoulders it was like an embrace, and she sighed. Her yearning grew until it was like a vast hunger in her, but for what she yearned she did not as yet know. She was soon to be enlightened, and disastrously.

CHAPTER 5

The athletic tutor for the maidens suddenly died and Thargelia went to the slave market for a suitable replacement. She came upon a male slave of remarkable beauty, all red pouting lips and smiles and mirthful blue eyes. He also had a mass of auburn curls and muscles beyond description and the body of a young god. He was as sleek as oil and as burnished as bronze and had engaging manners and a felicity of tongue and a gleeful and gladsome countenance.

What a treasure, thought Thargelia, with a warmth in her loins she had not experienced for a long time. She had tired, in this past year, of Echion and other of her mature lovers, who appeared to be suffering the fatigue of their middle years, while she, herself, was never fatigued by love. Sometimes they

57

fell asleep in her arms, leaving her sleepless and distraught, and without satisfaction.

However, she was a prudent woman and inquired why such a morsel of perfection was offered for sale, even though the price was high. The answer was that his master had discovered that Thalias was overly interested in the young sons of the household and so desired to sell him. Thargelia wondered why the master had not availed himself of such implied pleasures, then dismissed the thought. Would it not be possible for such a seductress as herself to educate him in the arts of normal affections? In any event, Thalias would be a safe athletic teacher for her guarded maidens.

What Thargelia did not know was that the report on Thalias was untrue. The young slave had availed himself of the charms of both the master's wife and his daughters, who had wept when he was taken away. He had also seduced all the women slaves, who wailed for days on his departure. Three were already pregnant. Thalias was a man of prowess, who was tirelessly erotic and potent. The master had thought of having him castrated, but his natural masculine nature revolted at this, fortunately for Thalias. As a castrated male Thalias would have no value except in an Oriental bazaar, and among effetes, and he was too valuable for this. So the master arranged for his sale—at a very high price—and discreetly kept the slave's proclivities to himself. Let the buyer beware.

Thargelia studied his athletic young body thoughtfully, both as the mistress of the courtesans and as a woman. She took him aside and questioned him. Her maidens must not develop muscles, for muscles on a woman were disgusting to men of discrimination. The athletics must be limited and intended only to round and firm a young female body. Thalias listened to this acutely, and his pretty eyes began to shine at the prospect, and being intelligent he held his tongue though his mouth watered. A veritable bower of beauties! He hoped they were also judicious. He told Thargelia fervently that he knew exactly what she desired, and Thargelia wryly remarked to herself that she anticipated that she could give him other desires, for herself. After all, she was most expert and had often turned the lovers of men into the lovers of women. She looked at his throat, like a brass tower, and at the muscles of his chest and his arms, and licked her lips. However, being cautious, she required that she examine him without his loincloth, to be certain that she would not be cheated. The inspection was all she could have desired. Thalias watched this inspection and understood perfectly. He would happily oblige

58

the lady, then go on to more luscious conquests. He was naturally of a cheerful nature, and accommodating, and he knew how to please women and make them ecstatic and his slaves. His former mistress had been a splendid teacher, and ardent, and her husband had a hetaira, and she had hungered. What Thalias did not know about women was insignificant.

Thargelia bought him. She bore him home in her own curtained litter and fondled him. He pretended to be modest and retiring but a certain phenomenon elated Thargelia, and she joyously deluded herself that her arts had aroused him as no woman had aroused him before, and that, therefore, after this, he would be her slave in her bed. She took him to bed at once in her house, and he shyly told her that she was the first woman who had made him aware of femininity, and that he doubted that any other could so awaken him. He performed excellently, and Thargelia sighed deeply with rapturous joy and contentment, and had his bed moved to her door. For a woman as astute as Thargelia this was amazing, but her female nature deceived her. She could not have enough of the young man, and her face bloomed and she felt young again and desirable. Thalias also enjoyed himself. When the curtains were drawn and the chamber scented, he hardly saw Thargelia's wrinkles, for she had an exquisite and youthful body and she also knew the arts of love and had peculiar appetites which he satisfied. In the meantime, Thalias surveyed the maidens he taught and enjoyed them in anticipation, particularly Aspasia.

Thargelia was candid with the young ladies, who listened to her with demurely cast-down eyes. Thalias, she said, was not interested in women, so they need not practice their arts upon him, however innocently. She also hinted that he was not quite a man. The girls listened, not believing a single word, for slaves gossiped and they had heard rumors of Thargelia's blissful cries in the night, and her vows of devotion. Moreover, Thalias wore a most complacent expression. It was evident that Thargelia could hardly bear him out of her sight, and would stroke his arm and his cheek even when she was among the maidens, and that her eyes would moisten with remembered exercises. She had gained an air of youth and vitality and sparkle and energy. The maidens noted this, and pondered, and looked at Thalias under their lowered eyelashes.

As for Aspasia, who loved beauty, she found him physically entrancing. His youth appealed to her, who saw no other young men. She studied his body, his face, his chest. She conversed with him briefly at recess during the athletic lessons and the lessons with the bow and the arrow. She thought him intelligent to some extent, but he could not meet her mind and he would stare at subtleties. However, he was a beautiful animal in her opinion, and his touch, when he directed her at the bow, caused a sharp thrill to run along her nerves.

What Thargelia did not know was that despite Aspasia's fondness for her she was in enormous interior conflict, and in furious silent revolt. So Aspasia both loved and hated her mentor, and at times was even afflicted with a wrath for nameless revenge. There was also the fact that her body, usually controlled and contained, was experiencing the pangs of adolescence and desire. Sometimes, at night, she imagined Thalias in her bed and would sweat, both to her disgust and her awakening passion, and her hands would fumble helplessly in the air and touch her body. The violet shadows increased under her eyes and made her more alluring and delectable. Thargelia, not knowing the reason, was elated. Aspasia's virginity would bring a tremendous price. There were Oriental potentates rich beyond imagining who would be infatuated with this wonderful maiden. Thargelia sent out delicate messages to the East. In the meantime Aspasia invoked her patron, Athene Parthenos, for a man of intellect and grace and understanding, and when she did so a coolness and remoteness invaded her body and she was content for a while, dreaming theories and abstractions, and long intellectual dissertations with a man of subtlety and philosophy. But she also thought of Thalias increasingly, for his flesh bedazzled her, to her distraction, and so her thoughts were in conflicting disarray, between corruption and intellect.

The child, Cleo, was accepted into the school of the hetairai, and was given the chamber next to Aspasia's. This was not to Aspasia's liking, for she had discovered that Cleo adored her as well as admired her, and she noticed that the younger girl had begun to copy all her manners and gestures and even the intonations of her voice, imitating a certain way Aspasia had of inclining her head with soft mockery and enlarging her eyes with amusement and touching her lower lip with her thumb. Cleo's big black eyes glimmered with strange lights when she looked at Aspasia. She had a pert appearance, most engaging, and a pouting pink mouth, which trembled when Aspasia spoke to her. She deferred slavishly to Aspasia, who found such sedulous attention irritating. When Cleo would touch her timidly her flesh would shiver, for girls did not attract her, and Cleo was not of notable intelligence in spite of a natural shrewdness. Others, more ruthless than Aspasia, would have taken advantage of this adoration. But Aspasia would have disdained to be so base.

Once Cleo crept behind her as she sat thinking alone in the gardens in the shade of a mass of cypress trees, and Cleo lifted a lock of her hair and kissed it. Revolted, Aspasia rose and struck the girl silently across the cheek and left her. Cleo fell to the ground in a paroxysm of grief and desire and tore up handfuls of the grass and writhed, and wept. Glancing back over her shoulder Aspasia saw this and made a mouth of disgust and aversion, for she was not innocent in her mind. She thought of reporting these things to Thargelia, but she had a strain of compassion in her heart and did not want Cleo sent to the dormitory where such girls were rigorously trained to give pleasure to women. For she had guessed that Cleo was attached to herself alone, and she hoped that the child would recover from this aberration.

When thinking of Thalias, Aspasia would also think of Cleo, but not with the same designs. For some time she shrank at the thought of exploiting the slavish younger girl in her own behalf. But as her desire for Thalias increased, despite efforts to suppress it, she gave Cleo more and more thought. The girl would do anything she would ask of her.

Aspasia knew that she did not love Thalias; it was impossible for her to love where her mind could not rest also. But now she lusted for him with increasing desire. She would gaze at his strong sun-browned arms and her loins would thrill and become hot and tense. She imagined his body on hers and would almost faint at the prospect and she would arch her back and shudder. She remembered that Thargelia had taught that a woman should feel no such response to a man, for then all was lost and she might love him, to her calamity.

One day Aspasia sought out Cleo and smiled at her with all her sensual and bewitching charm. Cleo, surprised at this condescension, was devastated and began to tremble and tears filled her eyes. Aspasia led her aside to the shade of a grove of green myrtle trees, hidden from the others, and she touched Cleo—though her own flesh winced—on the cheek and the throat. Cleo's eyes misted. She gazed at Aspasia as one would gaze humbly at a goddess and could not believe this strange and sudden tenderness from one who had been avoiding her. When Aspasia bent her tall head and kissed her gently on the lips the younger girl swayed, and Aspasia, making a wry mouth to herself and feeling subtly ashamed, caught her and held her against her own body.

She whispered in Cleo's ear. "Some night, my love, when our guardians have left us, you will come to me." Cleo trembled and timidly kissed Aspasia's throat. It was a child's kiss. What if she should permanently debauch Cleo's nature? Aspasia paused in herself and then she thought of Thalias. She conversed in her own mind. Were not all the maidens taught the arts of love, without shame? Let Thargelia bear the consequences.

After their athletic lessons in the afternoon, and their baths in perfumed oils and their massages, the maidens retired to their chambers to sleep, for sleep restored a woman's fatigued body. But before this retirement Aspasia became particularly provocative to Thalias one day, and the young man's thoughts became dizzy and he looked at her with a half-opened mouth and his face swelled and flushed deeply and he shivered. Aspasia smiled with all the arts she had been taught, and her eyes were ravishing. She leaned briefly against his shoulder, and let him see the swell of her young bosom, and she sighed. He closed his eyes and he shivered again, and seeing that they were alone he touched her breast and sweat drenched his countenance and his eyes became doglike both with passion and love. She permitted his hand to wander, and her own body responded with an ardor and a fire she had not even imagined before. Her eyelids drooped, her full red mouth moistened and her breasts swelled. She had an almost uncontrollable desire to draw him down to the green earth below them, but some maidens were approaching, laughing, with a teacher. She feigned to be interested in the adjustment of an arrow, aware of a cooling sweat along her brow. The sun blinded her and she felt that nothing existed but the middle of her palpitating body, which had become heavy, and at once languid and quickening. The imminence of Thalias was maddening, and there was suddenly nothing else in her world but her desire.

She whispered, "Tonight?"

He could not believe it. But he whispered almost inaudibly, "I share the chamber with Thargelia. In this garden then, in that grove of myrtles, under the moon, at midnight? Oh, my adorable one! It is not possible that you love me! Oh, by Castor and Pollux, that I might possess you even once—I would die of the joy! What is Artemis to you, or Aphrodite?"

"Live. Do not die," said Aspasia. The other maidens were chattering like a veritable swarm of swallows. "You are Adonis," she said, and when his hand touched her intimately

62

she felt as if she was bursting into flame and could hardly walk to leave him. Her flesh had grown ponderous and weak, clamoring for surrender and fulfillment.

A little later she drew Cleo apart and said to her, "My love, I am devoted to Artemis, the goddess of the moon, the eternally virgin, and tonight the moon is full and I would worship her in silence in the gardens. I fear I cannot give myself to any man, but be as Artemis, removed from the embraces of men. I must invoke her for her assistance. Therefore, my dear, arrange your bed so any of our guardians, passing in the night with their lanterns, believe you sleep there, then lie in my bed with your head covered so that they do not see the darkness of your hair. Murmur softly, as if restive in the dim light, as I do. Sigh deeply, as I do. They will be deceived. You will do this little service for me, dearest lovely child? Your reward will be commensurate."

Cleo's eyes were as adoring as those of Thalias, and as abject, and Aspasia felt chilled. She would keep her promise and give pleasure to this little one, after her own pleasure, and would restrain her aversion. She had been taught that one pays for everything in this life, and she intended to repay, however repugnant to herself or damaging to Cleo. She said, "Swear by the thunderbolts of Zeus that never will you betray me."

Cleo swore, in her child's light voice, and Aspasia was satisfied. She gently removed Cleo's little hand, which nestled against her breast, and left her. Aspasia had a very lively conscience, but she was learning that when a woman desires a man she has no conscience at all and only awareness of her appetites.

She lay, rigid and trembling and sweating, on her narrow couch in her chamber, to which there was no door—it was only a cubiculum—until the guards had shone the lantern dimly in upon her bed, and she murmured restively as if slightly disturbed. The lantern light retreated down the hall, wavering on white walls, then dying. She smiled to herself. Her window was open, high on the wall, and the moon, pure argent light, flooded over her feet, and there was a passionate scent of jasmine in the warm air and the fragrance of grass and the aromatic odor of pines and cypresses. The fountains sang to the moon and somewhere a nightingale trilled poignantly and an owl answered in dolorous accents. Hot stone exuded its own peculiar arid but exciting scent, and now the roses sent forth their perfume as if touched by the trailing garments of Artemis, herself, with her white hounds at her heels.

The guards would not make their rounds again for an hour, and by that time she would have returned. She waited a little, then silently rose from her bed and went to the chamber of Cleo. The young girl's eyes shimmered in the moonlight, as brilliant as black opals and as variable, and she rose at once and embraced Aspasia, and the older maid felt the heat of the child's body through her shift. She endured the embrace; she kissed the innocent brow, then disentangled herself, murmuring softly and even consolingly. A balmy wind had arisen, and now the sea could be heard, somnambulant and hypnotic, as if heavy eyelids had drooped over the eyes of Poseidon and he slept also.

Aspasia had wrapped herself in a dark cloak. She stole from her chamber, where Cleo now lay with covered hair, and moved like a moth down the hall. At a distance she could see the torches beyond the atrium, thrust into the walls, and the light of a far lamp, which smelled of ambergris. There was no sound at all except for the nightingale and the wind and the owl and the sea and the soft rustling of leaves.

A guard, a man, passed through the atrium, his sword in his hand, and Aspasia shrank against the wall, holding her breath. She waited until the sound of his sandals had died on stone, and then she fled as silently as the wing of a bird through the atrium and out into the night. Her bare feet were immediately wet with dew and she could smell the disturbed scent of grass, and she sped as lightly as Artemis over the warm and glittering earth. The moon stood at the apex of the sky, full and swelling, like an enormous plate of light against the blackness of the heavens. Avoiding all open places Aspasia bent double in the sharp darknesses, hardly breathing, and listening for an alarm or a movement. Her heart was thrumming and her body was trembling. She had covered her bright hair with the hood of her cloak and had dropped it over her face, so that she appeared part of the shadows themselves.

She reached the grove of myrtles, panting softly and quickly. The tops of the trees were blazing with moonlight, and, as the leaves stirred, they gleamed as if plated with shining and restless silver and their voices were as the movement of gentle silk. Beyond the gardens and the grass the sea heaved slowly, a plain of white light nearly motionless. The columns of the house behind Aspasia were lucent as alabaster, splashed by the ruddy light of an occasional torch which shifted over them like the shadow of burning leaves. The torches hissed a little and crackled and the odor of resin mingled with the fragrance of earth and flowers.

She paused in the deep shadow of the myrtles. There was still no sound of anyone abroad this night except herself and the guard. She crept deeper into the shade. She dared not call. Had Thalias been detained by his mistress? Had he been unable to slide from her bed? Then Aspasia felt the strong grip of a man's hand on her arm, and she started and almost cried out. Instantly a hot firm mouth was on hers; arms encircled her like arms of iron, and she sank to the grass in the embrace of Thalias and his breath was in her throat and his tongue pierced between her lips.

She was suddenly terrified of the unknown, though her flesh was singing a fierce and joyous song it had never sung before, like all the drums and the lutes in the whole universe, sweeter than life itself and as overwhelming, and strange and a little terrible. Feebly she tried to thrust Thalias from her, but he held her with one hard muscular arm and with his other hand he lifted her shift and then his lips were on her virgin breast and a rapturous languor overcame her and she lay still.

The crushed grass exhaled; the nightingale sang more poignantly, the plangent fountains splashed and then became the confused roar of a cataract, spilling fragrances, and the whispering myrtles, dancing with light, were a chamber of pleasure. There was the stammering moan of love in one of Aspasia's ears, the rising gasp of a man's passion, and she could not move, weighted down by a man's body upon hers, aware of the crispness of a man's hair against her cheek and the inexorable and rigid thrust between her soft thighs. The night swooned in its own melody.

Once there was the quick cry of a startled girl, swiftly silenced by demanding lips, and the ground appeared to rise and fall like the sea itself under Aspasia's body, moved to ecstasy, a fainting ecstasy which momentarily darkened the girl's consciousness. She felt herself not only in her own flesh but part of the flesh of the whole world, writhing in almost intolerable bliss. She felt that she was penetrating all secrets and that nothing she had learned before was of consequence, and she gave herself up to joy, incoherently murmurous, and weeping in the embrace which was both mutual and hotly entangled.

Somewhere there was a man's moan, a rapid groaning growing more tumultuous, and a savage and triumphant delight seized Aspasia, the delight of the conquered and yet the conqueror, and suddenly all was fire and shuddering transports beyond description.

CHAPTER 6

When Aspasia crept into the house she remembered her erotic promise to Cleo. Her flesh was still throbbing and her heart shaking and the thought of Cleo sickened her. Resolutely, however, she ran silently down the hall to her chamber, and, to her joy, she discovered that the child was sleeping heavily, her hand under her cheek. But she was in Aspasia's bed, and Aspasia paused, thinking. Finally she went to Cleo's chamber and lay down on the bed. Exhausted with delight, she fell instantly asleep, but not before covering her hair.

Before dawn she awakened, and went to her chamber and aroused Cleo. She whispered, "Do not speak. You have slept the night through, my dear one, and must return to your own chamber at once, for soon we will be called to arise."

Cleo's eyes filled with disappointed tears, and Aspasia suffered her embraces and caresses for a brief moment, then again whispering a warning she removed the girl's arms and forced her gently to leave, nodding promises for the future. She had hardly composed herself in her own bed when the guardians arrived to wake the maidens to another day.

She was in her mathematics class when she received a summons from Thargelia. This was most unusual, and the girl paled with apprehension. Following the slave, she came to Thargelia's chamber, to find the mistress of the hetairai in a cold rage. Never had she worn such a countenance before, pallid and tightened, her eyes glinting, and Aspasia thought, All is lost. I have been discovered. But, at Thargelia's silent gesture, she seated herself and folded her hands on her knee. If Thargelia had not been in such anger she would have been curious as to the reason for Aspasia's whiteness and the fear in her eyes.

The mistress said abruptly, "Did aught disturb you in the night, Aspasia?"

She is tormenting me, the girl said to herself. She wet her lips and mutely shook her head. While Thargelia stared at her implacably she prepared to speak and finally could do so. "I sleep very well, Thargelia. Little awakens me."

Thargelia played with her jeweled necklace and continued to stare at the girl. She said, "You are not one to betray a companion. I have discerned that before. But this is very serious. Did you not hear any furtive footsteps in the night or see a passing figure?"

Aspasia returned her stare and some of the fear left her. "Nothing. I saw and heard nothing."

"You saw none of your companions in the hall?"

"None. I slept through the night."

Thargelia did not remove her hard gaze. "One of the guardians looked into the chamber of Cleo, and discovered her absence. Very quietly, so as not to alarm others, the guardians searched the house, including the latrines. Cleo was not to be found. The guards outside and in the portico had seen no one. But one of some superstition swore that he had glimpsed a maiden in the moonlight, but when he pursued she vanished, and he is of the opinion that he had seen a nymph. He could not discern her features, but he swears that her face reflected the moon, and now he is convinced that he saw Artemis, herself." At this Thargelia's mouth writhed in scorn and fresh fury.

'Oh, gods,' thought Aspasia with new fear. Cleo! If she kept silent she would suffer terrible punishment, and be sent to work in the meanest of occupations. She was only a child, and therefore, in dread of such punishment she doubtless would tell the truth. Both probabilities were equally appalling. Aspasia said, in a shaking voice, "I have remembered something. Cleo, who is still a thoughtless child, came into my bed, whispering she had had a nightmare, and she was afraid. She remained for a while with me, while I comforted her."

Thargelia considered, while Aspasia gazed at her with strained eyes. Thargelia then said, "You are a poor liar, Aspasia, and it is possible you have never lied before. Why should you protect such as Cleo? I have seen no affection in you for the girl, and that you have avoided her. Yet you admitted her to your bed! A child, you say. She is but two years younger than yourself, and you are nubile. I will question her."

"She is about to pose again for Tmolus, Thargelia. It would not be well to interrupt his class."

Seeing that Thargelia was still studying her with reflection Aspasia continued: "Perhaps Cleo was restless, and the moon is full. Perhaps she was heated in the night—after she left me—and roamed in the gardens, as a child roams who cannot sleep."

Thargelia said, "Have you discerned any predilection on her part for any particular young male slave?"

"We have few here, and most are younger even than Cleo, and the others are of no great beauty and work in the gardens all day. No, Cleo has not looked at them with any attention."

She had a thought and then said boldly, "Why do you not have Echion examine her to confirm, or deny, her virginity?"

Thargelia pursed her lips. "That is an excellent suggestion. However, I mistrust Echion. He might destroy her virginity, himself, with his ruthless fingers, if not worse."

"Then, Thargelia, you must watch him, yourself."

Thargelia played with her necklace. "That, too, is a good suggestion. I will have that done. Echion is in the city and will return tomorrow morning. In the meantime, do not alarm Cleo, Aspasia. She might run away."

She dismissed Aspasia. Aspasia did not return to her class, for she was too overwhelmed by this calamity. Instead, she went to her small chamber. She sat on her bed in the silent dormitory and began to think with despair. The situation called for extreme decision. She could not let Cleo suffer for her own wantonness. Even if she, herself, confessed—and she trembled at the thought—Cleo would also be punished for her part in the escapade. Enough. There must be instant action.

She now considered Thalias for the first time. Discovery would entail the most drastic punishment a slave can receive: castration. She did not love him, but he had become her victim. She no longer remembered her ecstasies in his arms, and only determined that he must not suffer for her own abandon. She knelt by her bed and pulled out her small bronze chest of treasures from beneath it. The last gift of her dead young mother was still here, a purse of gold coins. She weighed it in her hand. It was very heavy.

Now she must seek out Thalias, who, before he was called to teach the maidens, spent his time gossiping with the other slaves in the kitchens. There was no one she could trust to send for him. But she must face the danger. She left her bedroom and wandered out to the gardens and to the spot where the maidens practiced archery under Thalias' direction. She found her bow and quiver and with apparent desultoriness shot at the target, and then expostulated aloud as if overcome with her own lack of skill. The gardeners covertly watched her and admired her beauty and the posture of her young body. Seeing this, she threw down her bow with exasperation, turned, tossed back her hair, and appeared to think. She let her eyes wander to an old gardener nearby, and she summoned him imperatively. He came at once.

She said, "I am about to engage in a competition with other of the maidens, and I am a poor archer, and this shames me.

Summon Thalias—that lazy and ever hungry slave—from the kitchen. He must help me at once."

The gardener bowed and touched his breast. He was stupid as well as old and Aspasia had chosen him well. She picked up her bow again, and though she was usually accurate and skillful she pretended that her missings of the target were in spite of her efforts. She sank on the grass dolefully, shaking her head, and fretfully pulling at the grass.

Thalias was suddenly at her elbow, his eyes ardent with memories. After furtively glancing at him she put her finger to her lips and he was immediately still. She rose and said loudly, "You must help me! I am worse today, with the bow, than ever before."

As he was moderately intelligent he became tense and acutely aware, and his browned cheeks paled. It was not approved that a maiden should see an instructor alone, and so he was aware that he was in danger. He helped Aspasia to her feet and whispered in her ear, as he bent to brush her clothing free of grass, "What is it, my adored one?"

"Silence," she said. She took the bow from his hand and fitted an arrow in it. "Become an actor," she murmured. "You are bored by my lack of dexterity. You will put your hand on mine as I draw the bow. You will lean against me from behind. You will reproach me loudly. Now."

The gardeners watched with amusement as the proud young hetaira was reproached by the slave, Thalias, for her clumsiness. They saw his vexation, for Thalias was by nature an actor. He was insulting, even to this most cherished one. None but Aspasia saw his paleness and his trembling hands nor saw the fright in his eyes. She no longer desired him. She only knew that he must be saved. She pushed the purse of gold into his hand, and immediately he dropped it into the pouch at his girdle without even an exclamation.

She whispered, "Do not ask me any questions. But you must flee at once. Do not wait for the night, when the guards are most attentive and pursue even shadows. Stroll down the road idly. They will not suspect, for are you not the pampered darling of Thargelia? I can only tell you that you are in the most desperate danger, and must not delay even another hour. You have much gold. Go to the harbor and take the first ship leaving the port, no matter its destination. You have not been branded as a slave, and gold answers all questions. Be at ease and haughty. In the city purchase a chest and fill it with garments, and induce a beggar to carry it for you to the vessel. It will be thought he is your slave."

His face was contorted with terror. She pushed his arm. "Array yourself in your finest tunic and sandals, and a cloak. Go at once. There is not a moment to be lost."

"We have been discovered," he said through his dry lips.

"Yes," she said with wild impatience.

Then he said, "But what of you, my sweet nymph?"

In spite of the extremity of her own fear she was touched, and she gazed at him. "Naught will be inflicted on me if you have fled," she answered.

With an oath he took the bow from her hands and threw it on the ground and the gardeners were more amused. He walked from her as if deeply outraged, muttering to himself. Aspasia looked after him with an air of anger and mortification. Then she stamped her foot and ran back into the house, shaking her hair off her neck and shoulders. It was a cloud of gold in the sunlight.

She returned to her chamber and again sank on her bed. She covered her face with her hands. She did not believe in the gods but she prayed to Aphrodite for Thalias' and Cleo's preservation. She had seduced both. They must not suffer for her. Cleo was in less danger now, and would be subjected only to Echion's rough examinations, which would reveal her virginity. Aspasia sighed out of the extremity of her emotions.

Later, after she had forced herself to attend her classes, she went to the gardens to join the other maidens who were chattering with excitement. Thalias had not appeared. One of the girls wished to run for the overseer of the hall to inform him. Aspasia, knowing that every moment was precious, said with contempt, "He is a mighty eater and drinker. No doubt he is lying in his chamber, drunk."

"Or in Thargelia's arms," one of the girls said, slyly.

The others tittered. "Then, of a surety, we must not disturb him," said Aspasia. "Come, let us practice our archery."

She had authority, and the girls obeyed her. Cleo was among them, with her innocent child's face. Seeing her, Aspasia was newly distressed. Nothing must hurt this little one.

The overseer of the hall, wandering out to the portico to watch the delectable sight of the young hetairai romping, noticed the absence of Thalias. He came to the maidens and asked, "Where is that rascal of a Thalias?"

"Thalias?" Aspasia asked, as if in wonder. "Was he not here a moment ago?"

To her dismay one of the maidens answered, "He has not been here at all."

"Then he is with Thargelia," said Aspasia. "Come. Let us toss and catch the ball."

The overseer became enchanted by all this young grace and the joyous laughter of the girls. He watched for a long time. He caught glimpses of their round young legs as they ran and as their long tunics lifted, and he saw delightful young bosoms heaving. He was certain that not even in Arcadia were the nymphs so beauteous and so perfect in face and form. He kept licking his lips as he watched. Then he remembered that Thalias had never been absent before. He went back to the house and Aspasia saw him go with anxiety.

When the maidens returned to the house they found everything in confusion. Slaves excitedly ran everywhere, and the house was filled with vehement babbling. Thargelia stood with the overseer of the hall in the atrium. Discerning Aspasia, her favorite, she exclaimed, "Have you seen Thalias?"

Aspasia halted and seemed to think, frowning. "But an hour ago," she said. The other maidens raised a chorus of fluting voices and declared he had not been seen at all today.

"Where did you see him, Aspasia?" asked the mistress, and Aspasia knew she had made a foolish mistake. She put her finger to her lips and considered. "It was after history class. He passed us in the hall."

"No!" cried the maidens, shaking their hair.

"Yes," said Aspasia. "He seemed intent on some errand and did not speak."

"I have heard," said Thargelia, "that he gave you a lesson in archery this morning."

"He did. I requested it."

Thargelia's eyes narrowed. "You, who are so proficient with the bow, Aspasia? You desired a lesson alone?"

"I desire to excell in all things. I am yet no Amazon."

Thargelia continued to regard her. "He has not been seen since one of the overseers saw him walking idly along the road to the city."

Aspasia shrugged. "He will return."

"Perhaps," said Thargelia, still watching. "He has no money. He has only jeweled trinkets which I have given him. They are gone." She pursed her lips. "I have sent slaves to the port, but none had seen him there. Nevertheless, he has run away."

"Alas," said Aspasia. "But I do not believe it. Why should he flee?"

"That is the question," said Thargelia in a grim voice. Her eyes went to Cleo, who returned her regard innocently and

71

Thargelia made a gesture of frustration. But she was a clever woman. Her gaze reverted to Aspasia. She bit her lip. The maiden had been very evasive.

Runaway slaves were not usual in Miletus, for all the punishments were dire and often resulted in death. But Thalias had been an indulged slave and the lover of Thargelia, who had adored him, and he had been given many privileges. Thargelia did not appear in the dining hall that night, and the maidens chattered discreetly among themselves, and laughed and winked. They knew that a wide search was being conducted for Thalias, and in the city itself, where officials had been informed. Thalias had been caught up into the air and had disappeared like a cloud of mist. Aspasia, listening, began to feel relieved. A gentleman, with a slave and a chest, richly attired, and arrogant of demeanor, would not be suspected as a fleeing slave. Moreover, Miletus was a busy port and multitudes of passengers boarded the vessels for many destinations.

Thargelia was beside herself. She loved Thalias, and he had been treated, in her house, as a free man, given gifts and tenderness and had dined with Thargelia and had slept in her bed. At no time had he appeared restive. Therefore, thought Thargelia, something extraordinary had occurred. Slaves like Thalias did not flee from delights and pamperings and all that they desired. He had shown his contentment and happiness. He was one who lived for the hour, and all his hours in this house had been filled with pleasure. He had been all laughter and gaiety and had come eagerly to Thargelia's bed. It was not possible that he had been seized by a desire for liberty—not such a man as Thalias! Thargelia was an authority on the ways of humanity, and so she knew that Thalias had not fled for freedom but from fear. Of what had he been afraid? There was but one answer: He had feared discovery.

Suddenly she thought of Aspasia, who had been so indifferent and had hastened to assure Thargelia that Thalias had not fled, and had seemed intent on persuading Thargelia that she had encountered Thalias in the hall. Thargelia felt a deep grief. Aspasia had never attempted to deceive her before. Why had she engaged in deception today?

The answer was terrible and devastating.

Thargelia began to think of what the guardians and the guards had reported of the night before, and she almost wept. Aspasia! Aspasia, who was the bright jewel of this house, loved and protected, with a great destiny—it was not possible. But Thargelia knew that all things were possible in this world.

Later, she discreetly sent a slave to summon Cleo to her. In the meantime she bathed her eyes in water of roses and composed herself. Cleo entered the chamber shyly, looking about her, for she had never been here before. She was awed at the beautiful mosaics on the wall, which seemed to move, so brilliant and precise were they, and at the painted statues in the corners of Hera and Artemis and Athene and Aphrodite. Persian rugs of intricate colors lay on the marble floor and there were many dainty tables of lemonwood and ebony and ivory and gilded chairs covered with cushions. Egyptian lamps of glass and silver and smooth gold hung from the ceiling or stood on the tables. They gave out the odor of roses and lilies and sandalwood. There were also delicate vases of exquisitely wrought glass near the walls, and a parrot in a golden cage hummed a ribald ditty to himself. In a small room beyond stood Thargelia's opulent bed with silken sheets and soft pillows, and woollen coverlets as fine as silk, itself. Everything glowed and sparkled voluptuously. The windows were open to the evening air and wind and through them came the tinkling soliloquies of fountains and the rustling murmur of the sea.

"Come, child," said Thargelia, touched unwillingly at the sight of this little one hardly out of childhood and in appearance as fresh as an almond blossom. The girl approached her timidly and lifted her dark eyes questioningly. All at once Thargelia knew with bitter certainty that Cleo had never left the house the night before. She said, in a voice she tried to make kind, "Cleo, you must answer me in truth or I shall be very displeased with you and my displeasure is not to be despised. Did you sleep well last night?"

Cleo looked at her and then suddenly her face was deeply flushed and Thargelia had a momentary hope that it had been Cleo who had gone to Thalias under the moon and not Aspasia. Cleo was nodding now, unable to speak.

Her hope made Thargelia say almost tenderly, "Do not be afraid. I want the truth. Did you leave this house at any time after you retired for the night?"

The girl shook her head with quick denial, and Thargelia knew that she was not lying and her own heart was again filled with grief, and also with formidable anger.

"I have heard from the guardians that your bed was empty at midnight, and that a maiden was seen in the gardens." She looked at Cleo and now her eyes had changed and had become relentless. Her hands clenched on her embroidered knees. "Was it you?"

Cleo uttered a faint dying cry and then dropped on her knees before the mistress of the courtesans, and she beat her

73

forehead on the floor in abject terror. Her black hair fell over her shoulders and covered her back. She wore the simple tunic of the hetairai with a girdle of ribbons, and the garment flowed over her child's body and every frail bone was outlined. Thargelia was rarely moved to pity, but now she pitied Cleo. However, she touched the girl as if spurning her with her foot. She repeated, "Was it you? Ah, you shake your hidden head. Where were you last night, Cleo?"

The girl whispered, "In Aspasia's bed."

Thargelia breathed deeply, and hope lived with her again. Was it possible that Aspasia had not deceived her after all and had told her the truth?

"Why?" she asked of Cleo. She had a disgusting thought concerning Aspasia and Cleo, then rejected it. She looked down at the trembling child who had begun to weep, her shoulders and back heaving. "Cleo," said Thargelia, "there is nothing reprehensible in that you crept into Aspasia's bed, for consolation or because of an evil dream."

Cleo crouched in stillness for a moment, then she sat up abruptly on her heels, throwing back her hair and her round wet face was bright with sudden relief and her eyes shone with the joy of one who had been delivered out of danger. "Yes, yes, Lady, that is what I did, and Aspasia comforted me!"

Thargelia studied her for a long moment and her experience told her that the child was lying, and she was sick with anger and sorrow. She clapped her hands for a servant and a slave woman moved aside a curtain and entered the chamber. Now a distant sound of lutes and girlish singing could be heard under the moon and in the outdoor portico. "Summon Aspasia to me at once," she said to the slave. The slave bowed and retreated. Thargelia gave her attention to Cleo again. The girl was as white as new bone, even to her lips, and she stared at Thargelia with utter dread between the long lengths of her black hair. She is as one who gazes upon a Gorgon, thought Thargelia, so fixedly does she gaze at me and with so intense a horror and fear. Thargelia could not bear the sight, for she was not a cruel woman. Cleo had been used by Aspasia without regard for the mortal fright Cleo was now enduring. Thargelia looked aside. All was silent in the chamber, except for the raucous parrot and the music and singing in the portico which had invaded the room. Thargelia did not know what emotion was the more overwhelming, her grief or the hot hatred she felt for Aspasia, who had not only deceived her wantonly but had seduced Thalias. She had no doubt that the seduction had taken place, for Aspasia was no soft maiden and Thalias was too cautious to make an overt approach. Now Thargelia hated him also and was filled with humiliation. Had he been in this house she would have ordered him flogged to death, or tortured to the same end. She vowed in her torn heart to find him if it cost her all her fortune. She would post a reward in all of Miletus, and at the port.

The curtain was moved aside and Aspasia entered, her face calm but rigid. She had dressed her hair in the Greek fashion, bound up in ribbons, and Thargelia, looking at her, was conscious, with tremendous fury, of the maiden's extraordinary beauty and youth and grace and regal air. These had seduced Thalias. Thargelia felt old and withered and undone and repulsive, and this increased her wrath. She was like a harpy in the presence of a nymph, a harpy who must buy love and not receive it ardently, and in truth.

Aspasia bowed, and then saw Thargelia's face and the child kneeling on the floor, and her heart clenched with terror. I am undone, she thought. But she was proud. In her stately fashion she approached Thargelia closer and looked down in silence into those eyes raised to hers, and she saw that Thargelia's eyes were vivid with hatred. I am to die, she said to herself. She had never been a slave, but this would not protect her from Thargelia's vengeance, for Thargelia knew too many powerful men in Miletus who were in her debt.

Thargelia saw and savored her favorite's helplessness, and she gloated and even smiled. The smile was hideous. What would this beauty be like after long flogging and torture? She envisioned Aspasia covered with blood, that exquisite body reduced to bleeding tatters, that face obliterated, those wondrous eyes blind with agony and death. She, Thargelia, would be avenged, and by a lift of her hand. She longed for the moments of destruction. She would watch in rapture. She felt no compassion for this maiden who had so humiliated and betrayed her.

Aspasia looked again at Cleo and she was sick with pity and regret. The gorgeous chamber appeared to swim before her eyes in a kaleidoscope of shifting and confusing colors, brightening, waning, fleeing, returning. Cleo gazed up piteously into Aspasia's eyes, imploring help, and then her little hand reached desperately for Aspasia's tunic and clung to it, winding her fingers in it. Contrition seized Aspasia so that her own eyes filled with tears. She would probably die, but nothing must harm this child. The very sight of the childish body, the faith in the round face, the small feet peering from beneath her tunic, the abjectness of her posture, moved Aspasia enormously. She said, as softly as a mother speaks to her little one, "Speak, Cleo. Tell the Lady Thargelia what transpired last night."

Cleo hesitated and Aspasia could not bear the sight of her countenance, for she saw that Cleo was not only afraid for herself but for her friend. "Speak," she repeated, "and all will be well."

Reassured, but not looking away from the one she adored, Cleo spoke in a half whisper. "You said, Aspasia, that you wished to worship Artemis under the moon. So you requested me to lie in your bed, with my dark hair covered, and arrange my bed clothes so it would seem I lay in my own. You then left me, and I fell asleep. You awakened me before dawn and I returned to my bed."

Ah, the sweet one is prudent even at her age, thought Aspasia. She will not repeat my promises of vileness to her. She placed her hand on Cleo's bent head and looked at Thargelia. "That is all," she said. "The girl is innocent of any wrong. If wrong there had been it was my doing, and my indiscretion. But I desired to look upon the moon. I was restless."

"You are often restless, Aspasia," said Thargelia, and laughed aloud in derision. Then she paused and regarded the girl with renewed love and hatred. Her intuition told her that she had heard the truth, and also lies. She looked down at Cleo, kneeling before her and weeping and she said, "You may leave us, child. I am no longer angry with you, for you have been victim and not transgressor. Go to your bed."

Cleo stood up slowly, wiping her tears with the palms of her hands, like an infant. Her lips quivered. She looked at Thargelia and then at Aspasia, and Aspasia smiled with reassurance, bent and kissed the girl then pushed her towards the curtain. Cleo fled, scampering, her feet slapping on rug and marble.

"Are you not ashamed," said Thargelia, "that you corrupted that child?"

"I did not corrupt her," Aspasia replied. "She told you the truth. As I have told you the truth."

"All of the truth, Aspasia?"

Though it did not seem possible that Aspasia could pale more she did so. She could only say, "Cleo and I have told you the truth."

"You lie," said Thargelia, calmly. "What of Thalias? You met him in the moonlight and for a purpose that I know. Do you deny this?"

Aspasia shut her eyes for a moment. Before she could speak Thargelia said, "He left me at midnight. He thought I slept. He did not return for some time. I believed he had gone to the latrines, or had strolled in the gardens, for the night was hot and the moon high." This was not true, but Thargelia was determined to know the whole of her mortification.

"You seduced my slave, Aspasia," said Thargelia. "He is young, and foolish, and you have been taught arts. Because of your infamy he will die, and painfully, and I will force you to be present to see what you have done."

Aspasia could not control herself. "He has been found?" she cried in a loud voice.

Thargelia did not answer for a moment, and then she said, "Yes. He attempted to board a vessel in the harbor, and was taken into custody. I heard but a short time ago. He will be delivered to this house in the morning. Prepare yourself for an interesting spectacle, Aspasia. Thalias is strong, but he will shriek for mercy and death. I can assure you of that, though he is a man."

Aspasia was young and so still possessed considerable credulity. Moreover, Thargelia had never lied to her before. She looked about her wildly, as if seeking succor. She was filled with despair. Then she sank to her knees before Thargelia and clasped her hands convulsively. Her beautiful white face was lifted and twinkled with sweat.

"Spare him," she said. "I alone am guilty. I seduced him because the heat of my desire was too much for me and had to be relieved. Any man would have sufficed. As you have said of Cleo, he, too, was my victim. You have taught us that men are seized with irrepressible passions which they cannot control, and that any woman to them then is desirable. I have also been taught the arts of seduction, and he is not experienced as I am, and not intelligent. It was a moment's madness to him, only. He is not guilty. He is only a man."

Thargelia's face twisted until it was extremely ugly, and the cosmetics on her face increased her wrinkles. Her dyed golden hair was a travesty. She saw her beloved Thalias in those round white arms; she saw him kissing that adorable breast. She saw him enter that body, and could hear his gaspings. They would be more delirious than in her own bed, for he had been embracing youth and divine loveliness. All that the girl was had been tended since her birth, and she had had a glorious destiny, which was now lost. Pain seized Thargelia then, pain for herself, pain for Thalias and even pain for this wanton, Aspasia, whom she had loved like an only daughter, and whose prospects had been destroyed. Thargelia rarely had wept in all her life but now she was taken with a desperate desire to weep. She controlled herself.

"How did Thalias flee?" she asked.

"I gave him the last of my mother's money." Then courage returned to Aspasia. "I told him to flee. I am not sorry, except that he will suffer for it. I wish he had escaped to safety! I should have that to remember with joy."

"Do not mourn," said Thargelia, with answering passion and fresh mortification. "He has not been taken, as yet. When he is I will send him only to the fields, for his punishment, in chains so that he cannot run again. Does that comfort you?"

Aspasia stood up and for the first time she regarded the mistress with loathing. "Then you have lied to me," she said. "And I trusted you."

Thargelia mocked her. " 'Then you have lied to me, and I trusted you.' Go to your bed, Aspasia. I will consider your fate tonight. I assure you it will not be a happy one. I may send you into the kitchens or the fields. I may have you flogged to death, or your beauty destroyed forever. You will know in the morning."

Aspasia knew that she had nothing to lose now. "I am not a slave," she said. "I was born free and am free. You can do nothing unlawful against a free woman, no matter your wrath. In the eyes of the laws of Miletus I have done little wrong, nothing to merit extreme punishment."

Thargelia had risen in dismissal of the maiden. Now she stopped and looked at the girl with contempt. "Do you think the law in Miletus will be concerned with the fate I mete out to a mere chit in my care, who has induced a slave to flee—a capital crime in itself? Ponder on that, insolent one."

"Let me go, tonight," said Aspasia. "We will see each other no more."

"Where will you go, you fool? On foot, with only the peplos on your body, and no money? Or would you sell yourself into slavery, which is all you deserve? Or become a public whore?"

"I know not what I shall do," said Aspasia, with the bursting wildness and recklessness of youth. "It is enough for me to go. I have long been rebellious of the fate you have designed for me. At least I will escape that, and with joy."

Thargelia considered. She said, "The fate you so despise was a fate of power and wealth and comfort and adoration and cosseting, the mistress of a selected and distinguished man. You would prefer the streets of Miletus and its noisome alleys and squalid dwellings, and the encounters with brutes of the ports and the slaughterhouses and the manufactories and the sea—for a handful of drachmas or a little bread and wine?"

Aspasia could not speak for a moment. Then she said, "I would be free to make my own fate, to live or to die."

"You speak like one born an imbecile," said Thargelia. "Go to your chamber. You have not interested me. I may set you, penniless and without even a cloak, on the streets of Miletus tomorrow. There you may use the arts you have been taught for a crust of bread."

"I may go to my father, for my mother told me his name," said Aspasia, who was quaking with an internal coldness. "For pity's sake, he may harbor me."

Thargelia laughed long and scornfully, throwing back her head so that the cords in her throat were prominent and ugly in the lamplight. "Audacious fool!" she cried. "He wished to destroy you, for you were female, and your mother saved you! You have known this. He would deny he is your father, for what man likes to confess that he has begotten a girl? He would do this—if he were alive."

"He is dead?" said Aspasia, her voice shaking.

"Go to. You never knew him. Certainly he is dead. He died but four months ago, of a fever. But you need not believe me. You will discover this tomorrow, perhaps, when I put you on the streets of Miletus."

She made an imperious gesture of dismissal, and Aspasia, still holding high her incomparable head, retired. Thargelia threw herself upon the bed and gave herself up to weeping, for her own anguish, for Thalias and Aspasia.

CHAPTER 7

In spite of the thick black kohl Thargelia's eyes were swollen and red in the morning, when she consulted Echion, who had listened with deep interest to the story she had told him. His mouth watered and he had to keep swallowing and his eyes had glistened. He wanted to say to Thargelia, "Give me the maiden, as a servant in my small house, or the tender of my garden, or my cook." But discretion warned him. So he shrugged.

He said, "Having lost her virginity she is now worthless."

Thargelia thought. She said, "We know the arts of deception so that even a wanton can simulate virginity."

"With the aid of a chicken's blood," laughed Echion, "and some clever simulations and cries of pain."

"It is true that men are fools and believe what they wish to believe," said Thargelia. "They always believe women, which is not perspicacious of them. They think women are too stupid to deceive effectually."

"Ah," said Echion, with an arch look.

He added, "The maiden is young and helpless. You can do with her what you will."

Being a cynic, he did not know that Thargelia had spent the night in pain pondering this very matter and that she had been desperately seeking for a way not to destroy Aspasia, but to save her. But it must be done with expedition. She could not remain in this house, under Thargelia's eye, to be a reminder of betrayal and shame. So this morning she had sent a slave to discover what foreign men of distinction had come from the vessels on affairs in Miletus, or on their way to Greece. The slave had not as yet returned.

"There is a possibility that she is still a virgin," said Echion, as if seriously considering. "After all, it is not easy to violate a virgin, and the man was a slave and may have been frightened, or, at the last, she may have struggled. Let me examine her in discreet privacy."

Thargelia narrowed her eyes at him. "I am certain she is no longer a virgin. I am experienced in these things." She laughed abruptly. "If Aspasia were still virgin she would not be after leaving you, Echion. Let us understand each other." They laughed together.

There had been many Greek and Ionian men who had been allowed to glimpse Aspasia in this house, without her knowledge. They also trusted Thargelia. To give them a violated hetaira, when they desired only a virgin, would be reprehensible and dangerous. (Many had ardently desired Aspasia and had offered Thargelia the most enormous sums, but she had been too loath, like a mother, to part with the girl as yet, and Aspasia had not completed her schooling.) Worst of all, Aspasia had been deflowered by a mean slave, a thing, and that was unpardonable.

Thargelia gave orders that Aspasia was to be enlightened in the art of simulating virginity, and at once and with all dispatch. Even foreign men, men from the East, were entitled to a kind deception, for they were notable for riches and extolled virginity in women more even than did the Ionians and the Greeks.

Aspasia at first resisted the information and the instructions. Then, as she was not a fool, she acceded. She was still pale and listless and full of pain for herself, and even for Thargelia, who had been as a mother to her. To her joy, however, she was permitted to resume her classes, for Thargelia wanted no scandal in her house, and Aspasia saw that little Cleo was not to be punished in any manner. For that Aspasia was deeply grateful, and she loved Thargelia again, if with reluctance and resentment. She, herself, was not to be punished severely, it would seem, though she understood that she could not long remain in this house, her home, suddenly dear to her. She wondered about her fate, and shrank from the unknown.

Thalias had not been caught, and again Aspasia was overjoyed. He was a rascal and would contrive to exist. She had no doubt of that. He knew the ways of the world, and was dexterous in many fashions. Aspasia envied him and again thought of the cruel restrictions on women which made them dependent on the whims of men. They had no status except as virtuous matrons or whores and to Aspasia each was undesirable. She said to herself, We have no position except as slaves, and she was angrily rebellious again and in revolt.

The slave Thargelia had sent to the port returned in a state of excitement. A Persian gentleman, accompanied by a rich retinue, had arrived that morning, and was now the guest of a famous man in Miletus, one Cadmus, who had long desired Aspasia. Thargelia was both elated and troubled. She could not offend Cadmus, but the Persian gentleman, Al Taliph, must be engaged. It was reputed that he was a familiar of Xerxes, himself, and enormously wealthy, so Aspasia would bring a great price. Cadmus, though rich, could not meet the price, as he had discovered to his regret a few months ago. Thargelia did not love the Persians, but a satrap like Al Taliph could be endured, and it was stupid to remember the Persian assaults on Greece. Xerxes, she thought, had been a noble gentleman after all.

Thargelia thought of Cleo. Once Cadmus had complained —the object being a reduction in price—that Aspasia was no longer young, being fifteen years of age, and so the price should be lowered. He preferred little girls and little boys. So Thargelia wrote a message to her dear friend, Cadmus, informing him that she had a young girl in her house, only twelve years old, though in fact Cleo was thirteen. She described Cleo, so like an almond blossom in the spring. The girl, she wrote, had not yet reached puberty, and that would be most desirable to Cadmus. Then, as if it were an afterthought, she invited Cadmus to bring his foreign guest to her house for dinner and revelry and music. Her dinners were famous, her maidens gifted in dance and song. Cadmus had always infinitely enjoyed these occasions and had always brought Thargelia lavish gifts in gratitude. He already had two of her hetairai in his house, as well as an assortment of beautiful female slaves. Yes, he would adore Cleo, in her innocence and virginity and, thought Thargelia, her stupidity. She had not as yet been taught all the subtle arts of seduction, but that would only enhance her in the eyes of Cadmus.

Certain that Cadmus would eagerly accept her invitation, she prepared her house, for the invitation was for this night. She sent orders to both Cleo and Aspasia that they must retire to their chambers for sleep, and then must elaborately array and dress themselves and perfume and oil their bodies.

Ah, thought Aspasia, then she will dispose of me. She was almost overcome with grief. Her vermillion complexion had paled during the events of the past days, and she was exhausted with her emotions. She hoped that the unknown man would find her undesirable and reject her. But the slaves were cunning in the arts of beauty. As for Cleo, she was elated, and Aspasia looked on her with pity, and listened to her excited babblings. Cleo had no doubts. She would enter the house of a rich man and there be pampered and adored and in many ways a mistress. What all this entailed was unknown to the child, and Aspasia sighed. The stupid were satisfied with any comfortable fate, where they would not be abused, and Cleo would be a happy concubine, unaware that she had a woman's soul. But many of the Greeks asserted that a woman had no soul and was therefore of the status of a dog or a slave.

The most colorful and perfect and fragrant of flowers were chosen for the house, and long garlands of ivy and ferns and laurel and myrtle branches. Pots of ambergris perfumed with attar of roses and sandalwood and other delightful odors were stood against the walls, later to be ignited to diffuse the aromas. Thargelia ordered the dinner herself. There would be artichoke hearts in oil and vinegar, the softest and whitest of breads, to be served on fresh green leaves, anchovies and sardines swimming in olive oil and spices, eels from Lake Copais, imported, shellfish and mussels in butter, squid in a pungent sauce, pickled and smoked meats, beef hearts stuffed with barley and liver, fowl, including a peacock roasted and dressed in its feathers, nightingale tongues broiled and seasoned with more exotic spices, suckling pigs, legs of lamb also roasted, game birds stewed in olive oil and garlic and thyme and mint, young goats' meat seethed in their mothers' milk, famous black broths filled with bits of pork and blood and salt and vinegar, many varieties of fresh fish, briny cabbage, ky-keon seasoned with pennyroyal, baked onions, cheeses of many kinds, green and black olives, maza—delicate pancakes flooded with honey—red and purple berries also sweetened with honey, lentils and beans prepared in many ways and fla-vored with smoked pork, grapes, figs, raisins, citrons and ap-ples, and above all, Syrian whiskey and the finest of wines, and fragile pastries filled with ground nuts and poppy seeds and soft goat's cheese.

This feast was only for distinguished and noble guests, but what remained was given to the young hetairai over several days. Their own diet was simple and frugal, Thargelia detest-ing fat though a dainty plumpness was not disdained. When the maidens heard, through the gossip of slaves, that Aspasia and Cleo were to be at the banquet they were filled with envy, for they knew that they had been chosen for the consideration of illustrious visitors. They embraced the two girls and Cleo laughed with glee but Aspasia's pale face was somber. She said nothing but only submitted when her eyes were enhanced by black kohl and her cheeks tinted with vermillion and her lovely mouth reddened with an oily paste. She was mute while slaves bathed her and rubbed her rosy body with scented oils and put golden sandals on her feet. Her hair was dressed with flowers and colored ribbons. The slaves threw a new peplos over her, green as a lake and girdled with silver set with pre-cious stones. A veil, as transparent as moonlight, was drawn modestly about her bare shoulders and arms, and the living flesh shone through it enticingly.

"A veritable Artemis!" cried the girls in extreme admira-tion, and clasping and clapping their hands, but Aspasia said nothing. "Let us pray a Paris chooses you," said the maidens, "for surely you are more beautiful than Helen of Troy." But Aspasia said nothing. She was filled with a stony agony of de-spair. She desired to flee but there was nowhere to flee, no habitation which would give her shelter, no compassionate friend who would harbor her. She thought of killing herself, but her youth revolted.

Cleo was in no wise of her mind. Clad in yellow with a gilt girdle, her long black hair braided with ribbons and left hang-ing down her back in a childish fashion, and with a string of small pearls at her amber throat, she was enchanted with her-self and laughed and jumped with elation. Her terror of the night before was completely forgotten. Her black eyes were like black glass, shining and dancing. Her full lips were a blooming rose. Her young body might have been that of a boy, so small were her budding breasts and so narrow still her hips and her thighs. This had all been carefully considered by Thargelia, knowing Cadmus' preference for young males, though he was not averse to females who had not reached puberty.

The girls most skillful in dancing and playing lutes and flutes were chosen to evoke soft music during the feast, and they were attired as woodland nymphs, with ivy in their hair and their feet naked. They wore translucent peploses the color of laurel leaves, and their vari-colored tresses flowed unrestrained over shoulders and breasts. Their virgin breasts gleamed through the fabric of the peploses, and the nipples had been stained a fragile pink. They had been chosen not only for their skill in music but also because, though lovely, they were less so than Cleo and Aspasia, and thus would not dim the beauty of the damsels to be offered.

The dining hall was the largest room in the house and decorated with small perfumed fountains, the finest of statues and Persian rugs, the most costly of lamps, and mosaics beyond compare. Baskets of roses hung from the ceiling, and roses were scattered in heaps on the table, which was covered with cloth of silver. The plates and platters were of silver also, and so were the spoons and knives, and the goblets, wreathed in ivy, were of the most expensive Egyptian glass and enameled with gold and set with amethysts and opals.

The windows were opened to the warm night, the green curtains undrawn, and so the rattle of palm trees and the sighing of sycamores and oaks and myrtle and cypresses, and the surging of the ever-present sea, could be heard clearly.

Thargelia greeted her guests in the atrium. She was attired in crimson and yellow with an enormous Egyptian necklace falling over her bosom, and she exhaled exotic perfumes with every movement of her slender body. Jewels glittered in her dyed yellow hair and on her arms and fingers. She was splendid and even heroic, and her white teeth flashed and her eyes glinted amiably. "Welcome to my poor house," she said to Cadmus and the Persian satrap, Al Taliph, and bowed deeply.

"It is hardly a poor house, dear Thargelia," said Cadmus, who had a voice like a squeaking mouse and effeminate gestures. He looked about him with pride and then at Al Taliph and was pleased that the other was visibly impressed. What! Had he expected a mean brothel? thought Cadmus. We may not be as opulent as Persia, but we are not peasants in Miletus! They repaired to the dining hall where the girls were already singing and playing and posturing in a slow dance at a farther wall. Al Taliph and Cadmus sat on a soft couch covered with brocaded silk, and Thargelia seated herself in an ivory chair opposite them. Two chairs awaited Cleo and Aspasia. Slaves, dressed like fauns, poured whiskey into small glasses and wine into the goblets, and Cadmus offered a libation to the gods. Al Taliph looked about him curiously. This house of courtesans was far more lavish than the house of Cadmus, who was himself a rich man, and everything was in the most perfect taste. If the damsel to be presented him was as fair as her surroundings and as exquisite, then she was greatly to be desired. Al Taliph, a man not in the least garrulous, listened smiling to the light chatter of his hostess and Cadmus, and sipped his whiskey and listened to the music and idly watched the slow dance of the maidens in the distance. He would have been pleased to have had all of them in his harem, especially those of white skin and light hair. His favorite concubine was from the island of Cos, and she had hair the color of silver touched with gold and eyes as blue as the legendary blue rose. But, alas, there were few such treasures as his favorite and he doubted that Thargelia's hetairai could compare with her, though, as promised by Cadmus, they were more seductive.

Thargelia knew that Cadmus still lusted for Aspasia, though she, at fifteen, was too old for him. So Thargelia said, "My dear Cadmus, I have a jewel for you, as I wrote you today, a mere infant, but like spring just budding into flower, and not yet a woman. Her name is Cleo and she was not born of slaves or mere peasants, but a distinguished father and his adorable concubine. I warn you, however, " she added with a coquettish smile, "that her price is high."

"Your prices are always high," grumbled Cadmus, motioning to a slave to refill his glass with whiskey. "But then, the maidens are exceptional."

The hall was permeated with swooning fragrances. The cheeks of the guests began to be flushed both with warmth and whiskey. They sat contentedly on the soft couch and smiled with anticipation.

Thargelia summoned Cleo and Aspasia to join her and to be seated one on each side of her. She looked at Al Taliph and liked his appearance. She hoped he would be kind to Aspasia, and she sighed, remembering that the Persians had an even greater contempt for women than did the Greeks.

The maidens struck up a more lively and louder melody at a gesture from Thargelia, and Aspasia and Cleo entered.

CHAPTER 8

Al Taliph, the satrap from Persia, looked at Aspasia as she silently walked to the table with averted eyes, and he thought, Ah, she is far more entrancing than my Narcissa, that lily from Cos, and she is also much younger. He could not believe that any woman could be so fair and so bewitching, and of such perfection of face and form. He stirred on the couch and his face became delicately lustful. As for Cadmus, after a first desiring glance at Aspasia, his eye was caught by the pristine charm of Cleo, who had a young boy's body and an infant's face, and who retained the tender awkwardness of childhood. He imagined her in his bed at once, this little virgin. No matter Thargelia's price, he must have this girl, and tonight. He would be gentle with her deflowering, for roughness might kill her, and then his money would be lost.

Cleo ate the unusual dishes with open and delighted pleasure. When Cadmus' hand would steal under her peplos she merely pushed it away so as not to be disturbed in her enjoyment. To her it had no more significance than a vexation. She was too engrossed to consider herself as his mistress as yet. He rubbed the palm of his hand over her breasts and said to Thargelia with satisfaction, "She is like a boy, still." Thargelia frowned. "I beg of you, Cadmus, not to annoy the child."

Aspasia ate almost nothing and sipped a glass of wine. She became more and more withdrawn in herself. From under her long silken lashes she had scrutinized both Cadmus and Al Taliph. She had seen Cadmus once at a distance and her first impression of him as a gigantic toad had not changed. He was very short and very wide with a great round head and bulging eyes and no hair. Everything about him was florid and oily and coarse, including his high fat ears and his lips. (He also sweated even in cold weather when the winter winds roared from the sea.) He constantly wiped his face and his short neck and big splayed hands, and he drank copiously of the chilled wine at the table as if it were water. His face thickened, his distended eyes reddened. He could not look away from Cleo. He was splendidly arrayed in scarlet and blue, and his hands wore as many rings as did the hands of Thargelia. He reeked of sweat and attar of roses. His wide heavy thighs sprawled as his desire for Cleo increased.

Aspasia shuddered in herself that such a man was to be given Cleo, the immature little bird. He will crush her to death, she thought, with the weight of his body. He will tear those frail limbs asunder. Ah, if I had but gold I would flee with this child and hide her. Gold answers all things. Without it we are helpless and the gods are deaf to our importunities, despite the pieties of philosophers. She saw Cadmus' hand fondling one of the budlike breasts of Cleo and Aspasia wished to kill him. Cleo irritably slapped his hand away and gave herself up to the voluptuous delights of the table. Her round face was rosy with wine.

Aspasia had never learned resignation but she was beginning to learn it now. There was nothing she could do to help Cleo, so she gave her full attention to Al Taliph, to whom she would be presented. She was not a slave, but Thargelia under the law was her guardian and she the ward of Thargelia, and what Thargelia willed for her would be legal and accepted. Thargelia desired Al Taliph to take her, Aspasia, and she must obey her guardian.

Al Taliph was not the man she had feared would resemble Cadmus. He was middle-aged, possibly thirty-five years old, and tall and slender, almost bony. He was magnificently arrayed in the Oriental fashion, and he wore a robe of intricate design in scarlet, blue, green, yellow, violet and gold, all in a pattern that had no beginning and no end. It was made of the finest silk, and glistened. His narrow waist was clasped by a girdle that resembled a living snake, with a jeweled head and an open mouth. A similar but smaller snake clasped his thin and sun-baked throat, and there were even smaller snakes on his arms and wrists. A short mantel of cloth of gold covered his shoulders, which were broad if thin. His sandals were of gold also, and the thong was in the form of a gemmed viper. There were many rings on his long dark hands, fabulous rings that glittered blindingly, and several of them were of the snake design also. He wore earrings, looped gold.

On his head he bore the first turban Aspasia had ever seen, of cloth of gold sprinkled with jewels. It was like a crown, high and wide, and gave him a look of majesty, lifting above his fine spare ears and his broad dark brow, which was also high and as unlined as brown marble.

But it was his face that engaged Aspasia's attention. Like his body his countenance was narrow and very attenuated, if nearly as black as an Ethiopian's. He had strange eyes which at one moment appeared brown and at another gray, and they were almost as large as Aspasia's, and glimmered and shone and changed with his thoughts. He had long black and silken lashes, and his eyebrows were like the wings of a bird, swooping upwards to his forehead; giving him a barbaric expression, and a delicately cruel one. His nose was short but beaked. His mouth was extremely mobile and satirical, and only faintly colored with red cosmetics. He had the hidden sneering air of the Persian aristocracy, and his whole face was subtle and occult beyond the comprehension of the western people. There was an aura of secret obscurity about him which, to her reluctance, exacted Aspasia's attention. She thought, Here is a man who reveals nothing of his thoughts or passions, and rules himself.

Those, she remembered from her lessons, who were in command of themselves were inevitably powerful and potent, beyond the hysteria and disastrous emotions of lesser men. Al Taliph, she thought with growing respect, would never permit vulgar vehemences in himself.

Despite her fear, Aspasia began to admire such a man, who had elegance and composure and spoke very little. At times a flicker of amusement flashed through his eyes and his lips curled as he listened to the conversation between Thargelia and Cadmus, which was becoming lewd. To him, Aspasia concluded, open coarseness was for the barnyard and not for cultivated men. When he glanced at Aspasia that glance was inscrutable and aloof; she thought he was weighing her and had found her of little importance. In this she was wrong, for Al Taliph was thinking, to his confusion, that here was a damsel of intelligence and subtlety. He did not know whether to be displeased or gratified. She had not spoken a word as yet, but he saw the planes of her face and the expression of her eyes. He was a man wise in the way of women, and Aspasia was unique to him, and he desired her. In contrast, Narcissa was a mere pretty animal. She would be a marvelous addition to his harem: A woman who possessed a mind, with whom he could converse. He laughed inwardly and remembered that he who debases himself and converses with a woman converses with a soulless creature, who merely babbles and does not know of what she babbles, and her conversation is madness.

Al Taliph had several wives and a huge harem. A man went to other men for intellectual understanding. He looked at Aspasia, to ponder, again, with conflicting thoughts, on her intelligence or her lack of intelligence. Could anything of consequence come from that adorable mouth? If so, it would be infinitely exciting.

He spoke to her for the first time and his voice, Aspasia thought, was not coarse and loud like Cadmus' but low and quiet and pleasing to the ear, almost like the sound of the sea. "I have heard that in this house the women are taught many things which other Ionian and Grecian women are not, and that their minds are respected."

"Yes, it is true," said Aspasia, and out of her bitterness she spoke loudly and clearly and the Persian was surprised at the resonance and fascination of her voice, though he deplored the strength of it. Women in Persia had soft whispering voices and when they spoke they meekly bent their heads and let their lashes fall. But Aspasia looked at him straightly, and he saw her eyes and marvelled, for liquid lights increased and shifted in them, as if they contained crystal waters in themselves. "But that does not help us. We are despised." In Persia men did not address women as they addressed men; they kept their eyes averted so as not to contaminate them by looking too long at a woman. However, he found himself, to his amused vexation, returning her regard. Then his gaze wandered once more over her body, at the swelling young breast, at the dainty waist and virginal hips.

She did not like that slow scrutiny of her person, to which she had never before been subjected; it was as if he were reflecting on the aspects of a slave he was considering purchasing. So in turn, flushing, she scrutinized him also, and he saw it and wanted to laugh. A fine young mare, he thought. It will be pleasurable to tame her.

A slave girl with a soft musical voice began to sing a ditty of the streets, and accompanied herself on a small harp:

"Do not try to make me love you,
For I swear by stars above you
That love like mine will always be untrue.
The moon was my undoing
When you seduced me—wooing,
But never was my heart possessed by you.

"The soul can love only,
And after that is lonely,
For love can come but once to any heart.
When fled, life's but for grieving,
All else is but deceiving,
Desire remains, yet always lives apart."

Aspasia had laughed at the ditty when first she had heard it, but now she said to herself, I will never love any man. I find this one not repulsive, and if he wishes me I shall have to

89

obey. She saw that he had been listening, too, over the laughter and conversation of Thargelia and Cadmus, and she saw him smiling a little. "Tell me," he said, "would you like to live in my country?"

She shrugged. "Does it matter where I live? I have no choice." Then she added, "Are you going to Greece, sire?"

He coughed slightly as if she had asked him a bold and embarrassing question. "In the midst of all these wars and turbulences, Aspasia? I doubt I would live long in Greece, if I were discovered. I do my affairs from this sanctuary in Miletus, where I meet with Greek merchants, lapidaries, manufacturers, weapon-makers, dealers in oils and excellent works of art, and many other things. Here we are pragmatic men and not enemies. Merchants are not emotional; it is gold, only," and he rubbed the fingers of his right hand together. "Is that not sensible?"

She considered this, and sipped her wine. "But is gold not the ultimate end of all wars?"

"The Greeks did not think so when we invaded their small country. But then, they who fought were not merchants. They loved freedom, it is said. That, too, is another delusion."

Aspasia looked at him, her face averted, and only her eyes shining with hostility, for always she had believed that freedom was the only thing for which men should fight. Seeing that he was scrutinizing her endowments again as if she were an animal, her thoughts became confused. She looked at his fine dark hands and thought of them on her body; to her surprise she did not shiver nor did she feel revulsion and dread. She had heard that in Persia women slept at the feet of their husbands or possessors, like cats, and she told herself that never would this happen to her even if he killed her for disobedience.

There was a sudden exclamation from Thargelia of annoyance mingled with drunken mirth. Cadmus had dexterously divested Cleo of her peplos and had swung the child onto his knees. He began to explore her little tawny body with rough hard fingers and Cleo started to cry, though she had drunk too much wine, herself. Without thinking Aspasia sprang from her chair and put her arms about Cleo, seeking to lift her from the huge knees on which she struggled in fear. Cadmus' hand reached out swiftly and he caught Aspasia by one of her breasts and squeezed it, laughing up in her face with a salacious light in his eyes. She cried out, strove to push away that gripping hand, but he held her breast tighter and his thumb rubbed her nipple painfully.

Later Al Taliph thought that he himself had behaved in a ridiculous fashion, for what was a woman and especially such as the hetairai? Aspasia, he was to think, had been presumptuous and forward in attempting to rescue that worthless little creature who had taken the fancy of a man, and who should have been grateful for it. It was probably Aspasia's cry which caused him to rise quickly, for he had already, in his mind, declared her his and it was intolerable to see another man touch his property.

So Aspasia saw a long lean hand dart like a striking snake at Cadmus' hand, which held her breast, and Cadmus uttered a short howl of pain and released the girl. Cleo fell from his knees and sprawled on the soft carpet and whimpered like a puppy.

Cadmus grasped his wrist and shrieked like a woman, half-rising. He looked up at Al Taliph's smiling face and he shouted, "You have broken my wrist, may the Furies seize you!"

Al Taliph spoke gently. "I do not think it is broken, though I struck it with the side of my palm, a Persian lesson from Cathay. Had I struck your throat so you would now be dead, my friend." He shook his head as if in reproof of his own impetuousness.

Aspasia fell on her knees beside the wailing Cleo and held her in her arms against her breast and she regarded Cadmus fiercely. Thargelia, amazed, stood up and was no longer drunk. She was filled with dismay. Never had this happened in her house before, no matter how intoxicated her clients. But above all she feared that this episode would result in the two men rejecting her hetairai for boldness, on Aspasia's part, and Cleo's absurd objections to Cadmus' caresses. She exclaimed to Cadmus, "I will send for unguents at once!" To Al Taliph, standing near her, she said, "I am humiliated at the actions of Aspasia. But she has the effrontery of youth. I implore you to forgive her, Cadmus," and she turned to the other man.

He said, through clenched yellow teeth, still holding his wrist, "Give her to me and I promise that every morning she will be flogged, as a punishment. What other man would have such a wench?" He looked at Aspasia with mingled hatred and desire, and sharply kicked her in the side with his sandaled foot.

Al Taliph caught his injured wrist and stared down into his eyes, smiling, and said, "Do not kick what is mine, dearest of friends." His voice was soft.

Cadmus shrank. He whimpered with pain, remembering

that he had dealings to do with Al Taliph and extremely profitable ones, and he was jeopardizing them. He swallowed his
hatred, and said, "Shall men quarrel for such as these? No. I
am ashamed."

Cleo was clinging to Aspasia, weeping into the older girl's
shoulder, and Aspasia was filled with despair. Thargelia's
bosom rose on a deep breath of relief. She said to Cadmus,
"You will take Cleo with you tonight?"

He scowled at her, biting one of his thick lips and his eyes
narrowed shrewdly. "I have discerned that she is close to puberty. Her price must be lowered, for in less than a year she
will be worthless to me."

"She is not a slave," said Thargelia, suddenly touched with
pity at the sight of the two girls sitting on the carpet. Moreover, Cadmus had dared spurn her darling, Aspasia, with his
foot as if she were a canine bitch. The singing and dancing
and playing maidens and the serving slaves had become still
and silent watching, "Cleo," Thargelia continued in a cold
voice, "was born free and is still free. When you have had
your pleasure and your fill of her return her to me." She
looked inflexibly at Cadmus who began to fear that never
again would he be invited to this house of joys and luxuries.

"You will also treat the child with care and gentleness,"
said Thargelia. "If ill comes to her, Cadmus, not all your
wealth will protect you from my wrath and the justice of the
authorities."

"You are insolent," he muttered. His wrist was swelling and
he was in pain, and he rubbed the wrist with the fingers of his
other hand. "Am I a heathen barbarian, a murderer? The girl
will be treated well in my house."

Thargelia clapped her hands and two male slaves came
obediently to her, and she said, "A bowl of hot water and
unguents and linen." Al Taliph had returned to his chair. He
looked down at Aspasia, saw her golden locks mingling with
the black locks of the child she held like a mother, heard her
murmurs of consolation. She was not weeping, as was Cleo.
Her face was like marble.

All at once Al Taliph was taken by a deep tenderness for
Aspasia, and he was so astonished by this unique emotion for
a woman that he almost burst out laughing in ridicule of himself. Yet, when he looked down into her eyes and saw the suffering in them he was moved in an unfamiliar fashion, for he
was not a man of pity and mercy was almost unknown to
him.

He touched her shoulder lightly, bending down to do so,

and she lifted her head and regarded him in a white silence. She saw his swarthy face and something curiously arcane in his subtle eyes. His reddened lips curled with incomprehensible thoughts. There were bronze lights on his cheeks, as hard as metal, which increased his appearance of virility.

I do not fear him, Aspasia thought in wonder. I will go with him and gladly, for I feel in my heart that he is not as other men. She said, "I pray you to take Cleo also." But he shook his head and removed his hand and turned away in grave rebuke. His burnished hooped earrings caught the lamplight.

"She is not mine to take," he replied, and glanced at Cadmus, whose wrist was being bound up by Echion, himself. Though Aspasia was again filled with despair she understood. Al Taliph was a man of honor.

CHAPTER 9

Kurda, the master of the eunuchs, and a eunuch himself, stared after the golden-haired woman with hatred. For three years now she, a detestable female, had ruled this household, this palace, with more power than a lawful queen, with certainly more power than the four noble wives of the lord—the ruler of the province. Not for this creature the confines of the harem, where lived two hundred young concubines and slaves! Not for her the cymbals and the flutes and the zithers and the dance, to please the lord, Al Taliph, during his weary relaxation after affairs of state! It was even rumored that she did not sleep at his feet, like a pampered dog or a silken cat. (Kurda was inclined not to believe this, for certainly no female would be permitted to confront her lord face to face in sleep on the same cushions! That was blasphemy, obscenity, unspeakable, disgusting—the Lord Al Taliph would never have permitted such. Never would he be guilty of defiling himself so.)

Kurda stood at the bronze gates leading into the hall of the palace and watched Aspasia's queenly and stately passage across the blue and white tiles of the courtyard, which was lighted by the ardent sun. She is not even young, he thought, with malevolence. It is said that she is eighteen years old, a withered leaf. She was as old as the oldest wife of the lord, who had already given birth to five children, all sons—for which the lady was honored. She was far older than the concubines of the harem, most of whom were not over fourteen years, for women began to fade at that age and the lord could not endure old women. Yet, he endured and suffered this one! Incredible! Shameful! Had she cast a western spell on him, to so derange his wits? If so, none in the palace was safe. Her golden hair was a web of evil, disastrous, in which the entire establishment was caught and helpless. Kurda, devoted to his master, for all Al Taliph was a Zoroastrian and not truly a Persian by descent, but a Mede, could have wept with fear and rage on every occasion when he encountered this daughter of Ahriman, the spirit of immortal wickedness, at war eternally with Mithras and man. Surely Mithras would soon visit calamity not only upon this household but on the whole Valley of the Polvar.

The multitudinous women of the palace unceasingly teased and even lightly tormented Kurda, and his eunuchs, but they feared him also, for at his will he could order whippings and other punishment for the women of the harem. Only the princesses—the wives of Al Taliph—and especial favorites—were safe from his malice and his detestation of their sex. But this western woman, who was neither princess nor true concubine, and not even a slave, pretended to be unaware of his very existence, he whose trousers were of silver or cloth of gold and embroidered with scarlet and blue and yellow and purple, with a vest equally magnificent and a turban even more so, and whose girdle was of gold studded with gems and who wore a curved sword of magnificent workmanship. He might have been a leashed jackal, for all her attention. She sought no favors or privileges from him, as did the young concubines and female slaves, nor did she reward him with a gold coin or a pretty gift when he was sometimes indulgent to women's foolish female whims. Once only had she looked at him directly, and with impatience, and she had lifted her lip at him and then had turned away. Ah, he had no testes, and for that she despised him! She, the impure, had dared to think herself superior to one who was pure. She had never seemed aware that even the uncastrated male slaves of the household, and the lesser free male servants, respected him for his power and that the lord Al Taliph often deferred to his opinions and asked his advice.

Ah, but she was growing old! It would not be long before she was banished to the lower stratum of the harem, to tend children and wash the feet of new favorites and oil their young bodies and serve them. Then he, Kurda, would have his revenge. He would order her flogged at sunrise every day until she died of it, and then he would have her body thrown to the pariah dogs who infested the mountains. None would mourn her. She was feared and hated not only by the noble wives but by the entire harem, who would rejoice in her final fate, this insolent and impertinent one who not only disdained Kurda but the wives, also, and the other concubines.

In the meantime, however, she was ominous and alien. Gloomily, Kurda watched her. She had traversed half the blue and white tiled courtyard, and was standing now by the jade fountain, an enormous bowl in which a white marble dolphin seemed gracefully to leap and dance in the iridescence of the springing waters. She put her hand in the rippling bowl, and smiled upwards at the dolphin, and Kurda saw her foreign profile and shuddered. Not for her the decent and decorous veil of a virtuous woman, which not only concealed features from the lustful gaze of random men but protected women's delicate complexions from the furious sun. Truly, Ahriman guarded his vile own! Her lips were like a pomegranate, her cheeks softly vermillion, her neck and forehead like milk, her nearly bare shoulders—obscene!—like the marble of the dolphin, itself. Nor was her nose the subtly curved nose of a patrician woman; it was straight and with an impudent tilt at the end. This betrayed her slavish origins. As for the wanton color of her hair—no woman ever possessed such fairness. It was certainly dyed, but that was expected of one of her advanced age. Al Taliph's mother had dyed her hair, but it had been black dye, which was permitted a woman. But the color of this woman's hair—like the hair of the displaced Greek woman from Cos (now returned to her home)—was obviously and flauntingly false. The western barbarian women had no regard for propriety. Ah, sorrowful and strange it was that the heroic emperor, Xerxes, had not conquered them! However, again, Ahriman protected his own, and Mithras was too patient and benign, even in the case of barbarians who did not know or honor him.

Kurda, more and more gloomy, observed that Aspasia was wearing a robe of scarlet, as scarlet as her mouth, draped cunningly and tightly across her lovely bosom and hips and then falling in lustrous silken folds and flares to her feet which were shod in golden and jeweled shoes. The robe was elaborately embroidered, but daintily so, and appeared less fabric than an airy gossamer woven in rainbows. She wore no covering on her head, and her fair hair lifted in a hot and perfumed wind coming through the myriad long pointed arches of the courtyard. The blue and white tiles of the floor reflected her; the water of the fountain threw radiant shadows on her face, and darting reflections. Her milk-white round arms were clasped with bracelets of gemmed vipers and there was a necklace of opals about her throat. Kurda was superstitious. He thought her an evil spirit, so strange was she and so potent in the affairs of the palace, and so inexplicable, and he made the sign to warn off demons. Sometimes he, the powerful Kurda, feared her, and he grovelled with shame in his mind at this indignity.

(Incredible and most alarming to him was the fact that she did not spend her time in the harem, nor did she sleep in one of the chambers assigned to the princesses. She slept with the lord Al Taliph—it was rumored, and Kurda could not debase himself enough to believe that—and she had a gorgeous chamber of her own, surpassing the chambers of the wives. She had ten female slaves to attend to her exclusively.)

The master of the eunuchs was an immensely tall and immensely fat man, with a huge belly and a great pallid face, as smooth as an infant's buttocks. His tiny black eyes were sunken in his facial flesh; he had a nose like a mushroom, a fat sullen mouth pouting like a peevish child's, and a number of chins so full that they concealed his neck. Aspasia could hardly refrain from smiling, so high and thin and girlish was his voice. But she knew at once how dangerous he was, how full of vindictiveness and malignance. She had heard that all eunuchs were like such as he, detesting women, murderous, lustful for the infliction of torture as other men were lustful for girls. But surely Kurda surpassed all his brothers in these attributes. She knew that though he hated all the other women in the palace, even the princesses he served so sedulously and guarded with such ardor, he hated her more than all others. At first she had been inclined to pity him, believing he mourned his mutilated state, but she soon learned that he was proud of it, accepting it as a superior endowment. His big belly, naked and hairless, protruded from between the sides of his patterned vest, and his navel was tinted rose, which Aspasia thought particularly obscene.

Once she had asked herself idly, Why does he loathe me more than the other women, and why does he fix his eyes upon me with such a desire to kill? It did not come to her for some time that this was because he had a woman's love for Al Taliph, and he had learned that the satrap loved Aspasia as he had never loved any other woman. Worse than all else, however, Aspasia was treated like an empress in this house, and never was she banished to that part where the women lived but sat at feasts with the satrap and his guests at the table, bold, shameless, conversing as men converse, and held all in fascinated attention. The guests did not disdain her or regard her as worthless, as they did even their own wives and daughters, and this inflamed the jealous Kurda. They gazed upon her like men under the spell of a golden moon set upon a mountain top.

Again, it was the privilege of the master of the eunuchs to strike a recalcitrant young concubine or slave girl who became mutinous in the harem, or punish her in some other corrective fashion, which did not mar her skin or bruise or truly injure her. Kurda understood that from the moment Aspasia entered this palace she was beyond his corrections and that he must speak to her with even more respect than he did Al Taliph's wives. How this was he did not know; hence his hatred and resentment of her, this alien barbarian woman.

She had a fascination for Kurda, also, the fascination of deadly hate, the fascination of a besotted woman who studies her flaunting rival. He did not think Aspasia beautiful; he told himself that she was repulsive and sighed over the blindness of his beloved satrap. Her very scent revolted him, for she did not use the heavy languorous musks of the east. A perfume as of hyacinths or lilies floated from her as if it were the natural exhalation of her body. She had but to appear to make him stare at her as if at a basilisk, unable to move until she was gone from his sight. Only her death or banishment would have satisfied him. His dreams were of such; he had only to wait for the hour when Al Taliph wearied of her. These were the dreams not only of Kurda but of the offended wives and the other ladies of the harem. They had thought Narcissa intolerable, for she had assumed, as the favorite, the airs of a sultana, and condescended even to the wives. This one was infinitely worse, as she was infinitely more beautiful. It was even rumored in the murmurous harem that Artaxerxes, himself, having glimpsed her in the palace, had desired her and had offered for her a sum equal to the ransom of a kingdom. But no woman of the harem believed this: only Kurda did so believe, for he knew it was true.

Watching her with fury today, as he always watched her, Kurda saw her, as usual, lifting her head from the fountain and looking ahead into the hypnotizing vista of the high blue and white pointed arches which led from the courtyard like the myriad diminishing reflections in a mirror. They seemed to extend into infinity, growing smaller with distance, one within another, an illusion of endlessness. They pierced the white fretted stone of intervening walls, stone so exquisitely carved and designed that it appeared made of intricate lace. They were floored with that glasslike tiling of blue and white which was never sullied with dust or even a fallen leaf, but only duplicated the passing colors and shapes of those who traversed them. To the right the floor and walls and arches ended in low white steps to the tremendous hanging gardens and grottoes and pools and tiny black bridges of ebony and beds of flowers and masses of oleanders and cypresses and palms and myrtle and oaks and strange fernlike trees and winding paths of red gravel. Here strutted peacocks and in the waters stood flamingoes, as rosy as dawn, and yellow and brown ducks and black and white swans, and herons with red beaks. The banks of the ponds, as green as emeralds, tumbled with cascades of flowers of massed hues, over which blew clouds of vari-colored butterflies. Rare birds of all colors hung in gilt cages from the branches of trees, and conversed with those free nearby. There was little if any grass here, and so the ground was covered with ivies and other creeping plants or left silvery bare with raked sand and sparkling white gravel. Here and there stood huge Chinese vases filled with flowering branches whose blossoms were like drops of blood or dripping gold, or lapis lazuli. Over all loomed a blazing sky of color of the peacocks' breasts, filled with a light so intense that the eye could not gaze upon it for long. It robbed shadows of any darkness, so that even those which lay on gravel or flowers or sand had only a fainter incandescence. The heat was dry and acrid, and so no scent rose from the earth except that of aromatic dust and stone which seemed to be on the point of igniting.

The very fountains appeared to be liquid stone and were very warm. In the colored bowls bright fish lazily swam or rose to the surface for air. Water lilies, pale or pink, were closed tightly against the sun on their pads of floating green leaves. There were few statues and these were of bronze rather than marble, and were of bizarre form, and startling to western eyes. Some depicted female deities with many twisted arms and hands and breasts, with frightening faces of malevolence and supernatural ferocity, and some were of turbaned male deities correspondingly fearful, with flames emerging from mouths or shoulders or embossed shields, and all possessed squat and muscular misshapen legs and bare feet with many toes. Aspasia found them horrifying and repulsive, especially those with jagged teeth protruding between Negroid lips. Occasionally she discovered one holding a severed head by the hair, and she would shudder. She had already discovered that the eastern mind was far more complicated and involved and obscure and unknowable than the western mind, which had a certain clarity and a straightforwardness of reasoning. That western mind proceeded from one logical point to another, but the eastern mind spiraled and twisted and was mysterious beyond her comprehension. Yet she found it interesting and tantalizing, for all its obscurity and hints of arcane darkness, and even its implications of things not in human context and beyond humanity, and its lack of directness. Once the old philosopher in Thargelia's house had said, "Nothing human is alien to me." Had he ventured here, Aspasia would think with some humor, he would not be so certain, or would conclude that there were things, superficially human, that could not be understood or which had emerged from some unseen sentient power which did not resemble humanity at all, but had the qualities of elementals or similar appalling natures.

It was only by ignoring the statues, which in some weird fashion echoed the Oriental mind, that Aspasia could enjoy the gardens at all. She preferred to cultivate the birds and the peacocks and the tame herons and flamingoes and parrots or look at the brazen or blue barren mountains which enclosed the green and fertile valley. She was endlessly fascinated by the hanging gardens which covered the walls of the gardens, themselves, dropping from the earth above the walls in billows of leaves and blossoms, all jeweled with unseen rills of water. But none was fragrant. It was only at night that unseen jasmine and roses breathed out sweetness under the moon. However, Aspasia, to her own amusement, preferred not to visit the gardens at night, for once, doing so, she had seen that the statues had acquired a kind of monstrous life of their own, fierce, distorted, and threatening, and she had been namelessly affrighted. She knew that her own people were not notable for compassion or disinterested tenderness, but the eastern mind, as exemplified in their works of art, had elements of complicated cruelty and indifference to agony repellent to the western spirit. "All men are the same," the philosopher had didactically stated. Now Aspasia emphatically disagreed.

It was not that the Oriental mind was inferior to the western. In many occult and subtle ways it was superior. But it had components unique to itself, elusive, and enigmatic, oblique and bewildering to the western intelligence. Often, in conversing with Al Taliph and his friends, she was aware of her own bafflement, for arguments were never concluded satisfactorily but seemed to continue on into labyrinths which she could not follow and which eluded her. They led nowhere which she could discern. To the Oriental, argument was only to enlarge mystic vistas but never to ultimately enlighten. Western man established the initial base for an argument, defined his terms, demolished his opponent with irrefutable logic or was demolished by his own ineptitude of reasoning.

"But we," Al Taliph had gently informed her, "argue more to confuse, or to display the elaborateness of our own intelligence for the admiration of others. It is an exercise in inscrutability. It is never dull like your western bald logic, which is barren of true imagination. We argue, not to inform or educate but to mystify. It is endlessly exciting and inspires our spirits as does wine, and is intoxicating."

"It never concludes," said Aspasia.

"Therefore, it has more validity than your restricted western conclusions, for nothing in heaven or earth is conclusive, but ever changes and is in flux, and never is graven on eternal stone."

"It does not possess the merits of law and order, lord."

"Nor does reality, Aspasia. There is no fixed reality, as you have averred yourself. There are realities within realities and those endlessly change form and context and never repeat themselves. Do you understand, my sun goddess?"

"No," Aspasia said, and laughed. But she was uneasy. She preferred boundaries even to imagination and conjecture, and all based on some acceptance of terms, however subjective they might be. "All else is chaos," she would say.

Al Taliph would shrug, highly diverted. "We know nothing beyond our mere existence and our feeble imaginings and hypotheses. Beyond this, it is apparent to us, live enormities and vast shapes which would affright us if we glimpsed them and which you would call chaos. We of the east suspect their being. You prefer your deities, or your supernaturals, to be recognizably human and governed by laws which also govern men. This is egotism of the most offensive kind. It is also childish." He informed her that the fearful deities in the gardens did not represent actual beings but rather the emanations of those beings, "or, if you will, their attributes or passions." But the beings themselves were not aware of humanity, or, if aware, were not concerned, or interested. They had their own identity, forever incomprehensible to man. Only their emotions, their natures, sometimes projected into the tiny realm of man, and then not by will but by accident.

Aspasia would then feel a tremor of terror which she could never explain to herself. She could only reject, for fear of insanity. However, the eastern mind accepted all this and did not stagger into madness. Perhaps, she would think, the Greeks were willing to die to halt the Persians, they half-realizing that if the east prevailed there would be no ground on which the west could stand and survive. The western mind would perish and all its reason and laws and acceptances of a common reality. Was the eastern mind corrupt? Not with the general meaning of corruption, certainly. But what else was it? She never knew though faintly she discerned, and retreated in her mind. All dealings with the east by the west must of necessity be superficial and based on some shallow compromise, acceptable to both, and profitable to both. Beyond that there was no meeting. No negotiations could be used on the basis of good will, for to the west such had one meaning and to the east it had another, and they were not compatible, and were rooted in immutable character.

"Men everywhere, east or west," said Al Taliph, "have one meeting ground, and that is gold. It is the universal touch, the universal understanding. We may differ on everything else—but not on gold." He had smiled at her. "You of the west find us devious. We fine you naive." She understood that he was not denigrating her, as a woman, but her whole race. Sometimes she was puzzled. The Persians and the Medes were of the Aryan peoples, as was she, herself—yet there was no complete comprehension. He would play with her wonderful hair and kiss it lingeringly, and she would smile. Men had another meeting place besides gold, she would think, and that was women. An astute woman of any race could meet a man of any race and subtly conquer him, east or west. However, she would admit, Al Taliph was never entirely conquered, as were the men of the west. Indulged, apparently loved and admired, and even respected, though she was, he could impatiently and abruptly dismiss her and ignore her, and not call her for days. He remained intact, invulnerable; for that reason alone he fascinated her. She did not love him as she understood love, yet she venerated him and often feared him, for he was a mystery to her. She was also grateful to him for many reasons, and she did not have to simulate passion for him. He was adroit in the ways of women and sometimes this humiliated her, for when she would use her taught blandishments on him he would watch her with a glint of amusement in his eyes, as one would watch a cunning child. He had power, and women, she would admit, adored power.

To the right of where Aspasia now stood in the courtyard were arched windows along the walls, not as pointed as the arches themselves but rounded. These were covered with bronze grills, like prison bars. Here was the life of the palace. The building was round, rather than square, with a domed roof of blazing whiteness, surrounded by tall and narrow turrets like soaring notched needles of stone. There was another secret courtyard, smaller than this, the courtyard that led from the harem and was used exclusively by the women of the palace and the eunuchs who guarded them. Aspasia sometimes went to that courtyard, where she was not welcomed, and endeavored to talk to the women and the wives.

Greeks extolled the body, as did all the western peoples, and worshipped athletes, pugilists, actors, dancers and prodigious wrestlers and racers and discus throwers. They were a physical people. But the Persians were not. The body was of less importance to them than the mind—with the exception of the bodies of their women, and their mighty soldiers. They had a certain indolence of character and deplored sweat and too much activity. The women of the harem were very plump and even fat, and this the men admired. It was strange that Al Taliph did not find Aspasia's slenderness and quickness deplorable. He would smooth her long slim flanks with his hands and fondle her tight firm breasts and concave belly, and she would wonder, even in her excitement, why this was so, considering the heavy plumpness of his wives and concubines. Sometimes she would think that this was because he was a Mede and not a Persian. Yet, when buying a new female slave he would consider only a woman who was fat.

Once she had complained to him, "I do not understand you in the least," to which he had replied fondly, "My white dove, feel grateful for that." He had intimated some terror in the eastern mind, and while she shrank she was enamored.

She was not unhappy. She had a tutor who sedulously taught her the language of Persia and the customs and she endeavored to learn, the better to please Al Taliph. She was endlessly curious, endlessly engrossed. She had access to Al Taliph's libraries and those areas exclusive to him, filled with art which at once repelled and captivated her. Yet sometimes she was depressed by the very ornateness of it, the inhuman aspects of carved jade and stone and lapis lazuli and bronze, the formal mosaics of one dimension only, the static postures that appeared to eliminate suppleness entirely. In short, they seemed to deny flesh and blood and the teeming heart and to be symbols only. "But I have caught you!" he once laughed at her. "Did you not once tell me that all in the universe is only symbols, my sweet Aurora?" She wanted to answer impatiently, but she had no words. He was far more conversant with the western mind than was she with the eastern, and he accepted the former with equanimity as a phenomenon of the world while she could not accept at all.

She believed that he loved her, if only as a novelty. Once she said to him, "Will you discard me when I am old, in a few years?" He had gazed at her with that amused tenderness which she sometimes found infuriating. "Lily of Shalimar," he had replied, "you will never grow old." He would then tell her of Egypt and India, their customs and religions, and her mind was divested and she was eager to learn. He said, "That is the attribute of those who are eternally young—they learn, their souls are ardent, their eyes, seeking, never fade, their bodies are never bent. My mother was such." That was the first and the last time that he ever spoke of his mother.

He asked her, "Are you lonely, my love?" When she answered that she had never truly known loneliness he had nodded as if deeply gratified and content. She had received priceless gifts from him, jewels and gold, and knew that she could leave him at any time she willed. But she did not want to leave. There were occasions when she felt the exhilaration of happiness.

Sometimes he would take her in his awninged chariot, blazing with brilliant enamel and embossed gems and drawn by black Arabian horses with harnesses of silver and driven by half-naked and turbaned Nubian slaves, to the furiously noisy and teeming bazaars on the outskirts of the city of Murghab. Here on an eye-blinding and sweltering plain below the barren blue and saffron mountains were endless rows of tents and booths reeking with mingled odors of spices and dung and sandalwood and nard and sand, and hot dust which blew in clouds over everything like billows of sunlit gold. Here were heaps of Indian chili powder, ranging from the palest gold to vehement scarlet, twisted tables and ornaments and jewelry of brass and silver set with semi-precious turquoise and flawed pearls and garnet, and bales of silk and embroidered tissues, exotic sweetmeats and jars of milk curds and carpets like flung flowers, and sandals and boots of the softest leather and straw. Here were merchants from Asia and Asia Minor and Cathay and Arabia and Egypt, all vociferous and unbearably vocal, and full of quarrels, laughter, oaths, as they visited from booth to booth, to study competitors, attempting to denigrate their wares, shaking treasures before their faces and haranguing them and sneering at their offerings. There were booths selling roasted meats and fowl, cakes, pastries, bottled wine and casks and beer and even Syrian whiskey. Others sold pickled olives in kegs, strings of onions, brined cabbage and cucumbers, strange breads coated with roasted and honeyed seeds and seething with flies. Camels, raising fresh dust, were dragged through the narrow passageways, screaming in peevish torment and eyeing the throngs with contempt and resisting masters, and clusters of dogs and scurrying cats, and tethered goats and cattle. Geese and chicken and ducks were confined in shaking crates of reeds, and their complaints competed with all the other hectic and disorderly sounds and sights. There were booths where knives, scimitars, swords and wrought silver daggers were sold, and which were filled with the hissing and grating shrills of grinding wheels. Yellow-skinned and sinewy men with shaved heads had booths of flowers, vegetables, woollen cloths and exquisitely carved ebony and teakwood chairs and tables inlaid with ivory and mother-of-pearl and little ceramics, and others sold pottery and porcelain ornaments, many of them of extreme artistry and extraordinary inlaid colors. There were beak-faced black men with cold and expressionless faces who opened small carved wooden boxes for the scrutiny of men only, and from under silk-hung tables, and they were surrounded by laughing male customers who elbowed each other and grinned in each other's face like naughty boys.

There were booths of money-changers, alert-eyed and drawn-faced men of all races, guarded by men with drawn swords, and there was a constant tinkle of gold and silver and bronze and brass, from locked chests behind chairs and chained drawers. The sellers remained calm and silently scornful, while customers blasphemed, shook fists, argued, slapped their hands on tables, thrust bags of coins in the faces of the bankers—who appeared aloof from all this and only whispered among themselves or threw back bags with gestures of dismissal, to the loud protestations of the sweating offerers. Some bankers merely recorded in open books, as quiet and studious as if they were in the sanctuaries of orderly banks, unaware of the masses that blew in and out of the guarded booths. Here the noise was stupendous.

"You will observe," said Al Taliph to Aspasia, who was both hooded and veiled in this melee and jungle of uproar and running and pushing men, "that men who deal with money are not to be discomposed or disconcerted. Gold and silver have a most sobering influence—for, do they not rule the world in spite of all the philosophers and priests who cry to the contrary? If I wished advice as unchangeable as the Medes' and the Persian law, and as adamant and sensible, I would go to a banker who is sealed in a crystal of reality and has no untidy passions. Certainly, I would go to no temple to consult the gods!"

"But gold and silver alike have value only in the subjective minds of men," said Aspasia. "They have no intrinsic glory of themselves. They were conceived by ideas, and those ideas could be shattered."

"I advise you to discuss this esoteric opinion with bankers," said Al Taliph, touching her veiled cheek as one would touch the cheek of a favored child. "I doubt, however, that they would agree with you."

"They are only symbols, and convenient ones—which men have accepted—of what is truly valuable: food, shelter, barter, land, possessions."

"Then men would, and do, give their lives only for symbols," said Al Taliph, laughing at her. "But, have you not said this, yourself, in your discussions with me. Yes."

When, embarrassed, she did not answer, he said, "You have asserted that our gods, too, are simply symbols of our hopes and despairs and longings, and possibly have no objective existence. However, we in the east believe that symbols are outward manifestations of unseeable and unknowable reality." Again he touched her cheek and smiled. "Alas, even philosophers who deride gold and priests who condemn the lust for it can only survive if they receive sustenance bought by the very thing which they despise! I have not discerned that they reject such sustenance; in truth, they are avid for it."

Aspasia, who possessed great humor, laughed in answer. "I have observed that it is rare to encounter a gaunt philosopher or a starveling priest. But they must eat, as they are men, or die."

"If they wish to prove their hypothesis that gold is worthless and the lust for it is wanton, then let them publicly starve in the market places as a worthy example to other men," said Al Taliph. "I love these idealists who denounce possessions but desire them for themselves!"

Awnings of every conceivable color and stripe and fabric lunged and flapped and fluttered and blew with the constant searing wind from the deserts. The mountains beyond were like hot lapis lazuli and brass against a sky the color of burnished bronze, and the sun within it was a hole and holocaust of flame. The crowds and throngs of customers and merchants, of men and squealing women, were jostled by hordes of children who raced between ranks of humanity and animals, brown, barefooted, naked children with ragged black hair and oily sly faces, holding hot breads and cakes and remnants of steaming meats in their hands, all of which they had stolen from brazier or table. Donkeys with laden baskets on their patient backs were beaten and pulled into the very midst of clotted bodies, and whips snarled and wheels grunted and hoarse oaths were yelled and heads were broken. All, with the exception of the children, were clothed in dusty black, crimson, yellow or blue, the men wearing headcloths bound with rope, and knotted, the women dirtily veiled with only their lustrous eyes darting everywhere.

Aspasia was not permitted to alight alone, but only in the company of Al Taliph and his band of eunuchs, headed by Kurda, and all carrying bared swords. Merchants would bring Aspasia ground lamb and mushrooms and barley roasted together and wrapped in green grape leaves, and acrid wine in metal goblets. Al Taliph, surrounded by his guard of eunuchs, would laugh when Aspasia declared that the meat was too spiced and hot for her taste and the wine too acid. He would laugh when she would eat or drink, however, and apparently enjoyed the strangeness and novelty. She once refused the soured milk, thick and bland in its earthen cups, but when persuaded she ate it and found it refreshing. At all times she sought to please Al Taliph, not only because she had been taught this but because she treasured his approval. He brought her unknown fruit which had a richness and emphasis beyond anything she had ever known. The hot cakes, filled with honeyed seeds and spices, or meats seasoned with coriander and cloves, excited her.

"I do not see pork," she said once.

His face changed, "We rarely eat pork," he said, and would not explain. She received raw fish in vinegar and onions with some trepidation but, urged, she would eat it from rough earthen platters, and found it delectable. There was also fried fish with capers and a pungent olive sauce which stung her tongue, and wine refreshed with the juice of lemons. Al Taliph was endlessly delighted during these experimentations and would laugh like a youth. He would always buy her some exquisite gold or silver trinket, necklaces or rings or earrings and bracelets, or some brazen vase or figure which she fancied. These she would hold in her hands, examining them, attempting to understand the east. Once he bought her a water lily of white jade, incredibly beautiful on its leaves of green jade, and this never left her possession. She believed it exhaled scent.

On another occasion he bought her a marble figurine taken from the tomb of some Egyptian noble, and there were many such in the booth of Egyptian rascals with black faces and black hidden eyes. She was repulsed by it. Turn it in her hands as she did it remained of one dimension, as if repudiating humanity and its warm aspects and contours. "Osiris," he explained to her. "The son of Isis, and also her husband. It is said that he, a most virtuous and sacred savior of his people, was murdered by his people, and then rose from the dead and ascended into heaven, from which he rules and loves humanity."

"The gods of Greece are handsomer and more sensible," she replied.

Again that inexplicable look came over his face, a look of gravity and withdrawal, which she could not interpret. Later he told her of the Egyptian religion, of Ptah, the God Almighty, who ruled all the endless universes, and was concerned with all creation. "The Greeks," she said, "are happiest when the gods forget them, for their attentions are frequently disastrous. We prefer to adore them—from a distance—and ask only their assistance when we need it."

Once again he looked grave and absent, and she was both intimidated and dismayed and wondered how she had offended him. She tried never to offend him, not out of fear but out of respect. And something which came perilously close to love, which she never suspected. A woman did not permit herself to love a man, she had been taught. That led to calamity and grief and despair, and the disintegration of a woman's dignity. She became a slave.

On still another occasion he gave her a large intricately carved ivory ball from Cathay. It had interstices and she discerned another smaller ball within it, and then turning it in her hands she discovered yet another ball within the second, and succeeding balls each smaller than the one which enclosed it. There was no joining, no indication of how each carved ball had entered the other, and she was puzzled. Al Taliph explained that the ball had originally been of one piece, the outer covering. "How, then, were the others carved?" she asked. He only shook his head. She marvelled, thrusting the tip of her finger, dyed in red in the eastern fashion, within the crevices. The inner balls rotated; they were not fixed.

Then, unaccountably, she was vexed. "You prefer solutions?" asked Al Taliph, watching her. He had made her seem absurd in her own opinion and she looked sharply at him, standing at his side. The hot sunlight struck her eyes and they smarted, but she continued to look at him, seeing how the light shifted on the dark bronzed planes of his lean face as on metal, lighted his large hooped earrings, but could not lighten his secret eyes. He had a brooding expression now, and she had seen it before and it had always perturbed her.

The jostling throngs were all about them, though kept at bay by the ring of lavishly attired eunuchs with their drawn swords. The men cursed them but sidled off at a respectful distance, for one knew that within that circle stood a man of consequence. So many milled nearby, clad in dirty and dusty robes of black and red and yellow, with striped head-coverings, clasped with knotted ropes, protecting their heads, their avid and blackish faces ravenous as jackals, their eyes glittering both with fawning abjectness and curiosity. They did not recognize this richly but quietly dressed man as their governor, for his own face was half-hidden within a hood and his mantle was of dark silk embroidered discreetly with gold. He never took these excursions with his own soldiers; he preferred to be without name in the market places, and without overt honor.

Then the burning wind from the desert partially lifted Aspasia's own hood and her veil, and a lock of her gilded hair streamed forth and the watching men came closer and raised a hoarse shout of wonder, seeing not only her hair but the whiteness and scarlet of her face, and her beauty. They pressed forward, the better to observe this unbelievable vision, and even crowded the eunuchs whose curved swords scintillated in the blinding light. Al Taliph gave no indication that he even saw the market rabble, but thrust Aspasia behind him —the usual position of a woman in the company of a man— and walked to the litter. Kurda's eyes jumped with hatred for this woman who had jeopardized his master. He followed Aspasia; the eunuchs, thrusting the air with their swords, guarded their retreat. Aspasia, glancing only once behind her, first saw Kurda with his face lustful for her death and beyond him the seething stalls of the market and the glaring faces of the market rabble, momentarily quiet, overcome with astonishment.

She was not frightened. It was only when she was in the litter with her lord that she felt some fear. He closed the thick silken curtains and they were in a hot gloom. The litter was lifted and they were borne away. Since then two weeks had passed and Al Taliph had not as yet taken her again to the markets. She never asked for a reason, for she learned that this irritated Al Taliph who did not believe that women were worthy of being given reasons for men's behavior.

But yesterday he had taken her to the site where Cyrus had defeated Astyages, last King of the Medes, from which battle he had entered on a career of conquest and power which ended only when he had succeeded in establishing himself as the mightiest emperor in all recorded history. He proclaimed himself the King of all the Persians and the Medes, thus uniting them in one empire, one ruthless power, extending his rule to all the lands between the Great Sea and Persia, and even to Egypt and Greece.

He had caused to be built on that site a great terraced palace, at the entrance to Fars, and a city had risen there to establish his glory. An enormous pillar had been raised beside the four-sided palace and on it, in three languages, Susian, Assyrian and Persian, had been inscribed: "I am Cyrus, the King, the Achaemenian!" The thick circular column, soaring to the incandescent blue sky, was embellished by a winged figure and an engraving of his tomb.

Silence stood all about them, the silence which inevitably followed the departure of the mighty and the illustrious, who are not as other men, and the desert wind blew fiercely into the valley. Aspasia was awed. She said, "He was an Achaemenian?"

"Yes," replied Al Taliph, gazing at the gigantic pillar. "He was also only a petty tribal chieftain, until he met the proud Median king, Astyages, and defeated him here."

Aspasia looked at her lord curiously. "You do not hate him?"

He returned her look with mingled amusement and exasperation. "How is that possible? He was godlike, King Cyrus, and though only the poor tributary ruler of Anshan he accomplished the incredible, the impossible, and made of Persians and the Medes, together, the jeweled and invincible crown of the world. We Medes reverence his memory, for he was a noble hero, and was merciful and just, honoring the women who had observed the battle." He smiled down at Aspasia. "Ponder. He was like one of your Greeks, who met Xerxes at Thermopylae and Salamis, with only crude weapons. He resembled your Spartan Leonidas—"

"I am an Ionian," said Aspasia, "not a Spartan or an Athenian."

He ignored this remark. He lifted his head and mused on the vast pillar. "The greatest of all virtues is courage, the most heroic. In the halls of courage even a petty chieftain is at one

109

with an emperor, and they bear the same banner. I have seen the tomb of Cyrus, the mausoleum where his golden vault lies, on an ascending terrace of white blocks of stone which resembles the pyramids of Egypt. His wife was an Egyptian. I have read the inscription on the tomb:

"'O man, whosoever thou art and from whencesoever thou comest (for that thou wilt come I know) I am Cyrus, who founded the empire of the Persians. Grudge not me then this little earth which covers my body.'"

His voice, in the profound stillness, was sonorous and commanding and even moving and Aspasia listened and was deeply stirred. He then turned away from her and went, in his usual baffling manner, towards his chariot, and Aspasia followed him in silence. Once in the chariot, with a slave protecting her from the sun with a scarlet umbrella, she said to Al Taliph, "'A little earth.' To that do kings and slaves return, and it is the end of glory and of slavery."

"It is also the end of a pariah dog," he answered, as one answers a child, and Aspasia flushed. "You think me ridiculous," she said.

"Alas. You are only a woman," he said and then seeing her affronted face and her mortification he lifted her hand and kissed it. "But are you women not the supreme conquerors, and we men only your slaves, even the mightiest among us?"

Had any other man of her own race, and of the west, said that to her she would have been placated. Now she could only think, in the heat of the garden: He mocks me, even with his kisses, his arcane smiles, and his gallant words. All men are strange, it is true, but he is the strangest of all. That was one of the times when I was afraid of him, for I do not understand him. He is capricious, at once tender and cruel, as a child is cruel, and then at other times he is lofty and grand and even more civilized than the Athenians. Sometimes he is as simple and direct as clear water, and sometimes he is as unsolvable as the ivory ball he gave me. Why did he desire me, in the house of Thargelia? I do not even know if he truly has affection for me. I believe that it is not my beauty, which he extols, which charms this most peculiar eastern man, yet I often fear he is not entranced by my intelligence and my learning and my arts, which he praises, for when I am most earnest and sincere he becomes hilarious. Would he grieve if I departed? I fear he would not, and I believe he would forget me the moment I was gone. Would I, in turn, mourn him? O gods, I fear I would!

She put her hands over her eyes and forbade herself to weep, for tears were smarting the rims of her eyes.

She had a hideous thought. Was it possible that she only diverted him, as a novelty would divert him for a time, and for that he cultivated her company and endured her presence? Did he display her to his guests as one would display an unusual but not human pet who had entertaining tricks, and charming ones, simulating humanity? Did she amuse those guests, as she amused her lord, and for the same reasons?

Mortification overcame her again. She vowed that at the next feast she would sit in silence, not even smiling, affecting stupidity. If Al Taliph became annoyed with her let him so be annoyed!

She began to think of her last visit to the tumultuous markets, and the booths where slaves were sold.

She always tried to avoid them and returned to the chariot, there to sit in melancholy under the white and red striped awnings, fanning herself with a jeweled and feathered fan, while Al Taliph bargained with the clamorous and gesticulating dealers. She had been surrounded in Thargelia's house by slaves, but since early childhood she had secretly protested against this degradation of human beings whom Greece considered only "things." Moreoever, she had sedulously studied the laws of Solon and his hope that slavery would eventually be banished by civilized nations. Slaves, however, were regarded as valuable property in Greece and her subject states, and had a measure of appreciation from their masters and were frequently loved and indulged, often educated if intelligent, and consulted.

This was not true of the east. Lords had the power of life and death over their slaves and could order their destruction at will, and with no more compunction than if those slaves had been rabid dogs or criminals. (In Greece there were some laws which protected the lives of slaves, and assured them some immunity from monstrous punishments.)

Only once or twice, seeing her reluctance, had Al Taliph demanded that Aspasia be present when considering the purchase of slaves. There, in large and shaded tents, and standing on a platform, were all conditions and ages of men, women and children, of many races from the blackest of Ethiopians and Arabs to the pale ivory of people from India and Cathay, and from barbaric nations as yet unnamed, with blue eyes and fair hair. They stood in mute resignation, like tethered animals, women with cookpots before them, signifying they were cooks and kitchen servants, naked little boys and girls with

111

faces covered with cosmetics to guard against the vehement sun, old women who could sew deftly, castrated boys conspicuously displayed in their mutilations and with faces like young girls, old men whose worn hands attested that they were gardeners and hewers of wood and drawers of water; beautiful maidens whose placards avowed their virginity, and without the smallest garments, their pubic hair plucked or shaven, their nipples tinted with henna; infants clasped desperately to their mothers' breasts, young strong men in chains, ready for the hardest labor, and middle-aged men carrying tablets and scrolls and styluses and pens who were obviously educated scribes; dancing girls with tambourines and as pretty as statues, and midwives with their stools and instruments.

All, without exception, bore that touching expression of resignation to fate, though sometimes, seeing one like Al Taliph, a distinguished lord of refinement, they would show a gleam of hope in their veiled eyes. He went from one to the other, considering, his dark finger against his lips. He would examine young girls as one would examine animals, parting their thighs and touching their parts expertly, and feeling the texture and firmness of their small breasts, or he would press the muscles of a sturdy young man, or contemplate the castrated boys shrewdly and eye their scars to be certain they bore no permanent disabilities or infection. He never spoke to the slaves but only to their dealers, questioning, bargaining, shrugging.

Aspasia had never been to a slave market before, and she was appalled. Al Taliph, so discriminating and fastidious in his house, here displayed a callousness which Aspasia could hardly believe. His handling of the slaves was not delicate; it was rough and expert. Worst of all, to Aspasia, the slaves did not wince or shrink from the indignities visited on them, some of which were intimate and ruthless. He did not refrain from examining some maidens to be certain of their virginity, and Aspasia closed her eyes and was sickened at the sight of the thrusting index finger. Often he would bring to the market some slaves he had found incompetent, or some girls of whom he had tired, and would sell them as one would sell cattle.

Then one day she had said to him, "Lord, you must not take me to the slave markets again. It is unendurable to me." He had raised his eyebrows with amusement and had studied her as one would study a curiosity. "Would you buy a horse or a cow without examining them for health and soundness?"

She had said, "They are human, even as you and I." He had laughed at her incredulously and then had turned

112

away in displeasure. She said, "Even if I vex you, lord, or even if you should exile me, I can come here no more." To her surprise, after a glance at her pale fixed face, he had shrugged. She was never forced to accompany him to the slave markets again.

She had decided, that night, that she hated and loathed him. She had not responded to his passion but had lain in his arms as mute as any slave and as unresisting. He had looked down into her face by the light of the gilt and crystal lamps, and had seen her revulsion and her averted face. A subtle and intuitive man, he had understood. He had turned away from her, and finally she had arisen and had gone to her chamber, her heart as cold as the winter snow on the mountains. He had taken no notice of her departure.

She had lain in her bed, sleepless, and dryly weeping, but whether in disgust or sadness she did not know. He did not call for her for a number of days, and each day was marked with suffering for her. When, one night, he had summoned her through one of his eunuchs, she had risen from her bed and had clad herself like a bride, trembling with joy. She felt shame also, but her delight finally overcame it and she went swiftly to his chamber with a smile so beautiful that he was struck once more by her marvelous loveliness and sat up in his bed and held out his arms to her. She ran to him. He removed the garment from her shoulders, reached into a bowl of fresh rose petals and sprinkled her breast with them, his swarthy face tender and pleased.

He had said, "You are very foolish, my white-breasted dove, my adorable one, but I have forgiven you. Come. Give me your lips, which are softer and sweeter than these roses."

She had given him passion before but tonight she excelled, half-sobbing under her breath, her snowy arms holding him as if with desperation. But when she returned to her chamber, and remembered, her face had become crimson both with remembrance and embarrassment.

She was thinking of these perplexing and devastating things today, in the garden, under the malignant eye of Kurda who watched her from the bronze doors of the palace. Seeing her bent head and saddened face with the acuteness of hatred he said to himself, "Ah, the foreign woman is sorrowful today. Has she offended my lord? Mithras grant it so, for then she will be banished!"

Feeling his gaze, Aspasia lifted her head and saw the gloating evil on his huge face, and a coldness, even in that heat, moved over her flesh and she felt alone as never she had felt alone before.

CHAPTER 10

Aspasia had considered the plight of Greek women evil enough but in Persia it was far more terrible. Free or slave, daughter or sister or matron, concubine or courtesan, sultana or mother or starveling whore: They were less than the dust before men, despised, ridiculed, hidden as shameful objects, suspected of the lowest instincts, as fickle as monkeys, as mindless as toads, as sexually virtueless as dogs, as stupidly vain as peacocks, treacherous as wild beasts, unclean, corrupt, soulless, sly, greedy as geese, quarrelsome, and instinctively malevolent and without true human qualities. They were also incapable of reasoning, and were mere prattlers and pretentious. They owned nothing, not even their own bodies. As Persia was a despotism, and did not possess even the dubious aspects of corrupt democracy, women had no appeal against the laws which considered them distinctly lower than a valuable animal. They had but one function, or parts of functions: to bring a dowry to husbands, to bear sons for husbands or masters, to work, to amuse, to give pleasure. If they possessed none of these attributes the law did not even protect their lives. If a female infant was unwanted she was not exposed for either death or adoption by some merciful childless matron, or taken by a slave-dealer. She was simply strangled and thrown upon a dung heap, to be eaten by wild dogs or jackals. As women were unclean, even as infants, the act of strangling was left to midwives, for not even a male slave would be expected to do this.

In Greece, if a matron was of a noble house or a wealthy or distinguished one, and if she possessed brothers and a father, she had much authority in her household and husbands sometimes feared her. Her dowry, though given to her husband, had to be accounted for to bankers and male members of her family, and if she were divorced or widowed it was returned to her with appropriate interest and any gains accrued by it. The mother of sons received considerable honor from a husband, and though she was relegated to the women's quarters and was not permitted to be seen by male strangers nor allowed beyond the portals except in the company of women attendants, not suffered at the table with her husband, she still had a certain status and respect. Then there was the hetaira, beautiful, educated and desired, and often extremely powerful, adored by men if hated by virtuous matrons.

Though legally under Greek law a woman was presumed to be incapable of managing personal affairs, she could, under dire provocation from her husband, such as cruelty or violence, send a written account of this to the Archon, the protector of such incapables as herself, who judged whether or not she was entitled to a divorce or separation from her husband, and the return of her dowry. Even the poorest and most humble of women had this privilege; the rich employed lawyers of eloquence, paid for by the family of the wife. In many cases the Archon agreed with the allegations and freed the woman from her marriage.

Indeed, in Minoan and Homeric times women had almost as much importance and weight with the law as did their men. It was not until Athens and her subordinate cities came under the rule of the Tyrants, and democracy, that women lost their status in public affairs. There had been, before this time, women who voted in elections, and who chose the husbands for their daughters and held property in their own right, and divorced their husbands at will, or decided on the man they would marry. They had authority over their sons also, and selected their wives. They had the right of inheritance from father or husband, and this was protected.

It was women like Aspasia, the hetairai, and wives of considerable intelligence, wealth and education, who were striving to raise the status of women throughout Greece and to return to them the old rights and privileges they had once possessed, and for which many were now clamoring.

But Persia had no such history as this, and Aspasia was revolted and in rebellion. It was true that she reigned over the household as not even the wives of Al Taliph reigned, and that all deferred to her wishes, with the exception of Al Taliph. However, she knew this was granted her not out of her inherent rights as a human being but as an indulged mistress whose privileges were tenuous and could be abrogated instantly at the command of her lord. Such had been the case with Narcissa, and Aspasia believed today that Narcissa's ultimate fate would very possibly be her own, when Al Taliph tired of her. She had dismally come to the conclusion, and this very recently, that Al Taliph had no real regard for either her or her mind, and was merely entertained by her, and secretly hilarious at her "presumptions" of being totally human, and that he enjoyed her love-making and the arts of love, including perversions, which she had been taught.

In this Aspasia was wrong, but she had no way to disprove it. For her lord complimented her only on her beauty or taste or dress or perfumes, and her seductions, and rarely if ever openly admired her aphorisms or opinions. It was not until much later that she realized that men, even such as Al Taliph, had an ancient and primordial fear of women. Thargelia had stated this often but Aspasia as yet had seen no evidence of it. That fear, Thargelia had taught, could be subtly used and manipulated by a woman to her advantage. Aspasia now did not believe it. It might be true of western men, but certainly it was not true in the east!

It did not occur to her, at eighteen, that men everywhere used punitive measures against women, and restrained and denigrated them and passed laws to contain and dehumanize and humiliate them, out of this primal fear.

Though knowing she was unwelcome in the harem, and that the women there regarded her as a suspected foreign woman and were envious of her and resented her and longed for her ultimate rejection, she went every morning to the quarters assigned to the women. The four wives would graciously visit the harem and sit among the concubines and slaves, listening to songs and harps and zithers and lutes and cymbals and tambourines and watch erotic dances, while munching on sweetmeats and pastries and drinking wine. They reclined on thick soft and silken cushions while slaves dressed their hair and the other women amused them. There was much gossip here also, and laughter and general happy contentment, and many lewd stories, and young children were brought to them by attendant slaves, and the wives and the concubines, who had also borne children to Al Taliph, played with the little ones and admired their beauty. Some erudite slaves, all women, would read their compositions in poetry to the fat and yawning beauties of the harem, and there would be a flow of delicious tears at some telling phrase concerning love and moonlight and golden rivers and the eternal partings of lovers.

Had Aspasia been older and wiser she would have understood that the women of the harem, and the wives, were quite complacent and contented in the harem, and longed for nothing but ease and comfort and the delights of the table and wine and music. They had known nothing else. They never bewailed their degraded state, for what more could a woman desire than this: protection and the favors of the lord, and joy in life? They accepted everything with serenity.

To Aspasia, this was incredible. She could not believe that none of these women ever secretly longed for dignity, for freedom, for the stature of humanity. Even the Greek women were stirring restively now, and the Archons were reluctantly listening. If the Greek women were nurturing increasing fire in their hearts at subordinations and masculine contempt, then surely these women of Al Taliph's household must possess such burnings also, for were not women of one breed and one desire, however suppressed? It was Aspasia's determination, especially lately, to increase this fire, this incipient rebellion, of her sex. She was inspired both by an instinctive fear for herself and by indignation, and, above all, by pride.

Over these three years she had remembered what Hesiod had said: "Even if you should lay up even a little upon a little, and should do this often, soon would even this become great." She believed that she had laid upon "a little upon a little" in the harem, and that eventually the wives and the concubines would understand their indignities and protest against them.

Therefore, she visited the harem every day, and ignored the giggles, the wondering blank eyes, the stares, the amused contempt, the resentment and even the hate and envy of the women, who thought her insolent and unwomanly and did not understand in the least her conversation and her exhortations. In truth, they had come to believe that in some way she was threatening their happy existence. In bed with Al Taliph, they murmured petulantly against her and deprecated her and tried to tell him that she was a disturbance and a fool and should be banished. They could not understand why he did not heed their meek warnings. Some proclaimed that she was a sorceress and had entangled their lord in a malefic spell, and some employed the astrologers and the conjurers in the palace to deliver Al Taliph from this malign enchantment. As the astrologers and the conjurers also despised and resented Aspasia, they were only too eager to comply. They cast Al Taliph's horoscope and warned him that misfortune would come to him from the foreign woman, who possessed a demon, and were outraged that he laughed at them.

"Would that there were many such enchantresses in the world," he would reply. "It would be a more delightful place."

Had they been told that he loved her—a secret withheld even from Aspasia for fear that she might exploit it—they would have thought they were listening to madness, for what man loved a woman except in poetry which was not part of life but only an amusement for idle hours and dreams?

On this early morning Aspasia, unattended, walked through the palace from her gorgeous chamber to the harem. She wore the eastern dress and not the tunic or peplos of Greece.

117

The robe was blue, a color Al Taliph preferred for it warned against evil spirits, tight and revealing over shoulders and breast and waist and belly, then unfolding into flares and pleats bordered with gold embroidery. She did not wear a headdress and her hair floated behind her in a pale bright cloud, and embraced her hips and thighs. Her arms were partially bare and clasped by many gemmed bracelets, and her sandals were also gemmed over white arches and painted toes. Her strong yet delicate face was set, even fixed, and her eyes, the color of topaz wine, were very sober. The eunuchs everywhere, and the guards, stared after her, the guards furtively desiring her and even the eunuchs feeling a faint stir in their mutilated loins. They all believed she was an evil spirit, for what human woman possessed such divine beauty, such grace, such fluid movements of hidden limbs, such whiteness and scarlet and gilt? Her very regality was a wonder, and foreign, and intimidating. They believed that she did not even eat, for she was not plump; demons did not eat human food. They dined on unmentionable abominations. It was rumored that she conversed like a man at the table with their lord, and that alone frightened the inhabitants of the palace, who whispered that she was not truly a woman but a demonic masculine apparition. So, she was unclean, and dangerous. Each man, eunuch and guard, made the sign against the evil eye when she appeared.

She passed through gleaming white halls whose arched doorways blew with blue or red or yellow silk curtains, and whose floors were strewn with colorful Persian carpets. Silken couches and Chinese tables lined the walls, and immense vases filled with flowers. Through the grilled archways facing the gardens there came the passionate smell of blossoms and water and resin, and the cries of parrots and the screams of peacocks and the quacking of ducks and the songs of the gardeners. Everywhere there were dancing reflections from fountains and sunlight, striking on floor and fretted stone walls and on mosiacs like strenuous paintings. There was the music of zithers and harps at a distance, and the far sound of women's smothered laughter or the slap of some hurrying slave's footsteps on marble.

It was still very early, yet the palace hummed with life and movement, and the presence of many people. Aspasia came to the bronze double-doorway which led to the harem, and which was guarded by six enormous eunuchs, hairless, fat, naked to the waist, arrayed in magnificent trousers and with turbans on their heads, their hands holding bared swords.

They wore golden chains about their thick necks and gold bracelets were clasped on their vast upper arms. Their shoes, of gilt leather, were turned up sharply at the toes. They eyed Aspasia without favor, and their eyes, sunken in fat, were sullen if respectful. She noticed that they made the sign against the evil eye, and she smiled and her beautiful white teeth sparkled. But she had to wait until the eunuchs opened the carved metal doors for her, and they did not hasten.

She entered the large room where the women of the harem disported themselves. Here it was dimmer, the light shaded by carved ebony screens from Cathay, the rugs thicker, one upon another, the walls hung with silken curtains, the floor scattered with heaped cushions of every hue, the divans soft and luxurious, the multitude of small brass tables from India covered with baskets and bowls of fruit and sweetmeats and cakes, the brazen urns redolent of wine even this early, and everywhere flowers on table and on floor so that the air here, hotter than in the halls, made the head swim with scent and musk and airlessness for all many slaves waved fans of ostrich plumes continually. There was also an odor of perfumed sweat, sickening to western senses. The overpowering luxury never failed to displease Aspasia, who thought it wanton and stale and deadening. It reeked of woman flesh, indolent and dissipated and oiled and sultry, and sensual. Aspasia thought of it as a voluptuous kennel of coddled bitches, constantly in heat and delivering litters. There had been a certain atmosphere of controlled and elegant austerity in the house of Thargelia, a civilized restraint, for all it had been sybaritic too.

She found the harem depraved with a spiritual depravity unknown in Miletus or Greece. She often thought that over-elaboration, the overly intricate and embroidered, the overly suffused with animal comforts, the too opulent, were not only decadent and cloying but hinted of dissolution and decay. Possessing the western mind she was revolted by redundance, by detail heaped on detail, as one is with exhaustive carnality —surfeited. She was never to come to terms with the eastern mind, the excessively ornate. In some peculiar fashion it wearied and oppressed her. She was aware of the hostility with which she was greeted.

The harem, as usual, was filled with women and babble and noise and clashing music and laughter. Some little naked children raced about, complaining and stuffing their mouths or flinging themselves upon their mothers with petulant cries and demands, or fighting. A few small monkeys swung from curtains and screeched, and a few cats yowled and leaped upon tables to devour the dainties there, and parrots shrieked from gilt cages. The hot dimmed air seemed to Aspasia the very atmosphere of Hades, reeking. There was a fetid smell, a sickening odor of overripe fruit, dates, figs, citrons and melons, all rotting away in beautifully painted and enameled Chinese bowls. Even the flowers had a sickly effluvium.

The fat oiled women, clad in rich trousers and tight bodices, reclined on cushions as bloated as themselves, or on soft divans, unveiled, languorous, smiling, gossiping, laughing, playing with the children or upbraiding slaves who were rough with their hairbrushes and combs, applying odoriferous cosmetics and perfumes, reddening their lips, scratching their hair or their voluptuous bodies, chattering, murmuring lewdly or slapping the more obstreperous children who were too exigent. The ostrich fans waved but could give no coolness nor for long banished the swarms of insistent flies which bit and polluted the sweetmeats and fruit. The music jangled on Aspasia's ear, for it seemed discordant to her and without coherence.

For a long time now Aspasia had endeavored to teach the younger concubines the skills of reading and writing and the appreciation of art, and even, unfortunate girl! philosophy. At first the young girls had appeared interested and had even learned a little. Then their natural indolence overcame them and they asked her, in their light pouting voices, of what use this would all be to them. She had replied, "It is your right as a human being to learn about the world and to comprehend it." At this the older women had laughed immoderately and had said, "It is enough for women to understand men." Aspasia reluctantly acknowledged, from her teachings at Thargelia's school, that that knowledge was the most important in the world, but there was also the question of a woman's mind and soul. When she would tell the women this they would stare at her risibly and shrug, as at the intrusion of barbaric ideas. They had everything a man could give them, and what more did they need or desire? Too, who had said that a woman had a mind and soul apart from men? They had never heard such absurdities. In the meantime, life was enjoyable and for that purpose were they not created? In the face of this mocking argument, this bland and superior amusement, this contempt for her "barbarian" ideas, she could only fume and despair.

Still, she persisted. Today, as she entered, to the familiar humming babble and broad and ridiculing smiles and the stuffing of mouths and the clamor of tambourine and zither and harp and flute and lyre, and the screaming of children, she saw, to her vague alarm, that Kurda, himself, was stationed here instead of the usual eunuchs. He stood half-hidden against a drapery and Aspasia unconsciously shrank, for all she despised him. His eyes gleamed like the eyes of a wild animal in the dusk. She could only ignore him; and the sight of his deliberately bared sword.

She waited until there was a comparative silence, trying to avoid noticing the smiling repudiation in the women's eyes, their overt envious scorn of her, their awaiting her next words and gestures as one awaits the antics of a comedian.

She said, "You have often remarked, ladies, that I am the favorite of our lord, the noble Al Taliph, and it has made you resentful and unhappy. Did you ever ask why he preferred me to you?"

They ruminated on that, exchanging mirthful sly glances. Then one of the wives, seated aside on a divan, said, "You make him laugh, and he needs laughter, as a king needs a fool to entertain him. We serve his deepest needs and passions, as you do not. What! You have never even borne him a child! Therefore, he has not regarded you as a woman but as a jester, a tumbler, a dancing girl of no importance." She spoke out of malice, for she knew Aspasia was treated as a queen in this house.

"I speak to his soul and his mind," said Aspasia, standing among them. Her face was proud and pale.

The women burst out laughing, throwing their heads on each other's shoulders, slapping each other's hands, feigning exhaustion of laughter, sprawling on their many colored cushions, and exhaling sighs of exquisite titillation. The slaves laughed also, and the children screamed with delight, not knowing why. The whole harem moved in a tumult of derisive joy. Kurda grinned at this evil woman. Only here did she find her proper position as a rejected slave.

One of the wives said, "Last night my lord called me to his bed and was pleased by my ministrations and I slept at his feet until dawn, and then he kindly rewarded me with a gift and a smile. Where were you last night, O Aspasia of Miletus?"

"This morning," said a concubine of about thirteen, "my lord summoned me for unusual pleasures and I gratified him and he said I was delicious. Where were you this morning, Lady?"

I was in his libraries, reading, thought Aspasia. Nevertheless, she was filled with angry humiliation, for all that she

121

knew of Al Taliph and his harem. He never spoke of these women to her and in her fashion she had thought them of no consequence to him.

"I am about to bear his third child," said the second wife. "Is your belly swollen, O Aspasia of Miletus, you his favorite?"

It is absurd to feel betrayal, thought Aspasia. I am a hetaira. I am his chief concubine. Why, then, should I feel degraded?

"He was weary when he came dusty from the city yesterday," said the third wife. "Did he summon you to his green marble bath, there to anoint him and massage him and clamber on his body for pleasure? Did he then slide into his pool and invite you to engage in more acts of love and tender consolations? Did you disport with him like a dolphin, a female dolphin pursued by her mate? Did you then enfold him in soft garments, give him wine while he reclined and sing to him softly until he slept? Where were you, O Aspasia, learned one?" She added: "I am again with child by him."

I was pondering on Hesiod, thought Aspasia, and she was mortified. Never had Al Taliph asked these things of her as he asked his wives and concubines. She was formally summoned to his bed when he desired her, and then fondled and loved, but in no other way was she asked to serve him out of her woman's heart. After the love-making he would discuss poetry and politics and art and science with her, and philosophy, while her head faced his on the pillow, and then he would sleep. She forgot that his arm would still embrace her as a treasure. Now she only thought of his disporting with his wives and his slaves, and laughing, and a terrible sorrow overcame her which she had come to fear was the sorrow of love.

Then her pride came to her rescue. She was an Ionian woman, and she had been educated and trained and was a human being, not a mere thing such as these women. It was a poor consolation, but she clung to it. Let him disport himself with these animals she had tried to raise to the status of humanity. She had his mind and respect—she hoped—and could entertain him with epigrams and stories and philosophies, and was that not the better part? She paused, doubtful.

She then noticed two little naked girls disporting themselves among the other children, and they were strangers to her. They were not more than seven years old, pretty olive-colored little girls far from puberty, and as hairless, except for their flowing black hair, as young pigs. Slaves kept catching them to massage their small bodies with scented oils and to comb and dress their long hair and weave pearls among it and brush it. Their infant bodies were smooth and vulnerable, their private parts closed and tender. Their only ornaments were earrings of pearl and enamel. Their childish eyes were smeared with kohl, their plump cheeks colored with unguents, their voices keen and babyish. They ran from ministrations and shrilled with the other children, until caught again. One was eating pomegranates with gusto, her chin running with scarlet. The other hugged a doll to her breastless chest, and kissed it lavishly and jingled its bells, holding it up for admiration. They were as newborn as lambs, and Aspasia was touched.

"I have never seen these little ones before," she said. "Who is the mother of these twin children?"

The women tittered, overcome with laughter. Then one of the wives said, "Our lord purchased them in the slave market yesterday, as a gift to a great merchant tonight, from Damascus."

Aspasia was appalled, and she thought of Cleo, who, at thirteen and still not nubile, had been given to Cadmus. She said, "As handmaidens, until they are of a proper age?"

The women were even more hilarious, rocking on their fat buttocks. "No," said one, "as concubines."

Aspasia disbelieved. "They will die," she said.

The eldest wife said with superiority over this barbarian: "They have been introduced today to phallic instruments of ivory."

For the first time Aspasia noticed small tricklings of blood on the children's round thighs. She put her hands to her cheeks and shuddered. The slaves, seeing her gaze, wiped away the blood indifferently, then smeared unguents on the parts. The children winced and whimpered, then ran off to play.

Aspasia turned to the four wives of Taliph. "Are not your maternal hearts in revolt against this desecration and deflowering and torture of children? Is it not abominable to you, you who are mothers of children, yourselves?"

They looked at her with fresh derision and wonder. "Is this not for what a woman was born, to give pleasure to men?" Thus spoke the oldest wife.

Then Aspasia realized fully, and for the first time, that the eastern concept of women was accepted by females, not denied, not rebelled against, but serenely recognized as their fate, against which it was unbelievable to protest, unthinkable to revolt.

The oldest wife, who did not detest Aspasia as much as the

others did, said to her almost gently, "Why would you destroy our happiness?"

Aspasia made a wide gesture with her white arms. "Is this happiness, to you?"

"Yes," said the wife. "What more could be given? Alas for you, poor foreign woman, your mind is beset by turbulent demons."

"I will protest this monstrous torture of little ones to my lord, tonight, and remove them from this noxious harem," said Aspasia, and left the room, her heart thudding with anger and sickness. She was followed by the high tinkling laughter of the women, and she felt unclean.

CHAPTER 11

Aspasia had been summoned for this night to attend a banquet given by Al Taliph for some illustrious guests. She was bathed and anointed and perfumed by her slaves, her long glistening hair brushed with fragrant lotions. Seething with rebellion and horror at what she had learned today in the harem she refused to wear eastern garments, and chose a white Greek tunic bordered with silver, and a full toga of the finest Egyptian linen the color of a faint hyacinth petal. She dressed her hair herself, binding it up in Greek fashion with ribbons of silver, and the tunic and toga revealed her white neck which was embraced by pearls. She put no armlets on her arms nor rings upon her fingers. She would not use more color upon her rosy lips nor cheeks. When she stood up before her polished mirror she was as untouched as Athene Parthenos, the virgin goddess of wisdom, and the slaves were intimidated. Her aspect was austere and remote. Her brown eyes had dangerous glints in them. She intended to rebuke Al Taliph in every gesture and intonation of her voice. She would confront him with western principles and her abhorrences, and, in his bed, she would reproach him coldly. Though she was supposed to conceal her hair under a light veil she now rejected it. She was a woman of learning and consequence and she was again determined to impress Al Taliph. She was his companion and not a compliant slave, concubine or wife. She could leave him at her will. She considered the wealth he had given her. With sickness in her heart, she reflected on leaving him, and almost wept.

She decided to recline upon a divan in her chamber to rest

and compose her mind before appearing in the dining hall. For once the sound of wind and tree and the scent of the gardens and the cries of the birds did not calm her. They were a hot discord, mocking. She understood fully now that eastern women had no more regard for human life than did their lords, or perhaps even less. The fate of those little girls was no more deplored than the fate of a fly or a locust or a rat.

She began to doze in the languid heat of the day despite herself. She suddenly started awake at a touch on her shoulder. A female slave said to her, "Lady, the lord Al Taliph wishes to see you at once in his chamber."

This was most unusual. He never desired to see her this early. She rose, arranged her garments and went to the satrap's chamber. The halls were unusually quiet, and she saw no one and heard nothing but the far sound of slaves singing and strumming on musical instruments.

A eunuch stood at the entrance to the chamber and he stared at her and then with insolent slowness he opened the door. She entered, bowing as customary. Al Taliph, whose chamber was royal and filled with treasures and perfumes, sat at a distance in a divan. He was splendidly clad in scarlet trousers and a silk shirt as white as snow and a vest of blue woven with gems. His turbaned head was majestic, his swarthy face unreadable. His whole posture was contained yet alert, as a panther, lying in shade, is alert. He did not respond to Aspasia's greeting. He merely observed her without expression. Then for the first time she saw Kurda near him, Kurda with a whip in his hand, Kurda gloating and grinning, his fat jowls gleaming.

"Lord," said Aspasia, her first start at the presence of Kurda subsiding.

"Stand before me," said Al Taliph in a voice she had never heard from him before. It was not angry or emotional nor raised. It was merely indifferent, as one who speaks to a slave. Aspasia halted. Was this cold and remote man the man who had held her in his arms and kissed her hands and called her his lily of the Shalimar, his rose of India, his moonlit blossom? For the first time she felt a thrill of apprehension and dismay. She glanced at Kurda again, and saw his hateful triumph. She raised her head proudly, and waited. Al Taliph continued to regard her as if she were a slave beyond his notice who had finally intruded her presence impertinently upon him.

"I have indulged you," he said. "I have heard for some time

that you have been vexing the women of my household with wild exhortations and fulminations against authority and the customs of our country. I did not protest. I even thought you would amuse them or awaken them to some liveliness that might entertain me. But they have finally appealed to me to bar you from their presence as a disturbing and unpleasant trespass. You have, they say, attempted to incite them against my pleasure and my comfort. They can no longer endure your blatant western barbarities, and from them I have now delivered my women. Never again must you visit unless you can control your tongue and be one with them."

Aspasia forgot her fear and her face colored deeply. "I am no barbarian, lord. I am a free woman, not a slave, not an unlettered concubine, not a fat and mindless wife whose sole joy is in eating and languishing on cushions and serving you at your will."

He inclined his head. "What are you?" he asked.

She felt her heart jump. "I am your companion, at your pleasure, to converse with you, at your will. I am freeborn, and have been educated, and my mind has been admired."

He lifted the lid of a box of sweetmeats, drew out a honeyed date and ate it slowly, watching her. Then he said, "What are these things to me, you bought woman of Miletus? I paid an enormous price to your mistress, Thargelia, for the alleged delights of your company. You no longer please me."

She was suddenly sick and dazed and something enormously sentient in her heart quailed. She felt tears in her eyes. But she lifted her head proudly. "Then," she said, "I will depart and no longer fatigue you with my presence nor bore you with my disputations. If you paid an enormous price for me I will return it."

"From the gifts I gave you," he said, in that same low and terrible voice.

She was silent. She felt as if she were dying both of shame and something else she could not comprehend.

"You are not even young any longer," he continued. "You are eighteen years old. I dismissed my Narcissa, and she was younger than you, seventeen, but she had become too old for me. Why, then, do I suffer you, the disturber of my peace, the turmoil of my women, the disorder of my household?"

Kurda gave a muffled chuckle of joy and victory, and Aspasia heard but did not look at him. The whole intensity of her eyes was fired on Al Taliph, as she stood before him like a white goddess, the color gone from her lips and cheeks.

"If I did these things which displease you, lord," she said, "it was because I could no longer bear to see my sex degraded, my womanhood shamed, my very existence made less than the existence of a dog."

He raised his sharp black eyebrows. "I have done so to you?"

"No," she said. "But you have done this to the women of your harem, and in their ignominy I have seen my own, however kind you have been to me."

He said, very slowly, as if with distaste, "You have learned that women are not considered truly human in civilized countries. Yet, you have set your face against this absolute truth. Are you not presumptuous, because I indulged you? You have not been treated in this house like a woman of the harem. I have proffered you honors which are unbelievable in my country; I have accepted you almost as an equal. For that you have not been grateful. You have tried to incite rebellion in my house, among creatures less valuable than a good horse."

"Some are mothers of your children!" cried Aspasia, goaded at the thought. "Or are your children less than the dust also, because they proceeded from 'a good horse' or a dog?"

"Your father considered you less worthy to live than a donkey," said Al Taliph. "Your mother rescued you and gave you to Thargelia; otherwise you would have perished as an infant. Are your men of more compassion and gentleness than I?"

At this, Aspasia was silent for a moment. Finally, she said, "If there was one thing for which I was born it is to elevate the stature of my sisters, and to deliver them from dishonor, to make them recognize that they are human also, with human prerogatives. Twice that was so, under the laws of Solon, and in the Homeric period. It is said that the women of Israël are honored by their men and respected by their sons."

"You are indeed learned—in the wrong things," said Al Taliph and now he smiled and the smile was more threatening than his voice. "You are my companion, you say—my bought companion. Do you not know that in the eyes of our laws you are only an animal? Yet, if you wish, I will have pity and release you, and you may go where you will. But without the gifts I have given you."

Aspasia was suddenly reminded of what Thargelia had threatened her with nearly four years ago, and she was filled with such despair that she instantly thought of suicide. There was no other deliverance. It was evident to her now that Al Taliph had wearied of her, though only two nights ago he had actually kissed one of the white arches of her feet, and, in passion, he declared that she was the moon of his delight and dearer to his heart than all his possessions and his position. But what a man swore in lust, Thargelia had taught her maidens, was not to be taken seriously, but only exploited at that moment before desire had become cool, or before it was satisfied.

Part of her mind contemplated her desperate condition but her heart was crushed with misery and longing and her white lips parted as if in an agony. She said, "Do with me what you will. It is no longer of significance to me."

He studied her as if probing her soul. He idly played with the golden tassel of his girdle. At last, he said, "I have heard that you pronounced some wild words upon discovering the women I have designated as a gift for my friend from Damascus tonight."

"They are infants, not women!" she cried.

"They are animals," he replied. "Would you have demurred so at a gift of twin lambs or a young colt?"

"They are human," she said.

He shrugged. "I have not discerned it. Aspasia, you have known for a long time that in the east human life is very cheap; it is worthless. It is not of any importance unless it is well-born, and even then, if female, it is not considered of any consequence. But an Arabian steed—ah, there is beauty and value. *There* is something admirable and to be cherished."

"Zoroaster did not come to animals, but to men," she said, becoming more broken by the moment. "Mithras, also."

"Let us not quibble," said Al Taliph, closing his eyes for a weary moment. "They came to men. They did not come to women, for women, in the east, have never been considered to have souls."

Kurda thought with hot impatience, Why does he even converse with this creature, as if she possessed a mind and an intellect?

Aspasia sighed with broken-hearted exhaustion. She repeated, "Do with me as you will."

"That I intend," he answered and held out his hand to Kurda. The eunuch responded swiftly and gave Al Taliph the whip he held. Al Taliph took it and idly slapped his knee with it and it made a sharp and crackling noise in the room. Aspasia could not believe what she saw. She glanced at Kurda with an appalled look and started.

"No," said Al Taliph, "I do not intend Kurda to flog you though for less I would command him to flog even my favorite wife. I do not intend for him to witness your punishment either. Kurda, leave us."

The eunuch was bitterly disappointed. He wanted to see this final crushing of the foreign creature, her absolute humiliation. He hesitated. Al Taliph raised his voice and said emphatically, "Begone, slave." Kurda bowed, and backed away and left the room and slowly closed the door behind him. Aspasia drew a deep and sobbing breath, seeing to the last his taunting and hating face.

Al Taliph rose and loomed above her. He said, "Remove your garments to your waist."

Aspasia glanced with terror at the thin but lethal whip. Never had she been struck before except once when receiving a mild slap from the impatient Thargelia. Despite her efforts her flesh quailed with mingled dread and shame. She looked up into Al Taliph's face for some sign of mercy, but there was none. It was incredible to her that those metallic lips had lain upon her own, that that hand had caressed her breast and fondled her body and given her delight. It was this incredulity rather than pride which held her still and mute.

With an oath he seized her hair with one hand and with the other, which held the whip, he stripped and tore the tunic and toga from her shoulders and forced her to her knees. He flung her forward so that she lay prone. But instantly she raised herself to his knees and clasped her hands to her breast and lifted her head in silent repudiation.

"As you will," he said. "It will be your last decision in this house."

He lifted the whip and it sang through the air and struck her across her shoulders and then her back. It was as if a hot knife had seared her. But she did not tremble; she did not utter a sound. She pressed her lips together and stared into the distance. The whip lifted and fell, whistling, and each stroke was of renewed fire and ferocity. Pain almost overwhelmed her; her tender white flesh quivered but did not shrink. Her hands protected her breasts from the curling weapon, but the sides of her palms were scorched. Then her whole back was in flames, in torment almost more than she could endure. Still the lash rose and fell with a steady hissing, and it was the only sound in the chamber. She did not cry, attempt to escape, or moan. She was like a marble image receiving blows it could not feel. Once she thought she would faint, but from that last indignity she held herself, nor did she groan for mercy.

At last he was done and he threw the whip from him with a sound like detestation. She pushed herself to her feet, her whole body in torment. She could feel a trickling of blood between her shoulder blades. Calmly, then, not looking at him, she attempted to cover her nakedness with the remnants of her torn clothing.

Then his hands were suddenly on her, and he was kissing the welts on her back and the broken flesh with a passion she had never known him to display before, even at the most ecstatic moments. He was uttering gasping words, incoherent, almost moaning. Dazed, she endured it. He brought a brazen bowl of water and a jar of unguents and dressed her wounds and soothed the swollen welts. His hands were as tender as a woman's.

"Ah, that you did this to me!" he cried.

Sick and dizzy and only half-conscious, she closed her eyes. Then she was in his arms and he was holding her against his breast and kissing her face, brow, cheek and lips and throat, and she could hear the thundering of his heart against hers. Without her own will her arms lifted and she put them about his neck and began to weep, and did not know why the pain in her breast, more awful than the pain in her flesh, subsided, leaving an anguished sweetness behind it.

CHAPTER 12

Though Aspasia was overcome by her emotions as she traversed the long blue and white halls to her own chamber she was aware of a peculiar pent silence in the palace, and understood that her humiliation at the hands of Al Taliph had flown through all corridors and rooms like a bird, and that, without her hearing a sound, all were maliciously gleeful and triumphant. Her body smarted unbearably, in spite of the unguents, and she held her torn garments about her and lifted her head, conscious of unseen and gloating eyes behind fretwork and curtain. Her hair hung about her in disorder, and she threw it back from her burning shoulders.

Calmly enough she told the slaves that she had decided on other dress, and they brought forth an eastern robe of scarlet and gold. She permitted the maidens to bathe her again and anoint her bruises and welts with unguents. She had not been relieved from attending the banquet given by Al Taliph. She perfumed herself with attar of jasmine and wore an Egyptian necklace of large stones and golden fringes and wound strands of pearls through her hair. She was deathly pale, the natural vermillion of her complexion and lips absent. She applied herself to the paint-pots and clasped her waist with a gilded girdle, which blazed.

She glanced through the barred arched window of her chamber and saw the brilliant and burning gold of sunset outlining the ochre mountains. The air was pervaded with aureate dust on the plain and the valley below, and shadows were purple. Everything seemed dreamlike to her, and unusually silent, and the violent colors of sky and earth and mountains became alien. She thought, I must leave him, and the next moment she said to herself, That I cannot do, for it may be that I love him while I hate him also. She could not understand her own conflicting agitations, at once infuriated and then composed, at once full of hatred and resentment, and then melting. She wanted to weep again but her eyelids had become dry and aching. Then something emerged from her chaotic thoughts:

When she left this place she would go to Athens and establish a school like Thargelia's, but not with its lustful teachings. It would be academe for girls of intelligence and gifts so that never would they be mere concubines with a smattering of learning to intrigue powerful men. The young ladies would be taught professions—Then Aaspasia thought, wearily: To what end, when women are so despised even in civilized Attica and their minds and souls deprecated? She had another thought, and it was exhilarating. An educated and learned woman, in the company of similar sisters, could be a force again in Greece, could come to terms—and not through lust—with the men with whom they associated. The power of their minds would be greater than the power of their beauty, for beauty was evanescent but the spirit grew in stature if nourished. It was said that in Egypt royal women had enormous influence on their Pharaoh husbands and in matters of state, and that well-born girls were almost as expertly educated as their brothers. It was not even denied women to be rulers of Egypt. In Greece there were priestesses, and in Egypt also, and in the latter country the goddess Isis was adored even more than Horus and Osiris, and she had special priests to attend her altars. Women were not considered unclean in Egypt, and if they had private quarters it was at their own wish and husbands and sons could not invade except by special permission.

If this was possible in other countries it could again be possible in Greece. As for Persia— Aspasia shrugged, then winced with pain. She put the matter far back in her consciousness and, serene as an eastern goddess, and as haughty,

131

she made her way to the banquet hall to join Al Taliph, who had just summoned her. The halls and corridors were now lighted by lamps and torches thrust into walls and the yellow and crimson shadows flickered over white and blue floors and on draperies of many colors. The gardens were now dark but the nightingales had begun to sing. Pots of incense smoldered in all the corners of the halls and the warm air was heavy with it, overcoming even the delicate scent of flowers in the huge Chinese vases. Aspasia saw no one except the figures of alert eunuchs. Now a desert wind came through the arches, parched, gustily hot, which did not cool but only enhanced the heat of stone and earth and mountain. It also carried with it an aromatic odor of pepper and spice as it blew over the land.

A eunuch held aside the curtains to the dining hall for her and she saw his smirk, only half-hidden. She entered the hall, which was large, its marble floor almost completely covered by Persian carpets of endless colors and patterns. The walls were alive with mosaics, and elaborate patterns of flowers and trees and hideous monsters, all lavishly painted. Al Taliph sat in his alcove on a divan heaped with cushions, so that he half-inclined in the small enclosure. The other guests sat cross-legged on vast cushions of silk on the floor, with very low individual brass tables before them laden with gilt wine vessels and Chinese plates and spoons and knives, in the eastern manner. At a distance there were musicians, all men, softly playing on flute and zither and harp. Large brazen lamps hung from the domed and frescoed ceiling, burning perfumed oils and throwing shifting light over the guests. Slaves were hurrying on muted feet with platters and jugs of wine.

Al Taliph was gorgeously arrayed in cloth of gold with a slash of red silk, embroidered heavily, and with gold tassels. He wore a headcloth of cloth of gold also, held by knots of jeweled cord. Never had he appeared so darkly handsome to Aspasia, nor so desirable, for all the fresh hatred she felt for him and the sick longing in her heart. He was conversing with his guests and did not halt at her entrance, but languidly summoned her to his divan in the recess with a wave of his hand. She made her way in silence to the divan and was permitted, as usual, to sit at his feet. For an instant she was dimly conscious of hearing a man gasp, then appear to choke. But as Al Taliph's guests were invariably astonished at her beauty it was of no immediate significance to her.

There were several men present, all resplendent in their robes, and turbans, eating and drinking with flattering voracity, and listening to their host. Aspasia hardly saw them. She was not permitted to speak unless addressed by Al Taliph, or his guests. She sat silently at his feet, all rose and gold and marble whiteness, and her hands were clasped in her lap. Occasionally, as if caressing a favored dog, Al Taliph would idly stroke her bare arm or shoulder or throat, or lift a lock of her hair, then would let the lock fall carelessly. For the first time her cheeks became hot and flushed at this treatment, but she did not shrink. It would only surprise and anger him, and she had come to fear his anger. Her flesh trembled, in spite of herself, at his touch, and she despised her own lack of control over her senses even while she yielded voluptuously to them. To divert herself she stared at the fabulous gemmed rings on his fingers until her eyes ached.

Al Taliph was not only governor of his province, he was also a very rich and astute merchant. He owned many bazaars in the city and also in other cities, fleets of vessels, caravans, a bank and countless olive groves, fields, orchards and meadows and multitudes of sheep and cattle and goats. He was invested in prosperous manufactories and was the possessor of jewelry and curio shops in profusion, including priceless objects of art. It was alleged he was a stern usurer in addition to all else, but never had he been accused of looting his province as did other governors, and his judgments, though severe, were invariably honorable. Not only was he received with respect at the court of Artaxerxes, but was famous in Samarkand, Persepolis, Naksh-i-Rustam, Kerman and Kashan, and in Damascus. All these things did Aspasia know, and she felt his power and both resented and adored it.

Surely she thought to herself as she sat at his feet and listened to the laughter and conversation—in multiple tongues —of the men, the glory and the lightning of the human soul should not be suppressed in women.

She glanced at the guests whom she had never seen before, but from their appearance she guessed that two were Babylonians, one was a Mede, two were Egyptians, three were Syrians, four were dark-skinned Arabians, two were Indians, one was a Greek, and the last, a young man with lascivious eyes and auburn curls—Her heart lifted in horror and panic and a dazed terror. She was gazing at Thalias, and in return he was gazing at her with the same appalled emotions, which she did not at first discern.

Al Taliph never introduced Aspasia to his guests, nor them to her. Her position was recognized at once: She was not a slave, she was something more than a favorite concubine, she was not a wife, for she was permitted to leave the women's quarters and allowed to speak when addressed. As the guests were invariably rich men of some learning and intelligence and travel, many remembered the hetairai of which they had heard or had seen for themselves, and not an inconsiderable number respected a hetaira for both her beauty and her intellect. They were women apart from both harems and prosaic marriages, and frequently they had power. So if some were offended by the presence of a woman at Al Taliph's dinner, the others were pleased to look upon Aspasia and even to listen to her conversation, and Al Taliph was often envied for possessing such a treasure.

He was an intuitive man, as well as subtle, and though he treated Aspasia when among his guests with none of the tender consideration and attentiveness he displayed to her in private, his awareness of her presence, the imminence of her body, her very breathing, was singularly acute. He knew when she suffered ennui, when she was distressed, weary or uninterested during these dinners in his dining hall. Her dignity and calm in spite of these things were admirable to him, and he thrilled with pride in her. Therefore, he now knew that she was deeply disturbed, that her flesh had become rigid, that something had assaulted her emotions, and that, mysteriously, she was frightened.

He continued to speak with one of the Egyptians, but he sharply glanced at her through the corner of his eye, and he wondered. She had not as yet been addressed; he had not spoken to her, himself. Was she in pain? It was true that her pallor made the vermillion cosmetics on her cheeks and lips too vivid, but there were no contractures of brow or chin which would indicate physical suffering. He had been conversing in the Egyptian language with one of his guests, a tongue with which she was not familiar, so she could have taken no offense though the conversation was delicately lewd. (Above all things Aspasia was never lewd.) She had not been suddenly seized by illness, for she was remarkably healthy. He saw her staring as at a basilisk at one of the guests, and then he saw her look away. A faint shudder ran through her and Al Taliph perceived this.

At whom had she been gazing? His eye studied all his guests, one by one, while he continued to talk and smile and eat the small portions of spiced and peppered lamb and artichokes on his plate. He even sipped a little wine. Had she recognized one of these men, his fellow merchants? That was impossible, for none were displaying any of the alarm she was so manifestly feeling, and all were attentive to their tables or exchanging little comments with a neighbor. Aspasia had seen but two or three of these guests before; the others were strangers. Yet, one had terrified her. How was that possible? It was true that two or three were old and gross at the table, but Aspasia was accustomed to this because of similar guests in the past. His curiosity became keener. She was sitting now with decorously downcast eyes, her hands folded on her knee. He knew she was exercising all the discipline she had been taught, all the control. Then to his surprise, she was smiling a little, her red lips curving.

For Aspasia was thinking: Thalias dare not betray me, for he is a runaway slave, for all his fine blue Grecian tunic and his wonderfully draped toga and his jewelry and fragrance. He is more frightened than I was, a few moments ago, for should I speak he would be seized and returned to Miletus for punishment, and he knows that surely. Now that her fear had subsided she was inclined to compassion for him, and she conjectured how he had come to this magnificence and position as an honored guest of Al Taliph. She had observed how handsome he was, how engaging in manner, how refined in gesture, and how obviously rich. She had not as yet heard his voice, did not know the name under which he lurked. She remembered that he had always been shrewd and intelligent and swift in answer to another's moods, and then, remembering his concern for her before he had fled Thargelia's house, she felt some suddenly amused affection for him. She desired, above all things, to convey to him that he was in no danger from her.

She is no longer afraid, thought Al Taliph. Aspasia drank from her silver goblet and then lifted a pungent morsel in her spoon and ate it. Her color had returned. Her hand was not trembling. Feeling that Al Taliph was studying her too closely she turned her head and smiled faintly at him, and her brown eyes were bland. For some involved and feminine reason she felt a vague triumph over him as if saying in herself, That man before you took from me the virginity you believed you deprived me of, my lord. I did not come to your bed immaculate. I lay with him within a grove of myrtles one hot summer night, when the leaves dripped moonlight on the dark earth, and he introduced me to joy. His kisses were the first I had ever known; his arms embraced me as strongly as ever yours did, and for an hour I loved him.

Her thoughts delighted her. She had never been so beautiful, and now her mouth dimpled with mischief.

135

Seeing this, Al Taliph frowned. He had never deceived himself that he knew all there was to know about Aspasia. Aspasia was full of mysteries to him, and that was why he found her forever entrancing. She withheld something from him, and he was always in chase and never did he seize upon her inmost thoughts.

Seeing her secret smile as she tranquilly ate and drank, he remembered that the hetairai had been rigorously taught all arts, and especially the arts of alluring deceptions. Was she trying to deceive him that his punishment of her was of no consequence to her, and that she felt herself the victor? He frowned again.

Thalias was scrutinizing her no less intently. Finally, as he was no fool, he began to understand that Aspasia would never betray him, as he would never, he said to himself with virtue, betray her. They had memories of one joyful night. Aspasia glanced up serenely and their eyes met and she smiled briefly then averted her gaze. Al Taliph saw that smile, but Aspasia frequently smiled in this manner at his guests and he saw no significance in it. She was trained to be silently amiable and charming.

Thalias, immeasurably relieved, felt all his not inconsiderable courage returning to him. He addressed his host with great courtesy and respect. "It is said, lord, that we have, throughout the world, entered upon a period of peace and enlightenment. Is your noble Emperor in agreement with this?"

"There will be peace," said Al Taliph, "only when all the world, my dear Damos, becomes one vast market place." He smiled cynically. "I never discuss wars, which are tedious. Wars interrupt the natural discourse between nations, for they diminish and constrict the markets of the world, and impoverish them. War has no victors but only victims, whether conqueror or conquered. But the market place is the only peaceful ground where all men can meet, argue, cheat, lie, purchase the pleasurable, exhibit simple honest greed without shame, arrange caravans and commerce, engage in sincere and vivacious conversation—except with customers—and disputations with rival merchants, plan expeditions, display novelties and beauteous objects from far countries, thus increasing understanding and admiration for that which is strange and felicitous, and so enhancing knowledge of one's fellow men. Even the hot uglinesses of the market place are a warmth to the spirit."

He paused to eat of a melon, a handful of cherries and some plums. A sudden cool gust of air came through the arches of the hall, for the year was drawing to a close and only the days now held scalding heat. Aspasia thought, So, our Thalias is now Damos, and where is his home, and why is he here in this house? Her sympathy for him and her affection increased, even as she listened to the conversation, which was now in Greek.

Al Taliph was smiling a little to himself. "I have seen merchants whose governments were at war speak amiably and with happy laughter to each other, in the market place. Commerce is the one subject on which all men can agree, and in which all men can engage, except for the philosophers who prefer to argue contentiously to prove superior activities of the mind. New ideas are not negotiable in the market place, and so possibly they are rightly despised." He directed his smile at the Indians, who looked aristocratically thoughtful, for India teemed with ideas and religions.

The host continued: "Commerce is the one activity in which customs and cultures from all over the world are regarded with amity, and therefore the market place is our only hope for peace. Merchants have the greatest respect for each other, for they deal in tangibles and realities. You, my dear Damos, and all our friends here tonight are merchants, and do we not converse in a common tongue? We compete, but we do not kill each other. That is left for ambitious governments and professional soldiers and such lesser beings. Tell me, Damos, have you not discovered that the roads of Persia, and all the caravan routes from your Damascus through Persia, are safe from robbers? You will see that even governments have the greatest regard for us merchants."

"But you, yourself, dear Al Taliph, are of the government," said one of the Indian merchants. He did not eat the meat served but only the vegetables and the fruit and the wine, for he was a Buddhist.

"True, I am governor of this province, and my Emperor is pleased to have a merchant here. Merchants rarely loot, and if they do it is taken with good nature by fellow merchants, who are prepared to do the same to them. Even on these occasions there is a certain frank honesty mixed with roguery, which we all understand. Merchants can only survive and gain a profit—and is not a profit profoundly admired?—in an atmosphere of trust and peacefulness. When profits are destroyed and in abeyance, as in a time of war, civilizations decline. Let us drink to the market place, where the rabble can meet merchant and prince in the utmost understanding and equality, without carnage or hatred."

So, thought Aspasia, with kind inner mirth, our Thalias is a merchant from Damascus. Al Taliph was absently stroking her neck, and the other merchants, having drunk from their goblets, watched with interest and concealed envy.

Now Al Taliph looked at Aspasia, and his large and brilliant eyes smiled upon her. He said in his remarkably rich voice, "Tell me, my love, what you think of this conversation?"

Thalias was the only man present who did not raise eyebrows in surprise at this question asked of a woman, however beautiful. Aspasia smiled at Al Taliph in return, with an acid sweetness that was very significant to him. "I am thinking of what a Greek philosopher has written of such as you, my lord, who pretend to be a mere simple merchant. 'We must look about under every stone, lest an orator bite us.' "

Some gasped at this impudence, but Al Taliph pretended to wince, and laughed. He lifted her hand and pressed his lips to it. "Ah," he said, "to be praised by such lips for my eloquence is more intoxicating than wine." He raised his own goblet and held it to her mouth, and she drank and then inclined her head.

He added, tweaking her ear, "Let me, in turn, quote from Euripides: 'A woman should be good for everything at home, but abroad good for nothing.' "

The guests laughed with appreciation, and Aspasia continued her acerbic if charming smile while she flushed.

"Permit me, my lord," she said, "to reply to you from what Herodotus has remarked of your nation: 'They are accustomed to deliberate on matters of the highest importance only when drunk. Whatever else they discuss when sober is always a second time examined after they have been drinking.' My lord, are you drunk or sober?"

All the guests sat as moveless as statues, holding their breath at this unpardonable insult to their host. But Al Taliph only laughed again, and laid his hand on Aspasia's shoulder. He addressed his guests: "You will observe that my pretty thing can quote from the philosophers—as a parrot repeats words without understanding them. Nevertheless, you have discovered that her remarks are astonishingly pertinent and her banter swift. So, here is the puzzle: Have I been a good teacher?" He put his hands over his face in mock horror. "Or, can she truly think?" He shook his head and shuddered. "From such, the gods deliver us!" The guests burst into laughter. Aspasia stared fully at him, a deliberate affront, and she was filled with such anger that she began to rise without permission to leave the hall. She was as white as bleached linen and her eyes were like the flashing of knife blades. The guests saw this. (Only Thalias thought, My poor Aspasia.)

As aware of her as always, without actually looking at her, Al Taliph darted his hand from his face and pressed it strongly on her thigh with such force and command that she sank down again on the divan. Her mortification was complete. She was certain now that she hated him. The slaves poured more wine, and pastries were brought and peaches the color of dawn. Al Taliph looked at Thalias, but Aspasia, as acute as himself, understood he was addressing her, for she recognized that certain tone of voice. She waited, her heart tumultuous, for calamity.

"Damos of Damascus, and Greece itself, I have a gift for you, for you and I have done profitable affairs together though never were you in this house before." He clapped his hands and a eunuch came running from an archway. Al Taliph said, "Bring to me the little maidens I purchased but two days ago."

Aspasia sickened. She thought of the small girls she had seen in the harem but this day. She closed her eyes briefly. Al Taliph said, "They are rare treasures, my dear Damos, and I chose them myself, thinking of you. For do not we all prefer the young and untouched?"

Thalias murmured in assent. "I promise you," said his host, "that they are mindless and can only babble pleasingly, and is that not to be desired, in a female, above all things?"

Thalias smiled uneasily, not glancing at Aspasia, who was now gazing at him fiercely. The guests repeated as one man, with smiles at each other, "Above all things!"

The little girl children were brought in together, and they held each other's hands tightly for protection, and it was obvious that they were frightened and had just been aroused from sleep. White linen tunics clung to their diminutive bodies, and their tiny feet were bare. But their fine sleep-dampened hair had been combed hastily and was tied with white silken cords so that their faces could be seen with all their appealing infanthood, their innocent vulnerability and bewilderment. They blinked in the light of the lamps. The guests murmured approvingly and a number with desire.

Their lips were the lips of babyhood, and without artifice, and their small olive-tinted arms and legs and complexions shone with perfumed oil and their defenseless throats were clasped with pearls as lustrous as themselves. Aspasia's eyes filled with tears and her mouth shook.

Al Taliph drew them to him as gently as a father, and then he lifted their tunics so that their hairless childish bodies and private parts could be seen clearly. He admired them elaborately. "They are twins," he said, "and as healthy as newborn lambs, without blemish or stain or the touch, so far, of a man's hands. Will they not grace your bed, Damos? It will be ten years—before they are too old for your taste. In the meantime, they are delightful as little boys, and do not you Greeks prefer such?"

Thalias was more uneasy than before. His cheeks colored. Now he felt the force of Aspasia's stare and he looked quickly at her.

She did the unpardonable: She spoke without first being addressed. She said, "They are slaves, and too young and helpless to run away. Who would succor them? Who would hide and comfort them—or give them gold?"

Thalias paled. He heard and understood the explicit threat in her raised clear voice, and he knew that she was prepared to destroy herself, and him, for the sake of these children. Moreover, he had no lust for such little ones and he was not depraved. He hesitated in confusion. He dared not refuse a gift from his host, and he wet his lips. He could feel Aspasia's wild and terrible challenge though she did not speak again. As for Al Taliph he ignored her as if she had not spoken at all. The guests were incredulous at his sufferance of this forward woman.

Thalias said, "I am deeply touched, lord, for your kindness and condescension." He paused. The guests nodded and moistened their own mouths.

Thalias continued: "My wife has given me one son, and longs for a female child or two, I will give these children to her, for she can bear no more, and she brought me an excellent dowry and has been most dutiful in all her ways."

Al Taliph's smile became fixed, and the guests exchanged glances of amazement. But Thalias' smile was brave.

"My wife," he went on, "is a lady of much virtue and the only offspring of her parents, and she was nurtured and tended and educated. One can understand this, for her people were brought out from Babylon by a leader of the name of Abraham and they now live in the land of Israel. They have a certain respect for women. Permit me, in my wife's name, to thank you, lord, and if it will not offend you I shall request her to send you a grateful message."

Al Taliph spoke with gravity, inclining his head. "They are yours, my dear friend, to do with as you will." He looked suddenly at Aspasia, saw the tears in her eyes and her trembling smile and he touched her knee with a caressing hand, and left that hand there. She sighed. She bent her head so that she would not weep openly. She pressed her knee, without volition, against Al Taliph's fingers, in an involuntary caress of her own. I have been forgiven, he thought, and laughed inwardly at himself. Yet, he was pleased.

He said, "The message from your lady will be received by me with pleasure. Let them be daughters to her, these little ones."

Later he summoned Aspasia to his bed and kissed the wounds he had inflicted on her, and she turned impulsively to him and laid her head on his breast and did not know why, in her turmoil of thoughts, she felt happiness and desire and a dangerous emotion she refused to examine.

He said, "Had you, today, asked me for those children as handmaidens for yourself, my empress, I should have given them to you at once. No, do not speak," and he laid his lips on hers and drew her down beside him.

CHAPTER 13

Al Taliph was about to go to Damascus with one of his caravans, and he had invited Thalias to accompany him and permit Thalias' overseer to guide his own caravan to the city. Thalias had heard of the splendor and foods and wines and girls who accompanied Al Taliph on these expeditions and eagerly accepted, thinking of huge Persian tents and luxuries, and of the dancing and singing women. He also thought of Aspasia and wondered if she accompanied her lord.

The satrap was still away this afternoon, just before sunset, and Thalias, who was always bored when not engaged in some activity, wandered out into the garden, chewing a handful of ripe dates. He found the palace oppressive with all its halls and fountains and its eastern air. He did not like Damascus, either, but he lived there on his business and with his wife— he had only one—and often longed for Miletus, or for Greece which he could visit at will, and in particular, Athens. As yet he had not dared to go to Miletus, where he had been born, for he might be recognized as a runaway slave and seized. In

Greece, however, he found refreshment from the hot turgidity of the east, and it was good to speak his own tongue among fellow merchants, who admired and respected him, and to enjoy, as he said, honest food.

He did not look at Kurda who appeared not to see him, for the eunuch was staring fixedly at someone in the garden, and Thalias looked with interest in that direction. There, in the shade of a group of date palms sat Aspasia on a marble bench whose arms were carved in the shape of Persian tigers. She was like a young and lonely girl, engaged with her thoughts, her flesh and tunic no darker than the white stone on which she sat. Thalias' heart tingled with pleasure, for often he remembered Aspasia even in the arms of his wife, and had loved her. He saw the quiet melancholy of her face. She was gazing at a fishpond but did not seem to see it. He went quickly across the path towards her, the gravel grating under his elegant shoes.

She lifted her head and looked at him absently, then her face changed. Kurda stiffened at the doors. Surely even the barbarian understood that no male guest approached a woman this openly, and in the absence of his host or the absence of slaves and attendants! But Thalias, acquainted though he was with the east, forgot everything in his desire to speak alone to Aspasia and to look more closely at her in this humid and shining light. She watched him approach, then glanced with alarm at Kurda, who had left the doors and was now standing on the low steps leading to the gardens, his fat face avid. She did not stir, but when Thalias, smiling like the sun, was almost upon her she said, in a very low voice, "This is most indiscreet, Thalias. Yonder eunuch is master of the other eunuchs, and he wishes to destroy me. He watches me constantly for something dangerous to report to Al Taliph."

Thalias halted, his smile disappearing. "Do not look at him," whispered Aspasia. "No, do not sit beside me." She rose, then indicated that he should seat himself, and he did, and she stood before him. "Let us pretend that we are strangers, and that you wish to amuse yourself for a moment with my company, and that you disdain me."

"Aspasia," he said, with sadness.

She assumed a humble attitude, and Thalias shook his head slightly. He said, "Alas, I am only a slave after all, and I have never forgotten you nor what you are in truth."

"What am I?" she said, with sudden bitterness. "I am the hired concubine of my lord, little more than a whore. Yet, I am without discontent." She half-turned from him and stared

142

at one of the bronze statues and he followed her eyes and said, "They are monstrous, are they not, and do they not resemble the east?"

"Tell me of Greece, and Athens, which I have never seen," she said.

"Ah, Athens!" he exclaimed, and she put her finger warningly to her lips. He dropped his voice. "It is foaming like the sea with thoughts and movements and great men! Have you heard of Pericles, the famed son of Xanthippus? The father many years ago was a power in Athens and its politics; he defeated the remnants of Xerxes' fleet at Mycale. Xanthippus was a heroic man, and his wife was Agariste, the niece of Cleisthenes, she was the mother of Pericles. Her family was connected with the former Tyrants of Sicyon and she was also of the family of the Alcmaeonidae. Surely, you have heard of the illustrious Pericles?"

"Pericles?" repeated Aspasia. She thought. "Ah, I believe that my lord has mentioned him with humor, for the Persians still believe the Greeks to be barbarians in spite of their victories over Xerxes. Is he not a politician?"

"He is more." Then Thalias added, "But Al Taliph quotes the Grecian philosophers with ease, so he can hardly believe Greece to be barbaric."

Aspasia said, "He believes that only Persia is entirely civilized, though he admits that Greek philosophers are now commanding attention throughout the world. He speaks to me little of modern history or the movements of nations. They bore him. He prefers things only of the mind," and her smile was bitter again as she remembered Al Taliph's harem. "His library is constantly replenished with the works of many philosophers, and he is convinced that the Persian ones are more subtle and mature, and certainly more profound. I am permitted to sit in his library and read what I will, and I have confined myself to the Greek philosophers, for my knowledge of other languages is not extraordinary."

"You are as confined here as when you were a maiden in the house of Thargelia," said Thalias, with pity.

"In a greater measure," said Aspasia. "I go only to the market place. I have no companions, no friends. Ah, do not look so compassionate, my Thalias. I have told you I am often happy."

"Yes, he is a man of mind," said Thalias, who was fascinated by Al Taliph. "But he is also a merchant, and very rich and discerning. Why does he not speak to you of what he sees and hears in the cities his caravans visit?"

143

"I am only a woman," said Aspasia, but she smiled. "But still, he converses with me on all things which do not concern the immediate present. We have very erudite conversations, when we are alone," and her smile was wry. "Tell me of this famous Pericles."

Pride was in Thalias' voice as he said, "He is a statesman, and more, and is married to the daughter of a noble house and has two sons, and is very rich. He was educated by Zeno of Elea, who taught him the power of dialectic, and by that most famed astronomer, Anaxagoras. So his eloquence can turn marble into flesh. He can even move that damnable Ecclesia. He helped to prosecute Cimon on a charge of bribery, after Cimon's Thasian campaign. He also attacked the Areopagus two years ago, and though his colleague, Ephialtes, has been given the credit of renouncing the Spartan alliance and the League with Thessaly and Argos, these were indeed the labor of Pericles, who deferred to his elder and allowed him to be celebrated for these acts. Pericles is a man of honor and discretion and tolerance."

"Alas," said Aspasia, "all these are but names to me. I have become an ignorant woman."

"Alas," Thalias echoed her. "I will continue. When Ephialtes was assassinated Pericles inherited the highest position in the State. He has not abandoned the dream of Ephialtes of making the citizens of Athens self-governing, and he is constantly challenging the Ecclesia, for he is not only bold but he is brave." Thalias looked at Aspasia reflectively.

"Pericles has a hetaira as a companion. Would that you were she, most beauteous Aspasia."

She laughed a little.

Thalias continued. "Pericles has a noble mind and is irked by the rule of the Ecclesia and its religious intolerance. It is said that he has confided to friends that Athens is in need of a rejuvenation of mind and soul. Many agree with him, but at the present it is not adding to his popularity. But he is like Zeus, not afraid to hurl thunderbolts, for he is Olympian of character and is famous for his composed bearing and his godlike dignity. He is also very handsome and proud." Thalias hesitated. "It is said his head is deformed and that is why he wears a towering helmet on almost every occasion, but that could be a slander."

Aspasia was silent and melancholy resumed its shadow on her face. Seeing this, the naturally warm-hearted Thalias said with impulsiveness, "Ah, that I could help you as you helped me, Aspasia!"

She made herself smile again. "I was not entirely generous, my dear Thalias. But you have not told me how you fared when you fled Miletus."

"I took the first vessel, and after long journeys, I arrived in Damascus. I became the friend of an elderly merchant, who had no sons. He was from the land of Israel and I married his daughter." He paused, and smiled widely. "I adopted their religion and I—" He paused again and Aspasia laughed aloud, and he laughed also. "I was duly circumcised and though I am still regarded with some suspicion by my father-in-law, who is very devout, he has no cause to complain. I also had considerable of the gold you gave me and I used it wisely and invested it with Ephriam. I am not unknown in Damascus," and he dropped his merry eyes in a parody of humility, and Aspasia again laughed.

"I am happy that you are so successful," she said.

He stood up and would have taken her hand but she shook her head with another warning. "It is best to leave me now, Thalias-Damos, and may the gods be with you." She glanced at Kurda, who was still standing on the steps, his hands on his hips and his legs spread apart in a virile attitude. He was staring with even more avidity at the girl and the young man at a distance and was still trying to hear what they had been saying. But their voices had remained low.

Thalias said, "May the gods—and also Jehovah—be with you, Aspasia. It may be that we shall meet again."

Mindful of Kurda she bowed to him formally and he bowed in return and left her. He passed Kurda with a genial smile but the eunuch scowled at him savagely and did not move, so that Thalias had to step around him. Aspasia resumed her seat on the bench, and she considered all that Thalias had told her and she thought, "I am immured here like a nymph caught in crystal, or I resemble Dryope, who was changed into a mute tree, and when I would grasp my hair to assure myself that I still live as a woman my hands are filled with leaves."

Then she laughed a little even as she sighed. "But the leaves are fragrant and shine like silver, and my fate could be worse."

Kurda went to Al Taliph, bowed his head almost to his knees and said, "Lord, the foreign woman has been indiscreet again."

Al Taliph frowned impatiently. "Has she been annoying my women despite my commands?"

"Ah, lord, if it were only that! It is much worse." Kurda assumed the face and posture of a tragedian and Al Taliph suppressed a smile.

"Tell me," he said.

Kurda hesitated. He knew that Thalias was an honored guest in this house, so he had prepared his story in advance. He said, "Your noble friend, lord, Damos, was walking in the garden just before sunset and the foreign woman approached him boldly in an open encounter and spoke with him. He would have left her but she forced him to sit upon a marble seat, and not desiring to give offense to one of your household, lord, he submitted and she stood before him and they conversed together. I tried to hear the conversation but they spoke very quietly."

Al Taliph's face was inscrutable. "The women of Miletus are not so immured as ours, and my guest is from Athens where women have greater freedom."

He dismissed Kurda who was sickened with disappointment. As for Al Taliph, he felt some vexation at Aspasia's indiscretion. Kurda, in spite of his malignance, had found nothing excessively wrong and Al Taliph, knowing Aspasia, did not believe that she had seized upon Damos shamelessly. As for Damos, he had married an Israelite woman and doubtless he was accustomed to a more tolerant attitude with regard to women. Aspasia often refused to wear a veil in the palace or the garden, as did the other women, and he, Al Taliph, had indulged her. She was a beautiful woman and had sat at his feet two nights ago and he had conversed with her before his guests, so Damos had probably guessed that she enjoyed a unique position in the household and had shown her courtesy. Al Taliph tapped his teeth with his finger and sent for Aspasia.

She soon entered his chamber and he held out his hand to her and she came to him at once and was drawn down to his feet. As always, her lovely face brightened in his presence. He poured a goblet of wine for her and put it into her hand gently, then kissed her wrist. She pressed her cheek to the top of his head and sighed. The light fragrance of lilies drifted from her body, and he was pleased, for it was his favorite scent.

"I have heard, my snowy swan, that you have been indiscreet today," he said.

Aspasia started and he saw this. Her thoughts fastened on

Kurda. Had he heard any word in the garden? Had he heard the words of affection and admiration which Thalias had uttered? She held herself from trembling and said, "How have I offended you, lord?"

"It is not our custom, Aspasia, for women to accost male strangers and to converse with them in secret."

She forced herself to laugh lightly. "Oh, that Kurda! He has the mind of a cesspool. And my conversation with—your guest—his name is Damos, is it not?—was concerned only with the children you gave to him, for his wife."

Al Taliph studied her closely. "And what was the conversation, my adored one?"

She said at once, "I told him that I prayed that his wife would love the little ones and accept them in her house, as a mother."

Al Taliph shook his head in amused exasperation. "You are very tenacious, are you not? You wished to assure yourself that the girls would not serve their original purpose?"

Aspasia knew that her best defense was boldness. She bent over him and kissed him deeply on the mouth. "Can any woman trust a man?" she asked. "It is true that I wished to reassure myself. Did I not deserve that at the least, for what you did to me in punishment?" She dropped her robe from her shoulders and back and let him see the healing wounds and then let the robe drop farther so that her beautiful breasts were fully displayed to him. She eyed him artlessly, as if this was an accident and his dark face flushed. He put his hand on her breast and felt the strong beating of her heart, and thought it passion and not fear.

"There are times," he said, "when I think you are a veritable child." He kissed the breast he held and Aspasia closed her eyes with relief, thanking Thargelia in her mind for having taught her wiles and control. "I forgive your forwardness," he said, then remembered what he had been considering all the day in the city.

"I must leave for Damascus tomorrow," he said. "I will be gone for some time. And it came to me how I would yearn for you, my sweet treasure, and would be wild with impatience to return to your arms. Therefore, I have decided not to deny myself the joy of gazing upon you and receiving your kisses. I shall take you with me."

Her amazed delight at this gratified him. She pressed his hand tightly to her breast and now she had no need to dissemble. "Lord," she said, "if you have yearned for me in that great city, surrounded though you were by your women, how

147

much more have I yearned for you, left here alone, alas, and dreaming of you in my bed and longing for your return!"

He heard the sincerity in her voice as well as her happiness, and it came to him that this was the first time he had been certain that she was not somewhat deceiving him with taught fervor. He was moved and was ashamed of his pleasure.

"But you will wear a veil at all times," he said, fondling her. "I have indulged you here in my house, but that cannot be on the journey nor in Damascus. I desire no one to gaze upon your face and contemplate slaughtering me and carrying you off."

"Like the bull who bore Europa away?" She laughed, and shook her head. "I have heard that the women of Damascus are great beauties."

"No, they are extremely ugly," he replied. "The men are handsome and corrupt, and the women are virtuous and an offense to the eye. Their veils, then, are less to conceal their faces than to spare men from looking upon them. Were the men of Damascus to glimpse your countenance, sweet Isis, they would lose their wits."

He drew her down beside him on the divan and she thought, as she clung to him, Alas, I love him, and this I see to my sorrow. But never shall he know.

CHAPTER 14

Aspasia had never seen a caravan. It was not until she was part of Al Taliph's own caravan that she realized how she had been so closely immured in his palace and how her mind, despite his libraries and the books he bought for her, had become stifled not only with luxury but with monotony and absence of communication with others. In Thargelia's house there had been the diversity and the teachings of tutors and visits to the ports and the shops and the presence of strangers who were friends of Thargelia. Always there had been stimulating conversations and controversies and the exchange of small or large thoughts. There had been news of the world from guests and Thargelia had encouraged her intelligent hetairai to ask questions, to give opinions, even to dispute amiably. Girl children were constantly arriving for scrutiny by the mistress of the courtesans, and decisions made. There had been laughter and games among the maidens, and frolics and discussions, and pranks and dancing and music.

But for over three years now Aspasia had had no access to

these things. She had seen nothing but the market place. She had entered no city. She had not seen the sea, but only a small river near the palace. She had been imprisoned behind walls, guarded constantly by eunuchs, never entertained except in the company of Al Taliph when he gave his dinners. She had talked only briefly with guests, who had admired her beauty but had often been disconcerted by her mind. I have been dead to the world, and the world to me, she thought. Time has gone by like the wind of the desert, coming from whence I do not know and going to mysterious places I never saw. I have lived suspended in a dream, and only now do I understand that the dream has smothered me. I awakened only when my lord summoned me at his pleasure, and then I fell asleep again and the world rolled without my knowledge or awareness. I see that I desperately struggled, in that dream, to be alive, but as the months and the years went on my struggles became fewer and my first uneasiness less. I have been a frog on a lily pad in a stagnant pool in a silent and deserted garden, blinking feebly at the sun, and rarely gazing about me. Flint does not create sparks unless struck against iron, and for a long time my mind has known no fire.

Her excitement, as the caravan set forth long before dawn this cool autumn morning, was so great that her heart thumped and she almost wept for joy. Veiled, wrapped in a warm crimson wool cloak, she was guided outside the walls by Al Taliph who smiled down at her glittering eyes as a father smiles. Torches had been forced into the sockets on the outside walls and they cast red shadows in the morning breeze and on the waiting caravan. Aspasia looked about her eagerly. It seemed to her that a multitude of loaded camels, mules and horses and donkeys extended from the fluttering light of the torches into the darkness and into infinity on each side. Now she heard the hubbub of men and beasts, the screams of the camels, the neighing of the horses, the complaints of the donkeys, and saw the enormous bustle of preparation. Men in long dark robes and cloaks and with headcloths covering both head and face rushed everywhere, carrying burdens to be hoisted to the packs on the animals, and as they hurried feverishly they chattered and cursed and laughed, and their eyes were alive in the torchlight. There was an air of desert barbarism about them and their loud voices were hoarse and impatient, and they yelled and bellowed as loud as the beasts they tended and dragged or struck. They also stank furiously and even the scent of the gardens behind the gates and the aromatic odor of the wind could not abate the stench of sweat, un-

149

washed hot bodies, damp wool, urine and manure. They had an animal rankness which Aspasia, the fastidious, found offensive. She leaned lightly against the arm and shoulder of Al Taliph, who was alertly watching, surrounded by guards with swords and lances.

Aspasia saw that the camels were linked together in lines of one hundred each, hair ropes attaching the rear of one to the neck of another, and all were heavily laden with merchandise. The leader, whimpering nearby and stamping his huge padded feet restlessly, was ornamented with colored cloths, fringes and tassels and tinkling bells. An ass, without a burden, was to guide the long strings of camels. He surveyed the scene philosophically, and seeing this and his wise eyes, Aspasia laughed and pointed him out to Al Taliph. "Ah, yes," he said, "he is a very clever creature and has deep thoughts of his own. He has no high opinion of camels, but they trust him." He left Aspasia, motioned aside his guards and went to the ass. "Hamshid," he said, "I am very proud of you. Again, you will protect us." The ass acknowledged this compliment with a grave whinny and rubbed his nose against Al Taliph, who patted him tenderly and who then returned to Aspasia. She was laughing behind her veil and her brown eyes with their gilt lashes were alight with mirth.

"Lord," she said, "I swear you love beasts more than you love any man or woman."

He answered her with seriousness. "Are they not honest and do they not work industriously? I respect them. They could survive without us but we cannot survive without them, and where is our vainglorious intelligence before that truth?"

Aspasia was momentarily abashed. She thought again, with a sigh, of how dull her mind had become, how stifled, how lacking in excitement and conjecture, behind those walls. She determined not to offend Al Taliph, for his displeasure dimmed her spirit and she wished to greet the world again with joy, as one delivered from a prison; tasting, feeling, smelling, touching, seeing, hearing. Moreover, if she pleased her lord he would take her again on other journeys, perhaps even to Greece.

For the first time she saw that he was armed, a long curved sword buckled to his girdle. Like the men about him he was clad in dark wool robes and a heavy cloak, and like them he wore a woollen headcloth secured with rope cords. The rough material covered not only his head but also his face from the nose down, and only his eyes could be seen, changing from gray to brown as the torchlight shifted, and his gaze ranged over the men and the animals. Aspasia had only seen him in elegance and grace, and as an aristocratic satrap. Now he was of the desert, as were his men, and he had the wild leanness of the desert-born, the acquaintance of far places and dangers and hazards and endless sands and storms. I do not know him, Aspasia thought. I have never known him. He suddenly looked down at her and though his face was hidden she could see that his eyes were smiling as if he had heard her thoughts and was amused. She leaned against him again.

The guards moved aside and Thalias approached, saluting. He, too, was clad as was Al Taliph, but his blue eyes were gay and young above the cloth that covered his face and a lock of auburn hair could be seen over his forehead. He glanced briefly at Aspasia. "My own caravan, lord," he said, "will leave tomorrow. It is very small compared with yours."

"You need fear no robbers in Persia," said Al Taliph. "But you have known that."

"True, lord, but we will not be always in Persia. I have been robbed before."

"My dear Damos, you will travel under my protection," said Al Taliph. "The banners we carry are royal, and not the boldest robbers between Persia and Damascus will trouble us. Nevertheless, we are armed also, as you will observe, if some savage band ignores our standards or does not recognize them."

Thalias' eyes were uneasy, "I have never killed a man," he said.

"I have killed many, and not only in war," said Al Taliph. "After the first murder the others are of no consequence." He spoke with indifference and with a touch of contempt for this Greek. His eyes became cold and haughty. "You will ride beside me," he added. "I have the strongest and the noblest of Idumean stallions who fear nothing except an irritable mare."

Thalias laughed, but he was still uneasy. He lifted his robe as if to examine his feet and Aspasia saw that he wore high leather boots, as did Al Taliph. Then he dropped his robes, saluted again, and went away. Al Taliph watched him go. "Our Damos," said Al Taliph, "has not only never killed a man but I fear he has not ridden many horses either."

"I, too, have never ridden a horse," said Aspasia. She heard him laugh. "My sweet nightingale," he said, "you will travel in comfort and in protection, as I have told you. No desert wind or sand or scorching sun will be permitted to injure your delectable complexion." He raised his hand and pushed aside the hood of her cloak and gently smoothed her hair. "Nor this glory, which is dearer to me than the bricks of gold which line the cellars of my banks."

She was vexed at this flippancy and he saw this and laughed again. Then he said, "Ah, here is my good Karawan-Serashkier, who will guard us all and deliver us and our merchandise safely, and settle all quarrels among my men. Even I, on such journeys, must follow his counsel and never dispute with him."

Aspasia watched the loping approach of the tallest and thinnest man she had ever seen, clad in black wool robes. He had pushed the cloth from his face and Aspasia saw his somber gauntness, the ferocity of his features, the fearless violence of his small vivid eyes, the eagle-like rapacity of his beaked nose, the cruelty of his almost lipless mouth. He bowed to Al Taliph.

"All is in readiness, lord," he said. His voice had the harshness of a hawk's utterance.

"Good, Raïs," said Al Taliph. He touched the man on his shoulder and they exchanged looks of mutual regard.

Now that the hour of departure had been reached the noise of man and animal rose to a higher pitch. It was discordant and deafening, yet Aspasia saw that the confusion had become order. The bright amber crescent of the moon was perched on the top of the highest mountain, which was as yet undefined except as a dark cloud against a lighter cloud. But in the east there was a bluish shadow. A group of veiled women approached the guards. Al Taliph nodded towards them and said abruptly to Aspasia, "Go. Do not be afraid."

Two of the women carried lanterns and Aspasia joined the silent group, knowing they were five of her own attendants, who would care for her. Al Taliph had not indicated how she would travel. She glanced back at him. He was talking to one of the guards and appeared to have forgotten her, as a creature of no importance to him. She did not speak to the women. They surrounded her and the women with the lanterns led the way past seemingly endless lines of camels, mules, horses and donkeys. The burning torches spluttered and hissed and smelled of hot resin. The men ignored the little group of females, for they were of less value to them than the beasts.

Now the caravan was only a vague movement in the dark, though Aspasia could hear snorts and complaints and the rude voices of men. The women held the lanterns high so that Aspasia would not stumble. She had a glimpse of the domed roof of the palace above the walls and it seemed to be formed of wan mist under the moon and the stars. Beneath that dome she had been imprisoned for long years. Now she was free. A sudden exultation came to her, and a renewed excitement, for she was young and had been delivered to the world she had longed for and had so loved. She looked about her with curiosity; the caravan was slowly beginning to move. The lantern light flickered on an eye here, a shape there, the muscular leg of an animal, a harness. Far to the front could be heard the jingling of bells on the lead camel. Somewhere a horn sounded, peremptorily. The women quickened their steps and Aspasia hurried with them. She feared they would be left.

They came upon a train of four long and wide platforms, each drawn by six black horses in silver harness and with plumes on their heads. Every platform supported a large tent of brown wool with closed flaps. The first, and the biggest, led the train and a nomad, carrying a pennant, rode one of the horses. "This tent is the tent of the lord," said one of the women, bowing her head in its direction. Even the spokes of the ironclad wheels were inlaid with silver and enamel. The second tent, somewhat smaller, had been assigned to Aspasia and two of her women; the others would sleep in the third tent until called to their duties. Among them, as Aspasia guessed, were a number of slave girls who were dancers and singers and tumblers and music-makers. The fourth also held women.

Aspasia climbed the platform to her tent, accompanied by two of the slave women. The flap was opened, and she entered and was amazed. Soft yellow glass lamps were affixed to walls and the walls themselves were completely covered with hangings of the most luxurious sort—ornamented silk of curious designs depicting colorful flowers, birds, trees and twisted patterns intertwined with gold and silver threads which glistened and sparkled in the lamplight. The floor of the platform was strewn with Persian and Indian rugs no less brilliant with color, and thick and soft under the foot. There were small brass tables and chests, and the famous crimson and blue Damascene huge cushions to sit and lie and sleep upon, all fringed with gold tassels, and many of them had afghans of wool and silk neatly folded to protect the sleeper or sitter from any desert or mountain chill. The whole tent was pervaded with the scent of sandalwood and nard. Aspasia felt the warmth in the tent and the fragrance was languid and somnolent. She was suddenly aware that she desired sleep, for she had lain for hours in the arms of Al Taliph, quivering with passion and excitement, and had not slept at all. The women removed her veil and cloak and other garments and dressed her in a white shift of linen, and she lay upon a cushion and fell almost instantly asleep, hardly conscious of the fact that an afghan had been placed upon her and that the other women had fallen upon cushions, themselves. The movement of the vehicle was lulling, the scent overpowering. Aspasia slept like one drugged.

But she was awake at dawn, after a short doze. Her women slept and moaned softly, their mouths agape. Aspasia threw a cloak over her shift and opened the flap of the tent and stood in the doorway. Then she was awed, and her old exaltation at the spectacle of beauty returned like a wanderer who had been banished and then had come home, rejoicing, intoxicated. Or, she was like one who had been blinded and then had been given sight again.

The caravan was traveling over a flat plain littered with small and large stones and heavy dust. But the eastern sky was a vast conflagration of palpitating gold and saffron streaked with scarlet and emerald green, and it seemed to extend forever from horizon to horizon. It threw yellow and purple shadows on the ash-colored ground. Boulders on the barren earth were ignited instant by instant and burned like gigantic cores of fire. There was no sound in that stupendous incandescence of the heavens except for the creaking of wagons and the rattle of harness. Then, at the rim of the world, the edge of the ruby sun began to mount in his panoply of awaiting banners, and the tent of the night, still high in the heavens, and the hue of hyacinths, folded and sank to the west.

Aspasia felt that she was seeing for the first time in her life. She clutched the sides of the fabric doorway and stared and her face was illuminated by the grandeur she gazed upon with distended eyes. Her hair blew about her in the morning wind. Then she heard the pound of horse's hoofs and there loomed beside the tent the figure of a horseman black as an iron statue against the wild storm of the sky. The horseman, mounted on a great stallion, was Al Taliph, his face covered with his headcloth, his eyes set ahead. He did not seem aware of the woman in the doorway.

He resembles a centaur, and is as unearthly, thought Aspasia. He rode beside the tent, silent and supple, tall and lithe. Never had he seemed so remote to Aspasia, so far removed from her, so alien, so strange, so in command of all about him. She felt a pang of fear as well as a thrill of pride. He touched his horse with his whip and the animal soared ahead, almost as if he were flying rather than running, like Pegasus,

154

and both man and beast were gone. A peculiar feeling of loneliness and melancholy came to Aspasia and she returned to her cushions but not sleep.

The caravan came to a halt. Aspasia rose, and her women rose with her, groaning. She opened the flap and saw that the caravan had stopped at a green oasis blowing with palm trees. Men were beginning to shout and fill pails and large baskets with spring water for the horses and camels. A fine golden dust floated in the warm air, for the sun had now completely risen, and heat touched Aspasia's cheek like a hot hand. She did not know if she were supposed to remain in her tent, or alight. Her women came to her and dressed her and covered her with veil and mantle, then, bowing, they indicated that she should follow them. She emerged from the tent and climbed down beside the women. As she did so she saw that an elderly woman, veiled and in dark clothing, was leading a girl child sternly by the hand. The child's face was uncovered though overlaid with cosmetics against the ardent light, and she was bewildered and frightened. She could have been hardly ten years old. Her robe was white and blue, her hair the color of brown wine. She pulled back once and the woman jerked her impatiently and said something in a tongue Aspasia did not know, and it was admonishing. The child cried again, a faint whimpering sound, then bowing her head she submitted.

The two approached the tent of Al Taliph, then climbed into it. Two of Al Taliph's men, who shared the tent with him, emerged and jumped to the ground and went to the spring. Aspasia's heart jolted and she was filled with anger and despair. Her women motioned to her to go with them, but she lingered. They patiently waited. Then Aspasia heard a muffled scream of agony within Al Taliph's tent and could barely restrain herself from running to it. She was sickened. The child within the tent screamed again, like a tormented animal, then Aspasia heard the sharp crack of a man's hand against childish flesh and the screams subsided to breathless moans of torment. Al Taliph's voice could now be heard, muttering and gasping and sometimes impatient.

But I always knew, thought Aspasia. Did I not know the fate of the women in the harem, the young girls, the children? Yet, she had not heard helpless cries until now. She was taken by pity and humiliation. Only a few hours ago Al Taliph's dusky body had lain on her white flesh, and she had embraced him and his voice had been loving. He had called her his light of life, his moon, his lily, his swan, his dove. But, had not Thargelia told her maidens that a man's vows, his protestations of eternal love, his devotion, were all lies and were intent only on deceiving the momentary woman and dazing her senses? Had she not been warned against loving any man, lest she be destroyed? A woman who loved became a victim of a man's brutal indifference, his deceptions, his betrayal. I hate him! she thought with deep rage, and I hate, above all things, what he is doing to that innocent child.

She tried to make her heart cold and still. She saw that her women had heard the sounds within the lord's tent and thought nothing of it. She followed them to the area set aside for the women's rest in the oasis. She was brought ice-cold water. A linen cloth was laid on the cool green grass before her, and upon it was placed a ewer of wine, sliced lamb, fruit, bread and cheese and oily artichokes and a pitcher of foaming goat's milk. All the women, a large company, sat around her in a circle, gossiping to each other. They had removed their veils. A wall of canvas had been erected about them to protect them from the men's gazes. Aspasia, as the favorite of the lord, was isolated but watched and tended. She could not eat. She drank only water. I am ridiculous, she told herself. I knew from the very beginning who and what he was. I knew he was pitiless and ruthless as well as kind and intellectual and full of power. Yet I deluded myself that he was superior to other men in appetites and passions. Had I not been warned by Thargelia? Alas, in this man's arms I was as melting wax and I believed his vows and rejoiced in his embraces! He did not deceive me. I deceived myself, because I desired the deception. However, from this moment on I shall be deceived no longer.

A sense of strength came to her, and even her despair lessened. She began to think. Could she steal away as Thalias had stolen away from Thargelia's house? Could she take with her the gold and the gems Al Taliph had given her, and go to Greece? Alas, she was a woman, and a woman traveling alone was in awful danger. But, I am strong and I was taught self-defense by the athletes in Thargelia's house, and I would not hesitate to kill if necessary. Her thoughts became somewhat confused as she realized the predicament of women in the modern world. Then she thought of Thalias. He had vowed to help her if she needed his help. He owed her much and was naturally benevolent, and he had loved her if only for a night. Yet, how much could a woman trust a man? Thargelia's cynical voice echoed in her ear: Take and take and seize and seize, while the man is still bemused by you, and then leave with your soul and your mind intact—for another man with

156

gifts. If a man marries you that is a different matter, for in his eyes a wife—even if betrayed or rejected—is still part of him in his own estimation, and must receive some honor and responsibility from him. That is his ego. But a woman without marriage is a woman without protection, except for herself. Remember that always. If you forget, you have forgotten to your deadly peril.

I must bind Thalias to me, for my use, thought Aspasia. Her women came to her, mutely offering the food on the cloth. She shook her head. If a woman, she thought, becomes as hard and cruel and merciless as a man she may prosper. But at what a price to her womanhood, her woman's soul, her woman's tenderness and softness and compassion! Aspasia's eyes remained dry but she wept within. Surely, she mused, in her pain, there are some men who can truly devote their passions and their dedications to a woman, and honor and respect her, while maintaining their own lives in the world of men. Surely love was not only lust to every man.

The vast company was now returning to the caravan in a bellow of noise, and Aspasia rose with her women. A deep weariness came to her, a heavy dejection. She passed the tent of Al Taliph. The flap opened and the elderly woman emerged, leading the little girl by the hand again. The child walked like a wounded and crippled lamb, staggering, bent over, holding her lower body in both her small hands. Aspasia could not control herself. She ran to the girl and enfolded her in her arms, to the astonishment of the women. She pressed the brown head to her breast. She murmured consolations, and the child cried and clung to her as to a mother. Then Al Taliph appeared on the platform, fastening his girdle.

Aspasia looked up at him and he saw her lifted glowing eyes. He saw her disgust and dread. But he said nothing. He did not even shrug. Yes, I am a fool, thought Aspasia. What is this child, or any other woman, to him? She smoothed the child's hair and returned her to her guardian. Al Taliph leapt from the platform and went to his men, and Aspasia watched him go. He did not even have contempt for her, and that was the worst of all. She had entered his world at her own consent, or the consent of Thargelia. She had known from the first that to Al Taliph she was only a woman.

By Castor and by Pollux, Aspasia swore solemnly, I will regain my self-control and never, from this moment on, will a man ever beguile me. I will deceive him as he has deceived other women; a woman is cleverer than a man.

Ah, but surely in this intricate and various world there can

157

truly be love between a man and a woman, and dignity and pride. And I will find such a man, even if I have to wander all the world. She wondered at her pain.

She did not know that Al Taliph loved her, and that to him other women were only a diversion and a necessity, and above all only a novelty. He had seen her revulsion and her disgust, and he was angered. She had spent over three years in his house and had seen many things there, and she remained blind and obdurate and without understanding. They had talked endless hours together, and it had come to nothing. He wanted to go to her and hold her in his arms—he fresh from the sweat and the blood of the nameless child. But Aspasia would not understand, though she was a hetaira. He, too, was filled with pain, as well as anger. She would never comprehend that he loved her, and he dared not try to convince her. Between men and women, even though they spoke the selfsame language, there remained an impassable chasm, hewn from their nature and their very lives.

While her women slept in the heat of the late afternoon Aspasia wrote to Thargelia, using the stylus and tablet she had brought with her in one of her chests.

"Greetings to Thargelia, my dearer than mother:

"In these years, sweetest of friends, we have exchanged no letters for none would have been permitted to be sent nor any given to me. I have not been unhappy in my situation. In truth, I have had much happiness. But now I find my circumstances untenable, insufferable. I have, in my mind, the thought of establishing a school for young girls in Athens, though not a school for courtesans. Do not laugh, dear friend and mother. I know you will not for always you knew what was in my soul even as a child, and my rebellion against the degradation of women. In Persia the degradation is far worse than in Miletus or Greece. Surely you are aware of this, for do you not know all things? Enough. I am sending this letter through the kind offices of one Damos of Damascus, a rich merchant. I implore you to help one you loved so tenderly when she was an infant in your house. When it is possible I will go to you and my former home, and in the meantime you will seek a house for me in Athens where I may live and establish my school. May Hermes, swift of winged foot and helmet, speed this letter to you and your reply through Damos of Damascus, who lives on the Street called Straight. Never have I forgotten you nor my sisters, and I long to embrace you, to throw myself, as a loved daughter, into your arms,

158

there to weep and tell you my story. I commend you to the protection of Athene Parthenos whom you have always worshipped and honored."

She was weeping as she signed and sealed the letter, then placed it in her bosom. The next step was most dangerous and her heart thumped with fear at the thought. She looked closely at her women; they still slept. The heat in the tent was most intolerable though it was nearing sunset. She drew her veil across her face and silently stepped through the flap of the tent and stood upon the platform, glancing fearfully about her and swaying with the motion of the wide platform. The men who drove the horses were half-slumbering on their seats, the pennant one held drooping in the fierce light. Aspasia crept along the side of the tent to the rear and found, as she had hoped, a narrow width of platform, which was covered with thick dust and sand. There she crouched, praying for the appearance of Thalias whom she knew rode at intervals with Al Taliph, and sometimes alone.

The western sky was, in its wideness and colors, even more stupendous than had been the dawn, and the bleak dead earth was crimson in the light of the falling sun, which was now an enormous globe of fire near the horizon. At a far distance there was a range of mountains like broken black teeth. Suddenly a mirage appeared on the desert, a mirage of a beautiful white city with towers and turrets and golden walls. So clear was the vision, so full of detail, in that ardent light, that Aspasia was half-convinced that the city was near at hand. Then it was gone.

She held her veil across her face to protect it from the sun. She heard the sound of an approaching horse and, thanking the gods, she saw that the rider was indeed Thalias and that he was alone. He discerned her sitting on the platform and reined his horse in astonishment. She threw aside her veil and pressed her lips with her finger, imploring quietness. He touched his horse with his heel and came closer. His blue eyes were uneasy and darted about him. He saw Aspasia's beautiful face, pale now and streaked with tears, and his generous heart was moved for all his dread of Al Taliph. He bent from his horse and said in a very low voice: "What is it, Aspasia?"

She stood up, the better to be close to him. The horse's breath was hot and parched against her cheek. She could see his great white teeth. She held up the letter to Thalias and he snatched it quickly. She whispered above the sound of hoofs, "Send it before Damascus, dear Thalias. I have asked that a reply be sent to you in the city."

He glanced down at the letter. He saw to whom it was addressed and looked afraid. "Do not fear," she said. "I have not betrayed you, my dear Thalias. I have given your new name to Thargelia, and the name of the street where you live in Damascus." She gazed at him with desperate appeal. "Help me," she pleaded, and clasped her hands tightly against her breast. "Help me as I helped you, for I am in danger."

He arched his eyebrows in amazement, and she nodded. "I am worse than a slave," she said. To herself she thought, Yes, I am worse than a slave for I would flee from a love which devours me and yet which I despise. Her large brown eyes, so filled with shifting stars and liquid brilliance, fixed themselves on Thalias with so much despair and sorrow that he forgot to be afraid. He thrust the letter into his robe and his eyes smiled with promise upon the girl. He dug his heels into the horse's side and the animal sprang forward and away.

Aspasia felt undone and weak. Thalias had not spoken in reply to her plea but she knew she could trust him, for all he was a cautious man. She sat again on the platform, calling upon her inner strength. Finally she rose and in that bloody light of sunset she re-entered the tent. Her women were stirring on their cushions, and yawning.

Al Taliph did not send for her that night, nor the night following, and Aspasia did not know whether to be relieved or to be crushed. She longed for him with a terrible longing, and she knew that this was just the beginning of pain and the darkness of grief and the unforgetting. But her resolution remained.

CHAPTER 15

The caravan climbed slowly and heavily to the great high plateau, between the valleys of the Tigris and the Indus, a vast basin surrounded by mountains, and fed by the Tigris and Euphrates rivers, and partially divided by a desert. The air of the plateau was cool, and the mountains were already turbaned by early snow. Here, on the immense wilderness lived lions and tigers, deer, lynxes, wolves, hyenas, jackals, hogs, porcupines, badgers, hares, martens and weasels, whose voices could be heard in shrieking chorus at night, in forests or on the plain. The day was profuse with the cries and screams of birds of uncountable variety. Sometimes the rare and beautiful Persian cats could be found, and frequently tamed, and were the pride of the ladies in the cities, who loved to stroke and fondle and comb them and whisper sweet words into those mysterious blue eyes. The rivers were thick with salmon, sturgeon, herring, perch and bream, especially in the estuaries.

The plateau seethed with the life of the beasts and the birds, and there were small settlements of that "manly and sturdy peasantry, healthy and brave," of which Darius had spoken with such admiration and pride, and who exemplified for him all that was sound and strong in a nation. "Let such a peasantry become urban and corrupt with civilization, and their country dies, and all its virtues, which sprang from the soil, the free air and the templed forests." He would also say of them with pride, "A Persian, the son of a Persian, an Aryan of Aryan stock, and shall not we Aryans inherit the earth? We come from the loins of a masculine race." To which several Grecian philosophers and soldiers had replied ironically. "We are called effeminate by the Persians—whose men redden their lips—but it was we who defeated them with our bows and our 'womanish' strength. It was we who began the destruction of that insatiable empire."

But a Persian philosopher said, also in reply, "We began to decline when we built enormous cities, and forgot our gods. The air of a city is stench, and the temples are corrupt. For cities are not the true habitats of a glorious race; they are its tombs."

Alone, isolated and almost ignored though Aspasia was, her newly awakened sense of life, of being, of again entering existence as from a moveless dream, of again being part of the world and its sights and sounds and rapturous changes and vitality, its hubbub and unpredictabilities, engaged her growing interest in spite of her sadness. So she had felt on leaving the shelter of Thargelia's house, but now in greater measure—for in the house of Al Taliph she had been completely immured —she felt a rising expectation, the radiance of hope, however feeble it still was and how accompanied by sorrow. She said to herself, paraphrasing a Greek philosopher: I observe, therefore I am. The natural vivacity of her nature slowly returned, resembling the tingling of a leg or an arm which had been compressed but which now was released.

Though she awaited a summons from Al Taliph, which did not come, she felt a little lessening of the wild despair she had originally suffered. She found that there were moments when she even forgot him, and could look upon mountains and rivers, forests and valleys, plains and cliffs and azure pools and cataracts, with eager marveling. She often thrust aside the flap of her tent, to stand in the aperture, gazing like a freed child on aspects she had never seen before. Once she saw a gigantic migration of butterflies in the lambent air, catching sunlight on crimson, black and golden wings, and rising and falling like a colored shawl from India which Al Taliph had once given her. On another occasion she watched the dance of birds against a silver dawn, and she was ecstatic and threw out her arms as if she would rise and join them. All about her were the scents, fragrances, odors and motionless luxury and montony. Cool green grass, dark trees whose names she did not know, scattered clusters of red and blue and yellow and snowy flowers, little streams bright and restless as mercury, thunderous green falls of water that shook the pure air and rumbled under the wheels of the caravan, sunsets and sunrises of incomparable majesty, circling ranks of mountains of somber green or ochre or even scarlet as the season advanced, rivers flashing like white fire as they raced under the sun, river islands tufted as if with enormous ostrich feathers, caverns with black mouths—all these she saw with a revived wonder and joy. The voices she heard from men and brutes and birds were new to her; the atmosphere was pervaded with resin and the scent of cold vegetation and colder stone and icy water. She felt she was breathing liquid and shining crystal and not strong air, and sometimes her lungs stung with the sweet unfamiliarity and the purity of it, and her eyes watered. The caravan would enter dim arcades of forests, and Aspasia was awed by the vaulting and living arches above her and the living columns that slowly moved past her. She understood for the first time that there is a subtle difference between knowledge and understanding. The first was taught, the second was a gift to the soul. She had a sudden new comprehension of life and the Godhead, and she was shaken with reverence. Once when she saw a narrow river the color of gold between dark and looming banks and another like a vein of deep purple stained with fire, she could hardly restrain her delight, and worship.

She was conscious again of still being young and alive, of having her eyes filled with constantly changing marvels. The fragile hope in her began to increase. This, then, is what men feared in women, she would think: They fear, if released from a man's arms and commands, we would see the world and desire to be part of it, and be not in a state of servitude and a victim of random passion, but a member of humanity, itself. So must an exultant slave feel when he discovers that in his heart he is free, despite his chains, and so must a master know fear when he discerns that though he can control the body of his slave he cannot control his spirit.

Her resolution for ultimate and absolute freedom became stronger hour by hour. It was only at midnight, when she slept alone, and the deep silence was about her, that she suffered torments of yearning and her tears wet her silken pillows.

One night the caravan halted at a caravanserai on a wide plain open to the sky. It was walled, square of form; the walls had thin small windows inserted in them, but the lower reaches had only insignificant openings for air. Within was an arcade, surrounded by storerooms; one wall was reserved for sleeping cubicles. The center was not roofed as were the outer sections, but contained a fountain and a well for men and beasts. There was but one entrance, tall and wide enough to admit camels, and was guarded by gates and strong doors. Stone benches were scattered about over the stone floor. Scores of camels and horses and mules could be harbored here and tended and relieved of their burdens for the night. On the second storey were cubicles, similar to the ones on the floor, for masters of caravans, whereas the drivers slept below.

Skilled guards patrolled the caravanserai, and were politely fed by those who owned the caravans, and treated with respect, for the safety of caravans depended on their watchfulness and bravery.

Aspasia saw the slow but steady entrance of camels, men, horses and mules within the gates, though the four tents did not enter. Only their horses were removed and taken inside for the night. Al Taliph's own armed guards remained without also, and, wrapping themselves in their cloaks after their evening meal—cooked outside over fires—they slept in the cool high grass with their swords in their hands. One sentry remained awake. The caravan fell asleep and there was no sound but the cry of night birds, the rustle of grass and myrtles and oaks and sycamores, and the occasional stamping of a restless camel or horse from within the walls. The enormous mystery of darkness lay upon all who slept, and a great amber moon climbed the amethystine stairs of heaven, and Aspasia thought of the virgin goddess, Artemis, ascending and ever serene and alert, carrying her lustrous shield on her arm.

The women attendants of Aspasia slept, and she let herself down from the platform and gazed enraptured on the heavens. Everywhere lay a deep purple shadow over the plain though far to the west there was still a faint scarlet burning as the sun withdrew his last banners behind him. Then, as Aspasia watched, she caught a single flash of bright green on the horizon, and the sun and his entourage left the sky. The silence and the darkness increased, and the moon became more resplendent and vivid. But it was the stars, not obscured by the hot yellow dust of Miletus or the fogs from the ocean, which caught at Aspasia's heart.

For never before had she seen such tremendous grandeur, such awesome majesty as that which was now revealed to her in the skies. She had thought the stars to be of a universal whiteness except for the pale crimson of Mars. Now she saw that they were of every brilliant color, amber, blue, cerise, aureate, topaz, rose, carbuncle, garnet and heliotrope, as well as blazing white. They were so gigantic that they appeared close enough to pluck like ripe dates, and some, in their passage, wore trains of fire. She thought that such a countless panoply of kings should be accompanied by retinues with trumpets and that all the world should resound with music and that all men should fall upon their knees and bury their heads in the dust, lest they offend by gazing. It is enough that I was born to see such splendor with these eyes, thought Aspasia. It is enough to live if only for an hour to know them; death, thereafter, would be nothing. What word of man could encompass these, one chord of earthly music do them honor? What prayer sufficient?

She heard a man's voice near at hand, grave and solemn: " 'The Heavens declare His glory, and the firmament shows His handiwork.' "

She started violently and saw a tall cloaked figure nearby, hooded. Then the voice spoke again: " 'What is man that You should be aware of him, and the son of man that You should visit him?' "

"Al Taliph," she whispered, and put her hands to her breast. She stood on the grass and trembled, and he came to her and held out his hand and she took it in silence. He led her a little apart and they stood side by side and regarded the incredible spectacle above them, and Aspasia was full of a tumult of joy.

"So the Jews, through one of their singers, questioned," he said, still looking at the sky. His fingers were warm and strong over hers and a deep content flowed over her. All her anger and disgust and sorrow were forgotten. He had remembered her. She also thought, Alas for the hearts of women. They betray us even in our souls and our resolutions. But the hearts of men are never betrayed thus. When men desert women they have deserted forever. But our souls are steeped in the bitter

164

waters of our tears and always we have our secret longings even if we love again.

She could feel Al Taliph, in the shadow of his hood, looking down at her tenderly as if they had parted only last night with last protestations of love. Now the revelation of God's glory above her was shattered by the tears in her eyes, so that all became a prism of many dancing colors floating in liquid salt.

Nearby the men slept rolled in their blankets, and a sentry passed after one respectful if curious glance at the man and the woman. Al Taliph said:

"Above us is the Life of the World, the Anima Mundi of the Greeks. He is the Life of all men, and no matter the religion men espouse, His command, above all else, is in them. The Taoists say, 'As you deem yourself, so deem others.' The Buddhists were told, 'Hurt not others with that which pains yourself.' The Indus say, 'This is the sum of Duty, that you do naught to others which if done to you would cause you pain.' The Jews have said, 'What is hurtful to yourself do not to your fellow man.' In all other things do almost all religions differ—but not in this. It is the Law. So Zoroaster has said, and Mithras—it is the Law."

He looked at the sky with an almost humble worship. But Aspasia could not refrain saying, "The Law, among men, does not apply in their dealings with women."

He answered, "You, my white dove, will never understand."

"I have been taught, Al Taliph, that this is the invariable reply men make to women, and it is meaningless even to themselves. Yet they utter those foolish words both in extenuation of their enormities, and to confuse."

She could feel him smiling, though his hand tightened on hers. "It is not lovable in a woman to refute a man with his own words. But I love you for all your sharp tongue." I have been forgiven, thought Aspasia wryly, for his own offense. But such are men. That I have been taught also.

Now she could see the heavens again clearly and they both gazed at them in silence that was more than speech. At last Al Taliph said, "Men and women do not speak the same language, as you have remarked before, my love, even if they use the same words. That is our curse or possibly a divine mercy. When I speak of God it is with the terrible awareness that I must deserve His own awareness of me. But when women speak of God it is with importunity for favors and a superb confidence that His Ear is open to them always and that He is even gratified that they remember Him. Enough. Let us live our lives as harmlessly as possible—even if we invariably fail. Who knows but what our intentions have weight also with Him, and that He understands?"

He dropped to his knees suddenly and bowed his head into the dust and grass, and was still, and Aspasia watched, marveling at his complexity, shaking her head the while. But her love for him was like a wild and renewed fire in her heart and she yielded to it. Was it possibly enough that one should love even if understanding failed? Had not a philosopher said, "Love or perish"? So, Eros like Justice, must remain blind and forgive always.

Al Taliph rose from his knees. The hood fell from his head and his dusky face was very moved yet still. Could it be, thought Aspasia, that the God of men and the God of women are two different Deities?

He held out his hand to her again and she took it, and he said, "Come." So she went with him to his tent and lay down beside him and returned his caresses. In the midst of them she again wondered at the treacherous hearts of women, who forgave all enormities against them because they loved and could not help the loving.

Before they parted at dawn Al Taliph said, as if their conversation had not been interrupted, "Empires, and men, to survive, must grow spiritually and intellectually, or die. That is the teaching of God and nature for all that lives. Once forgetting, they will be extinguished and only the vulture and the fox and the wild ass will inherit."

He went with her to the door of her tent and he looked at the eastern sky inscrutably. A huge crown of fire was slowly rising there and she knew that he had forgotten her in the mystery of his own being. She was not appeased, yet she was not offended. Above all, she was baffled, and remembered again that Thargelia had warned her maidens that it was impossible for the sexes to know each other. Did they embody the principle that no man can understand another, and all were walled up in their own flesh as a tree is walled mutely in its bark, no matter whether they were men or women? As men could never comprehend God then it was possible that no human creatures could completely perceive the motives and being of their fellows.

There was but one virtue above all others: compassion. For it was superior even to understanding, which could lead to stern judgment, and judgment was with God and it was His prerogative.

CHAPTER 16

The caravan came upon the ancient city of Damascus one early evening just before sunset. It seemed to Aspasia that the walled city approached the caravan rather than the caravan approaching it over the plain. The walls were golden and gleaming in the light of the descending sun, and piercing above them could be seen the glittering turrets and the tall thin towers and illuminated domes against a sky the color of heliotrope. Here, then, awaited the "Market of the Desert," so named by merchants, and famed for its Wine of Helbon, its delicate woollens, linens, dried fruit, damasks, exquisite and weblike silks of many colors, its Tyrian purples, cushions with golden and silver tassels, leather work of incredible intricacy, gemmed filigree work in gold and silver, enamels, inlaid wood and metals, its marvelous brocades, its incomparable Damascene steel weapons, its works of art in brass and copper, and its covered Street called Straight, wherein dwelt rich merchants and their shops, the banks and the bankers, many markets, fountains, and inns. It ran from the Damascan Gate from east to west, and few there were who had not heard of its wonders, its scenes, its opulences, its wealth, its commerce and its power. Older than the memory or records of man, Damascus had been assaulted many times by lustful enemies, Egyptians, Israelites, Assyrians and others, but she survived and was soon to be termed "immortal."

It was a fervid city, this jewel of the desert, hot, dusty, narrow of street, arched of gateways, violently colored, both perfumed and stinking, paved with stones polished by countless sandals and boots, teeming with men and camels, sleepless, blowing with red torches at night, glowing blindingly at noonday, restless, eager, sophisticated, cynical, and boasting the greatest craftsmen and artists in the world in endless profusion. Over all was the scent as of heated spices and burning stone and offal and urine of both men and beasts, and here were palaces of eastern splendor seen nowhere else in the world, and alleys noisome and noxious, and beggars and thieves and poets, and florid gods and winged Baals and the Ashtaroth—female deities—all with worshippers in an atmosphere of genial tolerance. It was a dazzling city, if without the grandeur of others, exciting and excitable, trembling always with the yellow dust that whirled over it, sometimes incandescent in the sun like golden particles, and pearly under

167

the moon. Here could be heard the tongues of many nations and many races, and every man hurried in spite of the heat, his face thrust forward as if he desired to run and not walk. Veiled women were everywhere, in stalls, selling flowers and sweetmeats and spiced morsels of meat and rice and wine and fabrics and vegetables and fruits and cheeses and ornaments, and their shrill cries and quarrels were louder than the complaints of streams of camels and horses and mules ever-flowing through the streets as caravans came and left. Almost every street held an inn, poor or lavish, for travelers and merchants. Faces could be seen in hue from the purest smooth white to the gleaming blackness of an Ethiopian or Nubian.

The bronze Gate of Damascus was opened swiftly by guards, who recognized the illustrious banners carried by the caravan of Al Taliph. Above the arch blew gay pennants and on the apex there was a crouching stone statue of an ambiguous creature, half lion, half woman, winged and crowned, with a beautiful and majestic face. Aspasia was enraptured as the caravan slowly passed through the gate, and entered a narrow rising street walled on both sides. On the tops of the walls stood throngs awaiting the cooler air of evening, chewing delicacies from their palms, arguing, laughing, curiously eyeing the caravan, joking, spitting and staring. Aspasia could hear music rising and falling everywhere, music alien to her ears. She had thought the market places of Miletus and Persia unbearably noisy. They were muted compared with the uproar that now assailed her, the sleepless uproar of a city beyond her imagination. When the caravan wound its way through the street men and women in vari-colored robes took refuge in slits in the walls. As the sun fell to the horizon torches began to sputter from sockets and lanterns began to move restlessly like illimitable stars.

Aspasia's women were discreetly amused at the girl's wonder and entrancement, for they had often been here before, and they smirked behind their veils. Her own veil was hot and suffocating on her face, but she did not draw it aside. She saw the countenances of the Damascan men and she acknowledged their handsomeness and their great lustrous eyes, ever moving. They saw the tall girl in the doorway of her tent, and marked the slenderness of her body even through her demure garments and showed their pleasure in smiles and inclinations of their heads. Once, in laughing defiance, she pulled aside her veil briefly, and the men who saw this struck postures of dazed admiration, and a few walked beside the tent until they were driven off by the guards uttering imprecations and displaying threatening whips.

Then, on the Street called Straight the caravan separated itself from the four tents, and the occupants alighted under guard at the entrance to a very large walled inn. They entered a courtyard in which was centered a tiny garden with a fountain. Windows peered down from all four walls, and were crowded with faces inspecting the new arrivals, especially the women, thinking many of them were beauteous slaves to be displayed tomorrow in the slave markets. A red light filled the courtyard, flittering from the torches, and the air was filled with insects and moths.

The turrets and towers and domes began to shine under a soaring moon, as if touched and plated with silver. Aspasia and her women were assigned two handsome chambers in the inn, rich with silks and brocades and divans and fat pillows and cushions, carved Chinese tables and ivoried chairs, the floors soft with rugs of many bright patterns. Aspasia discovered that the windows were barred by beautifully wrought iron in a vinelike shape. A dinner was brought to them of roasted lamb and vegetables simmering in garlic and olive oil, and dates and honey and soft pale bread and wine and assorted cheeses, and sauces and condiments of pungent odor and enticing aromas, and heaped fruits. She dined, listening to the music and the voices and the clamor of the city. Bells began to ring at random until all the air was pervaded with their dulcet or imperative tongues. Gaiety filled her, and excitement, and gratitude and love for Al Taliph who had condescended to give her such gratification. The vessels of oil flickered with light in the chambers, and were sweetly scented, partly to lull the senses and partly to cover the pervasive stench of latrines below.

Aspasia fell asleep on her cushions, after bathing in water redolent of jasmine, and she smiled in her sleep, her golden hair streaming about her. Her happy face had the innocence of a lily, and her women hated her and envied her.

In the morning Aspasia, after dining, was summoned to the chambers of Al Taliph. She was surprised, for he rarely summoned her before evening. She drew her veil across her face and arrayed herself in thin white linen and silver and went, attended by two of her women, to Al Taliph. His chambers were sumptuous, and he was half-reclining on a divan, appearing at ease and content. Near him stood Thalias who bowed at her entry, and Al Taliph smiled. He held out his hand to Aspasia and she sat, as usual, at his feet and looked at Thalias. Then she pushed aside her veil and he saw her face, fresh and curious if a little anxious. Almost imperceptibly he nodded his head. So, the letter had been sent many long days ago and Aspasia sighed.

"It would seem, my white rose, that my Damos and friend, has brought his wife to this inn to thank me for the little girls given to her, and to thank you also." A visible flash passed over his eyes. "She is in the next chamber, Hephzibah bas Ephraim. Do you desire to see her?"

"If my lord has no objections," replied Aspasia. Al Taliph laughed lightly and touched her cheek. "Your lord has no objections," he said, as if he mocked her. Thalias let his eyes drop as though embarrassed. A eunuch opened a door at a little distance and Aspasia rose and left the room, and also her women.

The chamber beyond was evidently used for dining and when Aspasia entered a young woman rose shyly, unveiled, and dressed very soberly, and her manner was both timid and sedate. She had a plain young face that was also appealing, as if she implored kindness. The two little girls sat side by side on cushions and happily devoured handfuls of a sweetmeat composed of honey and ground almonds, and they were rosy and clean and patient.

Hephzibah had beautiful blue eyes and her partly uncovered hair was soft and brown. She seemed a little abashed at the sight of Aspasia and her pale lips trembled a little. She said, in Aramaic, "I wished to thank you, Lady, for your great condescension in giving me these small daughters, whom I already cherish, though I saw them first this morning."

Aspasia was touched. "It was not I. It was Al Taliph who did so, a gift for you."

At the mention of that name Hephzibah's face changed, and Aspasia wondered. Hephzibah drew a deep breath and looked aside. "Yes," she said. "That is what my husband told me. He also told me something else." Now she looked directly at Aspasia. "Lady," she said, "you are not only as beautiful as Ruth or Rachel but as great of heart as any of the mothers of Israel."

Aspasia did not believe that Thalias had spoken of her beauty to Hephzibah, and she smiled gently. "Damos is fortunate in you, Hephzibah bas Ephraim, and you—" she paused, "are fortunate in him."

For another strange and unspoken reason the other woman's eyes glistened with tears. She took Aspasia's hand and kissed it. She whispered, "I thank you for Damos also."

Aspasia was alarmed. She glanced over her shoulder but no one stood there. She whispered in reply, "There are certain things a man should not tell his wife and I am surprised at Damos' indiscretion. Let us not speak of this, now or at any other time."

"What my husband tells me is ever safe in my bosom," said Hephzibah and lifted her head. "But if a man cannot confide in the woman who loves him to whom can he confide?"

When has Al Taliph ever confided in me? thought Aspasia with a pang of sadness. But she looked at the other woman with interest. Here was no woman whose husband despised her femaleness but gave her honor and all his secrets, and it seemed enviable to Aspasia and she was filled with longing. True, Al Taliph spoke with her always of philosophies and abstruse things, but never had he permitted her to see him as he was, himself, except for that night under the stars. Even then she had found him enigmatic. She yearned for a man who would trust her utterly as Damos apparently trusted his wife, and who put his very life into her hands. Truly then, and only then, could a woman be happy and content and proud, and never feel herself deprived or lonely or forgotten.

Hephzibah, though always she had been sheltered and loved and respected, had a woman's intuition and she was seized with confused pity for this beautiful girl who suddenly seemed so bereft and desolate. A bar of sunlight wavered over Aspasia's face, yet it only increased her air of melancholy. Hephzibah turned to the little girls, touched each fondly on the cheek and said, "This is Ruth, and this is Rachel, my daughters." The children leaned their heads briefly against her breast then ate another sweetmeat with childish voracity.

"They love you even now," said Aspasia, and Hephzibah smiled for the first time and her plain young face became radiant. "I love them dearly," she replied. "They will be sisters to my son."

Now both the women were silent. They could hear the vehicles rattling over the stones of the courtyard and the distant clamor of the city. They listened for a moment, but both were thinking their own thoughts. Aspasia said to herself, "This woman is happy as I was never happy, and I would change places with her with joy." Not for Hephzibah wild nights of ecstasy mingled with devastation. Yet not for her fear of ultimate rejection and abandonment, by either divorce or banish-

171

ing. For the first time in her life Aspasia saw another existence, infinitely gracious and serene and prideful. She saw that Hephzibah's hands showed evidence of toil at the loom and in the kitchen, among servants, Hephzibah singing tranquilly and eagerly awaiting the return of a husband who honored her and the visitation of a father who rejoiced in his ewe lamb. What are all my gems and opulences compared with this? she asked herself, and all my excitements and fevers? My heart bounds at the sound of Al Taliph's voice and I am joyful when I see his face, but always there is my dread and my fear. But Hephzibah is not tormented so, and she is blessed of the gods. When Thalias arrives home she is enfolded safely in his arms.

Hephzibah was gazing at her again and she discerned Aspasia's pain and she recalled what Damos had told of her, that she was a courtesan and the companion of Al Taliph. According to the Law women like this were frequently stoned to death for adultery or licentiousness. But Hephzibah suddenly wanted to embrace Aspasia and hold her to her breast with the same tenderness she had shown to the children, and to console and weep with her. This further confused her for never before had she seen or encountered a lewd woman, and why she should feel such compassion she did not know.

The young Jewish woman could not control her mournfulness at something she had only vaguely detected, but which was nevertheless poignant. She did not know the reason. She lifted an object wrapped in silk and tied with ribbons and placed it in Aspasia's hands. "It is a gift I have brought for you, in gratitude, Lady," she said. "My husband has declared it will please you, perhaps."

Aspasia said, "I must thank you, Hephzibah bas Ephraim." She began to unwrap the gift, but Hephzibah covered her eyes quickly with her hands and said, "No, I implore you. It is a graven image, so my husband has told me, and of the heathen. He bought it in the bazaar this morning, for your pleasure."

"You do not know what it is?" asked Aspasia in astonishment. The other woman shook her head and dropped her hands. "It is not permitted," she murmured. Aspasia was more astonished than ever. Had Damos bought her something obscene? Her cheeks flushed and seeing this Hephzibah said, "You must forgive me, but pious Jews do not gaze at graven images, and that is why I sit in my litter in the city with drawn curtains." She drew a deep breath. "I believe it is a statuette of a god."

Aspasia wanted to laugh a little. "You miss the excitement and the wonders of the city, then?"

"I have my household, and my children, and my women and my parents and my dear husband, my gardens and my roses and my friends. What more can a woman desire, Lady?"

What indeed? thought Aspasia, looking at the wrapped object in her hands. An awkwardness came to them, and there was nothing more to say between a woeful courtesan and a beloved wife. Then Hephzibah, who was rarely demonstrative, put her hands on Aspasia's shoulders and kissed her cheek and Aspasia, her eyes swimming in moisture, returned the embrace. In silence then she went to the chamber of Al Taliph.

Thalias was no longer with Al Taliph. The latter said indulgently, "What is this you bear in your hands, my sweet one?"

But Aspasia said, "I have seen what it is to be truly a woman." She began to unwrap the silk. She did not see Al Taliph's dark and ambiguous expression, nor did she see him move a little restlessly on his divan nor did she see the sharp somberness of his eyes. She said, "It is a gift from Hephzibah bas Ephraim, but she would not permit me to reveal it before her."

"Ah," said Al Taliph and sat up alertly. "Be certain it is either useful or edible. I know these Jews. If useful, what will you do with it? If edible, it will be delicious."

The silk fell from the gift and Aspasia's hands enclosed an exquisitely carved and detailed image of a fat and smiling god, of ivory, with a vast belly and with legs folded in a fashion she had observed among the Indus.

"Buddha," said Al Taliph, and held out his hand for it. He turned it carefully in his fingers and examined it with pleasure. "This was created by an exceptional artist," he remarked. "I have never seen anything so perfect. It must have cost our dear Damos a fortune, for doubtless he purchased it himself, that apostate Jew!" and he laughed.

He glanced at Aspasia and he no longer smiled. He balanced the object on the palm of his hand, the hand dusky against the ivory, which glimmered in the morning light and showed, in the intricacy of its carving, a faint golden light. "Buddha," he repeated. "The ineffable One. The ultimate in a non-embracement of the world. Sit beside me, my love." She did so and he said, "I have heard that if one rubs his belly and prays for what he desires, it will be granted. That is the superstition."

He held the image in his hands and presented it to Aspasia,

who, trying to smile, rubbed the belly of Buddha. Then, without her own volition, she prayed, "Let him love me as I love him!" She dropped her hand. She said, "What? Will you not rub him also, lord?"

"I am not superstitious," he said. Very carefully he placed the Buddha on the table before him and contemplated it. Again she saw that enigmatic expression she had observed under the stars.

As though speaking to himself only he said, "The Persians honor all gods, all manifestations of the Deity, Buddha, Lao T'zu, Zoroaster, Mithras, Zeus, Ahuramazda, Ptah, Osiris, Vishnu, and even the vengeful Jehovah of the Jews. We are on the best of terms with them all, for of what concern is it what name men call God? He has illimitable Faces and aspects, and reveals Himself in whatsoever guise He desires. It is enough, it is said, that men love Him."

A god who cared for the love of men was a strange thought to Aspasia. Then she thought of her impulses to adoration which she had experienced, and which had been most mysterious to her and had exalted her if only briefly.

Al Taliph continued to speak as if to himself. "I have heard that it is believed in all religions that God would be born to men in the form of a Man. I have heard that the Chaldeans await Him, and the Jews, and the Egyptians speak of the birth of Osiris. Is it not unfathomable that all religions carry with them the belief, though none knows the other?"

Aspasia said, "In all Greek temples there is a bare altar inscribed: 'To the Unknown God.' But He has no priests, no celebrations, no worshippers, no pageants, no offerings."

"Not yet," said Al Taliph, and he gently covered the Buddha with the silk again.

Aspasia was deeply interested in what he had said and the intonations of his voice and she marvelled again at the elusiveness and unknowableness of this man whom she loved so desperately. "But, He will come?" she asked.

"He will come," said Al Taliph. "Perhaps tomorrow, perhaps not for centuries. Time does not exist for Him."

"But it exists for mankind," Aspasia said with sadness.

"That is our illusion," he answered. He closed his eyes and she saw that he was suddenly weary and she rose and silently left the room, baffled.

Her women were absent and Aspasia felt a sweet freedom, for rare was it that she was alone. She went to the barred window and looked down at the crowded courtyard. Below her

174

Thalias was standing, looking up, evidently expecting her. He smiled like a loving gay brother and kissed his hand to her and nodded. Then he moved away swiftly and Aspasia followed him with her eyes and she was filled with warmth and gratitude. She forgot that he had once been a slave, for in his salutation was all understanding, all reassurance, all kindness, all promise.

CHAPTER 17

Aspasia accompanied Al Taliph to the bazaars of the city and she was like a child in her jubilation and staring excitement. Her eyes were wide and illuminated above her thick veil, seeking to encompass all the colorful movement and watch all things at once. Al Taliph took her to a jeweler and there, in the back room where an unveiled woman could not offend the eyes of men, he bought her a necklace of opals, all blue and rose and pearly fire in their restlessness. He clasped it about her neck himself, and she pushed back her hood and her hair fell about her face and the jeweler was entranced. He was a very rich man; he believed Aspasia to be a favorite slave, and he drew Al Taliph respectfully aside and offered a fortune for her. In the meantime she was regarding herself rapturously in a silver mirror. She heard Al Taliph utter a word or two that was half-angry and then half-amused. But the language was unknown to her.

He returned to her and regarded her as if with new eyes. "Does the bauble please you, my golden hibiscus?" he asked, and fondled both the necklace and her throat. She looked at him ardently and then he lost his smile and gazed at her with a stern earnestness she had seen but few times before and which had always puzzled her. It was as though he were trying to interpret her words or her gestures or her expressions, and was never certain. She said, "If only I pleased you, lord, as much as this pleases me then indeed I would be happy." He sighed and turned away.

He bought her embroidered and brocaded silks and jeweled slippers and sandals and carved jade and ivory containers for cosmetics and golden bangles and earrings of designs uncommon to her and reaching to her shoulders, yet as light as down. He bought her girdles of flexible gold and fretted silver, also set with gems. She had but to admire and it was hers. A mantle of argus-eyed peacock feathers charmed her, and he

175

flung it over her shoulders and it caressed her. He carefully told her the origin of all these and she exclaimed, "What a marvelous world is this, where so much beauty is revealed!"

"What men make is only a poor imitation of nature," he said with indulgence. "When those feathers were on the living bird they were far more splendid, as life is above artifice, however adorned, or excellent." When she looked grave and stroked the mantle he said, "You are fairer, Aspasia, than the most glorious statue of a goddess or a nymph, however artfully sculptured and painted."

She pretended to be flattered but in her heart she desired him to regard her, not as an object of bewitchment—whose loveliness would soon depart in the thieving hands of time— but as a woman and a soul and a mind. She thought of Hephzibah bas Ephraim and in her turn she sighed and turned away and the enchantments he had bought her lost their delight. They were not a tribute to her, she believed, but only an adornment of what in his eyes was delectable. When he wearied of her all these treasures would not entrance him but rather she would be but an artificial effigy for the display of them, fit only for a merchant's shop. He would desire them for a younger and a more novel woman, and she would be bereft not only of these but of her life, itself, for was not her life in him? Desolation came again to her; she felt her whole spirit becoming an arid desert in which there would never be an oasis but only death. She fingered the opals and now they were but stone.

"What is wrong?" he asked her seeing her pensive countenance.

"Naught, lord," she answered though in her heart she said, What you have given me is not truly what I desire. And what I desire is what all women desire and men can never give them, not in the measure of our desiring.

At night she knew that he went with companions to luxurious houses to dine and to be entertained by music and dancers and lascivious women. In the company of armed eunuchs and female attendants, all heavily veiled and cloaked as she was, herself, she was permitted to visit bazaars and temples without his presence. Still dazzled, she began to feel some satiation and depletion, however. As women did not eat in public she and her women were led to large rear rooms behind the shops selling sweetmeats and wines and pomegranates and pastries and spicy ground meat in grape leaves and flavorsome bread encrusted with sesame seeds and curious cakes filled with honeyed poppy seeds and nuts and dates, and there, sitting almost in silence, they devoured what they had bought. The rooms were invariably windowless and hot, though comfortably furnished, and smelled not only of the food but of incense. The famous Wine of Hebron was chilled and remained on the tongue like a sweet memory. It was also potent and Aspasia sometimes dozed in her litter and forgot, for a while, the now constant pain in her breast.

She would listen, sleepless, at night, until Al Taliph returned with his companions, laughing in the courtyard. Sometimes she would rise and run to her barred window to catch a sight of him under the moon and starlight, praying he would summon her. But the dawn would be igniting the east with fire and she knew that he had retired and had forgotten her, she immured in her chambers as she had been immured in his palace. I am a fool to weep, she would tell herself, for was this not my impacable end? Yet I still live and somewhere I can live again.

They were to remain for a considerable time in Damascus. The days went by for Aspasia like a repeated dream, changeless. She understood that Al Taliph sold the goods of his caravan and was replacing them with goods for his own shops and market places and bazaars. Very occasionally he invited her to dine with him at noonday. But he seemed increasingly weary and preoccupied, and often he would leave abruptly when a visitor arrived to consult him, and not return. Then she had a choice of sleeping in the afternoon, as most of Damascus slept during that period except for the busy merchants and bankers, or to venture out again with her guards and women for another view of a different part of the city. There is nothing more terrible than idleness, she would think, and I am an idle woman. She would try to read the books Al Taliph bought for her but the philosophies and poems were strange and elusive to her and the allusions cryptic.

She wondered if Hephzibah bas Ephraim had forgotten her, for Al Taliph had humorously mentioned that the Jewish lady would invite her soon to partake of a quiet dinner alone with her. However, no invitation came and Aspasia was filled with disappointed resentment. Doubtless Hephzibah regarded her as unclean and did not desire her house to be polluted by such a woman as herself.

She began to think of the house she would have in Athens, but even that was taking on the semblance of a lost dream. Al Taliph would never let her go until he tired of her, and the air of Damascus made her mind languid and without hope. She existed for the benefit of Al Taliph's pleasure; beyond that she had no existence, but was just a glass bubble aimlessly drifting in any random breeze, catching light and color though having none of these within herself. Where was the incandescent resolution she had possessed only a few months ago? Her listlessness increased and became animation only in the presence of Al Taliph.

One day she said to him, "I had hoped to see Hephzibah bas Ephraim again. She has forgotten her promise to me."

He averted his face and said, "Damos mentioned that she had been indisposed." He hesitated, then continued: "I know you have pleasure in seeing the city, but it is my desire that you not go forth again from this time on, but remain in your chambers."

She protested. "But that is my only diversion!"

He looked at her forbiddingly. "It is my command," he said and at first would not explain for all the bright anger in her eyes. "Also," he said, "drink not of the water from the well but only wine and eat no fruit but that it is washed and peeled by yourself, with your knife and fingers. Let no water reach your mouth, even for the cleaning of your teeth, and when you bathe close your lips tightly so that no water can enter, nor must it enter your nostrils."

Now a faint cold alarm came to her. "What is this of which you speak, lord?"

"There is a rumor that some illness is spreading through the city and the physicians fear it is carried in wells and rivers. That may be a superstition, yet it is wise to be prudent."

Her alarm grew stronger. "What of you, Al Taliph? Are you being prudent?"

He shrugged and smiled. "I must drink and eat what is given me in the houses of my friends and my fellow merchants, but their kitchens are fastidious and so no harm will come to me. This inn has a reputation for cleanliness. But you must remain within." He hesitated and said inwardly, Lest you come to harm and I would be desolated. He smiled at her again and said, "Does not a man guard his treasure and are you not mine?"

She answered with acerbity, "Until I am no longer your treasure but have become tarnished in your eyes."

Now her life became more restricted than ever before. She was not permitted to go down even to the courtyard, and she saw fright in her women's faces. She heard them whisper; she saw them fingering amulets. Once she said to them with impatience, "Of what are you afraid?" But they did not answer but

178

only peeped at her furtively, and she knew they feared to give their terror words lest it fall upon them like a Fury, as at a summoning. They were stupid and unlettered women, docile and sullen, and had no conversation and so they were not of any companionship to her nor could she understand them. They began to utter dissonant chants and rock on their buttocks on the floor, their faces strained with anxiety for themselves, and the sound was discordant to Aspasia and disagreeable to her ears. She knew they were imploring their own fearsome gods. But how had any rumor come to them unless the eunuchs had gossiped? Eunuchs were worse than women, Al Taliph had once said, for prattle and idle tongues. The eunuchs, however, rarely if ever spoke to her.

The women were also much older than herself and fat and repugnant to her eyes, and as none now left the chambers the rooms began to reek with the smell of sweat and increasing incense and rank perfumes. She noticed, from her window, that men were continually through the courtyard, swinging censers of burning fires in the corners and thus filling the air with acrid smoke, and chanting as the women chanted. Perhaps the season for the caravans was ending, for Aspasia saw few and even these were decreasing and often days passed when there were none at all. She, herself, began to feel fear, and longed for news.

At last she could bear it no longer and cried to Al Taliph, "You must tell me! What is this illness of which you have told me? Would you leave me a prey to fright? It is better to know than to be ignorant."

He appeared very tired. There were no more bronze lights on his cheeks, she saw with dread, and his nose seemed larger and his subtle mouth tighter. "Then, I will tell you," he said. "It is cholera."

At that fearful word Aspasia shivered and trembled. "Cholera," she whispered. "Are many ill—dead?"

"A fourth of the city is dead," he replied. "I thought to spare you the knowledge. The gates of the city are closed. None can leave nor can come in. Does it make you more at ease to know this?"

But she whispered again, "Cholera!"

"Even the physicians are dying," he said.

She put her cold palms to her face and closed her eyes briefly. "Almost all die, lord."

"True. I did not wish you to be afraid. You are safe here if you are careful in your food and your drink."

She exclaimed, as she had exclaimed before, but now with terror, "What of you, lord?" Her face had turned very white and her eyes enlarged.

"I am careful also," he said and tried to smile at her. "I tell you now so that you will understand why we are prisoners here. If not for this we should have departed three weeks ago. It is not my wish to keep you in a dungeon."

She reached out and seized his hand and she was trembling again. "Remain with me, lord! Do not go forth again, I implore you."

He regarded her curiously. "Do you fear that if I sicken and die you will be helpless here? Do not distress yourself, dear one. My men will convey you home." His tone was sardonic. "Your name, sweet blossom, is in my will."

She withdrew her hand and turned aside her head helplessly. She said, "Is the family of Damos well?"

"His wife died a month ago." He threw the words at her as if she had incontinently wounded him and he wished to wound her in return.

She cried out and clenched her hands together. "Hephzibah bas Ephraim? Gods, what of her children—and Damos?"

"The children sickened, but are recovering. Damos had cholera in his childhood, he has told me."

Aspasia wept for that loving young woman and covered her face with her hands. When she looked up at last she saw that Al Taliph had left her. Now her fear for him became frenzy and she returned to her chambers and walked up and down them wringing her hands and muttering her own incoherent prayers, though she felt them superstition and useless. The women, forgetting their own whimperings and fear, watched her sullenly and glanced at each other with unspoken questions. Was the foreign woman sickening? They drew together, huddling, for protection.

She paused before them suddenly and stared down at them and hated them for no reason but that they were witnesses to her uncontrolled anguish. "What is that amulet you wear, Serah?" she asked of one of them and pointed to the chain and object about the woman's fat creased neck.

Serah covered it with her hand, protecting it from Aspasia, for all knew that she had the evil eye. She cringed and whimpered and did not answer. In a rage she had rarely felt before Aspasia bent, flung aside the woman's clutching hand, and lifted the silver object in her fingers.

Once she had seen such an amulet about the neck of an Egyptian but it had not interested her then, though it had been of gold, and jeweled. The one she held now in her hands was the length of her little finger, and was a thin flat shaft; one third down there was a flat crossbar, of an equally thin size as the long bar. The end of the top bar was looped and through this there was a silver chain. It was not a pretty trinket as the one the Egyptian had worn, and it was cheap. Aspasia had seen many amulets before but only two of this. She said, "Whence did it come and what does it mean and what god can be invoked by it?"

Serah shrugged blankly. "I found it in a shop in Miletus and it is said to have great powers, and the Greek shopkeeper said it is the sign of the Unknown God, but Who that God is I do not know. It signifies eternal life and the resurrection of the dead."

"Oh, what folly! Eternal life. Resurrection of the dead!" Even in her misery Aspasia felt derision. Then she remembered that the Egyptians believed in the resurrection of the dead and eternal life; therefore, they were solicitous concerning the disposal of the bodies of those who died, particularly those of royal blood. But even poor families sold all they had to pay for such preservation of a member's body and had it embalmed. She had another thought, remembering her conversation with Al Taliph: the Unknown God, Whose altar still awaited Him in Greek temples, and the pervasive belief in His coming throughout all religions, particularly in the East.

She slowly let the object slide through her fingers, from which it dropped to Serah's breast, and the woman hastily thrust it under the cloth of her breast. "Does it guard against illness, Serah?"

Serah again shrugged. "That I do not know, Lady. The Greek said only it has great powers." She pressed her hand over its outlines. "What is more desirable than protection from evil and disease and death?"

"True," said Aspasia. "Do we all not desire that?" She turned away and resumed her pacing. She was not veiled in the chamber nor was her head covered. As she passed by the barred windows hot bars of sunlight alternately struck her then withdrew, and her pale golden hair was like a flame over her white brow and about her pale cheeks. She kept pressing her palms together tightly, until they sweated and she prayed in herself: "If You are indeed the Unknown God, do not let

181

my beloved die! Preserve him from evil. It is said You love mankind and desire the love of men and would be born of us. Therefore, You are compassionate as our gods are not compassionate. Have mercy, have mercy. For, if he dies I cannot live."

A faint coolness, or a numbness, touched her heart and she became calmer. It was then that she heard a light tinkling against one of the bars of the window. She went to the window and looked without. Thalias stood there below, clad in somber robes, his face shrunken and older, his eyes reddened. He tried to smile up at her, then bit his lip. There were but one or two men in the once-crowded courtyard and they were at a distance, talking together.

Aspasia hastily glanced behind her, but her women were rocking on their buttocks and chanting again. She leaned against the bars, her face full of pity and desire to communicate her sympathy to him. He understood. His once merry blue eyes became vivid with tears. He reached to his pouch and glanced about him, then withdrew a sealed letter and showed it to her. Aspasia's heart jumped. It could be only from Thargelia. Despairingly, she looked again at her women. They had as yet seen or heard nothing. Her thoughts flew through her head like distracted birds. Then her mind became clear. In the next chamber commodes had been prepared for her and the women so that they need not go down to the latrines in the courtyard. There was a small window there. She glanced down at her waist, which was clasped with a silver cord set with garnets and amethysts, a trifle she had fancied in a bazaar and which Al Taliph had bought for her. It was of several lengths so that it could be wound and twisted pliantly about her slender body and even about her breasts.

She looked down again at Thalias then pointed towards the window of the other chamber and turned back to the women. Sighing, she went into the adjoining chamber, which had no door but the one entering this. She closed the thick blue and gold curtains behind her then ran silently to the window. Thalias was standing below. Swiftly she unwound the gilded cord about her waist and, holding one end, she let the other through the bars of the small window very quickly, her breath tight in her throat, her eyes on the distant men.

Thalias deftly seized the end of the cord and speedily tied it about the letter. It flew up the dusty wall like a moth and Aspasia retrieved it. Then Thalias touched his forehead in farewell and wandered away, ostensibly to the latrines.

The thudding in Aspasia's breast was harder and more

painful. She looked at the closed curtains, moved to a wall and swiftly opened the letter, which read:

"Greetings to Aspasia, one dearer than a daughter:

"How joyous was I to receive a message from you, my beautiful child, for never are you out of my memory. How I cried with pleasure, for the hope of seeing you again. I shall do as you wish at once and seek a house for you, as you desire, in Athens, but it appears to me a strange house. I will not question you, for the messenger awaits my answer. You must come first to your home in Miletus where I will embrace you and hold you once more in my arms and we shall speak of many things. I await you and will invoke Hermes to bring you on wings to me."

Aspasia thrust the letter into her bosom. The disposal of it would be another problem. Nor did she think just then how she could leave Damascus and Al Taliph. That was for the future.

But still a lightness came to her, like a wind of freedom through the bars of a prison, and her resolution, so long in abeyance, began to open like a hidden rivulet within her, at first doubtful and muddy, then springing into crystal.

As the evenings were sharply cool after the heat of the day a brazier was lighted in the chamber where she slept with her women. Aspasia was able to drop the letter on the coals where it flared a moment and then was but ashes. However, like the Phoenix, there rose from them a renewed life. It was only later while her women slept that she thought, But even if he will let me go, how can I leave him? I will leave my heart and my love behind and all that I am, and henceforth I shall be but a shadow from Hades. But I must go before he tires of me and I wander like an apparition in the chambers of the rejected, unwanted and despairing of any summons, weeping and mournfully sighing in the endless nights.

CHAPTER 18

Al Taliph did not call for Aspasia for several nights, but she heard him coming and going in the courtyard, which now echoed for so few entered it from within the inn or without. So the fountain in the center could be heard clearly in the darkness and any voices. Sometimes she could hear Al Taliph's voice and it was increasingly slow and weary. Then she rose from her cushions and looked down at him in the light of the red torches, saw he walked with bent head. She wanted to call to him but her pride would not permit it. She was no importunate woman, whimpering for love like a dog, desiring above all things to grovel at his feet.

The motionless days repeated themselves. There was little noise from the city; it lay mute, cowed by fear. Then one morning Aspasia received a summons to go to the chambers of Al Taliph. She hastily drew a comb through her disheveled hair, for in these days she neglected her appearance. She rubbed her cheeks and lips with a red unguent; she had become pale and drawn in her sunless and imprisoned state. She dressed herself in a hyacinth-colored tunic and clasped a silver and amethyst necklace about her throat and touched herself with attar of roses. Then she hastened to Al Taliph's chambers. It was very early and this summons was most unusual. The two armed eunuchs at his door opened it for her in a dull silence, and she entered.

To her horror she saw Al Taliph reclining on his cushioned bed in an attitude of total collapse, his gray profile staring at the ceiling. Three slave girls huddled at a distant wall, and two strange men stood at the bedside, rubbing their chins and conversing together in low voices. They were Egyptians, she saw by their garb and their dusky features, and medical pouches were beside them. There was a horrific stink in the hot closed room of vomit and feces, and Aspasia stood and swayed and suddenly trembled. No one noticed her or marked her arrival. Almost creeping, she went to the bed and looked down at Al Taliph. She bent over him and he became aware of her scent and her presence, and he turned his face to her and tried to smile. His eyes were sunken far back into his skull and were dim. The bronze metallic shine had totally left his cheeks, which were sunken also. His mouth was dry as dust, and he panted. A heavy sweat covered him with glistening beads. His flesh had dwindled.

He lifted his hand feebly to her. She fell to her knees and took his hand and it was burningly hot as if she had touched a fire. In spite of her anguish this manifestation startled her, for it indicated very high fever. Al Taliph was obviously very ill and close to death. There is little fever in cholera, she recalled through the haze of her terror. She put her hand under the coverlets. His belly was swollen, and he winced and moaned though her pressure was gentle. The Egyptians looked down at her in surprise, and exchanged glances with upraised brows. Forgetting everything but her beloved's extremity Aspasia continued her examinations and for an instant his old ironic amusement shone in his eyes. The area on his right side was

184

especially prominent and had a thickened feeling under her fingers. Again she pressed gently on it and he exclaimed and pushed away her hand.

Aspasia flung back her loose hair and looked up at the physicians, and they attempted to smile disdainfully. Then they saw her large and wine-brown eyes, glowing like topazes with imperative authority. "He does not have cholera," she said, and her voice was strong and clear. "How long has he been ill?"

They were silent a moment and then one of the physicians said, "For several days, Lady. Why is it that you say it is not cholera?" But his voice was almost respectful and did not have the contempt in it for women which the Aryan peoples invariably displayed. One of the physicians thought, She appears as Isis, gold and white and rose, and resembles a priestess.

"I was taught considerable medicine by a famous physician in the house of Thargelia in Miletus, and it has been my abiding concern. Tell me, sirs. Has my lord had frequent bloody stools, and hard colic?"

The younger of the physicians moved closer to her with interest and now his expression was grave. "It is true," he said, almost as if she were a colleague. He saw the profound intelligence in her face and eyes and recalled that priestesses were frequently physicians in Egypt. He forgot that she was but a favorite concubine, a mistress, hardly possessing a status above an adored slave woman. "But this can occur in rare cases of cholera also."

"There is little fever in cholera," said Aspasia, addressing him while the older physician thoughtfully stroked his beard. "Does he vomit profusely, as in cholera?"

"He vomits, but not very frequently." The young physician's face quickened.

Aspasia, still holding Al Taliph's hand, sat back on her heels. "But in cholera, as we were taught, there is no thickening and swelling of the right region of the belly, and there are clear feces or brownish or murky, and no bloody ejaculations except in the most rare of instances. Tell me, is his urine deficient, or not present?"

Now the older physician drew closer to her also. "His production of urine is almost normal, despite his vomiting and diarrhea. Sometimes he retains water he has drunk."

"He is in deep pain," said Aspasia. "He cannot endure a touch on his belly. This is not true of cholera, which affects the bowels but little."

185

The older physician tried for indulgence. "What is your diagnosis, Lady?"

"The flux," said Aspasia. "It is very serious and can be fatal, but it is not so serious as cholera." She trembled again and held Al Taliph's hand tightly as if to imbue him with her own young strength and determination to live. Now her brow was wet with the intensity of her emotions.

"The flux?" said one physician, disbelieving. "We see that very often, and this seems not the flux."

"It could be, sirs, that it is because my lord has a virulent case of it. In Egypt, I have heard, it is endemic and so is more benign than in these regions where there is little defense against it, and it is therefore overwhelming." She clasped her hands together and lifted her face to the physicians imploringly. "I beg of you, lords, to let me treat Al Taliph, for the flux is not rare in the region where we live, among slaves and the poor. It is rare only among the rich and the comfortable. Let me treat him! He is almost in extremity. It can do no harm."

Al Taliph's hot hand lifted feebly to her throat then her cheek, as if both touched and rebuking. Again she gripped his hand and held it tightly. "What have you been giving him, lords, in treatment?"

"Purges," said the younger physician. "And herbal wine."

"O gods!" Aspasia murmured, and shuddered. Then she said, "I have your permission to order his treatment?"

They glanced at each other again, smiling, shrugging. "Love," said the younger, kindly, "can often accomplish what the most skilled physicians cannot. His case is desperate. Your care can do no harm."

"Aspasia," said Al Taliph in a very weak voice. But she looked at him fiercely. "You are in my hands!" she cried. "You shall obey me, or die!"

Intense astonishment touched his sunken face, and he said nothing.

Aspasia beckoned to the huddled slaves near the wall. "Open the windows, lest my lord stifle, and fan him gently. Fetch me cool water with Syrian whiskey, a full goblet of it, in the water, and soft cloths. Bring at once a large goblet of goat's milk, with three spoons of honey in it and a half spoon of salt. Order, from the kitchen, the boiled juice of beef in quantity. This, heated, must be given him every half hour, the milk and honey and salt every two hours. Hasten!"

The slaves remembered that this alien woman was a sorceress, and hurried to follow her commands, making the sign against the evil eye. The physicians said, "That is not the treatment for the flux, Lady. We give but boiled goat's milk and rice."

"I have said that in your country the flux is not so vehement, and is easily cured by rest and care. O gods! From what house did my lord contact this?"

He tried to laugh but it was a feeble thing. She nestled her hand against his cheek and he kissed the palm. "You must help me," she said. "You must not contradict my orders. You must struggle to retain what is fed to you. Thank the gods it is not cholera."

He looked at his eminent physicians with the old satiric glint on his face but to his amazement the physicians nodded. "We leave you, lord, in the most competent of hands," the older one said. "We shall see you at evening."

They hesitated. Then they each formally lifted Aspasia's free hand and kissed it deferentially. Al Taliph was more amazed. Aspasia acknowledged the accolade with a dignified inclination of her head, and an inner gratitude that she was not dealing with Aryan physicians who would have dismissed her like an impudent slave. They left her in a stately fashion, and she smiled at Al Taliph with tears in her eyes, and his fingers suddenly entwined themselves in the pale gilt of her hair, and she turned her head and kissed them.

The slaves brought the cool water and the strong whiskey in it, and Aspasia bathed Al Taliph with the mixture. She made him drink of the honey and milk and salt, then stared at him threateningly when he made a gagging sound. "You will only have to drink it again," she said, and she made a wry face. Within an hour she forced him to drink the pungent beef broth. While waiting she sat beside him on the floor and watched his face constantly and pressed her fingers against his wrist and his throat. The feverish pulse began to subside. Long before evening he slept in exhaustion.

At evening the physicians returned and examined their patient. Then they said to Aspasia, "Lady, you have brought your lord back from the gates of death, and we do not know if it is your solicitude or your treatment."

She never left him for many days, except to bathe and to partake of food for herself. She would not let a slave approach him without first washing hands and face with lye soap and wine. She watched his excretions. She fed him with her own hands, sternly admonishing him when he complained. She bathed him several times a day with the whiskey and water and his fever fell each time.

"Once," she said to him, "you remarked that I was a verita-

187

ble child. But women become mature humans and leave their childhoods behind them. However, this is not true of men, particularly when they are ill. They are the most petulant and intransigent of children."

His strength was so returning that he could say almost with his former power of voice, "That is a woman's illusion."

"What we see in men is also an illusion, the most fatal of all," she replied. "If Hera and Artemis and Demeter and Athene Parthenos did not guard us women, and comfort and guide us, mankind would have long disappeared from this earth."

"Would that have been so terrible?" he asked her, teasingly.

"Not at all," she said and they laughed together. Never had they been so tender, so dearly as one, not even in passion. But the resolution was gaining in Aspasia's mind. Her lips were taking on a new firmness. I am young no longer, she would remind herself. I am now nineteen years of age, and I must take up my life lest it be too late. The infirmities of age come quickly to women. Then her heart would become weak and heavy and she would weep when she was alone.

She said to him lightly on one gold and crimson evening, when he sat up in his bed to eat the food she had prepared for him, "I will return you in good health to your wives and your women, and for that they should be grateful."

He paused and looked at her intently. "You do not speak of yourself, my dearest one."

She looked at the windows where the sun lay redly in a lake of emerald, and she said, "I hear far winds and they echo in my soul."

He fondled her intimately, not understanding, and she smiled through her tears then fed him again. He could not have enough of her ministrations and when she slept on her cushions beside him he would rise on his elbow and look down on her pale face.

It came to him that she was no longer young but that she was more precious to him than life itself, and all other women were as naught. He could not speak of this to her. She would not comprehend, being a woman. She sighed in her sleep and he wondered why she sighed. "Far winds?" That was ambiguous but women were full of fancies and they meant nothing. He touched her hair and slept also, content.

CHAPTER 19

There was a great garden in the city, filled with birds and monkeys and fountains and many strange animals. The cholera had subsided and the city teemed again with noise and bazaars and caravans and music and shops and laughter, and bells, and the temples were crowded with those who gave thanksgiving that the plague had gone. Even those who sorrowed for the dead felt the quickening of the year, for the almond blossoms were blooming and the myrtle trees and the sycamores wore enameled green leaves. The olive trees were shining with new silver and the fruit trees were clouds of pink and white snow against a sky resembling an opal. Even the grumbling camels moved faster and the horses pranced.

Al Taliph and Aspasia sat side by side on a marble bench in this vast garden, watching the changeful colors of the fountains as they threw up their transparent arms in the sun. The armed enunuchs stood about them, and Aspasia's attending women. Their litter waited, its carved golden roof shining in the light. Aspasia was at once sad, weary, and hopeful. Al Taliph held her hand in his under the shelter of her crimson cloak, and her eyes, above the veil, smiled upon him. He was still weak and sometimes he had fits of shivering in the night, but it was obvious that he would soon be well. His gauntness was decreasing.

"In four weeks I shall be able to travel with my caravan," he said. "We shall return home."

She did not answer. She averted her eyes. "You will not be sorry to leave Damascus?" he asked.

She shook her head. A scarlet bird alighted near them, avid-eyed, then lifted its wings in the sun and was gone.

"I owe my life to you, beloved," he said. "Had it not been for you I should now have been gathered to my fathers."

She still did not speak, for there was a sudden drawing of unendurable pain in her heart. Then she said, "But have you not told me that all is ordained? If it had been fated for you to die you would have died, lord, and no ministrations of mine could have delayed you."

His laugh was almost as strong as before his illness. "I am not superstitious, nor do I believe in your Fates. I have told you, my rose of the valley, that nothing is fated and all that concerns man is an accident, for it is not possible that Deity is aware of our insignificance in the vastness of His domains."

Returning health made him feel like a youth again. Last night Aspasia had slept in his arms once more, surfeited, and he had held her so for a long time as men hold their life's treasure. No, she was not young, though still beautiful; he no longer thought of her beauty, remembering her ministrations and her devotion to him, and her tireless care. He thought of the hours when she had sat beside him, reading to him, anxiously watching every change of his expression. No task had been too repulsive for her, no aspect of his illness sickening or revolting. As a mother would have tended him so she had tended him, through nights of suffering and convulsive spasms in his belly, and though often he would urge her to rest she would only palely smile, and each day she had grown thinner and her eyes had enlarged in her translucent face. He never awoke but what she was there, bending over him. Sometimes she dozed in exhaustion, but her hand held his. His slightest movement had aroused her to full alertness, as a watchman is alerted at the most distant stir. She would permit no slave to attend him.

He said, remembering, and was gently moved, "Tomorrow, my beloved, I will take you to my jeweler and anything he possesses is yours. It is a poor sign of gratitude for my life, but it is the only recompense I can make."

She bowed her head and said to herself, Alas, is that all?

Then she said, "Lord, I want no more jewels, for I have much from your generosity."

"How, then, can I repay you, Aspasia?"

A cool sweat broke out over her body. She must speak now or never have the courage to speak again. She lifted eyes clouded with tears to him and from behind her veil she whispered, "Lord, let me go, in peace, with your blessing."

He was astounded. He turned so that he could more fully look down into her eyes. "Go, Aspasia? Where would you go, and why?" He could not believe it.

"I wish to return to my old home in Miletus for a space, and then go to Athens to open a school for young women who desire to be more than a mere bauble for men, and who wish to live as surely the gods intended a woman to live, for does not Athene labor endlessly, and Artemis, and doesn't Demeter attend the land, and is not Hera queen of Olympus and ever dutiful? The goddesses are potent in their sex. It was surely intended for earthly women to be important also, in their lives."

Al Taliph was still incredulous, but a pallor ran over his dark face like a shadow of a white wing.

"You desire to leave me?" he asked.

"Lord, I must." Now her tears ran over the edge of her veil, but her eyes were full upon him and straight.

There was a sick tightness in his chest, as if he had been wounded to the death. His hand left hers. He stared before him and she shut her eyes lest she weaken and implore him not to grant her wish.

He said, "How have I offended you, Aspasia, that you wish to desert me and leave me forever?"

Ah, she thought, if you had but loved me, even a little, I should not flee from you, core of my heart. But men cannot love to the measure of our hope, and that is their nature. Even if they love, the love is evanescent, and a new woman is a consolation and a forgetting. I do not reproach you, my darling; I reproach my own folly in that I have hoped when hope was impossible. I had forgotten what I had learned in the house of Thargelia and that was my grievous error. I am a woman.

Because she had not spoken he continued: "Then you tended me not out of love but as a slave would attend a master, a dedicated slave thinking of duty?"

She said in a low voice, "I have remembered our years together, and our affection and our joys, and you are a man of worth, lord, and must be preserved."

"For what, for whom?" he asked with bitterness.

"You have wives and sons. Are they nothing to you, sire?"

He thought of three of his sons, now young men, of whom he was proud, and who had fortunate futures and who loved him. Though fathers did not cherish their daughters there were two whose beauty and gentleness were dear to him.

Aspasia said, "Return to your family and their love for you. You are still their lord and their protection. Is that not enough?"

He did not speak. His eyes changed with his thoughts and with his rebellious passions. Then he said, "Is not what I have given you of any value, Aspasia?"

"Lord, it is of inestimable value. I will never forget you. But I must go."

He lifted her veil to look at her face and he saw there the marble resolution and did not see how her lower lip trembled. "It is regrettable that you are learned, Aspasia," he said in a hard voice. "Learning is not for women, for it makes of them not what nature intended."

"To be learned one must also be intelligent, lord," and she

was deeply offended. "Is the intelligence of women to be wasted?"

"It is the nature of women to love and nurture and serve. The market place is not for them, nor commerce, nor the affairs of the world."

"But you have not answered my question, lord."

"There is no answer to absurdities." He paused, and felt ill again and undone. "Is there naught I can do to persuade you to remain with me?"

Yes, she answered in herself. You can tell me that you love me—which would be a lie—and swear to me that above all things I am eternally dear to you. She said, almost inaudibly, "There is nothing which is in your power, lord, that can persuade me, for what I desire you cannot give me. It is true you can take back your jewels and set me defenseless on the streets, as once you threatened. How I shall live then I do not know. So I beg you to let me keep them and to set me free."

"You believe I am cruel and ungrateful?"

O gods, she cried inwardly, is gratitude all you know, my beloved? A heavy faintness came to her. "I ask for no gratitude, which is a poor and reluctant and resented thing. I did what I had to do. Let us not speak of it again. There is of a certainty one thing you can still give me: peace."

"You have known no peace with me?"

She put her hand to her throat where the pain was enormous. "No," she said.

He was silent. The pallor increased on his face, but when she touched him in alarm he flung off her hand, and she shrank.

"Peace is for the dead," he said. "Are you foolish enough to believe it is attainable for the living? Surely Thargelia taught you better!"

"We are, as usual, conversing, but we do not mean the same thing," she pleaded. "The peace I desire is not the peace you would understand."

He motioned to the litter-bearers. He said, "I only understand that you wish to leave me. I owe you much, Aspasia. I owe you several years of pleasure and conversation and the contemplation of your beauty. You have been my companion in my empty hours and have filled them with contentment and delight. No other woman has been to me what you have been, and I, too, will never forget."

"The world is full of complaisant women," she said, out of her pain. "I will not be hard to replace."

This wounded him more than anything else and he made an abrupt gesture. "I have a caravan leaving tomorrow. Do you wish to be part of it?"

Tomorrow! Then there would be no last parting, no last embraces. It was well, but it was also agonizing. "Yes," she said.

"I have servants who will then take you to where you desire to go. I trust that pleases you, Aspasia." He spoke dully and without emotion. "As for the jewels, they, too, are in gratitude, and I will also send to you a purse of gold coins." He paused and smiled at her somberly. "Go in peace, Aspasia, if that is what you desire above all else."

I do not desire that, beloved, she thought. But it is all that remains for me in this accursed world. It is a barren desire, the desire of the dying or the hopeless. But it is all I have.

They returned to the inn in a silence too sorrowful for words. That night he sent to her a large purse rich with gold coins—but no final word, no entreaty, no avowal. Her women gathered her possessions together and put them in her chests, gloating and smirking when she could not see them. They whispered to each other, "The foreign woman has been dismissed, and contentment will come to the lord's house again. She has the evil eye. We will all rejoice in the harem when she is absent."

The caravan departed, with Aspasia's tent. There was no last farewell from Al Taliph, no sign of his solicitude. Aspasia thought, He has already forgot me. She lay on her cushions in the tent and when the caravan began to move she rose and moved aside the flap on the tent and stood in the doorway. Al Taliph was not there. The gates of the inn closed after the caravan, and it started on its long journey. Had Al Taliph appeared she would have run to him and would have implored him not to let her go.

Unfortunate are we, she thought with crushing despair, when the gods grant our prayers! She lay on the cushions again and covered her face with a length of silk and gave herself up to torment and to suffering she had never experienced before. She was like a shell cast up on the seashore, bereft of the vital creature which had inhabited it. She was empty except for the dolorous woe that blew through the shell of herself and whispered of desolation, of the breaking of a heart, and the ending of life and immortal loneliness. She shed no tears. The dead do not weep for themselves. They can only remember.

CHAPTER 20

Autumn came again to Persia and the great caravans began to move to their many destinations. But Al Taliph accompanied none. "I am still recovering from a grave illness," he would say to his friends and his fellow merchants. "Too, I am no longer young." They accepted this explanation, for they were gentlemen. But it was whispered everywhere that the beauteous Aspasia, the crown of his harem, his adored one and the adorable, had disappeared from his house. Had he banished her or had she died in Damascus?

The women and the eunuchs gossiped. The women were happy that the sister of Ahriman had departed, and they were assiduous in their attempts to amuse their lord. His oldest wife suggested he acquire a new young wife from the slave markets of Greece, or Macedonia, where, it was said, there lived girls so fair that their hair was almost white and had eyes the color of hyacinths and flesh like pearl. Moreover, they were skilled in music and the dance, and were amiable and full of grace. The oldest wife, who loved her husband, felt alarm for him. He had become emaciated and his dark face, never lively or gay, was as somber as carved bronze. He accepted no invitations. He sat in the gardens, or alone in his chambers, and did not speak. He rarely frequented his library, once his pride above all his other treasures. He sent for no books. He received no visitors.

The women who had attended Aspasia in Damascus were eagerly sought out and had to repeat their story countless times. It was bare enough, but their malicious imaginations supplied factitious details. The lord had wearied of that woman's impudence. She had become too old and had borne him no child, and was idle and contentious. They had heard him quarrel with her many times. They even hinted that she had cast a malign spell on him and had mysteriously inflicted an illness upon him, with her incantations, so that she had brought him close to death. When he recovered, despite her malevolence, he had understood and had sent her away. She had been consigned to a small mean caravan, and no one had seen her since. "Rejoice," they said to the wives and the concubines and the slave girls, "that he was enlightened in time, for if Mithras—or Zoroaster—had not intervened he should have died."

The oldest wife was shrewd and a little more discerning. "Why, then, knowing all this, did he not have her murdered?"

"She had cast a spell on him. Did I not see it myself?" asked Serah.

"A veritable Circe," said one of the slave girls who was a Greek. She was forced to explain. The other women expressed horror, raising their hands and lifting their eyes to heaven. "She made a swine of our lord!" cried the youngest wife, holding her last baby to her breast and shivering.

The oldest wife said, "Nonsense. He adored her. Do I not know it? A woman who loves, as I love him, knows when another woman possesses his heart. It is given a loving woman to know it in her breast," and she touched that ample object. "I know also that she loved him. He murmured of her in his sleep when he slept beside me, in the most endearing words, and smiled in the moonlight. A man does not do that unless his love is returned. Do I not know?"

The others looked at her with disfavor, yet also with respect.

"Nevertheless," said the oldest wife, "it is well she does not disturb us longer. It is a mystery, with which we must be content. Let us go to the temples and offer thanksgiving and pray that he will forget her speedily."

"He permitted her to take with her all the fabulous jewels he had bestowed on her."

"Another spell!" cried the girl from Greece.

"Nonsense," said the oldest wife. "Spells cannot hurt our lord; he is too powerful for them. If he allowed her to do so then it was his will, which is inexplicable to us." She was annoyed at the mention of Aspasia's age, for she, herself was a year or more older. She sighed. "Who can understand a man? What they desire they do, and we women cannot comprehend."

But one of Aspasia's attendants in Damascus licked her lips. What she had to say was too important to be whispered in the harem. It was also valuable. It would bring a good price. Who would pay it? Eventually she thought of Kurda, who had not gone to Damascus. He would pay the price. But he disdained to gossip too much with the women of the harem, and he was busy in attendance on Al Taliph, as he loved him and was full of consternation at his appearance.

Then the rumor came that Al Taliph walked the long corridors, in starlight and moonlight, facing the gardens, pacing up and down like a man distraught and in great anguish of mind, and sleepless. His steps could be heard in the night, monotonously pacing, until the dawn. It was said he often uttered a groan and beat the palms of his hands together.

The attendants spoke of Aspasia's weeping in her tent, after her departure from Damascus. "She dropped like a lily, on the oasis, and never spoke." "Then," said the oldest wife, dejected, "they loved each other. Why did they part?"

Once when Al Taliph slept beside her, then awoke, she said to him with gentleness, "Lord, you returned to us, to my arms. The foreign woman was not for you, and well it is that you—banished—her. Men do not banish the woman they love, unless her conduct is heinous. Was her conduct so?"

"No," he said, touched by her love. "But we must not speak of this. What has gone has gone."

"You yearn for her, lord, and that is a grievous thing to me."

He left his bed and went to pace on the corridor which had been Aspasia's favorite walk, by night and day. He looked on the scenes she had looked upon. He sat where she had sat. Rumor again quickened. He spent hours in her chamber, where he had never gone before, and sat behind a shut door. He even slept in her bed.

Sometimes he hated her for the hot and unremitting desire for her. He waited for the sound of her voice, the scent of her perfume, her laughter, her rallying conversation, the touch of her white hands. He remembered how she had ministered to him and he would say aloud, in a hoarse voice, "Why, Aspasia, if you did not love me? Was it slyness on your part so you could cajole me to permit you to leave me, as once I refused?" But he knew that above all things Aspasia had never been sly. There had always been a forthright honesty about her, a clarity of character which nothing could cloud, a pride which scorned pettiness and lies. She had asked him to give her peace, and he had acceded. What was the peace she had desired? He did not know. He only knew that something in him writhed in agony and confusion, and that nothing could appease it. Time did not diminish it. Each day was a fresh confrontation with pain and despair, fury and loneliness. It was in vain that he told himself that she was only a woman, in a world of amiable women, and that she had been a hetaira and that he had bought her companionship from the notorious house of Thargelia. At moments he was seized by an almost uncontrollable desire to find her, to implore her return, to take her by force if necessary. But, knowing Aspasia, he knew this would be of no avail. The flown bird cannot be captured again, or, if captured, sickens in its cage however much the affection bestowed on it. At these thoughts he would grip his hair in his hands and roll his head in torment, and repeat her name over and over aloud like an incantation.

He despised himself for his agony, yet it remained. He had been too hasty, he would think. He had let her go without an avowal of his love, his need for her. He began to think that if he had made his avowal, had expressed his need, she would have remained out of pity alone. But, she had never loved him; the arts she had used to please him and give him almost unbearable pleasure were taught arts, and therefore did not come from her soul. The thought of a woman pitying him and remaining with him out of pity sickened his body as well as his mind. But there were moments when he felt as abject as a whipped slave, and it would have been enough for him but to see her and hold her in his arms.

It was useless for him to tell himself that he was a satrap, and a rich merchant, and often sat with Artaxerxes in his court, and Aspasia was nothing at all but a bought woman who was no longer young. It was not for his passion that he desired her with this awful desire. It was for her, herself. He had let her go and had not uttered one plea, one remonstrance. What were his wives to him, and all his women now? They were not the singular Aspasia, the incomparable. Beside her they were but crows in comparison with a glowing bird, or sparrows compared with a nightingale. I cherished her more than I knew, alas, he would think. I thought I would forget her in a week, a month. But her bright wraith is in every hall, in the garden, in all rooms of my house. I turn in the night to embrace her—and she is not there. Had she died I could not mourn her more.

He would not even see his children, whom he loved. They were not Aspasia, as his women were not Aspasia. Everything he had in the world was meaningless without her. His thick dark hair began to whiten at the temples and the anguish in his soul wearied his body and made him languid and inert.

Her face haunted him, smiling, serious, teasing, contemplative, or eager, like a child's. He saw her when she was discussing philosophy with him and obscure matters, and he had reluctantly admired her intellect which had been—he knew now—a spring of fresh water in a desert to him. It had been unique, sparkling, sharp as Damascene steel thrusting to a target, subtle. She had understood him as none had understood him before. He had found ease and entertainment in her presence, when they were not even clasped together in his bed. He had found contentment. He remembered how they had laughed together and jested. He had often been brutal with her and often rejecting, and had forgotten her on many occasions. Now he was aware that she had always been in his mind despite all these, and that he had returned to her like an unsatisfied lover who could not have enough of his beloved.

Alas, alas, that I let you go, my white swan, my adored one, he would repeat over and over to himself. I did not know what I possessed until you left me, and I returned to dull women who only chatter and have bodies. You had a body also, not distinguished from that of other women. Now I confess that it was not your body I loved but your soul, your mind, all that you were, my beloved one. Who can replace you? I see you everywhere, and all things remind me of you, and I cannot endure it, I who have had many women, and wives and am a man. Do men love only that which has forever fled? That is not true of me, for I always loved you. I should have held you close, gripped to me always, never forgetting.

He was abased in himself and sometimes disgusted. But the yearning remained and increased each day. He could hardly eat what was laid before him. He was distraught. He lived in a cloud, which made all things unreal to him. Aspasia had been with him but four years, and his wives had been with him for many more. Yet, in remembrance, it seemed to him that he had known her forever, had awaited for her through time.

His wives artfully sent their children to the gardens, but he no longer rejoiced in them nor admired them or desired their presence. Their prattle was the prattle of his wives and had as much import. He would return to his library and hold the books she had held, and once, to his horror, he stained a scroll with his tears.

Serah at last sought out Kurda, who listened with glistening eyes and a salivating mouth. He licked his lips. He gave Serah the gold coin she had demanded and even deigned to pat her shoulder approvingly, and with glee. Then he questioned the Raïs of the caravan, who questioned the men who had driven Aspasia's tent. After several week he found one of the men in the courtyard who had observed a peculiar matter, and still another.

Kurda pondered. How would his lord receive this information? With fury and denial and punishment? Or, with gratitude? Kurda would sit at night on his bed, rubbing his hairless chin and debating in himself the proper approach. At last he could wait no longer and sought out Al Taliph in his library. He entered silently and Al Taliph, gaunt and gloomy, looked at him with impatience. Kurda bowed. "Lord," he said, "I have news for you, if you can endure it, concerning the foreign woman whom you banished nearly a year ago."

Al Taliph started to his feet, and his bones became like hard metal under his skin. "Speak!" he cried, and there was a leaping and fluttering in his breast. Had Aspasia been found? Where could he seek her?

Kurda glanced about him, and hesitated. "It will anger you, lord, and I am fearful that your anger will fall upon me, who am guiltless, instead of the man with whom that woman betrayed you."

Al Taliph stood motionless. He stared at Kurda and his parched mouth became quiet and still. Finally he said, "There was no man, no lover. But tell me your idle tale—for I know you hated her—and I vow I will not punish you however absurd or vile the story."

Kurda looked at him beseechingly. He said, "The man is one of your companions, your friends, who has accompanied you on a caravan. He is Damos of Damascus, once a guest in your house."

Still staring at Kurda, Al Taliph slowly seated himself. He recalled the night when Damos had dined with him and he had offered Damos the little girls and Aspasia had intervened. He recalled that prior to this she had become agitated on her arrival in the dining hall, and he had wondered if she had recognized one of the guests. "Go on," he said to Kurda, and his dark hands clenched on his brocaded robe.

Kurda, despite his fear, told the story well, and in sequence. He had found one of the men who had driven Aspasia's tent. The man had seen Damos ride up to the platform, on which Aspasia was standing; the man had seen her leave the tent and creep to the rear. Curious, he had also crept along the other side of the tent and had observed that the foreign woman had given Damos a letter. They had whispered together, or spoken in low voices, and so the man had not been able to hear their rapid conversation. Aspasia had seemed to be imploring Damos.

"The driver spoke to his companion about this strange event," said Kurda, watching Al Taliph fearfully for any gesture of violence towards himself. "But the companion had only replied that as Damos was your friend, lord, and a guest in the caravan, the foreign woman was only sending you a

199

message, for it was known that you had not seen her for several nights. So the man shrugged, and forgot the incident, believing the explanation for it."

Al Taliph did not speak. Kurda's throat became dry; he could see but those terrible eyes fixed upon him.

The woman, Serah, one of Aspasia's attendants, had seen a far more serious incident in Damascus. She had told him, Kurda, of Aspasia's obvious restlessness, imprisoned as she was during the cholera. She had continually paced up and down her chambers like a demon, her expression growing wilder every day. Then one afternoon Serah, who was engaged in her prayers against the plague, had seen Aspasia suddenly halt near one of the windows and gaze downwards as if something or someone had attracted her attention. After a moment or two she had gone into the chamber where the commodes had been placed, and had carefully closed the curtains behind her. Serah had run first to the window and saw below the lord's friend, Damos, who was gazing upwards at the window of the smaller chamber beyond. To Serah's astonishment she saw that Aspasia had untied her jeweled cord and was extending it through the bars to Damos, and Damos instantly caught it and wound a letter in it. Aspasia then had swiftly drawn it upwards, and Damos had wandered away.

Serah had then run to the curtains and had drawn the edge of one aside and she discovered Aspasia in the act of reading the letter, which she then had thrust into her bosom. Serah did not speak of these odd matters to her sister attendants, being prudent and not desiring to be an idle gossip. But she had watched Aspasia and later saw her furtively drop the missive onto the coals of the brazier.

He, Kurda, on being informed of these events, had made inquiries and had not only heard the tale of Aspasia's giving Damos a letter or message while the caravan was on the road to Damascus, but had found two other men of the caravan who had been in the courtyard alone while Damos was furtively conveying the missive to Aspasia. They had pretended to see nothing. It was of little interest to them at the time, for they had not seen Aspasia clearly at the window, but had known Damos well, for had he not ridden beside the lord during the journey on many occasions? If he was making an assignation with a woman of what matter was it to them?

"Any of these revelations, alone, lord, would be serious though a possible explanation could be found for one," said Kurda. "But there are three events and combined they have unspeakable import."

Al Taliph was silent for a long time. He did not believe for an instant that Aspasia had been unfaithful to him. He recalled that Damos was a Greek and it was surely probable now that he had known Aspasia before, though he had denied ever living in Miletus, or of even visiting that city. Therefore, he had lied. Al Taliph remembered that Damos had invariably shown Aspasia deferential kindness, and that he had spoken of her to Al Taliph in the inn when Hephzibah had visited Aspasia. His voice had been gentle, as if he were speaking of a great lady, and not a courtesan, and had permitted his wife to converse alone with her, a peculiar thing for a virtuous Jew to permit. (Had he not taken those children to his wife instead of taking them to his bed?)

Had he been a random patron of Aspasia's when she was in the house of Thargelia? No. Thargelia delivered only virgins to distinguished or illustrious or wealthy men, and Aspasia had been a virgin in his, Al Taliph's bed, and of that he was convinced. There had also been a pristine quality about Aspasia, a freshness, an inexperience, which could not be assumed and certainly not to a man of Al Taliph's knowledge of women and their bodies.

Aspasia had been lured from her lord, or had induced Damos to assist her to flee, but for what reason Al Taliph did not know. Damos, deprived of a loved and loving wife, had remained in Damascus, nurturing and consoling his children and had wept when Al Taliph had bidden him farewell. Nothing could soothe his grief for the loss of Hephzibah, and his sorrow was genuine. He had not feigned his despair. Therefore, there had been no sensual communication between him and Aspasia.

Yet, but for him Aspasia would be in this house, and he, Al Taliph, would not be on the verge of madness. From whom had come those letters, sent, received, on the road to Damascus and in Damascus, itself? There was but one answer: Thargelia. Aspasia knew no one else, except for the damsels in Thargelia's house, and those she had known had long departed, for now it was nearly five years. Yes, it could only be Thargelia. Al Taliph felt the hot blood in his face, and rage. He would go to the house of Thargelia as soon as possible and would drag Aspasia from the infamous purlieus. Or, his rage subsiding in a tide of hope, he would induce her to return to him, even if she had gone to another protector.

There was still the matter of Damos, who had betrayed his friendship.

Kurda stood before his master, waiting, watching the

changeful expressions on Al Taliph's face, the arching and falling of his eyebrows as he thought, the red blood in his cheeks, the tightening of his mouth, then the loosening, then the paling of his color.

Al Taliph became aware of the eunuch waiting before him. He said, "Send to me Serah, and the men, who have not yet left for Syria."

Kurda almost ran, in relief, from the room. He heard nothing for a considerable time and then Al Taliph sent for him.

"I have a task for you, Kurda," he said, and his voice was smooth and calm. "But first let me present you with this purse, in token of my gratitude."

Kurda was overwhelmed with elation and love and kissed Al Taliph's hand. "Command me anything, lord!" he cried.

"You must go to Damascus, and you must contrive to have a man murdered quietly—Damos of Damascus. Do not do it yourself. Hire assassins. Do not return until the mission is accomplished."

"To hear is to obey you, lord!" cried Kurda, joyfully, and ran to prepare himself for the journey and to plot Damos' death so dexterously that he, Kurda, would never be suspected of the conspiracy.

Then Al Taliph went to Miletus and sought out the aged Thargelia. She received him with every graciousness and every evidence of pleasure. She said to him at once, "But why have you not brought my daughter, my loved Aspasia, to visit one who has such affection for her? Tell me, lord, how she fares in your house. Has she borne you children?"

Al Taliph regarded her with eyes like the points of daggers. He was sick with disappointment and the loss of his hope. He said, "Has she not written to you, Thargelia, you who loved and cherished her so much?"

"I have had no word from her, Al Taliph, since she left for your house, nor have I written her myself. Why do you gaze at me so strangely? Is not Aspasia well?" Her simulation of alarm and dread was excellent and he was deceived.

"She is well," he said to Thargelia and took his departure, refusing her offer to let him examine the young maidens in her house.

When he returned, after several months, he found Kurda at home. Kurda said nothing but only mutely nodded, with grinning satisfaction. Al Taliph gave him another purse.

Then he delivered himself up to despair for a long time.

PART TWO

Pericles

"Above all men, he was the most just."

ZENO OF ELEA

CHAPTER 1

After Zeno of Elea had seen Pericles, son of Xanthippus and Agariste, Xanthippus visited Zeno at his house. Concluding warm greetings, Xanthippus said, "My son's mother, who is interested in appearance, which she insists is the first door to power, complains that Pericles' skull rises too high above his brow and features."

"Does a great man mourn if he is not accepted by the acclamations of inferiors, the obscure, the unimportant? No. He rejoices, for what is commonly accepted is execrable and degrading and of little worth. A tumbler, an athlete, a jokester, a buffoon, a pugilist, a songster or an actor is applauded by the low multitude, whose appetites are the appetites of the barnyard. Who would wish to be applauded by such?"

"You are implying that my son is not of the mundane world?" said Xanthippus, with humor.

"Lord," said Zeno with dignity, "I was never mistaken in a pupil. Had I not looked into the calm, direct and radiant eyes of your son and had not seen what I have seen, I should not have consented to tutor him. He has a stately presence, even at his young age, and stateliness is to be much admired. I consider him the handsomest of youths, though he is but twelve years old. There is manhood in his demeanor, authority in his glance. I predict a future for him which will surmount the future of lower men, and which will ring through the ages."

"I implore the gods that he will be a great soldier," said the father.

"You speak as a soldier," said the teacher, and smiled with indulgence. "Your son, I believe, will be of military genius—I have observed him—but he will be the glory of his nation also. I have consulted the oracles at Delphi."

"But that is superstition," said the father, who was extremely superstitious though in many ways skeptical and pragmatic.

"It is said," the teacher remarked, "that superstition is the child of experience. Who know what controls the destiny and the affairs of men?"

The father thought, and stroked the fine white linen of his robe.

"You have mentioned 'the glory of his nation.' What is more glorious than a soldier?"

"It is said," the teacher murmured, "that history is the shadow of great men. Or, of monstrous men. Military genius is admirable, for it preserves a nation in its physical aspect. But there is another genius: the flame of intellect. Your son will possess both. As I have said, I have consulted the oracles of Delphi, and I swear that Apollo answered me."

The father was incredulous. "Apollo answered you, Zeno?"

The scholar averted his eyes, smiling, before the bright face of cynicism. "I believe so, or a reasonable power. I am not a hysterical woman, nor a man given to idiot dreams. I weigh. I ponder. But something in my soul informs me that your son is not of common cast, nor is he concerned with common aspirations."

Zeno of Elea, hailed by fellow philosophers as the creator of dialectic—that is, he proved that disputation has for its end not personal victory but the establishment of truth—was a young slight man of short stature, with a thin, white and pointed face in which his black eyes were great orbs of scintillating light, dominating all his features and giving his expression an extraordinary vividness and arresting power. One forgot his other insignificant attributes, such as a constantly wrinkling white brow, stiff coarse black hair cropped short and tickling the tops of huge ears, a little tilted nose and a nervous and unquiet mouth—which wrongly suggested an instability of temperament—when those vital and intensely living eyes were turned to the speaker. It was then that the suddenly abashed observer became aware of a presence, of a glow beyond the lesser glow of other eyes, and a focusing of enormous and restless power. Many felt that his fragile flesh would be consumed in that incandescence at any moment, and that it could not contain the core of flame that turned within it. Because his manner was simple and often shy and he never disputed in a loud voice nor displayed arrogance—but was invariably kind, interested in the opinions of others, and courteous—there were some who said he was not wise at all but only echoed the greater genius of his master, friend and teacher, Parmenides, who knew how to despise lesser intellects and had a derisive tongue. Some even found his eyes perfervid and ridiculed their enormous dominance, feigning to believe them hysterical or womanish, or the symptom of some physical or mental malady. They imitated his soft voice, which was somewhat high and diffident when he encountered arrogant disputers. They ridiculed his childish and thin pale arms, and ignored the large and beautiful hands.

But the perceptive listened to him with awe and rose when he entered a room or stopped to speak in a colonnade to students, and felt, when he had departed, that for a moment or two they had stood in the presence of an irresistible force, and that the very air had vibrated. His simplicity, they believed, was the simplicity of marble lighted by the sun, or, again, the simplicity of fire.

He had a considerable patrimony but lived without ostentation in the surburbs of Athens, content with a little square white house over which grew vine leaves on a lattice. He had no slaves, and attended to his own wants, even to making his own goat cheese and baking his bread and drinking the resinous wine of his own grapes. This austere way of living was not affectation, nor disdain for luxury, nor even his innate simplicity. He had discovered that the fewer needs and wants a man possesses the more independent he is, and that those needs and wants hamper the mind and are the servants of a ravenous physical body and are artificial, and should not be cultivated lest the spirit starve. But he had a love for land and his small house stood near a grove of olive trees and fruit trees, and there were smooth red gravel paths bordered by the dark green of cypresses and many flowers in their season, and had a view of the purple sea. He cultivated all that grew under his tender hands and often asserted—to the risibility of envious men—that what wisdom he possessed he had acquired from listening to his trees and to the earth.

He accepted but few private pupils, and then only one at a time and only when he was convinced that the pupil had unusual qualities of mind and spirit. Otherwise he preferred to converse in the cool luminescence of colonnades with the pupils of other philosophers and teachers, at sunset, never disparaging their mentors but deftly and eloquently enlarging the thoughts of young men. He stood among them in his coarse white or gray long linen tunic, belted by a simple chain of silver, which he rubbed with his fingers in the nervous mannerism of a man whose reflections are vaster and swifter than his fleshly tongue. But politics bored him, except when a principle of philosophy—universal yet unique—was involved. As these occasions were rare he preferred to ignore politics and once said that politicians should be abolished, a remark not calculated to add to his reputation for wisdom.

He was known as the master of paradoxes, and delighted in uttering them. He was also in frequent danger of the pious and orthodox authorities and priests of Athens, for he often asserted that but One had existence and that belief in Many was in error. "Yes, yes, Zeus, if the Unknowable can be given a name, but only Zeus," he would say, though he acknowledged that sublime poetry lived in the concept of Many, and that monotheism could not be truly comprehended by the finite minds of men. "If men cannot be simultaneously in ten thousand places, and have a universal awareness, then it is impossible for them to understand the omnipresence of Deity and omniscient consciousness, and instant and boundless cognisance." So far the priests had not overly tormented or harassed him, for they thought him mad and of no importance.

Xanthippus had visited him one past shining evening in his silver-decorated litter carried by six grandly attired slaves. He had never met Zeno before, though he was aware of his fame, as he was a powerful politician as well as a notable soldier who had been a captain of a squadron which had annihilated part of Xerxes' fleet at Mycale. An astute man, he was also aware that ostentation would not impress Zeno, but he was a man who loved luxury and the trappings of riches, and, as he had said humorously to his wife, Agariste, he was no pretentious hypocrite who visited a wise man on foot in dusty sandals. Zeno was inspecting his new olive trees when Xanthippus arrived, and he turned his head and mildly studied his visitor. He had seen Xanthippus at a distance on many occasions, and recognized him, and came to greet him without apology for his stained hands and the withered leaves on his narrow shoulders. There was soil on one of his sunken white cheeks. But nothing could diminish the black splendor of his eyes nor the sudden lucidity of his smile. Xanthippus was unaccountably touched and when he looked into those eyes he was moved as many men were moved.

So he alighted from his litter instead of reclining on his cushions and addressing Zeno through parted curtains. He held out his strong soldier's hand, and Zeno took it with childlike guilelessness. Yet the shrewd politician and soldier understood that Zeno was no simpleton and possessed little vulnerability. He was armored in his virtue.

In his turn Zeno studied his visitor, and was surprised, as always, by the face of Xanthippus, which denied his professions and his valor and genius as a military man. Xanthippus was tall for a Greek, and his body had the litheness of an athlete and the suppleness, and a peculiar swiftness of movement; he implied implicit power and masculinity. His face, long and narrow and pale and smooth, had the contemptuous delicacy of a Persian aristocrat. (In truth, he admired the

Persians whom he had defeated.) This gave his expression a subtle arrogance, which had made him a great favorite with women. He wore the pointed short black beard of the Persians, and his nose was thin and aquiline and his mouth sensual and red and full. But his eyes were the color of a Greek sky at noon, intensely and incredibly blue, if hard and clear. His eyebrows were black, as was his hair under the white hood of his robe, beginning too close at the inner corner of his eyes and then sweeping upwards the temples, giving him a cynical look that intimidated the less subtle.

"Greetings, Xanthippus, lord," said Zeno.

"You know me, Zeno of Elea?" asked Xanthippus, with some surprise.

"I have seen you at a distance, Master," replied the philosopher. He gestured towards his small white house, now smothered in the polished green of the spring grape vines. "May I offer you my own wine and cheese and bread and a portion of fruit?"

"I thank you," said Xanthippus. He gave Zeno a sharp and piercing glance of curiosity. Zeno's serenity and lack of tremulousness suggested that any explanation would inevitably come in good time from the other man and so needed but patience.

Xanthippus was accustomed to servility even from his equals, but Zeno was not servile. He stood aside to let Xanthippus precede him, but the soldier paused to look about him at the green land, the orchards, the groves, the high ground which permitted a view of the silver port of Piraeus, the acropolis with its crown of new low temples, and Athens, herself, white and rose-tinted in the first blush of sunset, and rising on her hills. Beyond lay the sea, flowing in aquamarine and streaks of running purple, and the ships at anchor, swaying in the breeze and the tide. Some were moving out to sea, and their white sails were full of blazing light. The soldier was not sentimental, though at secret heart he was a poet. As he gazed at the peace of the scene, and at Zeno's burst of gardens surrounding his little house, and at the goats grazing nearby, and inhaled the scent of the innocently lewd spring earth and grass and flowering tree, he felt the pride and humility and exultation of being a Greek. It was no wonder to him—though he did not believe in the gods—that the gods frequently preferred the noble earth of Greece to Olympus. And, most certainly, the daughters of the earth. The sea wind was as warm and pure as silk, as fresh as linen washed in the sun.

"This," said Xanthippus, "is a joyous place."

"Yes, so it is, and so it will be in the future. Joy and beauty, passion and delight, color and transparency, and absolute resonance of mind and spirit: I know it in my heart. I have had my visions."

"Ah," said Xanthippus. He distrusted visions, though he had his own. He entered the dusky coolness of the house and though he was a luxurious man he approved the austerity of the interior, its furniture which was enough but not more than enough, its white walls and plain stone floor, its books reverently occupying more than half the space, its smooth but unpolished benches, low chairs and one table. Beyond this one room he saw the little chamber of Zeno, the narrow bed and an Oriental chest, the only color in the house, with its enameled carvings and its ornate lock. Then, looking at that chest, Xanthippus, the soldier and the not-so-secret voluptuary, understood that there was in Zeno's spirit a vein of exaltation and a celebration of vivid life. Zeno entered the house and placed upon the table a jug of goats' milk, a plate of ripe cheese, olives, some coarse but sweet-smelling bread, a ewer of wine, a bowl of herbs, honey, and asparagus and young berries all tart and exciting in their fragrance. There was also a little bowl of fresh garlic and a pitcher of vinegar and a yellow mound of pungent goats' butter. The plates and the goblets were of the red clay of Greece, and were the utensils of peasants. The spoons and the knives were of the best of metals and the napkins of the roughest of linen.

"A feast," said Xanthippus. His words had been but courtesy but he was surprised to feel a deep and contented consent in his heart. He sat down on a bench at the table and Zeno poured a libation to the gods and Xanthippus raised his eyebrows. Zeno smiled, "If they exist, it will please them," he said. Xanthippus laughed a little.

The red sunset shone through the small high window as the men ate the comforting food, and during this interval Xanthippus shot glances of curiosity, interest and calculation at Zeno. He had thought his mission to be a simple one. Now he knew it was not. A contentment and tranquility—as pure and fathomless as water—filled the house.

He said to Zeno, "I have a son, twelve years old. Pericles. I need a tutor for him, and I have heard much of you, Zeno of Elea."

Zeno looked alarmed and anxious.

"Lord, I accept but few pupils, and only one at a time, and at my own desire."

"What are your requirements for a pupil, Zeno?"

Zeno hesitated. He looked about his room as if in apology and dismay. "Master, I take but unusual pupils, ones who intrigue my mind and excite my interest." He raised his extraordinary eyes fully to the face of the soldier. "Do you believe your son is such?"

Xanthippus pursed his mouth, then drank deeply of his goblet, which Zeno immediately refilled. The red sunlight struck on the face of Xanthippus and Zeno became interested, for he saw in full the half-disdainful, half-delicate formation of that subtle countenance.

"I believe my son has unusual qualities, even at his early age. He is grave. He is thoughtful. He has a certain reserve. He is interested in many strange things. He is disciplined, of himself. He needs no admonitions, no thrashings, no rebukes. He is of one piece, like the element of stone, like the configuration of marble."

"Alas," said Zeno.

Xanthippus was astonished and leaned back on his bench. "Alas?"

"Such men are dangerous," said Zeno. "They know from the womb what it is they desire and none can turn them from it. They are embued with destiny, and that is disastrous for other and lesser men."

Xanthippus was inordinately flattered and pleased. "It is possible," he said, "that I have exaggerated my son's qualities, as a father."

"I hope so, and yet I hope not," said Zeno, and he who was abstemious refilled his own goblet for the third time and drank hurriedly from it. He folded his large white hands, the hands of a sage, on the table and contemplated them. "I will see your son," he said.

"I will send a litter for you tomorrow," said the soldier. He rose and Zeno rose with him and accompanied him to the gate where the slaves awaited. When Xanthippus had left him Zeno leaned on the gate and stared into the distance and brooded and once or twice he shook his head as if both excited and despondent. The sun was now but a bloody thumbprint in the sky and the sea wind was cold.

He returned to his goats and said to a young male who butted him playfully, "Dear child, you are not in the least human, and for that give homage to the gods."

CHAPTER 2

Zeno looked between the embroidered curtains of the litter and at the hills of Athens already trembling with heat and radiance though it was still early morning, at the clustering white houses with their red tiled roofs and the lifting clouds of shining silver dust that wavered over everything, and at the passionate blue of the Grecian sky. Athens was so small a city. Hardly two years before she had been burned to the ground by Xerxes, except for a few suburban sections where Zeno and Xanthippus lived, yet, like the Phoenix, she had risen from her ashes with characteristic zeal and energy and had rebuilt herself. Her intellectual turbulence had been no greater than her inner strength and fiery determination and soon her blackened walls had been plastered, her temples renovated and refurbished and her orchards replanted. Still, she was not a pretty little city. The blazing countryside intruded once more into her narrow streets and was never far from even the most illustrious houses. It was quite usual to see herds of goats and sheep and geese and swine being driven below the very walls of the new houses and new government buildings and temples. They grazed and climbed and cried on the slopes of the still almost bare acropolis, while their herdsmen, forgetting the Persian and his torches, squatted in the shade of the crackling laurels and ate their bread and cheese and drank their repulsive resinous wine. The heart of the town, as before the fire, stank of latrines and the offal of animals.

It was the Spartans and the barefoot Thebans, with a few Athenians, men of no importance, who had defeated the mighty Xerxes at Mycale, and, greatest of all, at Salamis and later at Plataea. Why had Greece been saved only by an apparent miracle? At the last they had had, these Greeks, only their naked hands and bleeding feet and teeth and nails, when their thin spears and iron swords and weak little ships had splintered and had fallen and disintegrated. What great secret heart had moved them to fight thus, and had made them larger than other men, if only for a short time? What had inspired envious little souls and quarrelsome minds and had given them incredible courage?

The lust for liberty. Ah, thought Zeno, it is that lust which is greater in the souls of men than the lust for women or for gold and silver or for conquest. Yet, thought Zeno, as the litter began an ascent on another hill into a slight coolness and freshness, there was something else which had saved Greece when it seemed impossible that she could be saved. The priests spoke of the gods. Zeno reflected, though he believed in the Fates and only occasionally speculated on the hypothesis of the Godhead. Was it possible that Greece had been saved by design, and, if so, for what destiny? He smiled at this patriotic fancy, but his smile was not derisive and only slightly amused. If he could, simply, believe utterly in the gods! Then something profound moved in his heart, as if a golden serpent had stirred on a brassy rock, and Zeno felt a sweetness and a powerful emotion he had never known before.

The house of Xanthippus, spared from the fire, glittered white in the sun and the roof was like sparkling rubies. It was surrounded by a low white wall over which spilled a tide of red, purple, rose and white flowers and, beyond them, a barrier of pointed cypresses. But as the house was on a rise of land it was not entirely obscured. There was a slave at the gates attired as a soldier and he opened them and assumed a military posture. Now Zeno could see the grounds, all red graveled paths and flower beds and exotic shrubbery in bloom and enormous Chinese vases filled with blossoms, and polished green branches. The house was tall, of two storeys, with Ionian pillars which gleamed in the sunlight, and the atrium was cool with fountains and the scent of fern. It was among the most fastidious of the houses of little Athens, and all its appointments were elegant, and the artistic soul of Zeno approved.

He entered the coolness of the atrium and was greeted formally by Xanthippus who was dressed in a long blue tunic and an elaborate silver belt of Oriental origin, which held an Alexandrine dagger of ornate workmanship. His countenance seemed somewhat out of place in this noble example of Greek restrained architecture and appeared more fitting for the palace of a sultan. Xanthippus immediately suggested refreshments and the two men seated themselves in the shade of a wall of the outdoor portico and a slave brought a fine wine chilled in the waters of a spring, soft pale bread, fruit, excellent cheese, a plate of goose meat and one of cold pork in its own jelly, artichokes in olive oil and garlic, and new berries still wet with dew. Zeno saw that the plates were both of silver and of the best ceramic design and the goblets were Egyptian glass wreathed with silver vine leaves and grapes.

A slave stood behind him with a long fan of palm leaves which, as it waved, not only brought a cool breeze but kept off flies. Xanthippus poured a libation to the gods, and smiled at Zeno, who followed his example. A flock of doves, their wings catching golden fire in the sun, flew over their heads. Now, as the heat increased, there was the pervading dry yet aromatic odor of stone, dust and spice and warm earth. Zeno ate heartily. A babble of high female voices and laughter came from the rear of the house and the women's quarters, and the thrilling sound of a lyre. Xanthippus said, "My wife, Agariste, is not stupid and ignorant as are most of the Athenian wives, for she was tutored in her father's house and has," he paused and smiled, "an elevated opinion of herself and her intellect. Nevertheless, I have found her counsel felicitous on a number of occasions, and she has flashes of wisdom which can be daunting to a man. She has desired to see you after you see our son. I trust this will not offend you."

Zeno hesitated, then inclined his head. "I have visited the School of the Courtesans and have met there women of extraordinary intellect as well as beauty, and have conversed with them to my edification. Thargelia, who conducts such a school in Miletus at this time, is a woman of magnificent gifts of the mind and spirit, and it is a delight to visit her."

"Ah, yes," said Xanthippus, who possessed a mistress who had been a protégé of the School, "she is a paragon of what women should be but are not. Perhaps it is fortunate for our nation, for, it is written by the Sibyls, when women dominate a nation and their men and intrude their voices into politics and the arts of war and intellect that nation will decay and fall."

Zeno still hesitated. "However, it is a stupid waste of what is presented to man to ignore those few women whose minds are like ours or could even surpass them. When also," and he returned the smile of his host, "they possess beauty and charm and talent, they are formidable, and who can resist them?"

"Women need but one man, but men need many women. Nothing is so deadly to the mind as monotony."

"I find it stimulating," said Zeno, then seeing his host's surprise he added, "When the outward environment and life are not in turmoil and change, they do not distract the mind. But

214

if a man must attend to a thousand restless trivialities of existence—which pass as the shadow of clouds but seem at the moment to be imperative—it is impossible for him to meditate upon a hypothesis, a scientific theory, or an intricate elaboration of philosophy, or an idea of startling uniqueness. He must attend the little events as a peasant attends his cows, and after such attendance he is exhausted." He smiled deprecatingly at Xanthippus, who was looking amused.

A jeweled lizard ran along the stones of the portico and a slave would have struck the small creature with a stave, but Zeno said in a voice unusually sharp, "Let the beautiful thing live, for there is very little living beauty in this world. Besides, has he offended you? Has he bitten your toe or poisoned you? Has he not as godly a reason to live as you, and who are you to terminate his life?"

Then he flushed, for he had addressed a slave rebukingly in the presence of his master. But Xanthippus said in his very musical voice, "You have spoken truly. Who is man that he should decide what is baser than he? But the beasts surpass us in one thing: They have the virtue of their being and adhere to the laws given to them. We do not."

Zeno said, " 'Adhere to the laws of their being.' But could it not be that men are more intelligent than beasts because we constantly rebel against the laws of our own being?"

"We bring down Promethean fire," said Xanthippus. His sallow and narrow cheeks were bright with the stirrings of his mind and his eyes sparkled happily at Zeno. "However, is it not better that we possess dangerous fire as our servant than not to know fire at all? It is in man's rebelliousness that he can contemplate something greater than himself and know the gods, though they destroy him. Beasts do not rebel." He turned the goblet in his nervous hands and looked more and more excited. "There is no positive virtue in adhering to the laws of one's being."

Zeno smiled. "I will write a treatise on it, though the priests will not approve." Xanthippus nodded and said, "We speak as violent men and rebellion is deplored."

"There is much to be said for intelligent violence," said Zeno. "It is out of the furious vortex that the gods ascended, and out of holocaust that the worlds leapt."

Xanthippus clapped his hands for the overseer of the atrium. "So, we return to the ancient questions: As man is a disturbing and alien presence in this world, revolting against natural laws and one who invites endless chaos in consequence, would it not be better that he be eliminated?"

"The gods are violent," said Zeno, laughing. "Out of the fierce blaze of His Hands does God strike the universes, and out of the igniting rocks does He form continents. The seas convulse and throw up islands and rivers and lakes. Nature is turbulent and ever-changing, and perhaps in that we could learn a most momentous lesson."

"Most true," said Xanthippus, and frowned, leaning his elbow on the table and placing his bearded chin within his palm. "Yet, there are some politicians who say that if we had priest-kings and could command obedience of men and docile behavior, we would enter an immortal land of joy and fulfillment."

"In that event," said Zeno, "it would be the politicians who would rule and not their priest-kings. Priests are obsequious before the power of others, and are obedient to it."

The sly slaves were listening, and so even the brave and powerful soldier, Xanthippus, who despised the priests, said with haste, "Who has access to the gods but the priests?" He winked covertly at Zeno whose face became as quiet as marble, not with fear but with disgust at the world.

The overseer of the hall came and Xanthippus commanded the presence of his son, Pericles.

The young Pericles entered the portico with his attendant slave, an elderly man with a beard. Zeno looked at the child who was twelve years old, Pericles, son of Xanthippus, of the deme Cholargus of the tribe Acamantis, and Xanthippus looked at his son with smiling pride and said, "His mother, as you may know, Zeno of Elea, is the grandchild of Clisthenes, who drove out the sons of Pisistratas, and thus put an end to the Tyrants and attempted to return to the laws and principles of Solon. But that, as we know, was an impractical dream. My wife said to her slaves, being near her time of delivery of my son, that she was brought to bed of a lion." Xanthippus put his dexterous tongue into his cheek and winked at Zeno.

The sun in the portico was blinding and vivid even at this hour and the shadows were pointed and dark blue and very sharp and the sky was a resonant color as if formed of turquoise flame. Pericles stood in the reflected brilliance quietly and with containment, almost as if indifferent to the scrutiny of a stranger, and as if his thoughts were fixed on some distance. He was tall for one so young and slender but muscular.

216

He seemed much older than his years. He was clad in the short green tunic of preadolescence with the Greek key as its border on the bottom and about the sleeves, and his legs were slight but firm and his feet, in their sandals, long and narrow. His body and stillness had that elegance and grace much admired by the Athenians, and his skin was as fair as milk. His face showed the thinness but strength of his patrician bones, so subtly formed that they appeared to lie close to the flesh and to dominate it. His nose was slightly aquiline and his pink mouth was full and faintly sensual but finely carved and controlled. His eyes were of so pale a blue between pale lashes that it was almost as if they had no hue but were the eyes of a statue. His hair was the color of bright flax and curled at his nape and about his cheeks, and his white neck was long and thin and upright and flexible.

All this made for a certain exquisite and masculine beauty except for his brow, which though the color and rigidity of marble, rose to an unusual height as did the crown of his head, and gave an elongation out of proportion to the face, thus diminishing and dwarfing it. Such a grotesque height would have attracted the attention of the priests and authorities as being abnormal, and Pericles, had he been born of less illustrious parents, would have been allowed to die entombed in a large vase. For the authorities did not permit deviations in body or distortions of countenance or other grotesqueries to survive.

Zeno, in deference to the boy—for were not children susceptible to adult stares?—did not direct the full power of his eyes on Pericles, but fixed them at a point near the child's cheek.

"Greetings, Pericles, son of Xanthippus," said Zeno in his high kind voice.

The boy responded, "Greetings, Zeno of Elea." Zeno was surprised at the depth of Pericles' voice, for it was not the piping of children.

"I have told my son of you, Zeno," said Xanthippus, "and that I am attempting to persuade you to be his tutor."

For the first time Pericles looked fully at Zeno, and again Zeno was surprised, for it was not the wary and suspicious stare of a young boy but the calculation and weighing of a man, fearless yet cautious.

Zeno, gazing at the youth, knew with all his intuition that he had no need to question Pericles to discover his intelligence.

217

Those pale eyes were implicit with cold inner fire and intellect, with judiciousness and latent power, and glowed with that radiance which can come but from an unusually intelligent mind. Pericles had brought his attention to Zeno from a far place where his thoughts were engaged, yet when he had done so it was with a certain piercing and cogent vigor which was totally aware and focused, and not diffused or vague.

Truly, thought Zeno, a most remarkable child—if one can call him a child—and one with potential terribleness.

Zeno had never said this to another prospective student, but he said it now: "Do you accept me as your tutor, Pericles, son of Xanthippus?"

At this the youth smiled, urbanely, and flashed a glance at his father. "I do," he said, and Zeno, laughing a little inwardly at himself, thought: I have been given an accolade!

"He reads and writes adequately," said the subtle Xanthippus, who had understood the exchange and was gratified. He fingered his black and pointed beard and struck an attitude in his chair. "Then, it is settled," he said. "You will not find my son stupid, Zeno of Elea, but possessed of a mind of curiosity and eagerness to be enlightened and guided."

I doubt if he can ever be guided, except by a woman and then only on occasion, thought the wry Zeno.

"His mother has been educated by tutors in her father's house," said Xanthippus, "her father being deluded that women possess intellects." He smiled. He held out his hand negligently to his son, and Pericles went to him and took that hand and leaned against his father's shoulder.

Zeno could not restrain himself and he said, "Pericles, it is not in your nature to accept anyone immediately. Why have you accepted me?"

"I have read of your writings," said the youth.

Zeno raised his eyebrows. "And what did you think of them, my child?"

"They are lucid," said Pericles. He smiled at Zeno and it was as if he were a man, cognizant and a little amused.

Zeno became grave. "That is a compliment," he said. "If the young can understand a sage then he has succeeded in being intelligible."

He saw that Pericles was regarding him with that disturbing convergence of his which permitted no intruding thought at the moment.

Xanthippus dismissed his son with a kiss on his lips, and Pericles bowed formally to Zeno and took his departure with his slave. He did not run, flailing his limbs aimlessly, as did other children. He walked with the firmness and quiet of a man. Zeno said to Xanthippus, "Your son is not a child. He is a man, and I am honored to teach him." His eyes ached from the light and from his thoughts.

"Perhaps it is true that my wife was brought to bed by a lion," said Xanthippus, and laughed. "A white lion with a golden mane. Does not my son resemble such?"

Zeno did not answer frivolously as Xanthippus expected. He considered, and then he said, "Yes." He clasped his hands between his knees and gazed at the stones of the portico and absently took a sip of wine. Xanthippus looked at him dubiously, then he shrugged. He struck his hands for the overseer and when the slave entered the portico Xanthippus said, "Summon the Lady Agariste from the gynaikeion (women's quarters) to attend her husband immediately."

As Zeno was a man as well as a guest Agariste entered the portico attended by two female slaves with the customary short hair and simple long tunics and bare arms and feet. But Agariste wore a peplos of saffron linen with a golden girdle intricately wrought, and she was so tall that she had no need of the high-heeled shoes worn by other rich Athenian ladies. Her shoulder pins glittered with jewels and there were many jeweled rings on her long, white and very slender hands and bracelets on her narrow arms. She had a noble figure if one too thin for the taste of many men, and her bosom swelled under the folds of the peplos in a delightful fashion and it was evident that she had no necessary recourse to the strophion to elevate it. Her hair was naturally fair and of a fine gilt sheen, and so abundant and so full of tendrils and waves that she wore no false wigs or supplements to increase its bounty. It was bound with golden ribbons. Zeno saw that it was from his mother that Pericles had inherited the strong refinement of facial structure, the milky complexion, the carved mouth and aquiline nose and the almost colorless blue of the large eyes. But Agariste was haughty and cold whereas her young son was grave and stately. It was evident that she possessed enormous esteem for her person and her intelligence, for her glance was august and her manner suggested that she found even her husband—the notable soldier of much fame, and the politician of no mean ability—not entirely her equal. As for Zeno, whom she had desired to see, and with whose writings she was familiar, she saw before her a small man of no distinguished appearance and with crudely cropped hair and a childlike figure, and she was disappointed and in some curious way offended. Seeing this Zeno thought: Had she expected an Achilles, or Apollo or at least a Hercules, out of a Homeric poem?

"Zeno of Elea, the Lady of Agariste, the mistress of my house," said Xanthippus, who admired, respected but heartily disliked his wife. He loved her in his way for her gifts of character and her beauty and her family history; however, he frequently discovered her tedious for she had no humor at all but only arrogance.

She bowed slightly and coldly to Zeno and he saw the grace of her long body under the carefully arranged folds of the peplos. Xanthippus did not invite her to be seated and she could not sit without her husband's invitation. She glanced swiftly at an empty chair of ebony inlaid with pearl and when Xanthippus said nothing a slight flush ran over her transparent face and the pale eyes had, for a moment, the glitter of bare metal.

Studying her with a slight smile and in a little silence, Xanthippus finally said, "You wished to speak with Zeno of Elea, Lady, as you requested?" He leaned back in his chair, then negligently lifted a citron to his mouth and sucked at its juices.

Mortification heightened her color. She did not look at Zeno but addressed her husband: "Lord, you consider him an adequate tutor for our son?"

Zeno began to pity her. He said, "Lady Agariste, I find Pericles most exemplary, and I feel destiny in him. Therefore, I have consented to teach him."

Agariste, her humiliation growing, yet heard Zeno's voice and, more to her liking, his words. She turned her face to him though she kept her eyes averted. She had a voice as chill as snow and as colorful. She said, "Zeno of Elea, you repeat what I have heard in my dreams and have seen in my visions. I do not feel that you are exaggerating or flattering, but speak only the truth."

"It is true, Lady," said Zeno, and he began to feel annoyed that Xanthippus appeared to be absorbed in choosing a certain nut from a bowl of them, stirring them about noisily with a long lean finger as if looking for a favorite. So Zeno rose in a most courteous gesture to Agariste.

Xanthippus evidently found the nut he was seeking, and he cracked its thin shell between his strong white teeth and his eyes of that dark staring blue flickered with mirth.

"You are pleased, Agariste?" he asked, as if addressing a

superior favorite among his slave women. He shifted seductively in his chair.

Agariste, whose flushed face had suddenly whitened both with wrath and shame, inclined her head and Zeno had to admire her composure and dignity for all she was a woman of no pleasant ways.

"Good. Then you may retire," said her husband and waved his hand graciously.

He knew that she had intended to question Zeno sharply, and to impress on him the honor he had been offered, and that she had intended to cow him while she, too, studied his theories and his words. She had hoped to engage his mind and make him admire her attributes. Throwing up her noble head she turned and, accompanied by her maidens, left the presence of the men, her peplos as quiet as yellow stone. Xanthippus watched her leave and affected to study her figure and her movements as men study the gifts of the hetairai and are about to choose among them. Zeno did not find this risible.

Xanthippus saw this and he smiled. "The Lady Agariste is a female of many talents and not only beauty," he said. He paused. "Her conversation is chiselled out of granite."

Zeno could not help smiling. "I will return at dawn tomorrow to begin the instruction of my student," he said, and took his leave.

He believed the oracles at Delphi to be fraudulent and ridiculous and the imposture of priests hungry for lavish offerings from the superstitious and the gullible. In an unguarded moment or two he had quickly investigated the hollow caves. Still, an oracle had predicted the defeat of Xerxes and his barbarians when the very thought had been preposterous and even priests had fled their temples. Another had predicted the future fame and glory of Greece, and Zeno, not often mystical, believed that implicitly.

Twelve years ago they had announced the birth of a great hero who would bring down the imperial lightning from Olympus and from the hands of Zeus upon this small city of only forty thousand souls, the majority of whom were slaves, and would write the name of Athens in immortal marble for the blinkless stare of the centuries.

CHAPTER 3

"It has been asked from the beginning," said Zeno to his pupil, and with a courteous glance at Agariste who sat nearby, listening keenly and severely, " 'What is man?' The first brute in the skins of animals asked that when he suddenly contemplated himself in quiet pools in the primeval forests. 'Who am I?' he asked. 'I mate and live and breed and eat and defecate and die as do the animals which I hunt. Yet, I discern a difference. What is that difference which makes me a man?' He was less moral than the beasts of the jungles and the plains and the mountains. (He knew he was weak before the power of their teeth and their claws and their strength, and he was less agile.) He discerned that the beasts had their own code of morality, discipline and behavior, which could not be violated except at the cost of death or destruction.

"Was he less than the beasts after all? In all the capacities of their bestial nature they were superb, decisive, confident. He, himself, was not. We know that man possesses few instincts, and that he chooses by his own will, to a large extent, what he will think and what his future shall be. That is the crucial difference between man and the other beasts. The Choice. Does that ability make him an outlaw in the very natural world in which he was conceived, or does his disobedience to the law make him superior to them? He is not at peace with himself.

"We speak of the dominance of reason in ' men's affairs. Reason has been analysed. It is based, they say, on the observation of a common reality, an admission of what reality is. But what is reality to me is possibly not reality to you, Pericles, or to other men. If we are to know what man is, we have to know what reality is."

"On what, then, can we base our lives and sculpture our futures?" asked the young Pericles, who was now fifteen years old.

Zeno reflected. "It is necessary for objective laws, for we are a lawless and passionate and wicked and vindictive species. We have agreed that it is necessary for the survival of our tribe to have objective laws, though we are vehemently at war with law, both subjective and objective. We do not accept, as the beasts accept. Of what mysterious fruit have we eaten in that we are rebels even against ourselves, and challenge even the gods?"

He looked into the pale and thoughtful eyes of his pupil, which told him nothing except that the young Pericles was thinking.

"No one has truly defined what is a man. The answer may be in the mind of God. It certainly is not in ours, no matter how emphatic the priest or the philosopher or the scientist." Zeno smiled slightly, and ate a date.

"Young Anaxagoras has said that we are men because we have opposing thumbs. But so do various monkeys, and they have never raised a temple nor formulated a body of laws of their own. Others have said we are different because we think, that we are conscious of thinking, that we are conscious of ourselves. I have observed some dogs and notably the Egyptian cats. I am convinced they think, also." He laughed.

"You are inconsistent, Zeno of Elea," said Agariste, as she sat with her son and his tutor in the outside portico in the growing sunset. "You set paradoxes, and then smile at them as if with pleasure. You pose questions but never answer them. You hint of mysteries, propound them, then dismiss them as trivialities."

Zeno glanced at her with pity. She sat like a princess in her lemonwood chair inlaid with ivory, with her female slave behind her waving a long palm-leaf fan; her hair was like wheat in the late sun. She advanced her intelligence, not with calmness and modesty or as even an equal, but with a kind of triumphant defiance and overweening pride. In this, thought Zeno, she does not confirm the theory that women are intelligent. He smiled at Agariste gently.

"Lady," he said, and was somewhat vexed that the young Pericles was watching him with a spark of amusement in his eyes, "it is my intention to have my pupil ponder on my questions and paradoxes and seeming contradictions and inconsistencies, and formulate answers and theories of his own, which we will discuss."

"I believe it is the duty of a teacher to present facts and the reasons for the facts," said Agariste, with severity.

"Lady," said Zeno, "there is a vast difference between philosophy and what we have universally agreed is the truth."

"You do not agree that there is any absolute truth?"

Zeno hesitated. He studied the gardens about the home, the walls overflowing with color, and beyond them the silver ribs of the hills of Greece, thrusting out between the firs and the cypresses and olive groves that covered them like a mantle which quivered in the evening breeze. But the zenith yet was like blue fire.

"Absolute truth, Lady," he said at last, "is not to be known by men, just as no man can reach any truth by himself alone. The absolute truth, like absolute reality, is the prerogative of God and none other."

"You do not believe, then," said Agariste, "that men are like gods, though Homer has hinted of it?"

"I do not quarrel with Homer," replied Zeno, "for he was a poet and the majority of men are not poets. We are more akin to the beast of the field, and once we understand him we can begin the painful climb to our own mystery—from that mutual standing ground."

Agariste tossed her head. Pericles said to his tutor, offering him a blue and white bowl, "Refresh yourself with an apple, Zeno." Zeno looked at him sharply and saw a subtle gleam on the boy's face, and he wanted to laugh but refrained out of respect for Agariste.

"You do not deny the reality and truth of Thermopylae?" said Agariste, with umbrage.

"I know we held the Persians there to some extent," said Zeno. "But, as many in the east assert, perhaps all is illusion." He bit into the apple Pericles had given him and sipped a little wine. He stood at the table, rather than sat, for though like many sages he preferred to sit Agariste irritated even his gentle and serene state of mind.

"Illusion!" cried Agariste, moving strongly in her chair so that her pale blue robe was agitated, and her breast rose up and down in disquiet. "That is not only a foolishness, Zeno of Elea, but treason!"

Zeno closed his eyes briefly. He heard a faint chuckle near his elbow and knew that it came from Pericles, who was leaning back on his student's hard stool and enjoying himself at both his mother's expense and his tutor's.

"You do not even wear a dagger!" cried Agariste, exasperated by Zeno's silence, which she interpreted as a deprecation of her intellect as a woman. "What is a man without the smallest weapon with which to defend himself?"

Zeno deplored this. Agariste was a woman of mind, but she could descend to trivialities and personal attacks on those who offered a thought which conflicted with hers.

He said, with mildness, "From whom, and what, Lady, should I defend myself? I am a humble philosopher and teacher."

Then Pericles spoke. "Zeno, there are many who would attack you. You may believe yourself the most inoffensive of men, but a number of your ideas and words have aroused antagonism in the city." He beckoned to a slave near the doors of the house, and when the man approached he said with a sudden authority which surprised Zeno, "Bring the illustrious Zeno of Elea one of the lord Xanthippus' daggers at once."

He then looked intently at Zeno and said with firmness, "It is my decree."

The slave brought an Egyptian dagger of considerable value, set with turquoises and amethysts and deep red stones, some of them intricately carved. "This is very valuable, as well as beautiful," said Zeno. "Will not the lord Xanthippus object to this gift when he returns?"

"He has the highest regard for you," said Pericles. "He would deny you nothing."

Zeno fastened the dagger to his worn silver belt. It felt awkward against his thigh. Pericles observed him with a mocking smile, "I trust you to understand how to use a dagger, Zeno?"

Zeno became grave and his glowing face darkened. "I know how to use a sword also," he said.

Pericles raised his pale golden eyebrows. "In war?"

"In defense," said Zeno. He looked intently at Agariste, who was calculating the value of the dagger, and Pericles saw this. He turned with courtesy to his mother but also with imperiousness. "My mother," he said, "may I request that Zeno and I be left alone for a discussion?"

Agariste rose at once and her slave with her, but her lovely face was crimson. She exclaimed, "Am I of so inferior an intelligence that I cannot understand this—Zeno?"

"We will speak as men." Pericles turned from his mother, overtly expecting her obedience, and gave his attention to Zeno, who was embarrassed again for the poor woman. She left immediately, her head high, and again Zeno pitied her.

When Agariste had departed Zeno sat down, placed his sharp elbows on the table, and contemplated the cheese and wine and bread and honeycomb and fruit and olives before him. Zeno nibbled; he was not aware he was nibbling. His thoughts were far away.

The sun was setting to the west, a conflagration of scarlet and green, and the low roofs of Athens flared with it, and the white walls ran with red shadows. There were murmurous sounds in the air of men and animals, muted, and aromatic odors of stone and white and red earth, and the wild scent of jasmine. The palms began to rattle and open their fronds to the breeze. Somewhere there was a babble of high and rasping women's voices, and their shrill meaningless laughter. Now the zenith of the heavens was brightening into gold. The sound of the little city below was a long and insistent rumbling, hardly to be heard. The flowers of the garden exhaled. Pericles waited, his thin white arms folded on the table. He watched as Zeno nibbled, and once or twice he contemplatively chewed a date. Occasionally he turned his intense regard to the port and saw the sea racing in silver and dim purple. The skull of the moon was rising in the sky, pale as death, and frail.

Zeno finally spoke, but he looked at the harbor and saw the white sails leaving as the tide went out. He said, "It is strange that the government and the priests do not recognize an obvious evil, but seek out to denounce evils which do not truly exist, and only offend their distorted sensibilities."

"Yes?" said the young Pericles. "My father agrees with you. He believes governments are wicked by their nature, for who dominates other men will misuse his power, out of vanity and aggrandisement."

Zeno suddenly heard and looked piercingly at his pupil. "True," he said.

"Who, then, should rule?"

Zeno smiled wryly. "Who, indeed? When men become fully human—which I doubt will ever occur—they will rule themselves." He spit out an olive pit and gloomily drank a little wine. He said, "Animals have their rule of authority. The wisest and strongest control, in succession, the layers beneath them, which descend to the lowest level, and no one disputes. But there is growing in Athens the error of Demos—democracy—which is a retreat from rational government. All men are equal, say their philosophers. But, what is 'equal'? Equality under the law, or privileged 'equality' by furious demand of the inferior envious? You will find, Pericles, that politicians are the most cowardly of men. They seek votes."

Pericles waited. A big white moth hovered over the table and caught the brilliant sunset light on its wings, and it was a little lightning. Pericles was fascinated. How beautiful was nature in even its smallest manifestations! Pericles did not speak of his inmost dream to anyone, not even to Zeno.

Zeno lifted his eyes and studied his pupil. He thought over what he must convey to the youth. Many philosophers believed that man had an instinctive knowledge of private things, enhanced by the observation of domestic animals in their breeding, and that any hazards or errors or misunderstandings would be corrected by experience. These same philosophers—with some truth—said that it was not possible to give the young the value of the experiences of their elders, for youth scoffs at bitter knowledge, and wisdom and elderly sagacity, and prefers to make its own disasters and wreck its own life, as if none had lived before it. Alas, thought Zeno. The world is very old and is growing older and there will never be a "new" planet, but only repetition which will be hailed as novelty and progress, because the young ignore the ancient history of their inheritance.

Zeno looked at the gardens below and about him and saw the peacocks and the ducks on their pond, and roving domestic dogs and cats, and the shrilling birds. The sunset splashed him with ruddy light and Pericles, still waiting, thought that Zeno had the most noble appearance of any man he had ever known.

Zeno said, as if meditating to himself, "You have asked me if I am afraid of weapons. And I replied that once I carried a sword, but discarded it. I killed two men with my sword."

Pericles was amazed. He said, "But you refuse to be present when I take my fencing lessons!"

"True. It is my own remembrance. Many men deserve to be executed but it is a horror to the executioner. I cannot forget the men I killed—though they eminently deserved to die."

"We have a conscience," said Pericles, and made a mouth of derision which was also half-humorous.

"So do animals," said Zeno.

He looked again at the domestic animals. He said, "You have observed the mating instincts of these?"

Pericles said, "Yes."

"Then you know it is the way we human beings mate also."

Pericles was faintly amused. "Yes, that I know. Our bodies are as much animal as are the bodies of the beasts."

Zeno nodded. "It is when we depart from the profound instincts of our nature that we become less than the beasts."

Pericles frowned. "Elucidate," he said.

Zeno said, "There is a philosophy which is recent in our history, though it is ancient in practice. But we Greeks like to give a white cloak of morality to our sins, though older civilizations are more cynical and pragmatic. We Greeks say that our wives and our concubines do not entirely satisfy us, and that men cannot feel true love for a woman, who is lesser and inferior and has no mind or soul of any consequence. Therefore, we must seek out ideal love and perfection of understanding among our own sex, for exultant exchange of ideas. Do not men live by ideas and poetry and communication?"

Zeno continued. "If love between men, of the same sex, were confined to argument and ideas and conversation and the excitement of the exchange of theories, none would have objection."

Pericles was silent.

Zeno said, after a pause, "But when men substitute other men in the physical capacity of a woman, then they enter into a twilight world not only of perversion of nature, but in the perversion of their own minds and souls."

Pericles' light blue eyes widened innocently, and he said, "Is that possible?"

Zeno fixed his own eyes upon the youth and thought, "Ah, that feigned innocence!" He said to Pericles, "Let us be men. Let me say this: The love between a man and a woman, if really love, is a great mystery and a great glory. It exalts, it edifies, it elevates, it makes them one flesh, almost immune to outward calamity, steadfast, the deepest intimacy any human being can know, beyond friendship, beyond the mere breeding of children."

Pericles said, "You have not married," and there was pale blue lightning of amusement between his lashes.

"I have loved," said Zeno. "I have loved many women, but have found none whom I wished to marry. Women, by nature, as the sages have said, are of the earth and the concerns of the earth, including their own wombs, but that does not make them inferior, for who can live without the earth?"

He paused. "Some years ago I engaged a young scribe, for my friends wished what I wrote, and said, to be recorded. So, I found an erudite youth called Phelan, of much education and refinement and an intuitive and deductive mind. I took him into my house, where he could write down my musings and my sudden thoughts, as well as my dissertations and my theories."

Zeno rubbed his chin thoughtfully. "If I had been more discerning I should have noticed that Phelan was a youth of too much delicacy and sensitivity, and that he had a girlish appearance. He was also given to emotion and impulsiveness, and his responses were unseemly in a man. It is true that great poets and other artists can be moved to tears by the grandeur of a sunset or a statue or an epic—but Phelan could be deeply moved by the nuzzling of a lamb or a young goat, and would weep at the soft texture of linen or the sight of a young child bubbling saliva. These are womanish manifestations, but I hardly noticed them."

Zeno watched Pericles with an inscrutable but observant eye as he spoke in his quiet and harmonious voice.

But Phelan's extreme and even hysterical sensibility did not decrease with time, nor did his high ecstasies for all that Zeno said, even the most inconsequential. This was sometimes embarrassing to the sage, but he was by nature indulgent and kind. He, himself, had become so engrossed with the exhilarating excursions of his mind, and excursions into the minds of others, that he failed to see the obvious: Phelan was in love with him, as a woman loves a man.

"It is extraordinarily dangerous for a man to live by his mind alone," said Zeno to the listening Pericles, "for then he can stumble on the merest pebble in his path and break his neck, a pebble that even an infant would have avoided. It is true that Phelan often made me uneasy, with his obvious adoration and worship of me—which I unwisely attributed to his youth and to a gentle lack of sophistication. Then one day I said to him, 'You must not constantly follow me about, Phelan, as if precious rubies were falling from my lips when all I wish is to scratch my anus in private.' I had hoped to make him laugh, but he only blushed and looked at me with abject reverence and said, 'Rubies, Master, fall from your lips even when you are silent.' He turned his head suddenly and kissed my hand, then fell upon his knees, clasped his arms about my own knees, and confessed his love for me with such passion, such stammering candor, that repelled though I was I could not feel disgust but only pity and sadness."

Zeno sighed and drew his hands across his eyes and looked at the last red rays of the sun over the purpling western hills. "I should not have been so aghast, so startled. The evidence had been before me for a long time, and I could see it all at that moment, and despised myself for my blindness. I raised up Phelan as kindly as I could, speaking calmly, but he threw his arms about me and kissed me on the lips, as a wild girl would do. It was a wanton kiss, but still it had some innocence and a childlike recklessness." Zeno looked at Pericles, and said, almost inaudibly, "Do you understand, my pupil?"

"Yes," said Pericles. "I have heard of all this from my several companions, though not with the honesty you have shown, my teacher, nor the pity and understanding."

"Ah," said Zeno, and he was relieved. He said, "And what do you think of it, Pericles?"

The boy shrugged. "I find it neither repulsive nor attractive. But you have spoken of the attack on you by armed men."

"I find it difficult to come to an absolute decision and to act with authority," Zeno confessed. "So, though I sweated openly and cringed inwardly at the necessity, I discharged Phelan and sent him home to his father, writing the latter that I had come to the conclusion that my 'immortal words' were not worth the recording, and remarking on Phelan's extraordinary intelligence and competence and loyalty.

"Phelan left me in tears and with prayers to reconsider. Such men as Phelan have a woman's secret intuition. It took me hours to induce him to leave my house, whereas another man would have forced him to leave within moments. There are times," Zeno reflected, "when I believe that kindness is often cowardice rather than a noble virtue."

When Zeno had been a youth his father had sent him to the best fencing school in Athens. Though Athenians did not make the finest soldiers, they having too much humor and satirical intelligence, they could fight almost as valiantly as the Spartan when forced to do so. "It astonished my father even more than it astonished me," said Zeno to Pericles, "when I became an excellent swordsman, for both of us had believed that cold metal and I had no sympathy. When I was pronounced perfect by my fencing master my father gave me a fine sword of my own, keen as a razor, as viciously pointed as a woman's tongue. It had a gold hilt set with jewels. To please my father I wore it constantly."

He paused, and his face became melanchoy. "I slept with it in my bed, even when with a woman companion. It saved my life, shortly after I had dismissed Phelan.

"For, one moonlit night my house, which I occupy now, was invaded by two armed men in cloaks and hoods. They burst open my door and advanced upon me with daggers glittering and bare in the sharp moonlight. Fortunately I was still awake or I should have been murdered in my bed. Hesitation would have cost me my life. I sprang to my feet and seized my ready sword, and rushed at the nearest man and impaled him. He fell at once, his hood falling from his head, and he died without a sound. I saw it was Phelan.

"My horror at this almost caused my own death, for I stood mute and frozen for an instant or two, seeing the dark hot blood welling from my poor secretary's heart. Then, through the corner of my eye I saw the other man lunging upon me. I moved aside and he inflicted a slight wound on my left shoulder. A second earlier and it would have pierced my heart. Then I struck at him with my sword and it entered his belly, and he fell, clutching at himself and groaning, and his dagger flew from his hand.

"I knelt beside him and raised his head by his hair, and saw that he was some coarse ruffian or a slave, and I hated him as

I could not hate Phelan, who was still a youth and this was a man of middle age and brutal. I beat his head savagely on the floor and demanded an explanation. I did not recognize myself," Zeno added, smiling somberly, "but I believe it was Phelan's death that enraged me, and broke my heart. The fact that Phelan had desired my extinction seemed less heinous to me than that this man, a stranger, had desired it also.

"The brute confessed that he was a slave in the house of Phelan's father, and was devoted to the youth on whom he had lavished a father's affection. Phelan had told him that I had insulted him 'mortally,' had abused him before companions in the colonnades, had ridiculed him and reviled him as a man of no intellect. And then, with invective, had dismissed him, urging him to lower his ambitions to carrying wood for the baths. He had incited this slave to rage, then had begged for advice, and the slave had assured him that only my blood would wash out my iniquities against the son of an illustrious house. Phelan had then suggested that his slave accompany him to my own house for that very purpose. So, they had come."

Zeno was then silent for so long that Pericles finally said, "How was this explained to the city guards and the judges?"

Zeno rubbed his chin and looked towards the west where a racing purple cloud had begun to cover the falling sun, thus darkening the landscape so that the white houses and buildings shone like bare bones in the quickening gloom.

"It was of Phelan's father that I thought," said Zeno. "So I dragged the bodies far down the slope of my hillside and let them fall below, and I threw their daggers after them."

Pericles looked incredulously at the small stature and slightness of his teacher.

"It is remarkable what strength can be summoned in an emergency," said Zeno. "I was desperate not only to save the sensibilities of Phelan's father, a friend, but to conceal from him his son's aberration, for he is a proud man and an eminent soldier and would have died of grief to learn of his son's —peculiarity—and also to learn that that son, without provocation, had hired a slave and had accompanied him to kill a sleeping man. I returned to my house and washed my floor with lye and water to drive away the bloodstains. At dawn I went to the temple of Ares, who was never my favorite god, to offer sacrifice for the souls of the men I had been forced to kill, and to display my gratitude for the strength Ares had chosen to give me in those most awful moments.

"After the authorities had conducted their investigations

they declared that Phelan, and his slave, had been murdered by thieves when on Phelan's way to visit me."

Zeno fell silent again and Pericles waited. Then Zeno said, "Since that time I have never carried a sword, though it hangs on the wall of my house. I avoid circumstances and situations wherein I could be induced to display my swordsmanship in defense of my life."

"Such circumstances and situations cannot always be avoided," said Pericles. His fair hair shimmered like polished gold in the mingled light and darkness of the approaching storm. "You often walk to your house and refuse my father's litter. Suppose you were truly set upon by thieves and had no means of defense. Would you die meekly? Is that not cowardice in itself?"

Zeno reluctantly laughed. "I have taught you too much logic," he said. He looked down at the dagger fastened to his girdle. "I think I shall keep this weapon, after all, and wear it always, as do other Athenian men. Self-defense is no crime; to refuse to defend yourself is the instinct of a slave, not a man." He sighed. "Still, it is a monstrous comment on our times that sometimes we must kill in order not to be killed."

He suddenly stood up as if seized by restlessness and walked to the parapet outside the portico and stared at the murky west. Pericles slowly joined him and they gazed down at the city and up at the sky. All at once lightning struck a scarlet crevice in the heavens and soon thereafter thunder bellicosely roared in answer. For an instant Pericles was illuminated in vivid eerie light and Zeno looked at him with new comprehension. It was as if a white and gold statue had been precipitated into being. Thank the gods, thought Zeno. I had thought him too controlled, too much in command of himself, too removed. Thank the gods for men who can be moved to disquietude!

The storm increased and the palms lashed and the earth exhaled a hot odor as of both panic and desire, and dark and brilliant shadows raced over the city below. Zeno touched his pupil on the shoulder and said, "Do not be too much disturbed. Life will crush your heart or turn it to stone. It is inevitable. But, you have your choice."

Pericles lifted his eyes to the dusky height of the acropolis. "I have a dream," he said, as if he had not heard Zeno at all. Then he turned and smiled at his teacher. "A dream of marble, but it will be alive." From the women's quarters the slave girls had begun to sing, accompanied by the tinkling notes of lutes, and to Zeno it sounded very brave in the face of the rising storm. It is all the answer we can return, he thought. It is all we can say to the terrible gods. Courage.

CHAPTER 4

Xanthippus, though he had the aristocrat's and skeptic's aversion for the common people, also had the genial man's hatred for oppression from tyrants and governments. Once he said, "None can be free in a city unless all men are free. One slave nullifies the liberty of all." It was, in truth, the patrician's abstract love for freedom which drew him from the beginning to the Laws of Solon. Like many superior Athenians he knew that government must have a Constitution guaranteeing the rights of citizens. Athens had been in turmoil since the Tyrants, and Xanthippus desired to restore the pure Laws of Solon which had been appropriated by the Tyrants to oppress the people and to pervert the ideals of Solon, himself.

"The noblest concepts of men are invariably corrupted and interpreted in the light of self-serving, though the wicked are vociferous in their proclamations that they adhere to those concepts," he told his young son. "Whatever men touch they taint, even the feet of the gods. Solon's Constitution for our city was a document to free men from uncertainty and fear and to raise them to a rational just government, and to confer the benefits of liberty upon them, for it is only in the air of liberty that a nation can endure, prosper and increase. Law and order and the consent of the governed are what Solon desired for Athens, hence his Constitution. But you will perceive what wicked men have done to that Constitution while shouting their love for it."

As a fastidious man he resented all attempts of an oppressive government to regulate his own personal life with its laws. "We execute spies," he said to Pericles. "But governments are the most pervasive of spies, hence we must eternally be vigilant lest we be enslaved by bureaucrats and their busy pens and lust for power." He had been born with a mistrust for his fellow man, and this had expanded during his lifetime. Once he said, only half in jest, "It should be permitted citizens to decide, every year, who shall in government be executed publicly for his crimes against the people."

He called his son's attention to one of the precepts of Solon that "a well-governed State was when the people obey the ru-

233

lers and the rulers obey the laws." Alas, however, it always ended with the rulers demanding obedience to laws which they, themselves, enthusiastically disobeyed when it was to their own benefit and increase of wealth. "Do not think this is contradictory," said Xanthippus. "It is only human nature."

"How, then," asked the young Pericles, "can we enforce the rule of law on everyone, including governments?"

"Impossible," said the cynical Xanthippus. "But each generation must scrutinize its government and insist on precepts originally noble, which have been distorted out of exigency. Are you asking for a change in human nature, my son? A man is a hungry beast and thinks only of his stomach and his genitals, and so he must be periodically restrained by objective law."

He looked at the listening Pericles and pushed his tongue in his cheek. "We must struggle all our lives for the triumph of justice. You will remember that we were taught that when the gods removed themselves from habitations with men the goddess, Justice, was the last to leave. She will, no doubt, be the last to return." He smiled.

Sometimes his acrid tongue and his loathing for meek fraud and cruel expediency made him impatient and he lost his caution, and partially trusted friends with whom he had philosophic discussions. This came about when he attended dinners with considerable wine. Then his subtle character led him to imprudent dissertations, in which he only partially believed, himself. He would mock the gods, who were in the service of the priests, and he would mock the government which was only in its own service. He had a love for dialectics and paradoxes and he found humanity risible and was hilarious over its tendency to take itself seriously. This offended many, who pretended to be concerned men, with principles and virtues. They felt that his hard blue eyes, fixed on them, taunted them with their hidden knaveries and their hypocrisy, though in truth Xanthippus was often laughing only at himself.

He would say, "Solon's dream of a republic is the most glorious and godlike of all dreams, when good and intelligent men shall establish just law which will not distinguish between the man of riches and the man of no riches, and bestow liberty and the franchise on all those capable of exercising it. But alas, we have seen for ourselves that the dream of the republic has degenerated into the realities of a chaotic democracy, which oppresses all those who cannot buy it with gold, or with influence. What, then, should replace them? I have heard that benevolent despotisms are the best of all—but where shall we

234

find a benevolent despot who will not succumb to his human nature and become an evil dictator?"

"We must change human nature," the most perverted of his companions would say with a pious expression. "Man is capable of becoming more than man."

At this Xanthippus would laugh without restraint.

His dearest friends wrote discreetly to priests and government that Xanthippus was an impious man who mocked both gods and priests, and despised orderly government. His profane remarks were exaggerated; his tendency to cynic laughter was condemned as the mark of sacrilegiousness, and it was hinted, by reprobates, that he was the most licentious of men. The government began to take an inordinate interest not only in his "convictions" but in his taxes.

No one knew of his despairs except his delightful concubine who would cradle him in her fragrant arms and listen and console him. He would kiss her breast and say, "At the last, my divine one, only love is truth and delight and fulfillment—but even love can be perverted to lust and a desire for rewards. Kiss me. I will delude myself you love me, and that is the saddest delusion of all."

He was a very lonely man. But even at this he would laugh.

As a rich man he incited envy. As a patrician and soldier who had helped to save Greece he was resented by the inferior who had no aristocratic traditions but only pretensions. But as a confident man he dangerously underestimated his enemies and the malice of his friends, for, as he was later to say, "We cynics are the most naive of men. In our hearts we hope men are better than they are and that we, ourselves, will be refuted."

His mistrusted his own Athenians. Though they honored the memory of Solon, and though the tyrants like Pisistratus and Cleisthenes had sometimes actually enforced the Laws of Solon, the Athenians were too capricious and inconstant a people to demand that their rulers obey an unchangeable Constitution, for they suspected what they considered inflexibility even in perfect laws. Still, they cherished the dream of a perfect and noble republic, wherein an impersonal Constitution, immune to the attacks of vicious and greedy men, could be established like marble above the nature of mankind. Xanthippus did not find this a paradox or an inconsistency, as some of his more earnest friends did. "Dreams," he would say, "are often the matrix of the future, and who knows what coming generations may make them a shining reality?

"Considering the heroic laws of a republic which Solon established—and which our people honor but cannot obey—it is strange that Solon ever became an Archon of Athens and was not assassinated," he said to his wife, Agariste, when in a benevolent mood towards her.

But Agariste, whose ancestors had helped to depose the Tyrants, and who actually believed that an Athenian republic existed, was vexed. "What then, lord, do you believe our government is?"

"I should hate to lacerate your tender ears with my opinion, Agariste. But in spite of our boasts that we are a free people—which we are not—we are a slave civilization, though Solon desired to free the slaves. Our slaves and those who do not have the franchise compose the majority of our city-state. We honor Solon by revering him, but we ignore him."

Agariste thought this frivolous. Had not her fathers overcome the Tyrants? Where else in the world did there exist such perfection as the government and the mental climate of Athens? She began to suspect that Xanthippus had no deep respect and love for his city, and that he was no true patriot, and though she knew that men were executed by decree of priests or government for their opinions she was convinced that these were traitors, and that Solon would agree with her if he were alive.

"You are a very intelligent woman," said Xanthippus, who was still feeling benevolent, "but you have not understood one word of what I have said. Do you not revere Solon? Yet one of his convictions was that the influence of women was eternally pernicious, and though I have some disagreement with this at times I often contemplate what he said."

"There are many women who think like men!" exclaimed Agariste.

"Alas, then their genitals are dead," said Xanthippus, and now his benevolence had left him and he also left his wife, and went to his courtesan who received him with smiles of gladness and led him at once to her silken bed and poured wine for him. He looked up into her serene and beautiful face and all at once saw that her hazel eyes were sincere and that she loved him. He held out his hand to her and said, drawing her down beside him and caressing her breast, "Aphrodite was perhaps the wisest of all the gods, for out of love can spring all art and science and poetry and justice, while politics, though engaging the aspirations and philosophies of men, is an exercise in irrelevance in comparison."

Agariste was filled with bitter if silent rage when her husband left her for the arms of a disgraceful woman. She respected Xanthippus and sometimes admired him and was usually subservient to him, and well understood that he was of a distinguished family and a hero to many in Athens, though lately they seemed to forget. In the earlier years of their marriage he had appeared to delight in her intelligence and would converse for hours with her, while stroking her velvet cheek or her pale masses of hair. Yet now he found her tedious.

It was inevitable that Xanthippus come to the attention of both the priests and the government and that they should be extremely interested, for many envied him. Moreover, there were the letters from his discreet friends sadly denouncing him, and some were men of consequence, and had power and riches. Once he had been more discreet but lately, perhaps because of his son and the conversations with that son, he had clarified his own thoughts and had expanded them.

Xanthippus was politely invited to appear before the priests and the Ecclesia for a "consultation," for he was too respected a man to be seized and dragged before them, and he was rich and powerful. It was the intention of some of the priests and the judges merely to rebuke him and restrain him, but others wished his death though they feared him. The hero was not a mere chattering philosopher or fervent teacher, whose fatal disposition would cause little comment, yet that fact made him even the more dangerous.

When Xanthippus received the summons he requested the presence of his wife, and she came from the women's quarters with her two female slaves, joining her husband in the outdoor portico. He held a parchment in his hand and was studying it with an ironical half smile. He glanced up at Agariste and nodded to a chair near him and she sat down with dignity.

Then he said, without looking up, "I have received a summons from the Ecclesia and the Court of Justice, to appear before them tomorrow at noon, to explain certain convictions of mine." He threw the parchment on the marble floor and exclaimed, "Those accursed old priests! Those ignorant judges, fraudulent fools who know nothing but their prejudices! They are as valorous and understanding as a goat."

Agariste turned as white as linen, and her mouth opened on a gasp and terror and outrage blazed in her eyes. Seeing this, Xanthippus was surprised and intrigued, for he had never considered that his wife loved him.

Touched, and seeing that she was trembling, Xanthippus leaned towards her and said, "Do not fear, my love, for my safety and person. I am a match for the sons of Sisyphus, who, like their father, endlessly and futilely insist on thrusting a stone uphill only to have it recoil on them and fall to its source. But they persist in their folly and would remake law in their own image."

Agariste turned even paler, thinking of her slaves who were listening. Xanthippus took her hand with a gentleness she had not known for many years, and for an instant she was moved and tears moistened her haughty eyes. Then she withdrew her hand and folded it with the other on her knee and looked like a marble monument in the hot light of the sun.

"It is incredible, that this should happen to our name!" she said at last.

Xanthippus was taken aback for a moment, then he smiled sardonically to himself, and fixed his hard sparkling eyes on his wife in silence. Her fingers began to move slowly over each other and her long white throat was momentarily convulsed. Light shifted as palms and sycamores threw their fronds and leaf shadows over the white stone of the portico floor. Agariste became more agitated by the moment and stared blankly before her, her thoughts milling desperately. Then Xanthippus said, "Our name? My dear Agariste, there is more at stake than our name. There is my life."

But she continued with her spoken thoughts. "Never has there been a stain on the name of my family! We have lived honorable and noble and blameless lives in the service of our nation. We have been prouder, with reason, than kings. The annals of our history will live forever in the hearts and minds of men. But now there is a stain, an infamy—" .

"I am a very infamous man," said Xanthippus, and poured a goblet of wine for himself on the marble table near him. "I am a scoundrel, a base slave, a criminal. I have cast filth on the name of your family. Of a certainty, I have no family, myself! I am only a worthless soldier, a Helot."

His tone aroused Agariste and infuriated her. She said, "You have no regard for your own name, my husband!"

Xanthippus laughed aloud. He set down his goblet with a thump. "To you, my love, perhaps, yes. To me, no. I love the company of intelligent friends. I love my books, my gardens, my groves of olive trees, my ships. I love feasts and music. I love the morning and the night. I love the warm and scented breasts of desirable women, and I rejoice in their thighs. Their conversation, of course, is tedious, but their bodies are delicious, and for what else was a woman created?"

At this insult Agariste's white face turned dark red with humiliation.

Xanthippus continued. "For these, therefore, I shall fight for my life."

Agariste was no fool. She said, "You must not think, my husband, that I am insensible to your danger. Alas, you must have been indiscreet in wine. No doubt your hetaira must have betrayed you."

"Ah, no," said Xanthippus. "I have always paid my women well, and they are grateful, and when I discarded them I found them more youthful lovers and more virile, and gave them valuable jewels. You may remember the ruby necklace of my mother? I gave that to my hetaira a week ago, in gratitude for her understanding and affection and her concern for me."

Agariste had always lusted for that necklace. Her lips shook and her eyelashes quivered. "You torment me, Xanthippus," she said in a faint voice. "I do not believe much of what you have said, but there is a possibility that I have provoked you to such cruelty. Nevertheless, I think of my name —and your name," she added. "Is there no man of influence whom you could approach in your behalf, so that this shamefulness can pass from you?"

"No, my love," her husband replied. "I will confront the priests and the Court of Justice myself and laugh them down."

Agariste was aghast. "Think of your son, I beg of you, if you do not think of me and our names! A man undefended save by his own voice is lost. You should be too proud to appear before—such."

"Because they are—such," said Xanthippus, "I will confront them with detestation, even if it costs me my life, though I do not propose to surrender that. However, as you have said, death is preferable to infamy, and it would be infamous of me to bow to any decree of the Ecclesia or the judges, who have the taint of freedom about them for all their boasts, base fellows!" He smiled at her with no forgiveness. "You speak of our son. Would he be happy to know his father was a craven and had grovelled like his inferiors? Would you be happy also?"

"No," said Agariste, and for the first time he saw her tears. She covered her face with her long white hands and wept. But he had been too deeply offended and he rose and left her.

He went to his concubine in her beautiful small house which he had given her. Lying in her bed he told her of his predicament. She sat beside him, naked and rosy as Aphrodite newly risen from the sea, her tawny hair thrown back so none of her delights were hidden. Her nipples were like tight rosebuds and her mouth was a warm flame. While she listened gravely her agile mind was busy. Gaia knew a man of formidable influence in Athens, who greatly admired Xanthippus, and for an hour in her bed, unknown to Xanthippus, he would do her bidding and listen to her pleas.

"Tomorrow, at noon?" she murmured. "Then, I must hasten and pray in the temple of Pallas Athene who is all wisdom and protects the wise, and surely you are wise, my Xanthippus."

Xanthippus loved Gaia more dearly than he knew, and he was naturally indulgent towards women. So he shortly left her so she could go to the temple. He knew that by this time his dear friends would know of his summons and so he must avoid them to save both himself and them from embarrassment. He restlessly went to his groves of olive trees. After he had departed Gaia summoned one of her slaves and sent him with a message to the man who ardently desired her. She bathed in scented water and slaves rubbed her body with perfumed oils and brushed her hair until it shone like an autumn leaf in the sun. She arrayed herself in a soft blue peplos with one arm exposed, on which she fastened a bracelet which her heretofore disappointed suitor had sent her nestled in a bower of lilacs. She felt no pang of sacrifice or aversion. Men were men, and every man offered pleasure and took it with joy and gratitude, and she knew well how to please and all the arts of love. She pondered on which art he particularly liked, and which posture. She smiled. She loved Xanthippus, and this excursion would do him no harm but much good, and he would never know. She was a dexterous woman. She prepared to enjoy herself also, for a passive woman was no real lover. Slaves changed the silken sheets of her bed and sprayed perfume about her room and she studied her perfect body contemplatively. She would even endure the perversion of flogging for Xanthippus. She prayed that the man who would visit her would prefer more exotic and tender delights. However, a woman never knew a man until she had lain with him, for all a man's childlike simplicity. Or, she mused, was it really a brutish simplicity? No matter. She rubbed more scent on her loins and commanded a repast in the atrium when her visitor arrived. Her kitchen was famous.

"Ah, Athene," she said aloud, "you are the goddess of wisdom, sprung from the brow of Zeus in full apparel. But

Aphrodite is the most potent of all the gods, and everything that lives bows before her."

Xanthippus, who also admired Gaia's mind, for she had been well trained in that also, had given her a small alabaster statue of Athene Parthenos. She had it moved from her bedside and an indecent statue of Aphrodite and Adonis substituted. She smiled at the entwined lovers. She would ask no jewels; she would ask only for the life of Xanthippus. Later, if Teos desired a permanent arrangement, she would deal with that gracefully.

Xanthippus went to the Court of Justice on the Pnyx which was halfway up the acropolis. He disdained his litter and his chariot, and travelled on foot unattended. Consequently he was dusty, his feet stained and his garments disheveled when he arrived. Only his subtle countenance was serene and clear, and his carefully arranged hyacinthine locks. He wore no jewelry. He might have been a slave except for his face and his high head as he entered the court. He was smiling faintly as if remembering a jest.

The Ecclesia and the priests were waiting for him in a semi-circle in a small circular room of brown and white marble. They sat severely and solemnly in their chairs. The priests contemplated their clasped hands which lay on their knees, and they appeared to pray for wisdom and enlightenment. The judges appeared more brisk and portentous. All wore white robes, like statues. The noon sun fell in thin shafts from high small windows, and so the room was partly dim and the mosaics on the floor—white, rose and blue and yellow—were almost obscured. A large statue of blindfolded Justice with her scales stood behind the seated men and sunlight lay on her face and breast, though the rest was in shadow. Along one rounded wall was a row of marble benches for advocates and other interested men. Only two sat there today, and one was Zeno and one was Teos, one of the great dissolute citizens of Athens.

Soldiers stood at the bronze doors and one stood at the end of the row of priests and judges, and another stood at the other end. They were armed and armored and looked like still images, their eyes fixed ahead.

No one spoke when Xanthippus entered except for a robed man near the bronze double doors who announced in a voice like Nemesis: "The noble lord, Xanthippus, enters to be judged." Xanthippus paused for a moment for he recognized Zeno and Teos, and his black brows lifted. A philosopher and a lascivious man of Athens were all who cared enough for his fate to appear in his behalf, or at least to listen! His faint smile widened. None was so ineffective as a philosopher, and Teos, notorious for his fat living and his women and his gaiety and wealth and his lack of interest in politics, was certainly the strangest of advocates for an accused man!

Xanthippus was only casually acquainted with Teos, for they had nothing in common. They met occasionally in the houses of mutual friends, but Teos' light conversation, his elaborate attitude of ignorance of weighty matters and poetry and the arts of war, his refusal to engage in serious discussions and his obvious boredom with them, his sometimes crude jests, his flippant manner and his way of laughing boisterously at an exquisite epigram and shaking his head at gravity and his light dismissal of all injustices and his unattachments to anyone at all had sometimes offended Xanthippus who thought him light-minded and a fool and a rascal—for it was well known that Teos used bribery to manipulate government to grant his requests. He was no soldier, betrayed no concern for the fate of Athens, was good-natured to the point of ridiculousness, and appeared to prefer the company of low fellows, and even freedmen, to his peers, and could often be found drinking foul wine in dirty and crowded taverns among thieves and scoundrels from the waterfront and from filthy alleys of the city. Among such he was the merriest of companions, and when reproached by his friends for his company would say, "I have found more reality and more laughter among scoundrels than in your august presences, my dears."

He was a man of Xanthippus' age, handsome, slender, tall, and, to the soberer citizens of Athens, always disgustingly perfumed and manicured. Though he was no longer young his round face was as unlined as a boy's, with jovial and plump features and mirthful sparkling eyes and a very red full mouth like a woman's. His expression was alert and cheerful, as if he found life the gayest of experiences—which he did—and was constantly awaiting new jokes and new entertainments with an air of joyous expectation. His face never became blank or dull or sullen except when a companion uttered words of wisdom or an abstruse theory.

He wore the most elegant of clothing and was even known to affect the Egyptian fashion of elaborate gold and jeweled necklaces and his style of living in his ornate house was sybaritic and unconventional, and always filled with coarse jesting voices and shouts of laughter, and, of course, the most ribald of music. Unlike his friends, he had no library, and never wished for solitude and could not endure it, and was always surrounded by companions of his own libidinous mind and with his own taste in jokes and amusements and women. His round lively head wore an aureole of crisp black curls which sprang from his skull with seemingly an active life of their own.

He bored Xanthippus, who usually avoided him. "He is a perpetual youth," Xanthippus would say, "with desires like a satyr and the discriminations of the basest of slaves and the intelligence of a fish." Sometimes he had found himself impatiently disliking this happiest of men who never engaged in weighty matters and found existence without a purpose and who rejected any responsibility except for his own enjoyment. "There is a time for everything," Xanthippus would say, "and there is a time to be a fool, but not always." Xanthippus, who was genial enough himself, and often found life ridiculous and without an object, and liked a jest as well as any other man, was frequently angered that Teos seemed to find him heavy and ponderous and without humor. In fact, the sort of man he, Xanthippus, despised himself.

Yet here Teos, the irresponsible, the flagrant, the reprobate, the fool, the man without imagination or subtlety and who knew nothing of poetry or the intricacies of the law, sat with a profound philosopher like Zeno as advocate of Xanthippus! There was something humorous in the siuation, Xanthippus told himself, but he could not as yet discern it. Certainly Teos was no close friend of his and had never found his company entertaining or desirable. As for Zeno, he was suspected by the very priests and judges before whom he sat in silent dignity—and in his unimpressive appearance.

"Where is your advocate, lord?" asked one of the judges, a severe man of massive countenance and cold eyes.

Xanthippus stood before them, and all at once he wanted to laugh. He bowed to the lonely marble bench where sat Zeno and Teos. "These are my advocates," he said, and his neat black beard twitched. Three of the most important judges and priests studiously examined the parchments before them and their faces were sinister and momentous. They thought of their heavy purses.

"This is most irregular," said one of the lesser priests.

"The majority of things in this world are so," said Xanthippus.

He hated zealots, for they were the most stupid and cruel of men and would condemn a man who even slightly disagreed with them and invariably lusted for the blood of dissenters. They boasted of their love for tolerance, and asserted they would fight to the death for it, yet they were more intolerant than a mad bull who was provoked. They were the Helots of virtue, while at the same time being the most unvirtuous of men in aspects of the important affairs of life.

He looked at Teos again and Teos was smiling happily and playing with his Egyptian necklace. As for Zeno, he was full of distress and anxiety, and kept moistening his lips and twisting his philosopher's hands.

Someone cleared his throat noisily. A priest lifted a parchment.

"Lord, Xanthippus," he said, "you are accused of impiety and a disrespect for government and its just decisions. It is alleged that you do not believe in the gods and have no regard for their sanctity." He looked at his fellow priests. "For this, death is the only punishment. For, who has protected Athens and all of Greece but the gods, especially Athene Parthenos, our patroness? You are accused of jesting at her virginity and making lewd implications concerning it."

Again Xanthippus could not repress himself. He raised a long thin hand. "Surely that is a lie," he said in his pleasant voice. "Athene does not have a lovely countenance and is not alluring, for wisdom is forbidding and is not seductive in the least. What man desires wisdom above all things? I have yet to find such a man. Men prefer the thighs of women to any dissertation of philosophy or any theory—except if they are incapable. Wisdom, in short, is the refuge of impotence."

Even the bribed judges and priests could not prevent themselves from gasping.

One said in a hoarse voice, "You do not believe in the gods, lord?"

Xanthippus was beginning to enjoy himself, though it was a reckless and deadly game. He spread out his hands eloquently.

"Only a fool does not believe in something greater than man, for do not the stars obey inscrutable laws, and the sun and the moon? Who has laid down this law and this ineffable order? Men? But men are helpless insects, and have no knowledge of why they are here and what is their ultimate fate. Can they order, these insignificants, the wheeling of constellations and the Pleiades? What decree of man can forbid the rising of the sun and the illumination of the heavens? Who ordains the tides, and the seasons? Can any man demand of the mountains, 'Remove yourselves'? Can a man say to the sea, 'Retreat'? Who can order the fruitfulness of the olive trees and the fields and the palms? Who has given man awareness and harnessed the winds? Has any judge forbidden a volcano to explode, or a tempest not to disturb the waters? The moon changes by law, yet no body of men can regulate the phases of her. It is impudent of men to believe themselves all-powerful and in control of their merest existence."

Xanthippus had spoken with an eloquence and sudden passion which amazed even himself, and Zeno stared at him incredulously and for once Teos looked grave.

A priest said in a severe voice, "But it is alleged that you have jested at the very divinity which you now defend."

Zeno rose in his small stature and lifted his hands and all looked at him, as if startled that he was present.

"A wise man jests at the impertinence of ignorant men who would tear down the gods to their own meager level and make them equal to themselves or even less."

He looked at them and his brilliant eyes seemed to awaken light in the room and held the attention of everyone:

"Who has defined the attributes of Divinity or guessed at His nature? Who knows what is impiety to Him, or piety? A humble man who delights in the light of the sun or the moon and reverences life and marvels at the mystery of his being— though he names no gods—is surely more loved by Deity and more cherished than a sophisticated man who alleges he knows the attributes of Divinity and His nature and pompously demands that other men believe in his tiny concepts. It is through our lack of knowledge that we approach God, and through our ignorance that we begin our understanding. God has His laws, and only in humility can we perceive them, and only dimly."

"You do not believe that the gods have laid down a system of laws for the behavior and the obedience of men, Zeno of Elea?" asked one of the priests.

Zeno smiled. "I am not being judged," he replied. "But I will reply to your question, lord. We can find the will of God only through prayer and in solitude and in meditation. We can find His laws in the laws of nature, which He has ordained. What governs the humblest grain of sand or the merest sheaf of wheat also governs man. The law is of one piece. The suns obey Him and know His laws. Let us reflect on them. For law and order are of the nature of God, and are open to the innocent eyes of children and are confused and elaborated upon and made obscure only by the perverted sophistries of men."

He smiled at the priests and the judges. "My friend, Xanthippus, has been accused of impiety. But the true sacrilege is the making of God in the likeness and image of man and attributing to Him all the passions and errors of mankind, and all the savagery, and believing that we can comprehend Him in the slightest. Of this crime Xanthippus is innocent. Who among you, sires, is competent to say that he knows anything about the Unknowable? Xanthippus has repeatedly asserted that this is beyond our competence, and who can deny it in truth? To differ with this truth is to be truly impious."

"The gods have given us the capacity to comprehend them," said one of the priests. "Do you deny that, Zeno of Elea?"

"Who has said we can comprehend them?" asked Zeno. "The gods, themselves? No. Only arrogant men have declared that, men without intelligence."

He sat down, looked deeply at the silent priests and said in his sonorous voice, "Who among you dares to declare that he knows the attributes of the Godhead and is acquainted with His nature? Who dares to commit that blasphemy before the face of this august assemblage?"

The oldest of the judges, and the one most heavily bribed by Teos, was becoming impatient, thinking of the noontide meal which he had missed and for which he yearned. He pushed aside his parchment and said, "Zeno of Elea has put it cleverly and with precision. We are not presumptuous men; we would be presumptuous indeed to hold a dialogue concerning the gods with Xanthippus, who knows no more than we."

Xanthippus bowed and bent his head mockingly. "It is perhaps merciful that we are all ignorant men, for to know even a portion of the truth would be death to us."

But one of the judges, who had not been bribed, said, "There is the matter of insolence towards the law. I have here an accusation of an anonymous friend of the court to the effect that Xanthippus has declared his disrespect and ridicule of our democracy, and that he has not paid his just taxes." He glared at Xanthippus, for he hated the other's aristocracy and fame and riches. "Answer, lord," he continued. "What is your contention against the liberty you enjoy under your government, laid down by Solon?"

Xanthippus had a witty reply to this but for once he held his tongue. He assumed a thoughtful expression, but his thin and delicate face flushed with the anger he was repressing. He raised his eyebrows. "Are you asking me to define liberty, sire?" he asked.

The judge said, "That is my implication."

Xanthippus looked at him and his blue eyes became like bright and polished stone. "What is liberty? The right of a man to demand that his government let him be and refrain from meddling with his private affairs and his life, and regulating his conduct which offends no one nor interferes with the rights of his fellows. The right of a man to own property and to pay taxes upon it for the good of the commonweal and the protection of his property and his country from internal and external enemies. The right of a man to live in peace with himself and his neighbors and to enjoy the fruit of his hands and his intelligence. The right of a man to be a man, and to live unfettered by paternalism and the officiousness of petty bureaucrats. In short, the right not to be a slave. These are simple and honest rights. Anything more is oppression."

"You believe your government does not rise to these expectations?" asked one of the judges.

Xanthippus did not answer for a moment. Then he said in the softest voice, "Noble judge, do you believe our government rises to these expectations?"

The man shifted his eyes then thundered, "That is not only my belief but my knowledge!"

"Sire," said Xanthippus, "who am I, a mere soldier who offered his life for his country and have served it with blood and honor, to dispute you, who were never a soldier but instead a member of a more honorable profession? As for your knowledge, sire, I plead ignorance of it."

Teos chuckled aloud, and the priests and the judges glanced at each other, some with rage and frustration and some with only half-hidden amusement.

Then Xanthippus, the intrepid and the sophisticated, lost his precarious temper.

"You speak of Solon!" he cried. "But Solon envisioned a republic of just laws, under which all men would be free, and free, above all, from capricious and rapacious government. A nation where men could openly speak their dissent and plead for redress of wrongs—the wrongs of government against its people. We do not have such a republic, gentlemen. We do not have a republic at all. We have a degenerate democracy, the rule of the witless mob who have bellies but no minds. Under this condition we can be absolutely certain of but one thing: The world is ruled by fools, and this has always been and will be, for fools presume wisdom by their very overwhelming numbers, and what politician or judge will dispute numbers? You, gentlemen?"

Teos groaned inwardly. Now this Xanthippus had spoken

his death sentence. Those whom Teos had bribed also groaned inwardly. Once said sternly, "You differentiate between a republic and a democracy, Xanthippus? Are they not one and the same?"

"No," said Xanthippus with quiet emphasis. "One is representative government. The other is government by chaos. Which, gentlemen, do we have in Athens today?"

The priests and the judges studied their parchments. They had no reverence for a brave man who was also a notable soldier, and they knew that such as Xanthippus was dangerous to their very existence. Still, many feared him, and the others feared that Teos would ask for the return of his rich bribes. After a long silence a judge cleared his throat portentously and gave Xanthippus an ominous look.

"It is alleged that you have cheated on your taxes, Xanthippus. What is your reply to this?"

Xanthippus laughed softly. "Where is my accuser, sire? Bring him forth and let his records be examined with mine, and I will wager my life that drachma for drachma I have been more honest than he."

When they did not answer he added, "Or, is justice dead and not merely blind? Do we have government by vicious informers or government by impartial judgments?"

Again when they did not answer immediately, he said, "But only you can reply to that. That, too, is beyond my competence as a mere soldier."

The heaviest bribed judge said with eagerness, "Then, Xanthippus, you plead incompetence both as to the nature of divinity and the nature of law?"

Xanthippus bowed, "Sire," he said, "I am the most incompetent man present, and possibly the most ignorant, if that is possible."

The judge said with haste, "Your humility is worthy of you, Xanthippus, and is duly noted by the Ecclesia and this court and therefore the severity of your fate will be mitigated." He looked furtively at Teos who was slightly frowning. Teos had asked that at the most that Xanthippus be ostracized until he, Teos, had tired of the delightful hetaira, Gaia. In memory he tasted her lips again and smelled her perfume and remembered her embraces.

Seeing the frown of Teos the judge spoke with even more haste. "Therefore, it is the judgment of this court, and the Ecclesia, that you be ostracized from Athens until we, in our mercy, are inclined to recall you. We are not insensible to your fame, Xanthippus, which was justly earned, nor is your city ungrateful. You are not guiltless, and this you know in your heart—though your guilt was caused by ignorance and incompetence. Be thankful that you live under a just and benign democracy, which takes no vengeance on its—incompetent—enemies, who speak not from malice but from benightedness."

At this Xanthippus started to laugh aloud, but was seized quickly by both arms by Zeno and Teos, who led him towards the door. He threw off his friends on the marble steps and said to them with hilarity, "I have been saved by a philosopher and—" He halted and stared at Teos with sudden amazement. "And Teos. Why were you there, Teos, you who never interested yourself either in religion or justice?"

Teos smiled with the utmost cheerfulness. "Am I not your beloved friend, Xanthippus? Have I not always admired you?"

"No," said Xanthippus.

Teos took his arm again with a fond look. "My litter awaits. Permit me the honor of taking you to your house."

When Xanthippus arrived at his house he sent for his wife, gazed at her without emotion and with only indifference, and said, "I have been ostracized for an indeterminate period, but have not been deprived of any of my substance nor will I be imprisoned, or killed."

Agariste wept, but he did not stay to hear her protestations or her laments. He went to Gaia who received him with her customary joy and he was consoled in her warm round arms and with her kisses. He did not know why, but even as she smiled tears ran down her rosy cheeks.

From his villa on Cyprus he wrote to his son, Pericles:

"Above all things a man must love not only his own liberty but the liberty of others, or he is less than a man. True, liberty is an abstraction but is this not true of all perfect things? We must, however, strive towards it though never can we fully attain it. It is our noblest duty to love all that is perfect, for perfection is the Shadow of God and we may, at our will and desire, rest in it, though never seeing That which casts it."

Pericles was astonished at reading this from his urbane and mocking father, who had never revered the gods but had questioned their existence with laughter. He was deeply touched.

CHAPTER 5

Though Agariste believed that her son was all perfection, and even Xanthippus had feared that Pericles had too many virtues, Zeno suspected that the youth was more complex and intricate of character than was apparent. He had detected flashes in Pericles' eyes of impatience, contempt, hostility and intolerance on occasion, and once or twice there had been a gleam of amused brutality. Zeno did not admire perfection in humanity, which would then render it featureless and lifeless and without color, but he did admire Pericles' ability to control his tongue if not the sudden and unpleasant vivacity of his eyes when stirred to some less than admirable emotion. Then the pallor of his eyes was ignited to the whiteness of a vehement flame, and betrayed a capacity for rage and even fury.

Pericles was widely admired among the youths of his acquaintance, and by their parents, yet there was a remoteness about him which rejected intimacy while inspiring reverence in others and a desire to approach him nearer, a desire invariably frustrated. There was a Tantalus quality in his nature. When he left his fencing school, which was conducted by the expert freedman, Chilio, he never appeared anxious to have companions on his walk to his father's house, yet he was always surrounded by eager and fawning companions who often went out of their way to accompany him.

Finally Zeno came to the dismaying—to him—conclusion that Pericles possessed that mysterious gift of the gods: the power to move men's hearts as well as their minds, and to fire their imagination and their unpredictable emotions, which could be destructive.

Alas, Zeno would think, he has the attributes of a politician, and, as it is said, politicians are not born, they are excreted.

There was, in the fencing school of Chilio, a youth of sixteen who was scorned and ridiculed even by the master, though the youth was of a distinguished house and his father was a great soldier. His name was Ichthus, which meant fish, and this alone would have aroused hilarity among cruel youth. He was ashamed of the name, himself, but his mother, who claimed to be dedicated to Poseidon, and hinted that she had, as a maiden, been seduced by him, had insisted on the name. Moreover his character was gentle and elusive, and his movements flowing, and he lived in an aura of self-deprecation for he was very modest and not athletic of body. He absorbed learning like moss absorbing rain, and appeared to grow greener and fresher with every intellectual dew falling upon him, a faculty which did not endear him to his more robust fellows. Pericles, though he scorned the youth, never engaged in baiting him or laughing at him, but would watch him at a removed distance with an inexplicable expression, at once wondering and dismissing.

Ichthus was as tall as Pericles, who was taller than his fellows, and very slender and bony, and his skin had a peculiar pallid transparency which seemed to cover a body containing no blood. This gave him the appearance of chronic illness, for even his lips had no warm tint. His nose was overly large and emaciated and had a curious way—to the risibility of his mates—of turning bright pink at the tip when he was excited over a theory or a particularly interesting academic hypothesis. His very light brown eyes were almost completely round, and started hugely when he was confronted by a novel thought or word, and were lashless. His wide flat mouth was tremulous and betrayed too much sensibility. He stammered and would sometimes become speechless with shy fear of those about him. His thin retreating chin was not notable. His tutors and his mother loved him, and his father despised him as a weakling. Besides having tutors, he attended the same academe as Pericles. It was only his skill at fencing, which he detested, that brought him any measure of toleration from his mates. He had a high shaking voice like an adolescent girl's, which aroused mirth when he spoke quickly, and his light brown hair was straight and dull and blew in the wind, for it was very fine. He loped rather than walked and his garments never fitted him flatteringly.

He and Pericles were well matched as excellent swordsmen, and often he won a match. He would break into Pericles' polite congratulations with abject apologies and insistence that he was not the man Pericles was and his winning had only been an accident or an attack of preoccupation on the part of his antagonist. Pericles would leave him impatiently in the midst of his expostulations, Ichthus staring helplessly after him, hardly hearing the laughter of those who had watched the match.

There were times when Pericles felt a slight pity for Ichthus, and when the latter was beset too hard by his mates Pericles would interfere with a quiet word or a quelling glance. Sometimes the pity rose to the point of anger and protectiveness, which also annoyed Pericles. Ichthus was nothing to him, he would remind himself. He had no admiration for him except for his learning and his intelligence. When occasionally he found himself followed meekly at a distance by Ichthus, Pericles' vexation would heighten to the point of urging him to a cruel word, which he usually suppressed. Ichthus is a poor thing, the fifteen-year-old Pericles would think. Nevertheless, he has a right to an existence without harassment, as all men have, though his ridiculous name suits him well.

One day Pericles stayed later at his academe to discuss a point of logic with his teacher, with which he hoped to confound Zeno that night. He wished to prove that validity and truth have not much in common, and that validity could often be a sophistry, while truth was granite and not merely an exercise in syllogisms. His teacher was annoyed, being an academician and a pedagogue, but he had great respect for Pericles and his family. He conceded a point, without conviction, and the suddenly bored Pericles turned away. He then saw Ichthus at his bench writing swiftly on his parchment with a stabbing pen, and for once he was curious about the youth and his air of intense inner excitement. He strolled, in all his marble beauty, to the bench and looked over Ichthus' shoulder, and the other youth seemed unaware of his presence.

Ichthus had written in wild rushing words:

> *"O You Who are nameless, but gather all Names!*
> *The morning is Your mantle, the sunset Your heart,*
> *The winds live in Your garments and fire attends*
> *You,*
> *You possess no thrones but You are King of Thrones.*
> *The universes are Your habitations though You*
> *have no altars,*
> *You are the life, the sun, the core of flame*
> *creating stars.*
> *The gods adore You, but men are unaware of*
> *Your Being.*
>
> *Naught endures, not even breath or worlds, without*
> *Your knowledge,*
> *It is You Who alone know that the duration of a*
> *day-fly is equal*
> *To a mountain's, for time lives not with You,*
> *Who are Reality.*
> *When will You reveal Your Face to all men, and*
> *in thunder*

*Proclaim, "I am He Who was and is and eternally
shall be?
There was none before Me and none else."*

It is a poor poem, thought Pericles, but it is written with passion and adoration. What god does he address? Pericles smiled a little. Then Ichthus became aware of his presence and the tip of his nose flushed into scarlet and his eyes fled in confusion.

"I did not know you were a poet," said Pericles.

Ichthus, overcome by the condescension of Pericles, fell to stammering. "It—it is not a poem, Pericles. It is—it is only a —prayer."

"To whom?"

Ichthus' large brown eyes suddenly became ardent as if he had looked upon a vision. "To the Unknown God," he murmured.

"But that embraces them all," said Pericles, highly diverted.

Ichthus looked miserable and embarrassed, yet he had a certain tenacity of character. He shook his head. "There is but one God, the Unknown God, Who has a small altar in the temple of Zeus, inscribed to Him. It is waiting."

"For what, Ichthus?"

Ichthus' head dropped even lower. "I have heard a priest say for the day of revelation, when all men shall know Him, the Unknown God, and know there is none else."

"Monotheism is not a new religious concept," said Pericles, "though not popular with our priests. They call it a foreign aberration, for the Egyptians invented it centuries ago."

Ichthus was silent. Pericles waited. Then Ichthus whispered, "I adore Him. He invades my dreams, my thoughts, my life. I see His thumbprint in the sky at sunset. I hear His voice in thunder and wind and the rushing of rivers. I see His face reflected in the sea and carved in the clouds. The mountains tremble at His step, the earth shakes at His passing." He folded his lean hands together as if praying, and Pericles impatiently suspected he was.

"The priests would consider that a heresy," said Pericles.

"They are blind and evil men," replied Ichthus, with unusual emphasis.

Pericles glanced hastily at the teacher behind his desk, then said in a low voice, "I did not know you had such a dangerous tongue, Ichthus, and such dangerous thoughts. Keep them both to yourself." He hesitated. He did not know what made him touch Ichthus lightly on the shoulder before he walked away.

On the way to his father's house he began to muse on what Ichthus had said. He and Zeno had often discussed the injustice and indecency of priests and governments who would endure no opinion but their own, and persecuted the man who differed as a blasphemer or a danger to law and order. Pericles considered his father, and his white forehead tightened with anger. He then considered Ichthus and was astonished at the vehemence the mild and retreating youth had displayed. There is more there, thought Pericles, than we know of, and it is possible he is not a worthless thing after all. For the first time in his short confident life Pericles reflected that many judgments and opinions he, himself, held might well be open to honest scrutiny. Ah, but that would create bewilderment, distraction, and ultimately would paralyse a man! He had to be adamantine about his convictions even if some were manifestly absurd and false, and at this thought Pericles laughed aloud.

As he had delayed, his usual servile companions had left for their homes. Moreover it was a blustering day full of gray clouds so low they even obscured the top of the acropolis, and rain that resembled, in its stinging, the prickle of little shards of glass. It was near the time of the celebration of Chronos, and flakes of wet snow mingled with the rain. The silvery earth was ashen and ran with tiny black rivulets of water like dark veins. Lanterns were being lighted in the porticoes of houses, and lamps glimmered through windows, though it was still early afternoon. The wind clamored in pine and cypress and there was a thrumming sound in the bitter air. The hills were dim purple and imitated a giant reclining woman.

Pericles wrapped his warm woollen cloak about him tightly and pulled the cowl of it over his tall head. There were few abroad and those mostly in litters carried by shivering and running slaves or in covered chariots. Pericles began the descent down the hill from the school to begin the ascent to his father's house. Struggling with the gale he did not see that Ichthus, full of rapture that Pericles had condescended to him, and alight with love, was following him helplessly like a guarding slave. Pericles walked rapidly but Ichthus, with his long legs and light body, had no difficulty in keeping pace with him, though he lingered some distance behind, fearful of Pericles' displeasure at discovering him and not wishing to intrude on someone he regarded almost as a deity.

Athens lay below and the Agora also, crowded and beginning to shine with yellow lights as with stars. Pericles began the ascent to his father's house. He came upon a grove of dark cypresses, towering like spires and clustered together. He was almost past them when a large man, hooded and wrapped in his cloak, fell upon him with upraised dagger which glittered wanly in the dim light.

"Die, son of Xanthippus, traitor!" he shouted hoarsely. Pericles was athletic and agile, and he dodged the blow, springing to one side, the hood falling from his face and so exposing it to wind and rain. The man was much taller than he, and stronger, and his features were hidden, yet Pericles had the impression of ferocity and hate and swarthiness. In an instant he concluded that his best defense was flight and he was fast of foot. But the man was faster and powerful, and he seized Pericles by the hair and again raised his dagger.

I am lost, thought the youth, but though he was terror-stricken he began to fight for his life. He seized the upraised wrist with its weapon and clung to it with both hands. The man swung him off his feet like a monkey clinging to a branch and tried to dash him to the ground. Pericles curled up his legs, swinging helplessly but with determination. He tried to shout for help, but the wind bore away his voice. His feet scraped the ground and his knees were abraded by stones, yet all he knew was the screaming of his heart and the necessity to hold the murderous arm. In the meantime the assassin was belaboring him with the fist of his left hand over the head and the back, and blood spurted from Pericles' nose and from his forehead into his eyes.

Then suddenly he was dropped and fell heavily to the ground and he heard a cursing and a howling, muffled. Rising to his hands and knees he stared upwards, disbelieving. Ichthus danced near him. He had stripped off his big woollen cloak and had thrown it over the attacker's head and shoulders and body, and had drawn it tightly, holding it with one hand while with the other he was enthusiastically stabbing the stranger with his own drawn dagger through the folds of the garment. Ichthus' long tunic fluttered about him like the tunic of a dancer, and his long thin legs were active and swift. He resembled an emaciated Pan. All this Pericles saw in an instant or two. He pushed himself to his feet, drew his dagger and rushed upon his assailant also, stabbing recklessly and with cold rage.

The man sought to save himself, but the two youths were more than equal even to him, and he was blinded and smothered by the cloak. Frantically he kicked at the two he could not see, and blood ran down his legs. He began to weaken from the many wounds, one near his heart, and he groaned even as he struggled. Finally he reared upwards like a dying horse, and fell heavily to the earth, where he writhed for a few moments then lay still on his back.

The two youths stood over him, panting, their bloody daggers in their hands. They stared at him. They wiped the sweat from their brows with the back of their left hands. Their breath whistled shrilly. Then Pericles bent and pushed aside Ichthus' cloak and lifted the cowl of the murderer. The man was a complete stranger, with a black beard.

"He is dead," said the gentle Ichthus in a high and exultant voice, and he kicked the fallen man in the side.

"I do not know him," said Pericles. He could hardly speak from exhaustion and his breath was still fast. He watched Ichthus pull his stained cloak from under the man and wrap himself in it. Then Ichthus looked at Pericles and said, in a stammer, "You—you—are not injured, Pericles? Perhaps I hesitated a moment too long, and if so, forgive me."

Pericles heard this with incredulousness then began to laugh wildly and in short gasps. He flung his arms about Ichthus and staggered against his breast, for he felt weak and his head was whirling. Ichthus held him closely, and Pericles' head fell on his savior's shoulder and they stood like this until Pericles' heart slowed its agonized thumping. He stood in the circle of Ichthus' arms like a child against the chest of his rescuing father. At moments he was still convulsed with hysterical mirth at what Ichthus had said: "Perhaps I hesitated a moment too long, and if so, forgive me."

As for Ichthus, he was filled with delight and contentment and he wished he could remain like this, supporting Pericles, forever.

Pericles began to weep both with laughter and relief, and he removed himself from Ichthus' grasp, then embraced him, kissing him on each cheek. "You saved my life," he said. "For that, I am always, into eternity, grateful, my dear Ichthus."

"It was nothing," said Ichthus, his heart bounding with joy.

"Then it follows that my life was nothing," said Pericles with wryness. Seeing then that Ichthus was abashed and uncertain at his words, he embraced him again.

A city guard appeared out of the swirling storm with drawn sword, shouting. He seized Ichthus by the shoulder roughly, and Pericles said in a weak voice, "He rescued me from this unknown vagabond and thief and murderer, who attacked me, doubtless for my purse. He is my schoolmate, and I am Pericles, son of Xanthippus."

The suddenly craven guard then insisted that he accompany Pericles home. Instinctively, though he did not know Ichthus, he ignored him as always did others, and as if he had assumed the helmet dipped in the waters of Lethe, which makes men invisible. Ichthus stood aside shyly, accustomed to this treatment, and when Pericles looked over his shoulder and begged him to accompany him to his father's house Ichthus dumbly shook his head, and to save himself from further embarrassment he loped away as lightly as he had approached. Pericles watched him go, with wonder, affection and gratitude, and he said to the guard, "That is the bravest man I ever knew, and I owe him what I am and whatever I shall be."

He told his mother Agariste about the episode, and when she had recovered from her fright and indignation and anxiety, she said, "You would not have a slave accompany you, my son, as I wished!"

"I am no child," said Pericles with impatience. He was vexed that his mother had not yet expressed gratefulness to Ichthus. He said, "Nor is Ichthus," with meaning.

Agariste was in her turn impatient and she waved her long white hand dismissingly. "What else could he do but what he did for the son of Xanthippus and Agariste?"

Pericles stared at her, his pale eyes shining with hard wonderment in the lamplight. "He could have fled, for he put himself in the grasp of death also. But he did not flee. I know Ichthus. He would have saved anyone unjustly attacked, who was about to be murdered, for never was there a soul so filled with courage and kindness."

Agariste shook her wheat-colored locks, denying. "Doubtless he has courage, but you are the son of your parents and your illustrious ancestors, and though Ichthus is of a house not too unknown, he cannot compare with you. He helped to rescue you because you are what you are, my son, and hopes for glory and some future recompense."

"Does a man offer his life only for those?" asked Pericles, with contempt. He still stared at his mother. Was she really stupid under all her pretensions and her learning? Pericles pursed his lips as he thought, then turned on his heel and went to his own quarters, much perturbed. Even aristocrats, he reflected, could be base of soul and mean and full of laughable egotism.

It was a lesson he was never to forget. Under its influence he approached his companions quietly the next day and informed them that they must cease their baiting and ridicule of Ichthus, that the latter was under his protection, and that they were to honor him for his selflessness and bravery. They were astonished. Some were surly and resentful. For it came hard to them to realize that one so insignificant and so absurd as Ichthus, and so unlike themselves, could possibly possess any worth at all. Seeing this, Pericles was amused in spite of his outward sternness and resolution. He was beginning to find mankind incomprehensible when it was not dangerous.

Among those who walked with Pericles on his way home Ichthus was now the only one permitted to walk at his side. Pericles began to listen to the soft and hesitating words of Ichthus, presented to him humbly as if they were only field flowers offered a deity. Once Pericles said to Zeno, "You have taught me more than anyone else, my dear teacher, but there was one thing you did not teach me: How joyful it is to offer one's life for a friend, a friend who did not deserve that offering."

Out of his gratitude was born his appreciation of a tender and noble soul, and an intellect as shining as the reflection of silver. Later he was to say, "I have many of great spirit and mind who surround me like laurel leaves, and serve me and counsel me, but none are like Ichthus."

Ichthus wrote a little poem to Pericles which was not found until after the death of Ichthus:

> How fair and gracious is Pericles, son of Xanthippus!
> His condescensions are warmer than the sun, sweeter
> Than the light of Artemis. His soul is resplendent
> As is his face, and his heart is wrought of courage.
> Athens shall revere her son, and the ages will bless him.

When it was given to Pericles he hid his face in his hands and could only murmur, "Alas, alas, it is I who am nothing, and not Ichthus."

CHAPTER 6

Agariste said to her son with that haughty sternness which she had adopted towards him during the past years, for she feared that he found her less than interesting since the death of Xanthippus: "You are of an age to marry and beget sons in your father's memory."

Pericles was invariably kind and courteous to his mother

but he no longer took her seriously. "Alas," he said, "I might beget only daughters."

Agariste refused to recognize this lightness and said, "I have in mind my beloved niece, Dejanira."

Pericles did not have to pretend disbelief and aversion. "Dejanira! The widow of Hipponicus? She is older than I. She is at least twenty-six, and has a son, Callias—"

"Surnamed 'The Rich,' " said Agariste. "Riches are not to be despised, for all we are aristocrats."

They were sitting in the outdoor portico which overlooked Athens floating in the warm rosy light of approaching sunset. The distant hills were jade and lavender and some were silvery, and held Athens as in an enameled bowl.

"You are jesting, my mother," said Pericles who was clad only in a short tunic because of the heat. He crossed his long white legs and surveyed his mother with what he hoped was indulgent affection. "Not only is Dejanira older than I, a widow with a son, but she is stupid and ugly, short and fat, and has a face like a pouting sow. Her voice is like the string of a lyre which is out of tune, shrill and twanging, and to hear her speak is an assault on the ears. Certainly you are jesting."

Agariste's face, still severely beautiful and august, flushed with anger. "You prefer your hetaira, that ignoble and shameless woman who is a physician?"

"She is at least intelligent and lovely to behold, my Helena, and she is my own age and has a merry tongue, while Dejanira's conversation, like Medusa's head, can turn anyone to stone out of sheer fatigue. When she is not complaining she is whimpering, and when doing neither she is eating or sleeping. Moreover, she sweats and smells and not even the attar of roses which she so lavishly uses can obliterate it. Does she not ever bathe? Her garments, too, swell over her body as over a keg, as if she were perpetually pregnant, and her peploses and tunics, though costly, appear to be the clothing of a slave girl who works in the fields and they are stained. She also waddles."

He stood up as if to dismiss the conversation as absurd. He even laughed a little and twinkled at his mother. But Agariste had the persistence of a bee lured by a dish of honey and the more she was resisted the more stubborn she became. "Your remarks are obscene, my son," she said, "and revolting, and unworthy of an aristocratic man. Does appearance seem to you of the utmost importance?"

"You have always said, Mother, that appearance is most important, yet now you imply it is not." He was becoming slightly irascible not only because of Dejanira but because he was afraid to annoy his mother too much, for had not his beloved Helena said that her heart was affected, as was evident to Helena by Agariste's new bluish pallor and the throbbing of vessels in her long white throat when she was in the least agitated? Pericles loved his mother still, though of late she was making him increasingly irritable with her pretensions and arrogance. Too, he was a notable soldier but he was becoming involved in politics in which he was not as yet notably successful.

Agariste said, ignoring her son's last remark, "You forget that her father is an Archon of Athens at this time and can be of invaluable assistance to you."

Pericles regarded his mother in silence. He was somewhat surprised as he always was when she revealed a sharp shrewdness concerning the ambitions and the thoughts of others. At these times he was reminded that his mother might be a fool in some respects, and utter absurdities, but she also had a mind and was intelligent. He had not as yet informed her that politics attracted him immensely, yet in some way she knew, though he had not confided his intentions to anyone else, with the exception of Anaxagoras, whom his mother loathed.

"He must have bribed well to be elected," he said.

"My brother would bribe no one!" cried Agariste, turning very pale and trembling. "We are of an honorable house!"

"Even aristocrats love power, and their second love is money, however vulgar that appears, and they will use the second for the first without hesitation." But he hardly believed that the Archon, who was a proud and repellently virtuous man, had bought votes. He would use influence, yes, to procure what he wished, but gross gold never, not truly because he despised money but because influence was more dainty and did not publicly smell. Moreover, influence could not be traced, a fact which the prudent Archon must have considered long and carefully. Pericles had never liked his uncle and Xanthippus had detested him and had often mimicked him for the entertainment of Pericles.

Argariste was protesting Pericles' observation about his uncle but Pericles did not listen. He was thinking; he made wry mouths. Was the abominable Dejanira his rapid path in the streaming fields of politics? He shuddered at the thought of her, but Pericles was inordinately ambitious. He reviled the Ecclesia for their oppressiveness, their stultifying of Athens, their crass and degenerate democracy. He believed that, in politics, he could affect the liberation of Athens and her new empire, make her great and free her for mighty things. At times he felt he could actually feel her throbbing but stifled heart under his feet; he yearned to give it room for expansion, for glory. The military man had little influence over the government. A man of resolution, determined that his loved country would spread shining wings over the world, had one access to the needed power: politics. Even the profound Anaxagoras had so admitted, with sadness, while deploring the fact.

Can I endure Dejanira even for Athens? he thought, and he knew the answer. He could avoid her bed, but this would anger her father. But how could he father her children when she was so repulsive to him and even to impoverished aristocrats who needed money? I should have to stuff my nostrils with lint, he reflected, when I would bed her. What of the sons I would beget on her? Would they resemble pigs, as does their mother? Is Athens worth such sons? Alas, he already knew the answer. Athens was worth anything a man could offer her, his adored country; any sacrifice would be as nothing. His stomach turned, but he said to his mother, "Let me consider it. Perhaps you could induce her to wash, my mother, and reduce her stink, at least for the wedding night."

"Your remark is not only disgusting, it is unkind," said Agariste. But she knew she had won, and she smiled her frigid but delicate smile. "Dejanira is a healthy young woman and you are not accustomed to the fragrance of health. You prefer the odors of closed chambers where you and your companions drown yourselves in wines and garlic and romp with lewd women. Such as your Helena, who has no respect for her sex but must engage in the abattoirs of surgeons and dabble in filth and forget that she is a woman."

Pericles laughed. "I have not observed that she ever forgets she is a woman," he said, and Agariste blushed at the implications of this and averted her head as if to avoid seeing something unspeakably lascivious. She lifted her hand to protect herself from any further mention of Helena, a gesture which Pericles found not only annoying but affected. Helena was like a rose that bloomed ebulliently and lustily and she was as candid as any unsophisticated youth for all her intellect and humor and sometimes bitter understanding of mankind. Robust, tall and somewhat plump, Helena was to Pericles a young Hera but without Hera's petulances and jealousies. Her laugh was loud and strong, and she loved a jest more than anything else, and did not pretend horror at a rude joke fresh from the military camps. Rather, she enjoyed it and would add an epigram to it besides.

I can forget Dejanira in Helena's arms, thought Pericles, smiling fondly, though Helena is owned by no man and is herself only and her bed is available to me seldom.

Agariste was acutely watching her son. How like a young Apollo he is! she thought. Despite that towering brow, which is somewhat grotesque and overshadows his perfect features, he is the handsomest man in Athens and his profile implies potency as well as thought. Who can compare with my son? His future is assured. Dejanira resembles a daughter of Erisichthon, who ate his own flesh out of his insatiable greed for food, and does not Dejanira adore the table as the altar to her fat body? This is true, but she is very rich and my brother is powerful and will help Pericles. Dejanira will not distress him overmuch, for men are men and seek their consolations among many women. Beauty is not necessary in a wife and is not much esteemed after a few years by a husband, for men grow accustomed to wives and desert them, no matter how lovely. Did not my husband prefer a hetaira to me?

Zeno of Elea had retired to his small estate, and thankfully. His place in the life of Pericles was taken by Anaxagoras as a companion and a very dear friend, and from Anaxagoras Pericles learned much asceticism and the ability at all times to maintain a personal dignity even under intense provocation. Anaxagoras was born in Clazomenae, ten years before the birth of Pericles, and at this time was some thirty-three years old. He had arrived in Athens from Asia Minor only a year ago, lured to the Grecian city by its culture and its fame as the home of philosophers, though the latter were rapidly becoming the victims of the Ecclesia, which was increasingly more ruthless and cruel in its persecution and extermination of all who disagreed with it.

Anaxagoras was a tall and slender man with an elongated and serious face, a very sensitive mouth, and a thin long nose with a sharp tip. His brow was smooth and invariably calm, his cheekbones distinct and broad, and above them was a pair of the largest and bluest eyes Pericles had ever seen, radiant with intellect and a magnificent sense of the ridiculous. Though middle-aged, he walked with the awkward grace of youth. His gestures were disciplined but eloquent. His dark hair seemed painted on his fragile skull and his ears, though unusually large, were translucent, so that they appeared rosy against the natural paleness of his complexion.

His fame as a mathematician and astronomer had reached Athens long before he arrived there, and he was received with accolades and affection from his Athenian colleagues, even if the never-sleeping Ecclesia was able to restrain its enthusiasm without much difficulty. So he came under its stringent eye because of his scientific knowledge and teachings and writings. Contrary to the convictions of the Ecclesia, whose ideas of Deity were extremely limited, fixed and dogmatic, and therefore all the more vehement and passionate, Anaxagoras was guilty of posing questions, advancing dubious hypotheses and drawing unorthodox conclusions. His one fault was his impatience with fools, unlike the gentle Zeno who only pitied them, and he could be abrupt with asininity no matter the source, and would remove himself without apology. He was particularly, and bitterly, incensed that the Ecclesia, once a noble body representative of the voting citizenry, as established by Solon, had become a quarrelsome and ignoble body of inquisitors, open to any public or private accusation against disliked figures. While containing few priests it was more or less dominated by them and was in fear of their alleged thaumaturgy and their intimacy with the gods. "Liberty," he would say, "is the most desirable possession of man, followed only by knowledge and wisdom which cannot exist without freedom. But liberty, unless safeguarded by an unchanging Constitution, can become the tool of tyrants who use their own liberty to destroy that of others."

Many of the Ecclesia were ignorant men whose only claim to pride was that they were freemen and voting citizens of Athens, and that they were pious conformists. When Anaxagoras, introducing his scientific method, declared he could predict eclipses, and that eclipses were not a sudden whim of the gods, the Ecclesia were horrified, and debated whether or not to pronounce the curses "against those who would deceive the people." Anaxagoras had not been in Athens two years before the debate began. "It is well to be prudent," said Pericles to him at one time. "Prudence," said Anaxagoras, "is the last refuge of the coward. Though," he added, seeing Pericles' youthful smile, "it is a virtue in the brave man. I do not speak in paradoxes, as does your late teacher, Zeno, for science does not recognize paradoxes as a characteristic of Deity but as a natural problem that challenges and can hold a solution which can explain that no paradoxes exist at all but churn only in

263

the minds of uninformed men. Pious marvellings have no place in the realm of science, but only facts."

"There is still the mystery of man," said Pericles.

"Then let us ponder it and perhaps reach an explanation," said his friend. Like all scientists he was certain that there are no mysteries and that by the employment of scientific exploration the veils would fall one by one. In a way he was a dogmatist himself, and this Pericles understood. If Anaxagoras had any weakness at all it was his insistence that the scientific method, and scientists, would prevent chaos. Despite all opposition he did introduce scientific inquiry to Athens from Ionia, and was later to influence Socrates.

He believed that the body of knowledge was already complete but that in some degenerate manner man had lost the ability to penetrate far into it. "So you do believe in Deity, which has held this body of knowledge for the use of man," said Pericles. At this question the blue eyes of Anaxagoras became grave. "A scientist who is not aware of the Anima Mundi is as petty as the Ecclesia, itself, and can hardly be called a learned man," he replied.

His marvellings over what he discovered, he would say, was at the wonders which research revealed, and their perfection. "No man should approach science without a spirit of reverence, for without reverence there is only arrogance and vainglory and conceit, and these destroy the true soul of scientific inquiry." At each new discovery he was exalted. There was a gentleness in him also, and he pitied humanity and was charity itself. Pericles considered him the most magnanimous and wisest of men and he had the strongest influence over the younger man, and was the only one who even neared true excellence.

Anaxagoras taught not only in the colonnades to young men and students but had a small academe of his own, for which he charged a minor fee for attendance. He would quickly expel youths whose intelligence disappointed him, and totally materialistic ones also. "It is true that all things are governed by natural laws," he would say, "but law implies a Lawmaker and he who thinks all comes from blind Chance is as idiotic as he who denies there is any Chance at all." "Then Deity is capricious," Pericles would laugh, to which Anaxagoras would reply, "Deity, too, has a sense of humor. One has only to observe animals at play. I am not speaking of man's contrived play, but the spontaneous capers of the innocent ones."

He taught that there was a Oneness in all the universes,

from the suns to the smallest field flower, and variability among species and the infinite variety manifest even to the dullest of men were manifestations of the divine Mind which ruled the apparent chaos, and was illimitable and incomprehensible. "That Mind is endlessly in motion," he would teach, "and out of that motion evolves all things, from the marvelous configurations of a sea shell to the movement of the stars. If that Mind should cease its motions, which are creativity, then everything would disappear and be no more. All would be void, and nothingness."

When he was accused of impiety in insisting on "mechanism" in the universe, he would reply that this was an exercise in semantics, and "mechanism" was the law of the Divine Mind, and he was then accused of inconsistency, for did not "mechanism" imply a machine ungoverned by the creative Mind? He would throw up his hands in despair.

He found mathematics not a boring subject but an inquiry into the workings and the law of the Anima Mundi, and a marvelous mystery. He introduced an implication of esoterism into mathematics. He was confronted by his own sayings that there were no mysteries and he would answer that his definition of mystery was not the definition of other men. Like Zeno of Elea he said that speculation was the first step towards the understanding of common mysteries, and their solutions. But the Mystery of the Godhead was not to be understood by men. The Ecclesia said that he was indeed a danger to the people, for everything that he said not only confused philosophy—as they understood it—but frightened "simpler minds." When he said that "simpler minds" had no place in philosophy he was accused of the very arrogance he despised and condemned. The Ecclesia said that this showed an imperviousness towards and contempt of the common people, and so he was their "enemy." At this Anaxagoras would laugh ruefully. "It would seem that I threaten the Ecclesia, itself, for surely there are no uncommon people among them."

He had no tolerance for those who would oppose inquiry, no matter how "impious" it seemed. "The only impiety," he would say, "is a denial that the Divine Mind is larger than the mind of man."

Pericles would attend his classes and he would experience, as always, an exaltation of spirit and excitement as he listened to this majestic man's teachings. He would feel an enlargement in himself, a quickening of consciousness. Anaxagoras perfected and colored his dreams for Greece above all other teachers. It was Anaxagoras who told him that he had become too engrossed with the arts of war and politics. Pericles joked, "Can a man's mind contain all things?" to which the philosopher replied, "There is no limit to a man's mind, no end to his speculation, if he is not lazy and does not tell himself that his mind can contain only so many matters, and that it is necessary to judge what is important and what not. Who are we to decide the importance of anything?"

"Except truth," Pericles would reply with mock solemnity. "Have you not said that yourself, you scientist?" Anaxagoras replied, "Even truth has its amusing variables, and we scientists recognize that—if we are truly scientists." He added, "Even reality changes or is transformed when man perceives it."

Pericles had heard of Pheidias, who was the same age as Anaxagoras, but busy as he was he had not yet encountered him. Anaxagoras soon changed that. He took Pericles to the studio of the sculptor, who now had a considerable fame. He had already executed the incomparable chryselephantine Athene for Pellene and the Marathon memorial at Delphi. The mighty bronze statue of Athene, which towered on the acropolis and was a landsight for sailors, had been designed and cast by him. He had many students; some of the more gifted imitated him expertly.

He was an Athenian, son of Charmides, and though still fairly young he was balding, and he had a shy sweet smile infinitely touching and self-deprecating. His body was slight and bending like a young sapling, but his face was plump and rosy and frank, which gave him an appealing aspect. His workshop was as modest as himself, and as dusty, and as stained with paint and the shavings of metal, but as noisy as he was quiet. He greeted Anaxagoras with affection, touching him gently on the shoulder and smiling bashfully into his eyes. He gave the impression that he felt that Anaxagoras was demeaning himself by visiting him, Pheidias, and he was humbly grateful in consequence. He looked at Pericles with some timidity, for he was afraid of strangers. He had seen Pericles at a distance, at the theatre and in the halls of the Ecclesia, and at the games, and knew who he was.

"My friend, Pericles, who is a notable soldier and, alas, a blossoming politician, has been very anxious to know you, dear friend," said Anaxagoras. Anaxagoras was dressed as humbly as the famous sculptor but nothing could reduce his aspect of self-containment and grandeur. Pheidias led his two visitors outside his workshop and into the midday. Here there was a small but perfect garden of myrtles and oaks and sycamores surrounding graveled walks and one single flowerbed centered with a fountain in which stood one of his own works: a little but exquisite bronze statuette of Psyche with a butterfly on her shoulder, her wings outspread, one delicate foot poised on her pedestal. The metal had been polished by the water which flowed over her so that she was bright gold in the hot sunlight and airy. It was so finely wrought, that statuette, that it appeared alive and pulsing, and the infinitesimal veins on her hands and ankles seemed to palpitate with moving blood. A smile of eager and virginal seeking was on the lovely little face, an ardent desire for love. Pericles went to the fountain to admire this work and to long for it. Pheidias watched him with an expression of gratification, and he thought: Though this young man is obviously somewhat pompous in manner and speech, and even assuming, there is something splendid about him, something massively stately and sincere. As if Pericles had heard this thought he turned suddenly and encountered Pheidias' gaze and he said to himself that here was a great man who understood more than one could guess, however simple his demeanor. Now Pericles himself understood what Zeno had meant when he had said that it was only the base fellow who swaggered and spoke importantly and had a high opinion of himself. Alas, however, the truly great were frequently ignored by the rabble, and even by government and prominent men, for they had no pretensions. He, himself, Pericles, acknowledged that he was not guiltless at times of open scorn, and that he slighted others when impatient.

A student brought wine and cheese and olives and honey and bread to a rough plain table under the shade of an oak, and a dish of dates and figs. Pheidias made no hypocritical apology for the simplicity of this light meal and as the three sat and ate and drank Pericles gathered that food was of small importance to the sculptor and to Anaxagoras also. The wine was execrable, and cheap, yet Pheidias was not a poor man. It is probable, thought Pericles, that he has as meager a regard for food and wine as he has of money. In the background, from the workshop, there came a constant hammering and the sound of youthful voices.

"It is my dream," said Pheidias in his hesitating voice which implored forgiveness for his words, "to see Athens the supreme centre of beauty as well as philosophy and science." He glanced up at the acropolis, and mused and his face became sublime with dreams. "I can see a temple there, to Athene Parthenos, and a statue of her before it of ivory and gold, a vast statue facing the dawn, heroic and terrible and commanding, bathed in the light of Aurora, and gleaming against the blue sky."

"It is not an impossible dream," said Pericles, and Pheidias was pleased again by the sonorous quality of his voice. "I, too, wished for the glory of Greece and though Anaxagoras here despises politicians it is necessary to be one to obtain the money to bring a dream into reality."

"But we have a ramshackle democracy," said Anaxagoras, "which is too solicitous for the bellies of the citizens to care for the glory of the nation. Only republics, and empires, can rise above the gutter and execute splendor. But democracies are feminine and republics and empires are masculine, and therein lies the difference between mediocrity and sublimity."

He began, as usual, to inveigh against the Ecclesia and the judges, not with rancor but with regret. Pheidias listened, sighing. "Even the arts, which are immortal, must stand aside for the greedy appetites of the mob," he said. "You are correct, my Anaxagoras, in believing that the spirit is of more importance than the body. But it is impossible to tell government that. Or, they are afraid to acknowledge it in the search for votes."

He led his guests into the workshop. "I perceive little or no marble here," said Pericles. "Do you work only in gold and ivory or bronze?"

"I find marble too ponderous," said Pheidias, again with that air of fearing to give offense. "But I dream of the acropolis crowned with marble, as pure as light, as powerful in aspect as a mountain."

"Which you will grace with your genius," said Anaxagoras. "How beautiful are the elements of nature, ivory, gold, metals, marble! They speak in the voices of silence, which are holy."

Pericles watched in fascination as Pheidias took up a knife and began to work on a statuette of Zeus. The knife flashed and cut as through butter, and Pericles marvelled at such elegant and fastidious power. The small countenance began to emerge, regnant and endowed with godly lineaments. "One day," said Pheidias, as if thinking aloud, "it may be that I will enlarge this small thing into superhuman stature, not only for my own delight but for the greater delight of those who will see." His face saddened a little as if he feared that such a dream had small hope of emerging into reality.

When Pericles and Anaxagoras left Pheidias, Pericles carried with him a gift from the sculptor, an ivory figurine no longer than his index finger, and it was of a lovely woman with a clear and radiant face. She had the body of a young goddess, yet was mature of aspect. Her hair was dressed in the Grecian fashion and bound with ribbons, which Pheidias had colored with gold. One arm was lifted in a gesture of pinning her robe on her right shoulder, and one perfect leg was half-revealed. Her expression was musing but firm and there was a slight indication of humor about her mouth. Pericles held it on the palm of his hand and said, "Where is such a woman endowed not only with beauty but, better, with character and subtlety? Yes, I have my pretty courtesan, and she is like a mirror to me, reflecting back what I say. She has graces. But she is not as womanly as this, so bravely tender of appearance, so human yet so divine, indicating profundity of mind."

"You are speaking of Helena, the physician?" asked Anaxagoras with surprise, for he knew Helena.

"No," said Pericles. "Helena belongs to no man, not even to me, though she is often my companion. I speak of my Pomona, my nymph."

He studied the figurine again as it seemed to him that she moved on his palm and was about to speak. He put his hand in his pouch and withdrew a silken kerchief and carefully wrapped the figurine in it and returned both to his pouch.

"If I do find such a woman—which is impossible, of course —she will be more to me than my life." As they walked on down to the Angora, Pericles said, as though continuing a conversation with himself, "Yes, the dreams of Pheidias will emerge into reality. I know it in my soul."

He put the figurine on the chest at his bedside and would gaze at it for long periods, filled with yearning and desire. Once he dreamt that she grew and stepped down from the chest and was a tall woman and that she smiled at him and bent over him and whispered, "I have hoped for a man like you. We will find each other." When he awoke he was comforted and thereafter spent years seeking for her in every assemblage and in every temple. He was always disappointed yet he never ceased to search.

CHAPTER 7

It had not been Pericles' serious intention to marry early in life, and he had often hoped to escape marriage entirely. As to the latter he was discreet enough not to discuss it in the presence of potential enemies or random friends. For he was in politics and it was dangerous to dissent against popular custom, especially in the case of a man who had no older brothers to continue the family line. He had idly played with the thought after two years' ephebia, or military service, when his mother had hinted of his duty to the family. He had had his choice of the camp followers when he was a young officer, and there had been pretty slave girls in his father's house, and a concubine or two. He had fallen in love with the hearty Helena, a former hetaira, and now a physician much deplored in Athens. Helena, however, was a happy companion to any man who attracted her—another violence against the public virtue—but she loved none except her former protector who had been a noted physician, himself, and who had trained her in the arts of medicine. Upon his death she had been disconsolate, but she was very healthy and natively cheerful and liked men and so later gave her favors as she chose and at her own will and desire. It was she who had introduced Pericles to Pomona, a young hetaira, and had furthered the alliance. Helena was naturally benign and affectionate and she arranged the affair partly because of fondness she had for both Pericles and the young girl, and partly to distract Pericles from her own person and to free herself from his importunities.

In short, he had wanted her only for himself and Helena considered that both tedious and self-assuming. Yet, she did not hurt his feelings and his passion for her by dismissing him abruptly. She let him occupy her bed occasionally but did not encourage his devotion. She accepted his gifts joyously, smiling her rosy smile of genuine pleasure. She also appreciated his genuine regard for a woman who was intelligent, and who did not despise her as did other Athenian men. As a woman of sense she also knew that there were many times when even such a proud and sufficient woman like herself needed the protection and influence of a prominent man, and particularly a politician and a man of riches. Too, Pericles was very handsome and when he was not pompous he was a merry companion. She trained him not to take himself and public matters too seriously, as he was inclined to do, and introduced him to men of famous wit and ribaldry in her house at her sumptuous dinners. (She could eat and drink like a man, and as zealously, and did not consider asceticism a virtue. Accordingly her tall figure was voluptuous, but not fat.) Above all things she had an enormous sense of humor, rollicking and sometimes even rude and a little coarse, and she had enlightened the astringent and acid-tipped tongue of Pericles so that his natural impatience did not break out into arrogant insult too often, insults that invariably exposed the other man's secret foibles or weaknesses to the laughing eyes of others. "One thing I have learned," she told Pericles, "is that fools sometimes attain power and they can be dangerous. Moreover a little kindness never hurt the giver. The predicament of humanity is sorrowful and tragic enough without making it more onerous, even when justly exasperated." She brought reluctant compassion into his life.

She had a round pink face and full red lips, a small impertinent nose and gray eyes fringed with lashes the same auburn tint of her hair, which, in the sun, turned to the color of copper. She could laugh like a jovial man, and usually did. When she discovered that Pericles had become sensitive over his towering brow she suggested the nobility of a helmet to be worn in public at all times. She laughed when he did so, for her suggestion had been half jest. It was her spontaneous kindness and her handsomeness which made Pericles adore her, and her intellect, untainted by the insistences and haughty fretfulness of his mother. She taught medicine to young men as well as practiced it and had her own infirmia, left to her in the will of the one man she had truly loved. Her friends were devoted, her enemies, fierce—the latter did not distress her for she was courageous, and neither sought good will nor placated a foe. Though only the age of Pericles she had something endearingly maternal about her. To the women of Athens, with her freedom and her free ways, she was a revolting scandal, a fact that did not disturb her. Her only female friends were the hetairai.

"One day," she said to Pericles, "intelligent women will not be classed with whores as they are now, but will be respected and honored. And you, my beloved, will help to advance this felicitous state of affairs." "And you shall be the first to be honored," he said in answer.

He went to her one night saying that exigency and his mother's prayers and arguments had induced him to enter into an engyesis (giving of a pledge into the hand) between himself and his cousin, Dejanira, through the offices of the Archon, Daedalus, her father. (Rather, it was a pledge between two men, the suitor and the kyrios, the father, if still alive.) "She will bring me a handsome dowry from both Daedalus and her unlamented husband," he told Helena. "Better still, she will bring me influence and power through her father, and I have no time to waste."

Helena's full face sobered and she gazed at Pericles with

unusual intensity, her gray eyes flickering with thought. "I have seen Dejanira in wedding processions," she said, "and in her litter, when accompanied by her father."

"She is, undoubtedly, not beautiful," said Pericles, making a face. "Nor can she claim that Athena ever gifted her with a touch of intelligence."

"Ah, well," said Helena, shrugging her plump shoulders. "I suppose a man must marry, to continue the line of his fathers, and I hear that Dejanira is a matron of many virtues and is assiduous in the managing of a household. Also, though you are rich, my Apollo, more riches are not to be despised."

"I agree that a married man can ask no more," said Pericles. "I had hoped, however, to escape marriage entirely and devote my life to my country."

"It has been my observation that married men do not loiter about their households with any zest," Helena said with a smile. "They leave such things to their wives, and wives can be useful in many ways. You could do worse."

"At least she will have to take the ritual bridal bath," said Pericles.

"Do not be unkind, O Apollo. Order your slaves to sprinkle the nuptial chamber with nard."

She had spoken lightly, but she was perturbed not only for Pericles but over Dejanira also. She had heard of Dejanira's stupidity and her other defects of character, and she knew that Daedalus went to the brothels not only in what he considered complete secrecy but as one went to a physician with a serious disease, hating the necessity and almost hating the healer for that necessity. His wife was a woman singularly like her daughter. Helena would have pitied him had he not been so coldly contemptuous and condemning of those who lacked his own dedication, sincere and passionate and without hypocrisy, to public and private rectitude. "He detests himself for what he cannot help possibly more than he detests others with fewer or no qualms," Helena would say. "He is like one who resents the actions of his bowels but must drive himself to a latrine, holding his nose against the smell. One understands such men, but one cannot forgive them for their harshness towards others, and their vindictiveness. In castigating their fellows they castigate themselves and suffer larger pain."

Pericles was less charitable towards Daedalus, whom he found repellent. "He is as lean as a skeleton and has a skull-like face and a mouth like a dried date, without its oozing sweetness. When I shook his hand at the time of the engyesis ⸱ was like shaking fingers formed of brittle parchment, so little life does it have. His whole power lies in his voice, which is like a horn, and his manner which expresses civic virtue. He is also honest, which is a rarity among us Athenians, and actually believes what he says. His word needs no oath to seal it, and I suppose that can be counted in his favor. How my beautiful mother could have such a kinsman is one of the seven extraordinary wonders of the world."

"I have seen him, alas," said Helena. "My unfortunate Pericles! Yet, I believe this marriage to be advantageous to you, and there are always consolations, are there not?"

Pericles' pale eyes shone on her with such ardent tenderness that she embraced him, sighing while she smiled. She wondered why she could not love him and had only a deep affection for him. Was he not the most desirable man in Athens and did he not possess attitudes of mind and character to enthrall any woman, and was he not virile and gentle and considerate in her arms? But she had loved once and could not bring herself to love any other man, no matter how illustrious. As if in extenuation she ate alone with him tonight in her beautiful little house, and arranged that her dinner table held only his favorite dishes and the best of wines. While they dined she would talk seriously of nothing, but amused him with naughty gossip of the city and new raucous jests she had heard.

Pericles secretly hoped that something dire would happen to prevent his marriage to Dejanira. But the winter day in the month of Gamelion dawned crisp and especially bright and vigorous, which Agariste said was a good omen, but Pericles considered it disastrous. He had seen Dejanira at family festivals, when her husband was still alive, and he had had the heartiest, if derisive, sympathy for him. He remembered that Dejanira had never had the slightest prettiness even as a child and young girl and now, as a widow, she seemed particularly abhorrent to him. Before her marriage she had had, at least, a slender figure and kept herself reasonably hygienic with the help of slaves. Even these had departed.

Ah, well, he said to himself on this day Agariste proclaimed was auspicious, I suppose worse things can happen to a man than marriage, though at the moment I do not believe it. He had chosen Anaxagoras as his parochos (best man) to the fury of Agariste, and she was further incensed that his wedding party was "composed of all the ragamuffin philosophers from the dirtiest of the arcades," and not the men of distinction Pericles ought to have chosen. She had never liked Zeno of Elea at the best of moments. He was another of Pericles' attendants. She was convinced that her son had done these things to vex her. Only the fact that her brother had dubiously informed her that these "ragtags" were bringing fame to Athens could mollify her anger. She admitted that they had intellect; however, were they not very poor and wore coarse garments and, if they possessed shoes, did they not wear them only to dinners in order to preserve them as long as possible? On hearing this Pericles said, "Better bare of feet than barren of brains."

Coldly, and to annoy his mother more, he insisted on hearing the details of Dejanira's purificatory ceremony the night before the wedding which Agariste had attended. The women of the bride's house, and her female relatives, had formed a procession to obtain the water from the fountain called Callirhoë. They had all carried torches, and there had been two flute-players, instead of one, leading the woman who carried the special buckets for the water—the loutrophoras. The bride, in the women's quarters, was then ceremoniously undressed—"What a delectable sight that must have been!" said Pericles with gloom. She had been rubbed and cleansed with perfumed oil then clothed in pale linen, and, with her relatives and bridal attendants, had appeared at her father's side where the sacrifice was offered up to Zeus, Hera, Apollo, Artemis and Peitho. (Gamelion was considered to be particularly a choice month in which to be married, as it was the month of Hera, goddess of marriage.) For the second time—as though she were a virgin bride—she had offered up her childhood toys and her dolls. "Alas, that she could not offer up her son!" said Pericles, to his mother's wrath. "I thought such a ceremony was only for a virgin. Is it possible that she never lay with her husband at all but produced her son—who resembles her remarkably—by some parthenogenesis?"

Agariste, too outraged to reply to this, went to supervise the decorating of her house with garlands of olive and laurel leaves, as the house of Daedalus was being decorated on this bridal morning. The bridal chamber, which Pericles refused to inspect, was also being garnished with olive and laurel leaves and flowers. As the weather was shiningly cold, braziers stood in every room and curtains were drawn over windows and lamps were lighted, though the sun outside was brilliant. Pericles, who was never restless, was restless today, and he strolled outside to breathe the sharp chill air and look down on his beloved city. He said to it, "I am doing this for you. I am offering myself as a sacrifice." He stared up at the bronze statue which Pheidias had created and murmured to it, "Athene Parthenos, my patroness, grant that what I am about to do will enhance your glory." The statue on the acropolis gazed sternly to the east and the morning light glittered on her mighty and severe face. But her face was no more stern than was Pericles' and his light eyes had the blind look of a statue, statue which Pheidias had created and murmured toit, "Athene he wore a helmet which concealed the extraordinary height of his brow and head. He shivered in the blazing cold and wrapped his cloak more tightly about him. He decided to get drunk, though as a rule he was careful in his drinking.

By noon he was sleeping in his chamber, snoring, and though Agariste, on hearing this, tightened her mouth, she had to admit to herself that perhaps he had reason, considering Dejanira, about whom she had no delusions. But Dejanira was rich and her father powerful, and a man could do worse than marry her, especially an ambitious man like Pericles.

As Pericles slept in an aura of sour wine he dreamed again that the beautiful little figurine Pheidias had presented him enlarged to the height of a tall and slender woman, and that again she bent over him. But this time she kissed his lips and laid her hand tenderly against his neck and whispered, "I am coming to you, O my beloved!" He felt the warmth of her mouth; it was as fragrant as a lily, and soft as a heather, and her hair, silver-gold, fell over his throat and his shoulders and hands. Her eyes, so close to his, were as brown as choice autumn wine, tinted and flecked with gilt and sparkles of changing light. She seemed radiant to him and vital and she smiled. He came abruptly awake, searching for her in the dimness of his chamber, his eyes strained and enlarged, so real had she appeared, so imminent. He was certain that he could smell the odor of lilies. He turned on his side, his heart beating fiercely with yearning for what was only, surely, a dream. He was as desolate as a man newly deprived of his loved bride before even the consummation of marriage. The thought of Dejanira now was unbearably repugnant to him so that he had to restrain himself from rising and fleeing his house and the city of Athens, itself, to roam the world for the vision he had dreamed. At length, groaning, he put the figurine against his lips and kissed it, then placed it under his pillow and slept again until almost sunset. When he awoke he felt dulled and numb and without feeling, which, he thought, was fortunate. Then he laughed at himself. What was marriage after all but a convenience to produce sons? He was taking this matter too seriously and was not Helena always admonishing him that he did so in all things?

"There are only two things worthy of solemnity," she had said, only three nights ago. "Birth—and death. Between them, if one is wise, lies hilarity, for is not life hilarious, even when tragic?" Pericles did not answer this. There were occasions when he suspected that Helena, despite her wisdom, could be light-minded, and so, on that night, he had been so surly with her that she had dismissed him in exasperation, and, unpardonably, had advised him to go to his espoused bride.

At sunset he was his apparently calm, stately and rigidly dignified self. His face, under his helmet, was so without expression that it appeared less flesh than white stone. This was due not to his dread of marriage to Dejanira but to Anaxagoras' teaching that at all times a true man is self-disciplined, especially during acute events or under stress. "Disorder of mind," he had said, "is unpardonable."

"Zeno of Elea thought I was too self-controlled," Pericles had replied to this.

"Ah, there is a subtle but profound difference between an *appearance* of self-control and the physical and mental effort and anguish this involves, and the true self-discipline which orders the emotions within and the appearance without. The latter produces peace of mind, for it is absolute dominance of one's self. The first produces, at the end, physical and spiritual collapse, for nothing is more deadly than lack of command over one's own weaknesses. Composure is in the mind, if one has dominion of his thoughts. Without such, a man is a victim of random emotions which come and go and can destroy him, and are wild and savage and animalistic."

Anaxagoras had smiled kindly at the young man. "You have extraordinary serenity and steadfastness of appearance. But this must seep into your mind and your emotions. When I was attacked on the streets by howling and disheveled young men who violently disagreed with my theories I felt no fear or anger or heat at all, and certainly no indignation! I knew they were only echoes from our primitive and chaotic past and were of no consequence."

On this, his wedding day, Pericles reflected on what Anaxagoras had said: Objective and *apparent* emotions could be used deftly by a politician to impress voters—if one cared for public office. However, thought Pericles dismally, I am only flesh and blood and true serenity is far from me. Was it better, in this appalling world, to resemble marble within and without than to feel passions? Or, was marble alive, as Pheidias had said? (Zeno had once remarked that all things have being: To be is to feel, and stone, itself, grew and therefore had sentience.) Pericles felt more than a slight confusion in his mind. It came to him, with no originality, that life was very perplexing and dark and enigmatic, and not, as Helena had said, hilarious, unless one found earthquakes humorous and mysteriously tormented humanity infinitely ridiculous and mirthful. Anaxagoras had declared that a true man did not just rise above calamity. He remained impervious to it. Pericles shook his head. There were occasions when a man must weep or die. Blood was blood, no matter what the philosophers said. A man could not escape himself, nor his human heritage. Perhaps even God was the Victim of His own Nature. Alas, thought Pericles, what of us mere mortals, if that is so? We must all deal with tangibles, God or man, even if they are not of our own making. Reality confronts us all. Unlike the east, the west is pragmatic.

CHAPTER 8

Among the wedding guests was the shy and emotional Ichthus, who was, from a calm and philosophic view, deplorable in his lack of self-restraint. His feelings were ever visible, in the constant slight trembling of his face and in his ardent and fervid eyes. He seemed always on the verge of flight; his sensitivity was that of a man who has been flayed. A felicitous word or a kind smile could provoke him to tears. He haunted the colonnades, following the philosophers and listening, and sometimes he would cry out as if unbearably moved. The philosophers found this gratifying, if amusing. Their students did not. They did not know that here was an undefiled soul who yearned for beauty and justice and truth and could not understand a world in which these were so terribly lacking. (Worse, he could not express in eloquent speech the majesty he perceived, and so could only mumble though his spirit vibrated. His tongue was as if paralysed.)

However, he could write. He wrote anonymously, and broadcast his writing throughout Athens, employing young lads to toss pieces of parchment in public places, and against the doors of houses. His poems were poor if touching. But his polemics were potent and galvanic. They rang with passion and eloquence and fire. He questioned everything, but with humility, if it pertained to the Godhead. However, when he questioned government it was as if a volcano had broken its stony fastnesses and was pouring lava and flame over the city, full of wrath.

His particular hatred was for the hypocritical democracy of Athens, which pretended to serve the people but only served politicians. "The Founding Father of our once-beneficent laws, Solon of holy memory, sought to establish a just republic, wherein there would be no slaves and all men would be equal under the law, and all would have recourse to government if offended or deprived of their rights. No privileged man would be above the law nor too humble to evoke it. The Tyrants proclaimed that they followed the laws of Solon; they perverted them for their own advantage and almost destroyed Athens with their venality, their craftiness and exigency. Virtue's own spotless raiment was assumed, and is still assumed, in which to envelop demons and give them an air of authority and sanctity. Harpies swooping with the white wings of justice! Where is the man in Athens today, no matter his station, who can declare in all honesty, 'I am a free man?' Onerous taxes destroy ambition and create listlessness in the strong and mendicancy in the weak. No man knows this very hour whether his land belongs to him or if the government will seize it tomorrow for evil purposes. The Ecclesia is a den of thieves; it is a congregation of liars and oppressors! It deprives honorable men of their goods or their lives. It elevates Cerberuses to be the guardians of the people! The River Styx flows through Athens and her dominions. Who will build a bridge upon it over which free men can flee and be safe?"

The Ecclesia affected to be ignorant of these writings, or if someone brought them to their attention they laughed indulgently. "A hot-head, a fool, a disgruntled idiot," they said. "Who but slaves would read such nonsense—if slaves can read? Is not Athens rich and strong and proud, filled with artists and philosophers, the wonder of the modern world? Such could not flourish if Athens were oppressed by its government or restricted or muted. There will always be dissenters. If their cause is just we will listen. But when their cause is stupid or mad we must ignore them."

But the Ecclesia did not ignore the writings of Ichthus. They set their spies searching for him. Only one person was convinced that he knew the author of these fiery writings which were disturbing the minds of the people and forcing them to think of their government even above their petty daily affairs. That man was Pericles. He was determined that he must speak to Ichthus for the latter's own sake. Prudence,

prudence, he said to himself, as if addressing his shy friend. Then he would add with bitterness, "Dear Ichthus, the truth is a deadly spice and can poison the administrator. I agree with you, but the time is not yet. Prudence, no. Patience, yes." Then he would ridicule himself for his own discretion. More nations, he thought, were destroyed by indifferent patience on the part of the people than by perhaps any other destroyer. A people which had too much tolerance for evil deserved to die in its own leniency. There was a difference between indulgence for natural faultiness and indulgence for wickedness. The first was civilized, the second perfidious.

Then Pericles reflected that there was nothing more invincible than a just and uncorrupted man who set out to right wrongs. Gentle and timid though Ichthus was he had the soul of a Hercules bent on cleaning out the Augean Stables though he died for it. Rightful anger was a frightful weapon, stronger than Damascene steel, and he who used it must beware that it did not turn in his hand and slay him. Pericles decided that at some time during the wedding festivities he would speak quietly to Ichthus and urge—what? Self-preservation? Such was the cave in which shivering cowards died of their own inertia. If men had any reason for living at all it was for truth and honor and justice. For anything less, for compromise, a man was only a devouring beast intent on his miserable security and appetites

Pericles thought of his father, Xanthippus, and his heart burned. What should he say to Ichthus which would not be a soothing lie?

Pericles, with his best man and his other friends, went to the house of Daedalus to the wedding ceremonies. He was so preoccupied with his dream of the beautiful mythical woman and the problems of Ichthus that any thought of his own state was numbed. Seeing his abstraction his friends became silent.

The house of Daedalus was already seething with gay guests, and was wreathed in laurel and olive leaves and somewhat dejected flowers wilting in the cold air. The Ecclesia, many of them, wore the bland and smiling faces of politicians and greeted everyone as if they were the honored. At last a signal was given and all repaired to the banqueting hall, where tables were set aside for the men, including the bridegroom and his attendants, and others in the rear for the women. Daedalus, though very rich, was frugal and so the cloths on the table were of the coarsest linen and the spoons and knives thinly plated with silver. Here were no rugs or precious murals but only small statues of the household gods on wall pedestals. The bare stone floor was icy. There were no silken curtains at the windows; heavy dull wool hung there instead. No braziers warmed the air except for a thrifty one in the center of the hall. The Archon boasted of his austerity; Pericles decided he was less austere than mean. The vases in the corners of the hall were slightly filled with drooping branches, unflowered.

Pericles saw his bride at a distance, clad in a demure tunic of blue linen with a toga over it of a darker blue. She was veiled and had a wreath on her overly large round head which appeared to be set solidly on her shoulders with no neck intervening. Her friends sat about her, chattering happily, but she was stolidly silent as always except that occasionally her thin voice, laden with complaint on this, her wedding night, could be heard over the voices of the other women. As she was the most important person among the women today some gave her complaints attention, for all they were meaningless and irrelevant and did not express true dissatisfaction with anything. Her mother, as stoutly shapeless as herself, and with the same hard round head and heavy stupid features, sat sullenly at her side. Semele was very pleased by this marriage of her daughter to the handsome and distinguished Pericles. But if one were to judge by her wary and sulky expression one would have guessed that she was in ill-temper and morose. Her graying hair was lank by nature, though for these festivities it had been painfully curled and waved and bound in red ribbons. Her clothing was brown; she wore no jewelry. Like her daughter, she had a truly snout-like nose, with large gross nostrils, a low sallow forehead and sallower fat cheeks, a thick mouth sharply downturned, and very small sunken black eyes constantly darting with suspicion of all things. Her chin was greasy.

Agariste looked upon Semele and Dejanira and sighed. She glanced across the hall at her son, and felt a sick compunction. She prayed to her patroness, Athene, that Pericles would beget children, if not beautiful, at least with some of his intelligence.

As for Pericles he sat among the men, at Daedalus' right hand, and he was filled with dark gloom. He looked at his veiled bride and at her mother, who she incredibly resembled, and shuddered inwardly. He usually drank with care and moderation but now he resolutely strove for drunkenness. The wine was execrable if strong. Fortunately Daedalus had thought to provide Syrian whiskey and Pericles, wincing, drank it down, then hastily ate a piece of brown rough bread. He had become accustomed to army food during his campaigns, otherwise the dinner would have revolted him. There were suckling pigs prepared carelessly and without flavor, and game and fowl and fish—without a sauce, and a mound of mashed beans and lentils cooked with no felicity and tasting of rancid pork. There were wilted onions indifferently roasted, and olives both green and ripe, and they tasted of too much brine. The cheeses were dry and hard and cracked, with thick rinds. The pastries had no delicacy. The fruit was wizened and had spots of decay upon them. Even in the country the peasants fared better than this. The wedding feast would have been despised by slaves in the house of Xanthippus. Pericles drank more whiskey. Finally a warm haze enveloped him from the potions and a dreamlike apathy flowed over him. Voices seemed louder and incoherent. The forced laughter of the men became jovial to his ears. He thought to himself, Nothing lasts forever. He could forget this nightmare tomorrow, this visitation of harpies, this presence of Medusas.

Daedalus, who prided himself on his controlled appetite, ate sparingly, and when guests were served more wine he watched closely, calculating the cost. He saw the two leather bottles of whiskey being emptied, and frowned. He detested immoderation. He also disliked frivolity but Semele had insisted on music, so a male slave—no pretty dancing girls!—played alternately on flute and lyre with a pathetic lack of talent. Pericles, subsiding more and more into drunkenness, believed that he was listening to the wailings in Hades. He no longer cared. His handsome face flushed. His helmet tilted over one ear. His wedding garments of silk became stained with wine and grease, he who was so fastidious. He looked across at Anaxagoras who was, with his exquisite politeness and unshaken courtesy, eating a little. Pericles winked openly at him, and at Pheidias. They began to avoid his eyes. Ichthus, who cared nothing for flavors or culinary delights, looked about to burst into a polemic, and Pericles kicked him deftly under the table. His friend glared at him, confused and bewildered. But something in those pale eyes directed at him kept him silent. He hated the Archon who to him embodied all the crimes of the Ecclesia. His overly sensitive mouth quivered; yet he obeyed Pericles, his idol, who, in turn, possessed all the heroic virtues. The hanging lamps looked down at the wedding party unshaded, and without fragrance. A cold wind swept through the hall at intervals and the one brazier in the

281

center of the room spluttered and gave out little warmth. The few slaves scurried, sweating, overwhelmed by the presence of too many guests for their services.

A young male slave listlessly moved among the guests carrying a basket of sesame cakes and intoning, as was traditional, "I have eschewed the worse, I have found the better." Ho, thought Pericles, and felt a wild impulse to roar with laughter. He looked at the table where his bride sat. Dejanira still wore her veil, but she was avidly stuffing her mouth under it, greedily, as if starving. Her whining voice drifted to him occasionally and he thought, I hope I am not moved to strangle her tonight. Would that not be rude of me? Tut, tut, I am a gentleman. The whiskey permeated his mind mercifully at last and he wanted to sleep. There was an acrid odor in the air which he disliked. He did not know that it came from the whiskey in his goblet and on his clothes. Daedalus scowled. His son-in-law was certainly behaving strangely. The Archon did not delude himself—for he had eyes—that his daughter was desirable except for her money and position. However, he resented this open display of intoxication on the part of Pericles. If he continued to drink that abominable whiskey he would become unconscious and that would be a scandal. The whiskey was also costly and was being wasted. He motioned away a slave who would have filled Pericles' goblet again but Pericles seized the bottle himself and poured the contents into the receptacle and drank it down in one gulp as if it were army wine. He began to shake with laughter, and his friends were alarmed. Open public laughter was foreign to Pericles who had a stately decorum at all times.

Then came the presentation of gifts to the bride. She and her mother eagerly inspected all, cleverly guessing at their price. Then they were satisfied, looking at each other with satisfaction. The guests had not forgotten that the bride was the daughter of an Archon, who could be a malevolent and dangerous enemy. Pheidias had presented a figurine of Hera so charmingly cast in shining bronze, and with details that were so incredibly living, that the guests exclaimed in sincere admiration. Pish, though the Archon. It is a nothing. It is worth but a few drachmas. The sculptor had fame; he ought to have presented a figurine of ivory and gold at the very least. Daedalus was insulted. He looked at Pheidias surlily under his tight eyelids. Fame! For such cheap trivia? Bah. He, Daedalus, would remember this offense.

It was now the time for the procession to take the bride to her new home. The marriage wagon was prepared; two white horses were attached to it. Anaxagoras, as the best man of the bridegroom, was, by tradition, obliged to drive it. He had forgotten this contingency, and was much alarmed until Pheidias offered his services also. Pericles never remembered how he, staggering and laughing, was got into the vehicle beside his still-veiled bride, but it vaguely seemed to him that something of sturdy bulk was his support and against which he helplessly sagged as the wagon proceeded over the cobblestones of the city, swaying and lurching. It was early night, and the stones glistened whitely with frost and a full moon was a cold and blazing ball skipping through thin black clouds. People rushed to their doors to see the procession, which was very large and noisy as it followed the wagon. The whole wedding party was on foot, carrying flaring red torches; flutes and lyres could hardly be heard over the roaring of the marriage hymn. Little boys began to follow the procession, capering like fauns, and the guests threw coins at them and sweetmeats.

Agariste had left the house of Daedalus to return to her own house, there to greet the bride and bridegroom. She looked about the perfection of the house, comparing it with the chill meagreness of her brother's, and gave orders to slaves who were splendidly dressed. She waited, pale and composed in her rosy robes, her shoulder and hair pins sparkling in the light of fragrant lamps, her golden hair seemingly carved on her head. She was satisfied with the decorations of the atrium. The house was embellished with laurel, olive and myrtle leaves and late flowers, and there were many handsome braziers warming every room. An odor of nard drifted through the house as if on a balmy breeze.

A slave brought her a torch and a myrtle wreath. The wreath was carefully placed on her head. She sighed, thinking of Xanthippus who should be wearing the wreath while she alone held the torch. Then she heard the noise of the procession and went calmly to the doors. The overseer of the hall, bowing, flung them open for her. The cold wind stirred her garments and she shivered. The procession was now at the doorstep, the wagon leading. Male slaves ran out to assist the bride and her groom. Dejanira heavily lumbered down, her veil flowing. The slaves had some difficulty with Pericles, to the laughter of the guests. They had to lift him down and then hold him upright. He had begun to sing a ribald ditty of the city streets and this increased the hilarity of the guests, who joined in—to Agariste's humiliation. She was not certain of the meaning of some of the coarser words but she guessed their import. Dejanira stolidly and silently walked at the groom's left hand, trudging like a milkmaid. Daedalus ignored the lewd singing for many of the singers were his friends, but Semele muttered.

On entering the atrium, Dejanira was showered, as was traditional, with dried figs and nuts. Her little black eyes darted under her veil, surveying the festive scene but above all the luxury of the house which she considered too costly. Agariste was apparently prodigal with money. Dejanira, having been reared in a frugal household where every drachma was counted twice before being reluctantly relinquished, was busily deciding in her mind that as she was now the mistress of her husband's house she would be firm in its management. There were too many slaves; there was too much lavishness. The beautiful rugs would be rolled up and carefully set aside except for occasions of festivity. The murals would be covered with cloths to preserve their lustre. She did not admire her aunt, whom she considered pretentious and unwomanly in her learning, and Agariste would soon learn who was mistress in this house. As she thought these things she munched on the bridal cake of sesame and honey, the crumbs littering her veil and falling on her bloated breast. The juice of the quince she had been given ran down her chin.

Pericles was glazed of eye and deeply red of face. The guests propped him upright. It was evident that he was not very conscious. He was led to the bridal chamber and dropped on the bed, where he sprawled. The bedside lamp was glowing with golden light, and it shone on the figurine which Pheidias had given him. The bride entered, still munching. The door was closed behind her and she was alone with her groom. In the atrium Daedalus formally bestowed Dejanira's dowry upon her husband's surrogate.

Dejanira lifted her veil and regarded Pericles and now her large face flushed and her black eyes gleamed. Having been married before she knew how to deal with a drunken husband. She slowly removed all Pericles' clothing, strongly moving him from side to side until he was a fallen white statue on the bed. She stood for some time, surveying him. She was smiling and her breast began to heave. Dear love, she said in her mind, I have adored you since first I saw you at a family festival, and you were but a child and I was little older. My dream of marriage to you has come true at last. Now I shall lie beside you and hold you in my arms as I have longed to do for many years.

On the other side of the door one of the bridegroom's friends stood formally on guard. The guests raised their voices in a nuptial hymn with such enthusiasm that the house rang. This was intended to ward off any evil spirits which might be prowling to do mischief.

Dejanira, no novice to these ceremonies, divested herself of her clothing until she stood only in her shift. She hesitated, then removed the shift and stood in the short massiveness of her nudity. The lamp glimmered on the bulges and ripples of her fat expanses. Her more than ample breasts swelled and tightened, her shapelessness quivered, and her obese thighs, thickly veined in purple, trembled. She gleamed with oil. She took the pins from her hair and the black and lightless mass fell over her shoulders and back and breasts. She blew out the lamp and climbed into the bed beside her sleeping and snoring husband.

She put her hand on his chest and pressed her head against his shoulder. She began to pant deeply. Her hands roved. Now she did not hear the singing uproar beyond the door. Her breath was burning on Pericles' flesh.

He was dreaming again of the lovely figurine which was rapidly becoming the supple form of a woman. He could see her face as if illuminated by the moon. She was lying beside him and murmuring endearments in his ear; he could feel her breath on his mouth, his cheek, his belly. "Love, love," she whispered. "My own beloved. I am beside you. Take me." Her hand was hotter and hotter, and roamed deliciously, and he began to shake with delight.

"Heart of my heart!" he cried aloud and Dejanira closed her eyes on a spasm of joy. He rolled upon her, groaning with ecstasy, clasping her tightly in his arms. He saw his love's red lips and brown eyes, smiling up at him in ethereal moonlight which existed only in his intoxicated mind. A fragrance of lilies floated up to his nostrils. "Sweetness of my soul," he said.

And so the marriage was consummated but Dejanira did not know that it was a woman of a dream with whom it was consummated, in the blackness of the chamber.

CHAPTER 9

One day, some years later, Pericles, in his official offices in the Agora, meditated on the incredible confusion, duplication to the last degree, chaos in the administration of government, the multiplication of mindless bureaucrats, the numerous Archons, the Areopagus, the Assemblies, the teeming magistrates of various titles, the Council of Five Hundred, the Eleven, the Heliaia, the Dikastai, the milling courts and tribunals where there were juries of from five hundred to two thousand men all convinced that their opinions and judgments were the truth and only the truth, and who shouted accordingly during sessions, and the Boule—which democracy had brought in Athens in the "name of the people."

He, himself, had fought the Areopagus, which had attempted to restore its authority to appoint only cultured aristocrats to positions of power in the government, and sometimes he ruefully reflected that perhaps he had been wrong in this. Perhaps anything was better than the tumult and turmoil in every department of government, hoarse with the base voices of the mob and masses and their sykophantai (informers), lowborn judges who resented men of superior intelligence and education and family, and the general corruption of democracy.

Government by asses! he said to himself with gloom. Such was democracy, which now governed Athens. (But he mistrusted his fellow aristocrats only a little less, for such led to tyranny by a few contrasted with the tyranny of the mobs.)

He contrasted all this with the simple Republic which Solon had envisioned, where a firm Constitution which all men must obey guided government and judges. Alas, that the vehement and volatile nature of Athenians in general had made this impossible, for they were always screeching for "new laws for new times," and the government invariably obliged, in the name of votes. Good and just men were now being ostracized, especially when they attempted to restore order and the rationality of a republic or protested the tyranny of the mob-elected government. At least half the electorate—"democracy!"—were illiterate. Solon had said that only men of some education and common sense and integrity should be permitted to vote, but later statesmen had called this "discrimination against the free citizens of Athens." They had known, in their contriving and wicked and exigent hearts, that if the kind of voter suggested by Solon was alone permitted to vote they, themselves, would never attain public office.

Republics were stable, forthright, and organized and cautiously prudent in respect to wild and irresponsible proposals for new laws. They were as humanly impartial as was possible in a naturally unequal world. Republics dealt with probity with every man, under a Constitution; favoritism had no place in republics. Republics had the masculine nature of strength, firmness, cold justice, reason and mistrust of emotionalism and had a horror of the passionate and seething anarchy of mob rule. For mobs were first of all intent on the satisfaction of base appetites and little mean pleasures. Republics were truly equitable in the administration of law; they held no distinction among malefactors, whether wellborn or peasant. Republics were discreet and wary when dealing with other nations, always aware that men are men and so could not be trusted when their emotions—and not law and order—were concerned. Republics were not imperialistic, for they were concerned only with the welfare of their own people; hence, republics entered into war only after profound reluctance had been overcome and the national safety was imperiled. Republics had the masculine love for conservatism in all things and a discreet suspicion of dangerous innovations. Law, to them, was sacrosanct, the distillation of the wisdom and experience of mankind. When they built they were certain that the building was based on stone. Above all things, Republics were mature.

But democracies were feminine, in that they were propelled only by fierce and passing emotions, concern for the immediate, unduly ambitious because they were vain, were many-tongued and chaotic, devious, passionate over trifles, ruled by bellies and not by mind and reason, discordant and arrogant, feuding and conceited, swayed by gossip, heedless and exigent, immature and often childish, caring nothing for integrity but only for instant satisfactions, anxious for amusements and laughter and transient concerns, eager for titillations. They had no concern for the future, and the concepts of law and order made them impatient and the enforcements of such led them to revolutionary rebellion. Republics could be trusted as much as any human institution could be trusted. But democracies were hazardous not only to themselves but to all the world, for in them lived terrorism and the seeds of their own violent death. Democracies, governed only by passions and unreason, loved wars. In short, Republics were ruled by law, democracies by the lawless.

Pericles began to dream of Solon's Republic, and his position and power under it.

When Ephialtes had been assassinated Pericles had been given, or had assumed, the position of leadership in the government. His eloquence was hypnotic. He was credited for the expansion of the State and in the continuance of Cimon's policy. He had sent two hundred ships to support the Egyptian rebels against the Persians, and had ordered detachments against Phoenicia and Cyprus. He was more or less forced to carry on the ambitions of the democracy of Athens and he had acquiesced in wars against Greece, proper. (He had the

287

thought of consolidating the various factions and rebels into one cohesive nation.) He had allied Athens with the Megarians, who had been threatened by Corinth, and had gained the hostility of Corinth. He knew that there would be more war and bloodshed before his hope for a united nation could be realized. Perhaps, under such a nation, peace and commerce would come into being and Athens would be the sun of the western world. He had not been deterred by the cool cynicism of Anaxagoras and the timidity of Zeno, his dear friends. There were times when a powerful man must act alone.

"I did not create these situations," he would argue with Anaxagoras. "But I must contend with them. Only when passions are subordinated to reason can a nation hope for freedom, the rise of the arts and sciences, and just government."

"You would, then, meet force with force?" asked Anaxagoras.

"When confronting a tiger one does not sing sweet songs," Pericles had replied. "I am no Orpheus. I must look at things as they are and not a chimaera of delusion. Hope is a liar when she does not deal with reality. Have you not said this yourself?"

"I have also said that the greatest art of man is meditation," said Anaxagoras.

"A dead man cannot meditate. Therefore, I intend to remain alive," the younger man had answered. "Later, I will meditate—when confusion dies."

He knew that his leadership in Athens was precarious. He was dealing with a vagrant democracy and not the republic of Solon. He was dealing with judges and bureaucrats and the unpredictable Archons and all the other Myrmidons of a corrupt mob-controlled government. He might be assassinated as Ephialtes had been assassinated. But he had long ago decided that too much prudence would result in inertia. He did not have the philosophers' fatalism or renunciation. He was driven by a vital dream, as he had been driven from childhood. He loved his country. He would rescue her from the rule of the base, the disorder of mindless rebels. Often he would gaze up at the acropolis and imagine there a crown of light, a diadem of brilliance, the rise of the free western world as opposed to the elaborate despotisms of the east. Athene Parthenos was his patroness, and in Chronos his hope.

He talked of this with Helena, his random mistress. She listened not only with sympathy but with understanding. "You need a hetaira of mind and greatness of heart," she told him. He tried to embrace her, laughing, but she moved out of his arms and said, "I belong to no man, and am not your hetaira, beloved. You must have a woman solely dedicated to you and not to a dead love."

She pondered, and then her face became cheerful. "I think I know the lady," she said, looking at him with brightening mischief. "A young woman, a protégée of Thargelia of Miletus, most beautiful, most accomplished. She has opened a school for girls of good family, wealth and position, here in Athens. Surely you must have heard of her."

"Aspasia?" he said, and made a mouth of distaste. "She is notorious. She has fashioned her school on the school of Sappho of Lesbos. What would I have to do with a Lesbian?"

"Sappho has been unjustly maligned," said Helena with reproof. "But why is it more reprehensible for a woman to love another woman, than a man to love a man?"

"You would not understand," said Pericles, smiling. She slapped him lightly on his bare shoulder and said, "That is the foolish reply of all men to an acute question from a woman. It tells us nothing except you will tell us nothing. Let us return to Aspasia. She was once the companion, the mistress, of a Persian satrap. She left him two years ago, heavy with jewelry and gold. The oppression of women in Persia is even worse than it is in Greece, and she is determined on the eventual emancipation of all women, as am I. If you laugh, my love, I shall drive you from my house. Your attention, please.

"I have heard from Aspasia, and from old Thargelia of Miletus, too, that from early youth it has been the dream of Aspasia that women's minds must be respected as well as their bodies loved, or lusted for, and that they have a mission in this world as well as a duty to bear sons to their husbands. They have talents unique to them, and who knows how many female geniuses have died in childbed? We have souls as well as genitals."

"I have never denied that," said Pericles. "I have an intelligent mother of many attributes, though she is growing waspish in her age. This is no wonder. Dejanira is the sole authority in the house and it is a case of older arrogance meeting younger arrogance, and Dejanira's vindictiveness is awesome—and dangerous—to encounter. So even my poor mother is silenced by her and I console her frequently, reminding her that it was she, not I, who desired this disastrous marriage."

"Do not distract me from the subject of Aspasia, Pericles. Aspasia is no Lesbian. It is reputed that she is very discriminating in the choice of lovers. It is said that she has had many, but this I do not believe, for she is fastidious and is concerned only with her school. Many of your more enlightened friends have placed their daughters under her tutelage. She not only teaches them the arts of song and dance and music but gives them an excellent education besides, equal to that of men. Zeno of Elea teaches them at intervals; philosophy and dialectics."

"For what end?" asked Pericles, with a gravity that pleased Helena. "What can an educated and intelligent woman do in this world?"

"I am a physician," said Helena, running her fingers through her auburn hair, which streamed over her bare breasts and shoulders. "It is true that I am considered infamous, but that is not of great moment to me. Many of my patients are men of distinction—and money, for I have a reputation, and a school of medicine and a large infirmia. I am very rich. I am not alone among my sisters, and many of the hetairai have married noble and famous men, men of family, who have regard for a woman's intellect and gifts. Have you not promised me that you will help women to attain their status in life, and so be regarded as human and with respect?"

"I have sworn it," said Pericles. "If I had daughters instead of two sons I could not be more determined."

"Good." She gave him a rewarding kiss. "I will give a dinner for Aspasia, and you will be one of my guests."

Pericles became weary. It was one of his convictions that, with the exception of Helena and a few more of the hetairai, women of intellect cared nothing for personal beauty and did not cultivate it in themselves and regarded it as trivial. He had been careful not to let Helena guess this opinion, which he held in common with other men. His mother, too, had been an exception. He said, "What is her appearance?"

She regarded him closely with her large blue eyes. "Is that of importance?"

"I dislike harpies," he said. "No one, man or woman, should neglect a pleasing aspect."

Helena sighed. "Aspasia is considered the most beauteous woman in Athens, for all she is no longer young, being twenty-two years old. Have you not heard of her loveliness?"

"I have heard she is a Gorgon."

"From men who have never seen her. For a powerful man who hears and sees everything you have been very ignorant. I will give that dinner in my house and you must come. Aspasia's voice is as lovely as her appearance, though it is no soft or gentle one, and not fluting. It resembles the singing in a sea shell, and men are captivated by it. She is also very amusing."

"A paragon," said Pericles. "Still, you have not told me of her appearance, except that she is beautiful. I have discovered that when a woman says a woman of her acquaintance is charming she is invariably no rival and is repulsive to men."

"You are speaking of mean and trivial women who have minds like pigs," said Helena. "When I say a woman is beautiful she is truly beautiful. Aspasia is as tall as I, but slender while I am robust, and her body would make Aphrodite envious. She has hair of so pale a color that it appears spun from both moonlight and sunlight. Why are you suddenly gazing at me so intently, Pericles?"

"I am but listening," said Pericles.

"She has an oval face, a complexion of milk and vermillion, and a mouth like a pomegranate. There is no aspect of her which is not perfect. Pheidias has already cast her in bronze from the memory he has of a small figurine he created. Why do you start so strongly, my love?"

"Did I start?" he replied. But he had paled. Anxiously she felt his forehead for fever, touched his pulse and was alarmed to feel it racing. She reached to the bedside table and poured him more wine and held it to his lips.

"I am not ill," he said. He drank the wine; his expression was abstracted. Then excitement seized him. "I must meet this famous Aspasia," he said.

She smiled in relief. Her description of her younger friend had stirred him and she was gratified for both Aspasia and Pericles, for she had a kind and loving heart. She forgot that she was a free woman and a physician of much renown and began to plot. The more she thought of Aspasia and Pericles together the more enthusiastic she was and the more determined.

"I will tell Aspasia that she is to meet the most powerful man in Athens," she said, laughing gleefully.

"Except for the damnable Archons and the rest of this government," he said.

"Dear love, you have forgotten that Pericles is also of the government."

That conversation with Helena had occurred last night, and he had almost forgotten it, for his mind was too disturbed today as he sat in his hot offices in the Agora and considered Athens and her government. Because of the discipline of his mind he could focus his thoughts on any subject and give it his full concern to the exclusion of other matters. Nothing distracted him from a reflection in which he was engaged. He had removed his toga of office and was clad only in a short tunic of yellow linen, without sleeves. He had folded his white strong arms across his chest and had lifted his sandaled feet upon his desk. As usual, he wore his tall helmet for he was still very sensitive on the subject of his towering brow and skull. His handsome face was full of brooding. Books and parchments and tablets and pens were strewn on the desk before him, awaiting his attention. Why are bureaucrats, he thought with loathing, always so zealous with pens and parchments, as if what bustled in their tiny minds was of importance? There was no one so busy as a man of no station and no consequence. I find it pathetic, this belief of theirs that what they record, or suggest, will have immortality, especially in oppressive laws.

He could hear the roar of the heavy traffic on the streets which surrounded the Agora, and the clamor of thousands of impatient voices. Common Athenians were noisy and insistent, unlike the aristocrats among them. This was not surprising; the market rabble in every country were alike. In other countries, however, the market rabble did not vote, except for the rising city-state of Rome, in Italy. Pericles promised himself to visit Rome, which was reputed to have been founded on a fratricide, but which was also reputed to be sternly moral and virtuous and full of industry, and whose great hero was Cincinnatus, the Father of his Country. It was said that Rome also had a representative government and this savored of a republic, in embryo at least. He had already received a request from the Roman Senate to permit it to send him a commission which desired to study the laws of Solon and his legislation.

I am afraid that they will be disappointed in the government we have! he thought, moving his buttocks restlessly on his chair. But it will do no harm to inspire a young nation with the dream of Solon, though we have not achieved it ourselves. A shaft of burning sunlight struck through the high narrow window and with it came a cloud of bright dust and the usual smell of a heated city—compounded of hot stone and latrines and animal offal and stale air and nameless astringent and dusty scents. A swarm of flies gushed through the windows and Pericles slapped at them irritably. Many of them settled on his desk and particularly on the rim of his wine goblet which was full of dregs. Some crawled on his white and muscular thighs. He snatched up a rolled parchment and killed them. That, he said to himself, is the sole usefulness of messages from a bureaucrat. He brushed the bodies from his flesh and flung the parchment from him.

A guard in plumed helmet and leather armor knocked on the bronze door then opened it tentatively. Seeing Pericles' glare he almost retreated; then his courage rose. "Lord, the noble thesmothetai Archon, Daedalus, is here to consult you on a grave matter."

Pericles muttered something particularly obscene and pithy concerning his father-in-law, then rose and nodded at the guard. He put his thumbs in each side of his silver girdle and cautioned himself to discipline his vexed thoughts. When Daedalus entered with his usual harsh quick glancing-about, Pericles greeted him amiably enough and led him to a chair. Daedalus was drier and more wizened than ever, and leaner of body and more skull-like of facial appearance, and his brown long robes were dusty.

He had never had a pleasant expression that Pericles could recall and age was making his skeleton's face more disagreeable every day. He was soured that he had not attained the position of King-Archon with extraordinary powers, for he was an ambitious man, ambitious for self-aggrandizement and not for his country. For this Pericles could not forgive him, among many other things he could not forgive Daedalus, including having begotten Dejanira.

Daedalus regarded his son-in-law's stateliness of form and his dignity of countenance. He both secretly respected and resented Pericles, who always appeared incomprehensible to him. Pericles puzzled him also, for though invariably serene and calm and firm he avoided any serious conversations with Daedalus. So the latter had come to the conclusion that Pericles, for all his fame as a soldier and a statesman, was innately frivolous. Pericles usually assumed a lightness in all dealings with Daedalus, because he held Dejanira's father in low esteem and unworthy of an intelligent man's time. Daedalus was never unconscious of Pericles' power, but there were powers he could not seize, thank the gods, and those certain powers belonged to the Archons. They were safe from Pericles, for did not the people honor them and vote for them?

Still, Daedalus was proud that Pericles had married his daughter and he would boast of him to his fellow Archons when he was alone with them. But he incessantly complained of him to Dejanira who agreed with him that Pericles was a difficult man, if a kind husband and indulgent father, and that he lacked the proper respect for an Archon.

"How may I serve you, Daedalus?" Pericles asked. "Cool wine, bread and cheese and fruit? I have some fresh plums and grapes in that closet yonder."

Daedalus waved away these suggestions. "I have no time for dallying, Pericles. I come to you on a matter of great importance."

Pericles doubted this but he inclined his helmeted head gravely and seated himself on a corner of his desk, and waited. Daedalus wished he would sit down in a chair, for Pericles' presence was overpowering when too close. This quality in him had intimidated larger men than Daedalus and Daedalus was suddenly furious that he felt that force in Pericles, that imminence which often appeared silently threatening. Daedalus swallowed his fury though his bony cheeks crimsoned.

"You have heard of one Ichthus?" said the older man in his grating voice.

Pericles widened his pale eyes and again they attained the aspect of a statue's eyes, blind and hidden. This usually affrighted more subtle and intelligent and powerful men than Daedalus, but the latter thought it merely unpleasant. It was as if Pericles had removed himself to a distance, and Daedalus was vexed.

"You know I have not only heard of Ichthus, Daedalus," said Pericles in a gently perilous voice, "but you know he is one of my dearest friends and that he saved my life when we were young." He paused because he was suddenly alarmed; he hid the alarm from his detestable father-in-law, but he grasped his elbows tightly. "Ichthus is of a most distinguished family, as you know, Daedalus, almost as distinguished as mine," and certainly more honorable than yours, he added to himself.

Daedalus, always careful of himself, heard the warning in Pericles' voice. But he was a malicious man, and sharp malice made him less afraid of Pericles today than he customarily was. Pericles, he reminded himself, was not entirely invulnerable. There were still things he could not do in spite of his position.

"I know all about Ichthus' family," said Daedalus. "His father was ostracized for heretical opinions and died in exile. Despite your gracious opinion of Ichthus, Pericles, the family is not notable. Nor is it rich."

Pericles still fixed those blind eyes on the other man and did not answer. He only waited.

"Ichthus wasted his patrimony by buying and freeing worthless slaves, and on his activities, which are both imperious and subversive of government."

Daedalus watched Pericles closely but Pericles' face remained impervious. "I know of Ichthus' dedication to the freeing of slaves," he said. "I find it admirable, for did not Solon demand this also? It is not unlawful, this bestowing of liberty on the unfortunate who are suffering under the whips and tortures of cruel masters. Mercy is not to be despised. You have mentioned my friend's 'activities.' What are they?"

Daedalus lifted a hand which appeared fleshless. "He is your friend, is he not, Pericles? Surely you must know that he is the author of seditious writings denouncing the government and accusing us of all vileness and oppression, of corruption and defilement of the laws of Solon, of faithlessness toward the people of Athens, and crying for our overthrow."

He still watched Pericles, but Pericles remained as if uninterested.

"Your friend," said Daedalus, in a weighty tone. "Do his activities not offend you?"

"I do not believe he does these things," said Pericles. His remark was apparently idle and amused. "If he did what you have accused him of, then surely I would know. He was a guest at my wedding. We were schoolboys together. I count him closer than a brother. No, I do not believe the foolish charges against him. The world is full of malevolent men. Ichthus probably offended one of them without intention, for he is timid and retiring and gives the impression of weakness. Therefore he is open to enmity; in particular the enmity of the brutal."

Daedalus lost his temper. "If he is truly your friend, then you are in danger, yourself, Pericles! I have only this advice to give you, for you are the husband of my daughter, and you are ambitious: Deny that you know much of him. Declare, if asked, that he is but a slight acquaintance, from childhood. If pressed and reminded that he is often seen in your company, denounce him, and feign horror when told of his writings."

Pericles' heart was a heavy thumping in his chest. But he maintained his attitude of serenity. He knew that Daedalus hated him, for all his pride in him. He also knew that Daedalus' position as an Archon would come under scrutiny, for was he not the father of Pericles' wife? So Daedalus was impelled to protect both his own station and the station of Pericles, however he might resent the latter.

Pericles said in the most detached voice, "Have public charges been made against Ichthus?"

"Seven thousand ostraka have been received," said Daedalus, again watching Pericles closely.

But Pericles laughed aloud and slapped one of his knees. "I doubt if Ichthus knows *seven* men in Athens! What absurdity is this?" Then he made his face serious. "Those who signed those potsherds are liars and libelers, and should be prosecuted for defaming the gentle character of a harmless and merciful man."

He stood up and began to pace the room indignantly, breathing loudly so that the outraged sound would reach Daedalus' ears. "Illiterate peasants from the country, who must have friends sign the ostraka for them! It is not unknown that many men have been ostracized or even executed by the Assembly, upon receiving forged potsherds produced in the thousands at the command of a venomous man who desired some revenge on another man, or had malignance in his soul. It is not unknown that citizens have been suborned and bribed to send in the ostraka, if a criminal desires the fortune of the accused man, or his position, or envies him for one reason or another."

Daedalus cried, "Are you accusing the Assembly of corruption, of being the creature of designing and evil men?"

I can accuse them of much worse, thought Pericles, his teeth clenching together. He stopped his pacing, his back to Daedalus, and pondered. The situation was terrible. At all costs Ichthus must be saved.

Daedalus said, seeing that Pericles would not reply to his question, "You did not know that we have discovered, through confidential and unimpeachable sources, that Ichthus is really being condemned for his writings, and that the Ecclesia has hundreds of such writings in its possession. Ichthus has not denied the writings, when confronted."

Pericles held himself very still. What a fool was Ichthus for not denying the authorship of the inflammatory writings! But what a man of fearless integrity lived under that inoffensive exterior, that retiring demeanor! Athens would be free and saved if only two thousand of his kind lived in the city.

"This is in addition to the ostraka," Daedalus added, exasperated by Pericles' silence and his turned back. "Have you nothing to say, husband of my daughter?"

Pericles slowly faced his father-in-law and for an instant Daedalus was frightened, though Pericles' features were still serene and the light eyes still indifferently blank.

"I have this to say, Daedalus," he said in a slow and steadfast voice. "I will defend him before the ostrakophoria and the Ecclesia."

Daedalus started to his feet, holding his arms above his head, and his countenance was distorted. But before he could speak Pericles abruptly left the room.

CHAPTER 10

Pericles loved his sons, Xanthippus, eight years old, and Paralus, two years younger. Miraculously, neither resembled their mother, Dejanira, for which favor Pericles had sacrificed on their births. Xanthippus resembled his grandfather of the same name and Paralus, though he had Dejanira's black eyes, had Pericles' coloring and stature. Xanthippus had his grandfather's high sense of humor and mischief and quick intellect and slight and elegant body and was already famous for his vivacious wit. Paralus was more serious, somewhat inflexible of character, took life, even at six, as a sober affair and rarely laughed or played pranks, was stronger than his older brother and taller, and moved ponderously. Xanthippus excelled in such athletics as the bow and light fencing and playing with balls, and was dexterous and fast. Paralus excelled in discus-throwing, wrestling and pugilism. Xanthippus was as fluid as water, Paralus tenacious and fixed in opinions and also very determined.

It was Pericles' custom to join the lads at sunset, before dining alone, for an hour of discussion and play and comments on their tutors. Sometimes Xanthippus, the elder, was permitted to dine with his father, but Paralus was still too young and ate his meals with his mother in the women's quarters. They were both fond of their mother, Dejanira, though Xanthippus teased her frequently, for she had no gift of drollery and could only stare, frowning, at him and try to understand his sallies. Paralus sympathized with her, for often Xanthippus teased him also though usually he could reply to his brother in a slow bantering fashion. Of the two, Dejanira preferred Paralus not only because he resembled Pericles but because he appeared to be kinder and of a tender sensibility.

There were no other children, for Pericles had not called his wife to his bed since the birth of Paralus. He was afraid that the gods might not be so benign with other children and that they might be born looking like their mother and with her immovable obtuseness. Moreover, Dejanira became more and more repugnant to him, more unbearable to his nostrils. Worse still, she adored him and would look at him with imploring eyes when she saw him, and he pitied her the more execrable she became to him. Therefore he avoided her, though admitting that she was most able in household affairs and was increasing his fortune through frugality and expert managing.

He never interfered with household matters though he had refused to permit Dejanira to make his house into a replica of her father's and had demanded that she treat Agariste with deference and listen to her advice concerning the meals he ate and the preparations for guests. Dejanira, abjectly worshipful, obeyed him in all instances though she detested Agariste and considered her an idle woman. She, herself, almost lived in the kitchen, overseeing the kitchen slaves and the cook, and watching every fragment of food and every drachma. Delicacies were for Pericles only, and she silently deplored his extravagant tastes and his demands for the best of wines. When Agariste protested that she now dined on the food of slaves Pericles intervened in her behalf and Agariste ate at her own table while Dejanira and her sons dined apart, Dejanira sniffing loudly in derision at the expensive items on Agariste's plate, the good wine, the fine dishes. Once she said loudly, in her whining voice, "We shall be bankrupt." To which Agariste had replied, "In the meantime we shall dine as human beings and not as pigs."

Dejanira's son by Hipponicus, Callias, was now sixteen years of age, and was a male replica of his mother, being short and massive and fat and disagreeable of temperament. He sullenly resented his brothers for their appearance and their accomplishments, and would console himself that he was surnamed "The Rich," for he had been his father's heir. He was as miserly as his mother and dressed as meanly as a slave and his tutors despaired of him. He was no athlete. He preferred cock-fights, the bloodier the better. He also liked to gamble, but as he was not averse to cheating he was rarely invited to participate with the companions at his academe. They called him, invidiously, the Dog, referring to the treble kybos, or three ones at dice. He also annoyed them by infrequently throwing the kybos and by winning regularly. He brought his own dice to games, and they were loaded, and so none would play with him unless he consented to the common dice, when he would win as sporadically as the others. This would throw him into a temper, and as he was strong as well as fat few cared to contend with him. His fighting was as shameless as his cheating and he was infamous for driving his knee into groins.

He hated Pericles and ridiculed him to his mother when she would permit it, and after Pericles had rejected her again and she was sore at heart and grieving. Though usually sluggish of mind he seemed to be able to perceive when contemptuous remarks would not be forbidden by her. He would then grin snottily at his brothers, who despised him and openly scorned him and pretended to be deaf at the slurs on their father. He would chuckle hoarsely. He had attempted to treat the younger boys brutally on more than one occasion, until Pericles had thrashed him in the presence of Xanthippus and Paralus, and Dejanira, who had stood aside whimpering and wringing her hands. But she loved Callias far less than she did the younger boys and was reluctantly relieved when he would order his slave to pack his chest for a prolonged visit to Daedalus' house. Daedalus preferred him to his younger grandsons.

During the past few months Pericles had conferred with his bankers concerning Dejanira's dowry and the increase in it, for he had come to the conclusion that he must divorce his wife. Though seeing her seldom and rarely close by, he found her presence in his house more and more intolerable. He saw the misery of his mother, who had no escape from Dejanira as he did, with his hetaira and other women of even less repute. He saw the mutinous expressions of his slaves who resented Dejanira and who complained to the overseer of their bad food and crowded quarters, and the overseer complained to Pericles in their interest. For Pericles was a kind master and treated them as paid servants rather than slaves, and often rewarded them lavishly and if petitioned enough he would free them, warning them, however, of the perils of freedom. When, at Dejanira's secret orders, distinguished guests had been served a poor wine in richly ornamented bottles, he had decided that he could endure Dejanira no longer. That wine was symbolic of the climate of his house. He had upbraided Dejanira for his mortification and she had burst into tears, had tried to embrace him, and had wept, "I only sought to save you money, lord." He had spurned her then as one spurns an importunate and untrained dog.

Not even the fact that his sons had considerable affection for their mother could deter him any longer from divorcing her. They could see her in the house of Daedalus at regular intervals. He was afraid that some of her coarseness might be conveyed to them and he loathed Callias as much as Callias hated him. Pericles, always pragmatic, feared that Callias might infect his sons in some fashion. As for Dejanira's own feelings, he did not consider them, for he doubted she possessed any capacity for devotion though she had been repellently passionate towards him when he had called her to his bed out of a sense of duty and compassion. He no longer pitied her. He must rid himself of her and as quickly as possible. As yet the unfortunate woman had no premonition that her husband's lawyers were already preparing for the suit.

On this evening after Daedalus' visit to Pericles' office Pericles did not call for his sons. He wished to be alone while he considered the deadly danger to his friend and how he must protect and save him, for, on inquiry among his friends in the Agora, he had learned that not mere ostracism was contemplated for Ichthus, but death. The King Archon had been consulted but two hours before, and even Daedalus had not known, though he had been informed of it an hour after he had left Pericles.

Pericles did not know that at the very time that he was attempting to eat his dinner Daedalus was in terrified and raging consultation with Dejanira.

"He will destroy us all if he defends that Chilon!" he cried to his daughter. "He is already in bad favor among men of influence, who not only mention his resemblance to the Tyrant, Pisistratus, but assert that he is aiming at arbitrary power. He has been accused of cynicism in that he, an aristocrat, has set himself aside from his fellow aristocrats, and espouses the humble merely to make his position secure. It is noted that though he pretends to be the friend of the common people he keeps far from their presence and lets them see him rarely. He is too ambitious, sinister, ambiguous, to have many influential friends. It is no secret that he was the instigator of the banishment of Cimon, who was truly beloved, for he coveted Cimon's power. Yet, my daughter, he connived with Cimon later to have Cimon appointed commander of the fleet while he ruthlessly plotted with him to gain power in Athens for himself, with Cimon's consent. It is even rumored that he had procured the murder of Ephialtes, the great and popular statesman!"

Dejanira whimpered and wrung her fat hands together and squinted through her tears. "I know of none of this, my father, and it is possible they are lies inspired by envy."

"Hah!" exclaimed Daedalus fiercely. "I believe it all,

though he is the husband of my daughter! He desires to be a monarch! The aristocratical party justly fears and hates him, for they consider him a traitor to his nation and his family, and his ancestors. They rightly fear his power, which he unlawfully took upon himself—"

Dejanira said with a spirit unusual with her, "Father, that is not true! The citizens of Athens raised him by his merits."

"Silence, woman!" cried infuriated Daedalus, lifting his hand as if to strike her. She subsided and renewed her whimperings, shrinking from her father.

"The aristocratical party has induced Thucydides the Alopece, kinsman of Cimon, to oppose him, a good and intrepid man. He will succeed! Thucydides is no hypocrite, to woo the people to advance his own power. You have not read the writings on the walls of Athens, infamous accusations against Pericles scrawled by the very people he defends against the aristocrats. I tell you he lusts to be king and that Athens will not endure!"

Dejanira could only sniffle forlornly. Her father regarded her with exasperation. "He is your husband," he said. "He is the father of your sons. You must prevail upon him to listen to you, that if he continues his plan to defend Ichthus not only he may be destroyed, but you and your children also."

Dejanira broke into fresh tears, and her face turned very red. She averted her face and said, "I have no influence on Pericles, my father. Rarely do I encounter him. He avoids me. I fear he despises me. I enter his chamber no more, not since the birth of Paralus. He has abandoned me for dissolute women. You have said that when you spoke to him today he turned on his heel and left you, after daunting words. You are an Archon, a man of position. If he will not listen to his father-in-law, why should he listen to me?"

Daedalus stood up, shaking with rage. He looked down at his stricken daughter and he, who rarely felt pity, felt it now. He laid his hand on her head and said in a trembling voice, "My daughter, I did not know of this indignity laid upon you, and your mother did not know for she would have told me. There is but one solution: You must leave him and petition for a divorce, and return to your father's house with your children. Only then will the people realize that you are blameless, that you renounced your husband for his treason, and removed your children from his house lest they be dishonored and punished in their father's name."

"Leave Pericles?" wailed Dejanira, her small black eyes

bulging with grief. "He is my husband! I love him, no matter the humiliations he has heaped upon me, and in the presence of the very slaves."

Daedalus seized her fat shoulder and shook it. "Have you thought of your parents, my daughter? I am an Archon. Do you not realize that not only you and your children will be destroyed by the impetuous actions of this man but your parents also? Five innocent people! You will let us all die, or be exiled and our fortunes confiscated? You will serenely permit yourself, and your family, to live in dire poverty far from Athens, on some barbarous island? Have I begotten a human daughter, or a female Cyclops who sees with but one eye but who is blind to those she should dutifully love?"

Dejanira stared up at Daedalus through her tears and saw that her father was truly desperate and affrighted, and the color fled from her face and it was a yellowish white. Daedalus nodded at her grimly. "Our fortunes, if not our lives, are in deadly danger from the man you call your husband. Dare you defend him, and remain with him until we sink into the Styx?"

She could not speak for her own terror and anguish. She wrung her hands and sobbed deep in her breast.

"Speak to him!" her father commanded. "Speak to him this night. If he is adamant, send me a message and I will dispatch litters for you and your children and you will return to your father's house and will procure a divorce. Tell him this."

Dejanira pressed her hands to her breast and her stolid face was contorted with fear and suffering and hopeless love. She whispered, "I will try. I swear by Hera that I will try. That is all I can promise. If I fail," she paused and wept louder, "I will return to your house, my father, and that tomorrow."

"And he will be forced to return your dowry and what has accrued to it," said Daedalus, sighing with relief. It seemed to him, as a covetous man, that the loss of Dejanira's dowry would be a worse blow to Pericles than the loss of his family.

Dejanira said almost inaudibly, "He loves his sons. He may not permit their removal."

"Then, once you have left his house, and he is ruined, we will petition for the return of your children from the nefarious influence of their father. Do not be distressed, my daughter. Attempt, as your duty, to prevail upon him to reconsider. If not, then you must flee at any cost." He rubbed his bony hand over his face and sighed. "I am a man not without influence. Your children will be given to me as their guardian. I would that I had never consented to this marriage, but my sister besought me to consent."

Dejanira was not without shrewdness. She knew it was her father who had proposed the marriage and not Agariste. She thought of Agariste with a sudden venom, Agariste who did not conceal from her her contempt for her daughter-in-law.

"It was through me that he was assisted to power," said the Archon. "One must never forget it. Would that the Furies had paralysed my tongue before I did that!"

He embraced his daughter and departed, and after long and shivering thought Dejanira sent a slave to Pericles, beseeching him to permit his wife to visit him immediately. While she waited for his reply she bathed her reddened eyes, combed her hair and changed her rumpled garments and rubbed her eyes and throat with attar of roses. Dismally, she looked into her silver mirror and for the first time confessed to herself that she had no graces and no beauty and no attributes to enchant a man, especially a man like Pericles. She had thought herself desirable for her money and her father's position in Athens. Now she vaguely comprehended that Pericles did not need her money, and that he was far more powerful than her father. Hence, she could not appeal to him on these grounds. Ah, if I had but beauty and were young! she cried in herself. But I am ugly, and I am old, and there are white hairs on my head and I have three chins. She was devastated as never she had been before.

Still, she consoled herself with the thought that Pericles might listen to wise counsel for the sake of his sons if not for her sake. There was also his mother, who would be in deadly peril.

Dejanira paused, the glittering and jeweled mirror in her hand, and stared into space. Agariste. Much as she disliked the older woman and much as she had tried to relegate her to an inferior position, Agariste, at the last, might be a formidable ally. Waddling fast and ponderously, she went to Agariste's quarters.

Agariste had not surrendered her own exquisite and tasteful rooms to the new mistress of the house. After dining at night she would retire to her chamber and go to bed, for she was increasingly infirm and physicians spoke of her heart. She could not forget her husband, Xanthippus, and found him enlarging in stature and virtues through the years. She often accused herself of stupidity in not understanding him, and her pride, for upbraiding him. He had loved her even if he had disliked her. He had seen her at a distance and so theirs had not been an arranged marriage in the true meaning of the word. He had, himself, gone to her father and beseeched him to consent to the marriage, declaring his love. In his way he had honored her for several years and had not resorted to a hetaira or any other woman. It was I who drove him from me, she would say in the sleepless midnights, with my presumptions and my vanity. I was too insistent that he admire me for my intelligence. I did not know until after he died that he did so admire me for it, even if he never confessed that to me.

It came to her, sadly, that one never gained wisdom until it was too late. The gods were malign.

She very seldom slept deeply but only drowsed, to awaken to gaspings for breath and a piercing pain in her heart. She had fallen into a sick doze when a slave entered her chamber softly and said, "Lady, the Lady Dejanira would speak to you for a moment on a matter of the most extreme importance."

Agariste, blinking in the soft light of the lamps, forced herself to sit upright. Her breath was loud and struggling in the fine chamber. A warm night wind scented with roses blew into the room through the open window. She stared at the slave. What would Dejanira have with her, she who had never entered these rooms and had never been invited? The two women avoided each other as much as possible. Dejanira had never asked her advice except on a few occasions. Whenever they did speak together Dejanira would gaze at Agariste with sullen resentment and, as always, would try to impose her authority as mistress of the household on Agariste. She was invariably and coldly rejected by the older woman, but still she persisted in her stubborn way. Only yesterday they had had a quarrel, Agariste disdainful and aloof, Dejanira stammering with surly anger and insistence. At last Agariste had said, "You may be the daughter of my brother, the Archon, but to me you have the manners of a kitchen wench, and an insolent one. Your father is my brother, and so is descended from a noble house, but your mother is as vulgar as you and had only money to distinguish herself. She has taught you well and you are as insufferable as she." Dejanira had heavily stamped away, muttering and helpless.

Agariste said to the slave woman, "The Lady Dejanira wishes to speak to me? Is one of my grandsons ill?" She pushed herself even higher on the bed and was frightened, for her son's children were very dear to her.

"I do not know, Lady," said the slave woman. "But the Lady Dejanira implores you to receive and listen to her."

Only a great emergency could have driven Dejanira to her, and Agariste sipped at the cup of medicine at her bedside, and trembled inwardly as she awaited the coming of her daughter-in-law. She pulled her shift more easily over her still beautiful breasts, but her face was haggard and lined with pain and very white, and her golden hair had long lost its lustre and was dull and streaked with gray. An agonizing pang shot through her heart and she gasped and leaned back on her cushions, and a cold sweat of apprehension and mortality bathed her whole body. It seemed to her that an icy wind swept through the warm chamber. Her colorless lips dried and she thought she tasted blood.

Dejanira entered the chamber, sobbing. But she had the shallowness of mind of the stupid and was easily distracted by trifles even when in great distress. She glanced about her curiously while the tears ran down her fat cheeks. She almost forgot, at least for a moment or two, the mission which had brought her here, as her swollen black eyes darted disapprovingly about the room and noted the costly lemonwood tables with their delicate lamps of gold and Egyptian glass, and the Damascene brocades at the window, the chairs of ivory and ebony inlaid with enamels, the painted walls depicting Pan and fauns in woodland settings, the flowers in tall and graceful vases of inestimable value, the thick Persian rugs on the marble floor. The bed was not the plain bed of the usual Greek chamber, but opulent with silk, and wool of such fine weave that the coverings appeared woven of air and gossamer. There were many small marble statues about in niches, all of incomparable workmanship. There are several fortunes here, thought Dejanira, fortunes which should be invested in ships and cargoes and banks, and she was filled with vexation and umbrage. Then she sank, unasked, onto a fragile chair—which creaked ominously with her weight—and began to wail loudly.

"In the name of the gods, tell me!" cried Agariste and turned even paler. Dejanira was stolid and without much emotion, so Agariste assumed that the news she brought was appalling. She wanted to strike that shapeless woman in her anxiety.

Dejanira said, "We are ruined, we are destroyed, and all with us!" Her voice was hoarse and harsh and she rocked on her massive buttocks and her tears streamed. "Pericles has brought the Furies down upon us, and we are lost!"

Agariste regarded her incredulously. Her impassive son, so remote and self-disciplined and laconic in speech except when addressing the Assembly, could hardly have been so impetuous and reckless as Dejanira indicated. She sank back on her cushions and said in a cold and peremptory voice, "Tell me."

It was almost impossible for Dejanira to tell a coherent story for her thoughts invariably flittered onto irrelevances. So Agariste was forced to strain her attention upon the flood of stammering words which poured from that thick wet mouth. Loud sobs interrupted the flow; Dejanira spoke of the honor of her parents, the delinquencies of the slaves in her husband's house, the depredations of the cooks on the larder and the money, the fate of her sons, her threatened self, her father's fear and offer, his importunities that she talk with Pericles, her general dissatisfaction with the ordering of the household, her fright, impending bankruptcy, her premonitions of disaster which had haunted her for many months, Pericles' indiscretion and his mistresses, her unfortunate fate which marriage had brought upon her, the failure of Pericles' last investment in ships to Egypt, her meekness and virtue under insufferable trials in this house, the lack of appreciation she received for all her scrupulousness and thrift, and sundry other things.

Agariste wanted to scream. She reached out her thin hand and clutched Dejanira's enormous wrist. "Tell me!" she almost shouted. "You fool! Can you not bring your feeble wits to order and enlighten me? What has all this to do with the disaster you spoke of?"

The flood of meaningless complaints came to an abrupt halt, and Dejanira was outraged by her aunt's voice and the fierce seizing of her wrist. She strove for dignity. "Have I not been telling you, Agariste?" she said. "But you will never listen to me! We are undone."

But Agariste's eyes were quelling and enlarged, so Dejanira dropped her head and her moist face became sullen. She could hardly remember her father's specific denunciations of Pericles, for she was always confused by rapid speech, which she could not follow. But Agariste, sitting stiffly upright on her bed, was finally able to grasp a little of what Daedalus had imparted to his daughter. At last she dropped the wrist she had been clutching and lay back on her pillows, panting. She stared at the gilded and painted ceiling for a long time after that whining and sniveling voice had ceased and broken sobs had replaced it.

The lamplight, golden and soft, fluttered over the walls and the furniture and a nightingale began to sing in the gardens in sad and poignant music. Agariste thought rapidly. Surely

Pericles was not insensible to the peril and jeopardy into which he was hurling his family. He was not volatile or heedless. His emotions, however stirred, did not rush him into fatalities. His friendships were temperate if strong. Anaxagoras had taught him that; but he was innately prudent. Agariste was again incredulous, though she knew that Dejanira had so little imagination that it was impossible for her to be inventive, and exaggerate.

She broke into Dejanira's sobbing and said, "I can hardly believe this of my son. I will go with you to his chambers, for your slave woman has announced that he will see you." She glanced at Dejanira contemptuously and rose with difficulty and threw a white toga over her nightdress. Her heart was painfully thumping but her countenance was composed. "Come," she said, and led the way from her chamber, and Dejanira followed her like a servant, moaning over and over. Agariste walked like a goddess, proudly suppressing her pain, and thinking, and Dejanira trailed after her like an obese shadow, sniffling.

Pericles was sitting in his library, but he was not reading. His face was closed and intent. He looked up at the two women and frowned, but he directed his attention at once on his mother. He saw her translucent pallor and requested her to seat herself, but he did not invite his wife to do likewise.

"I was informed that only Dejanira wished to see me," he said, but his tone was gentle towards his mother. "You are ill; why have you risen to visit me this night?"

Agariste waved her hand in the direction of Dejanira but did not look at her. In a few concise words she repeated what Dejanira had told her, and the threats of Daedalus. She had an orderly mind and could speak shortly and clearly. As she did so she watched Pericles' face. It had become impassive again, a marble mask which concealed his thoughts. When Agariste had stopped speaking he leaned back in his chair and was silent. His mother waited. Dejanira's sobs and random exclamations filled the library. Her black hair was disheveled, for she had been running her fingers through it constantly in her distraught state. Her cheeks were blotched, her eyes and nose red. She mumbled over and over about bankruptcy, her father's position as Archon, ruin, exile, confiscations of estates. But neither Pericles nor Agariste heeded her.

Then Pericles said to his mother, "It is all true, that I must defend Ichthus, for he is a simple, just and good man, and he speaks the truth. He also, unfortunately, writes it, and broadcasts it."

"You understand the consequences if you fail, my son?"

"I have weighed them. I shall not fail. I must only induce Ichthus to recant and plead for mercy, for he values my opinion and guidance. He is a man of fervor, but tractable. I have been thinking of all this for hours, and I have come to the conclusion that a brief ostracism will be his only punishment."

Pericles was not so confident as he appeared, but he wished to allay his mother's fears and to soothe her.

Agariste sighed with relief. Her son was the most powerful man in Athens. She thought of Xanthippus, who would defend a man and his principles, however he deplored them. But Xanthippus had been heedless on many occasions, while Pericles was never heedless. Nevertheless, father and son were both exemplary in public virtue and never failed to do their duty. Agariste sighed again, sorrowfully.

Then Pericles turned to his wife for the first time and his face was even more impassive and hard. "I must inform you, Dejanira, that I am about to divorce you. You have made my house untenable and caused disorder and dissension in it. You must leave my house tomorrow and return to your father, taking your son, Callias, with you, but my own sons must remain."

Dejanira's lumbering thoughts were stirred into disjointed confusion. She was also filled with despair. She broke into loud and hysterical weeping. She attempted to go to her husband but Agariste restrained her. The mother said to her son in a dispassionate voice, "This is for the best. We have been an unhappy household since your marriage, Pericles. Unhappiness is not to be suffered if it can be removed."

She stood up and took Dejanira firmly by the arm and forced the younger woman to look at her. "You will have observed that none of us is in danger, and it is all your father's fevered imagination. Go to your quarters at once, there to prepare to leave this house in the morning."

Dejanira struggled with her briefly, while Pericles watched, then subsided. She burst out into a storm of denunciations, complaints, pleas, importunities, incongruous arguments. Pericles closed his eyes wearily. Sweating, Dejanira exuded an offensive smell and the fastidious Pericles drew in his nostrils, as did his mother hers.

"Come," said Agariste. But she pitied Dejanira who had been so brutally dismissed and rejected. "There is no use in crying this way. Tomorrow is time for reflection and decision." Dejanira stared at her with bulging eyes, and licked away the moisture on her upper lip. She thought that Agariste was assuring her that she would not have to leave this house. Her breast heaved and she permitted Agariste to lead her away.

She said to the silent woman as they walked through the halls, "I love Pericles. He is my life, my love. On our wedding night he called me his sweetness. I have never forgot it. He embraced me not only with passion but with joy."

Agariste raised her eyebrows, disbelieving. She was also surprised that Dejanira could love in this manner, and with such vehemence. Again, she pitied the younger woman and her touch on Dejanira's arm was kind and comforting. Yet she knew that Pericles' decisions were inexorable.

CHAPTER 11

Though Anaxagoras had told Pericles that a man who could not command his body and his emotions to his will was not a full man at all, Pericles found that he could not sleep that night. He had disciplined himself to make firm decisions and then act upon them with no regret and no wistful glances back over his shoulders. A strong decision, which later proved catastrophic, was far better than vacillation, which weakened a man. One was action, the other inaction; one was life, the other a dim death. Pericles had long before decided to divorce his wife. Still, he had not been insensible to her wild grief and protestations of love, and her lamentations. These had not shaken his decision; compassion was often cowardice, which one later regretted. Or, one became hostile and angered, knowing that he had succumbed to artful manipulation, and had been betrayed by maudlin deceit on the part of others.

To him, the situation of Ichthus was far more grave. Unable to sleep, unable to reach a decision—he was innately a prudent man for all his resolution and character—he rose long before dawn and sent a message to the barracks that he would be leaving immediately. A sleepy slave brought him a cool melon, a delicately broiled fish, light bread and wine for his breakfast. He ate, brooding, and tapped the table with his fingers. At moments he was furious with his endangered friend for his indiscretion; Ichthus had also placed his few friends in jeopardy, and his widowed mother and his relatives. But in the next moment Pericles would say to himself: He is a brave man, and courage is more to be desired than any other virture. He did what he must. That is all a man can do.

Pericles stared at the smoking lamp on the table, which

flickered in the darkness of the small dining hall, and he cursed the government of which he was a part for its oppressiveness. He cursed the Archons and the Assembly and the Ecclesia. Though Daedalus had accused him of pampering and wheeling the market rabble, no aristocrat in Athens despised that rabble more than Pericles, himself. He had not been reluctant to express his detestation, and he had admitted his fear of the rabble, which was incontinent, vociferous, irrationally passionate, stupid, the prey of sly demagogues, greedy, demanding, thinking with the area below the navel and never from the chin up. To Pericles, they were the peril of the nation, for they lacked heroism and patriotic fervor and the spirit of self-denial. The immediate was their only concern, and their base animal appetites. By the very weight of their overwhelming numbers they were dangerous to the State and to law and order. They invited chaos. The athlete or the Statesman they fawned on today they would render apart tomorrow and with the same lack of discrimination, and with the same absence of considered judgment. That which displeased other men but slightly, stirred anarchy among the rabble, and destruction, and the lust for murder. Yes, it was well to fear them.

The aristocrats, in the main, did not distinguish between the rabble and those whom Cyrus the Great had so extolled: The sturdy peasantry, the small merchants, the industrious manufacturers, the shopkeepers, the artisans, the builders and the conscientious workers, the scribes and the clerks, the officers of the army and the navies, the cooks, the innkeepers, the weavers and the blacksmiths, the prudent little investors, the wine-makers, the shipbuilders and the mill owners, and many others on whom the very existence of a nation depended. But Pericles distinguished between them and the rabble. It was his hope that the rising middle class between the rabble and the aristocrats would grow in strength and influence, and so he cultivated it. To him they were the heart of a country and their judgments, though often simple and rarely complex, were usually sound and sensible. They also had a profound mistrust of government and their elected officials, which Pericles considered very perspicacious. Unlike the rabble, which adored power, the middle class suspected it. They paid their enforced taxes ruefully—the rabble usually paid no taxes— and grumbled loudly. They voted glumly but with care. The rabble voted for any pretty face or eloquent liar.

To his fellow aristocrats Pericles was ambiguous; some of them hinted he was a traitor to his ancestors. To the rabble he was accursed, an oppressor. But the middle class admired and revered him. They knew he was concerned with them and admired them in turn. He had been able to relieve them of many customs duties when they engaged in trade and imported or exported. It was no secret in Athens that he desired to make of his city a place of beauty and glory for the joy of the multitude and honor abroad. But his enemies—and they were a multitude in themselves—condemned him for removing the common treasury of Greece from the island of Delos into Athens, herself, where it could be available for the construction of temples and beautiful public buildings, and theatres and the extirpation of noisome alleys and houses and stinking old streets. He wished to encourage all the arts and all learning, and his rich enemies hated him for this, for was not their money more valuable than all the music and the paintings and the statues and the murals and the theatres in the world? The middle class rejoiced in his plans. The aristocrats and the powerful and miserly stirred up the rabble against him. He was taking bread from the mouths of the poor and driving them from their "modest" habitations. What were art and gracious buildings compared with the belly? The middle class, though not quite understanding the grandeur he proposed, had a vague vision of majesty and they were proud and they trusted him. In truth, he was the only man in government they did not fear and suspect.

It was this middle class whom Ichthus had caused to stir and to think and to ponder, to turn for long moments from their ceaseless and prideful industry, and to consider their government. He was a menace. Ichthus had declared that a nation became great only when it encouraged a variety of opinions and protected all religions and listened to judicious dissent. But a city cowed into conformity of thought, and which became only an assemblage of meek and timid sheep under the staff of government, was a dead city in which no ideal or splendor or nobility could flourish. It became the lair of wolves at the top and jackals at the bottom. For these sentiments Ichthus must die.

Pericles' guard of six mounted soldiers, helmeted and armored in leather, arrived and he rose and went to join them. His chariot waited outside, with two fine white horses. He always drove it, himself. It was not the splendid car of the aristocrats, all gilt and enamel, but Pericles was no man for personal ostentation, for all he had one of the most lovely houses in Athens. He jumped into the chariot and took the reins from a slave, to whom he spoke kindly, thanking him. He was unaware that his mother had died peacefully in her bed in the night. Even the household did not know it as yet.

As the cavalcade swept down the hill, the soldiers carrying torches, Pericles glanced at Piraeus, the port of Athens. Some red torches still burned there, and there was some sluggish movement of lanterns. Athens still slept. However, as Pericles looked at the port and then beyond it, he saw a line of purple fire, flickering and brightening, at the horizon of the dark sea, which was formless and almost soundless. A round and tarnished moon sloped slowly to the west and the stars seemed to race in attendance. A cool and acrid breeze touched Pericles' face, smelling of clean pepper and clean earth and water and freshening grass and flowering plants.

He wrapped his cloak more closely about him and his helmet was a dancing red moon, itself, in the flare of the streaming torches. The horses' hoofs and the rattle of the chariot wheels on stone aroused echoes from the sleeping sides of houses and other buildings. The line of purple fire on the watery horizon spread rapidly towards the land, a brilliant carpet thrown down before the entrance of a king. Very soon Phoebus would drive his incandescent chariot into the sky and Athens would awaken. His gold and roseate shadow was already mounting against the somber sky and the opposite hills were suddenly outlined in quickening light. Now the breeze on Pericles' face blew warmer moment by moment. No longer was Athens spectral, a pale and diffused blur. Her flat and crowded roofs began to shimmer with silver and rose as she lay among her heliotrope hills. The small white temples on the acropolis slowly sparkled, moved into vision one by one, shyly, as through mist. Birds swooped and fluttered over the cavalcade, which disturbed their nestlings, and they cried out shrilly. A shepherd with his crook and sheep caused the company to halt, and the guarding dogs barked at them.

The great white Agora was still below Pericles, its tiled roof beginning to redden in the rapidly growing dawn, its white walls and columns faintly gleaming. The upper tiers of the theatre emerged from shadows. All at once vehicles moved into view, rattling, wagons, cars, carts, and the sound of voices rose sharply in the freshness of the morning.

The chariot and horsemen reached the street of the Agora, the largest meeting place of Athens, which seethed from dawn to long after midnight. Here could be found the gymnasia, very popular with the effete who needed exercise, and especially the sedentary members of the government. Here also were many shops and offices, and the Odeon, the music hall where concerts were regularly held, and bazaars and small taverns where men gathered to dine at noon and drink wine and incessantly argue and play dice or backgammon or draughts and exchange gossip and rumor and scandal and news, and to tell the latest lewd jokes. Here were barber shops and textile shops and little jewelers and many others. Flower-stalls brightened the passageways and the streets about the Agora, and here could be found in profusion low actors, mountebanks and tumblers and jugglers, magicians, ragged dancers and astrologers, all shrilling for a chance drachma for which they would perform in the very midst of the crowds or on the steps of the colonnades, or on the surrounding streets. Workrooms of all sorts were jumbled together in the Agora, and throngs filled them, and the shops, whether or not they were customers, there to gather for long discussions with ve-hement gestures, or to inspect wares they had no intention of buying. At noon one had to scramble and use elbows and knees to find a seat in the taverns, which smelled of spilt wine and beer and whiskey and sweat and roasting meat and frying fish and baking bread. Waves of heat, at midday, almost visi-bly rose above the Agora, especially in the warm months.

Many government officials had their offices in the Agora, and Pericles was one of them. Although of an aloof nature, and possessed of a preference for his own company, he liked to hear the uproar of crowds about him, and to feel the heart-beat of his beloved city in the streets and colonnades outside.

Now the company had reached the level of the Agora. Peri-cles began to wonder why he had arrived so long before his usual time, forgetting his sleepless hours and his sense of pres-sure and unease and anxiety. Ichthus, he thought wryly, would not die before noon, if he died at all. There was the matter of his trial. He brought his horses up short with a sharp command as a young man suddenly appeared on the road before him. The young man dodged and danced lightly up on the pavement, and he turned an antic smiling face on Pericles and half-mockingly saluted. He had a Pan-like ap-pearance, and there was an air of goatish agility about him. He had a very ugly little face with a nose that resembled a persimmon and was most undistinguished, a thatch of roughly cut hair, and an incongruous little beard trimmed to a casual point. His big ears stood out from his head like the handles of jugs.

But his eyes were extraordinarily brilliant and dancing and

313

full of vitality, and on looking in them one forgot the small figure, bony, seemingly deformed though it was not in truth, and the poor garments. Those eyes were gray, almost as colorless as Pericles' own, yet they were so ablaze, so radiant, that it was as if color had been burned from them leaving nothing but light behind.

Pericles recognized him though he had never exchanged a word with this young man who was already noted for his arguments and his philosophies and his teachings in the colonnades of the Agora and near the temples. Anaxagoras spoke approvingly of him, and with some little amusement, as an elder. But Athens teemed with philosophers, all hungry and vehement and self-assured even if humbly dressed and often barefoot.

The morning light lay in his eyes as he contemplated the halted company and Pericles, who rarely smiled, found himself smiling. "Were you coveting death, Socrates?" he asked, flicking his whip idly.

"Do we not all, even the happiest of us?" returned Socrates with an impudent grin. He was not awed by this most powerful man in Athens, whom he had often seen in the Agora. "And why should death be feared? If it is an endless sleep, do we not woo sleep? If there is life beyond it, then that too is good. Death is not to be abhorred."

"It is too early in the day for philosophy," said Pericles, and Socrates grinned again, inclining his head. The company went on. Socrates watched it go, scratching his armpits abstractedly. Then, as rapid as a cricket, he disappeared into a wineshop. He sat down at the table and said to the innkeeper, "I have just encountered Pericles, son of Xanthippus. He is entirely too grave and too cold. Yet, he is not an old man. One must laugh at this world or perish."

In the meantime Pericles had reached his offices and went to his separate room through a mass of petty officials and scribes who were just beginning to arrive. He sat down at his desk and began to frown and to ponder. A huge restlessness seized him, nameless and unformed. He faced the problems of Ichthus fully. His mind was fresher than it had been during the dark hours of night. But he was conscious of a physical weariness. He went silently over the arguments he had prepared for his friend, and clarified some of them. At some he winced; however, he knew them to be sensible. The trouble was that Ichthus was rarely if ever sensible and had no terrors for himself. Accursed zealots, thought Pericles, sighing. Yet, without them, would the turgid waters ever move or flow or

314

become clear? In their deaths they acquired a stature they never had in life, and that, thought Pericles, is something to reflect upon.

A young scribe silently brought a bowl of fruit and a goblet and a small jug of wine and set it down before him. Pericles nodded without speaking. He glumly drank a little wine and ate an apple. The door opened and Anaxagoras entered, a man of grandeur for all his simple long tunic. He sat down opposite Pericles and said, "Our friend, Ichthus, is to be tried tomorrow before the Ecclesia." He poured a little wine for himself in a goblet Pericles silently offered. "He will," said Anaxagoras, "surely be condemned to death. On that the Ecclesia is determined."

When Pericles said nothing, Anaxagoras continued: "The time is at hand when no man will be permitted to criticise government, however mildly, nor speculate on the gods. Above all things, the government fears enlightened or controversial men. Dictatorship by one man is bad enough; he usually acquires enough enemies to cause him to be somewhat cautious. But dictatorship by a whole government is greatly to be feared. There is nothing worse than inferior men in absolute power. They support each other, obey each other's directives, and hate and fear the people, whom they regard as their common enemy, and a threat to their power. Bureaucrats are the hungry jackals of society. This, I believe, is what unfortunate Ichthus has been proclaiming—to his disaster."

When Pericles still did not speak but despondently refilled his goblet, his friend went on. "You are a controversial man, Pericles."

Pericles shrugged. "That I know. So are you, Anaxagoras."

"Yes. The government does not believe in the scientific method, which deals with reality and not emotions. Facts are abhorrent to the government, and its minions, the market rabble. They prefer fantasies, and theories which are not based on facts and human nature. That is madness, of course. I do not expect to reach a grand old age."

Pericles looked up sharply and Anaxagoras nodded, faintly smiling. "I will be a victim of truth. For truth is greatly hated by bureaucrats and the emotional rabble. You and I know that dreams are deceivers, and bureaucrats deal in dreams. For their own advantage and advancement. Yes, surely, this is an age of madness. I know you have tried to establish a transcendental religion, a monotheism, based both on reverence and reality. So, you are in danger also, my dear friend."

"You were speaking of Ichthus. I intend to go to the prison

315

this morning. I will attempt to persuade him to be cautious, and not to blurt out damning facts about himself, nor orate in defense of freedom."

"You say that, you a man who constantly speaks in behalf of freedom of the individual? You say that, who have said that without freedom a man is less than a beast?"

Pericles made a slight, impatient and weary gesture. "There comes a time when the warrior's best defense and offense is prudence—for the sake of his battle. And his life. If he perishes—what of his convictions, and what of his arguments? They die, also."

"No," said Anaxagoras. "It is reduced, then, to will a man choose between deathless truth, even if he dies for it, or compromise."

"Zeno of Elea has sometimes said that compromise is a means of gaining time."

Anaxagoras sighed. "Zeno is an intellectual man. But now we have no time—for compromise. What will you tell Ichthus then?"

Pericles felt a faint anger, for what Anaxagoras had said were his own convictions, with which he was struggling futilely. He said with some exasperation, "Perhaps you, not I, should consult with Ichthus!"

Anaxagoras waited, looking at Pericles with his noble eyes. Pericles stood up and began to pace the room, cursing half under his breath. "I will try to persuade him, for his own sake, and the sake of his family, to be discreet. Discretion is not to be despised, when a man's life and the lives of his family are endangered. If I fail—"

He stopped. Anaxagoras still waited. "If I fail," said Pericles, "I have but one recourse: to defend him before the Ecclesia, even if I have to say that he is mad and so is not responsible for his writings."

"But the Ecclesia desires his death above all other things. If you persuade them he is mad, they will incarcerate him for life."

Pericles, who had begun to sweat in his extremity, removed his helmet and wiped his damp hair. "You pose no solutions," he said.

"In life, there are no solutions. A man can only do the best he can with the guidance of his reason. I grant you that Ichthus is not notable for reason. He is no philosopher. He is only a man who loves his nation and would die for it."

"I love it also. But I must deal with bureaucrats, and may the Furies seize them!"

Anaxagoras rose. He leaned the palms of his hands on the table and fixed Pericles with his eyes. "You might pray," he said, with kindness. Pericles gave a short laugh. "You, who believe only in truth and scientific facts, can say that?"

"I have never denied God," said Anaxagoras. "For truth, and the truth science reveals, proclaim His existence."

Seeing that Pericles was in no mood for abstruse arguments, Anaxagoras left him. The morning sun shot through the high small window in hot beams floating with golden dust. Pericles suddenly felt sick and drained. Was prudence only self-serving, or was it the course of a wise man? It was a riddle that no philosopher had reasonably solved, nor, in fact, any religion. Was it better to live in cautious peace or to die for a principle which might not survive tomorrow's scrutiny? What, in fact, was ultimate truth? Perhaps it lived with God, but it certainly did not live with man!

Pericles called for his chariot and his guards. He passed the wineshop where Socrates was still slowly drinking and musing, and Socrates saw his face. There is a man, he thought, who is beset. When a man is so beset it is best for him to withdraw from the uproar of life, and conflicting arguments, and to think coldly and clearly, and without emotions. He must define his own terms in the light of reason, then act upon them, even if they wound his heart, and sensibilities. This is a sorrowful world, indeed. Often a man believes he is acting with reason when he is in truth acting only from his hidden desires and his uncontrollable impulses. What self-deceivers we all are! Often when we believe we are acting from the purest of altruisms we are, in fact, acting only from the instinct of self-preservation. Socrates sighed, and said to the innkeeper, "Refill my goblet. Sometimes we must take our refuge in wine, if we are not to go mad."

"The Persians," said the innkeeper, "say that only when a man is drunk can he see the truth with clarity." Socrates laughed, a high thin whinny, and shook his head. "Wine is a deceiver, it is said," and he drank deeply of his goblet. "But, a pleasant one. If the gods had not desired us to get drunk occasionally, then why did they teach us the arts of fermentation? To destroy us, or to give us a momentary peace?"

"The gods do not desire our destruction, Socrates," said the innkeeper with an air of pious virtue, he being mindful that his shop was filling up with new customers, who were listening.

"Who knows?" said Socrates. "There are times when I believe the gods regret that they made us." Yes, it was a dolorous world and full of enigmas. Was it better to be ruthless in this world, or to melt in pity and so be destroyed? To survive was to be good. The destroyed, therefore, were not good. It was a valid argument, but, was it moral; was it truthful? It was an argument to be debated. There was a great difference between validity and truth.

Pericles drove up the acropolis to the prison of "the Eleven," or the Criminal Commissioners, where Ichthus was confined. It was a formidable and grim place, and only heinous prisoners, suspected of being enemies of the State, were incarcerated there.

Now the sun was very hot and the sky was incandescent with blue fire. The sea beyond the port glittered as a plain of blazing white light. Athens was embraced in her bowl of hills, which enclosed her with ochre arms. Groves of olive trees ran up their sides in a wave of fretted silver. In the distance were small green valleys, palpitating in the heat in a glimmer of emerald, and beyond them clusters of cypresses and palms and karob trees and sycamores and oaks, and orchards. Sheep and cattle were dotted there, little moving spots on the landscape.

The guards were awed when they saw Pericles and his company. He was readily admitted, and with incredulous wonder, by the guards, to the cell of Ichthus. What had this powerful man to do with a criminal?

As Ichthus was not only a citizen of Athens but was of a notable family his cell was commodious and light and clean. A member of his family had brought a soft carpet to cover the stone floor, and some light furniture and a comfortable bed. But Ichthus was not a man to enjoy comforts or notice or care about them. He sat on his bed in deep thought, his hands clasped between his knees. His overly sensitive face twitched and his gentle mouth was mournful. A less dangerous man, Pericles thought, was not to be found in all Athens. Yet, he was dangerous, for he was a good man and loved his country, and for that he must be punished. He also did not compromise with truth. Yes, truly a threatening man to governments. He disturbed the tranquil death of slavery.

Pericles motioned to the guard not to open the barred door as yet, and he stood there and looked through the iron bars at his friend. Like many men of strong and ardent passions Ichthus had not aged much, and appeared almost as the youth Pericles remembered, who had saved his life. However, the years had appeared to enlarge those huge brown eyes, to have increased his transparency of flesh, to have elongated that tremulous nose, to have made firmer that emotional mouth. The fine brown hair had retreated on his delicate skull so that his brow, always high and wide, seemed to dominate his whole face. Many of his old schoolmates jeered, and still jeered, at what they described as his "weak, vacillating chin," which receded below his lower lip. But Pericles knew, with fresh despair, that here indeed was a valorous man who would never be turned from what he believed his duty.

Pericles studied him for long moments, his fair brows drawn together in pain, his helmet faintly illuminated by the lanterns which hung from the walls of the corridors. Then he motioned to the guard to open the door, and he said with stern authority, "I will call you when I wish to depart." The guard saluted, Pericles entered the cell, and waited impatiently for the sound of the guard's retreating footsteps.

Ichthus had started at the sound of Pericles' voice, and then had slowly risen to his long and emaciated height, uttering a faint sound deep in his thin throat, but whether of protest or welcome it was impossible to know. A lamp burned on the table beside which he had been sitting, and there were numerous books on the table also.

Then Ichthus exclaimed, "Pericles! Oh, never should you have come to this place!" His high voice was still almost feminine in its intonations.

Pericles hesitated, then held out his hand and Ichthus took it. Tears shimmered in his eyes, and Pericles looked away. "Why should I not have come?" he asked. "Am I not your friend?"

Ichthus glanced at the barred door with a sort of terror and he raised his voice and said with loud emphasis, "No, never were you my friend, Pericles, son of Xanthippus! We knew each other slightly, but that only." He drew a trembling breath. "If you have kindness, lord, please leave me at once and forget"—he could not speak for a second or two—"forget you ever saw me."

Pericles understood at once. His enemies were always accusing him of possessing a heart of marble, for he was almost invariably cold and distant in his manner, unlike the majority of his clamorous fellow Athenians. But now his strongly disciplined face softened and he felt a plunge of pain. He put his hand on Ichthus' shivering shoulder, pressed it firmly, and Ichthus sat down on the bed again in a posture of anguish. Pericles drew up another chair and sat near him and once again studied him, and now with gentleness.

"Ichthus, my friend," he said, in that sonorous voice which

could always move the emotions of others, "you have come to a sad pass, against which I warned you years ago."

"Yes," said Ichthus, who could not move his eyes from the face he loved so much and adored almost slavishly, "you have warned me."

"You did not listen," said Pericles.

Ichthus made a desperate motion with his long and sensitive hands. "I obeyed One I loved much dearer."

"The Unknown God," said Pericles.

Ichthus nodded. "What is my life?" he said. "It is nothing besides that obedience."

Pericles made a wry mouth. "Have the gods communicated to you their desires, Ichthus? Have they spoken to you in the night, and especially Pallas Athene? Is that not presumptuous? How do you know their commands, their wishes?"

Ichthus put his hand on his slight breast. "I hear the voice of God in my heart. God is the enemy of tyranny, of all that oppresses man, and to obey God is better than to obey an unconscionable government."

Pericles frowned. It might be possible to save this pathetic and innocent man, this fervent and honest man, but he would always be in danger of retribution. At the end, he would be murdered. Pericles rubbed his chin, and the rings on his fingers twinkled in the rising and falling light of the lamp. He moved nearer to Ichthus and lowered his voice.

"You have a mother," he said. "You have sisters, and cousins, all who love you. Do you know their fate if you are found guilty by the Ecclesia of heresy and treason?"

Ichthus briefly closed his eyes on a spasm and the lids wrinkled. Then he opened his eyes and regarded Pericles straightly, and Pericles saw the valor in them, the steadfast light shining like a star.

"They know what I must do," he said. "They know I can but obey, and fight for my country, that she might be free again, and a sun to the world of men."

"Do you understand that it is very probable that all your goods and lands and money will be seized, your family dispersed or ostracized, if you pursue your course?"

"I know," said Ichthus, and Pericles could hardly hear him.

Pericles said, and with some painful exasperation, "It is very heroic, and very honorable, Ichthus, but it is a sacrifice no man should ask of his family!"

He stood up and began to pace the cell with rapid and clanging footsteps, and Ichthus watched him mournfully.

Ichthus said, "I have talked of all this to my family, and they know I must do as I must do." When Pericles did not reply but only increased the rapidity of his pacing, Ichthus said, "What would you do, my dearest of friends?"

Pericles abruptly paused. He faced the little high window of the cell, his back to Ichthus. He was silent for a long time. He had clasped the elbows of his arms in his favorite gesture, and his fingers tightened on them until they were as white as stone. Then he slowly turned to Ichthus, and said with that cold and brutal candor so well known to the citizens of Athens: "I do not know, Ichthus, by Castor and Pollux, I do not know."

He resumed his seat and rested his hands on his bare knees. He gazed at Ichthus and the older man could not read his face, for it was impassive.

"I often think that nations are ungrateful," he said. "Brave men have died for their country, and were joyous so to die. They have fought for their people—and their people have forgotten. Perhaps it is better to be a living weasel than a dead lion. The gratitude and the memory of nations are all too brief. Should a man die for such ephemeral things?"

Ichthus made a sad gesture of resignation. He repeated, "I can only do what I must do." When Pericles did not speak, he said, "What would you have me do?"

This time Pericles hesitated for so long that it might have been that he had not heard. But Ichthus saw his eyes, the tightening of his face.

Pericles hated the ugly words he felt he must say, "You can recant."

Ichthus started to his feet. He looked down at Pericles, who averted his head. "Recant?" cried Ichthus. "You would urge me to such a base thing, to the denial of all I love and honor, to the repudiation of my whole convictions and my life, itself?"

"Let me say this," said Pericles, not looking at him, "is any cause worth your life, your family, your peace, Ichthus?"

Ichthus sat down as if his knees had failed him. He leaned towards Pericles and said imploringly, "I have known you long, my friend, and have bowed before your wisdom and your integrity and your love for your country, for they are greater than mine. This I know in my heart," and he struck his breast with his fragile fist. "In my place you would not recant—"

But Pericles said, as if speaking to himself, "I do not know. No man can trust himself utterly, or guess what he would do under danger of death or dishonor. To proclaim he can is to be a liar, full of self-delusion."

Ichthus put his hands over his face as if to shut out some terrible sight, and Pericles saw the gesture. Then Ichthus said in a low voice, "I have faced all that can be faced, except the ultimate end, and I have not turned away from it. Better it is to die than to betray one's self, and all that is a man."

Pericles hated his next words even more, "Better it is to buy a breathing space, then fight again more adroitly, more subtly, and with a keener weapon, understanding the enemy fully."

Ichthus dropped his hands. "You would do this, Pericles?"

"I have said, I do not know. That is the only answer I can give you in the deepest honesty."

He could not bear Ichthus' face which had taken on the aspect of death, and had become dull and expressionless. Ichthus slowly averted his head. It was as if all that he loved, all that on which he had anchored his life, had disintegrated and had been swallowed by soundless waves.

"I would not have you die," said Pericles. "You are one of the few men of probity I know, one of the few I can trust. You saved my life. For that alone I shall always be grateful. But more than that you taught me a tremendous lesson. You are my friend, and I can say that of only a small number."

The fervent light slowly began to return to Ichthus' face and he turned eagerly towards Pericles. "Then, you would despise me if I betrayed all that for which I have lived! And all that is mighty to you, yourself, Pericles!"

Pericles was silent. He felt old and heavy and very tired and sick. He thought of Anaxagoras and what the latter would have felt at this conversation. Pericles could see those piercing and noble eyes. They seemed to have fixed themselves on him, in this cell, glowing and unwavering.

Ichthus spoke again and again imploringly. "What would my life be worth to me if I lied to myself, if I ignobly recanted and if I were permitted to slink away like a beaten dog? How could I live with myself? How could you live with yourself, Pericles, if you followed your own advice?"

Pericles sighed. He did not stop his pacing. He fingered the sharp Damascene steel dagger at his girdle, and felt the faceted gems in the hilt.

He stopped before Ichthus. "I fear I could not live with myself," he said. Ichthus clasped his hands together and his eyes were radiant and full of reverence.

"So," said Pericles, "I have but one recourse. I will defend you before the Ecclesia."

The radiance died instantly from Ichthus' eyes. Terror and alarm suffused his face, which had become deathly yellow. His mouth opened on a great cry.

"No! That you must not do, Pericles! You have formidable enemies. They would use your defense of me to your destruction, your ruin, and even your life!" Horror gripped him, and confused agony.

"All through the night," said Pericles in so stern a voice that even the distraught Ichthus caught his breath, "I have pondered this and have come to the conclusion that I must defend you, if you refused to be discreet. Let us speak no more of this. I, too, Ichthus, must do as I must do."

Ichthus fell on his knees before his friend and raised his clasped hands to him. He almost grovelled.

"No! I will not accept this monstrous sacrifice! I will not permit it! Who am I, compared with you, Pericles, son of Xanthippus, the glory of our country?"

"You are my friend," said Pericles. "You are even more: You are a brave man."

He reached down to lift Ichthus to his feet. Ichthus' eyes stared wildly in his extremity of dread and suffering, then roamed about the cell, then returned to Pericles. He swallowed visibly. Tears began to flood from his eyes. He flung aside Pericles' hands and moaned over and over, "No, no, no. This you must not do! Athens needs you. You must not die for me, an insignificant man!"

Then, before Pericles could move, Ichthus' hand darted out and seized the hilt of Pericles' dagger. He leapt to his feet and sprang back from the other man, and he smiled deeply, a heartbreaking smile, the dagger high in his uplifted hand.

"Farewell, dearest of friends! Live for Athens!"

Before the startled Pericles could move one foot Ichthus had plunged the dagger into his breast. The blood spurted forth, and Ichthus staggered. Pericles caught him in his arms and swayed with the weight that had become heavy and flaccid.

Pericles lowered him on his bed, and his hoarse panting filled the cell. "Gods," he muttered. He leaned over Ichthus, who lay on his bed with a beatific smile on his face, a smile of love and triumph. Pericles looked at the dagger which stood upright from Ichthus' chest. Blood flowed all about it. Pericles began to tremble. The jewels on the hilt glittered in the lamplight.

Ichthus tried to speak, but he died, still smiling that ecstatic smile of loving triumph. At the very last he had touched Pericles' hand consolingly.

Pericles, never looking away from the piteous countenance, so gently victorious, so dauntless, forced himself to stand upright, though all his flesh was shaken.

Again, Ichthus had saved his life. He covered his eyes with his hand and began to weep.

CHAPTER 12

The King Archon looked at Daedalus with an inscrutable expression. He said, "You have brought grave charges against the Head of State, Pericles, son of Xanthippus. It is true that the Head of State must be beyond reproach, even if he is just a man as are the rest of us. In his official position he must not be guilty of malfeasance, however he may be only a human being in his private life. You are enraged, my friend, that when your daughter refused to divorce him he brought suit for annulment." The King Archon raised his hand. "Let us not be emotional. Your cries have been hysterical. Bear with me. The affairs of your daughter, Dejanira, have no bearing on the conduct of Pericles. Many men divorce their wives or seek annulment. The government is not concerned with the domestic problems of their members.

"You wish to have your grandsons, Xanthippus and Paralus, returned to the custody of their mother, under your guardianship. Pericles is their father. Men have full disposal of their children, and this must not be denied Pericles. The children are content with their father, and adore him. Let us not be concerned with children, who are insignificant. It is womanish to consider children; they are nothing until they are men. Before that they are unripe, and disorderly. There is no room in our national life for such. Their future belongs to their fathers and not their raging mothers, who think with their wombs and not with their minds—if they have any.

"What are your other impetuous charges? Ichthus died in his cell by his own hand, with the dagger of Pericles. You deny this. You have said that Pericles, the notable Head of State, deliberately murdered Ichthus to prevent that unhappy man from 'betraying' his connections with Pericles! Had Pericles wished the death of Ichthus he could have had him quietly poisoned with the hemlock cup. Or, he could have repudiated him with contempt. Why, then, murder? It is ridiculous to believe for an instant that Pericles, the Head of State, reduced himself to the status of a common alley murderer!"

"I hate him!" cried Daedalus.

The King Archon frowned. "Government has no room for personal sentiments. Government is orderly—or should be—and detached from the aberrations of female instability. As Solon said, women should not be permitted to interfere with affairs of State. Go to. If you would not be prosecuted for libel, my Daedalus, you will control your tongue and your twitters. It was you who arranged the marriage between your daughter and the noble Pericles. Now, for some reason known only to you, you wish to destroy him, he, the Head of State. I do not admire Pericles, but I know what is ridiculous. Let us be done with this nonsense."

Daedalus rose in all his skeleton height, his teeth clenched.

"I will have vengeance!" he said.

The King Archon shrugged. "If Pericles is mysteriously assassinated I will remember your words." He added, "I am not in agreement with the design of Pericles to waste the public money on the raising of monuments and temples to the glory of Athens. I am not in agreement with his policies. I do not admire his defense of what he calls 'the middle' between the aristocrats and the rabble. The rabble is only the offal of a society. It needs to be controlled at all times. I do not distinguish between the market rabble and Pericles' advancement of merchants and shopkeepers and artisans and skilled labor, and the mean professions of physicians and lawyers. What are the people? Dogs. Nevertheless, he has been a prudent and determined administrator. His opinions are his own. Only time will tell whether he has been right. The sober people of Athens love him, and the sober are not to be despised. Let us wait. In the meantime, my friend, control yourself."

"May Hecate and the Furies devour him!"

Again the King Archon shrugged. "The gods have their ways, and they are not known to us. If Pericles flourish or die, that is their judgment. Please leave me. I am wearied with your outbursts and denunciations, none of which are relevant."

When Daedalus had departed the King Archon reflected on the confusion which results from confusing politics with emotions. Men should refrain from introducing their penises into affairs of State, and their violent emotions with the conduct of orderly government. Perhaps it was too much to expect. It was no mystery, then, that governments were vehement and shouting. Even the gods were not immune from passions.

Pericles did not know for whom he mourned most deeply—his mother or Ichthus. Agariste, despite her preening and pretensions, had been an excellent and devoted mother, a woman of realism even if she had long asserted that she had been brought to bed by a white lion with a golden mane—ostensibly the father of her son. It was her small conceit and no one had taken it seriously. She had had much intelligence which she had flaunted; she had also been kind, a trait she had hidden as a mark of weakness but which often burst forth spontaneously, much to her later chagrin. She had been a stern mistress of her household, but her slaves had respected both her justice and her authority. She had been a chaste wife, and had loved her husband and had mourned him sincerely and had been proud of him, for all her sharp tongue and insistence on the honor of her family. Alas, she had had no sense of humor, which had made Xanthippus avoid her and had often irritated Pericles.

It is not, unfortunately, the attributes of the dead which we remember, thought Pericles, but their easy smiles, their words of love however false, their amiability or lack of it. Trivialities engross us; the noblest man is not recalled with affection and reverence if he had possessed a shrewd cynicism concerning his fellow man or had had a brusque manner and an undeviating honesty. A man who spoke the truth was hated in his lifetime and forgotten after his death. We prefer affable liars, even if they had wounded us and deceived us.

He was filled with hatred of the faceless man who had betrayed Ichthus. Ichthus had written his broadcasts anonymously. Therefore, only one he had loved and trusted could have delivered him to his enemies. But, was that not always so? Who was it who had said that a malicious enemy was less to be feared than an avowed friend, full of protestations of loyalty? He, Pericles, had few friends, not only because he was a politician but because he repudiated all fawnings, all declarations of dedication to him, all vows of eternal faithfulness. He was especially suspicious of the latter. Yes, friends were to be feared.

He was determined to discover the dear friend, the trusted and loyal friend, who had been the cause of Ichthus' arrest and death. No doubt, if apprehended, he would virtuously protest that what he had done was in the interest of his country, which came above friendship. Of such stuff were liars made. Malice was the one dread and terrible trait which all human beings possessed, though they differed in other traits.

It was inspired by envy, private cruel ridicule of the victim, greed, or some petty imagined offense the victim had inflicted on his destroyer. Often it was only the result of the heroic character of the victim; men can endure anything but profound virtue in another. For some reason virtue inflamed hate among mankind, just as vice receives its secret admiration. We are an evil species, thought Pericles, and why the gods do not eliminate us must be due either to their indifference to our fate, or their benignity.

Now he sought the beloved and trusted friend of Ichthus. He could not be denounced publicly, for the government would praise his loyalty to it. He must be murdered and before his murder he must be told why he was being done to death.

Anaxagoras said, "Will that return Ichthus to life? Let God judge the betrayer."

"God," said Pericles, "is forgetful. Who knows if we live after death? But a man who knows he is facing it suffers enormously and even goes mad. Let that be his fate."

Men, Pericles had noticed, are not to be bought by friendship but only by money, and sometimes by fear. Fear, perhaps, was best, for there was always someone else who could raise the higher bribe of money. So, night and day he pondered on the identity of the avowed friend of Ichthus. Then he would exert fear on one he would employ to kill that friend. He went to the mother of Ichthus, who was ill with grief. She was a woman of a large-hearted countenance, and a dignified demeanor. She joined Pericles in the atrium of her house and though her face was ghastly with sorrow she was calm. She was clothed in black and her eyes were afire in the apparent tranquility of her features.

"Who was my son's best friend, lord? You were, though you saw him seldom. He would have died for you. His closest associate? An old schoolmate, Turnus, whom my son pathetically loved. He has been with me often, consoling me, offering me his selfless services—"

"Ah," said Pericles. He remembered the ancient myth of another Turnus, who, on defeating Pallas, had acquired his gold girdle, inlaid with gems, and other valuables. Pericles said, "Did Ichthus leave, in his will, any treasure to Turnus, son of Patroclus, who is one of the Archons?"

"Yes," said the bereaved mother. Despite her composure her face twitched. "He left him one-third of his patrimony."

Money is always an inducement to betrayal, thought Pericles with intense hate and bitterness. He remembered Turnus in his youth; he was of a most earnest countenance, a serious youth who always proclaimed his virtue and his steadfastness and his loyalty to his friends, a youth with big serious eyes which he would fix on others, testifying to his sincerity. Sincerity! The cloak of scoundrels. Honest men frequently had the aspect of rogues. Turnus, son of Patroclus, the Archon, was a very grave man now indeed, filled with ostensible charity and always active in behalf of his friends—as he declared, himself. Pericles questioned the mother further. Yes, Turnus had been the only one who had encouraged Ichthus in his attacks on the venal government. He had even helped Ichthus with the preparation of his broadcasts. He had been like a son to her, the mother of Ichthus.

Pericles recalled that Patroclus was as miserly as Daedalus, and very severe with his only son, who was rumored profligate and who had disposed of his wife's dowry with alacrity. She had appealed for a divorce, on which Turnus would have had to return her dowry with interest. But—he had no money and his father would give him none, disapproving of his son's conduct. Turnus was a very busy man, according to Pericles' remembrance of him. All his ventures came to nothing. He was also a gambler and could always be found in the Agora shaking the dice or playing backgammon and chess and draughts with others of his kind. His sincere voice echoed everywhere. He advised friends on investments which later proved disastrous, but not to Turnus who had lured them into the investments. Huge and veracious of eye, animated in his dealings, enthusiastic in his persuasions, he had convinced many, and even those he had deceived still were certain that he was an honorable man and that it was only bad luck when the ventures failed, and certainly not the fault of Turnus, who condoled and wept with them.

Pericles left the unhappy mother, saddened by her distress; he was burning with renewed anger and determination. He made some inquiries concerning Turnus and discovered something secret which enraged him further.

He then explored the backgrounds of his friends. Who was the one who feared him most? Pericles thought, ruthlessly.

He sent for Jason, son of an illustrious father, who was not only a bureaucrat of formidable power but was tied to Pericles' service by the most potent respect. He was a tall quiet man of middle age and of a gentle manner and scrupulous in his duties, not, in this case by fear, but because of his character. He was famous for his natural magnanimity, which was not a pretense, and his sympathetic attitude, again not a pretense. He had never been known to do a cruel or unjust act;

his probity was beyond any doubt. He and Pericles had been schoolmates together, and both the youths had protected Ichthus. He was also a patriot and loved Athens little less than did Pericles. Pericles had considerable fondness for him and often consulted him on difficult matters. However, without any hesitation Pericles chose him as the destroyer of Turnus, whom Jason despised.

Jason not only respected Pericles, but returned his affection. Pericles counted him as one of his few friends. He greeted Jason with his usual restraint, but smiled at him and gave him his hand in the privacy of his house. Pericles ordered wine and pastries for his friend, and while they drank and ate together they discussed these affairs of state. Jason was somewhat puzzled. They had discussed these affairs only yesterday. Jason fixed his gray eyes on Pericles with curiosity, but being a courteous man he did not ask why he had been summoned almost at sunset from his office.

Pericles' manner abruptly changed and his eyes took on that blind look which was so daunting to others. He said in a low voice, "I have thought, today, of your murder of your wife, Calypso, two years ago."

Jason turned very pale and his refined features tightened. He stared, without speaking, at Pericles.

"It is true that she deserved to be murdered," said Pericles, in a soothing tone, and nodded. "She was notable for her evil temper and viciousness. Did she not abuse you and your children by your dead first wife? Did she not lie to you so that they would not inherit your estate? Did she not attempt to degrade your daughter in your esteem? Did she not, at the last, betray you, for she was a woman of considerable beauty? But, you loved her, and trusted her despite her enormous defects of character. So do our hearts betray us, and we are helpless when we are pierced by the arrows of Eros, even when evidence proves that the one we love has deceived and reviled and injured us."

Jason's mouth and throat became so dry that he made a retching sound. After an attempt or two he found his voice. "Why do you recall this to me, Pericles?"

Pericles said as if Jason had not spoken, "Love and trust—and perish. That is always inevitable, as I have observed. We become absurd in the regard of those we love and trust, for we are pitiable objects and enslaved by unmanly passions. Who does not scorn such?"

Again those blind eyes turned themselves on Jason, who had begun to tremble. "Yes," said Pericles, "your wife deserved to die. Yet, you could not kill her, yourself. You hired an assassin, and paid him well. Then he began to torment you, demanding more than his fee on the threat of betrayal. He would write a confession, he said to you, and then would flee back to his native Arabia to escape punishment himself.

"You came to me, your friend, in despair, for you knew I was discreet and remembered friendship. You laid your case before me. You thought of hiring another assassin to dispose of the Arabian. However, you feared that he would also betray you. Murder is an endless chain. The assassin did not know that I was your friend. I had him investigated. He was a thief, though he had concealed the fact well, and he had murdered others. Yet, there was no valid evidence against him, for he was clever and adroit. Now, I had the evidence. He was duly executed."

"Yes," whispered Jason. For the first time he saw a baleful glow in the depths of those unreadable eyes.

Pericles sighed and leaned back in his chair as if wearied. "There is one dread thing I have learned in this world of men, which I did not make. I keep full dossiers on friend or foe, sworn to most solemnly by myself. It is known that I am not malicious—but I trust few if any men, even yourself, Jason. Do not be offended. I consider that friendship is a very frail thing, and friends unpredictable. The brother today can become your most mortal enemy, with or without provocation, tomorrow. It is human nature."

Again Jason whispered; he felt that he was dying. "Are you my enemy, Pericles?"

Pericles smiled slightly, though his conscience was troubling him. "Not yet, Jason," he said frankly. "But I have a dossier on you which I hoped I would never need to use. I must protect myself. I trust I will never need to use it and deliver you to executioners. But, as the Egyptians say, who knows what tomorrow will bring?"

"You are going to use that dossier against me, Pericles?"

"Not unless you force me to do so, either by becoming my enemy or by any violation of your duties. You can trust me a little better than you can trust others. Tell me. You have the name and know the whereabouts of the second professional assassin whom you considered employing against the first?"

Jason swallowed. "I do," he said.

Pericles nodded. Jason said, "You wish someone murdered, Pericles?"

"Yes. Turnus, the son of Patroclus. I have discovered that it was he who betrayed our poor friend, Ichthus, to the authorities. Love and trust? What enormities follow such! Perhaps they are justified. No matter. I want Turnus dead, as quickly and as secretly as possible. It might be that your assassin can contrive an accident for him, as the first contrived it for your wife."

"Turnus, the son of Patroclus, the Archon!" Jason's face almost disintegrated with shock. "He betrayed Ichthus? That is indeed a crime of calamitous proportions. His father is very powerful. He will not lightly accept an accident to his son. He will investigate. Woe is me!"

"Do not be distressed. He will be disposed of swiftly, the assassin. I have another thought. He will be caught in the act of murder, and will be dispatched at once before he can speak. I promise you that. I will order this. The details will be arranged most meticulously."

Trembling more than ever, Jason bent his head and pondered. After a while he looked at Pericles straightly. "Why can I not give you his name and you arrange the—murder—yourself, my friend?"

Again Pericles smiled. "I am the Head of State."

Jason clasped his hands together convulsively. "I detest murder."

"So do I. But sometimes it is—effective—and necessary. Was it not so in the case of your deplorable wife?"

Jason winced. "I was driven almost to madness. But murder leads to murder—"

"I disagree—my friend." He withdrew a large purse of gold coins from his girdle and laid it on the table between himself and Jason. "I would not have you bribe the murderer yourself, Jason. This is my money. There is another matter. Before the assassin kills, in whatever manner he devises, he must say to Turnus, 'This is vengeance for Ichthus.' Let Turnus think of that before he dies. Otherwise the murder will be pointless."

When Jason did not speak Pericles said, "The first assassin was truly inventive. Calypso was inadvertently hanged by her rich necklace of pearls, which she accidentally caught on a hook in her bedroom. I trust the second assassin is as inventive. Only you can know. But you must not tell me."

Still Jason did not speak. Pericles sighed. "If Turnus is not executed—we must call it a just execution—then I will be forced, in honor, to make public my dossier on you, my poor friend."

Jason spoke weakly. "Then you will be asked why you had not shown the dossier heretofore."

Now Pericles' eyes became young and candid. "My dear Jason, I was only thorough in my investigations and did not wish to prematurely accuse you! The dossier was completed only yesterday!"

"I never thought you would injure me, Pericles, or ruin me."

"Have I done so? Never will I do it unless you become my enemy, or fail in your authority."

"That I will never do, and so you know it, Pericles."

Pericles shrugged. "Make no rash promises, Jason, for you are only a man and also possess malice, the one evil which all men, regardless of virtue or station, possess. I trust you as much as I am capable of trusting—which I confess is very little. Sometimes men are driven to malice, against their very scruples. Tell me, Jason. Is not Turnus deserving of—execution?"

"Yes, that is true," said Jason with reluctant honesty.

"Think of it, then, not as murder, but as a justified execution. If someone murdered you, Jason, I would have the assassin executed. As you know, I am a determined man on the subject of law and order. But there are some things beyond the reach of the law. I am not advocating private justice, though sometimes it is very necessary. The heinous crime must be expiated. Law is often dilatory, even if the crime is obvious. There is the rule of evidence, which must be explicit. However, often the worst crimes are so cleverly wrought that evidence cannot be found, and the judges are frustrated. We are now the judges of Turnus, who not only is beyond the vengeance of conventional law; he would be extolled for his act of 'patriotism' by government."

Jason half-covered his eyes with his hand. "Why did Turnus betray Ichthus?"

Pericles looked impatient. "I thought I had told you that. Ichthus loved and trusted him, and that inspired his ridicule and his malice. He also sought profit. The government cancelled his debts."

"O gods," groaned Jason. "How wicked is man!"

"I never disputed that. Our iniquity calls for vengeance by the gods, themselves."

Jason stood up, slowly, his hands visibly shaking. He

looked down at the purse of gold for a long time and Pericles watched him. Then Jason took the purse. Suddenly he was resolute. "It will be done," he said.

Pericles embraced him. "Do you think this is an idle petty judgment on my part, and that I rejoice in it? No. I am not only Head of State. I do not know any assassins."

"You will destroy your dossier on me when this is done, Pericles?"

Pericles was silent for a moment and then he shook his head with true regret. "No, Jason. That I cannot promise you. One day you may become my enemy. I pray this will not happen, for I love you."

When the distraught Jason had departed Pericles was filled with gloom. He had been ruthless, even more ruthless than customary with him. He disliked himself for the misery he had imposed on Jason. But Jason was only a weapon in behalf of justice. Justice, that much abused goddess, must be appeased. The gods, themselves, often chose men to wreak retribution on the wicked.

Five days later Turnus suddenly arose from a dice game with his friends and called for his chariot in a condition of great agitation. He then raced off in the direction of his father's house. The horses mysteriously bolted, or he had whipped them in too great a frenzy, and he was thrown from the chariot and killed, smashing his head against a marble column. His friends spoke of his sudden pallor at the gaming table, his staring eyes, then his flight. Among them was Jason.

Pericles sent for Jason, who came into the offices silently, his face gray and still. Pericles closed the door and said, "Nemesis rode with him."

"Yes," said Jason. He briefly closed his eyes. Pericles said, "Your assassin is very clever. Unfortunately, my agents had no time to eliminate him, for I had had no word from you."

Jason was silent. He bent his head and gazed at the floor. Pericles continued: "We must know his name and where he lives."

Jason shook his head. "He will never speak—that assassin." Now he looked up at Pericles and his tired eyes were still and intent. He repeated, "He will never speak." He laid the purse of gold Pericles had given him, on the table.

Pericles stared at the purse for a long time. He was filled with pity. At last he said, "You must tell me nothing." He went to his closet, unlocked a brass chest and withdrew a sheaf of papers rolled and sealed. He put them into Jason's hand. "I, too, will never speak. Here is your dossier, my friend. Destroy it as soon as possible." I hope I do not regret this, Pericles thought to himself somewhat ruefully.

Jason said in a faint voice, "He was a most iniquitous man."

The next day Anaxagoras said to Pericles, "God took His own way in avenging Ichthus."

Pericles smiled at him blandly. "Was it not fortunate? I did not have to intervene."

Anaxagoras answered the smile with his own, though reluctantly. "Who shall limit the instruments of God? He often employs men to carry out His will." He drank from a goblet of wine and said, "However, do not presume too often, Pericles, in deciding that what you do is His will. He may have other plans."

CHAPTER 13

Pericles arrived at the house of his beloved Helena, who greeted him with her usual robust and rosy smile, and embraced him. "I fear I shall lose you tonight, O Apollo."

"Never, my Hebe," he said, kissing her soundly and stroking her auburn hair in which were diamond pins he had given her. They were no brighter than her eyes. He smacked her rump and she led him from the atrium into the dining hall, laughing. She whispered a short lascivious joke to him, and he smiled in appreciation though he did not admire lewdness in women except in the bedchamber. But physicians were famous for their improper jests.

The dining hall was already filled with guests, though they had not yet seated themselves. Slaves went among them with wine, beer and whiskey and various savory tidbits. The silken curtains at doors and windows moved in a brisk breeze and there was a sullen stalking of thunder in the hills and an occasional flash of blue lightning. Beautiful Egyptian and Damascan lamps of glass and gold and silver stood on the long waiting dining table, and hung from the frescoed ceiling where nymphs and satyrs and fauns frolicked in intense colors. The table was strewn with late roses and lilies and ferns in delicate patterns and the air of the dining hall was suffused with their fragrance. The chairs and the divans, both at the table and against the yellow marble walls, were rich with silk and velvet of many hues, which were all harmonious. Even the Chinese vases, overflowing with blossoms in the corners and against the walls, had been chosen with meticulous taste for their form and their decorations. Helena was a physician; she was also a woman of great artistry and discrimination.

Helena rarely if ever entertained dull and stolid matrons so Pericles knew that the beauteous women present were rich and courted and beguiling courtesans, all selected for their appearance, wit and intelligence and gifts of entertainment. With pleasure he observed that his friends, Zeno of Elea and Anaxagoras, were among those present. But with surprise he saw the roughly clad young man, Socrates, with his goatlike beard and vivacity and ugly face. Even more to his surprise, Pericles saw that Zeno and Anaxagoras were listening to him intently and with evident pleasure. Also present was the shy sculptor, Pheidias.

Pericles had halted in the archway with Helena and so he surveyed the guests, particularly the women, before entering the hall. Beautiful women were no novelty to him; he knew most of them present and had enjoyed their loveliness and their conversation. Then he saw the stranger, and his heart rose like a fountain in him and he was lost.

She was the woman of his figurine and of his dreams, with whom, in a drunken fantasy, he had consummated his marriage with Dejanira. She was not young; she was in her early twenties and so had lost the first freshness of youth. But she had the maturity of a ripe pear, of opalescent grapes ready for the treading. She was speaking gravely to Pheidias, a goblet in her hand, and the sculptor appeared entranced. She was much taller than Pheidias, and, unlike the other women's her hair, a cobweb of silvery gold, flowed simply down her back and almost to her knees. She wore a garland of pink rosebuds. She had the easy grace and slenderness of a trained courtesan, and the courtesan's elegance of movement and gesture. Her robe was of green silk, Pericles' favorite color, and seemed to flow about her body like tinted water rather than fabric, and so outlined her incredibly perfect body. Her breasts were high and full, her waist delicate and fragile, her hips swelling daintily. Her waist was entwined with a girdle of gold, blazing with gems, and there were armlets clasped about her round white arms and bracelets about her small wrists and a multitude of flashing rings on her adorable hands. She wore golden shoes, also ablaze with jewels, and when she moved a little Pericles saw her ankles, as beautifully wrought as a statue's. There was, to Pericles, a strange air about her, a lack of personal consciousness, a lack of artifice, in spite of the splendor of her garments and her jewels, in particular a necklace of incomparable opals set in rubies and diamonds. Her intimate attention was not on herself, unlike other women, but upon Pheidias to whom she listened with intensity and respect. The sculptor seemed almost animated in her presence, forgetful of his shyness, his eyes glowing eagerly. He had lost his stammer; his gestures were vehement; he shone with excitement, and Pericles marveled.

Pericles looked at her face, disbelieving that any countenance could reveal so faultless a contour, whether she was in profile or facing him.

Her face, like her arms and shoulders and neck, had a translucence, as if light went through them rather than around them. Her cheeks and lips were a natural vermillion, her brown eyes like wine, her nose and her brow clear and pure, as was her dimpled chin. Her mouth, Pericles said, had a certain lovely sternness about it, as if she had suffered much, and she had a tranquility which was not assumed but natural. She appeared composed and restrained, and betrayed discipline. Sometimes she threw back her hair with a pretty impatience, but never stopped listening to Pheidias whom she apparently found magical. Once she smiled and dimples raced over her cheeks and about her mouth. Above all was her aspect of extreme intelligence.

"Aspasia," whispered Helena, smiling broadly. "The harpy, the Medusa."

Pericles confusedly thought of Helen of Troy, of nymphs and dryads, of green water and moonlight, of fire and flame and snow, of hushed restful glades, and of storms. This woman was all women in one person. Yet, she did not have the appearance of pliancy and complaisance, for all her feminine attributes. She was a woman of convictions, of certitude, of mind, and he, well acquainted with human nature, knew that she could be bent through love but never broken. Passions might rule her briefly, but never would they destroy her. Always, she would remain herself, intact and invulnerable. There was something formidable about this, something that warned against vulgar intrusion, for she implied explicit aristocracy.

Once or twice she turned her head and looked at Pericles, but as if she did not really see him. He saw that her eyes were lustrous and autumn topaz and filled with brilliant lights like moving water in the sun. Still, they were unreadable, starred with golden lashes. He thought of a forest pool, shifting with shadows as wind blew the trees, holding secrets, seeing nothing but its own being.

In that he was wrong. Aspasia, though listening with all her attention to Pheidias, had noticed Pericles immediately and knew who he was. An instant glance had revealed his tall stature to her, his strength of compact body, his tawny mane of hair like a lion's, his air of power and assurance, not flaunting but immediate. She had seen his face, calm and impassive and rigorously controlled, his strong straight nose, his carved severe lips. She also saw his helmet, which he invariably wore even on festive occasions, and which hid his towering brow and skull. He wore a tunic of green and a toga of white linen and a silver girdle and there were silver armlets on his arms and he wore one jewel on his finger, a sapphire as blue and as iridescent as a Grecian sky. He is puissant, she thought, a man of men, and Helena had not exaggerated in her buoyant enthusiasm. He had eyes so very pale that they seemed to have no focus at all. She doubted that they ever overlooked anything, even of the smallest importance. Above all, he had Olympian grandeur.

She was stirred for the first time since she had left Al Taliph, and she was annoyed with herself. She had vowed never to look again on a man with interest or provocation. How different they were, the man of the unknowable and intricate east, and this western man who had the appearance of immovable marble. She saw that his eyes were fixed on her, those inexplicable eyes which revealed nothing. No doubt to him she was just another beautiful woman, ripe for exploitation. She would enlighten him. Helena had assured her that Pericles was not as other men, but the skeptical Aspasia had not believed this.

She permitted a slave to refill her goblet with Syrian whiskey. She drank with almost the same gusto as Helena. She glanced briefly at Pericles. He did not display any distaste or disapproval. Now Helena and Pericles were advancing on her and she showed them a face without expression, and not even a smile. She said to Pheidias, in her lovely voice, "We must continue this conversation, for I, too, think of Athens as the glory of Greece." She turned to Helena and Pericles and her eyes were merely expectant and courteous. Helena had told her, "Pericles is a man who respects women and does not regard them as animals fit only for breeding, or stupid. When you know him you may be able to exert influence on him." Aspasia had smiled cynically to herself. Helena was an intelligent woman but Aspasia suspected her of being too ardent in her relations with men, and too gullible, for Helena had boasted of her lovers, all of whom, according to her, were men of intellect as well as distinction, and who had regard for women. Aspasia was now mistrustful of all men, remembering Al Taliph. She had led an ascetic life since leaving him, despite the malicious rumors in Athens. She had promised herself over and over never to love another man. That way led to destruction. Thargelia had been correct.

But still she loved and anguished after Al Taliph, and yearned for his kisses and arms.

Helena embraced Aspasia, as she had embraced her earlier, and exclaimed, "You grow more entrancing every moment, my dear friend! Behold! Pericles, son of Xanthippus, Head of State, has deigned to grace our dinner tonight. I have told you much of him." She glanced humorously at Pericles, who took Aspasia's hand, bowing, and kissed it.

"Rumor has not lied of you, Lady," he said, and she was pleased by his eloquent voice.

"Of what has it said concerning me?" she asked, and he saw the bright watery lights in her eyes dancing.

"Only that which was laudatory," he replied. He still held her hand and smiled down at her.

"You are gracious, lord," she said. "But I do not believe you." He saw that she had a mischievous look, almost saucy, and that she suddenly appeared as a young girl. He held her hand tighter, when she tried to withdraw it. She frowned slightly and her smile disappeared. She felt a tremor through her body; where his lips had touched her hand there was a burning, a smarting, which ran up her arm. She had not felt this for two years and she was frightened. She was confused; she saw the pallor of his eyes and knew him to be inexorable, and all at once she was excited and the tremor was stronger in her flesh.

"I have heard of your school, Lady," he said.

"That is good, lord. I educate young ladies from the age of twelve to seventeen, so that they may be worthy citizens of Athens." She waited for a jocular remark, for a shrug. But he was regarding her seriously. "Alas," he said, "they cannot vote."

"Once, in Homeric times, they did, lord. Surely a woman is as worthy to vote as the market rabble!"

His powerful interest in her heightened. Here was no light woman; his first opinion of her was confirmed. "I agree with you, Lady. I had a very intelligent mother, who was worth ten thousand of the street men."

He smiled over his shoulder at Pheidias, who was shyly trying to retire. "Pheidias," he said, "I have much to discuss with you, and your plans to glorify our city."

"Ah, yes, Pericles, I am at your service. I have sketches drawn, for the Parthenon." Pheidias' face was illuminated. "I hope you will approve of them."

Pericles nodded, then turned to Aspasia again, whose hand he still held. "Tell me," he said, "what do you teach your young ladies in your school, which has acquired some renown?"

"History, science, art, mathematics, medicine, patriotism, poetry, literature, responsibility, esteem for one's self, astronomy, architecture—whatever path their native talents suggest." She waited for an upraised eyebrow, but Pericles was still serious. She continued, "Not domestic duties, which are the province of their mothers, nor religion, which is the province of their priests."

"Not dancing, not singing?"

"No. The arts of entertaining are to be taught by their mothers." Now Aspasia's dimples reappeared. "Surely their mothers are expert in that, having husbands!"

"Are all your young ladies intelligent, Aspasia?"

"I accept none whom I have not personally questioned, and chosen. I want no fools in my class, to exasperate teachers and to degrade the teaching rooms. My school is not a place for frivolities and chatter and gossip. I also teach gymnastics, for the health of the girls and to develop their bodies. As the Greeks say, a sound mind needs a sound body, if it is to be effective."

"I have seen many great men who were not sound of body, Aspasia. And many men of sound bodies who have the minds of pigs."

"True, lord. They both labor under misadventure. I do what I can in my school. I have two young ladies who have deformed limbs, who are extremely intelligent. How they escaped infanticide I do not know, except that they were rescued by their mothers."

"It is a most extraordinary school," Helena said, noting that despite Aspasia's small struggles Pericles did not relinquish her hand. "You must send earnest men to observe it."

"I will remember," said Pericles. It was a polite remark but Aspasia believed that he spoke the truth and not idly.

"I have heard that you are an Ionian and that you have spent some years in Persia," said Pericles.

So, she thought, he knows much about me. She looked at

339

him directly with her luminous eyes. "I was the companion of a Persian satrap for nearly five years. No, he was a Mede."

"He let you leave him?" he asked in an incredulous tone.

"No. I left him." She drew a quick breath, and her eyes did not avert themselves. "It broke my heart, but I had to leave him, for never shall I understand the east. Two years ago he died, and left me a vast fortune. He had sought me earlier but could not find me." Her eyes were suddenly filled with mist. "His lawyers were more successful. I am using his money in my school, though he would hardly have approved of that."

She did not speak as the Greek and other women spoke, timidly and fearfully, averting their eyes when addressing a male stranger. She spoke, rather, with the forthrightness of a man, and with simplicity. There was an absolute fearlessness about her; she had his own assurance.

So, thought Pericles, she still loves her satrap, and love is women's armor against other men. Here, he reflected, was a woman who once giving her heart gives it passionately and perhaps for life. For some reason this vexed him. Despite what Helena had told him of Aspasia he had believed that she would be delighted to fall into his arms, he the Head of State, and a rich and handsome man. After all, she was a courtesan. Now he was uncertain, and his yearning for her increased. She was no longer even faintly smiling at him. Her face had paled a little, as if at memory, and with sorrow. Seeing this, he felt a deep respect for her, and a gentleness, and he longed to hold her and console her, not with passion but with a tender understanding he had never felt for a woman before.

The thunder which had been snarling in the mountains now advanced on the city and the lightning glittered and flared at every window and door and the wind rose and shouted against the walls. Slaves scurried to close every portal and window, drawing curtains, securing bolts. But outside, the trees began to roar and whiten in the approaching storm.

"You must tell me of your Persian, or Mede," Pericles said. "They are a mighty people, brave beyond imagining, with a magnificent history. I revere them, for all I am a Greek."

"They are beyond our understanding, they being of the east," Aspasia replied, and a sigh lifted her breast. All at once he saw her grief fully.

The guests repaired to the dining table, laughing and vehemently arguing, and Pericles, forgetting even his Helena, led Aspasia to the chair which stood beside the ornate divan reserved for him as the most distinguished guest. He could smell her perfume, that of lilies, and he wondered if that had pleased the Persian satrap, and that she wore it in memory of him. He felt a pang of jealousy. Nard became her more, or heliotrope. She was the most beautiful woman he had ever seen, though he saw that she was not deliberately voluptuous, and used no conscious arts or seductions. There was a certain pure clarity about her, almost virginal, for all she had been a courtesan. He no longer believed in the vile rumors about her. She had put from her, like a garment, the lessons she had been taught by Thargelia, the artifices and smirks and graces destined to lure and hold a man. If she had any passions now it was for her school. He had heard that she had had lovers in order to obtain money for her young ladies' tutoring. He knew it was not true. The satrap had left her a fortune. He must have loved her dearly, Pericles thought, with a stronger pang than before, and now with resentment. He decided he hated the satrap who had brought her to his bed from Thargelia's house.

The guests began to seat themselves, still arguing. Suddenly the thunder became a deeper, heavier sound, a subterranean rumbling, and the earth moved and the lamps and curtains in the dining hall swayed. The guests looked at each other with dismay. "Pluto," said one, "is stirring on his black bed. Doubtless Proserpine lies in his arms." Some laughed, though uneasiness had them. They waited for another ominous rumble, but it did not come. The curtains fell into place, and the chattering of plates and cutlery and glass ceased.

"It is strange," said Socrates in his high and piping voice, "that the forces of nature disturb us more than do the utmost ferocities of men. That is because we cannot control nature but we can exhibit even worse ferocity to enemies."

"It is said by us scientists," Anaxagoras remarked, "that one day we shall control nature."

Socrates lifted pious and antic eyes. "That will be an even worse calamity than the uncontrolled furies of nature. I do not trust my beloved fellows. We are more inventive than nature, and with malice. Nature, at least, is without discrimination and knows no evil passions."

"You are a Sophist," said Zeno.

"No," said Socrates. "I am a Stoic. I endure all things, even humanity, which is the hardest of all disasters to endure." And he laughed with good temper, and his absurd little beard wagged.

The storm broke over the city. They could hear the wildness of the wind, the thunder, the rush of trees, the slashing of rain against the walls. A slave fearfully drew aside a window

341

drapery and through the glass they could see the marching steel rods of the falling water in the lights of the lamps.

The women sat in their chairs like tall bright birds, their jewels twinkling, their beautiful faces alert to please, their mouths ready to converse, their hair, auburn, black, yellow or chestnut, sleek and glossy, their robes of many colors. The men sat comfortably on their divans, fondling the women's hands, touching their cheeks, whispering to them. But Pericles did not touch Aspasia. Helena, watching, was satisfied. However, she saw that Aspasia had become sad of countenance again, and she knew the reason. Aspasia had confided to her, on receiving the fortune from Al Taliph, "Alas, I know now that he loved me. I believed he did not. Had I but known I should never have left him." To which Helena had replied sensibly, "But the east revolted you. You would have left in any event, or Al Taliph would have tired of you as you aged. Had he tired of you and dismissed you he would not have left you that money and the many treasures which adorn your house. One must reflect on that."

"Money does not answer all things," Aspasia had replied. At this Helena had laughed incredulously.

"When you discover only one, my dear, you must tell me!"

Pericles also saw the abstracted sadness on Aspasia's face, which seemed like a pale veil over her features. He guessed the reason—that she was remembering the Persian satrap; he knew that if he touched her now, even slightly, she would recoil from him. Also, she was a woman of fastidiousness, and an overt approach would offend her. He knew that he loved her as he had never loved before, and knew all her qualities. He also believed that she was drawn to him, however reluctantly.

A group of young women slaves at the rear of the dining hall began to strike their harps and to sing softly. The rain had become a gentle hissing against glass and wall, and the wind began to fall. Intermittent lightning flashed, but the thunder was growling in retreat. The scent of flowers and grass and leaf flowed refreshingly through an open door, and the perfumed lamps flickered.

Helena's dinners were notable not for gross quantity but for artful flavors and textures. Her wine was incomparable, her whiskey undiluted. Her friends said her dinners were Epicurean delights, stimulating both the mouth and satisfying the soul. They were not dinners for frankly hungry people, who desired only to appease rumbling stomachs, but for men who regarded a fine dish as a work of art, to be gazed upon with anticipation and delight, and then slowly enjoyed. Above all, conversation was the important sauce, whether it was frivolous or serious. All things, lamps, beautiful plates and cutlery and cloths and food, were the auxiliaries to speech, the joy of the exchange of ideas. For this reason Helena had no distractions such as dancing girls or tumblers or jokesters in the dining hall. Needless to say, she rarely if ever invited dull or pedestrian people who could contribute no mental exhilaration to the gathering. Even the entrancing music of harp and lute and voice was only the soothing background to conversation, and never intruded.

Slowly Aspasia began to be more acutely aware of Pericles, in spite of her despondent thoughts of Al Taliph. She began to glance at him sideways, and saw the clear hardness of his features, which had no hints of softness or sentimentality. Almost imperceptibly his expression would change, while he conversed with others. It was not as subtle as Al Taliph's or as elusive and elliptical, and had more discreet control and sharpness. If he had passions they were not overt. He had command, not only by inspiring fear—which she guessed he would do but rarely—but by the cold force of his personality, his aura of authority. He was the least impetuous man; yet she knew that he could be moved by terrible anger when aroused. It would not be violent, that anger. Its very restraint was all the more intimidating. But at moments she discerned a certain silent disquiet about him, which only the most astute eye could see. Helena had been right. Here was a formidable man, a man of men, a man of chill thoughts, a man who reflected objectively, whose decisions were wrought in stone after long internal argument. He was also a man of passion.

So involuntarily had she been concentrating on him that she had become unaware of the conversation near her, and she was vexed, for all looked to her for opinions. He would not, like Al Taliph, goad her to epigrams for his amusement, or demand that she display her intelligence before guests. He had accepted that she was intelligent; he would never urge her to intellectual exercises for his sole entertainment. She could not imagine this man prostrating himself before Deity as Al Taliph had done, for he was proud if, perhaps, reverent. She knew, from many remarks from Helena, that he had been trying to lead the Athenian religion into monotheism, which had inflamed the priests. Yet, this was not inconsistent or devious. He had a respect for humanity even if he deplored its excesses, its wildness and savagery, its turbulence and perilous nature, its childish unpredictability.

She became frightened by her own fascination with him, and turned to listen to others. The conversation had advanced from whispered and intimate remarks with adjoining neighbors, and had become centered on the approaching three-day festival of plays, and other arts.

Sophocles, that gentle poet and writer of plays, had introduced three actors on the stage simultaneously, and he was famous for his delicate discrimination as well as for the power of his work. His play, *Oedipus Rex*, was to be produced again this year during the festivals, though some priests had protested that there was little religious dialogue or direction in the play.

"I have talked with him concerning a sequel to Oedipus," said Zeno of Elea. "It would concern a man's expiation of evil through penance and understanding of his own evil. He thought of it long and said he would remember our conversation and that he might, at some later date, write a sequel."

"I respect Sophocles," said Socrates, the light of controversy glittering in his brilliant and colorless eyes. "I grant you that expiation of a crime is most desirable. But the perpetrator of such a crime must be a man who undertook evil deliberately and with complete knowledge and will and malice. Oedipus was not such. His crime was an innocent one, in that he did not know he was committing it, did not do so with deliberation and will and malice, was not aware that his wife was his mother and that the hostile stranger he had encountered and killed was his father. He gouged out his own eyes for a crime of which he was intrinsically blameless, however we may find it horrifying. That was absurd of him, as was his self-exile."

He smiled at the listening company. "In one way, I am a Sophist. Truth, as they say, is often a matter of individual opinion, and varies with cultures and philosophies and religions, and, with governments. We can, therefore, call it subjective. The agreed truth is that Oedipus committed a crime against nature and law and order. But, the truth also is that he did not know he had committed a crime. Why, then, should he have expiated anything? Why should he even have engaged in an agonizing dialogue with himself, which led to his destruction?"

"But you, yourself, Socrates," said Zeno, "have said that ultimate truth is attainable through dialogue and the defining of terms."

"I have said," Socrates replied, "or I meant, that an agreed-upon truth can be arrived at. But who knows it is the ultimate truth, however many agree? The terms we think we define exactly are often a mere accord on semantics, for a word which means something to one man may mean nothing to another. Therefore, in the very agreement we must admit that that agreement, itself, is subjective, and each man will retain his own version on what has been agreed."

"You are disagreeing with yourself," said Pericles, smiling.

"But, that is the function of philosophy! To assert a hypotheis, then demolish it!" He laughed his high piping laughter, at himself. "I affirm nothing, not even that I affirm nothing." He continued: "If Oedipus had been a prudent man, given to reflection, he would have discerned that he was not truly guilty of anything at all. But he did not examine himself, and the unexamined life is not worth living."

He turned his faun's face on Pericles. "And what is our politician thinking of all this?"

"Do not mock politics," said Pericles, with a slight edge of reproof in his words. "Would you tell me that politics are nothing to the man of mind? I do not say that a man who takes no interest in politics minds his own business. I say he had no business here at all."

"Ah," said Socrates. "That is true. I did not mean to offend." He looked merrily at Aspasia. "Was it only two nights ago, Lady Aspasia, that we were discussing politics in your house? Will you repeat what you have said of government so that this company can not only have the pleasure of gazing at your face but of listening to your words?"

Aspasia blushed, and Pericles thought this most charming, for, again, she resembled a young girl. "It was nothing, Socrates," she said. "But, if you wish, I will repeat it: Republics suppress aristocracy, democracies, freedom. What, then, is the best government? I have heard it said, from one who was a governor, that a benign despotism is the best, but as there are few benign men and despotism is abhorred by such, my—friend—was wrong. It is my belief that an aristocratic Republic is the best, though that may seem a contradiction in terms. Democracies are the worst; they become tyrannies, for the reason that when every man speaks, whether or not he is a fool or a wise man, chaos and shouting take over government and inevitably a strong if dangerous man assumes power. The man on horseback."

Pericles looked at her fully and smiled at her with amusement. "You do not like our form of government?"

She hesitated, looking for mockery in him, but there was none. "I see it in its present form, as a disaster to Athens."

Pericles drank from his goblet and then said, "So do I."

He thought of Ichthus, whom he still mourned unceasingly, and so did not see the look of surprise on some of the guests' faces. But Anaxagoras nodded, and so did Zeno, and then Socrates. Pericles said, "There is a great clamor among politicians in Athens now that my plans to make her the diadem of the world, in art and poetry, in science and in marble and in learning, should be abandoned for 'the domestic necessities of the people.' In short, to pamper all the appetites of the mob, as one pampers cattle—for their milk. Votes. The tearful critics who shrill at me proclaim that their own plans arise from their love of humanity, but it has been the experience of history that when government pretends benevolence it really means it intends to abolish freedom. We have little enough now, the gods know. We shall have even less if those who prate of the purity of their intentions and their hearts prevail. An official who truly loves mankind seeks to elevate it through beauty and knowledge. An official who thinks only of bellies degrades mankind."

He looked at his old teacher, Zeno, and said with respect, "What does the speaker in paradox think of this?"

Zeno considered. Then he sighed. "I am growing old, Pericles, and I discover more and more paradoxes, and no longer do they seem consistent to me. For instance, we long for that which is alien to our natures. The violent man craves peace, the coward, bravery. The dissonant speak of harmony, the placid, enterprise. The husbandman dreams of cities; the urban man of grass. He who cannot love admires love; the loving would often hate. Not in self-deceit are these. They are the unattainable, and therefore the stuff of poets. We philosophers, alas, are less astute. I no longer understand this world."

Helena, seeing that her guests had taken on melancholy countenances, said with her robust smile and laugh, "Pindar has said the best of healers is good cheer, so let us drink to this night and this gathering, for this moment is all we have."

Aspasia gave her a look of fondness and for the first time she truly smiled and said, "Aeschylus has remarked that the pleasantest of all ties is the tie between host and guest. And so, let us drink to our dearest Helena, who condescends to teach one of my classes twice a week, in the art of medicine."

After the toast had been drunk and the singers and harps had struck a lighter note, Pericles said to Aspasia, "Tell me of Persia, for I admire the Persians."

Again she hesitated, and the pale veil of sadness drew down

over her features. Then she began to speak to him alone in a quiet voice, as the guests had begun to jest among themselves and Helena was telling some of her more indelicate stories. Aspasia spoke of Al Taliph with difficulty yet with candor. As she became more eloquent, and saw that Pericles was regarding her with disconcertingly intent eyes, she was less constrained. A warmth pervaded her. She discovered she could now speak of Al Taliph without the overwhelming pain she had endured for several years. In fact she laughed gently now and then as she related some tale of his unpredictabilities and his acrid conversation. Yet she was not able to conceal from Pericles the sombreness of the aristocratic Mede, the bitterness under his sallies.

"I should have liked to have known him," said Pericles, when she fell silent, smiling to herself at some memory. She looked up, started, and said as if with amazement, "He should have liked to have known you also, Pericles!" She knew this was true, and was even more astonished.

"In his terrible way, he was a great man," she added, and now without any sorrow at all but only with admiration. "He never said a crafty or deceptive word, yet he was most elusive and inexplicable. He could be frightful, and then the kindest of men. We did not understand each other, yet—"

"You loved each other," said Pericles. His jealousy seized his throat. "How fortunate was he to have had your love, Aspasia!"

"He was spared a deep suffering: He never knew I loved him," she replied, and all at once her face was no longer young but grave with years.

"You speak in mysteries, Lady. Do you not believe in the real rapture of the love between a man and woman?"

"I have not found it. I think it is the imagination of poets." She looked restive. She knew he was scrutinizing her with too deep an intensity, and it disturbed her. She did not know how she felt concerning this man; she did not want to be concerned with him at all, yet there was a powerful struggling in her, and an overwhelming fear. She said, "I must content myself with my school, in the hope that women will be recognized as human and be permitted to acknowledge talents. The world is poorer for lack of this recognition."

She thought, in her confusion, to turn him away, but he said, "I hope this also. It was not so in Persia, was it? Did its women submit to their servitude?"

She was horrified at his perceptiveness, for she had not

347

spoken of the monstrous oppression of women in Persia nor the women's bland acceptance of their fate. She stammered, "Without a single protest!"

He said, "But the women of Athens have been protesting, though futilely, since Solon. At least a number of them are so doing. Athens is the richer for your presence, Aspasia."

She murmured her thanks. She was more and more frightened. She could feel the warmth of his body, now so close to hers, and the scent of fern which rose from his garments. It was all like a threat—or an embracing—and she feared both. She half-started to her feet, involuntarily, in instinctive flight, then sank down again and a bright haze seemed to cover her eyes and she felt weak and undone. She looked timidly into his face and saw there only kindness and approval, and she thought again that there was something Olympian about him, something splendid, and a soft melting came to her and for some reason she wished to weep. She saw his strong white hand near hers. She longed for him to touch her, yet she shrank. Never had she experienced such an inner trembling, such a tumult of feeling, and she did not understand it. This was entirely different from her passion for Al Taliph, and she endured no pang of betrayal.

When Pericles and Helena were alone Helena said with an arch smile, "So, you have fallen in love with my beauteous Aspasia? Ah, do not suddenly look so stiff and annoyed. I have watched your face for hours. She loves lilies and the scent of them. Send her a sheaf tomorrow. You have touched her heart."

"She is like a nymph who has never been awakened," said Pericles.

The cynical Helena said with demureness, "Then, awaken her. For the last time, my Hercules, you may enter my bed tonight, in a farewell. I am not unhappy. My heart rejoices in your future happiness. But Aspasia will be hard to woo. I must pray especially to Aphrodite tonight."

Pericles, lying with Helena in her bed, found that he could embrace her, not as a lover, but only as a tender brother or passionless friend. With alarm, he thought of impotence. However, Helena understood and kissed him with cool tenderness. For the first time, she thought, he had truly loved a woman and therefore—for a time at least—he would be indifferent to other women. Yes, I understand, she reflected, for when I had my beloved I saw no charms in other men, but alas, as I am a faithful woman, I still find few charms in them, remembering my love.

Aspasia lay sleepless in her chaste bed in her small and delightful house adjoining her austere school. The moon stood in her window, as white and pure as Artemis, and as cold. She turned from it, restlessly. She could think of nothing but Pericles, not as yet with joy, but with yearning and fearful agony. Al Taliph had been like a sleek and sinuous leopard, revealing eyes which reflected secret emotions but which would not answer an inquisitive glance. Pericles was like a lion, stately and regnant, deliberate and lonely, resembling a mountain. The man of the east and the man of the west were singular in that both possessed enormous strength, yet one had the strength of the unknowable and the other the strength of steel, flashing yet icy. One moved with subtle grace, the other with overt power.

She thought of a fragment which Sappho of Lesbos had written: "Now Love masters my limbs and shakes me, fatal creature, bittersweet."

Again, she was frightened and was full of the instinct for flight. Then a deep sweetness came to her, a surrendering sweetness, and she wept and smiled, then slept, and dreamt that she was a girl again in a moonlit grove of myrtles.

PART THREE

Pericles and Aspasia

"Not houses finely roofed or the stones of walls well-builded, nay, nor canals and dockyards, make the City. But men able to use their opportunity."

ALCAEUS (611—580 B.C.)

CHAPTER 1

Daedalus, father of Dejanira, stood before the King Archon, shaking with hysterical rage, and cried, "It is infamous! A man in his position, who takes a notorious harlot, an open courtesan, to his bed and often to his house, should be impeached by virtuous citizens! At the very least, the ostraka should be used against him. He is a public outrage; he is a spendthrift; he is devious and unapproachable. He is robbing the treasury of the labor of the people, for his fantasies in architecture and his patronage of low artists and sculptors and barefoot philosophers!" Daedalus almost choked with his rage; he had become incoherent. When he could find his breath he burst out again: "A harlot, a notorious and infamous woman, who flaunts the modest feminine decencies and flaunts herself in public and debauches young girls! There is not a woman of immaculate morals who does not avert her eyes at the mention of her imperious name! The people despise Pericles and demand redress and his removal from public office."

The King Archon stroked his beard and reflected on such as Daedalus, who demand civic virtue at all times but have their secret and not so dainty vices. Was there envy here, and inner torment, as well as rage? Those who proclaimed their humility, like Daedalus, were frequently inordinately proud, though they had little reason for pride. The King Archon, always seeking to know the weaknesses and the characters of men, understood that what a man denounced were his own wickednesses. In denouncing them in others he absolved himself of his own guilt. Daedalus would bear watching.

The King Archon said in a conspicuously moderate voice, to express his disapproval of Daedalus' excesses, "Go to. There is not a man of any distinction, or wealth, who does not have a hetaira. This is accepted. Do we not all marry stupid or illiterate women of family and money to breed us sons and enhance our wealth and govern our households? And do we not all, in flight from what we have married, acquire us a beautiful and loving and intelligent woman to soothe our exacerbated senses? Who can blame us? Custom forces upon us less than delectable wives, with less than the intelligence of donkeys but who know the measure of every pot and a thousand ways to cook beans and keep records of expenditures. They may be virtuous—but gods! how they bore us!—and this may be the unpardonable sin of virtue. We may be sure that the sons they bear us are truly our sons; beyond that, their mothers are intolerable. Then our priests prate of 'the constant elevation of mankind through each generation.'! What liars and fools. A donkey breeds a donkey. There will be no 'elevation' of mankind until the time a man carefully selects a wife who has more than money or kitchen aptitudes, and has a mind. Then, indeed, shall we breed superior sons and daughters and not mundane animals who cannot distinguish between the light of the sun and darkness. So far the human race recognizes darkness only because it augurs their mindless slumbers, and the sunlight only that it increases their crops.

"Pericles is like all of us. He has fled from stolid women and their meek whinings, and their shrill little rages. Why, then, should he be singled out for blame? It is hypocrisy to do so. To denounce him is to betray our own iniquities." He smiled at Daedalus slyly, and the other's skeleton features flushed with harsh scarlet.

The King Archon continued: "You may deplore Aspasia. At the very least she is educating young ladies who will not merely stink of the kitchen, the barnyard and the breeding pens. They will be a joy to their husbands. They even may make their husbands so fascinated by them that they will eschew the hetairai and even harlots. As Pericles has said, women belong to the human race also, a saying that some may doubt, considering their wives. At the best, intelligent women may give us sons fit to be called members of humanity, and daughters who will not only possess beauty but be entertaining. Let me ask you this, Daedalus: Do you consider your wife to be enthralling?"

Daedalus suddenly looked sick. Yet he became even more infuriated, and his mouth kept opening and shutting soundlessly, which the King Archon thought a blessing.

"You have called Aspasia impious, Daedalus. In what manner? She is teaching the girls in her school to question and not merely to accept. If that is impiety, let us have more of it, especially among our sons.

"We publicly deplore love between men and men, and have penalties against it, though it flourishes. Have you ever considered why? Again, it is a flight from our women, who have nothing to say of relevance, but babble only of slaves, records, fashions, children or other inconsequentials. Would you prefer the perversion of the love between those of the same sex to the open preference for that which is ordained by nature: the love between a man and a woman? I confess I prefer the latter. I have my own hetaira.

"You have said that the people despise and hate Pericles, our Head of State, that they demand his impeachment or ostracism. Who are the people you speak of, Daedalus? The market rabble, who want no monuments to glory and history and the gods, but only the satisfactions of their bellies? Shall we descend to the pigpens which infest our society, or shall we raise our eyes to the dreams of Pericles? Is a fat and well-fed beggar, who lives on the industry of others, preferable to a man of vision, a man who works in honor and sobriety, and loves his country not for what his country can do for him but what he can do for his country? Those who regard their country only as a smelly trough in which they can wallow and devour are a terrible danger to all of us. A man should justify his birth by his life and his accomplishments, even if they are humble. The world did not ask him to be born. So, he must prove that he has a right to live, not by the capers of his parents in their bed, but by the quality of his existence.

"Those who love Pericles and would defend him to the death are not only intellectual aristocrats but men who earn their own living with pride and work and dedication, whether it be at the loom or in the field, in the manufactories or in the shops or the vineyards. These we dare not offend, for they are the life of our nation, our city-state. They are the hope of our survival through the ages. But the market rabble are our death."

Daedalus swallowed with difficulty and found his voice. "There is always the ostraka to be used against officials or persons like Pericles."

The King Archon sighed both with exasperation and disgust. "If it were possible, and left solely to my judgment, I would not permit the ostraka to be employed by men who cannot read or write, and so have no clarity as to the significance of their votes. I would permit a citizen to vote only if he has been measured for his intelligence, his awareness of why and for whom he votes, and is literate. Voting is an awesome duty and a momentous privilege. It should be confined to the responsible who see less their own advantage and more

355

the advantage of their country. I fear, alas, that this is an impossible dream."

He saw that Daedalus was still having difficulty in speaking, and he waited with obvious patience. He saw that Daedalus had not listened to him in the least, and that he was concerned only with his furies and his emotions.

So the King Archon, who was a benevolent man for all his stern principles, said, "Let me refill your goblet with this good wine from my own vineyards. Wine is the blood of our age."

"I am no drunkard!" cried Daedalus, with an offensive gesture.

The King Archon refilled his own goblet. "Nor am I," he said in an equable tone which did not entirely cover his anger. "Moderation in all things. Is that not the saying of us Greeks? I am never immoderate," and he looked meaningly at Daedalus. But the latter had never considered himself immoderate so the rebuke did not touch him.

Daedalus said, clenching his fists on the table before him, "Pericles, it is said, would marry that woman—that woman for whom he had his marriage to my daughter annulled! If that is not a public scandal then nothing is!"

The King Archon smiled. "Have no fear of a marriage between them. Had not Pericles, himself, a few years ago, ordained, with the approval of the assembly, that no Athenian citizen may marry a foreign woman? Aspasia is an Ionian. Therefore, he cannot marry her. He is a prudent statesman; for him to repudiate his own law would indeed cause an outcry, and justly so, for many are the Athenians who cannot marry the women they love, for they are foreigners. They have obeyed the law. Therefore, Pericles must obey the law. When rulers flout the laws they have personally fostered they are criminals. Pericles is no criminal."

Then his kind face became stern and hard. "There is the matter of your grandson, Callias. He has been proscribed from the meanest and lowest of gaming tables, and taverns, and from nearly every establishment in the Agora. That is because of his furious conduct, his arrogance, his reliance on his riches—"

"He is but a youth!" shouted Daedalus, forgetting the superior position of the King Archon. "It is but his high spirits, his young exuberance!"

"Youth is the time for discipline, for the exercise of self-control," said the King Archon, and his eyes darkened. "If a man does not learn these in his youth, he will never learn them. You speak of high spirits and young exuberance. Was it those which caused him almost to murder a man in a tavern? Had he not been rich, as you have mentioned, and had you not interceded, he would have gone to prison. For the honor of his own sons, the half brother of Callias, Pericles also interceded, though, I believe, with reluctance." He shook his head. "That is the one thing which vexed me concerning Pericles."

"You have always, lord, had a high regard for him!" said Daedalus, forgetting his own prudence for a moment.

"Of a certainty. He is a man of public justice, of civic virtue, in larger matters. I would have done as he has done." He became weary of Daedalus.

Daedalus stood up. "I will have vengeance," he blurted, and without permission he almost ran from the room, despite his rage, his robes flowing back from his emaciated figure. The King Archon laughed a little, and called for his scribes and for the lawyers, who had more important matters to discuss with him.

"Was that the Archon, Daedalus, who blew from here like Boreas, lord?" asked a young lawyer.

"It was. He is an old man. Yet he sprang from this room as if pursued by Nemesis," said another.

"I fear he was," said the King Archon, smiling. Then he thought of Callias, whose petty crimes and insane assumptions and malignities, his cunning and coarseness, his joy in cruelties, his swaggerings and roughness, had earned him a dissolute fame of his own in Athens. Only his riches, and his family, protected him from the wrath of many. They often saw him drunken on the streets, or belaboring the slaves who carried his elaborate litter, or stabbing innocent street dogs, or reeling after young maidens accompanied only by women attendants. He was infamous and avoided, and this inflamed him.

The King Archon said, "It is often that from a man's own loins comes his ruin."

It was only with his mother and his grandparents in the house of Daedalus that Callias was accorded any tolerance. His rude appearance, his bulky body, his stolid countenance were exceptionally like his mother's, but he did not have her docility, her capacity to love and to endure. He heard her

357

wails over her lost sons, Xanthippus and Paralus, and he hated his brothers, for he wanted all attention and affection on himself, though he had none to give, himself. He knew that Dejanira preferred her other children above him, those youths who were the sons of Pericles. Often he had fantasies in the night of murdering them. He listened to the stammering diatribes of his grandfather against Pericles, and the weeping denunciations of his grandmother, and he pondered. Not only had he loathed Pericles and envied his half brothers for their beauty, but the father had shown his detestation of him while he had lived in the house of Pericles. He had enormous vanity; he was convinced that his aspect was that of a prince, and that his intellect surpassed that of anyone in Athens. Though tutors had despaired of him, and though students had driven him from the colonnades of the Agora where they were listening to philosophers, he considered them lamentable fools, and had cursed them for their shouts of derision. His tongue was full of blasphemies, and threats. He had already killed two inoffensive slaves, one an old man, the other a child. Though Athenians did not regard slaves as human, but only as things, they were appalled. Callias believed that all envied him, which pleased him, and he was the bitterest enemy of all who dared to belittle or laugh at him. Both these crimes against him he had encountered in the house of Pericles, in the person of Pericles, himself, and his half brothers.

His deepest hatred was concentrated on the lofty Head of State. He became certain that not only was Pericles his enemy but that Pericles was hated by the whole of Athens. So, for many midnights, he pondered on Pericles, after listening in the dining hall to the imprecations of Daedalus on his former son-in-law. What would cause Pericles the agony he deserved? To lift one's hand against the Head of State or even an official of government meant execution. Even an open threat was punishable. Callias believed himself as invincible as Hercules, so great was his egotism. But something warned him not even to speak of Pericles with so much as an oath, in public or in private, among his debauched companions. Pericles was famous for his ruthlessness.

So Callias concentrated on Pericles, and listened to the outcries of Daedalus against him, and the whore, Aspasia, who had displaced his mother, as he had been taught to believe. The shame of Dejanira became his. How dared such a woman sit on the chairs his mother had sat upon, and lie in the bed of

Pericles? Dejanira's degradation became his. Was not Aspasia the infamy of Athens, as well as a notorious courtesan, of whom the lewdest stories were told? She was also impious, it was openly declared, and the mortification of all pure women. Pericles loved her. It was enough.

Callias began to plot. Should he cause the death of Aspasia it would not only mortally wound Pericles but it would bring accolades from Athenians on her assassin. At one stroke he would avenge himself on Pericles and become the hero of Athens. Pericles would not dare to seek revenge on him, no matter the loftiness of his position. So Callias believed.

But how contrive the opportunity of murdering her? She had guards about her house and her abominable school, which had inspired the indignation of good citizens. She never went abroad unattended. Virtuous Athenians might find her contemptible, and comic poets might lash at her with witty verses on the stage and in the taverns—even before Pericles, himself—yet she was feared as the mistress of the most potent Head of State. She was also courted and admired by the patrons of her dinners. No one, not even her most intense enemies, could deprecate her beauty, which was renowned in Athens.

Her beauty. To destroy that was to destroy the woman, herself, make her repulsive to Pericles, visit him with mourning and despair, cause even the most devoted to turn from her with pity and revulsion. Slow though the wits of Callias were, they were also cunning and dogged. He went, hooded and alone, to the dark abode of an old woman notable for her brews and her potions. Many called her Hecate, and she had even preened herself on the name, and had cackled. Her house was avoided, not only at night but by day also, for it was rumored that she could cast evil spells. Nevertheless, she had her customers who went to her for love philters and amulets and curses upon their enemies. Barren women visited her, and became fertile. She told fortunes, and multitudes whispered that she was a seeress. Officials considered her mad and so did not apprehend her, for they had heard that she was lavish with gifts to the temples. She was rich, if not honored. There were those who said she was one of the Sibyls in disguise. Her house was set in a grove of heavy sycamores and guarded by fierce dogs on chains, which she could loose in an instant—it was said—by uttering a single guttural word. The house, though small, was luxurious and filled with treasures given to her by grateful patrons. Daedalus, who proclaimed himself above superstition, had execrated her, calling her the scandal of Athens.

Callias trusted no one, so he did not send a slave to acquaint Hecate that she was about to be visited by a noble lord. Slaves babbled. If his grandfather heard that his grandson had visited such an ominous woman he would be wrathful, even with him, and declare him a disgrace. Besides, Daedalus was an Archon, who had public responsibilities, and was a cautious man. Callias knew that Daedalus had tried to injure Pericles through Aspasia, but only by way of legal channels, and that furtively.

It must be done by the utmost stealth, so that none would suspect the son of an aristocratic house.

Callias, though rich, was frugal. He thought of intimidating Hecate with threats, when he found himself, still hooded, in her house, his features hidden, and so to force her to accept only a gold coin or two. But she insisted on fifty gold crowns, and when he complained that he was a poor man, she laughed at him and offered to set one of her snarling wolflike dogs on him and drive him off. He had worn humble clothing, but she saw that his large hands had never labored, but were soft and fat, and she heard his voice, which, though coarse, was not the voice of a peasant or small shopkeeper.

She threw back her haggard and disheveled locks, which resembled gray snakes, and said, "It is not only the acid which you buy, but my silence. That has never been broken, though I have been threatened with torture more than once." She grinned at him like an evil mask in the theatre, and cracked her gaunt knuckles. Her house smelled of incense, and the walls were covered with ghastly murals of harpies and furies and Gorgons and serpents and dragons, all lit by the light of brass lamps, and all surging with frightening colors. Callias had a thought of murdering her with his dagger after he had received the acid, thus retrieving his purse and leaving no witness behind him, but as if she heard his threat—though she could not see his malevolent face—she loosed two dogs who sat before her and made the most sinister sounds, their red eyes fixed upon him. He shrank, and she cackled, and she knew she had guessed his intentions.

Her carved brass chest of large proportions stood by her side, as she crouched on her silken chair. Callias, with an oath, flung his purse onto her bony knees, and she opened it and counted the coins. She nodded her head with satisfaction, opened the chest and withdrew from it a glass vial filled with a murky crimson liquid. "Throw this upon your enemy's face, and never will he see again, and none will dare look upon his countenance for very horror. It will be more dreadful than the face of Medusa. The acid will burn like a fire that never was, and will consume all it touches. Flee from it immediately after it has been flung."

Callias, without speaking again, left her with exultation, the vial carefully wrapped in parchment, and then in leather. He now had only to arrange an encounter with Aspasia, to come close enough to her to throw the acid fully into her face. She would not die, but she would pray for death then and later. It was a most fitting revenge on Pericles, who adored her, it was said, as if she were a goddess who had condescended to love and lie with him.

For a number of days he skulked about her house and her school, wary of guards, clad humbly as if he were a workman or a man from the fields, his face hooded, his gait slouching, his head bent meekly. He saw slaves coming and going, and guests whose famous faces he recognized, and none noticed him, not even the guards. Once he saw Aspasia's litter, but it was guarded also, and the curtains were closed against the hot sun which could injure her celebrated complexion. It was reported that in the city she showed her bold face at night, without shame, and her eyes stared fearlessly before her and were not averted. But Callias knew that she was always surrounded by admirers who could seize him in a moment, and doubtless slaughter him.

It was impossible to get into her house, guarded as it was. As Callias was forced to wait his frustration made him frenzied and even inclined him to recklessness. He thought of becoming the hero of Athens, even if he died for it. But always he recoiled from that end, and always he knew he must be anonymous. That infuriated him against Aspasia. He desired glory, but the price was too high, though his act no doubt would be applauded. He lost interest in being a hero, if he would not be here to be acclaimed. He had also learned that Aspasia had many powerful friends who would avenge her, no matter how much the citizens of Athens might approve of his act.

He told himself that he must be fearless, for the honor of his family. But he was afraid. He forced himself to the first real and concentrated thinking of his life, and he sweated with the monstrous labor of it.

Eventually, after long days he came on a plan which was all folly, but from its boldness it might succeed. What had he heard Daedalus say sourly one night? "Money is all things, and with it one can even seduce the gods—who created it." Callias had found this eminently true, and for a unique hour he wildly pledged to himself that he would not be frugal, as was his nature, but throw with golden dice.

He went to the lowest quarter of the city where lived and prowled the most audacious and venturesome rascals, criminals hiding from the law, willing to face all things for money, and as heedless of mercy as the vultures they resembled— bloody men armed in their spirits with congenital evil. Not only would money lure them, but wickedness itself, for that was their climate.

Callias knew their taverns and frequented them, but never did they know his name, for he feared his grandfather as he feared no other. He called himself, to them, Hector. He roistered with them, drank with them, and they recognized him as one with their own natures, and so did not rob him or murder him. They guessed that he was not of their birth, and this flattered them, as he sought their company. Moreover, he bought wine for them, out of gratitude that they accepted him. Some considered that in an extremity he might come to their aid through influential friends. He often implied this, boasting. He and they knew that should they be arrested they would be immediately executed, for some of them were escaped murderers as well as thieves.

He entered the sinister tavern they preferred, lit with sullen candles, and filthy beyond imagination, and reeking with sweat, vice, vermin and crude wine and spirits. The tavern, as usual, was filled with scoundrels with contorted faces, their daggers always loosened, their garments soiled and dusty and torn, their sandaled feet dirty. They hailed him with pleasure and crowded about him, their arms on his shoulders. Their breath was fetid, their yellowed and broken teeth displayed, their features villainous. He responded to them, not with aversion, but almost with affection. They were his own, though they had no money.

He flung a purse of spilling gold on the table before the wine merchant, who was as evil as his customer. "Spare no wine tonight!" he shouted. "I have plans of greatness, of fortune, for a number of you!"

They shouted with joy and delight, and scrambled for the coins and Callias watched, satisfied. Then he asked for Io, a harlot who catered to these men, a very young girl not more than thirteen who had the face of a dryad, as innocent as a lily, and with pure blue eyes. She was a favorite of Callias, who often slept with her on her squalid bed, and she liked him for he gave her a gold coin instead of a copper one. They sent for her at once, dragging her from her bed where she lay with a malefactor. She was in her short shift, which revealed her gleaming white thighs and her child's arms and part of her budding breast. Her hair was black as a sable wing, her mouth soft and rosy, her countenance virginal. She was also very dull and of little wit, and as obedient as a puppy. No one had ever heard her speak, though she heard, and the only sounds she could make were squeals and gasps and small shrieks. She was most beguiling in appearance. She might have been the daughter of an aristocrat, for she had strangely delicate gestures, for all the grime of her flesh and garments and feet.

Callias studied her, and knew his judgment and memory had not failed him. She was perfect for his purpose. She would ask no questions, for she possessed neither curiosity nor understanding. She had only a stainless beauty untouched by her propensities, which were as vile as her face was untainted. She exhaled sweetness despite the rankness of her surroundings. She had been found as an infant, wandering the noisome streets, and had been taken as a slave by the wine merchant's wife.

"Io, my love," said Callias, fondling her immature breast, "you are about to attain fine garments, and soap, and fragrances."

CHAPTER 2

In the two years Aspasia had been his mistress—or, as the surlier Athenians called her, "his harlot"—Pericles had never wearied of her for an instant, but was constantly in a state of joyous wonder that she always seemed to possess a new countenance, a new variety of character, a new and startling revelation, for him. He would leave her in a state of gravity, and when he saw her next she was scintillating with mischief and humor, or, if gay, she would show him a temperament of such seriousness the next time that he was reminded, again, that she was not a light woman but a woman of profundity. There were moments, especially when she was wearied, that she presented to him a face almost plain, and pale and thoughtful, even old, and tomorrow she would be a blaze of loveliness, shining with color, and as young as an untouched maiden. She would on one night spend hours discussing the plans of Pheidias with him, and the next time she would throw her round white arms about him and say, "Kiss me. It is a night for love." It was, Pericles would think, as if he possessed a harem of entirely different women, all of whom worshipped him and were adorably complaisant though in different manners.

She combined the delicious arts of a courtesan, with all the rapture and ecstasy and beguilements of that condition, with the tenderness and devotion and solicitude of a beloved wife. But careful, as always, having been sedulously taught by Thargelia, never to bore him, never to engage in tedious conversation or complaint, and never give herself totally to any human creature. Between her and Pericles blew a fragrant veil, and when he pursued ardently the veil quivered freshly in his face. He found this both tantalizing and exciting, especially that when he moved the veil briefly aside he found he had been pursuing a stranger, who laughed at him softly. She could be exquisitely playful, like a very young girl, and in a twinkling she was a composed woman who discussed philosophy with him.

She was indeed, in all aspects, the woman of the figurine, but also of warm flesh, at once yielding and resistant. But no matter her changefulness he knew that she loved him as deeply as he loved her, and often, in the very midst of addressing the Assembly, the Archons or the Ecclesia, he would think of her with an inner trembling, a bliss, a longing, an absolute belief in her integrity and her steadfastness.

As for Aspasia, she had been taught by Thargelia that to protect herself she must not love utterly, or at all, because men tired of women and looked for novelty, and were as restless as hares in spring, or deer at mating time. Thus, a woman who loved was vulnerable, and when discarded pined to death or into old age, and never knew happiness or joy again. Men, Thargelia would say, despite the poets, loved women but never a woman, whereas women, unfortunate creatures, loved a man but never all men. A woman in passion must love, even if little and briefly—and always personally—before she can surrender herself, but to men any charming woman was desirable and love was not considered during a new encounter. Women, by nature, desired the established, the sure, the secure, but these made men restive.

It was not for over a year that Aspasia could feel herself safe in Pericles' love, and could trust him and love him fully, and this was a warm and secret joy and happiness to her. She could speak to him from her heart and her moods, not always mindful that she must invariably please him; she could speak as one human soul to another, confident of protection and sympathy and tenderness and reassurance. She knew that such a love between a man and a woman—never fearful of deceit or betrayal—was the most precious gift of the gods, and must be cherished and kept alive like a Vestal fire, for it was holy and blessed. She lay in the haven of Pericles' love for her, never anxious, never afraid, never moved to silly pretenses, though always careful to let him believe that there was more of her than she had already revealed.

She saw that his utmost desire was to please her, to hold her closer to him, and that in her presence he was wholly himself and never doubted her, and she pleased him in return, and what he said when he was in bed with her was never confided to another. She knew the burdens of his state, his enemies, his struggles, his frustrations, his desires, his hatreds and his cold furies, and he and she knew that his confessions and his outbursts would never travel beyond this chamber where they lay in each other's arms, head to breast, hands clasped, or lips together in the hot and scented heat of midnight. Ah, she would think, what it is to trust, and how few can we trust! If we have one, it is enough; it is more than enough; it is the water of life for a whole existence. It is nurture to our spirits, a garrison against vicissitudes of chance, the precariousness of living.

Once he said to her, "I will repeal the law I have made, that no Athenian citizen can marry a foreign woman." Above all things, he desired her for his wife, fearing the inconstancy of human beings. But she said, "That would give a mortal lance to your enemies, and especially to those men who love but cannot marry an alien woman." To herself she said, "Many men are more faithful to their mistresses than to their wives, for whom they invent faults in excuse for their betrayals. But a free woman can leave them at any hour, and this they know, and so must be faithful lest beloved women leave them first for men more tender and considerate and bountiful." If her reflections seemed cynical to her she also knew that they were relevant and based on reality and human nature. To hold Pericles, who was, after all, only a man, she must withhold also. On further reflection she knew this was true of all human encounter. To give all, except perhaps to God, was to lay one's self open to disaster.

So in her beautiful gardens she erected a bare marble altar under a marble roof and surrounded by marble columns in the calm Doric design, and without walls. The altar stood in the center and was inscribed: "To the Unknown God." It was a small temple but with the purity of snow and silence, and on each side there were iridescent fountains with leaping dolphins within, spouting rainbows so that the columns dripped with shaking light under sun or moon. Surrounding all were beds of lilies and roses and jasmine, and a circular walk of red gravel. She did not know how it was—for it seemed fanciful to her—but the area about the little temple possessed a great and quiet peace, a promise of refuge and eternity, enhanced by a square of dark and pointing cypresses beyond the flowers and the paths. It was like a small grove, sanctified, to be approached only by those who were seeking, and who were filled with awe and reverence. It was a favorite spot for the girls in the school, but rarely did they venture to the steps of the marble floor. They would stand at a distance, in unspeaking motionlessness. They asked no questions. It appeared that in their young hearts they understood. It was Pheidias who had designed this with love and passion, and who had said, "One day He will have thousands of altars and thousands of temples, and all will know who He is."

Also, in her garden, in a secluded place, was a plain marble plinth with the words graved on it, "Al Taliph, who taught me, Aspasia, many things of joy and many things of pain. Who can discern the difference?" Pericles had come upon it once and had felt that cold anger of his, and a sharp jealousy, but he had never spoken of it to Aspasia. He had his secrets and she had hers, and both respected them. It was another of those hidden things which bound them together, more than if all had been revealed in the bitter light of day. Bareness could be ennui, and perfect revealment, like nakedness, unenticing. Mystery, like the shadows of the moon, could create visions and awaken Poesy. Above all else, he found Aspasia mysterious and never to be held in entirety.

They entertained their friends in Aspasia's house, rather than in his, though Aspasia's house was smaller even if more beautiful in a very austere and elegant way. She was perpetually in revolt against the opulence and crowded intricacies of the east, and she liked the aspect of unadorned marble walls reflecting the rosy light of sunset or the shards of palm trees, and the gleaming reflections of polished marble floors. But her statues were incomparable and many of them had been created by Pheidias, though he preferred to work in ivory and gold and bronze. They too had the grandeur of heroic simplicity, and were gravely dignified. Over everything lay a numinous peace, a noble quietude.

The house adjoined the school, a square building surrounded by colonnades where the girls could study and read and converse and walk and look upon the composed beauty of the gardens. The girls lived in the school's dormitories, under the guidance of their teachers, and guards. At sunset the gardens echoed with their laughter as they played ball or practiced archery or threw the discus or splashed in the pools. To Aspasia, it was a lovely sound and she often joined the maidens in their play, for though now twenty-five years old, she still miraculously possessed the suppleness and swiftness of youth. The maidens reverenced her; it was their ambition to resemble her in all ways. "Excellence," she would tell them, "cannot be utterly attained, but with diligence and devotion it can be approached. One must never be content with mediocrity, for that is the complacency of low minds. Strive always. Compete always, as in the Great Games of the Olympiad. Only this pleases God."

Zeno of Elea had often told Pericles that happiness was the dream of cattle, and not to be attained by thinking men, for thought bore with it the understanding of the tragic predicament of mankind. "It is said," he once remarked, "that Prometheus brought down fire from Olympus to mankind, and for that he was direly punished. But it is my belief that was an allegory; he brought thought to men, which most certainly is a fire! In so doing he made them conscious creatures. Perhaps it might have been best had we remained baboons."

"The majority of mankind is still baboons," Pericles had replied. "I am no idiot democrat who believes that men are created equal in any fashion."

He found the only real happiness he had ever known with Aspasia, and even that was fitful. For he was filled with the terror all true lovers know: the terror of losing that which was most dear, through death or disaster. Anaxagoras had said, "Enjoy the moment, rejoice in it, for we have lost yesterday and the future is not yet ours. Think not of evil or loss in the coming days. That sours the present hour as rich wine is soured into vinegar." But still, Pericles was not of the nature to enjoy only the present. The future is formed by the present, he would think, and not to think of it would result in stagnation, and nothing would be built or created and we would live in a wilderness like beasts. Thoughts of the future could bring pain; that was true. However, one was armed in advance. So, he had insisted on more guards over Aspasia's house and school. She had not wanted walls about her buildings; he demanded them, with locked iron gates beautifully wrought, and guarded day and night by burly men.

Callias had meticulously surveyed walls and gates. His desire to destroy Aspasia, and thus destroy Pericles, grew daily. His first plan had been to throw the acid into Aspasia's face, himself. But like all physically powerful, bullying and loud-voiced men, he was a coward. He studied all possibilities and had finally concluded his plans down to the smallest detail, for he had the cunning mind of the stupid and malicious. He had been told that Pericles spent at least three nights a week in Aspasia's house. When his cutthroat friends informed him that Pericles would not sleep that night with Aspasia, that he had spent the night before with her, and that he was due to address the Assembly this morning, he completed his plans. He did not know that Aspasia and Pericles had entertained guests the last night, that Pericles had been somewhat overcome with wine and conversation, and had remained in her house, from which he would go to the acropolis.

This morning, as usual, they walked together through the gardens just after dawn. Though high summer, it was still pleasantly cool before the sun rose too high, and the grass dripped dew as prismatic as a rainbow and the flowers exhaled sweetly in a medley of fragrance. The dark cypresses pointed against a sky as yet only a pale blue. The fountains rustled, speaking to themselves. The hills surrounding the city had burned to sepia, over which the climbing olive trees were a pattern of fretted silver against the brown and yellow earth. The temples scattered on the acropolis seemed formed of delicate white bones against the darker background and had already caught the first aureate light. The little temple to the unknown God stood in its beatitude of isolated quiet, the unadorned altar waiting. Birds were busily conversing in the myrtles and sycamores and palms and the air was full of musical sound. It was the hour which pleased Pericles more, though Aspasia preferred the night.

"I have received a letter, some days ago, from a very rich young man who lives in Corinth," said Aspasia, holding Pericles' hand in her soft fingers, like a trusting child. "His parents died of the flux just recently, and he has been left with a little sister, thirteen years old. As he is often absent from his house

368

he fears for her safety. Her name is Io. He has slaves to attend her, but is sedulous regarding her welfare. He has heard of my school, and wishes her to be with me, and so he is bringing her to see me. He spoke of her shyness and vulnerability, for she has been unusually protected, even more than is usual among the Greeks. He will arrive with his sister either today or tomorrow, for my inspection. He mentioned that she has had tutors and is considered very intelligent, in spite of her youth and inability to converse with strangers."

"I hope she is handsomer than most of your young ladies," said Pericles.

Aspasia laughed. "My maidens are not chosen for comeliness of countenance, but for their intellect. My house is not a house for the training of courtesans. However, many of my girls are pretty. It is just that I do not teach personal adornment, but insist on a severity of dress and hair, so they will not be distracted. The arts of luring a man are best taught by their mothers."

"But what is more enchanting than beauty with intelligence?" asked Pericles, and bent his helmeted head to touch her lips lightly with his own.

"Ah, I am a rare vessel," said Aspasia. Peace filled her; Pericles' hand was strong and firm and protective, as it held hers. She sighed. She never doubted his love for her, his intense concern for her happiness, his devotion. She had dreamed of him during her years with Al Taliph, that inexplicable man whose moods were never reassuring, who could be furious at one moment then tender the next, leaving her always in a state of trepidation and uncertainty. Sometimes she was glad that she had never known that he had loved her, for then she would have stayed with him, to her calamity. There were other times when she remembered him with a gentle sorrow and a dim longing, even when she was with Pericles. A woman's heart, once given, cannot be taken back without bleeding and pain.

The sun was rising higher. It was time for Pericles to leave. Aspasia never asked him when he would return, for this made men impatient and gave them an uncomfortable feeling of restraint, deadly to love. Pericles, on visiting Aspasia, brought with him but two guards, mounted like himself. He went to join them, after a last embrace with Aspasia, and disappeared behind the school. She stood there, enjoying the morning, and gazing about her with pleasure and comfort. Even when she was old, she thought, she would love all this and remember. She looked idly at the distant gates and the walls. Two guards stood inside the gates, well armed. She smiled. Pericles protected her thus, not that he truly considered she was in any danger, but because it gave him confidence.

A company stopped outside the gates, a handsome chariot with an awning, in which sat a young man and a young girl. It was accompanied by four horsemen, helmeted and armed. They sat on their horses like soldiers and the early morning light glanced off silver harness and helmet and made the hides of the animals glimmer sleekly. So the girl, Io, had arrived with her brother, with considerable ceremony. Aspasia walked slowly down the red gravel path, then paused. The guards were talking with the company. Then one came towards her and said, "Lady, the lord from Corinth, one Nereus, and his sister, Io, have arrived. They crave an interview with you."

"Let them enter," said Aspasia, and stood, waiting. The guard returned to the gates and opened them. The occupants of the chariot climbed down, and the chariot with its white horses, and the accompanying soldiers, remained outside the gates. The young man and the girl entered the gardens alone, which Aspasia idly thought was a little curious. She looked kindly on the approaching young people. The brother, Nereus, was fair and tall and dressed richly if quietly in a robe of crimson silk with a girdle of gold and a mantle the color of his robe. His smooth head was gilt; he did not affect the hyacinthine curls of the Athenians. Aspasia's attention was directed at the girl, and she saw before her a child of an absolutely pure countenance, smooth as a lily, and as sweetly pale, with thick black hair, unbound, under a veil of blue the color of her wide and staring eyes. Her dress was white linen, bound with silver, and her mantle was of blue traced with a silver design. Her feet were shod in sandals of silver, twinkling with gems. In her hand she bore a small object wrapped in a red and blue silk cloth.

Callias, on his horse outside the gates, gloatingly observed that Aspasia was alone in the gardens, with not even a distant slave in evidence, or a gardener. His men outnumbered the guards; still, he was afraid, as a coward, of entering the purlieus of the house and the school. If the guards, after the fearful act, attempted to seize him and his companions, they would be unhesitatingly slaughtered. As for the two within the gardens, they were of no moment to him. They might be able to flee and rejoin the company. If not, then let them perish. This he had not told the spurious Nereus, who had been reassured that the company would wait and bear the two off in safety.

Nereus, who was a thief and a murderer, though young and fair, had heard of the beauty of Aspasia, but even he was surprised at the tall stateliness of her, her aspect of a statue wrought in marble and tinted deliciously. Her silvery-gold hair was not dressed; it blew about her in a radiant cloud in the morning breeze. For an instant his nefarious heart hesitated, thinking of the coming devastation of that face, that exquisite form, for he had been gently bred and had been forced from his father's house for his incorrigible conduct. Callias had shrewdly chosen him well, for he had patrician manners and an educated tongue.

Nereus greeted Aspasia with a proper bow and said in his cultivated voice, "Lady, it is gracious of you to receive us, and we are humbly grateful. Here is my sister, Io, of whom I have written to you. I pray you will receive and nurture her, though she is shy and seldom speaks. She will observe her childish silence."

Aspasia bent her head and smiled tenderly at the young girl, for always she was moved by youth. She saw the fixed eyes, and then she hesitated, for there was no intelligence in them, but just an empty staring which their beauteous color and form could not conceal. She said, "You say she has been tutored well, Nereus?"

"Well indeed," he said. "But she has not been exposed to public gaze, and so does not speak readily to strangers."

His left hand pinched Io's upper arm, and this was her signal, which she had rehearsed many times under the brutal guidance of Callias. She began to unwind the silk which concealed the deadly vial of fuming acid. She did not look away from Aspasia, who said, "Let us withdraw to the outdoor portico, where we can converse. Then I will show you, Nereus, my school." It was her thought to question Io, about whom she had become uncertain. The girl had an infant's eyes, blank and uninhabited. She reminded Aspasia of Cleo, who, despite her lack of intellect, was now the tyrant mistress of an intimidated Cadmus, a fact which invariably amused Aspasia. There was no one more rigid in demands and rules than the stupid. Moment by moment Aspasia was becoming convinced, regretfully, that Io was not a candidate for her school. Still, she had been mistaken before. She would not dismiss the two until she was completely convinced of Io's unsuitability.

She turned to lead the way to the outdoor portico of her

house, but Nereus said, "My little sister has brought a gift for you, Lady, and wishes to present it to you now."

Aspasia faced them again, smiling. The last fold of the silk fell from the vial and Io gripped the vessel in her hand, staring at Aspasia's face. She had lifted the top from it with a swift movement. At that instant a buzzing wasp flew before Aspasia's face and she quickly stepped aside and waved her hand at the menacing insect. It was this that saved her, for even as she moved and made her gesture the girl flung the contents of the vial in the direction where she had been standing.

Hissing, and flaring redly, the acid arched in the early sun, and fell on the grass near Aspasia, where it burst into flames and exuded a stench which was intolerable. Aspasia recoiled with a cry of terror.

Nereus had received his orders. If, by some unseen misadventure, the acid failed he was to stab Aspasia in the heart as rapidly as possible. He saw the blazing acid on the grass; it was creeping in a thin serpent of fire through it, away from Aspasia. He drew his dagger and furiously advanced upon the shivering and horrified woman, while Io merely stood there, blankly staring and expressionless. At that moment Pericles and his men rounded the side of the building. Nereus saw them. He was a brave murderer, however, and would have completed his task had not Aspasia, herself, seized his wrist and flung his arm upright and had brought her knee swiftly to his groin. She screamed wildly; Nereus dropped his dagger and doubled over with a yell of pain. Pericles struck his horse with his whip and rushed towards the three, seeing the crawling flame, and the struggles of Aspasia, for though agonized Nereus had gripped one of her ankles and was twisting it, intending to bring her down where he could the more easily kill her.

Callias saw all this from his safety beyond the gates. He made a signal and the empty chariot and his horsemen began to roar away. However, Pericles' men raced after them, though they were outnumbered. They had one advantage which they did not know as yet: Callias' men were not soldiers and though they carried swords they hardly knew how to use them with any dexterity. So, they all fled. Pericles' horsemen pursued, and the guards at the gate ran in their wake with drawn swords.

Pericles shouted for more guards, and he seized Nereus by the hair and pulled him from Aspasia. Io simply sat down on the grass and began to fold and unfold the discarded silken kerchief, and gaze about her unwonderingly. It was not Pericles' intention to kill Nereus, who was much slighter and smaller than himself, and so he had to control his murderous rage, for he wanted information about the assassins. He caught Nereus about the throat and choked him into submission, then threw him on the ground and held him there with his booted foot. He looked over his shoulder at Aspasia, who was hugging herself with her arms and shuddering and weeping. He said, in a very calm voice, "It is over. Do not fear, beloved. Return to your house and await me."

"They wished to destroy me," she said.

"That I know. I will soon discover why, and they shall be punished."

She repeated over and over, "They wished to destroy me. Why?"

"Go into your house," he said with terrible sternness, and then she obeyed, her head bent, her face in her hands, her hair lifted about her in the wind. Pericles' face had drawn itself into formidable lines. Nereus feebly tried to stir, and creep from under that inexorable foot, and Pericles deftly kicked him in the temple. Nereus sprawled laxly, unconscious.

In the meantime the house guards appeared, running over the grass, swords drawn. The acid had stopped its crawling, and now was just a small smoking trench in the grass, without fire, and only with smoldering sparks here and there. Pericles said, "Take this murderer and lock him in some room and guard him constantly. Do not injure him. He must be questioned."

Alone, and waiting, Pericles looked down at the black trench in the grass and for the first time he, too, began to tremble both with rage and horror. He felt undone. He looked at the sitting girl, Io, who had begun to hum softly to herself, winding the multi-colored scarf about her wrist and raising it now and then to see the glimmer of it. Pericles' first impulse was to kill her, and then he saw the vacancy of her young face, the untenanted aspect of her eyes. She was no more guilty of this atrocity than the birds in the trees, he thought. He said to her, tempering the roughness of his voice, "Who sent you here, wench?"

She heard him, with her slow wits, then she lifted her face and gazed at him. She only knew that he was a man; she had been taught seductiveness. She inclined her head and regarded him with blue eyes as shallow as a puddle deposited briefly by rain. She said in an infant's voice, "Hector. Do you—bed, lord?" Her voice was uncertain, like the voice of a very young child. She began to gurgle incoherently, and Pericles frowned. To Pericles the imbecility of the girl impressed him with a kind of frightfulness, as if she were an elemental and not a human being. He saw that she had no conception of the enormity she had tried to complete. She was beyond good or evil, for she had no soul. Pericles felt himself in the presence of something innocently appalling yet supranatural, from which the human spirit must recoil.

A female slave came into the outdoor portico and Pericles called to her and she came running. "Take this child to your quarters," he said, indicating Io. The slave led Io away by the hand, and Io went with docility and unasking, and without resistance. Pericles shuddered. The garden was bright and lonely about him, smiling in the risen sun, but there was only tumult and fury in his heart. The garden seemed to mock him and he realized that nature was completely uninterested in the turmoil of humanity and its tragedies and therefore was direful in itself. Alas, he thought, we desire that even nature partake of our passions and despairs and fears, and when it does not it confuses and alarms us. We are insignificant before its forces and its own brutal designs, which are without thought or emotion. The Fates spun their webs with no tremors, no sympathies, no engagement with those they raised or destroyed. They were as indifferent as Io, and therefore as much to be feared. How presumptuous it is of us to think that the abysmal depths of some huge unknown consciousness is aware of us!

He looked at the temple to the Unknown God and he felt considerable bitterness, as if he had been betrayed. He dared not think of what Aspasia had escaped, as yet. His whole mind was set upon vengeance.

The soldiers and the guards, panting and dusty, returned with but one man, who was slightly bloody and disheveled. That man was Callias, surnamed "The Rich." The others had been slain after a hard battle. The only reason the guards had not killed him was because he had cried, "I am the grandson of the Archon, Daedalus, Callias, and if you murder me you will pay to the last drop of blood! Take me to Pericles, for my mother was married to him." To the last he was a coward, thinking only of his own life, and never of his grandfather or his mother, who could be crushed under this scandal and attempt at murder or worse. He thought himself above the law, as all the stupid did, and therefore had privileges. He also believed that Pericles would spare him.

Pericles wondered at his own lack of surprise when Callias was dragged before him into the atrium, bleeding from several superficial wounds, and as grimy as a peasant. His face was bestial and defiant, though his eyes flickered when he saw Pericles.

Pericles contemplated him as one contemplates something unspeakably obscene. He said to the guards, "Take him away, and put the brand of slavery on his forehead." Callias shrieked and struggled futilely, but the guards overpowered him and bore him away. Sudden nausea took Pericles. He bent his head to his knees for a moment or two, then accepted the iced wine a male slave mutely offered him. He found he was sweating coldly; the walls of the atrium appeared to move about him like white sails. He thought of Daedalus and Dejanira with enormous hatred and considered the pleasure he would feel when his soldiers flung Callias at their feet with the shameful brand of slavery on his brow. Forever he would be marked as a thing, and not a man. This was more desirable than any other punishment.

Aspasia, as pale as death still, came into the atrium and stood mutely before him, seeing his silent and mingled rage and hate and emotion. He was leaning back in his chair now, his eyes closed. After a little he became aware of her presence and looked up at her. She watched him as she said, "I have taken the liberty, lord, of countermanding your order to have Callias branded a slave."

He sat there and gazed at her and she had never seen the face he now presented to her, the blind and menacing face, and she stepped back, frightened. But he said quietly enough, "You dared to do this thing, Aspasia? You dared to disobey me?"

"Yes, lord." She clasped her hands tightly to her breast and felt her first terror of him. Never had he seemed so imperial in his short white tunic, his helmeted head, his fixed expression, and never so dangerous. She had often been afraid of Al Taliph; in comparison that fear was nothing to what she felt now. She trembled visibly, but kept her features as still as possible.

"You doubtless have an explanation for this mortal affront, woman?"

Never had he addressed her in such a voice and with such chill insult. She bowed her head and said, hardly audible, "I do, lord. You have two sons, and they are brothers of this Callias. Would you have Xanthippus and Paralus kinsmen of a slave?"

He had not thought of this. He considered what she had said with profound shock. She continued, "Would you also have it laughed through Athens, by your enemies, that you had been married to the mother of a slave?"

He stood up and slowly paced up and down the atrium, his hands clasped behind his back, his head bent. She watched him and said in a shaking voice, "The disgrace would be bad enough. But the punishment you decreed for him is beneath you, lord."

He stopped with his back to her and said in a tone hard with scorn, "What would you suggest, O Sibyl?"

She went to him and touched his bare arm imploringly. He did not turn to her and she saw the inflexible profile. "I suggest that he be beaten soundly by my overseer of the hall, before my slaves, then taken in chains before the King Archon, who is your friend. Let Callias be exiled for life. Are you not Head of State, even above the King Archon? He will not deny your demand."

"Callias is pestilential," said Pericles. But he was thinking; he rubbed his jaw with his hand and stared before him. "He deserves death. Would it not be better to have him killed and then buried in some unknown spot?"

"It is beneath you, lord," she repeated.

He thought of Turnus and smiled grimly. He knew that Aspasia was appealing to his pride and not to his justice. She was a woman and thought as a woman. Wise as she was, she did not fully understand a man. He said, "Had that wasp not saved you, Aspasia, you would be deformed for life, hideous to the eye, or you would have been murdered. Yet you appeal to me for mercy for the assassin who would have done these things to you!"

"I am not insensible to what I escaped, lord," she said, and tried to get him to look at her, but he would not. "I, too, have imagination. I am not as weakly compassionate as you may think. I was less his intended victim than you. He wished to strike at you, through my destruction. For, have I offended him in any way? No. For what he tried to do to you death is too feeble. My suggestion is far more ghastly. When he is thrown before the King Archon, command that Daedalus be present. Daedalus is your enemy, and mine. He will never

376

outlive the shame, that his grandson attempted murder, that Callias is a miserable demon, worthy of the utter contempt of honorable men, that he stood before an assemblage in chains, like a common criminal."

He looked at her now and she saw the tight ruthlessness of his smile. "You are very artful, beloved. Still, there is much merit in what you have said. Let it be done." He clapped his hands loudly and the overseer of the hall entered the atrium, and slowly and carefully Pericles gave his orders. The slave bowed. Pericles said, "Bring to me one Nereus, who is under your guard."

Nereus was dragged into the atrium, manacled, and flung on the floor before Pericles, who spurned him with his foot. Then Nereus rose, and he had the quiet manner of the born aristocrat, for all his face was bruised and bloody. His eyes momentarily struck Aspasia. She saw disdain in them.

"What have you to say for yourself, O son of a female Cyclops?" asked Pericles.

But Nereus said nothing. He wiped blood from his mouth with one of his chained hands. Pericles contemplated him, his eyes narrowing. "I know your father," he said, "one of my friends, and he is of a noble house and a man of probity and honor. I recognize him in your face, and I saw you as a child. Your father drove you from his house, with grief and despair and just anger. I know your crimes."

Aspasia listened to this with astonishment.

"You are more nefarious than Callias, who is a pig, a fool, and a gross creature," Pericles continued. "For you chose your evil life. You darkened your father's house. He is still suffering from the infamy. How shall I punish you, so that men will know and avoid you for the rest of your life?"

He glanced at Aspasia, and she said, "Let him be branded, and not even his father will have one pang of pain. Then deliver him into the hands of a slavemaster, who will send him far from Greece. He has kept his silence, for he is a man of birth. He will not defame his father further."

Nereus' mouth shook, and yet he did not speak. When the overseer led him away by his chains he walked proudly. "No," said Pericles, "he will never give his name, and never will his father know. There is some advantage in being an aristocrat. At the last they suffer punishment without whimpering or an outcry."

He went to Aspasia and took her gently in his arms and kissed her brow and her lips. She rested against his breast, but she was still afraid, remembering his aspect when he had upbraided her. As if to console her he said, "Your advice was excellent, and I am grateful, my beloved one." Her fear left her as she thought that Al Taliph would never have spoken so to a woman; he would have felt no gratitude for this offense to his pride, however judicious. She clung to Pericles, and for the first time in this day of horrors she wept. He held her tenderly.

"I will have Pheidias design a giant wasp in marble, for your garden," he said, "with eyes of turquoise. It will be a warning to you, my sweetest one, never to trust a stranger. In truth, never trust anyone absolutely."

"Not even you, lord?" she asked, smiling through her tears.

He kissed her again. "Not even I—perhaps," he said, and for a moment she was desolate. He lifted her hand and pressed his lips against her palm. "For some day I must die, and must leave you."

"I pray that I will die first," she said.

"Never have you spoken to me so cruelly," he replied, and she saw the gravity of his eyes. "For what is life to me without you, Aspasia?"

A few days later the King Archon visited Pericles in his chambers.

"It has been done to Callias as you commanded, Pericles," he said, as he seated himself. "But it has not increased your popularity among the rabble, and even your fellow aristocrats are outraged." He hesitated. "A multitude believes that Callias was justified—in avenging the repudiation of his mother by you. Moreover, they say that the Lady Aspasia—"

"It is a scandal," said Pericles, when the King Archon did not finish his sentence. "And that she was trained as a courtesan. Yes, I have already heard what is being said. It matters nothing to me."

The King Archon was an old man, and he had loved many women. Still, he reflected that even such as Pericles was not immune to Eros, and in this he was like countless other men. Empires had fallen at the touch of the soft hand of a woman. Men had abandoned honor and position and even life for women they had loved. There is a lot to be said for the theory of some philosophers, thought the King Archon, that a man in a great position should be deprived of his testes, so that his people will not perish.

CHAPTER 3

"Alas," said Aspasia to her friend, Helena, as they sat in the outdoor portico of Helena's house, "perhaps it had been better that I perished than Pericles suffer the present calumny and vituperative attacks. Would I not give my life for him? Of what moment is my life compared with his benevolence, his love for his country and his desire to create beauty for her, his rule of law and justice, his intellect and understanding, his hatred of the vile and the hypocritical, his calm judgment, his patronage of the arts and the sciences, his lofty detachment from all that is emotional and hysterical, his loathing for the fervent and the zealous, his contempt for politicians and government and bureaucrats—in short, all that Pericles is. He is the crown of Athens. But, I am nothing."

Helena saw her friend's tears, but she could not resist saying with some irony, "You have made Pericles superior to Zeus. Beware that Zeus may be listening! You will remember that the gods hate, above all things, pride in human beings and they punish it severely."

In spite of her anxiety and distress Aspasia was forced to laugh.

Helena continued: "The gods would have us grovel in the muck of the earth and pour dust and ashes on our heads and never contemplate the stars. We have committed the crime of pride and have become higher than the beasts of the field—a most terrible effrontery to the gods. I have always said, as did my dear mentor, that without pride a man is simply an animal, but in his challenges to the gods he becomes heroic. Enough. Pericles is inexorable as well as kind. If he believed that only by dismissing you he could retain rule of Athens he would do so."

"You do not believe, dearest Helena, that a man might sacrifice himself and his dreams for a woman?"

"I do not believe," said Helena. "Yes, there have been some instances in history, but the men were fools, ruled by their genitals and not their minds—an unpardonable thing in both men and women. An active penis or vagina is no substitute for the stuff of a human being's soul, no matter what the hedonists say, and the adorers of Dionysius. Nor can they comfort a man in the dark night of the soul, which comes to all of us, except to the happy grinners of the market place, who are less than human. A romp in bed with a woman can never console a man for the loss of his honor and his position—and his advantage. So, do not fear. Pericles loves you; he will hold you to him, not in recklessness and disregard for his whole life, but because he knows he is stronger than his enemies and can defy them. Never, sweetest friend, deify a man. Admire him, if he is worthy of admiration, but never adore him."

"You are truly a protégée of Thargelia," said Aspasia, with a slight resentment. "I thought Pericles would give up all his life for me!" And she burst out laughing, as did Helena. Then Aspasia said with more anxiety, "But, he is in danger, not only because of what he is but because of me, also."

"He is also in danger because of his associations with philosophers and scientists—accused of impiety—such as Anaxagoras and Zeno and Pheidias and Socrates, to name but a few. The Archons, the Ecclesia, the Assembly, and all the dreary scum of government hate him for using the public treasury to enhance and glorify Athens. They would prefer to pocket the gold, themselves, or to advance what they call the public welfare, which means, in the raw reality, the buying of votes for themselves. Be not proud, Aspasia. Pericles would not destroy Athens and himself for you, or any other woman. In that, you can take pride in him, for he is no womanish man, the victim and slave of emotions, and what the vulgar call love."

Helena was as rosy and robust as ever, and as always her counsel was sensible, if filled with cynicism. Aspasia, despite her own experiences, acknowledged that Helena was less vulnerable than herself and sturdier of spirit and for this she loved her. Rather than feeling sad because of Helena's exposition of Pericles' character and ambitions, Aspasia was comforted. He would not be destroyed because Aspasia was his mistress. She was merely the passing excuse for the demands of the rowdy market rabble—which unfortunately could vote —for his impeachment and removal from office. They saw in Pericles a threat to their hope of an easier and more abundant life, at the expense of taxpayers. They hated him in that he had told them that a man should earn his bread with his industry, and not with mendicancy. They knew he despised them openly, and regarded them as a peril to their country.

The rabble knew that Pericles respected and supported the new middle class, who believed that work was both honorable and prayerful, and that a lazy man, though free, was less than an industrious slave. Had they, the rabble, not a right to live, too? they had asked of the Archons. To which Pericles had replied, "No. Not unless you have justified your right to live —which you have not."

They seized on Aspasia—they the filthiest of fornicators and adulterers at every opportunity—as an example both of impiety and of lasciviousness. They cried that she influenced Pericles in his office. She was a degraded woman, a courtesan, and never a matron. She was scandalous, in that she corrupted young women with learning. She entertained suspect philosophers—who sneered at the gods, and scientists who debated the existence of the gods—in her own house. It was said that she had a temple to some Oriental deity in her gardens, on which a spell had been laid, so that any who approached His altar became impotent, mindless, frenzied or blasphemous, and challenged Olympus, itself. The Unknown God, of Whom some priests and philosophers spoke? He was unknown because He possesses no holy attributes, no adherents. Zeus has not acknowledged Him. Therefore, Pericles and Aspasia have insulted Zeus. If Pericles was not deposed the gods would avenge themselves on Athens. Woe!

Daedalus said to the King Archon, with hysterical fury, "He would have branded my grandson, of a noble house, as a slave! Had it not been for some merciful slaves, who smuggled him out of that detestable woman's house, he would have been disfigured for life! Now my beloved grandson, Callias, has been exiled; such was the decree of Aspasia, the whore of Athens, who rules us in the name of Pericles. Is that not monstrous, that a harlot is more important than the government, itself?"

When the King Archon did not answer, Daedalus screamed, "Who is Aspasia, that she dominates our lives? My grandson was only attempting to redeem his mother, his house, his pride of family, his position. Had he killed or deformed her it would have been only justice. For his manly intentions, for all he holds dear, he is a vagabond on Cyprus, and can no longer return to his loved family, and his weeping mother. For the sake of a harlot Pericles has debased my family, my daughter, my grandson, and his own sons. He has defamed his house. He has disgraced his position, and all of Greece laughs at him. The comic poets compose pentameters in ridicule of him and his harlot, and the playwrights are hilarious."

The King Archon considered him thoughtfully as he stroked his beard. He said, "Yes. 'To find him a Juno, the goddess of lust bore that harlot past shame, Aspasia by name.'

Infinitely hilarious, is it not? I do not find it so. Daedalus, you and I are old men, and often our memories fail us but our prejudices, on the contrary, become more fiery. If I am wrong, correct me: If I remember, your grandson was not smuggled out of Aspasia's house by righteous and merciful slaves. He was brought in chains, after a flogging, to the court of the Assembly by Pericles' soldiers. The Assembly does not love Aspasia, just as they do not love Pericles, but they are men frequently just—though that appears a mere blunder at times and not deliberated opinion! They were appalled at the attack on a woman who had done your grandson no wrong, and who, though despite her faults and her convictions, is not only a beautiful woman but a learned one. I do not admire her, you will understand, for women are contentious enough without an education, and learning could make them even more disagreeable." He stroked his beard again and fixed Daedalus with bright intent eyes like a bird. "I am informed that it was Aspasia who prevented Callias from being branded with the brand of a slave.

"Nevertheless, she had been seduced by a ruse your grandson had concocted. He intended murder, through his companions, or at the least the mutilation of a defenseless woman. A moment, please," and he lifted his hand to stop the bursting words of rage already on Daedalus' tongue. "Let me continue. Pericles had demanded a divorce from his wife long before he knew Aspasia. When Dejanira refused, he had the marriage annulled. As for Pericles 'defaming' his name, his house, his family, his position, by protecting a hetaira—who among us has not loved such?" He watched the bruised scarlet run over Daedalus' aged and sunken cheeks. "Shall we denounce in him our own—peculiarities? What Athenian gentleman can endure his wife? There are very few tender marriages. At least Pericles is faithful to his Aspasia. He has wanted to marry her, but will not break his own law. He is an honorable man.

"Daedalus, your grandson had no reason for malice towards Aspasia, except that I have heard he is naturally malicious. He was striking at Pericles. It was Pericles' own plea that this not be brought too strongly to the attention of the Assembly, and the Archons and the Ecclesia. You know, most certainly, what the punishment is for an attempted injury against the Head of State?"

This was a somewhat specious remark, and the King Archon knew it. He also knew that Daedalus' fury would prevent him from detecting the adroit fallacy. Daedalus could now only stand and shiver with rage and clench his hands at his sides and glare at the King Archon with mingled fear and blinding temper. He thrust his face forward as though he could not see well and fixed his eyes on the King Archon's features as if to imprint them ominously on his mind.

Finding his voice at last he almost yelled, "Lord, it is common talk in Athens, and in all of Greece, even in Sparta, that Aspasia is impious, that she teaches the deluded girls in her school that the gods do not exist, or if they do they are not cognizant of man and therefore honor given to them is a delusion!"

The King Archon became grave. "Who has told you this, Daedalus?"

"It is common knowledge, lord!"

"What is 'common knowledge,' Daedalus, is a common lie, in my experience. Are we men or old women who idle away the hours in slander? When you have some authentic evidence against Aspasia, bring it to me and I will give it all my attention. Now you must leave me. I have matters of *consequence* to consider."

So he dismissed Daedalus. However, he was more concerned than he had appeared. He admired Pericles; as a young man he had known Xanthippus. Even some members of the devoted middle class were expressing criticism of Pericles. It was one thing to keep a hetaira; it was quite another thing for a man as powerful and as famous as Pericles to flaunt her in public, as Pericles seemed to flaunt Aspasia. It was known that his new laws giving women more freedom in Athens, and more rights of property, and more consideration and privileges, were inspired by Aspasia, she of the notorious school. (Scandalous things were said of her school, by those who knew nothing about it.) Pericles, as a politician, should know more about the hypocrisy of the people than he appeared to know. Governments must, at all times, be aware of that hypocrisy and respect it, and must avow that it is virtue and not contemptible pretense. What was being rumored and said about Pericles by his enemies was doubtless honey to the slavering lips of men, who desired to believe all enormities concerning public figures. More good men had been destroyed by sanctimonious liars than the sentimental would admit.

The old King Archon said aloud, "Ah, Virtue! What virtues have been done to death in your name!"

Privately, the King Archon thought that it would have been wiser of Pericles merely to have had Callias murdered and buried far out at sea or in some isolated spot. Then there would have been no public scandal—something no politician can afford. But, he had chosen the honorable way. The King Archon sighed. Sometimes honor could well be confused with folly, and was often less excusable. It was also very dangerous.

Pheidias sat in the cool atrium of Pericles' house, where the center fountain made a plangent sound against the night silence, which was broken only occasionally by the rippling and poignant music of nightingales. Even the trees were still and the moonlight seemed to come from an unmoving orb of alabaster. The dried brown grass of summer exhaled an odor of aromatic dust, pervasive as smoke. The hour was late; even the vociferous Athenians were now in bed and, to Pericles, blessedly quiet.

The two men sat at a table over which hung a lamp, and they were leaning forward to study the scrolls Pheidias had spread before them. The shy sculptor's gentle face glowed with eagerness. Pericles had removed his helmet, and his towering skull and mane of light tawny hair were damp with the sweat of excitement. Yet he did not betray that excitement, not even to Pheidias, for years of conscious control had become an involuntary habit. Occasionally he refilled the sculptor's goblet with excellent wine, while he, himself, drank chilled beer. He did not wear his toga of dignity, but a short tunic of brown linen, and his feet were bare. He had long forgotten he was weary. In less than two hours the city would be roaring again as the dawn flared over the eastern hills. The house slept; there was not even a slave on duty, and only the soldiers moved about the house and its grounds, their helmets and swords and belts glittering in the stagnant moonlight.

"It is fortunate, Pericles," said Pheidias, "that the vast superstructure for the Parthenon was completed long ago, though for another temple. Our repairs and the completing of the buttresses required but little effort. Now, these are my architects' plans for the Parthenon—Ictinus and Callicrates." He smiled softly. "At the moment they are not speaking to each other. Such are artists! Ictinus insists that the temple to Athene be considerably shorter in length and considerably wider than Callicrates as determinedly insists. There is much argument about proportion, vistas, aspects, the casting of shadows. I have told them, in an effort at pacification, that the temple must not be built solely to exalt the spirit of man but to please the eyes of the gods from their loftier abode, as they look down on the world. For a while, at least, they were so active in scorning my opinions and deriding my mysticism, as

384

they called it, that they became brothers in arms against a perfidious foe—me."

Pericles marvelled, as always, at the genuine humility of genius. It was not that a gifted man considered his creative power of no consequence, but he himself as the unworthy priest at the altar of that sacred gift. He served his genius with a profound objectivity while he brought to it all his attributes of subjectivity. It was only the mediocre man, of small talent, who was pompous and overweening, and demanded that he be honored as adorning what meagre endowment he possessed. Yet, how often, reflected Pericles, did the world of men not give honor to the possessor of mighty genius—because that possessor had a holy humility which convinced others that he was intrinsically worthless, and his genius an incredible accident of nature. But the arrogant and conceited man of little aptitude, who noisily called attention to himself with eccentricities and pride, was usually honored. He had such a tremendous appreciation of himself! So on this night Pericles became for a time engrossed more with Pheidias' shining face, his joyous descriptions, his passionate ardor, than with his plans, and Pericles' cold and judicious heart was deeply moved as rarely it was moved.

Pheidias sighed with exhausted delight. "It will be perfect, a most glorious example of the Doric order." He hesitated. "I remember, lord, that you said you preferred Corinthian columns."

"I do not—now," said Pericles. "It could be nothing but Doric." Then he, too, hesitated. "The cella— There is the base in these plans for the gigantic statue of Athene Parthenos. You still believe that the statue should be of ivory and gold?"

Some of the light went from the face of Pheidias. "I am not successful, at least to myself, when I work in marble. It has a rigidity which demands a certain ruthlessness and power. A man must have rule over his materials; he must command them. Marble intimidates me. It has a monumental challenge which only the strongest can answer with a greater challenge. But the gentler materials, the more fluid and compliant, the kinder, are to my hands living, and our souls are in sympathy. However, lord, I have students who are greatly gifted, and will work in marble under my direction, including the statue of Athene Parthenos."

He could not understand Pericles' slight smile. "No," said Pericles, "it will be as you desire, a gold and ivory statue."

Pheidias was joyous again. Then he was suddenly dejected.

"It will cost far more than a marble statue, for it will be a towering work, and gold is very precious. The treasury may refuse it."

"They will not refuse me," said Pericles, with some of that haughty and overbearing manner which his enemies detested.

They went on to discuss each metope in detail, and the chariot of the goddess and the painted friezes. Sometimes Pericles winced, thinking of the cost, and the miserable little men of the treasury who would bay like wolves to the moon of the public's avarice. But as the light of the false dawn made the east dim as a pearl he was overpowered by the massive dream of Pheidias. He could see the terraces and fountains and gardens which would adorn the grounds of the rising acropolis to the huge temple of Athene Parthenos, and the lesser temples scattered about and below it. It would resemble a fortressed mountainous city of marble and color and flowers and dark cypresses, soaring and gleaming and blazing, not only over Athens but over all the world. The climbing white stairways, broad and polished, would know the feet of great men who would come to see and remain to adore, and to walk dazed among all those golden sun-struck colonnades and stand refreshed at the profusion of fountains, and look down upon the silver city on the violet sea. They, and all others after them, the multitudes who would come here through the centuries, would know the glory that was Greece. The vision overcame Pericles, for it was as though he had heard a solemn prophecy.

"It will be almost worthy of God," he said. "He will know it is the most glorious offering that a race can humbly present to Him, in His honor. He will not despise it."

"He who loves the blood-red little poppy of the springtime despises nothing," said Pheidias, and he was touched by the cool passion of the skeptical Pericles. "True, is it not, that the poppy holds all mysteries and has a grandeur beyond marble or gold or ivory or gems or statues? For it contains the Life of God, whereas stone contains only the dreams of men. The poppy renews itself forever, even in the barren places; what we create is, from the moment of its conception, doomed to decay. The splendor, which the poppy possesses, is yet unassuming and eternal, but all that we have wrought with our hands is mortal and drifts into desert silence."

He looked into space and his eyes enlarged radiantly. "When the Parthenon is only the white dust of marble and its colonnades lie shattered under the indifferent moon, the poppy will resurrect itself on the dead fields of spring and proclaim the Glory of God, making the heart of man glad with its intimations of immortality, its holy and invincible power to endure."

He waited for Pericles to comment, but when he did not Pheidias continued gently, "But, who can compete with God? Even our noblest dreams are sent by Him. The man who sees the poppy of the field and is not stunned with reverence and awe is a man whose spirit is dead. He may honor us who raise stone and statues and temples, but he honors, therefore, only the passing and the dying."

He saw the stern shadow of melancholy on Pericles' face and touched his hand in comfort. "For a little while men will know that Pericles has made visible our small dreams, and never shall he be forgotten."

"It is Pheidias who shall never be forgotten," said Pericles. "For never shall there be another like him."

Pheidias shook his head. "Men can excel only in imitation. God alone creates anew." He tried to lift the melancholy of his friend. "Rejoice—for God never repeats Himself in man, either. We are all unique. Therefore, we are valuable to Him. We are as loved by Him as He loves the poppy, and so are immortal and as dearly designed."

CHAPTER 4

The youths, Xanthippus and Paralus, sons of Pericles, were infatuated with Aspasia, and loved her. Pericles was pleased by this, for never, therefore, would his sons marry inferior or stupid women but would demand of a woman not only a pleasing form and countenance but a superior mind also. In truth, the latter was the more desirable, for any young girl, unless deformed or gross of appetite, could present a comely face to the world and an enticing figure, if just for a few brief years. Pericles wished his loved sons to be as happy as it was possible for mortals to be—which was very little. Beauty passed as rapidly as did spring. In the summer or autumn or winter of life the woman of intellect was infinitely protean and variable and fascinating, no matter her age. She retained an eternal youth of the spirit, and humor, and was never petty or hysterical. Pericles had seen women of seventy and even eighty, former hetairai, who entranced men of all ages with their wit and conversation and knowledge and wisdom. They were like gold which had been used and worn through the years, thus gaining a patina of brilliance.

It had been Pericles' observation that those men who roamed with increasing hunger and dissatisfaction among many women, particularly the very young, had invariably married materialistic women of little intelligence and who were mundane and greedy and petulant. But a man never tired of a superior woman, even if he frequently quarreled with her—as he rarely did with a stupid wife. Flint needed steel to throw off sparks and fire. But it was never ignited by contact with mutton. He, himself, often quarreled with Aspasia and said she was a contentious woman and declared that he found no peace with her. But when parted from her he thought of her helplessly, and though sometimes she was at fault, and not he, he would return with a gift and a bounding of joy. He found in her arms, not only extreme passion, but a renewal of spirit and ambition. He knew that with Aspasia he would never grow old and senile and apathetic, for all he complained that she brought him little tranquility, which, he would angrily declare, was treasured by men.

"Go to the cemeteries, then," she would say with some asperity. "So long as I live, my beloved, I will not be a corpse." When he was good-tempered he would laugh and reply, "I come to you in the ashes men have reduced me to, but I rise like the Phoenix in your arms, for all you often have a tongue like an asp. Or when dreary men in the government have gelded me or burdened me like a mule, I become potent again in your bed, to soar like Pegasus in the morning, and confront the sun once more." The true peace and tranquility he found with Aspasia were not the things of the grave.

Once immovable and even implacable and overly opinionated and intolerant in many ways, he became, under the influence of Aspasia, less inflexible, less coldly impatient, less rude with inferiors. So he gained the reputation of mellowing. Men who had feared and avoided him found him amazingly more congenial, more willing to listen, less sardonic and bitter. Even the despised bureaucrats spoke of him with reluctant appreciation. The Archons, with the exception of Daedalus, were now less afraid of his aristocratic arrogance, and the Assembly, which once had sat like bound and resentful slaves when he addressed them, began to anticipate his speeches and his suggestions with pleasure. However, once he had become an enemy he never deviated from his detestation. Nor would he suffer fools. "They should be castrated," he would often say, "for they bestow folly on their sons, and are more terrible than Helots, and are like the dragons' teeth." Consequently the fools in the government—and they were in the majority, as was inevitable—hated him with the deadly hatred of the simpleton. He laughed openly at their power, and derided it, though knowing it was theirs, and fought it ruthlessly and often successfully.

So, he was delighted that his sons loved and reverenced Aspasia and found her company irresistible. She could quell the cynical and sometimes cruel wit of Xanthippus, and make him more thoughtful and considerate of others, for he respected her and wished her regard. She could move the adamantine character of Paralus to a less intolerant reflectiveness. "It is good to have sound convictions," she would tell him, "and noble principles. But the majority of men are neither sound nor of any intellectual principles at all. They are confused; they suffer the predicament of mankind, in that they are bewildered by the world in which they find themselves. Have mercy on them. But indiscriminate compassion is not only perilous. It is maudlin, and is often the attribute of the secret destroyers of mankind. Rather have pity of your fellow men, and seek to lead them with tenderness and understanding, but never with the conviction that you know what is best for them. We are all but human. To believe that we know more than our brother is the supreme arrogance."

"But surely my father knows more than do his associates," Paralus would protest, to the glee of Xanthippus.

Aspasia would dimple at this, and the youths would be enchanted. "Your father," she would reply, "is very rare indeed. He even admits this, himself."

She loved both the youths like a mother. She was often afraid for Xanthippus, whose tongue was like a double-edged sword, heedless of the wounds he inflicted and careless of the wounds he suffered in consequence. He was born to infuriate those of lesser minds, and he had realized that much earlier, and with enthusiasm. "It is not necessary to placate fools," Aspasia would say. "Avoid them. But to hurt potential friends and make them enemies, just for a moment's sharp epigram, is folly. An acid witticism is a high price to pay for the loss of a friend. A man needs all the devoted friends he can acquire."

"My father has few," Xanthippus would say, with a taunting but affectionate twinkle.

"Ah, but they are true friends! They would die for him. Choose your friends as you would choose a jewel of great price. He who says he has many friends, and boasts of them, is laughable and to be pitied, for he is deluded. A pleasing presence at his table, who drinks his wine copiously and assures him of love, often laughs at him in private as a naive fool, and is ready with slander either out of envy or malice."

As Xanthippus was approaching marriageable age, for he was seventeen, Aspasia would introduce him to some of her maiden students in the gardens of her house. Athens professed to be outraged at this impropriety. A young man of family did not choose his bride. That was the prerogative of his parents, and the parents of the girl. However, the parents of Aspasia's students did not object, for was not Xanthippus the son of Pericles? Moreover, were they, the parents, not themselves enlightened? Too, Aspasia never permitted Xanthippus to be alone with any of her students. This was not because of seemliness but because she knew human nature, and remembered Thalias. Youth was hot enough without providing it with encouraging opportunities, and the maidens had been entrusted to her care.

Daedalus, hearing through the gossip of slaves that his grandsons were being taught impiety and corruption by Aspasia, brought himself to confront Pericles in Pericles' own house. It had been the first impulse of Pericles to refuse him an audience, then he relented and received Daedalus with iced courtesy and offered him refreshments. But Daedalus, more vitriolic with age, furiously declined. "I will not dine in this infamous house!" he shrieked. "I have degraded myself in behalf of my grandsons, and it is a vomit in my mouth."

"Visit the latrines, then. I will wait," replied Pericles. "I am Head of State. You are but an Archon, and I have politely granted you permission to speak to me."

They both stood in the atrium, for Daedalus would not sit. His usual high color had paled to a deathliness. Pericles felt some pity for this old man, and so stood in a waiting attitude, his arms folded over his chest.

"My grandson, Xanthippus, visits the young courtesans in the house of that unspeakable woman, Aspasia! It is rumored that he will even marry one of them!"

Pericles' mouth became fixed as marble. "The young ladies in Aspasia's school are of aristocratic names and of impeccable houses. Shall I inform the parents of those maidens that you have slandered them, have called them concubines and harlots? Their fathers are powerful, as you are not powerful, and they would destroy you."

Daedalus trembled with fear. He flung out his arms. "I do

not mean the students," he stammered. "It is said that Xanthippus is induced to consort with the female slaves in that house."

"Of a certainty, that is a lie, and that you know, Daedalus."

"I would believe anything of that woman!"

Pericles controlled himself. "The Lady Aspasia has enabled Xanthippus to know the daughters of great families and to choose a bride for himself. He has taste and discrimination. Of a surety, if he chooses a maiden who is a student of Aspasia's, he will not commit the appalling folly of marrying a stupid and ugly woman. His son will be no Callias, whose name is infamous in Athens, so much so that no gentleman will consider him as a husband for his daughter, in spite of his inherited riches."

"His name is not infamous! He has been the victim of pestilential people! If he has done foolish things it is because he was distraught over the dishonor done to his family! Has he not vitals, not emotions, that he cannot be overcome with shame and sorrow? His riches have been held against him. No matter. He is living in loneliness and sadness on Cyprus, and this is the only reason he cannot marry an Athenian maiden, for what parents would permit their daughter to share exile?"

Pericles laughed lightly. "I know he is living in luxury in Cyprus. He is flattered there and fawned upon. He is no wandering vagabond. His house is magnificent, and full of slaves. He entertains lavishly. Many an Athenian maiden of a great house would be permitted to marry him and with alacrity. He does not desire marriage. He has concubines. I have sent emissaries to Cyprus to hint that if he desires he may be recalled to Athens. He has repudiated them. He can commit license in Cyprus which he could not commit here. What! You did not know this?"

"I do not believe it!" cried Daedalus. "We receive mournful letters from him, stained with his tears, for he longs for his family."

"You believe I am lying?" asked Pericles in a dangerous voice. Daedalus flinched, and retreated a step before that face.

"Perhaps he is exaggerating," he said. "But what man does not want to return to his loving family?"

"Callias," said Pericles.

Daedalus cast down his eyes and he trembled. Then he looked up to see the mingled derision and sympathy in Pericles' eyes.

Pericles said, "I have told you. He could marry—if he wished." He paused. "He could return soon—if he wished. He does not wish."

Daedalus was distracted. He flung out his arms, despairingly. "You have called my daughter, Dejanira, stupid and ugly. She is virtuous and faithful. Are these not gracious attributes?"

Pericles closed his eyes for a moment, wearied. "I grant you that Dejanira has virtues. They do not appeal to me. I am grateful to her for my sons. I respect her name. We had no quarrels. But all that is past. I have given you time, and it is precious to me. I must ask you to leave."

Daedalus started away, then swung around, his garments flurried. "I will not forget!" he exclaimed, raising his hand in an oath. "I will not forget! I implore the vengeance of the gods—in whom you and that woman do not believe! They will not be mocked."

He trotted from the atrium and into the outdoor portico, where his litter awaited him. Once behind the curtains he burst into tears, and his mouth moved with imprecations. He was not without power, and Pericles had many enemies. He began to plot. His old face twisted and contorted with hatred.

Aspasia took Pericles by the hand at sunset and led him into the cool tranquility of her gardens. There, near the altar to the Unknown God, stood the huge marble statue of a wasp, which Pheidias had personally designed two years ago. Seeing this, Pericles was again disturbed, remembering what Aspasia had escaped. He held her in his arms and said, "I will defend you, my beloved, against all evils."

"Do you expect evils?" she asked, looking up into his eyes.

He hesitated. "Man is intrinsically evil—all men. I have heard it said, by the Jews, that man is evil from his birth and wicked from his youth. It was asserted by their fabulous Solomon. I believe it. A man who is not alert to the innate viciousness of his brothers is a fool. Men are iniquitous by nature. They do wrong not because they have been wronged, but because it gives them pleasure and satisfaction. If they do not have enemies they invent them. This is true of nations as well as mankind."

Aspasia looked at the myrtle trees whose leaves were plated gold in the sunset. "It is a beautiful world," she murmured. "Why is it that only man is unregenerate?"

"It is his nature," said Pericles. He paused. "The Jews say that God will be born to this world in a near century." He laughed a little. "Be sure that men will murder Him, as they murdered Osiris, for virtue is the one crime that men cannot endure."

Aspasia saddened. "You have no faith in your fellow man, beloved."

"That is because I know him, only too well. Enough. The plans for the acropolis have all been completed. The marble is ready. I have given orders that only free men must build the temples, for temples raised by slaves are abhorrent to me. God did not intend that men be slaves. Solon deplored slavery. So do I. But it has come to me that multitudes of men crave that they be slaves of government, in order that they may not be forced to think and act with responsibility and order their own lives. It is easier to crouch on your knees and be fed by government than it is to stand on your feet and find your own sustenance. Was it not Anaxagoras who said that nature takes the path of least resistance? So do men. To resist government is arduous and perilous. To obey is to eat in slavish peace, and be forgotten by bureaucrats. That is no mean advantage in itself!"

Aspasia said, as she had said many times before, "Why is it, then, that you remain as Head of State?"

He answered as he had answered before, "I must do my best for my dream of a united Greece. City-states are always in danger, especially from each other. They can also be divided, too, by exterior enemies, who are lustful for treasure. A united nation is strong. I do not admire Sparta, nor Macedonia. But wise men can compromise and come to terms, whatever their differences. Did we not once in our near past cleave together to fight off the Persian? If we can do that in emergency we can do that again as reasonable men. Athenians stood with Leonidas, the Spartan, and we despise Spartans for their rigorous discipline and their iron determination to order the lives of all their people, men and women, male and female children. Who among us has not laughed at Spartan maidens, who compete with their brothers in athletics and work? They wear male tunics. They have muscles, and their skins are brown with the sun, and coarsened. They have grim faces. Laugh though we do, we must remember that we are not empowered by the gods to order the affairs of other nations. That is preening assumption. Let each nation live in peace with the government it desires. That does not negate union against enemies, or commerce."

There are always wars, thought Aspasia. The Greek city-states were always in dispute with their sister states. It is wea-

risome to remember all the petty but cruel wars. Let Homer glorify them, and speak of the arts of war. They are only tragedies. However, only women with sons and husbands realize this. She thought of Lysistrata and her women who had refused their beds to their husbands unless they concluded peace. She thought of the barbarian Roman women, who, captured by the Sabines, and who had had children by them, threw their infants before the horses of the Romans and the Sabines and defied them to trample on the childish flesh. What had restrained their men, fevered and exalted by the hope of battle? Was it the power of women, after all? Aspasia pondered. Thargelia had said that the hope of the world was in women's hands. Aspasia did not entirely believe this, except that men could be seduced in the beds of women, if the women were artful enough. Certainly men were not merciful enough to spare children. Aspasia sighed. She loved Pericles with a passion and a devotion she had not known for Al Taliph. Still, as he was a man, she did not entirely trust him to know the urges of a woman's heart. Then she smiled. The father of gods and men, Zeus, was afraid of his wife, Hera, who ruled him as he ruled the world.

"Why do you smile, my golden one?" asked Pericles.

"I am thinking of our son," she replied.

He was astonished, and seized her arm. "Our son?" he exclaimed.

She bent her head.

"I have waited to tell you, lord. I am with child. I am certain it will be a son—your son and mine."

When he did not speak but only gazed at her with enlarged pale eyes, she said, "We will call him Pericles, after his illustrious father."

He frowned, released her arm, and removed himself a pace. "He will not be legitimate."

Aspasia touched his arm. "You can adopt him, sire. Then he will be truly yours." She felt some anxiety. Was he not pleased? Was he angered that she had been careless during one heated night?

Then he turned to her, his face lighted, and he took her in his arms. "I am thinking of your danger, my sweetest. After all, you are in your thirties now. Have you consulted Helena?"

"Yes." Aspasia was moved. She had misjudged him, as the sexes always misjudged each other. Had Pandora released this confusion as well as other confusions and distractions? "Despite my age, she has said I am in the most supreme health. She will tend me, herself. She has had many instructions from the young Hippocrates, who has visited her school and her infirmia."

"I must see this Hippocrates," said Pericles, but he was frowning again, alarmed for Aspasia.

"Do not disturb yourself, lord. It will be well. But, tell me. Are you pleased that I am to bear your son?"

"It may be a daughter," and Pericles laughed. "If she resembles her mother I will adore her."

"And—if it is a son?"

"I will discipline him. He will be a worthy son of Athens."

What did a man mean when he said "worthy"? Worth, too, was subjective.

"A woman in her thirties, old enough to be a grandmother, should not have young children. Do not sigh, my Pericles. Our son will be like a god."

They held each other, breast against breast. But, we are not truly one, thought Aspasia. A woman's thoughts are far from the thoughts of men. Who had ordained this in mischief, or perhaps with wisdom?

They looked at the top of the acropolis. The great Doric pillars of the Parthenon were flushed with the rose of the dying sun. They stood like pylons, unroofed as yet, against the scarlet sky. On the lower reaches of the acropolis were smaller groups of columns. Walls were rising like ramparts. White wide steps led nowhere but upwards, awaiting a completed building. The sides of the acropolis were heavily buttressed and terraced, and cypresses were already planted and earth placed for gardens and fountains. Long thin pipes of lead, for water, writhed over bare spots on the hill like tormented serpents, still uncovered. On the other hills olive trees were bright with silver in the clear and translucent light. The theatre below was filled with purple shadows, the circling seats empty, the stage—once an altar—soundless and untenanted. Nightingales began to sing, and a flock of gulls, from the sea, caught the last radiance in gold on their wings. The myrtles and sycamores and cypresses of Aspasia's gardens had become dark and were starting to whisper in a new breeze. The temple to the Unknown God shimmered dimly in its shadows. A curved crescent of the new moon was like a fingernail of pearl glimmering slowly up the sky in the east.

There was a deep peace in the garden. Pericles stood and looked up at the acropolis, his hands on his hips, his strong legs apart, his helmeted head raised. There were shadows of silver in his hair now, but his face was still gravely beautiful and dignified though his eyes dreamed.

Aspasia knew that he had momentarily forgotten her. He was seeing his visions wrought of stone on the tall hill, and a faintly exultant smile lay on his lips. He was not thinking of wars or affairs of state. What he saw was more splendid than any victory, more exalted than treasures. It was as if he gazed on the works of gods. Still, thought Aspasia, men have created this and soon, one day, the acropolis would shine in white and gilt, peopled with temples, crowded with pillared colonnades like a marble forest, alive with statues, and winged figures on columns soaring skyward. The innate glory of mankind was emerging and lifting from its murky and villainous flesh, like a bird rising from the stinking morass of a swamp in which evil things flourished. Man was a demon; he was also like the gods, as glorious as he was vile.

As if he had heard her thoughts Pericles said, "Athens is joyous now that a dream is becoming a reality, and is proud of what is being created there. But she forgets that there are few Socrateses, very few men like Pheidias and Zeno and Anaxagoras, and not many like Sophocles. However, in these men the common man believes he sees himself and that he has a share in their glory. He says, 'We are great,' and not 'He is great.' He takes upon himself, to cover his drab flesh, the raiment of the immortals, and struts and cries, 'How glorious are we!' He does not understand that Socrates and Protagoras and Pheidias and Zeno and Anaxagoras and Herodotus and Sophocles, to name but a shining few, are like stars that briefly and rarely flash through the black skies of the world, and are not of this world at all."

"Still," said Aspasia, "the few are an inspiration to the rest of mankind, and a hope that man can become perfect and heroic. Without a dream we are only animals, so, lord, let us dream," and she smiled.

Pericles returned her smile indulgently. His white tunic paled as the night advanced and the crescent moon lifted more brilliantly, like the bow of Artemis reflecting the fallen sun. The temples of the acropolis became ghostly and unsubstantial.

Aspasia leaned against the breast of Pericles and he put his warm arms about her and kissed the top of her head. But her thoughts were troubled. Pericles was now being called the man on horseback, the dictator, and the comic poets were becoming more ribald and bold in their attacks on him on the stage. She cared nothing for calumny directed against her, but she deeply feared for Pericles. As she had fled for her own sake from Al Taliph so she often considered fleeing from Pericles for his sake.

She was hated, derided, accused of unspeakable things, and she knew this was because of Pericles' association with her, and his passion for her.

"Why do you sigh, my love?" asked Pericles, lifting aside a lock of her hair and peering down, in the growing darkness, to see her face.

"Did I sigh?" she said. "It is the nature of women to sigh, for do we not love men even though you do not deserve it?" They laughed together, for Aspasia had never forgotten that Thargelia had said that a melancholy woman was disliked by men and left to her miserable sorrows, and that a woman must always pretend that her sighs were pleasure or teasing or trivial and meant nothing. Even though she knew that Pericles loved her and would defend her with his life and often comforted her, Aspasia also knew that she must not be melancholy too long. Men might be moved by a woman's tears, but not if they were chronic, and Pericles was a man after all.

They went into the house together, hand in hand, to dine and then to go to Aspasia's chamber to love and sleep under the moon. When Pericles slept beside her, surfeited, Aspasia pondered again on the fate of women, and felt, again, the old rebelliousness. Her new fears returned and she stared, sleepless, into the dark. Whether a woman's destiny was due to custom or innate nature was impossible to know.

CHAPTER 5

"The true purpose of education," Aspasia would explain patiently to inquirers, "is not to enable a man or a woman to make money or attain high position and self-aggrandisement. It is to enlarge the soul, to widen the mind, to stimulate wonder, to give a new vision and understanding of the world, to excite the intellect, to awaken dormant faculties for the exultation of the possessor. In short, to reveal new vistas of thought and comprehension so that enjoyment of life is enhanced. An ignorant man or woman is half-blind, and does not truly hear, and so existence is narrow and limited."

She would add, "Alas, it is true that the gods endow few men with extraordinary minds and talents and genius, for they are frugal with their gifts, and the gifts cannot be bestowed on offspring. It is a great mystery. The majority of men are born with constricted understanding and circumscribed intellect. So intensive education would not only be useless in their case but would only confuse and frustrate them, and incite them to anger and resentment. In education, as in everything, we must be merciful and acknowledge that men are not born equally endowed with intelligence and health and character. However, all men are born with their own potential and a certain power to become better than they are, within their own limits of aptitudes, and so education, like cloth, should be measured to fit the individual. I do this in my own school, though I will not accept a student of definitely meagre mind and small capacity to learn. She is better with her mother who can train her simply."

She would conclude, "But let us not despise that vast majority which is not gifted and has closed borders of intellect. They, too, have their own hierarchy in nature and it is not a mean one. It is more valuable than we know, and the humble and industrious should be respected and honored. Without them the intellectuals could not exist; they would starve or die for lack of shelter or raiment. They would stifle for insufficiency of time to develop themselves." She would smile. "The humble worker can well and comfortably live without our art and science and philosophies and books. But we cannot exist without them!"

A number of her students became the pupils of Helena and were trained in her infirmia under the tutelage of the new school of Hippocrates. They became physicians but the majority of them had to leave for Egypt on graduation, where they became priestesses, for only priests and priestesses could practice medicine there. However a few remained with Helena, to teach others, both men and women. The balance became instructors in mathematics and science and literature in other schools now rapidly opening under the influence of Aspasia, who, in this matter at least, was influential with Pericles.

Hence her infamous name with the outraged women of Athens, who claimed that the emancipated hetairai were corrupting their daughters, whether or not those daughters were educated or kept illiterate as custom decreed. Custom, to them, was almost as sacred as religion, and in this delusion they were encouraged by the priests, who, above all things, detested ferment. They desired only a stable society which did not question anything at all. They desired serenity alone. Understanding this, Aspasia would say with scorn, "It is the serenity and order of the tomb."

The enemies of Pericles were divided. Many insisted that they were secretly ruled, not by Pericles, but by a disgraceful woman. Others declared that Aspasia was only the weapon of Pericles against the people.

Pericles believed that through the Delian League of city-states he could bring about a united Greece, invincible against enemies. He sent out many cleruchs to the city-states, and he candidly admitted that he also had for his purpose the consolidating of strategic points for Athens and securing land for the industrious workers of the cities. The latter was done by the remitting of tribute and taxes. The more numerous of the cleruchs went to Naxos, Imbros, Brea in Thrace, Lemnos, Andros, Oreus and Eretria.

Had the enemies of Pericles thought of these things themselves they would have demanded public gratitude and honors as patriots and thoughtful statesmen. But in the affair of Pericles these enemies had sudden attacks of what they declared was world-conscience and a proper regard for the autonomy of other states. No matter that Athens was herself strengthened and that benefits to the members of the League were tremendous. Pericles, they shouted, not only desired to rule Athens in an absolute despotism and dictatorship but wished to extend his lusted empire. He was the worst tyrant ever to afflict Athens. In his ambitions he would destroy his country; he was mad at the very least. His concern for free workers and the rising new middle class was only hypocrisy. He sought votes and public approval, and wished to delude and confuse. He not only was bankrupting the treasury in his absurd and exorbitant plans for the acropolis, but had as his real intention the glorification of himself. He would elevate himself as a god, they shouted, for the blasphemous worship of the people. In these denunciations they were joined by the priests who feared, above all things, the enlightenment of the populace, for that would threaten their own positions. They feared expansion of benign power. Pericles' own military establishment and naval officers came under the attack of his enemies. Peace would not ensue from alliances and mutual assistance to other city-states, no matter what Pericles said. He wished military and naval force to advance his secret ambitions and make subjects of his allies under his imperial command. His egotism must enrage the gods, who were too patient respecting him. They quoted the ancient proverb to the effect that they whom the gods would destroy they first made mad.

But for all these exhortations—and they were shouted in the Assembly and among the Archons and the Ecclesia and the Nine—the Athenians, in the great majority, were infuriatingly complacent with regard to Pericles. They trusted him. When calls were made for his impeachment and the revocation of his office the people remained calm and could not be incited. "Clods!" said the Archons to each other in rage and hatred, though the King Archon made some satirical epigrams concerning the public avowals of their love for their people and their private remarks. He was particularly ironic among the Archons, for Pericles had decreed that the poorer citizens must benefit through the establishment of the theorikon fund, which enabled them to attend the dramas presented by the Dionysia. "Shall culture and beauty be the total province only of those who can afford these things?" he had demanded. "God has surely intended that all men should be aware of the glory of art, and feast at its altars, according to their capacity to enjoy the feast."

His aristocratic enemies declared that he was blaspheming the whole meaning of the Dionysia by encouraging the masses to invade, "like wild asses," the purlieus of sanctity. Others insisted that he was at heart an anarchist and desired to create false and voracious appetites in the mob so that they would be incited to seize what was not lawfully theirs, and, in gratitude, raise him to the throne of a king. Had not Sophocles—no favorite of theirs under normal circumstances—asserted, "There lives no greater fiend than Anarchy. She ruins states, turns houses out of doors." He had even demanded a remuneration of two obols a day for all jurymen, a cynical procedure for the sake of votes, it was sworn, for was it not a privilege to serve on juries and should jurymen be paid? The honor was enough. "Men cannot eat honor," Pericles had replied. "When you demand the services of jurymen you have removed them from the fields and the shops, where they make their living, and so have deprived them of a certain sustenance." So he was called a gross materialist.

The Athenians naturally detested Sparta, who was either their ally or their enemy, depending on politics or self-interest. Sparta's way of life was hilarious to them, for were the Spartans not only dim of wit but demanded of women the toil they demanded of men, and did they not despise culture though they had pretensions to it? They were hardly more than animals, with their militarism and their interest only in the mechanics of living. Yet when Pericles fought against the militancy and encroachment of "barbarians," the government had another of its periodic attacks of conscience and affirmed that Pericles was only ambitious and that he wished to direct attention of the people away from domestic problems in engagements and wars abroad. He was not truly protecting Athens and her legitimate interests. He was protecting his own power and the enlargement of it by ruthless naval and military involvements in areas not pertinent to the welfare of Athens. He was implacably murdering the "flower of the youth of Athens."

In short, no matter what he did he was denounced for it by his enemies. "You cannot appease a tiger when it is determined to devour you," he said to Aspasia. "All governments are tigers; the people are their prey. If populaces once learned that terrible fact they would sleeplessly watch their governments, their natural adversaries."

His face daily became tighter and leaner with his anger. Despite his self-control he frequently found himself exasperated, not by the denunciations of his government, but because of their malice and stupidity and determination to ruin him, and above all by their hypocrisy. Once Aspasia said to him, "Al Taliph was the governor of his province, and never did his officials dare to dispute with him or denigrate him or defy him, or defame his name among the people. That had its advantages."

Pericles laughed grimly at this. "But, his was a despotism under a higher despot. We Athenians have a democracy—of sorts. Better this confusion of malevolent and envious voices than despotism. It is a sign of considerable freedom of speech, and that, above all, is the very soul of liberty. God knows our liberties are daily becoming more restricted. But even the few remaining are rubies above price. Therefore, let my enemies shout. Should they halt their imprecations I should be seriously disturbed and would seek to know in what manner I have suppressed their freedom to criticise, curse and censure. I would then reverse it."

"But they will not permit you the liberty you grant to them," said Aspasia.

He shrugged. "Traitors cry for liberty—for themselves. But they will vehemently attack opponents who also desire that same liberty. It is the old story of tyranny."

Writhing with rage over a populace that did not heed their exhortations against Pericles the government sought another way to destroy or mortally wound him. It had been seeking for years. They newly scrutinized his associates, particularly Anaxagoras and Socrates and Zeno and Pheidias, and, above all, Aspasia. Were they not all impious, heretical and a menace to the order of the State? A hetaira of despicable repute, and barefoot philosophers and challengers of orthodox religion! They were worthy of imprisonment, death or exile. They were inciting the people to rebellions against priests and authority, all capital crimes. The middle class was demanding reductions in taxes and tribute. The workers were demanding a larger voice in government. The very slaves were seething. Athens was in a dangerous position and the government was determined to save her. Their virtue inflamed them to excesses, at which Pericles only laughed. He also ignored them, or publicly jeered at their bureaucrats and humorously addressed the Assembly and said that bureaucrats were the excreta of civilization. Perhaps, he would say, they were sometimes necessary lest a nation become constipated, but one must always remember that they were only feces, with a smelly function.

His friend Jason said to him, "But who will do the record-keeping and the paperwork, for there must be order, as you know, in government."

Pericles said, "I do not dispute that, but bureaucrats have a way of proliferating, to increase their powers and importance. But when they become more onerous than government itself that is the time to decimate them and restore to them the truth that they are only menials and do not rule us, for all their busy pens and their endless rivers of interpretations."

In retaliation—which he usually despised—he ordered officials to reduce their bureaucrats by one-third at once. "Athens," he said, "cannot afford this waste of money and the removal of workers from private employment, where they are needed." He assumed a countenance of virtue, in mimicry and mockery of his enemies. "Above all," he said, "let us save money. Are you not demanding this, yourselves?"

Only one part of the populace listened to the government, and that was the market rabble who hated Pericles for daring to call them less than slaves and exhorting them to work. Among them was the class of professional criminals, incendiaries, murderers and thieves. They were also for hire by government, which was an old story. Governments had, through history, used them to intimidate citizens who showed signs of indignation, just as they had always used bureaucrats.

What Daedalus lacked in personal power he made up in vituperations against Pericles, whom he now hated with a frenzied hatred. His fellow Archons began to be wearied by him, though they agreed with him and hated Pericles hardly less than he did. But while he merely frothed they consulted how best to depose Pericles and obtain his exile as an overweening and dictatorial Head of State. He was not invulnerable, so far. They dared not, as yet, pass resolutions against him and consult openly with the others of the government how to bring about his fall. They could only insidiously discuss with the many others the situation of his extravagance and his outrageous contempt for the weighty and heavy pendulum of government and its confusions and vacillations. "It is true that he is Head of State," they would say, "but that does not make him a god, not in our form of democratic government! Nor does it give him the power of a despot. He is answerable to us," and they added as an afterthought, "and to the people who elected us." He sought to be king, with absolute powers and had not Solon, himself, warned of ambitious men?

Daedalus urged his daughter, Dejanira, to marry again, for she had many mercenary suitors who were also of noble if impoverished families. But she shuddered away from him, weeping, and declared that she loved only Pericles and still considered herself his wife, and that if he would permit her she would creep like a dog to his feet. Daedalus loved his daughter; therefore he was scandalized at this abjectness, and ashamed. So, he upbraided her, only to be answered by loud sobbing and a wringing of her hands. Once she even said to him, "Callias deserved his fate; I do not pity him, though I love him as my son. He received only a measure of justice. Another man would have been executed for that act." Daedalus did not see the certain nobility of Dejanira's words—for she had lost a measure of her obtuseness. He was only aghast and accused her of being an unnatural mother.

She believed herself blameless for the dissolution of her marriage, for had not Pericles on their wedding night declared his passion for her and had he not embraced her with desire? What had she done to deserve banishment from his house? But still she said to her father, "I despise such as Aspasia, but he had forced me from his bed long before he saw her. She is only a hetaira, and Pericles is of an illustrious house. I do not believe he loves her, for how could such an abandoned woman be respected by such as my husband? No, she is a passing fancy; there will be others."

Daedalus, beside himself, shouted at her, "Do you not hear the gossip that she is with his child?"

Dejanira closed her eyes suddenly with grief and anguish. Daedalus went on: "He is not only not ashamed that he has lacerated the sensibilities of decent men. He flaunts her condition to all who will listen. Yes, I know that the hetairai often bear children to their lovers, though it is loathsome in the eyes of the virtuous. But at least their lovers do not boast of the vileness as does Pericles."

Dejanira opened her tearful eyes. "It is not in Pericles' nature to boast, my father."

"Hah! And how do you know this thing? Pericles was perhaps speaking the truth when he said to me that you were stupid."

Seeing her suffering, and seeing her shrinking, he felt some compunction. But the next moment he was again incensed that Pericles had made his daughter suffer such despair. When Xanthippus and Paralus next visited his house he said to them, "Are you not ashamed that your father has begotten an illegitimate child by his hetaira, his whore? Have you considered what this will do to your name, his lawful offspring?"

"What will it do?" asked Xanthippus, a bland expression on his lively face. Paralus nudged him in his side, for he saw the brilliant mischief in his brother's eyes and he was innately more compassionate than the irrepressible Xanthippus. But Xanthippus said, "We honor Aspasia, for she is not only the most beautiful woman in Athens, but is kind and loves us. She adores our father, and gives him laughter and consolations. Her situation is quite common and there are few outcries against it."

"You do not care for the humiliations of your mother?"

Paralus said with his father's own gravity, "My mother is no longer the wife of my father. What he does does not injure her in the esteem of others, for she has no part in any of his affairs."

Daedalus seized on this with hope. "You do not, then, approve of your father?"

Paralus had more respect for his grandfather than did the youthful satyr, Xanthippus. So he replied, "I did not say that. Forgive me. I meant that what my father does, or my mother, is not the concern of either. They are not one."

Xanthippus struck an orator's attitude and quoted from Homer: " 'There is nothing stronger and nobler than when man and wife are of one heart and mind in a house. A grief to their foes, and to their friends great joy. But their own hearts know it best.'" He grinned at Daedalus. "That best describes my father and our beloved Aspasia."

Paralus did not like this baiting of the aged Daedalus who stood blinking, now, trying to comprehend with his senile wits. So he said, while frowning formidably at Xanthippus, and resembling his father acutely, "Do not mind Xanthippus, Grandfather. He loves to tease. He means nothing by it."

"I never say a word which is not pertinent," said Xanthippus, who affectionately made fists at his brother and stood in the attitude of a pugilist.

After Callias, Daedalus loved Paralus best. He was afraid of Xanthippus and his acid wit, and so disliked him while still loving him.

He said, "Pindar has asserted, 'Strive not to become a god. Mortal aims befit mortal men.'" (He had heard this in the Assembly only yesterday.) He added, "Your father strives to become a god before the people, for their worship. Men are but mortal; they are as dust before the gods, something your father does not realize."

Xanthippus shook his naughty head and imitating Paralus' gravity he proclaimed, "Sophocles has said, 'Wonders are many, but none is more wonderful than man.' My father is a wonder. Therefore, he is as wonderful as the gods."

"Your syllogism lacks something," said the temperate Paralus. "My father is not mad; he is above the folly of considering himself divine and his decrees are not infallible." He smiled. "One should not quote philosophers as the ultimate authority, for they dispute with each other and are frequently contentious. They are also not quite sane, in our own dull interpretation of sanity."

"It is true," said Xanthippus, "that you are frequently dull, my brother," and they laughed in each other's eyes and pushed each other. "You should encounter Pan!"

Daedalus was not following their quick exchange. He said with bitterness, "Your father is trying to lead us into war again. Who profits by war, except tyrants such as he?"

"Hah!" cried Xanthippus. "Has not Homer said, 'All dreadful glared the iron face of war, but touched with joy the bosoms of the brave'?"

Paralus said quickly, "Poets, too, often disagree with each other—as do the gods. I doubt, Grandfather, that our father is warlike, though he is a soldier. He is trying to unify Greece, and if he appears devious at times we must trust him."

Daedalus was incredulous and his eyes bulged. "Trust your father? I should prefer to trust the harpies!"

"It is a matter of taste," said Xanthippus, and was thrust from the room by the more forceful Paralus, to join their mother. While they travelled down a corridor Paralus said to his brother, "Why do you torment that poor old man, who has nothing but his hatred to feed him in his age?"

"Hatred is the bread of Hades to which he is destined," said Xanthippus, who knew little mercy and found life ridiculous. He did not have the cold control of either his father or brother. He had only wit and intellect, and a huge sense of humor which others found infuriating. Above all things he loathed stupidity, and could not forgive it, though Paralus often told him, "Blame stupidity not on the intransigent nature of him who possesses it, but on his fathers who bequeathed it to him and on the gods who decreed it. Does a swine ordain his snout, and the monkey his lice, and the vulture his stink? We are what we are, not by our own desire, but from the loins of our fathers and the wombs of our mothers, and nothing can change that, not government, not alms, not learning, nor prayer. We are fixed in our natures from our conception, and we cannot escape our fate."

"We can try," said Xanthippus. "At least it is in our power to order the filthiest aspects of ourselves. Do we defecate in the streets? No, we go to latrines. Let the stupid go to theirs and learn discretion, so that they do not offend others."

"We can perhaps teach the stupid," said Paralus, sighing, "even though they destroy those who would teach them," to which Xanthippus disagreed and said, "You have refuted your own argument."

They loved each other dearly, they so dissimilar, and they entered their mother's quarters in amiability, and arm in arm. Dejanira was overjoyed to see them. They visited her at least once weekly but she greeted them as if she had not seen them for years, with embraces and smiling tears. She did not immediately inquire about their health but asked about their father with an eagerness they both found moving. Their grandmother lurked in the background sullenly with an air of chronic disapproval. She listened to the conversation, grunting, and as she, like other Greek women, did not believe in idleness, she was sewing industriously. But her eyes, black and small, darted about like cockroaches. She had affection for the sons of Pericles, though her love was for her grandson, Callias. So she felt some sullenness towards Xanthippus and Paralus, who did not resemble her or her daughter in the least. Her animosity toward Pericles extended to his sons, if not with the hatred she had for the father. This conflict of emotions made her irascible and her grunts always became very loud in the presence of the youths. Though they showed her the courtesy she deserved as their grandmother they ignored her after the greetings.

The youths conversed with their mother in an atmosphere of ease and love. She stroked their arms and fixed her eyes on their countenances, seeking for signs of Pericles. She asked about their academe. She had heard that Xanthippus was almost espoused to the daughter of a great house. Xanthippus shrugged. "I have met the maiden in the school of Aspasia, and she is sweet and kind. Why is it necessary for a man to marry? Is marriage all?"

To which his teased mother replied earnestly, "Yes, it is all."

Xanthippus was about to enter on his military service and he affected to find it onerous, but he was the son of Pericles and the grandson of Xanthippus, and he always thought of this with a pride he was careful to conceal. He talked with his mother, but he was easily bored with those whose minds were lesser than his, and he was soon yawning despite the stern glances Paralus gave him. At last, in spite of Dejanira's entreaties, both youths protested that they must return to their father's house, as the hour was late and they had a military guard waiting in the courtyard. The poor woman clung to them, kissing them and leaving her tears on their cheeks, and imploring them to visit her as soon as possible.

They mounted their horses. An abnormally large orange moon stood in the dark sky and gave the earth a curious illumination, so that every pillar and wall shone with a saffron light and every shadow was sharp and black. The hills were bathed in a wash of lemon yellow and the crowded and rising columns of the acropolis temples appeared to be made of gold. Athens, below, glittered with red torches and lanterns and lamps, restless and unsleeping. The autumn air was pungent and the wind cool. Fallen leaves rattled on the road and scurried before the horses like brittle small animals. Xanthippus began to sing the newest ribald ditty of the streets, to the amusement of the guard, and he added a few more stanzas of his own which were even more lewd. The horses pranced a little; hoofs clattered on stone. Xanthippus was in high spirits, as usual, while his brother merely smiled and made reproving sounds which were not entirely sincere.

The military guard carried torches and rode close to the brothers, watching every door and alley. They glanced at rooftops, for the light of the moon was very vivid. But they did not see the archer who was awaiting them, crouched on a roof and hidden by shadows. He did not rise until the company was directly below him, and he stood for an instant or two like a black faceless demon from Hades against the orange moon. A guard uttered a loud cry. But the archer was swift and skilled and he had chosen his target.

There was a whirring sound in the air, as deadly as that of a hawk, and the arrow found its lethal way into the right eye of Paralus, and he fell into the path of the horseman behind him.

Instantly, all was uproar and shoutings and the screaming of horses, and the hissing of fallen torches, which spewed off showers of red sparks on the stone. Horses wheeled frantically and reared. Xanthippus, careless of danger, swung down from his horse and threw himself on the body of his brother, and felt the blow of a horse's hoof on his left arm. Everything became confusion and oaths; men and horses crashed into each other. One horseman veered about and raced towards the house, dark and closed, on which the archer had stood. But he had disappeared, vanished like a phantom.

CHAPTER 6

Helena would not permit visitors to her patients in the infirmia, in order to limit meddling and noise. "The patient's welfare is more important than your curiosity, or even your love," she would tell anxious relatives. "He must rest if he is to recover. Who knows what diseases you may bring to him unwittingly? I have studied with Hippocrates, who says that the well may carry with them infections which will overcome the sick or the feeble."

She had a pleasant room for relatives and friends outside the infirmia itself, scented with flowers and a fragrant fountain, and with comfortable chairs. There she would converse with the visitors and tell them evil news or good. Her physicians would sometimes accompany her, with an air of deference when she spoke. In this room her voice was firm and strong. When visitors lamented the fate of the sick she would say, "Sophocles has said that it is better never to have been born at all in this world. Why do we grieve if one dies? Socrates says that a good man has nothing to fear in this world or the next—if it exists, and that death is only sleep, and who does not desire sleep? Death is our portion; it comes to us late or soon and none can escape it. We must accept it, as we accept life. The wise law-giver of Athens, Solon, has advised us never to call a man's life happy until it is over. Think on these things, and you may envy the dying."

For these remarks, delivered to the relatives of an expiring patient, she was considered heartless and without sympathy. She told her friends, sighing, that if a physician became one with his patients he would not be able to practice his art and would spend his days in fruitless tears. At all times, he must be as remote as Olympus, if his mind and intellect were not to be clouded by emotion, and yet must understand human suffering and grief. But they must be objective, not subjective, lest the patient himself suffer.

She would not permit alleged sorcerers or miracle-workers into her infirmia, nor would she allow a patient's neck to be garlanded with amulets. "It is true," she would say, "that the mind rules the body more than the body rules the mind, and sometimes superstition is as strong as a draught of medicine. But let me and my other physicians decide whether a man or woman is ill of the soul or of the flesh. If of the soul, you may bring amulets—for the soul is easily persuaded and is subjective. But if he has an illness of the body an amulet will not cure cancer or cut for the stone or deliver a child in difficulties. The body is objective, and does not believe in amulets."

Still she was beginning, more and more, to believe that a man's will to survive was most potent. She said to Pericles, "Your son will live, but he has lost the sight of his eye and nothing can restore it, not even the gods. It is miraculous that he is not dead or paralysed, for the point of the arrow pierced his brain. He is a valorous youth. He is determined to live and does not spend his painful hours bewailing that his sight will now be only partial. He is glad that he is not blind. As for Xanthippus, you may take him to your house, for he had but a broken arm and shoulder. He will not be comfortable for some time. However, he is more disturbed about his brother than is Paralus, himself, and vows vengeance." Helena's high color faded and her face, usually robustly cheerful, darkened.

"It is being sought," said Pericles, and his voice, though quiet, had a terribleness in it. "This was not a private vengeance or a sudden impulse, the attack on my son. The attack was directed at me. I have no foes but political ones. Even if the King Archon himself is responsible for this, he will suffer."

Paralus was the first person of high family to be a patient in the infirmia, for all households had their own physicians. But Pericles believed Helena to be the most learned of them all.

Paralus had been brought here at Pericles' request, almost in a state of extremis, and he was in one of Helena's handsome private quarters, guarded at all times, both within the chamber and outside the infirmia, and in every corridor by armed men with drawn swords. Not a morsel of food or a goblet of wine or water was permitted to enter his mouth without its first being tested for poison. His favorite dog slept at his side, as alert as the guards at any sound it did not recognize. In the next chamber Xanthippus had been housed. The brothers had been here a week.

Pericles said to Helena, "Aspasia pleads to be allowed to visit Paralus."

"Of a certainty my dear friend may visit one she loves so dearly, who is like a son to her."

"I am fearful her grief may affect her in her pregnancy."

Helena laughed shortly. "A pregnant woman is doubly protected, and she is as strong as a span of horses. Nature protects burgeoning life more than she protects those already born. Let Aspasia come, to relieve her anxiety. Her very countenance will soothe and delight Paralus." She hesitated. "Aspasia is well guarded, also?"

"I have doubled the guard—in my house. I have taken her from her own. She does not breathe without being heard. I lie beside her with my drawn sword in my hand."

Helena said, "The attack upon Aspasia was a private malice, though directed at you. The attack on your son was doubtless political, as you have said. Therefore, it is more dangerous, and more formidable. I doubt that your political enemies will attempt to injure you through Aspasia, for they regard women as trivial and insignificant, no matter who loves them. Guard your son, Xanthippus, as closely as Paralus is guarded. Guard yourself above all."

"Base dogs!" Pericles exclaimed. "They dared not attack me, myself! They knew it would arouse the rage of those who trust me. They therefore struck at me through my son, in order to frighten and intimidate me, and cause me distraction, and give me a warning. They wish me to withdraw in fear for my family, because though they whisper of impeachment and my ouster from office they know the people are with me. I will not withdraw! But I will find the perpetrators of this mischief and will ruin them."

"They may be too many," said Helena, thinking that a civil war could well be precipitated. She said, "Let me advise you, my dearest Pericles. Do not cry out publicly that this is a political matter, lest you open the gates of hell, to the injury of

Athens. Say always it was some dastardly criminal, who wished to rob or who had a private spite against you. Demand openly that Athens employ more street guards in order that blameless citizens might be safe from murder and theft."

"What pusillanimous advice!" said Pericles.

She smiled. "Perhaps. But think on it for a moment or two. My advice is wise. You will lull your enemies into complacence, while you search them out. An open attack on them will invite an open attack on you, whatever the consequences to themselves, for they are desperate."

Pericles considered. As he was rarely if ever moved by emotion he began to see the wisdom of Helena's advice, though it galled him and angered him.

"I suggest," said Helena, watching his white face closely, "that you proclaim a high reward for the discovery of the 'single criminal.' Make the reward so high that the hired assassin will be more than tempted to betray those who employed him. Offer him sanctuary, if he comes to you, which he possibly will. Money, with death, is no temptation. In the meantime, breathe no word of your true suspicions. Accept the condolences and the sympathy which the government is offering you, and do not search each face fiercely with your eyes. They must suspect nothing, though it is most possible that the greater the vehemence of indignation expressed the greater the probability of guilt."

Frowning, and running his fingers through his hair, Pericles said, "Some of my horsemen have sworn that they saw not a single archer, but others on other rooftops, waiting to see if the first succeeded. I do know that arrows were found in the shoulder of Xanthippus' horse. Had he not flung himself instantly on the body of Paralus he would have been murdered. Only the second arrows convinced me that my men were not hysterical."

"Then, above all, say publicly that it was but a single criminal who had attacked your company, and your enemies will be deceived. But I will wager that after you offer your reward there will be an unusual number of dead criminals found in alleys. Your enemies dare not let them live."

"What it is to be a politician!" said Pericles, with bitterness. "If a man seeks to help and glorify his country and make her strong before her enemies his own people will leap at his throat and call him malefactor, a thief, a mountebank, a liar! Better it is to smile and smile and smile upon the people and show a shining countenance than to raise them above the ruck."

"But, is that not an ancient story of heroes?" said Helena, and refilled his goblet. They sat in the blue twilight in the outdoor portico for, though it was autumn, it had been a warm and golden day. "My dear Pericles, you will remember the ancient proverb concerning powerful men: 'Walk softly among your enemies—with a sleeping sword.' Do you desire the fate of noble men? Exile or death or maledictions or contempt or hatred? Heroism is splendid, and candor, but there is also judiciousness in all things—if a man would serve his country as well as possible."

When he did not reply she laughed and put her warm hand on his knee. "This you have told me always. Am I not a good pupil? I repeat to you your own words. Reveal yourself as a just and angry man before your people and they will laugh at you."

Pericles had difficulty in removing Xanthippus from the infirmia, for the youth did not trust even Pericles' most trusted guards. Pericles was forced to exert all his parental authority to take his son to his house.

Helena, despite her convictions, had permitted the weeping Dejanira to visit her stricken sons. Dejanira volubly and tearfully questioned Helena about the identity of the assassin. Who would wish to injure her children? What was the power of Pericles if such could attack her sons amidst their guards? Athens had become a den of thieves who flaunted the law, and murderers who could kill at will. Where had been the city guards, that none were present? Helena, restraining her impatience, replied, "These are evil days, as always the world has evil days. We must acknowledge this. Mankind is a race of barbarians, of primeval animals."

"My father," Dejanira replied, her face red and swollen with weeping, "declares that it is Pericles who has been too tender towards criminals and the judges too merciful, and that we need a stronger man as Head of State. He is distraught. He has taken to his bed, my poor father."

Helena was too kind to explain to this unfortunate and stupid woman that her father's incessant ravings and denunciations had assisted and encouraged the attack on Paralus. She could only shrug and repeat that these were evil days. "No one is ever safe in this world," she said. "Those who seek safety and security are deluded, just as those who fight for peace inevitably must face war."

Friends and enemies in the government all extended words of wrath and condolence to Pericles, and he watched their faces, friend and foe alike, seeking for those who had plotted his son's death. "It is outrageous," said the Archons, and Pericles smiled cynically but accepted their remarks with grace and apparent gratitude. They congratulated him on offering the huge reward for the apprehension of the assassin. Many offered a purse of their own also. It was a paradox which only Zeno appreciated, that Pericles' worst enemies were the most lavish in their offerings, and the loudest in their expressions of ire. But he knew that among themselves they were pleased, and sniggered, and that they whispered against him.

He said to Aspasia, "My dear one, I am going to remove you, before the birth of our child, to one of my most secluded farms near Athens, with guards."

Aspasia said, "No. I must remain with you, lest fear destroy me. I am guarded here." She gazed at him desperately. "I have my part in your present persecution. Would it not be well if you did not see me again?"

He was both touched and irritated and said, "Shall the lions flee before the jackals? Shall they whimper at shadows? You must obey me, for my peace of mind. You will leave for my farm tomorrow, at dawn, and none must know where you are save Helena and myself."

He dared not accompany her to the remote and peaceful farm lest it be noted, so she left in the morning before the sun came up and few were on the roads. She was accompanied by strong and trusted slaves and soldiers, who were to remain with her. "If the Lady Aspasia comes to harm," he said to them, "I will exact the utmost penalty not on one of you, but all. Therefore, you must watch each other sleeplessly, and report the smallest dereliction to me."

Helena promised him that when the hour of the child's birth was imminent she would go to Aspasia, though ostensibly she was going to Epidaurus to pray in the temple of Asclepius, son of Apollo, who had been educated by Chiron, the centaur. There she would also attend a meeting of the new followers of Hippocrates, and study his methods and his teachings. "He has removed medicine from the realm of magic and thaumaturgy," she said to Pericles. "He is loftier than any Egyptian teacher. Have you ever wondered, my dear Pericles, why so much genius has been born and has arisen in this brief time in Greece? If I were a devout woman and believed in the gods I would say that they have looked down upon us from Parnassus and have blessed us. For truly this is a miracle."

Zeno, too, believed in the miracle. "God has chosen Greece for a great and majestic destiny," he said to Pericles. "What other race in our history and memory has been so deluged with glory and ferment and genius?"

Even Pericles, worn and coldly enraged and embittered now, conceded that something mysterious had occurred to cause the lightning to strike this little land with such brilliance and concentrated gifts. He said, "Anaxagoras has declared that the Universal Mind is not remote and indifferent, but chooses, not at random, to open His hands in blessing upon a nation or a race, for His own purposes, and Pheidias asserts that this is the hour of Greece and when even Athens is in ruins her spirit will dominate the world."

"In spite of our deplorable government," said Anaxagoras. "But what have governments to do with a nation? They are catastrophes rather than patrons of that which has splendor."

Pericles, on Aspasia's departure, was bereft. He visited Helena for comfort and encouragement, and inevitably, to soothe him, she took him to her bed. She was a sensible woman; she knew she was not violating his love for Aspasia, and that men needed the consolations and the soft words and hands of a woman in their extremity. Moreover, she was not afraid for him, as Aspasia was afraid. "Love makes cowards of the most valiant," she told him. "Aspasia is a woman of valor and never knew true fear before, but now she is as weak as the daisy of the field for dread for you. I write her constantly that you are flourishing, though," she added with a smile, "I do not inform her that you find surcease in my arms. You and I are old friends, Pericles, but Aspasia, being a woman abjectly in love with you, would not understand for all her intelligence. We could not explain to her that we do not love each other, except as friends, and that our festivals in bed have no true meaning."

One day Pericles received a sealed missive delivered by a cloaked and hooded man who put the letter into the hand of one of Pericles' scribes then fled swiftly into the crowds of the Agora. The scribe said with indulgence, "Lord, the vagabond was very elusive and had a voice of import. Doubtless he wishes alms, or this missive contains a denunciation against you."

Pericles smiled and opened the letter. It was written in a peculiar hand, hardly legible, but the wording was that of a cultured man. "If the noble Pericles would like news of those who instigated the attack upon his son, Paralus, he will come at midnight tonight to a certain tavern which will be closed and locked but which, upon five knocks, repeated three times with a short interval between, will be opened to him. He may bring guards, if he so desires, but he must not permit them to cross the threshold of the tavern. He must enter alone. He will find it silent and deserted with but one candle burning on a central table. As he is an honorable man, and after perceiving a letter addressed to him on that table, he will leave a purse of gold, as promised, in the place of the letter." The tavern was named; it was situated near the sea in a desolate and notorious section where few dared to venture except criminals.

Pericles, trembling inwardly, read and reread the missive. Was it a plot to lead him to his own death? Was it a snare to rob him of money? Was it fraudulent? A criminal could give a few names. Would they be, in truth, names of those who had paid for the attack on his son, in order to strike at his most vulnerable spot? He studied the letter over and over, gnawing his lip, rubbing his brow. He had an impulse to destroy the letter. The next moment he again read it. He had nothing to lose but a sum of money. On the other hand he had much to gain. He would tell his soldiers to surround the tavern so that if he were injured they could capture the criminals at once. There would be no escape for the traitor or the thief. Too, if Daedalus was named he would know that the message was mere trickery. Malice had done worse than to name an innocent man.

Then he had another thought. He sent for his most trusted officer, a brave young man whose courage and honor he had tested many times. His name was Iphis, and he was a distinguished soldier, short and massive, with glittering brown eyes and a square face under his helmet. Because of his small but powerful legs he waddled and planted his feet heavily, yet he could move like the darting of a sword.

He saluted Pericles and stood before him, waiting. Pericles gazed at him thoughtfully. Then he said, "My dear Iphis, you know of the reward I have offered for the name of the assassin who attacked my son, Paralus."

"Yes, noble Pericles."

Pericles held out the letter to Iphis who took it and read it. The young man's face became as still and carved and hard as

415

stone. He stood in silence for several moments then carefully placed the letter on the table before Pericles and stared down at it.

"Well?" said Pericles at last.

"Lord, it may be an ambush. You cannot go." He looked directly into Pericles' eyes. "I will go. I am not of your height, but I will wear a cloak with a hood and be seated on your horse, surrounded by my men, also on horseback. I will obey the instructions in that letter."

Pericles placed a finger against his lips and looked down at the letter. Iphis said sternly, "You are too important to Athens, lord, and you are Head of State, and the people trust you. To go as directed, yourself, would jeopardize not only your person but Athens as well. It may be that this letter is sincere and the rascal seeking money. We dare not miss the opportunity, however suspicious."

Pericles was always frank with his soldiers and so they trusted him without question. He could be most severe and then most kind. He said, "I hoped you would suggest this, Iphis, but I would not have suggested it myself. You may be in grave danger of death by going in my place. Do you understand this?"

"Yes, noble Pericles. But I will be armed, and will surround the tavern with my men, and I am a notable swordsman." His complexion was browned with the sun and had the texture and folds of leather for all his youth, and his eyes were clear and penetrating as he gazed at Pericles. He had an aura of resolution. He added, "I have no wife, no children, no kin. I have nothing to lose, but you have our country and your family. Who am I compared with you?"

Pericles stood then and embraced him, much moved. He withdrew a flashing ring from his finger and said, "This ring is famous in Athens and I never am seen without it. When you ride at midnight, let it be conspicuous, so that it will deceive any watcher. Go to my house at once; you will be seen emerging on horseback at midnight, through my gates. I, myself, will go to my house within the hour, but will leave for the house of Helena, the physician, so that even my most trusted slaves will believe I am with her."

He added, "Do not return to my house when you have procured the promised letter. Seek me in the house of Helena, where I will be waiting."

Iphis saluted. "What shall I tell the overseer of your hall, sir?"

"Tell him you have a message which you must deliver to me, and to me alone. Then, at midnight, with your soldiers, leave in yawning impatience and say that you will return at dawn."

When Iphis had left him Pericles pursed his lips and walked up and down his office, shaking his head. Iphis was indeed a notable swordsman, while he, Pericles, had not attended a fencing match for nearly two years. Iphis was also young while he was middle-aged. If danger there was, then it would be acute. Iphis was wary, and he had been warned. He would not give up his life easily, and his men would be there to guard him.

Before I had known Aspasia I would not have considered letting another man take my place in peril, he thought. But love makes us weak, even if we are powerful, and cowardly even if we are brave. What are even my sons compared with Aspasia? Iphis was right. I must also think of Athens. Those who trust me would be inconsolable, and my enemies would caper with delight if I were murdered. I stand between them and my country. Too, generals do not expose themselves carelessly to danger, for then their armies would be in disarray.

But he was still troubled.

Helena said to him in her house, "You acted with wisdom. Iphis is intrepid. Athens is greater than you, and she is in your charge. Do not look so uncertain. Come. I have a most delectable dinner for you tonight and I will amuse you until Iphis returns."

"You are too sensible," he said, and began to smile.

She regarded him gravely without an answering smile. "When you have the names—and they may be illustrious ones in government—what will you do with them? Have you considered this? You cannot punish those men openly, for then, in return, your enemies will become more united and more vengeful."

"I have considered," he replied. "But I will find a way to eliminate them, without open accusations. However, I must be convinced. It is not my way to act with haste, and that you know."

CHAPTER 7

Shortly after midnight, at the height of Pericles' apprehensions, Iphis rode up to the house of Helena where every lamp was burning. He bowed deeply to Pericles and bowed slightly to Helena as the friend of Pericles only and not to be considered seriously, though she was a physician of renown.

"Lord," he said, "it was as written in the letter. I knocked three times, as declared. There was no answer. I pressed against the door and it opened silently. None was there. On a single table, lighted with a candle, was a letter, which I have in my possession. A search of the tavern was futile. There was no sign of life or recent occupancy, though we searched." He smiled grimly. "It is apparent no one trusted us. I left the purse of gold on the table."

He gave the letter to Pericles; it was sealed. He opened it and read it with astonishment. There were four names. One was the Eponymous Archon, Philemon, and the second was the Polemarchos Archon, Leander, the third a member of the Supreme Court (called Heliaia), Tithonous, and the fourth, also a member of the Supreme Court and the Boule, Polites.

These four men had appeared to be his kindest and most devoted friends, serious, bearded and thoughtful. Philemon, Leander, Tithonous and Polites! It was incredible; it was impossible. But nothing, he reminded himself, was impossible in this worst of all possible worlds. A man's enemies were frequently discovered as his friends, his friends, his enemies. He had even expected to see the name of the King Archon, who always greeted him formally and coldly, though with respect. The fact that his name had been omitted, and that of Daedalus, gave credence to the letter. He had anticipated the names of those whom he believed were his overt foes. They were not here.

He had more than expected to see the name of Thucydides, his arch foe. He was not named.

He showed the missive to Helena, who read it carefully. She said, "I believe every word. These men have been in my house. They always expressed their devotion and loyalty to you. This made me suspicious from the beginning. The more a man protests the more he is to be mistrusted." She added, "The man who wrote this missive was no tyro, no mere vagabond. He knew the truth."

"I have dossiers on them all," said Pericles, but his heart was weighted. "I will study them tomorrow. It was only yesterday that Polites came to my house to speak with Paralus and bring him gifts of sympathy. As for the others, they surrounded me, weeping, and vowed that the dastardly assassin must be brought to justice. They pleaded with me to allow them their assistance."

"The more reason for you to suspect them, Pericles," said Helena.

"But what if the writer had a grudge against them and wished revenge?"

"You must study their dossiers," said Helena. "You may find truth there. If I remember, they are easy and elegant men, with sincere faces, and airs of integrity. Such should be doubted and watched."

Pericles was very perturbed. He stared at the letter and said, "I trust your judgment, but not always. I have known these men in my youth, in my childhood and early manhood."

"So," said Helena, "they are envious of you. They saw your rise and your popularity. They ask themselves, 'Why is he Head of State and not I? Was he more distinguished than I at our academe? Was he praised more by our teacher than I? Was he more industrious at learning, and did he receive prizes, as I received them? Is his house more notable? Is he richer? No! Therefore, why is he Head of State? Has he bribed voters and politicians? Has he poured out treasure to be elected, when I am more justified? Doubtless. Therefore, he bought office which I, as an honest man, would not have deigned to do. I am virtuous. He is heinous. He deserves punishment.' "

"They were my comrades in arms," said Pericles, and knew fresh grief.

"Hah!" said Helena, with a cynical face. "So, they believe themselves to be at least your equal. Did you not defecate and urinate with them and exchange lewd camp jests and sleep among them? Who are you, then, to be loftier? That is their reasoning. I have discovered that when a man is accessible and amiable to his companions he is denigrated in their estimation. He is not only on a level with them but possibly inferior. He is not to rise above them; that is unpardonable. If they guess inherent superiority they are sleepless in their hatred."

Pericles was silent. He said to himself, Is a woman wiser than a man? She has what Socrates has said—an innate sensibility and intuition, the gods' gifts to women! No wonder we men fear them! They are all Sibyls. Zeus hides himself in his amorous adventures, but Hera discovers them all. How? I do not know. He looked at Helena, who was gazing at him with her large blue eyes and a tender smile, as a woman gazes at a child. He touched her shoulder and said, "I will consider what you have told me. I fear you are correct." He thought of his

419

beloved Aspasia, who read his speeches before they were delivered, and who censored them, adding emphasis here, reducing emphasis there.

He said to Helena now, "I hate no man but an evil and stupid one. How, then, could these men be my enemies? Your explanation wounds my heart, my wise one."

"Think on your wounds," she replied. "They are not only valid; they bleed."

The wounds we receive in mere living! thought Pericles. The wounds we do not invite but which are inflicted on us—by men, our brothers. No wonder that Justice was the last goddess to leave this world, and has not yet returned. She may never return. The terrible offense to other men is to show them that the superior is not of them, that he has other impulses and other goals. We must all be sweet and democratic and pretend that we are only animals among other animals. If we do that, to God, who gave us gifts, we insult Him. If we do not do that, we offend our neighbor. Better it is to serve God than man, though that is perilous, and our brothers will destroy us. My brother—my enemy. Never my friend. Only my enemy.

The next day he summoned the King Archon to meet him in his offices. The King Archon came with his retinue, elderly, composed and as alert as the old bird he resembled. Pericles received him with ceremony and seated him and ordered refreshments. The King Archon knew this was a grave occasion, and waited patiently, looking at Pericles thoughtfully and with an expression that told nothing. In his turn Pericles studied the old man, for whom he had small respect as he had small respect for all other members of his government. But now he saw that the King Archon had a kingly aspect, and that it was possible he was a man of verity. How unique it is, thought Pericles, to discover a man of probity in any government!

He lifted a sheaf of papers on the table between them. He then gazed at the King Archon with his pale eyes that could take on a baleful look.

"My son, Paralus, was wounded almost to the death by an assassin, or assassins," he said to the King Archon. "But this you know. I have four names here, which are alleged to be those of the men who bribed criminals to kill my son. I also have their dossiers."

The King Archon inclined his head. "Yes," he said. "I have heard of your dossiers, Pericles, son of Xanthippus." He paused. "You would not have called me here if you did not trust me."

Pericles dropped his eyes. "I trust no man absolutely, not even myself. But I trust you as much as I can, which, I assure you," and he smiled faintly, "is not in extraordinary measure."

The King Archon smiled a little and again inclined his head. He drank some wine and ate a ripe fig or two.

Pericles gave him the missive Iphis had brought to him. The King Archon read it. He began to frown, and his bearded cheeks turned sallow with shock. At last he lifted his eyes and looked in aghast but quiet silence at Pericles.

"You do not expostulate," said Pericles.

The King Archon shook his head. "I can believe anything of mankind," he said. "Tell me. What do your dossiers show?"

"The Archon, Philemon: He is your cousin's husband. A few years ago he was accused of bribing the charioteers of Athens in the Olympic Games. He had much invested. Our charioteers lost to Sparta. Though accused, he was never brought to trial, because of your high position, and the name of his house. The news was quietly suppressed. You will observe that the charioteers confessed, under holy oath. You will see that I have corroboration."

He waited for a comment but the King Archon made none. "Ah," said Pericles, "then you did not know." The King Archon tried to speak but could not and Pericles looked at him in sympathy. "After all, it is considered a terrible crime to bribe anyone in the Great Games."

The King Archon said nothing. Pericles sighed and continued.

"The Polemarchos Archon, Leander. He is in charge of metics, foreigners. For a large fee he had documents forged to show that many Ionians, not to speak of Persians, had their names inscribed in our public records as Athenians born in Athens. He did this because he had to return his wife's dowry, and he had spent her money in unwise investments, which had all melted away like butter under the sun. It is curious," said Pericles, "but he has been most stringent in his attacks on foreigners who were poor and desired only to come to Athens to work and practice their arts and live virtuously. Many of them, poor good men, were forced to leave our city, and lost all they had, which was very little in the very beginning. That was to assure his fellow Athenians that he held our city to be inviolate and not to be polluted by aliens."

The King Archon retained his composure but his eyes flickered with pain. Pericles looked at the papers in his hands and said, "Tithonous, a respected member of the Heliaia, the Supreme Court, from which there is no appeal. He has persuaded many of his innocent fellow judges—by his vote and oratory—that various dangerous criminals were innocent, if they came of rich families or had political influence. He would weep over their 'wrongs' or say that they were young and heedless and meant no overt transgressions. He castigated fathers for the plight of their sons. The criminals went free. He received large sums from grateful parents for this."

The King Archon closed his eyes as if he could not endure listening, but must.

Pericles said, still quietly, "Another member of the Supreme Court, Polites. His wife, of whom he had tired, died under mysterious circumstances. He is rich and powerful. You will observe the names of the men who swore that he was with them far away when she was stabbed to death in her chamber. They did that, not out of venality, but because it was unthinkable to them that a man of such a blameless character and sober mien could have arranged the murder of his wife. But, you will observe, I have received letters from the murderers, themselves, from their sanctuary in Syria. Even murderers, it would seem, have consciences, occasionally. Or, perhaps, they had received less money than they expected. Their letters are beyond doubt. They described the actual murder as only participants could do, for many of the vile facts were unknown except to officers of our police."

There was a long silence in the office. The King Archon spread his hands, palm down, on the table in a gesture of misery. Then he said, "Pericles, you are not without guilt. These men should have been brought to justice. You did not speak."

Pericles leaned back in his chair. "I am a politician. Moreover, these men did not commit further crimes. To expose them would have destroyed the trust, more or less, our citizens have for politicians—and I am a politician."

"They did not commit further crimes because they feared that someone knew the truth about them."

Pericles lifted his eyebrows. "True. But they did not know that I was the one. You asked me why I did not speak. Again, I must repeat I am a politician, and I have kept these dossiers for the day when I might need them. The day has come."

The King Archon lifted his spotted hands and covered his face with them, leaning his elbows on the table, and Pericles felt compassion for him, for the old man was honorable. The

King Archon said, "I, too, am a politician, but I would have spoken."

"I do not doubt it," said Pericles. "Perhaps you love Athens less than I do. It is also true that politicians keep their fellows in order, under threat of exposure. We scratch each other's backs."

The King Archon dropped his hands and his bright and youthful eyes were lucent. He said, "You scratch no one's back, Pericles, and no one scratches yours. I have watched you for many years. I knew your father well. He was a hero."

Pericles looked aside. "I am no hero, and have no pretensions to be one. My public life has been as clean as possible. I am guilty of no crimes against my country. Still, I am a politician."

The King Archon rose and walked slowly and heavily up and down the room. Then he came to a halt before Pericles and said in a sick voice, "What would you have me do?"

"Summon these men, tell them that you are aware of their capital crimes, and that they must go into exile at once, for life."

"You wish me to tell them of your dossiers?"

Pericles bent his head. "Yes, if you will. Tell them that if they depart without incident, without speaking, the dossiers will not be made public. Tell them I showed you the dossiers out of spirit of public service, only."

"They will know it is revenge."

"They have no way of knowing how I came by this information, nor that I suspect them of bribing murderers to attack my son. How could they know? Let them suspect, in their exile. They have no proof."

"Why do you not confront them yourself, Pericles?"

Pericles' smile was bitter and arrogant. "I am Head of State. I would not demean myself to accuse my fellow politicians, of inferior station. That is your function, not mine. Again, I was moved to inform you only because my conscience began to annoy me—though I came on this information only recently."

"That is not the truth, Pericles."

"No, it is not. But you will not be lying to them. You do not know how long I have had this information." He paused. "I implore you to space the sentences of voluntary exile. I say, voluntary. Thirty days, at least, must expire between each rascal's invitation to leave Athens forever."

He pushed the papers towards the King Archon. "These are copies. I will retain the others."

The King Archon looked at the papers as a man looks at vipers. "Would it not be better if I did not reveal the source of them?"

Pericles shrugged. "Perhaps. But I am only human. I should like them to ponder the rest of their lives and wonder if the information was given to you because I knew of their bribery to murderers, or," and he smiled coldly, "that I was moved by civic virtue. It will make their years of exile interesting."

"Knowing you, Pericles, I fear they will think it is civic virtue."

"Perhaps. After all, they were my companions in arms. Let them believe that Nemesis overtook them. I will not know their thoughts, and that, to me, is regrettable."

The King Archon took up the papers. "I am an old man," he said. "I love my country. I have done no wrong to her, or her laws. This is very grievous to me. Had I had this information the malefactors would have been driven into exile long ago."

"You are no politician, then."

The King Archon bent his head and shook it slowly and heavily. "I have heard that before, from my beloved hetaira. She has assured me that no honest man enters politics."

"Let us encourage the honest men, then. Let us make it possible for honorable men, though poor, to enter politics. But that is only a dream of the perfect state, and no state is perfect."

The King Archon sighed deeply. "I often think of Solon," he said.

"So do I," Pericles replied. "As much as the people allow me I attempt to enforce his laws. But, we must deal with the people and they are capricious!"

"And we fear them. Pericles, I will move as swiftly and as discreetly as possible. These men will be exiled—for their crime against your son—though they will believe it is for another reason." He paused. "Why is it not possible to accuse them openly of the attempt on the life of Paralus?"

"On the unsigned word of an informer? Sire, who would believe it of such notable and ostensibly good public servants?"

"And you desire not to increase the mistrust of the citizenry for their government."

"True. Not all politicians are venal. Incredibly, some of

them are honorable men, and it is very hard for a man to remain honorable before a treacherous citizenry, who are, themselves, as fraudulent as their leaders."

He added, when the King Archon was silent, "I could have had these men murdered, and they deserve death. You will observe that I am merciful."

The King Archon smiled strangely. "No. I observe only that you love your country and would not have her plunged into chaos because of evil men." He looked long at Pericles. "I, too, look at the acropolis in the moonlight. For the sake of Athens and her glory and beauty you would do anything, except the dishonorable."

He took his departure, walking as weightily as a very old sick man and Pericles watched him go and his face was somber. He thought: The King Archon is wrong. I would do anything for my country, honorable or dishonorable.

CHAPTER 8

Pericles had believed the King Archon to be neither friend nor foe, but only a just man. His coldness and formality were even more notable than his, though he was never pompous. Therefore, he had few acquaintances and fewer friends. What he thought in private was never revealed, not even to his hetaira.

When alone in his office with the damning papers before him the King Archon thought long and intensely. Pericles would have been amazed had he known of the respect and admiration the King Archon had for him, and how often he had rebuked his fellow Archons who had expressed rage or hate for or envy of the Head of State. The King Archon did not consider it wise to make personal friends of fellow politicians. That way led to subornation and the mutual "scratching of backs," and was a betrayal of justice and of the people who trusted them. Justice and friendship, he would often think, are what Socrates would call a contradiction in terms. They who would serve justice publicly should keep aloof from human entanglements. So, he was a lonely old man, distant and cool even to his sons and daughters. If one of his sons had committed a crime he would have punished him as severely as any other criminal, with no outward aspect of distress.

He thought, as he sat alone in his private chambers: Pericles, after all, is only human. He would like these men, who are to be exiled, to know he was the avenger and the instigator, or, rather, suspect it for the rest of their lives. But that is most perilous for Athens, Pericles, and his family. These men have many powerful friends, and many male relatives of valor, and they would avenge the four, and they would eventually find means of destroying Athens through the destruction of Pericles. No, this must not happen.

He summoned Polites, Polites who had had his gentle young wife murdered—he, a member of the Supreme Court. The King Archon did not believe in lengthy explanations and accusations. Moreover, he must be sure that what had been revealed in the letter was true. So when Polites arrived, a man of fifty with a fine and aristocratic face, perfect manners and a candid expression, the King Archon, in silence, laid his dossier before him, and acutely watched his face. It turned a mortal white; his eyelids quivered; he seemed to grow old rapidly. So, it is true, thought the King Archon in despair. Polites finally looked up at him and said, "Lord, do you believe this libel?"

"Yes," said the King Archon, at once. "But, I am merciful. Rather than give this information to the proper authorities I will keep my silence, provided you leave Athens forever, within two weeks."

Polites cried out in anguish. The King Archon lifted his hand. "Your trial could be prolonged, in the way of the law, but the people would believe it, as they are inclined to believe anything of public officials. Truth will out, though many do not believe this. Long investigation would bring your case to the light of day. I have said: I am merciful. If you challenge this dossier you will be ruined. You are accused of a capital crime. You would be put to death, and your estates confiscated. Be silent, then. Tell your friends that you are leaving our city for a considerable period—for the sake of your health. You may then keep your estates and your family can abide with you."

Polites said, "Who made this dossier?"

"It is not pertinent. In mercy, I do not advise you to challenge it. If you do, other accusations will be brought against you—I promise—and this time you would not escape justice as you escaped it before."

Almost beside himself, Polites quickly named several men who were his enemies, execrating them, but the name of Pericles was not among them, a fact which made the old face of the King Archon ironic. He merely kept shaking his head, and repeating, "I shall not tell you." He dismissed Polites, who left him with an almost staggering gait, and he then summoned each of the other three in turn.

In every case guilt appeared on their countenances though they protested their innocence, even vowing the most sacred of oaths, that of Castor and Pollux. The King Archon closed his eyes in weariness and lifted his hand. "Let that oath not condemn you before the gods," he said. "If you wish to withdraw it, do so now."

After some hesitation the oath was withdrawn and the King Archon, who had prayed that at least one of the men had been falsely accused, was sickened. They had always declared their deep love for Pericles; they were his comrades in arms. They had voted with him almost invariably. Men of family, and proud of their city, they had approved of the Parthenon and other costly temples on the acropolis. They had frequently dined, and with pleasure and accord, with Pericles, and he had visited their own houses often. Two were of his own tribe. Why, then, had they attempted to kill his son and cast him into sorrow and misery? Malice and envy, the ancient human crimes, the old Archon thought. A man, even the best of friends, will forgive anything but that a friend rise above him and attain fame. Pericles had understood that, and the King Archon reflected on Pericles' own sorrow that his friends had betrayed him, had tried to plunge his heart into grief, and by no justification except that he had proved himself their natural superior. We are a wicked and incorrigible race, thought the old Archon, and why the gods endure us is a great mystery.

He contemplated the paradox of love and hatred lodging simultaneously in the minds of these men. They loved Pericles; they also hated him. Had he fought on the battlefield with them they would have given their lives for him, as heroes. But when it was a matter of public acclaim and power, they would destroy him, not as their friend, Pericles, but as the symbol of their jealousy. Their love for him had kept them from murdering him, themselves. Their hatred had chosen a lesser object but whose loss would devastate Pericles. Over and over the King Archon shook his head, sad but with wonder. As their friend, with whom they were in entire agreement in matters of policy, they would preserve Pericles' life with diligence. As his enemies, they would rejoice in his suffering. They would even regard it as retribution. The manifold intricacies of the human soul! the old Archon thought. Not even Penelope could unravel the threads and the designs of a single human mind. The pattern of that most diligent weaver could never encompass the spirit of a man, and portray it.

The King Archon, even more discreet than Pericles himself, did not send word of the results of his accusations to the Head of State. The news would reach Pericles soon enough. One man had said he would leave Athens soon to manage his estates in Cyprus; another claimed the air of Athens had injured his lungs—he must flee for his health's sake; another had said he was weary of public office, and would retire to the country; still another said his beloved wife wished to be with her family in Cos. Not one hinted that his absence was exile, forced upon him under threat. The King Archon, hearing all this, was deeply depressed, knowing now, beyond all doubt, that they were guilty.

Each of the four men went, weeping, to Pericles, to announce his imminent departure from Athens. They confided to him that they had been forced into exile because of false accusations, "which would endanger the State, if I challenged them." Pericles, who had trained himself, as a politician, to be somewhat of an actor, against all his principles, said in apparent wonder and concern, "But, if you are innocent, why not seek to prove it?" Their silence, their dolorous sighs, filled him with hate and he could scarce restrain himself. "Let me help you," he said, and none heard the iron under his words. They replied, "It would imperil you, yourself, dearest of friends." He heard sincerity in their voices, and marvelled. They truly meant it. Pericles, and now with sour humor, suspected that the King Archon had never mentioned his name.

He almost pitied them, and he especially pitied Polites who had been a valiant lieutenant under Pericles' command, and who had proved his loyalty and love under dire circumstances. But Pericles had only to look at the sunken right eye of his handsome son, Paralus, to feel the return of his furious hatred. Paralus said to him, "I live. I can see, if only in a flattened state. I am fortunate to be alive, and to have some sight. For a time my other eye was threatened, but Helena saved both my life and my vision. Alas, though, I shall never be a soldier as you were, my father."

"Nor will you have comrades-in-arms," said Pericles, and Paralus, who thought he knew his father better than did even Aspasia, was puzzled at the profound bitterness in his father's voice, and the look of terrible anger. When he said those words he would turn away from his son and stare blindly into space.

Xanthippus, the acute, said to his brother, "Our father

knows something we do not know, and never will he tell us."
But Paralus shook his head. "There is nothing to know. My
attackers will never be found."

Xanthippus, now healed, proclaimed his discontent that he
would have to serve his two years in the army. He did this to
spare Paralus, who longed to be a soldier, and Paralus said,
soothingly, "The time will pass soon, and I will think of you
as taking my place, for you must have the strength of two
men." His brother was now espoused to the young girl whom
he had met in Aspasia's house, and the marriage would take
place soon. Xanthippus was very happy. He sighed, and said,
"I would prefer not to marry, but it is my duty. I am like a
virgin heifer led to sacrifice." His dark face beamed.

Helena informed Pericles that the time for the birth of his
child had arrived. He insisted, against her advice, in being in
that remote farmhouse with Aspasia, and so she left one
morning alone, except for two young physicians who would
aid her, and he, Pericles, left the next day. He took with him
only Iphis and a subaltern who was devoted to Iphis, for it
was not his wish that he attract attention. The farm, though
secluded, was but a four-hour journey on horseback. The
roads were very poor, the Athenians declaring that good
roads were not necessary outside the city. "We do not travel,"
they said, grandly, "for where is there a spot more beautiful
and important or renowned than Athens? If we wish to see
the world and engage in commerce with other nations, the sea
is our road." So a land journey that should, on horseback,
have taken but an hour or so took far more than that, over
cattle paths, and over deer trails climbing hills and sometimes
wandering into thickets of thistles and choked forests. The
spring sun was hot and burning, ablaze with incandescent blue
skies and clouds of silver dust catching the light. The little
poppy grew on field and hill, a thrown carpet of vivid scarlet,
moving gently with the wind. The brown and withered shards
of the palm trees were falling, and new fronds were appearing, brilliantly green, and flowering, and the sycamores stood
in a haze of emerald and the blossoms of the myrtle were a
shower of soft purple and the fruit trees had burst into fountains of pink and white in the orchards. Little goats and new
lambs romped innocently and unafraid in the brightening
meadows, and young colts ran to the sides of the deplorable
roads and raced with the horsemen, tossing their delicate
manes and neighing. The olive trees were burnished with a
fresh silver, and corn was thrusting moist green tips out of the
earth and into the sun. Children played outside of the small

square and white cubes of their houses, and the grapevines which grew up the sides of the houses were exploding with new tendrils, the garlands of Dionysius. The red mud ran with mercurial brooks, reflecting the sky. The ponds teemed with fish, and so did the rivers.

It is a goodly season in which to be born, thought Pericles, whose fair skin had begun to smart with the heat and the sun. It is a promise. He hoped for another son, but even a daughter would be welcome, a daughter who resembled Aspasia. Now he had reached his own fields and meadows and he knew the pride of owning land and thought that every man should possess a little measure of it for the sake of his nature. No man should be landless, as so many of the urban Athenians were. As Socrates had said, small villages and the land bred noble men, but cities bred effete creatures, criminals and merchants, and, alas, necessary commerce. But a man should have a retreat from that which was artificial and fevered and vehement so that he could contemplate his soul in silence and sunlight and moonlight and not be distracted by the claims and uproar of the cities. "Who looks at the stars in the city?" Socrates had asked Pericles. "In the country, at night, there is nowhere else to look, and awe comes to man and he knows his littleness and feels an inclination to worship that which is greater than he. In the understanding of his smallness and insignificance comes wisdom and clarity of thought."

Peace, now known so seldom by Pericles, came to him. He saw his white farmhouse in the distance, surrounded by cypresses and sycamores; he saw his olive groves and his sheep and lambs and goats and cattle and horses, and he felt more pride than when he addressed the Assembly, which rose in a rustle of garments at his entry, and bowed before him. He could even forget hatred here and the hot sickness that often assailed him. Above all, politicians needed a retreat where they could observe their unimportance, and feel, however vaguely, the Presence of God, not the dutiful gesture to the Godhead which was expected of them in public, but the immanent Presence which touched the heart and the spirit with verity, and only in solitude.

Aspasia, with Helena at her side, greeted Pericles joyfully. He embraced her with hunger and delight, careful of her swollen body. Her face shone like the moon; never had he seen her so beautiful, so young, so radiant. She took his hand and kissed it, and pressed it to her breast. She gazed at him adoringly. She was in transports. She threw back her pale golden hair and laughed, and there were tears in her brown eyes. She even babbled incoherently, and never had he heard this before, and he held her again as one more precious to him than his own life. Helena watched them with indulgent affection and humor. One was a trained and experienced courtesan; the other was the most powerful man in Greece. Yet they were as bride and groom, awaiting their first child, parents as simple as peasants, and as innocent and unknown.

The food of the farm was theirs, as the three dined together: new cheese, dark rich bread, little carrots and lettuce drenched with oil and vinegar, young roasted lamb, broiled fresh fish from the river nearby, fowl fried in olive oil and tender as butter, soup of green peas with pork—and, always, the wine from his autumn hillsides. The food had a taste not to be found in cities, though it was coarse and had no pungent sauces. It was like life, itself, fragrant and satisfying and poignant, yet hearty. Pericles thought, It is well I sent her here where life is, and health, and simplicity. He could even forget that he was Head of State in this tranquil and pellucid spot, and he felt like a robust peasant who had worked with his brown hands in the earth and had produced this warm bounty. He looked at the bowl of poppies and apple blossoms on the bare wooden table, and at the last sunlight illuminating everything with rosy gold, and he heard the sweet silence about him, and forgot he was a politician. He was a country man, under his white roof. A nightingale began to sing, and in the zenith Jupiter rode in sparkling majesty. A horse neighed; cows passing into paddocks let their bells tinkle. A melancholy dulcitude came to Pericles. He had removed his helmet. In his brown tunic he was only a farmer, but he had his land and that made him a king. I should come here more often, he thought, to escape the hot breaths of men and their shrill exigencies.

He was accustomed to talk politics and affairs of State with Aspasia. Now with ease he spoke as a countryman, of crops and orchards and farm animals and weather, and she smiled at him like a farm wife glad to have her husband home from the fields and partaking of the fruits of his own land. Contentment welled between them, and peace. Helena's firm cheeks were reddened; Aspasia's face bloomed like a flower, vermillion and white. She told Pericles she had picked the vegetables herself, and the blossoms. She showed him her lovely hands with pride, because the pink nails held the honest earth which she had been unable to remove. When Pericles had poured the libation to the gods her eyes had glittered with reverent tears. "God is close to us on His land," she said. "It is hard to discern Him in the city."

"He is drowned out in the voices of men," said Helena, the skeptic. "Pheidias tells me he has to retire to his garden in order to evoke majesty, and to think, and see glory. He cannot do that in the Agora. Philosophy, it is apparent, and the arts, grow with the pace of turnips in the field." She laughed. They looked at her affectionately, their hands clasped together.

Later, they retired to their rough chamber, where the walls were of unpolished wood, and pale gold. The floor was of stone; it was covered by no carpets, and was cool to the foot. The blankets were coarse, the linen prickling, and it was not bleached. Pericles held Aspasia in his arms; he would put his hand on her belly, to feel the kicking of his child. It was as if he had no other wife, no other children. The uncurtained windows were bare and open and they could smell the carnal passion of the warming earth and could hear nothing but the nightingales, the shrilling of insect voices and the night wind. Pericles had blown out the lamp. Stars gazed through the windows.

Aspasia slept, her head on his shoulder, her hands entwined with his, her round limbs seeking him, her breasts full and warm and preparing milk. Her hair was fragrant with the aroma of grass and sun. Her shift was of linen, and simple. She wore no scent. He felt her soft silken hair against his chin, and he kissed it. She sighed happily in her sleep, and murmured like a maiden awakened to love. Athens became unreal to him; his problems and his distresses were of no significance. He held the whole world in his arms, the world of life and labor and veritable joy. A dog barked sleepily; a cow lowed in the barns. A horse stamped. The only discordant note was the voice of a guard speaking to another guard. The wedge of the rising moon peered in the window. Pericles slept.

The next morning, clad as a countryman, Pericles rode with his men and slaves over his land. This farm was not his most profitable; it was, in truth, a peasant's farm, including the farmhouse. His other farms were almost opulent in comparison, with villas for the visits of the owner. But he preferred this, a return to simplicity.

Aspasia was in the kitchen peeling onions for a soup when Helena joined her, and Helena smiled a little mockingly at her friend's humble occupation. Aspasia said with an almost childlike joy, "Oh, if but Pericles and I could live here always,

432

in such peace and such unaffected plainness! How happy we would be."

"Nonsense," said Helena, critically selecting a citron from a reed basket on the table and beginning to remove the peel. "This is a novelty for you, dear. Go to. What, no Agora, no banks, no shops, no booksellers, no music, no dinners with philosophers and artists, no dancing, no pleasant luxury, no jewelry or fine robes, no solicitous services of slaves in the baths, no gossip, no excitement, no stimulation of the mind, no sophisticated conversation, no politics, no discussions of the arts, no meeting of thoughts? Pah. I agree that every man should have a little quiet land of his own to which he can escape and renew his peace of mind and be freed from the burden of thinking." She laughed, her blue eyes sparkling. "Oh, I can see you and Pericles here for all time, until you gnaw your knuckles for very ennui and dullness and too much quiet!"

Aspasia was at first offended, then she laughed and wiped her eyes with the back of one of her hands. "How we pretend to ourselves!" she said. "I have known nothing but opulence all my life and daintiness and excellent food and wine, and I admit I do not despise them. But, for a space, this is good. Let Pericles and I have this pretense for a little while." She then asked of her friends in Athens.

"Anaxagoras is coming under attack, and I fear for him," said Helena. "All of Pericles' friends are being scrutinized, including me."

Aspasia stopped smiling. "You, Helena, who have given your life to the saving of others and the mitigation of their diseases?" She was incredulous.

"Ah, but I am a dissolute woman! My lack of virtue is beyond dispute. I am a black example to modest wives and daughters. I am unchaste, and impious. I go publicly into the market place with no attendants; I am the companion of many men. I wear no veils of discretion. I do not titter and cast down my eyes and say childish things, as do other women. Therefore, I am a disgrace, the shame of Athens." She paused. "As for Anaxagoras, and the others of Pericles' friends, they, too, are impious. They question not only government, but religion and superstition. They are leading the youth of Athens to disaster and rebellion against authority; they ask youth to think as well as merely to obey. These are capital crimes, of a certainty." She sucked at the citron and her eyes were darkly serious. "On one hand we hear talk of the splendor and glory burgeoning in Greece, and worship it.

On the other hand we would destroy those who have brought this splendor and glory to our country. It is not a new tale; it is the history of every nation. But we never learn. After we kill heroes we elevate them among the stars. But the gods do that also, so what can we expect from men?"

Aspasia looked through the window at the warm and pellucid sky, at the far wide peace of the fields, at the stands of dark cypresses, at the orchards and the cattle and the lambs and the goats and horses, all exuberant in the spring air. Birds swooped and darted like colored arrows in the lucent light. She was about to say something when she caught Helena's mocking eye, and so was silent.

"Of a certainty," said Helena, "a man who thinks will be forever unhappy, for who can come to terms with this world except the stupid? Still, it is better to think and conjecture and be unhappy than it is to be happy in ignorance. The divine discontent—it creates glory. Contentment? That is for the tomb."

Aspasia said, her thoughts still with her dear friend, "You are not afraid for yourself, Helena?"

The physician shrugged. "Of what avail is fear? If one ponders on it long enough one becomes cautious, and caution has blinded and deafened and made impotent too many who should have been bold. I despise prudence—to some extent. I do not court death or any other punishment. But I must live as I must, according to my nature, or expire, one way or another. What is it?" she asked quickly.

For Aspasia had suddenly put her hand to her belly and had gasped. Her face had paled and sweat had broken out on her brow. "A pain, a great pain," she stammered, and all at once she was afraid. But Helena was calm. "The child is due. Let us repair to your chamber, where I have placed the birthing stool and my instruments. Let the slave woman continue with this preparation of food."

"Pericles," Aspasia murmured, as another pain seized her, causing her to bend deeply.

"Nonsense," Helena said with briskness. "How can he assist? Men are only a trouble when women give birth. They become hysterical, and they dither. Let him look at his growing turnips and cabbages and talk of manure to his slaves; let him examine the new corn. Let us pray he does not return soon."

She conducted Aspasia to her austere chamber and told the slave women to prepare towels and linens and oils and heat water and wine. She put Aspasia on the birthing stool and sat down placidly near her. If she were concerned about Aspasia's age—she was thirty-four—and this a first child, she did not reveal it. She talked genially of Athens and their friends and politics, but ever watchful, counting the contractions. They were still not very fast. Occasionally she rose and wiped the sweat from Aspasia's face with a cool cloth dipped in water of nard. She made no comment on this. She still conversed as she felt the other woman's pulse. Her conversation was matter-of-fact; she did not discuss the coming birth. When she saw Aspasia was in pain, she told her a lewd joke, and Aspasia laughed. The sunlight came through the window, and the fresh scent of the jubilant earth. A bird, whose feathers were blue and gold, lighted on the window-sill and sang. "It is a good omen," said Helena.

Aspasia began to writhe on the stool. Helena said, "It is not a good thing for a woman in labor to lie in bed. Now you must stand and walk." She took Aspasia's arm and led her up and down the chamber. Two slave women, crouching in a corner, wide-eyed, stared at the two. The garden slaves were singing; a fragrance of grass and lilacs blew into the room. A bee flew through the window and buzzed against a wall. A slave woman would have killed it but Helena said, "Let there be no death here. It is an industrious thing, the bee, and we should honor it."

Helena permitted Aspasia to lie on her bed for a few moments while she examined her. She said, with satisfaction, "The head is already presenting itself. There are some physicians who hasten labor. I do not. Nature knows more than we. In your case, my dear, there will be little difficulty."

Aspasia gasped. "What women must endure!" she said.

Helena forced a yawn. "It is no high tragedy," she replied. "Do we not all endure travail in our lives? Besides, in the case of giving birth it is not only women who suffer. We suffer with other female animals, who assign no importance to it." However, she was somewhat concerned. The enclosed child's head was indeed presenting itself at the cervix, but the birth bag had not yet broken.

She made Aspasia walk again. Then she let her lie on her bed, and forced her legs apart. She hid a small instrument in her hand and then inserted her hand into the birth canal. She punctured the bag. Aspasia cried out as a gush of fluid mingled with blood ran from her. Helena was satisfied. Now the birth could proceed. She put Aspasia on the birthing stool again and knelt before her, her instruments at her side, and the high forceps which Hippocrates had invented. At her command a slave woman brought a pail of hot water and soap

435

and Helena, as Hippocrates had taught her, washed the instruments and her hands over and over and then dried them on clean towels. The air was becoming warmer, more fervid. Helena, herself, might have been a hearty and very plump countrywoman herself, as she knelt before her patient, her brow wet and streaming, her auburn hair darkening with water. When a strong contraction came she pressed gently on Aspasia's belly, pushing down. Aspasia's gasps and groans became louder. "Do not draw deep breaths," said Helena. "It delays birth. Press down as I press, even if it increases the pain."

Aspasia was very pale and drawn. Helena studied her. Then she rose and mixed a murky liquid in wine. "Drink this," she said. "It will ease you."

Aspasia, beyond speech now, drank obediently. Her mouth contorted. "Opium," said Helena. "I give it seldom for it inclines to delay the birth and the child is also affected. So says Hippocrates. However, you are near delivery, so it will not injure you or your child."

The opium rapidly affected Aspasia, and she entered a dreaming state. At one moment everything was bathed in too much hurtful clarity, so that each object in the room and even Helena wore a bright outline and every mote of dust was painfully shining, and at the next moment everything was still and quiet and at a distance. Aspasia's mind became confused. She was not separate from her pain; she was agony itself and no longer a distinct personality. Darkness sometimes fell over her straining eyes. Someone was panting in the room, or, was it eternity and not a room? Little bright moons swam before her; she tried to watch their passage; they too were physical anguish. She willed them to move more rapidly, to leave her in peace. They merely mocked her by increasing and dancing. Once she thought—and even her thoughts seemed far out in space—what we pay for an hour's delight! It seemed to her that she had come on a profound truth which no one else had ever discerned, and she was for a moment elated. She must write it down, and talk of it with Pericles, who would marvel.

Now in the darkness before her she discovered a far and brilliant star and she watched it moving and waxing and waning. All at once she told herself that now she was embowed with all wisdom, that the star was a revelation of infinite and immortal Being, with whom her own soul was intermingled. Nothing was hidden from her. She possessed all knowledge, and a strange ecstasy seized her. She thought that she was speaking the words of Sibyls, but she was only muttering incoherently. Now she could see Helena in a haze. It seemed to her that she must impart what she knew to this woman, this friend, lest it disappear forever.

Helena's voice came to her in a strong and peremptory fashion. "Do not sleep. Press down your belly."

But what have I to do with my flesh? Aspasia asked herself with superb amusement. It surprised her that Helena could be so obtuse. A sudden unbearable pain tore her, but it was still apart from her. She gazed at the star again. She felt hands take her roughly, lift her, put her on her bed. There was one appalling convulsion, which slowly died away into night. She slept.

It was sunset, red and burning, when she awoke, flaccid and exhausted. She was in her bed and Pericles was bending over her, smiling. He was holding her hand. She looked up at him and said, "I have seen all things." She heard Helena laugh.

"We have a son," said Pericles, "a beautiful son, with hair of gold and with blue eyes, and he is very fat. He is perfect."

She clung to his hand. She said, "Pericles," and she spoke of both her lover and her child. She slept again, her cheek in the palm of Pericles' hand, and she sighed with joy that the pain was over and that her bed was soft and that her beloved would never leave her.

To Aspasia, her child was a miracle. No other woman had ever given birth to such excellence, such beauty. She was amazed at him; she examined him with awe. It was morning and Pericles sat beside her in his rude countryman's tunic, his knees already burned by the sun, his stern face youthful. "Never was there such a wonder," she said to him, and he smiled. Helena, standing near him, said, "Life is always a wonder, and marvelous and full of mystery." Aspasia knew compassion for her friend, Helena, who had never given birth. She felt the strong sucking of her son at her breast, and she was overcome with happiness. She said to Helena, "Oh, beloved, if only you had given birth to a child!"

"The gods have been kind to me," said Helena in a satirical voice, and she pushed Pericles' shoulder.

She and Pericles went outside into the lyrical morning light. "What is it?" she asked of Pericles. "I heard a messenger ride up to this house just before dawn, and I see that you are greatly disturbed."

Pericles said, "I have just received a message that Anaxagoras has been arrested, on the accusation that he has been teaching impiety and heresy, and that death has been recommended for him."

Helena made a sound of angry protest. "What will you do?" she asked.

"I must return to Athens at once, and save him."

"Yes, you must go," she said. "Do not fear for Aspasia. Fear for Greece."

"Do I not always? The gods have struck her with lightning and glory, but there are always men! We must invariably fight our brothers that even they may survive and not be the victims of their own crimes and stupidity."

She put her hand on his arm and said with gentle affection, "Go at once. Do not see Aspasia again, lest she be troubled. I will tell her later."

CHAPTER 9

Pericles found Anaxagoras in the same prison where Ichthus had been incarcerated and had died. But Anaxagoras was not in a pleasant cell, for he was poor and only a philosopher. A dim lantern hung on the sweating walls of the corridor and shone fitfully into the cell, where Anaxagoras was lying on a bed of straw. Pericles had come directly from the road to this noisome place and was covered with silvery dust and was weary. Before he even spoke to his friend he said in cold rage to the guards, "Remove my friend immediately to a large cell with a window, and bring him wine and fruit and cheese and bread." He had seen a brown plate on the floor with a repulsive mixture on it, which Anaxagoras had not eaten.

Anaxagoras opened his great blue eyes and he started and gazed at Pericles with pleasure and raised himself on his elbow. His magnificent face was gaunt and drawn, but he had retained his air of utter serenity. He rose slowly to his feet while the guards unlocked the door of the cell. Pericles took him by the arm and, led by the guards, they proceeded to a larger, warmer and airier cell. A guard went for the ordered food and returned, placing it on a bare wooden table. During this interval Anaxagoras and Pericles did not speak, but only exchanged smiling glances.

When the astonished but respectful guards had left, saluting, Anaxagoras embraced Pericles and said, "I am overjoyed to see you, beloved friend, but you should not have come here. You endanger yourself."

"The time has come," said Pericles, "when one should not consider such danger, but how to preserve what small freedom we yet retain. Now, you must tell me the charges." He sat down at the table and poured wine for Anaxagoras and broke bread and cheese for him. They began to eat and drink together. Anaxagoras sank into thought and looked dreamily at the wall. Then he said, "I do not know. I was teaching in my small academe when the government guards arrested me. They told me I had committed an offense against the State, by impiety, heresy and corruption of youth, and so was an enemy of the people. On query they said the charges had been placed against me by Daedalus, the Archon."

"So," said Pericles. He had removed his dust-covered mantle and helmet. The light of the lantern flittered over his hard face and lofty forehead.

"I will, tomorrow, appear before the Assembly to defend you."

"I beg of you, no," said Anaxagoras, and his eyes filled with sharp anxiety. "Your former father-in-law will halt at nothing. He has powerful friends in the government."

"In short, they are striking at me through you," said Pericles. His weary face flushed with rage, but his voice remained quiet. "I will, then, be defending myself and my office against these scoundrels." He thought of his son, Paralus, and Aspasia, who had been wantonly attacked in order to injure him. "Do not protest. Had you not known me you should not now be in this predicament."

Anaxagoras shook his head. "You are wrong, dear friend. It would have happened to me eventually, even if you had not known me, as it has happened before to others."

But Pericles was frowning in thought. "Have they witnesses against you?"

Anaxagoras spread out his hands. "Who knows? My students? My friends, with whom I have conversed often? It is impossible to know."

"Be sure they have witnesses who will eagerly aid them to exile or imprison you or kill you. Doubtless, they are avowed friends."

Anaxagoras regarded him with compassion.

"Tell me," said Pericles, "have you been expounding some new theories which conflict with the accepted religious dogmas?"

Anaxagoras sank into thought. Finally he said, "They were extensions of what I have already been teaching. Only recently I repeated that there were no magical or supernatural or

439

godlike interventions in eclipses, meteors, rainbows or comets. They were only manifestations of the eternal order, founded by God, and could be predicted. You will remember I predicted an eclipse of the moon three weeks before it occurred, and related that it is but the shadow of the earth between the moon and the sun. This enraged the authorities, who, on the eclipse, called upon the people to pray that the moon would not be obliterated. They sent criers through the streets, shouting, armed with torches and carrying statues of the gods. My students laughed. This was unpardonable, of a certainty. The priests were particularly enraged. Had they been a little more stupid they would have declared that I, Anaxagoras, through sorcery, had caused the eclipse, but then the whole populace would have laughed."

He, himself, laughed gently, but Pericles remained somber.

"I wrote a thesis," said Anaxagoras, and Pericles winced. The written word was far more dangerous than the spoken. "I said it was my belief that all things that exist now had existed from eternity, and would continue to exist, whether it was the material of the stars and their planets or the life of living organisms. Not their immediate manifestations, but in other forms. While all is flux and change, the innate patterns remain, though giving rise to either more intricate manifestations or simpler on the base of their original matrix. This was because, I wrote, all matter, whether of stars or a blade of grass, are only an illusion of form, for all things are composed of infinite particles which are not matter at all, but only energy. In short, all things, suns, planets, galaxies, dust, trees, the earth itself, constellations, flowers, men, birds, insects, wheat, water, wine, houses and temples, mountains and marble, furniture and statues and murals, oceans and continents, are but one dynamic force and are indications of one endless pattern of energy which can change itself—perhaps by accident or by the will of God. There is only a Oneness in all that we see, hear, feel, touch, taste and smell, despite the apparent differentiations, and so variety of apparent objectivities is only an illusion. I even ventured," said Anaxagoras, "that nothing really exists but the Mind of God, which contains all manifestations and apparencies, and therefore is subjective."

When Pericles did not comment, Anaxagoras said, "To put it more simply, everything that exists is only in the Mind of God, and in His dreams, and there is nothing but His Mind."

Pericles put his head in his hands and groaned. "That neatly disposes of the gods, who, our priests say, are overt and material." He laughed grimly. "In short, as you surmise, the gods themselves are subjective."

Anaxagoras looked depressed. "That was possibly the conclusion of the priests." He added, "But, was my thesis blasphemous? God contains everything and all things. Surely that reveals His majesty. For He is all, and there is nothing else. He is Energy, itself, and weaves, like a weaver, patterns without end, and evokes changes which are yet the same. He cannot disobey His own divine Laws, which He established from eternity. If He once disobeyed His own Laws, then all would be chaos and darkness. He is the Law. If the Law disintegrates, nothing would exist any longer."

"I see," said Pericles. "Our gods constantly disobey the laws of decency, morals and justice and mercy. Therefore, they do not exist—except in particles of mindless energy," and he laughed without mirth.

"That is the interpretation of the priests of what I have taught. It is not mine."

"Did you truly expect that the average man would understand your thesis?"

"One can only try," replied Anaxagoras. "It is the duty of those who teach to speak the truth, though all teachers know only a small portion of what they teach. There is such a thing as integrity."

"Which is very rare," said Pericles.

Anaxagoras looked down at his veined and elegant hands. "I also wrote, in that thesis, that there is but one God, and not a variety of male and female antagonists."

"How thoroughly you disposed of all the goddesses," said Pericles, "and most of our gods."

"Who were created in our own image—by men," said Anaxagoras. He looked again into space. "There is but one God, in Whom all things exist. I wrote, in my thesis, that the endless color and forms of nature, in both land and sea, exist because He moved over the world in music, and in the diversities of His music rose the varieties which we discern, the multitude of varieties." His blue eyes sparked with fervor. "Who shall limit God to the dimensions of men? Only blasphemers."

"True," said Pericles, "therefore you must recant the truth."

"If I do, then am I myself destroyed and there is no meaning to my existence." His eyes glowed. "I believe in one God, eternal and unchanging, even if manifestations appear to change, as a lute and a lyre and a drum change tempo though remaining themselves as entities, unchanging."

He looked at Pericles earnestly. "Do you understand what I am saying?"

"I am no philosopher, Anaxagoras. I am only a politician. I discern, dimly, what you mean, but only dimly. Zeno would understand you more."

Anaxagoras sighed. "Philosophers are also egotists. They deny all philosophies but their own, which they believe is divine revelation."

"Including yours?"

Anaxagoras chuckled. "Including mine." Then his face became grave. "I do believe, however, that future ages will understand what I have been saying. Perhaps to their glory. Perhaps to their death. When men grasp the fact that all apparent things are only energy, and that energy can be manipulated— it may be the end." He was graver than before. "I do not dispute with God. But would it be wise to give man the secret of the universe?"

"Perhaps," said Pericles, "God is weary of man and his stupidities and his evils. Therefore, He will give the secret so that man can choose between life and death."

Pericles stood up and began to pace the cell. "That is a terrible and momentous choice, considering the limitations of men's capacities. It is as though we gave the secret of guiding a fleet into the hands of children." He looked at his friend. "Our minds approach the universal but our tongues are the gross tongues of apes. We communicate with each other in the meagre language of the jungle, even while our thoughts are afire. That is the tragedy of mankind."

"We must find a different mode of communication, then, Pericles. Mind to mind, and not tongue to tongue. For, despite what Socrates has said, there is no defining of terms which are relevant to every man. Our emotions intrude." He smiled faintly. "In the midst of discussions, sometimes flaming and exalted, my students have to repair to the latrines. When they have taken care of their animal needs the divine flame has left them."

"Perhaps that is the curse which God has inflicted on man." Pericles laughed. "It is possible that God, Himself, does not wish us to complete our knowledge, so our intestines demand our attention."

Anaxagoras said, "In the middle of an elevated conversation I spilled a plate of beans on my lap, and that ended the

442

discussion, as my students hovered about me—picking up the beans and commiserating and wiping the debris from my garments."

"It was possibly a relief for them. You terminated their thinking."

He refilled Anaxagoras' goblet and leaned back in his chair. The friends were much refreshed not only by the wine and food but by their conversation. Pericles said, "If I let this pass, and they exile or kill you, then I am guilty of betraying my country. So, I will not let this pass." He looked at his friend, who was about to protest. "I assume, for the sake of peace and your freedom and your life, that you will not recant, and beg the pardon of the government?"

"Of a certainty, no!" exclaimed Anaxagoras, astonished. "I cannot deny the truth I know."

"Hmm. Do you recall what Sophocles has told us: 'Truly, to tell lies is not honorable, but, when the truth entails tremendous ruin, to speak dishonorably is pardonable'? I agree. Again, it is not you who is on trial, Anaxagoras. It is the freedom of Athens."

"You believe that Athens, and freedom, can be saved by lies?"

Pericles shrugged. "When I was younger I would have denied that. Now I am a middle-aged man and no longer young and I know that in the cause of truth lies are sometimes necessary, paradoxical though that seems."

"Did you tell that to Ichthus?"

"I did. But he was too emotional to listen and to understand."

"And so he died for truth."

Pericles shrugged again. "It would have been better if he had lived, by a lie, so that he could later utter the truth and perhaps with impunity."

Anaxagoras pondered. He was no passionate young man like Ichthus. Pericles said, "Would you at least hold your tongue while I defend you?"

The older man began to smile. "It may be a good comedy."

"What, in life, is not?" Pericles was relieved. "If truth is so dear to you then you have no right to condemn it to death. It deserves to live—to flourish again in another time. You are no tragedian, Anaxagoras, who makes a sublime gesture in the face of the gods, and defies them. You are more discreet. Therefore, again, in the name of truth, live."

"You are very eloquent and persuasive, dear friend. Perhaps Sophocles is right. Gestures may be heroic, but it is possibly better to be silent. Gestures are for the stage." He sighed deeply. "I do not lust to be a martyr, and certainly not a sacrificial bull for the priests and the government."

His face saddened. "But can I live with myself? My students would no longer believe what I said. They would think I betrayed them, and that my words had been foolish."

"The true ones among them will understand. The others will only be satisfied, and the self-satisfaction of rascals is amusing in itself. For they never believed you anyway."

Anaxagoras burst out, "The moral purity of the immoral corrupt! That is what we are fighting! The sanctimony of the base!"

Pericles picked up his mantle and shook it. "I have not told you. I have a son, as young as the morning, and as beautiful."

Anaxagoras rose and embraced him. "He will be a glory to you and to Aspasia."

"Who knows? You will see I am again melancholy. The dark Sisters, the Fates, have the thread of his life in their hands, for good or evil, and who can know what pattern they are weaving for my son?" He added, "Or for me, or for you?"

Pericles left with a lighter heart than he had come. Anaxagoras was a sensible man. He had immediately discerned that he need not deny the truth. He had only to be quiet. Truth should not be shouted from the rooftops; it should move with the wise subtlety of the serpent, and often in silence. Then it was potent.

When Pericles had left, Anaxagoras sat thinking. Years ago he had rebuked Pericles for his proposed plan to save Ichthus. But age brought more hesitation, more weighing of facts, more thought for the future and its consequences. Too, Ichthus would have condemned himself openly before the Assembly and the Ecclesia, and that would have endangered Pericles beyond hope. Pericles, at that time, had not been above gestures, himself! Anaxagoras smiled wryly.

Before going to the place of judgment, before the King Archon, Pericles first went to his offices and studied some of his dossiers. He wrote some short notes on a tablet and put them in his pouch. He had dressed himself soberly, in a blue tunic and a gray toga and he wore black shoes. His helmet had been polished diligently. He had gargled with honey and water so that the full power of his sonorous and eloquent voice would not be impaired. Composing himself, for at intervals his cold and bitter internal rage became unusually intense, he went to the place of judgment. He knew that the King Archon, a noble and just man, would listen with gravity and detachment to the accusation and defense of Anaxagoras, but if he was convinced that Anaxagoras was indeed an enemy of the people and State, and a corrupter of youth, he would not refrain from ordering even the extreme punishment. Pericles had rarely seen him smile, for he took all things seriously.

The huge jury was already assembled, and Pericles, somewhat to his dismay, found that many members of the Assembly and the Eleven, and the Ecclesia were there also, all avid, like men in the theatre awaiting a bloody drama. The spring day was hot. The judgment hall was crowded and very warm, and the high small windows let in shafts of smarting sun and the effluvium of the Agora. When the stately Pericles entered, all eyes turned upon him, and he knew, as he had guessed before, that Anaxagoras was not the chief accused, but himself. Some of his friends were there, also, standing against the ochre walls, a number of them with foreboding that one day, sooner or later, they would be the accused and suffer ostraka or death. They watched Pericles' approach before the high seat and bench of the King Archon, and their quiet eyes were anxious.

Also before the bench was the Archon, Daedalus. Pericles turned very slowly and studied him as a gentleman studies some obnoxious sight—that is, with an expression of faint incredulity, faint astonishment, and cool aversion. The aged Archon, bent and even more skeleton-like than he had been at the marriage of Pericles and Dejanira, returned Pericles' gaze with venom, his face writhing and wrinkling so that he resembled an ancient ape with jaundice. His sunken eyes were fiery, vindictive and almost insanely fierce, and his mouth twisted as if he wished to spit but his throat was too dry. He trembled visibly with his hatred; his hands appeared palsied. All looked at both the men, some gloating and anticipatory, some with alarm. Anaxagoras became insignificant before these two mortal antagonists, who loathed each other.

At a silent gesture from the King Archon, Anaxagoras was brought into the hall, walking as tall and regnant as a king, for all chains dripped from his wrists. His wonderful head was lifted. He moved with serenity and that dignity which only men who do not fear death can bring to cover them like an invincible armor. He was thrust before the bench, between Pericles and Daedalus. He bowed courteously to the King Archon. He smiled gently on Pericles and did not give Daedalus, his accuser, a single glance. Now the hall became very still, and all leaned forward so as not to miss a word or a gesture.

The King Archon spoke: "Daedalus, you have brought charges against the teacher and philosopher, Anaxagoras, who stands before us. Repeat the charges you have made to me." The King Archon's folded hands were clasped together on the bench before him.

Now Daedalus shook as if a wind had struck him. Some thought he would fall. Others believed he had been seized by a fit and would hurl himself to the floor, foaming and twisting in all his limbs. His dull garments of brown actually blew over his emaciated body. The King Archon observed this with silent detachment, waiting. Pericles pretended that he saw nothing. He was studying his notes. Quickly he glanced at some of the members of the government whom he knew hated him and had come here as to a slaughter. His face had taken on that deadly and daunting expression, and they saw it and a few moved uneasily. They were all powerful men.

Daedalus found his voice, as cawing as a crow. He pointed his finger at Anaxagoras and said, "I accuse this man of impiety and heresy and the corruption of our youth! I have heard him speak, myself, to the innocent boys and other students, and my heart and soul were shaken with wrath and outrage, and, yes, fear of the gods whom he had so insulted!"

"You must be specific," said the King Archon in a steadfast voice. "Tell me. What has the prisoner said in your hearing?"

"That the gods do not exist, that they are fantasies of mist, that they have no being!" The caw rose to a loud croak, and a stammering. "He denied the verity of the gods. With these ears I heard it, and that I swear by the sacred names of Castor and Pollux."

Pericles' enemies affected to be horrified, and a loud groaning filled the hall and men looked, as if astounded and aghast, into each other's eyes. Pericles smiled faintly and with obvious contempt at them.

The King Archon motioned to Pericles, who gave Anaxagoras, who seemed about to speak, a quelling glance. Then Pericles smiled broadly and shook his head as though he found the charge absurd and fit only for laughter.

His voice, clear and strong and vivid, rose when he turned fully to Daedalus. His brows lifted in pretended amazement and his smile was the indulgent one that one gives to a child or a senile old man. All listened acutely.

"My dear Daedalus, most honored Daedalus, surely you do not believe that the gods are of our gross flesh and material, and are only enlarged men? You do not believe they are mortal and will suffer death?"

"No!" screamed Daedalus, in a frenzy.

"No?" repeated Pericles, in surprise. "But that is what you imply. Homer has written that the gods ride on the wind, are often invisible and impalpable, can pass through matter and substance as if matter and substance did not exist, can change form and shape. They are protean. Do you deny this?"

"No!" howled Daedalus with fury.

"No?" said Pericles. "Then you agree with Anaxagoras that the Godhead is immaterial Mind and that all apparent things dwell in It. For that is what he maintains, and I, too, have heard him often."

Daedalus could not speak. Pericles said with kindness, "You do agree with Anaxagoras in this?"

Daedalus still did not speak. He was shaking again. The King Archon said sternly, "Answer, Daedalus."

Daedalus wrung his hands. His eyes darted frantically. Pericles said, "Perhaps it is you, dear friend, who defames the gods and would bring them down to the earthly gutter in which we all wallow?"

Daedalus spoke hoarsely, "If that is what Anaxagoras maintains, I must agree with him."

"You thought that when Anaxagoras compared them with radiant mist, with the deepest and most subjective adoration a man can feel, and that when he implied that they are not in our context of existence, you believed he was denying their being?"

When Daedalus was speechless again Pericles smiled at him tenderly. "It is all a matter of semantics. You are not to blame, dear friend. We all misunderstand each other, for words are clumsy stones and they lie heavily in our mouths."

"Do you wish to withdraw the charge of impiety, Daedalus?" asked the King Archon and his beard about his mouth stirred a little, as if with a smile.

"In that one instance," Daedalus muttered. His bony cheeks had become dusky.

Pericles let the silence of the hall expand while he appeared to muse kindly on Daedalus, who looked at him with a helpless if ferocious malignity.

The King Archon said to the jury, "The charge of impiety —that the gods do not exist—is removed from Anaxagoras." He said to Daedalus, with some sternness, "Do you wish to continue with your other charges?"

Daedalus gathered himself together as a vulture gathers himself, preparing to pounce. He pointed to Anaxagoras, who seemed to have withdrawn to a great distance and was meditating.

"This creature," Daedalus said, "has declared that eclipses are not supernatural manifestations of the gods, but are natural phenomena, and therefore are not omens, as our religious teachers have taught us! He has even declared that they can be predicted!"

Pericles' pale eyes enlarged in amazement. He stared at Daedalus as one stares disbelievingly when hearing incredible things. He said, "But Anaxagoras did predict an eclipse of the moon very recently."

Daedalus shrilled at him, "Who can explain that? Was it chance? Was it some dire magic? Did some malevolent demon whisper it to him? Only he can tell!"

Pericles shook his head, incredulously, and turned to the King Archon. "Lord," he said, "we Greeks boast, and with some reason, that we have a grand new age not only of the arts and philosophy, but also of science. I only pray to God, and with due reverence for Athens, that the Egyptians and the Chaldeans do not hear of this trial, and the words of Daedalus! How they would laugh at what they would call our pretensions to glory and reason!"

A deep growling roved through the hall and angry eyes focused now on Pericles, and men exchanged outraged glances. The King Archon remained calm. He stroked his beard thoughtfully. He said, "Noble Pericles, we should like to hear you elucidate more on this matter."

Silence fell again. Hundreds of eyes glared at Pericles.

He said, "Lord, the Egyptians and Chaldeans through their wise men, their scientists, have been predicting eclipses almost to the exact moment for hundreds of years. Before Anaxagoras came to Athens he studied among those scientists." Anaxagoras made a quick movement, as if to protest, but Pericles ignored the gesture and raised his voice. Now it was grave, earnest, almost confidential, even pleading.

"Let us pray that they do not hear of this folly. They are already envious of what we are accomplishing here. Let us give them no reason to jeer at us and call us barbarians, as they have done in the past. Their scientists would be appalled at the ignorance of—Daedalus. But one must excuse him. He is a very old man and has not had the advantages of an extended education in science."

The King Archon almost imperceptibly smiled. The hall was hushed.

Pericles continued, "So, let us not spread the word of what

has been said in this august chamber, for surely every Greek would be embarrassed, and with excellent justification." He cast down his eyes as if with shame, and a heavy murmur rose from the assembled men, sullen yet uneasy.

"Sorcery!" shrieked Daedalus. "It is only sorcery!"

Pericles shook his head sadly. "So unlearned men through the ages have proclaimed, when confronted with something which refutes their prejudices, their unreason. But, we are Greeks. We have reached the Age of true Enlightenment, and what our elders believed was the truth we now see as superstition or obtuseness."

"Heresy," said Daedalus and flung out his arms.

Pericles now became stern. "What is heresy?" he demanded. "Is it not the impotent cry of those who do not know what true heresy is? True heresy is that which refuses to accept truth, which limits the capacity of man to think, which belittles our nature, which denies that we are more than animals, which would blind us to knowledge and prevent us from increasing our stature, which stands at the portals of learning with a savage sword, which will not let us enter the temples to look upon the manifestations of the Godhead, which fears the light and declares that it is darkness and an illusion. In truth, heresy is a denial of God, Himself! All that inhibits the increase of human knowledge, human wisdom, human reverence, human achievement, human awareness of God, human glory, is heresy. Heresy is that which cramps the soul and the spirit of man, those which emerged from God's breath. Heresy is that which would force us to walk in the dust and not lift our eyes to the heavens. Heresy is that which would fill up the footsteps of the gods with mud, and declares that all things are dead and nothing is sentient, especially not the human mind. Heresy is that which worships stone and not that which the stone represents—the Being of God, His visage."

His eloquent voice held everyone as still as the stone of which he had spoken. He turned to Daedalus with a gesture of repudiation, as if he were trying to control his indignation.

"It is you, Daedalus, who, by your own words, are a heretic! You would enclose the soul of Greece in clay and obliterate her features! If that is not heresy against God and man—" He stopped, evidently overcome, and his loud breath was heard in the silent hall.

Daedalus shrank. He had not understood much of what Pericles had said, but now he was aware that he was in some danger, himself, and he could feel vexed and umbrageous eyes upon him from every quarter. The King Archon gently pulled his own beard and looked at the old man.

"Speak, Daedalus," he said.

Pericles raised a respectful hand. "Lord, he is an old man and his wits are confused and he does not recognize heresy when he hears it. Let us not be without mercy, without understanding. He has not had the advantages of this age of Athens. His youth was constricted, narrow. He accepted the word of ignorant men as the truth, of stupid teachers, as learning. Must we condemn him for what he did not know, for what he was not taught? If he has offended God, surely He has compassion, understanding the limits of Daedalus' mind."

Daedalus clenched his withered fists and cried, leaning towards Pericles, "I spit on you, wily liar and deceiver, who with words can addle the thoughts of just men!"

Pericles was never so dignified and aloof as when he wiped the spittle from his cheek. He looked imploringly at the King Archon, who rubbed his lips to quiet the involuntary smile which had begun to move them. But he said to Daedalus, with severity, "This is unpardonable. We are reasonable men in this chamber. We are here to listen to arguments, and not to spit like unweaned children. If this occurs again, Daedalus, I will order the police to seize and confine you."

As all honored the King Archon they were moved to reluctant vexation against Daedalus, and even Pericles' enemies felt admiration for his dexterity and eloquence. Daedalus shrank; purple pulses beat visibly in his temples. He almost whimpered, "Lord, King Archon, I forgot myself in my sincere anger against this Anaxagoras and against him who dares occupy the highest position in Athens while profaning her name and her gods."

A faint murmur of amusement trembled in the hot air of the chamber, and smiles were exchanged among the jury.

The King Archon said, "Let us continue. Your next charge, Daedalus?"

The frail breast of Daedalus heaved. He looked about to expire, but his glance at Anaxagoras was strangely violent.

"I have heard him say, with these ears, that in Greece wise men spoke but fools decided! He defamed our government—"

Pericles gave such an exaggerated start, and looked so aghast that Daedalus stopped speaking. Then Pericles turned to Anaxagoras with a countenance full of pale reproach. All were then immediately attentive.

"My dear friend," said Pericles to Anaxagoras, "I cannot believe this of you, that you did not give the credit for those

450

salient words to their author, Anacharsis, the Scythian philosopher, to his beloved friend, Solon, the sacred father of our incomparable laws! With Anacharsis did Solon agree, and in sadness. How is it possible that you did not attribute the words you spoke to Anacharsis?"

"I did," said Anaxagoras, and his great blue eyes glinted with mirth. "But it is probable that Daedalus had never heard of Anacharsis."

Pericles covered his eyes with his hand and sorrowfully shook his head. When he dropped his hand there were actual tears in his eyes. Now he looked fully at the jury and then at the whole assemblage, which was showing signs of acute embarrassment.

"Alas," said Pericles, "this august company has been presented another evidence of piteous ignorance. Again, let us be compassionate."

Daedalus almost went mad with rage. He even struck the sides of his cheeks with his clenched fists, and some of the jury involuntarily laughed until halted by the imposing frown of the King Archon. "Let us have no levity here," he said. "This is the court of justice," and he glanced at Pericles, " 'founded by the sacred father of our incomparable laws.' "

The friends of Pericles stifled their happy chuckles and the jury and the members of the government assumed an air of gravity, though inwardly they seethed against Pericles and Anaxagoras.

The King Archon let his weariness become plainly seen. He said to Daedalus, "Your next charge."

"Pederasty," Daedalus squeaked. "The foulest crime against nature!"

No one moved. But Pericles turned and with slow glances like shards of ice he fixed one man after another with his eyes, and each man who encountered his glances shrank and huddled himself in his robes. But Pericles held them with those cold and rigorous looks and they could not turn away. Many were almost overcome with terror.

"Pederasty," said Pericles, with loathing. "No doubt every man in this chamber is horrified at the very word, and recalls his own virtue to mind. No doubt that every man here is guiltless of such an act, and shudders even as it is mentioned."

He, himself, shuddered elaborately. Then he took his notes from his pouch and studied them carefully, letting his brows lift to the rim of his helmet, and letting murmurs of shocked disgust rise from his lips. And each man, watching him, felt his terror increase, and each wondered what names were listed on those notes in Pericles' hand, praying that his own was not among them. The King Archon watched their faces and tight lines appeared about his eyes.

Pericles raised his eyes and said to Daedalus, "And who was Anaxagoras' eromenos (male adolescent lover)?"

Daedalus' frantic eyes went at once to one of the Archons, who had two adolescent lovers, and what he saw on the face of his friend made him quiver, for the other Archon was a man of remorseless vengeance when offended.

Pericles patiently repeated his question, then added, "You have accused Anaxagoras of corrupting our youth, and have said that he is the erastes (older male lover of an adolescent male) of at least one boy. It is true that our laws forbid pederasty, which openly flourishes in Sparta. But we are Athenians, and do not practice perversions. I have heard rumors, however—Let us continue with Anaxagoras. You have said that he is the erastes of a youth, or youths. You have not named names, Daedalus, though we have been patient. Is it possible, too, that you know those among us who do practice pederasty? If so, it is your duty to name them immediately."

He looked at the King Archon with deep seriousness. "Is it not his duty to accuse others, also, of the crime of which he accuses Anaxagoras?"

"It is his duty," affirmed the King Archon.

Fear nearly caused Daedalus' collapse on the spot, for he felt at least a dozen pairs of threatening eyes upon him. He tried to moisten his gray lips, but he could not speak.

"If a man accuses another man of a crime, and speaks his name, and knows of the same crime among others of his acquaintance, then in justice he should name them all," said Pericles. "Is that not so, lord?" he asked the King Archon.

"It is also the law," said the King Archon. He looked at Daedalus. "If you have the name of any eromenos of Anaxagoras', speak now, and also speak the names of those who are also guilty."

Daedalus dropped his head on his breast. "It is possibly only a rumor—"

"A court of law is not the place for rumor," said the King Archon. "You have uttered a vile slander against Anaxagoras, which is punishable. Therefore, you are fined five talents, Daedalus."

When Daedalus was struck dumb the King Archon said, "I have observed your countenance. You know of men here who are truly guilty, for I have followed your eyes. Speak then, their names."

It was then that the relentless Archon rose with a rustle of his robes and bowed to the King Archon. "Lord," he said, "my fellow Archons and I have come to the conclusion that all that Daedalus has said is a slander, the foolish wet mouthings of a senile and pathetic old man."

The King Archon gazed at him for a long time, then looked at several others, who tried to avoid his eyes.

He said, "I agree with you, Hyperbolus. We have wasted precious hours of our time in this chamber. But when one of the position of Daedalus makes reckless charges against another we are compelled to listen, for is he not an Archon?" He paused and said with quiet meaning, "And are we not all honorable men?"

He let his glance rove slowly over the jury. "To what conclusion have you gentlemen come?"

Several members of the jury rose and said with reluctance, "We agree that Anaxagoras is not guilty of any of the charges brought against him by Daedalus. We do not approve of Anaxagoras, but he has done no obvious wrong."

The King Archon next turned to Pericles. "Is there aught you wish to say, Pericles, son of Xanthippus?"

Pericles sighed, and wiped away non-existent sweat from his forehead. It was as if he were very tired. Then he addressed the whole assemblage, and only the King Archon and Anaxagoras heard the irony in his resonant voice.

"I have always been proud, as Head of State, of the nobility and balanced judgment of the men of Athens. We are all but human, yet sometimes we rise to grandeur, as the acropolis is now rising. What stands there, what is being built there, is a poor if beautiful reflection of the Athenian soul, the glory of that soul. Let no man now or in the future denigrate Athens, her integrity, her holy passion and reverence for beauty, her arts, her scientists, her philosophers. But above all, let all admire, in every corner of this world, the spectacle of our matchless impartiality, our craving for the orderly processes of law which were given to us by Solon. Where else in the world do such processes exist? Who can be compared with us? Despotisms abound, tyrannies which will not let a man speak the truth or lift his head as a man and not a slave, and who exact the last coin of tribute from their helpless people.

"But in Athens a man is free. His opinions may not be honored or regarded highly, but he may speak them—as you have

453

permitted Anaxagoras to speak. You have refuted slanders with that mighty sense of justice which only Athenians possess. There are some among us, I admit, who possess the tarnish of a despot's evil urges, but only a few. Only a few. But from those few may the gods deliver us!"

Even his enemies felt their hearts swell with emotion at this subtle flattery of themselves, and they experienced a thrill of gratitude for Pericles who had so elevated them in their own estimations. For a brief moment or two they actually loved him and forgot their enmity. As for the men who had known terror, they sweated with relief and were grateful to Pericles for delivering them from open accusations. Some of them said to themselves: "That fool of a Daedalus nearly destroyed us. We must warn him to hold his tongue hereafter."

The King Archon ordered the chains to be struck from the wrists and ankles of Anaxagoras, who stood there eying Pericles with a most peculiar smile. The King Archon then rose and all bowed to him, even the Head of State, Pericles himself. The King Archon retired from the chamber and a loud buzzing of voices rose as a storm of bees in the hall. No one noticed that Daedalus, staggering, was leaving like a gaunt shadow.

Pericles himself led Anaxagoras from the chamber. "Come with me to my offices, for a little refreshment," said Pericles. "My throat is dry."

"I do not doubt it," said Anaxagoras. "My dear friend, you are worthy of the most prominent role on the stage."

"Tut," said Pericles. "Do I not always speak the truth?"

"No," said Anaxagoras, smiling. Then his face changed. "But I am afraid I have not heard the last of this."

That night the unfortunate Daedalus, consumed by his own rage and defeat, had a seizure and died before dawn. To the last he cursed Pericles.

Dejanira, his daughter, wrote to her son in Cyprus: "My dearest Callias, what calamity has fallen on this house! My beloved father, and your grandfather, has died in his bed, in our arms, weeping. Alas, it was his own fury against Pericles which killed him." She then related what Daedalus had incoherently gasped before he succumbed.

On receiving her letter Callias lifted his hand in an oath and said, "We will be avenged! Of a certainty, we will be avenged!"

CHAPTER 10

Socrates said to Pericles, "This, of course, is not the end."

"In the meantime," replied Pericles, "let us not anticipate trouble before it arrives. Each day we live is a day gained."

"We, your friends, are alarmed for you, Pericles."

"So am I," said Pericles, laughing.

"You are an orator," said Zeno of Elea.

"Have I not had an excellent teacher—you?"

"Alas, what a world this is," said Pheidias.

"When was it not? It was and ever will be a dangerous and precarious planet, full of evil and contention, of malice and envy, of death and fury, of murder and pillage, of lies and hatred. Human nature is, was, and always will be detestable and unchangeable. We are a monstrous species."

He looked at his friends and added, "With rare exceptions. But you are in this world but not of it. There is a difference. Future ages will proclaim your names, forgetting that you were outlaws among your contemporaries, just as they will persecute their own contemporaries who are superior, leaving them for future generations to extol."

Zeno of Elea said, somewhat sadly, "You grow more caustic and embittered with time, my dear Pericles. But then, you are not a philosopher."

"Thank the gods! I, therefore, will not perish."

His enemies in the government, however, declined to sanction the name of his illegitimate son, the infant Pericles, and refused that name on its records.

Aspasia was too wise a woman to attempt to soothe Pericles with the metaphorical substitute of a honeyed tit, as one soothes a fractious or frightened infant. She said, "Our son is Pericles, in our minds and our hearts, and so he will be called among us and in our houses. The malice of governments is always present, and its attempts to punish its adversaries or those who criticise it. It should not be pertinent to our own lives. We should remember who and what it is, and disdain it."

"Unfortunately, it has the power to defame, exile, depose and even kill," said Pericles, who was both humiliated and angered at the insult. He knew now why some men like himself desire to be dictators, when inflamed, mortified or impatient with lesser functionaries of government. He knew that his own government, and many of the rabble, were accusing him of plotting to become a monarch or at least a dictator. He told this to Aspasia. She touched his cheek gently with her soft hand. She smiled and dimpled.

"That, too, has its worth, for it is only when the lesser functionaries of government, and the rabble, fawn unanimously on a man that he can attain depotism."

He laughed. "So I am kept in salutary check! I do, at times, have an imperative impulse to override the rules and regulations of the functionaries and the bureaucrats with one powerful gesture—which, I am certain—would cow them. Adversaries, I see, cannot only be abrasive and irritating, but can make a man pause and take measure of himself, unpleasant though that is."

Aspasia now lived almost always in his house, for he feared for her since the birth of his son. They resumed their dinners for their friends and the long and exciting conversations which ensued during them. Only Aspasia observed that Anaxagoras was unusually silent these nights, or started when someone addressed him. Since his trial and exoneration he had become melancholy, though he continued to have his academe and to speak in the colonnades. However, it was as if some vital virtue had either been wounded in him, or lost. Each time she saw him Aspasia became more anxious, for he was aging. Sometimes his hands trembled. There were rumors that he was mocked and threatened on the streets even more than usual, and that his little modest house was stoned. If this were true he did not speak of it.

Xanthippus, the enthusiastic soldier, and Paralus, an avid student, loved their infant brother and played with him at all opportunities, remarking how much he resembled their adored father. The child had a merry temperament, like Aspasia, and his father's stateliness also. He was strong and vigorous. "What an athlete for the Olympian Games he will be," said Xanthippus. "And what a soldier."

The young men were now permitted to join the dinners and discussions in the house of their father. They saw that not only were gifted and beautiful hetairai present but the advanced wives of many of Pericles' friends. The dinners, because of Aspasia who presided, were becoming more and more famous throughout Athens, and hundreds of wives became rebellious against their husbands who kept them in subservience, and hundreds of daughters demanded the education given their brothers. The young ladies, graduates of Aspasia's school, often refused the husbands chosen for them and insisted on their right to choose their own. They did not encounter much opposition, however, for their parents had sent them to Aspasia. But the girls' influence extended to their friends, who had not had their own opportunities, and this outraged more conservative parents.

In the meanwhile Pericles was being attacked covertly in the theatre, to the hilarity even of his adherents. Cratinus, the poet and playwright, had an actor declaim:

> *"Here's Pericles, our own squill-headed Zeus.*
> *Where did he buy that hat? What, what excuse?*
> *It's new head-cover in Odeum style,*
> *Late storms of censure hardly left a tile."*

Not only then did he mockingly liken Pericles to Zeus, as did other poets and playwrights. In his *Chiron* he derided:

> *"Strife and old father Chronus went together to bed*
> *And gave birth to the mightiest tyrant,*
> *Whom the gods call Head-gatherer."*

(This, referring to Pericles' towering brow and helmet.)

Pericles, however much he despised his fellow aristocrats and the market rabble (who appeared to have too many things in common), had no desire to be a tyrant, not even over his mockers and foes. He might, in his secret anger, wish to bang their heads together and to order them to refrain from their iniquities, and command them, but his emotions were never translated into action. He only watched them assiduously. If others found it strange that the aristocratic nobles of Athens, fastidious and discriminatory, and the odoriferous rabble had a deep accord, Pericles did not. The aristocrats (though they figuratively and sometimes literally held their noses) consorted in private with the rabble. They pretended to deplore the "tyranny" of Pericles, who opposed all laws giving the rabble free bread and meat and cheese and housing and demanded that they work for a living. "He has no compassion on the unfortunate," the aristocrats would say to leaders of the rabble. "He has no mercy on the deprived and the humble. He despises those in want, and would have them starve. What is the treasury and gold of a people compared with a single human life? Should not taxes be used to alleviate distress and illness and starvation among our people? Are we not equal in our humanity? What pains Pericles in his flesh and belly pains the people of Athens also. He has physicians and medicine and fine food and shelter. You, our poor friends, have none of these. He builds grandiloquent temples and wastes your substance. While a gold and ivory statue is being raised in the Parthenon your children cry for bread, and you desire the barest amenities of living and have them not. Who can compare the house of Pericles with your huts? Our hearts bleed for you."

None of the rabble appeared to notice that their friends, the aristocrats, parted not with a single drachma to relieve their alleged miserable state. When Hippocrates' influence persuaded physicians that infirmias for the destitute should be built, the very "friends of the humble" opposed them, for such infirmias would cost them money in increased taxes. When Pericles insisted that the noisome hovels of the poor should be destroyed and more agreeable housing be built, his fellow aristocrats raised an outcry over his "extravagance, and his hypocritical desire to be known, unrighteously, as a humanitarian."

Pericles, bitterly, understood the motives of the wealthy aristocrats. They were using the rabble against him, to impeach him. If, he would say, these gilded traitors attained their object and became omnipotent, they would at once enslave and subjugate the poor whom they pretended to respect and pity. They, the lovers of the poor, the champions of the afflicted, lusted for power above all things. They, in their souls, hated the populace, and despised them.

Daily the rage of the rabble increased and became more vociferous and audible against Pericles. The aristocrats smiled happily under their noses. The middle class was alarmed at the growing hostility against the man they so deeply admired and trusted. They knew that he stood between them and exploitation by the lazy and worthless, and between them and their natural enemies—the rich patricians. They sent him delegates to extend their love to him, their trust, their faith. Though these were not scholars their deep instincts warned them that their destruction was being plotted by the aristocrats through their minions, the rabble. If they did not know that the aristocrats called them "upstarts, who are inimical to the glory of Greece and would subdue her to the rule of dull merchants and shopkeepers," they dimly suspected the truth. But they sensed, in their strong spirits, that if they disappeared and the aristocrats were solely in authority and the rabble were slaves, Greece would become a despotism.

Sometimes Pericles pondered: "Who had said that a despotism meant wolves on the top and jackals on the bottom?"

Aspasia said, "I think you did, beloved," to which he responded with gloom, "It does sound like me."

His endless troubles with Sparta and other city-states were increasing, but he was now so obsessed with the saving of Athens and the buildings on the acropolis and the dilemma of his intellectual friends that he had little time to think of them. His government seemed to be apathetic and offered no suggestions and no assistance—and this made him suspicious. Sparta, believing he had become weak, daily became more aggressive, and incited other sister cities against him. Aspasia, who was not tormented daily as was her lover by the hostile government and the aristocrats, heard of Sparta and her determination to take over trade and commerce from Athens, and subjugate her. Because Pericles came to her and their son with smiles and embraces and jests, she tried to believe that he had complete control over all things. Thargelia would have smiled at this, saying, "Women attribute prescience to the men they love, which can be a mortal error."

In the midst of all his worries the young city-state of Italy, Rome, sent a commission to him, through her Senate, of three earnest Romans, "in order that you, lord, can instruct them in the creation of a perfect and just Republic, as established by your great law-giver, Solon, and which has made Greece the wonder of the world." Pericles, on receiving the message announcing the imminent arrival of the Romans, laughed with mirthless and cynical hilarity. But Aspasia said, "Why disillusion these honest men with the truth? Let them establish their republic, according to Solon, and perhaps they will realize the dream which Athens never attained, a dream which other nations may make into a glorious reality."

"But these barbarian Romans are also men, and inevitably, despite their labors, they will become corrupt and establish a democracy and hence a despotism." Yet secretly he felt a deep pity for the Romans and a sadness for their hopes. He prepared to receive them with solemn respect, and ceremony. This made the aristocrats restive and contemptuous. "He will honor barbarians," they said, "barbarians without an aristocratic tradition, and entertain them lavishly at governmental expense, which will come out of the pockets of the working poor."

Pericles addressed the Assembly: "We have been laughing at this small and virtuously ambitious city-state in Italy, but who knows what the future will bring? They may be only farmers and little wine-makers and shopkeepers; it is possible

459

that tomorrow, if they remain industrious and pious and honor God and humanity and patriotism and justice, they may become, too, of a grand stature." This highly amused many of the Assembly and the Archons and the Eleven and the Ecclesia. "He is growing senile," they said among themselves. "The values he extols are the petty follies of the middle class. He apparently does not know that the world is now sophisticated and that most of us have discarded those so-called virtues as the prejudices of our humble fathers who had no advantages and no wide learning." With superb tolerance they consented to give the Roman barbarians some deference, for were they, themselves, not educated and indulgent gentlemen? As cultivated men they would not insult even foreign savages, who yearned to imitate them.

"We have heard they are a village of grocers," one man said to Pericles, who replied, "Grocers are estimable. Let us not despise men who work." He added, "We of Athens have come to belittle labor as fit only for slaves, but I tell you that white hands never built a nation or maintained it. Labor is the cornerstone of grandeur, and he who denies that is not worthy of his bread."

He personally met and greeted the Romans at the port, clad in ceremonial attire, with an honor guard headed by his trusted lieutenant, Iphis. When the three Romans left the ship drums were sounded, trumpets flared and colors were dipped. Pericles advanced, bowing, then extended his hand solemnly to each Roman in turn. His perceptive eye swept them, and he felt a warm impulse of approval. They were short but bulky men, not fat though muscular, and about forty years old. They had strong and serious faces with large noses, dark eyes and firm full lips, and their hands were calloused and familiar with work. Their hair was severely cropped, their dress sober, and they wore no jewelry. They looked like farmers, for their faces were browned by sun, and their shoulders were massive. They wore plain leather shoes, crudely but sturdily made. Pericles saw clear intelligence in their eyes, though he detected from their sincere expressions that they lacked the urbane humor of Athenians. Each carried one small chest, and none had attendants. They walked weightily as men walk who have trudged the earth and have sweated, and have guided plows and have builded houses. They were men with a purpose, and Pericles trusted them immediately. It was obvious they were peasants.

He took them to his house in his large awninged car, which was drawn by four magnificent white Arabian horses bright with silver harness. They watched everything with grave and alert eyes, and did not pretend that they were not impressed as the car passed grand houses and elaborate government buildings. When they glimpsed the acropolis and the now-completed Parthenon—shining like silver gilt in the morning sun—they audibly drew deep breaths of awe and admiration. Their knowledge of Greek was poor, and their voices were hoarse and loud, as are the voices who call to cattle and swine. They had the genuine dignity of simple men who esteem themselves without vanity, and who honor themselves and their country. Pericles loved them more and more. He pointed out spots of historic interest. They had, at first, been somewhat taciturn with him, as a superior man, but his manners, his kindness, his obvious respect for them as the men they were, reassured them and they spoke to him in the spirit of equality as members of government. They were not ignorant. In slow sentences they mentioned the history of Athens; they were conversant with the civilizations of Egypt also, and other eastern nations.

In short, they were such men as once lived in Greece, proud and steadfast. Alas, thought Pericles, their tribe will disappear as our tribe of husbandmen disappeared, and their children's children will dishonor their memory and call them simpletons.

They knew much of Sparta, and questioned Pericles. He smiled. "This is a most auspicious and pleasant occasion for me," he said. "I pray that you will not darken it." They laughed loudly, an honest and knowing laughter. "We Romans, too, have trouble with city-states in Italy," they said. "We wish to live and flourish in peace and in trade, but others challenge us."

"It is the way of all men," said Pericles, without originality.

They told him of Cincinnatus, the Father of his Country, who had left his flocks and his fields to defend Rome, and to give it a government which all could revere and respect. "Dusty he came from the meadows, walking barefooted through our streets, his noble head high, his beard flecked with straw, his stride the stride of a man who cannot be turned from principle. When he spoke it was as though a trumpet sounded, for he was a man of truth. Even evil men were silenced by the sound of that voice, the voice of patriotic

461

fervor and conviction. He honored the gods with devotion, as a man of integrity must. For what can destroy a nation if God is with her?"

Pericles had a pungent reply to that, which, out of mercy, he refrained from voicing.

"We are a tribal people," one said with pride.

"So once were we," replied Pericles. "Now we are complicated and urban. Every man is his own philosopher in Athens."

They detected cynicism in his voice and were concerned. But again his smile reassured them. They thought him beautiful and godlike, and his graciousness evoked a response of fraternity in their countrymen's hearts. They felt sympathy for him but why they did not know. They began to speak of their sons, of their parents, whom they reverenced, and even of their wives, whom Pericles suspected were as frugal, simple and sturdy as themselves. He thought of his father, Xanthippus, and his elegance, and of his mother, Agariste, who would have disdained these men, at least when she had been younger.

They inquired with true interest of Pericles' family, and he told them of his sons. "My youngest is named for me, and he is an infant still," he said. Now he became thoughtful. He could not speak of Aspasia as his mistress, and his son as illegitimate, for they would have been shocked to the very heart. He cursed himself for not earlier thinking of this emergency, for he already knew that though Romans respected and loved their wives they kept them secluded, and mistresses secret. How would he explain Aspasia to them, for it was not possible to keep them in ignorance long; they would meet others in government besides himself. So he said, "I have a lovely wife of much intelligence, but Athenians do not regard her as my wife for she is a foreigner born in Miletus."

He was both pleased and surprised when they laughed in comradeship, and spoke of the Sabine women whom their fathers had abducted and brought to Rome and made wives of them. "To this day," they said, "many Romans do not acknowledge that those of Sabine ancestry are their equals. Are not men foolish?"

"Of a certainty," said Pericles.

He was relieved. But what would these Romans think of Aspasia when she joined them at his dinners? Like Athenian wives, Roman wives could dine with their husbands only when they were alone. How could he explain the hetairai to them, for surely they would hear of the ornamental and learned courtesans. They would also learn that Aspasia had been one of that adorable company. He said, "My beloved wife has been gifted with intelligence, and so she was educated highly. In consequence, she has come under suspicion as a woman of immoral character."

One Roman hesitated, then said with candor, "I have four sons, in whom my heart rejoices, but I have a daughter who is the sweet core of my heart. My sons are valorous and are soldiers, but their minds are not of great consequence. My daughter has the wit of a man, and I have a tutor for her, though my wife disapproves, being an 'old' Roman. My daughter, Calabria, swears she will not marry a man except of her choosing, and though this is reprehensible in a mere chit," and he bridled with pride, "I agree with her, for I saw her mother in the market and loved her at once and asked her consent after her parents had given me their heartiest approval. Had my wife refused me I would have withdrawn, in spite of my love for her, for she had a beauteous face. But Venus was kind and her son, Cupid, had pierced my wife's soul with his arrow."

Pericles knew that the Romans had changed the names of the Greek gods, and he understood that his guest meant Aphrodite and Eros. So he said, as the host, "Your wife was fortunate, and your daughter must be a veritable Minerva." The brown countryman's face flushed with gratification, but he said somewhat sheepishly, "She is a mere chit."

But what would they think when Aspasia greeted them in the atrium? Would they consider her an outrageous and forward woman whom no man could respect? As they neared the acropolis they exclaimed at the sight of Pheidias' Athene Parthenos, glittering with gilt fire and august majesty in the sun. They were overcome with wonder and reverence. "Minerva," said Pericles. "The patroness of our city." They nodded solemnly.

The guard of honor on their horses trotted briskly beside the car, and crowds stopped to stare at the company, and many hailed Pericles in joyful voices while some merely remained sullen and silent. This surprised the Romans, for they were accustomed to respect given to the head of the government. Perceiving this Pericles said, "We Athenians are very lively, and often are abusive to the Head of State, at least in language, and we are not disturbed. We accept it as evidence of freedom."

However, it was apparent that the Romans did not approve of this. One had honor for a man who had been voted into the highest office, and only heinous conduct could deprive him of that honor. "Freedom," one said with a certain severity, "is not license. If a citizen does not respect his government, for which his fellows have voted even if he had not, whom will he respect?"

As Pericles had a paradoxical attitude towards government, especially his own, he merely nodded. The complexity of his thoughts would not be understood by these men of rectitude. But alas, he thought, their children's children will have other opinions. It is inevitable.

When they arrived at his house, which the Romans considered a magnificent palace of possibly too opulent a taste—judging from their expressions—Pericles was happy to see that Aspasia was not in the atrium but only the overseer of the hall and the most handsome of the male slaves, all dressed exquisitely. Ah, I have not given her credit for her reticence and discretion and wisdom, he thought with tenderness. The house had been garlanded with laurel and wreaths of flowers, in honor of the guests, and it resounded with soft music and gently singing voices of unseen female slaves. Once more it was evident that the Romans thought this somewhat effete, and Pericles smiled inwardly. The overseer conducted the Romans to their assigned chambers and Pericles wondered what they would think of silken coverlets and delicate alabaster statues and Egyptian glass lamps and marvelous mosaics and Persian rugs, not to mention exotic scents and painted walls delineating nymphs and satyrs in somewhat liberated postures. One chamber wall depicted Aphrodite and Adonis coupled together in voluptuous enjoyment, both rosily naked, and Pericles went to his own chamber, laughing, and wished that he could overhear any scandalized comments.

When they emerged to join him he could scarcely refrain from mirth, for their faces were openly embarrassed. But they were men with manners, however recently learned, and they thanked him for his hospitality, even if at first their voices were constrained, and even if they avoided each other's eyes for a while. In his heart he did not deride them as ingenuous farmers, for so his own ancestors had been in a time less corrupt than this. He told himself that he must not, even in wine, tell them any lewd jests of the city, but must impress them as a man of gravity and open sincerity, for they expected this of him.

He conducted them to the dining hall, and they stared at its lavishness, which was yet tasteful. But they averted their eyes from the bawdy paintings on the walls and pretended that they did not exist. One furtively fingered, with hardly suppressed disapproval, the rich texture of the tablecloth, and one examined the knives and spoons, of beautifully wrought design, and another gazed at the silver plates. But as they were innately courteous, as were most men of the earth, they did not exchange meaningful glances. He could almost hear their thoughts: This is truly inexcusable luxury, which we Romans dislike. However, one must remember that Greeks are not Romans, and Romans are not rich. The gods forbid that ever our children's children will become so decadent! Ah, thought Pericles, but they will, they will, when they reach affluence through your labors! In the meantime, may God bless your austerity, for it is like the clean air of mountains above a murky city.

One said, unaware he was voicing Pericles' thoughts, "I have been in Egypt and it is very depraved, and very extravagant and—sensual." When he colored at what he considered unpardonable and covert criticism, Pericles said quickly, "That is the history of nations when they become wealthy and debauched. We, in Greece, have not as yet become so, but I fear we will." He shook his head sadly. "Of a certainty, we will."

He added, "When a nation is agricultural, and cities are small, they are virtuous and ascetic. We have a philosopher in Athens, Socrates, who avers that cities breed infamous men, but the land breeds heroes."

"We have heard of your Socrates," said one of the guests, relieved that Pericles had not taken offense. "We should like to see and to listen to him, for surely he is a great and honored man in Athens."

Pericles' mouth twisted a little. He said, "Socrates is an immured man, by his own will, and it is difficult to approach him." He could hear the shrill laughter of Socrates in his own mind at these words. "Yes, he is honored, though few understand him, among his students. He has said that the unexamined life is not worth living."

The Romans nodded in assent. "We examine our lives each morning, during our prayers, and search our consciences, for is that not our duty to God and our fellow men?"

"Indeed," said Pericles with a most solemn face.

He was pleased when he saw the simplicity of the meal which the astute Aspasia had ordered. Yet the goblets were ornate and jeweled, and the Romans were openly taken aback and touched them dubiously. Cool beer was poured in the goblets and once again Pericles thought of Aspasia with gratitude. The following wine was one of which Dejanira, in her meagreness, would have approved. Pericles wondered where Aspasia had found it, and he drank it very sparingly.

There were no dishes with sauces, cunningly flavored. The fish had been broiled simply, the tough meat was stewed, the vegetables were heavily burdened with garlic, and there was a dish of beans with robust pork. Pericles thought it all execrable and was again reminded of the frugal Dejanira. Aspasia, unlike himself, had known exactly what Pericles' guests would appreciate, and he marvelled, and saw that the Romans heartily enjoyed what was set before them. The meal was of their taste and their lives. He could hear their thoughts: Our host is not ostentatious or depraved. His table is commendable, if not his house. Moreover, his appetite is not voracious. He eats but little.

The Romans expanded. They gazed at Pericles with fondness. For all his house, he was one of their own, a man of asceticism and prudence. No doubt his wife has been indulged too much, and she had chosen what we have seen. Or possibly she had brought him an enormous dowry and licentious articles from her father's house. Perhaps he loves her too much, this handsome and elevated Head of State, and lets her have her female way. It is probable that she is very young and willful in addition, and extremely beautiful. Such are hard to resist and oppose.

They smiled wisely at Pericles, as at a brother. They began to ask him questions.

CHAPTER 11

Pericles conveyed his Roman friends to the Agora, where they would meet the Assembly and the Archons. He said to them, "You have spoken of a perfect government which would meet the needs and aspirations of all its citizens. In theory, a perfect government is possible. But it is not possible in reality. We must always remember human nature, which is not in the least exemplary."

"However, if a nation is founded on a firm Constitution, and its leaders bound to that Constitution, which they will not dare disobey, what ill can come to a republic?" asked one of the Romans.

"You will always be able to find some politician who has a unique interpretation of any Constitution," said Pericles, "and one which will serve his own purpose and the purposes of his friends, or some other exigency."

"Not," said another of the Romans, "if the Constitution is so written that it is not equivocal, and its language is so clear that no expediency can misinterpret it."

Though Pericles was dubious he reminded himself that Athens did not have a Constitution such as these Romans understood was necessary for the foundation of a republic. He said, "It is possible that the Constitution you envisage could be so soundly written on immortal stone that none would dare to misinterpret it, that is, the law would carry an extreme penalty for any manipulation of the Constitution to further the ends of any man or group of men. But let us suppose that Rome creates such a Constitution today. Other eras might arise when venal men would use that very Constitution in the light of their present ambitions."

When the Romans looked a little baffled, he said, "Let us suppose that certain crimes in the Constitution you are now planning carry the capital penalty. And let us then suppose that future generations of politicians shall say, 'That is not exactly what our fathers intended in that particular table of law.' Or, 'They really intended such and such.' Who can then refute the politicians? Who among you would be alive to insist that indeed the old meaning was intended? In short, different ages would have different interpretations for their own purposes."

One of the Romans shook his head decidedly. "That would not be possible."

Pericles was a little impatient. "Let us say that your Constitution carries the penalty of death for treason. But later politicians and judges might inquire, 'What was our father's definition of treason? Indeed, what is treason? It must be defined in today's meaning of the term.' "

The Romans were silently thoughtful and forgot to look at the sights of Athens for a few moments. Then one said, "I see clearly the extent of your argument. Other ages, other interpretations."

"Yes," said Pericles. "Today's patriotism may be tomorrow's treason, if it serves any judge or politician. And so it would go with any statute you might define today, no matter how explicit the terms. Let us suppose that a future Roman Head of State is a plotting and ambitious man, and a liar. He can only become all-powerful if he is a traitor to his country. So he might say to his people, 'I love my country and in the

467

name of that love I propose such and such an amendment to the Constitution, of which our fathers would have approved in the light of today's needs and changing circumstances. In truth, the Constitution of our fathers really means so-and-so.' I assure you, gentlemen, that he will already have a band of fellow traitors who will uphold him, and help to confuse the citizens. Then, if any patriot would oppose him the traitor will denounce him for treason! You can be certain, then, that the unfortunate patriot would suffer the penalty for the alleged crime."

The Romans were depressed. Pericles pitied them. So he said, "But you must remember that Athens is not a republic, with a firmly written Constitution, as Solon intended. She is a democracy, and democracies can be manipulated at will by any demagogue or traitor or exigent man. Democracies carry within themselves the seeds of their own death; they are not rule by judicious and virtuous men, but rule by the mob, which is neither judicious nor virtuous, and is inspired only by its own belly and lusts and greeds."

"You are implying that democracies are chaos, Pericles?"

"Exactly," he replied. "That is why they can never long survive."

One of the Romans was gazing about him and then up at the acropolis. "But observe what your own democracy has created here in Athens, where lives freedom, a reverence for beauty and law, among the common men."

Pericles could no longer restrain his bitterness. "Democracy, as such, did not create this beauty nor does it reverence any law at all. Beauty and law rise from the souls of only a few men in any nation of the world. They are visitations of God, through His chosen vessels."

"However that is true," said a Roman, "beauty and law could not flourish in a hostile environment. Therefore, the climate of Athens is not hostile."

My dear innocent friend, thought Pericles. Your syllogism is not apt, not valid, not true. Most often your famous beauty and law survive not because of, but in spite of, governments and their mobs. And often they are trampled and despised. That they persist is not due to the goodness of human nature —for that goodness is very doubtful—but due to the immortal designs of the Godhead. He said, "Only in a republic, or a Constitutional monarchy, can beauty and law truly expand and continue to exist and be reverenced."

He laughed a little, remembering Aspasia's counsel. He said, "In your Constitution you must exact the extreme penalty for any man who would subvert one iota of it, no matter his claims to love of country or 'changing times.' "

"That we shall do," said one of the guests in a strong and determined voice. "As your Solon has said, there must be rule by law and not rule by men and their whims and exigencies."

Pericles, on advice from Aspasia, had written a message to the King Archon; he was beginning to believe, however tentatively, that the old Archon was not unfriendly to him. He had written:

"Our friends from Rome are desirous of meeting our government. They reverence the laws of Solon—which, regrettably, we do not obey. The Romans are under the misapprehension that we have a perfect government, based on the laws of Solon. Therefore, their aspirations for their own government are very high, and they dream of an excellent republic. It would be most cruel to disillusion them while they are in Athens. If we deceive them well enough they will return to Rome and found a republic worthy of the honor of honorable men. The eldest is one Diodorus who is a member of the Roman Senate. They are all men of principle and conviction and the sternest probity. Senator Diodorus has expressed a desire to address our government in solemn session. I pray that the Assembly will not be too rowdy and will control any spasm of risibility before these simple but stately men, and will answer their questions in all due sobriety, remembering always that they are our guests."

Of a certainty, he thought, I am praying.

The Romans were intrigued by the Agora even if they found it somewhat noisy and boisterous. It was evident that they were accustomed to a more decorous way of commerce and shops and markets and offices. Pericles, seeing this, said, "The Athenians, as I told you before, are very animated and quick and vehement. If they appear to be quarreling, it is only their way of doing business and conducting negotiations."

The Roman Senator said, giving him a grave glance of admiration, "It is not so with you, Pericles. Jove could not be more steadfast and serious."

Pericles considered Zeus, whom the Romans had named Jove, or Jupiter. He was amused that the Romans had not, apparently, when adopting the Greek gods, also condoned Zeus' livelier aspects concerning seductive maidens. Or it was possible that virtuous men averted their eyes at the implications, preferring to view the father of gods and men as white as Macedonian snows, which, thought Pericles, would make for a very dreary life on Olympus. Virtue, like truth, should

469

have its discreet limits. These good men make me feel like a veritable reprobate and voluptuary, said Pericles to himself. May they return to Rome with their illusions intact!

The King Archon, and the lesser Archons and the Assembly and Ecclesia, met Pericles and the Romans with all ceremony and composure. Elaborate compliments were exchanged. Once Pericles caught the eye of the King Archon, who rarely smiled. But now there was a grandfatherly twinkle in his eyes which Pericles enjoyed but hoped the Romans had not discerned.

Pericles wished that Aspasia had had the ordering of the feast which was set before the Romans. The latter were astonished and somewhat appalled at the rich dishes, the profusion of different wines, the Syrian whiskey, the wreathed goblets of Egyptian glass glittering with jewels. They gazed at everything; they studied the fine tunics and togas of the other men, their gemmed armlets and rings and necklaces. Several wore a single gold earring set with bright stones, in the Egyptian manner. Many were perfumed. The Romans, frankly, did not know what to do with the silver bowls, floating with petals, which were set before them for the dipping of their fingers. They watched and followed suit, and looked dumbly at each other. Singing girls, indecorously dressed, played lutes and lyres and flutes, and smiled openly at any man who glanced at them. Pericles saw the Romans wince. The King Archon said to Pericles, "This is none of my doing, but our friends wish to impress the Romans, whom they consider country bumpkins."

"I believe, alas," Pericles replied, "that the Romans fear we are decadent."

"And, in a measure, are we not?" asked the King Archon, to which Pericles had no answer. The King Archon said, "It might have been well had they visited Sparta instead of Athens."

The Romans reservedly ate of the fine food, and drank very little of the wine and none of the whiskey. Their neighbors conversed with them in polite phrases and asked many questions of Rome and inclined their heads when answered. The Romans relaxed somewhat under all this pleasantness, and spoke of industrious Rome and the nobility of labor and commerce. They were proud of their engineers and their new aqueducts, and of the arch which they had perfected. At no time did they mention music or statues or poetry or philosophy. The Athenians looked at their calloused hands, at nails worn in the pursuit of productive work, and raised their own eyebrows. Manual labor was, to the Athenian, the province of slaves and not free men, who preferred to discuss politics and theories and philosophies and the theatre and the Olympiads. But sports, to the Romans, was not an aesthetic pursuit, during which one admired beautiful precision and physical perfection and dexterity. They viewed sports as a robust spectacle where the strongest won and not the most artistic, and skillful. Worse still, to the Athenians, was the Roman habit of admiring bloody gladiators.

Pericles was relieved when the moment had come for Senator Diodorus to address the assemblage. He rose in his subdued garments and looked about him in a sedate fashion. The Athenians had become somewhat vehement with wine, but when they saw the temperate, if weighty, countenance of the Senator they fell into reasonable attention.

He spoke without grandiloquence. "We Romans," he said, "have founded a republic according to what we have heard of your holy Solon. Our knowledge was small until we came to your glorious city," and he glanced kindly at Pericles, who bowed in his chair. "Now our knowledge is vastly increased, and we are full of admiration and respect.

"Our Constitution is not yet complete. But we are establishing a system of checks and balances. We intend to diffuse power so that no one body of Romans can assume tyranny over others. I will say it more plainly: We intend to protect all Romans against their government by establishing agents in government who will assiduously watch each other, so no one group will become too potent."

The Athenians exchanged amused if careful glances, as do adults when an immature child speaks, but they saw that the Archon was looking at them sternly.

"Under that Constitution we are in the process of completing, there will be strong emphasis on the unity and sanctity of family life, of patriotism, of the inculcating of our children with reverence for their parents, the inviolate status of a man's solemn word, self-control at all times, and, above all, the profound relationship between man and God.

"We Romans believe that the man who labors is the foundation of every just society, and by labor we mean every endeavor in which a man uses his mind and his hands, and respects the earth from which we have sprung. At no time will any man be permitted to oppress his neighbor, to exploit him, to defame him, to demean him. We will, at all times, strive for greatness and justice in our public and private lives, not the

471

greatness of riches but the greatness of the familiar virtues. For he who is a good man, however humble, is more to be honored than a king.

"We know that all men are born free and that it is the sacred duty of government to protect that freedom before the Face of God. That is the foremost duty of government. When that duty is despised or obliterated all else will be lost, for nothing can flourish in the absence of liberty. Our courts will be courts to which any citizen can appeal if any of his rights are threatened. We will teach our people that self-rule and self-sacrifice are the marks of a dignified man who reveres his God, his country and his humanity, and that the man who does not possess these is not a man at all.

"We prize industry and honest commerce. We will strive to live at peace with our neighbors and not war against them unless we are attacked. We will have no foreign alliances which can lead to wars and dissensions and bankruptcy. We will treat other states with deference but avoid entanglements with them. We will not permit any politician or other unscrupulous man to rob one section of our citizens for the benefit of another section, through the seizing of their property which they have earned and giving it to others less prudent and industrious. If a man will not work, then he must starve, and no politician will be allowed to alleviate his state at the expense of others. For we hold that what a man earns by his own labor belongs solely to him, and he shall not be plundered of it. It does not belong to the government; it does not belong to his neighbor. The rights of property will be protected at all times. If it becomes necessary for government to use a man's land, for the building of aqueducts or other public services, then that government must pay that man in full. If he does not assent even then, he will be allowed to take his case to the courts.

"Remembering that ancient nations were destroyed by crushing taxes, we shall tax our people for only what is necessary for our military services, for the guarding of our city through a system of police, for clean water and streets, for the support of the courts, for sanitaria, for sound buildings, for fighters against fire. The stipends for those in public service will always be modest; the honor is almost enough."

He looked earnestly at his audience; many were carefully studying their jeweled hands.

"Riches," he said, "are not to be despised if they are acquired by superior work and intelligence. But the man who becomes rich by thievery and malfeasance in office or crafty dealings will be treated with contempt. He is a disgrace to his nation.

"In conclusion, then, we will build a state on the laws of your Solon, and the Constitution he desired will be ours. Frugality and thrift and open respect for neighbors will be taught our sons, and they will also be taught that law and order must rule lest we all perish in a welter of crime, and venal politicians become our masters."

He sat down, after bowing to his audience. They looked to the King Archon for a signal. All near him saw tears in his aged eyes. He lifted his hands and clapped them in applause and the audience, however reluctant, and highly amused, joined him.

He turned to the Romans and said, "May your city flourish under God, and may your children's children remember you with piety and gratitude and honor, and may they never forget what you will write on your Twelve Tables of Law. Your republic, I prophesy, will become the wonder of the world. So long as your people adhere to those Tables they will never decline nor will dust choke up your temples nor foul men rise to power, nor any just man become the slave of his avaricious neighbor."

He turned to Pericles, and Pericles rose and bowed to the Romans and said in a voice no one had ever heard before, so moved was it:

"Go with God."

When the Romans had departed Athens, heavy with gifts, Pericles said to Aspasia, "No. I did not introduce them to our philosophers, not even Anaxagoras, whom they would have admired for his very appearance if not for his theories. Nor did I introduce them to Socrates. But Pheidias visited them and they walked on the acropolis, which rendered them dumb for a space. Beloved, I kept them from our philosophers who only think and teach, estimable things without doubt, but not the kind which would have been appreciated by our Roman friends, who reverence work almost as much as they do their gods, and suspect theories and abstract ideas. Whether or not they will produce artists in their future I do not know. But they are men of a different character than ours. Who knows? They may become the rulers of the world, which would benefit most of us—if they keep to their Constitution."

CHAPTER 12

Pericles had told the Romans, "You have asked me of Sparta. Spartans devote their lives to war, Athenians to politics."

"But they are an industrious people," Senator Diodorus had remarked.

"They are also lightless, grim, unrelenting, suspicious and their lives are unimaginative. Their government is all-powerful, an oligarchy, and so their people are virtual slaves, always in terror of those who rule them with so much gloom and ponderousness. I admit they are valorous and patriotic; but their existence is one of monotony, endless labor without the reward of laughter or any ease. Their surliness is famous. Their women do the work of men, the children are never permitted to be children. They are afflicted by a conviction that the rest of Greece is conspiring against them, whereas they, themselves, are conspiring to dominate our country. There is a kind of madness in their souls, a darkness of spirit. They believe they are superior to all other Greeks, and their tread is the tread of iron. They have no humor and I confess I am terrified of humorless men. They are dangerous. You have spoken of freedom as the breath of life. The Spartans do not regard freedom as desirable for their citizens, nor, in fact, for any other state. If they have any cherished belief it is that they are ordained to force their manner of living on the whole world."

He thought of Sparta for a moment or two and then said, "I fear them, not so much for their arms but for their philosophy. They are both savage and spare, and they punish the slightest infractions of their stupefying laws with the utmost barbarism. They are becoming more and more aggressive; they have discovered that they can best conquer the world through commerce and trade, so now they are devoting all their energies—which are vast—to commerce and trade. Their singlemindedness is affrighting."

"But you have said, Pericles, that the Spartans devote their lives to war."

"True. And there are more ways to war against envied neighbors than by the force of arms. That the Spartans have now learned. I honor labor as you honor it, but not the grinding labor of the Spartans directed against us."

Years before this, Pericles knew that Sparta was not alone in envying and resenting Athenian maritime supremacy.

Corinth and Megara, members of the Peloponnesian Confederacy, who were certain that Athens intended to drive them off the seas, listened to Spartan propaganda about the avarice of effete Athens. Sparta, herself, had had no desire to go to war with Athens at that particular time, but she goaded her allies to that end, preferring to pick up much of the spoils of any conflict, and keep her growing wealth and city and men safe. Knowing of this Pericles once said, "It reminds me of the old fable of a dog who had a rigorous master who denied him entrance at will to the pen of fat rabbits. On the other hand the wolves of the forest would chase the dog from their hunting territory. So the dog plotted and went to his master and said, 'Lord, I listened last night when the moon was full to the wolves who are the rulers of the forest, and they conspired against you so that when you are in the fields they will attack and kill you and seize your domain.' He then went to the wolves, cringing and fawning, and said, to the leader of the wolves, 'Sire, I am of your kind though I live in the kennel of a man, and I heard him plotting with his wife that when the moon is waning he will come into your realm with arrow and sword and spear and kill you, and take your forest.' So the man went forth with weapons to slay the wolves, and the wolves met him to dispatch him, and the man was slaughtered and the king of the wolves also, and the other wolves fled. Then the dog took over the pen of the fat rabbits and the domain of the man and drove off his wife. That dog is Sparta."

This was inevitably repeated to the Spartans, and their oligarchy was enraged. The older Spartans were still gloating in memory of the defeat of Athens by Sparta and her allies, at Tanagra, when Pericles was still a young man. The oligarchy, that oppressive body of men which ruled Sparta, began to address their people in inflammatory language, and even the very young men who had not been born at the time of Tanagra or had been little children began to burn with fury against Athens, though she was also a member of the Peloponnesian Confederacy. The oligarchy had accused the younger Pericles of lusting for empire over all of the members of the Confederacy, and had declared that he was a bloody tyrant and vainly ambitious. Not only did the average Spartan believe this without doubts, but the other city-states believed it also, because of their envy. "If," said the Spartans to their allies, "we defeated Athens before, we can do it again and once and for all quell her bold aspirations."

So began the miserable sequence of erratic if desperate wars against Athens by members of the Confederacy, and which had plagued Pericles over many years. Sparta had confined herself to sporadic raids into Attica almost annually, while inciting her allies against Athens. Corinth and Megara were firmly and relentlessly crushed. Eventually Athens retired from the Confederacy. In the meantime Sparta, who had suffered little during those long years, dreamed of driving Athens from the sea which was her domain, not by war but by seizing Athens' ascendancy in commerce and trade.

To this end she fused all the energies of her men, demanding endless sacrifices of them and endless labor, stringent physical training and self-denial. Several generations ago she had been acknowledged the leader of Hellas because of her military superiority over her sister-states, and the magnificent valor of her fighting men. The Spartan people had never known freedom in the sense that Solon had intended for Athens. At one time the oligarchy had forbidden Spartans the possession of gold and silver and substituted iron for barter. Inevitably, wealth reached a few cunning hands, and the intended equalization of property was a failure. The oligarchies had been defeated by human nature, and for this they had become the laughter of Athens. Zeno of Elea, when instructing the young Pericles, had brought this emphatically to his pupil's attention. "This should be a lesson for governments, but governments never learn anything and remember nothing. You cannot equalize men unless you chop off the higher heads and stretch, on a rack, those of lower mental stature. Both efforts are fatal."

But still the later oligarchies thought longingly of the old days when there was a prohibition against the bequeathing or the gifting of land, and when lowly helots worked the land for a few selected and powerful Spartans. Still they lamented the fact that many citizens now owned precious metals. As the members of the oligarchy were only human also, they had no objection to acquiring fortunes for themselves though desiring that only they should possess them. "Are we a nation who loves banks, like the Athenians, and vast accumulations of wealth like them also—and the Persians, not to mention the Egyptians who coat their dead with gold? We are a stern and upright people. We believe in the equality of men, provided they are sound of body and mind. Why should any man aspire to rise above his fellows and gain greater rewards? It is a wicked injustice."

When hearing of this the older Pericles remembered what Zeno had taught him—that men are born unequal by nature, though they should be equal before the government, so that no man is penalized for being poor and no man, however rich, can escape the punishment of law. Opportunity should not be forbidden the superior in soul and character, nor false opportunity given to the inferior who would prefer to be without the responsibility of it.

Now the Spartans were directing all their determination against the older Pericles, who had far more power than when he had first come to the attention of Sparta, and had made Athens the supreme maritime queen of the seas. They jeered at his desire to make Athens also the empire of the mind through the help of his artists, his sculptors, his architects, his philosophers. "Has it not been said," they asked, "that he whom the gods would destroy they first make mad? Pericles is a madman, an overweening dictator and tyrant." So now they were fixed with the resolution of stubborn and narrow men that they must seize the maritime power of Athens. Labor, once held the province only of helots, became the duty of all men—except, of course, the oligarchy and the few aristocrats.

This, then, was the present anxiety of Pericles, who was weary of the constant small but costly and enervating wars and distractions. He knew that among his own Athenians there were rich and potent men who were sending emissaries or spies to Sparta, out of hatred for him. He knew that they were also secretly inciting the rabble against him, so that through his destruction they could assume authority. The word "impeachment" was constantly on their lips in private. Only the accursed middle class of shopkeepers and little merchants and industrious men stood in their way, and these loved Pericles. Pericles called his foes traitors, openly, and they laughed at him.

Aspasia said to him in concern, "Is there no way to reach an accord with Sparta and assure her that there is enough trade and commerce in the world for all cities?"

"No. Sparta has never relinquished her ambition and purpose to be all-powerful in Hellas, as once she was through military might. Dreams take various shapes and war is but one of them. It is now trade—the rule of the world through commerce. It is the same goal: conquest."

On a few occasions he sent his own trusted emissaries to Sparta, to conciliate her and to assure her that Athens had no imperial designs upon her, and that surely reasonable men could reach an amicable understanding in the name of peace. Sparta received those emissaries with what they could only report as brutal courtesy and a lightly controlled rudeness. Her demands for an agreement were absurd, and so Pericles was forced to refuse. "These foolish little wars will continue," he said, with mingled wrath and despair. "Sparta is determined to subjugate Athens as she has subjugated her allies. Our treasury is ominously depleted and we may soon have to debase our currency. The debasement of currency invariably means the decline of a nation, and so Sparta is compelling us to do that."

Aspasia said, "A final confrontation with Sparta, then, is inevitable?"

"I fear so," he replied. "In the meantime we will try to avoid that confrontation as long as possible. I only pray that it will not come in my lifetime." But he suspected that it would and often he would pace his chamber at night futilely searching for a way either to conciliate the irreconcilable or to threaten Sparta in one open and exasperated challenge.

His enemies were now accusing him of "goading" Sparta to attack, or of inciting her through unjust suspicions of her motives, motives which Sparta candidly and consistently proclaimed. "He is, first of all, a soldier," his enemies told the rabble, "and soldiers are not famous for hating war; they love war even for its own sake. His imperial ambitions grow hourly and Sparta knows that and fears us. If we war strongly against her she will retaliate as strongly and peace in our world will be a lost vision." They appealed to the pusillanimity of the market rabble, its fearful self-love. The rabble scribbled lies and threats and libels on the walls of Athens. When they saw Pericles in the Agora they either were sullenly silent or shouted at him before fleeing.

Pericles' enemies struck at him again and again through Aspasia. They said that she was the real power behind Pericles, that she was insisting that Sparta be attacked or made subservient, that her school was only a disguise for the procurement of free women for unspeakable purposes, that she induced young girls to engage in perversions with the ageing Pericles, and that, worst of all, she was impious. The comic poet, Hermippus, publicly accused her of these things. "If I were a tyrant, as my enemies and Sparta say I am," Pericles told Aspasia, "I would have him quietly murdered or thrown into prison."

"I do not fear lies," Aspasia answered him.

He raised his eyebrows humorously at her. "Then, my sweet, you are still an innocent, and I am amazed. Lies are far more potent than the truth, and far more dangerous. They have caused the death of more good men than any deadly truth has done. For human nature is inherently evil and it prefers lies, and delights in the suffering of the just which it has inflicted."

"Then," said Aspasia, "we must remain serene and indifferent to evil, as Anaxagoras does, in spite of the pain imposed on him by the mobs." She added, disturbed by Pericles' suddenly darkened face, "Future ages will give him honor, as they will give you honor, beloved."

"Unfortunately," said Pericles, "neither Anaxagoras nor I will be aware of that."

Anaxagoras was growing old and tired. The repeated stoning of his little house and the disruptions of his academe and in the colonnades by the rabble were finally exhausting him. His voice no longer had the power to rise above derisive shouts and taunts, and the serenity and indifference which his friends so admired in him were giving place to deep inner sadness and a desire for even a precarious peace of mind and spirit.

One day he went to see Pericles in the latter's offices. The natural high dignity which had always distinguished him had not disappeared, nor his calm glance and composure. But his hair and his beard were white and his wonderful blue eyes had faded, and his fine hands were tremulous. Pericles had not seen him for three weeks, and Anaxagoras' aspect today alarmed him, for it seemed to him that the philosopher-scientist had aged greatly even in that short time. But Anaxagoras smiled at him with his usual sweetness and embraced him. Yet Pericles, to his dread, saw that there were tears in his friend's eyes.

He poured wine for Anaxagoras, who gently refused other refreshments. He was long in speaking; he swirled the wine about in his goblet and absently studied it. Pericles was more alarmed.

"Do you bring me bad news, my friend?"

Anaxagoras hesitated, and seeing this Pericles said, "Do not refrain from telling me. There is not a morning that comes to me with hope, but only with aversion, these days. I must armor myself afresh each day by deliberate will."

"But you are much younger than I, Pericles."

"You must remember I am a politician." Pericles tried to laugh. "Well, you must tell me. I assure you that my enemies have not as yet castrated me, try though they do."

Anaxagoras still hesitated. Then he sighed. "I must leave Athens."

Pericles looked at him with astonishment. "You would flee from your own enemies?"

Again Anaxagoras sighed. "There comes a time in a man's life when he is weary of fighting, of struggle—when, in truth, he finds it too hard to endure and becomes tired of living. That time has come to me."

"You are tired of living?"

Anaxagoras raised his eyes and looked at Pericles fully. "Yes. If I am not to come to the desperate conclusion that no life is worth living then I must leave Athens, however dearly I love her." Seeing Pericles' misery he added, "It is my age, dear friend. I would have a little peace in my last years."

"You were never a coward," said Pericles, hoping to perturb that calmness and restore spirit to Anaxagoras. But Anaxagoras merely smiled.

"Is a longing for tranquility in an old man cowardice? Even an old soldier eventually retires from the battlefield and the sound of drums does not quicken his blood."

When Pericles did not speak, Anaxagoras reached out and placed his hand on the back of the other's hand. "Do not sorrow for me," he said. "The gods have not endowed us with perpetual youth, and the high heart of young men must become subdued in late years. Would you have me a cynic, and speak with acid in my mouth? Would that not be worse than —flight? When I am no longer in Athens I may start to believe, again, that I am with God and that His peace is with me, and that in time men will become truly human."

"I cannot endure that I will never see you again," said Pericles. "Now will all your friends be devastated."

"You must explain to them," said Anaxagoras. "I have my limits of endurance, too. I have spoken of this only to you, for if I see the others and listen to their pleas I may weaken in my resolve and remain. At the end that would be a little death for me. It would be the end of all my hope."

"Where will you go?" asked Pericles, and now he was most anxious.

Anaxagoras shook his head slightly. "That I will not tell you for you may seek me out, and seeing you will cause me suffering and a longing to return."

Pericles rubbed his suddenly tired eyes and his mouth and chin. "You have little money, that I know. Will you at least permit me to give you a purse of talents as a gift? I should like to have that small pleasure."

"I need very little," said Anaxagoras, looking at him with compassion. "But, yes, if it will truly please you."

Pericles went to an iron locked chest in his cabinet and took out a heavy purse. He laid it before his friend. They both stared at it. A deep silence fell between them. It had been many years, too long to count, since Pericles had felt a desire to weep, but he felt it now, and with that impulse his growing bitterness was increased and his growing despair. He was always striving against hatred in himself even for his enemies. Now it was rising beyond his control.

Anaxagoras was pushing himself heavily to his feet and Pericles stood up also. Anaxagoras put his hands on Pericles' shoulders. "Give me peace," he pleaded. "For I say to you, may the peace of God be with you, dear friend."

"Go in peace, then," said Pericles, but his expression was harsh.

"Do not grieve for me, Pericles. My hour for silence has arrived, as it will, unfortunately, arrive for you. We cannot escape our mortality."

When Anaxagoras had departed Pericles felt a great wound in his soul, a tremendous emptiness and loss. His reason told him that the loss of beloved friends, and the emptiness which follows, cannot be avoided, but his heart rebelled. Why could not Anaxagoras have lived out his few remaining years in tranquility among his pupils and those who loved him? He had been driven away by evil, for all his explanation that he was only weary and old.

Aspasia wept when Pericles told her of Anaxagoras' departure.

"Who will replace him?" she asked.

"No one. A good man can never be replaced."

"We have that to console us, Pericles. Bad men die and no one sorrows for them."

Now Pericles spoke to her impatiently, he who was rarely impatient with her. "But their evil endures after them. Have you forgotten history? The good descend into their graves, lamented only by their friends, or, if history does record them, it is only briefly. But the memory of evil men is too often glorified. How many statues are erected to good men? But forests of statues are erected to ruthless conquerors."

"That is a sad commentary on human nature."

Pericles shrugged. "But a true one." He paused. "That one such as Anaxagoras was finally forced to flee is enough of a commentary."

The friends of Anaxagoras were broken-hearted. Only Socrates kept his composure. "At least they did not murder him," he said. He smiled. "He has escaped that honor." He laughed, his high whinnying laughter. "But I feel that I shall receive that honor one day, for which I am already grateful."

They all tried to console themselves that Anaxagoras had probably found the peace he so deeply desired. But his absence tortured them. A vital element had departed from their lives, and it would never return. They were poorer. A golden coin had been forever lost from their purses; the light of their existence had darkened in a profound measure. The sun would never shine for them as once it had shined, and their hope had lessened.

They never saw Anaxagoras again nor did they receive any message which might have consoled them, nor did they know where he was nor when he died. But one day Socrates said to Pericles, "Our dearest old friend, Anaxagoras, left this world yesterday or the day before."

"How do you know?"

Socrates' satyr eyes were sorrowful. "How do I know? I do not know. Did I dream it and have I forgotten the dream? Or did his spirit pause beside me one night to bid me farewell? I do not know. I only know that I know."

Pericles did not doubt him. Acrid tears came to his eyes and Socrates looked at him in commiseration. "But does not death come to all of us? I say to you now, as I have said it before, a good man needs not fear death, for if it be eternal sleep is not sleep pleasant? If he lives beyond his grave, then God will surely receive him with love, and embrace him."

When Pericles' despairing face did not lighten, Socrates said, "Let us compare death with a ship full of passengers. The ship leaves its harbor and we weep and say, 'She departs, and never shall we see our friends again.' But perhaps in another harbor a glad shout is raised, and the waiting ones say, 'Here she arrives, and our friends with her!' "

It was then that Pericles could not restrain himself and he broke down and wept, weeping as he had not wept since his father had died.

Socrates thought, When a great man is moved to tears the world should so be moved also. Alas, it never is. We save our tears for mountebanks and liars and oppressors, when they die, and we hail them as saviors and heroes.

CHAPTER 13

Thucydides, son of Melesias, was called the Old Oligarch because of his insistent and querulous dogmatism and pursuit of those he hated. Had not Pericles had him once or twice prosecuted for usurious practices he still would have hated the Head of State. Pericles was all he despised. The character of Pericles infuriated him. Among his friends he mocked Pericles' stateliness, his composure, his aversion for the mean and petty, his intense patriotism, his patronage of artists and philosophers, his Aspasia, and the illegitimacy of his son. Avaricious though Thucydides was, he spent his money almost lavishly to inspire outbreaks among the rabble against Pericles, cunningly aware that there was almost nothing the populace loved more than the ridicule of the prominent and the powerful, and especially the noble. Well-knowing that mobs were naturally hysterical and believed any vicious rumors, he accused Pericles of not only prolonging the hostility between Sparta and Athens but of using that hostility to "hide his derelictions and the depletion of our treasury." The ignorant masses, Thucydides knew, were womanishly excitable and always solicitous for themselves, and that no matter what ill came to Athens they were eager to believe the fault was in their leader. Thucydides bribed comic poets and orators to blame Athenian troubles on Pericles' alleged indifference to the gods, "which remains unpunished." Was he not known to neglect them? Had he not been heard to say that "there is only God," when it was obvious there were many gods and goddesses? His patronage of Pheidias and his approval of the enormous gold and ivory statue of Athene Parthenos on the acropolis was not the result of piety, for though it was complete it had not yet been dedicated. Moreover, it was shamefully expensive.

"Look at all those other statues and extravagant temples and gardens and terraces on the acropolis!" Thucydides would complain. "No, it is not piety. It is self-aggrandisement on the part of Pericles. He also wished to enrich his sculptor friends, particularly Pheidias. Pericles' association with such pestential ragamuffins like Socrates is a disgrace to Athens. Where is our former sobriety in financial matters, and our prudence and responsibility? Pericles has corrupted them all with his vanity and his desire to be known as the leader of culture and philosophy in Athens. Let us return to his sacrilege: He permitted Pheidias to represent him, and Pheidias, on the shield of Athene Parthenos, bold enough for any eye to discern! If Athene does not destroy Athens with an earthquake such as afflicted Sparta years ago it is only because she is merciful, or she is waiting for Athenians to avenge the insult to her."

The envious rabble, who were already persuaded that Pericles should have spent the gold in the treasury "on your abject needs and laudable aspirations for a better life," were daily becoming more mutinous. Pericles lived in luxury. Why should they not, too, be more adequately sheltered and given other sustenance? To them Pericles embodied all the wealthy and the aristocratic. He, and he alone, was accused of delighting in "the suffering of the poor," and in instigating it. He was selfish; he was too ambitious; he detested the lowly; he was a dictator; he was endlessly greedy; doubtless he had misappropriated funds from the treasury—to which they had never contributed through taxes—for his own enrichment. The jewels of Aspasia were famous. From what lowly pockets had the money come for these? He had plundered Athens for the adornment of a harlot, whose habits were shameful, and who was known for her own impiety. He was attempting to divert the attention of the outraged citizenry from his crimes against it by goading Sparta to outright war. "It is well known," said Thucydides, "that this has often been, in the history of nations, a tactic used by tyrants." As an investor in various enterprises engaged in the manufacture of war material, and from which he, Thucydides, had enriched himself, Thucydides was careful never to attack those enterprises or his wealthy friends who were also invested in them.

As the masses do not think, they were easily persuaded that Pericles had a personal treasury of his own, gained by war and investments in war. They lusted for this imaginary treasure. That there were many men in Athens far richer than Pericles they did not consider, for did not several of them agree sadly with Thucydides and also accuse Pericles of the same crimes and were they not always loudly proclaiming their love "for the meek and exploited?" Where was the hero who would rescue them from this cruel and merciless man?

On the death of his uncle, Daedalus, Pericles had permitted his sons, Xanthippus and Paralus, to attend the funeral of their grandfather. Moreover, he had encouraged them. He had sent the kindest of regards and condolences to Dejanira, which had caused her to weep more copiously than she had over her father's death. She had then written to Pericles imploring him to have her son, Callias, recalled from exile, unaware that on several occasions he had been so invited through the agents of Pericles on the latter's orders. Callias, for many years, had revelled in his exile, for he had escaped his reputation in Athens and there were no disapproving faces to annoy him. But he pretended, to his mother, in tearful letters, that he was languishing in exile. In some manner he had come across the information that Pericles, out of pity for Dejanira, had kept her ignorant of her son's refusal to return to Athens. This had made him gleeful.

But now he had learned of the more virulent attacks on the hated Pericles, his mistress and his friends, and Callias' vengefulness increased. He allowed himself to be persuaded to return to Athens. His mother, very fat and gray, and cumbersome in all her movements, greeted him with incoherent joy and embraces. "I have been so lonely, so sorrowful!" she cried, covering his rough face with kisses. "Yes," he replied, "that I know. I will not tell you of my own sufferings, dearest of mothers, and how I longed to return to this house, and my midnight tears. But behold: I am here, and I will never leave you—unless I am again forced into exile."

Within a few days of his return to Athens he went to the house of Thucydides, which was almost as frugal as the house of Daedalus, and he offered his own money, and his talents, in the plot to ruin Pericles or at least drive him into exile "with his harlot." He was elated that the hatred of Thucydides and the latter's friends almost surpassed his own. The rich aristocrats in the plot thought him personally loathsome and obnoxious and disreputable, but they pretended to be overjoyed and grateful to him for joining them. He preened over their protestations of admiration for him, and their enthusiastic friendship, and became more conceited than ever, for when he had been young these patricians had avoided him, had publicly shown their contempt for him, and had openly held their noses when they had encountered him. Never had he been admitted to their houses or sat at any table with them. Even his riches had not been enough for any of them to offer him their daughters in marriage.

"He caused the death of my beloved grandfather," he said to them, with meretricious tears in his eyes, and they nodded solemnly while they laughed inwardly. "He exiled me, kept me from the affection of my dearest of mothers," he would continue, and again they would nod with commiseration and sympathy. "I will be avenged for the crimes against my house, and the crimes against my city," he said, and they were intensely interested. What suggestions had he to offer? One must remember that Pericles had saved Anaxagoras.

"Who is now dead," said Callias, "after he was forced to flee Athens."

"Pericles is more powerful than ever among his detestable middle class," said his new friends.

Callias had a suggestion which at first revolted his friends with its crudity. Then when Callias was absent one observed, "Its very bold uncouthness might make it possible of success. The old King Archon is dead, and the new King Archon hates Pericles as much as we do. Pericles is absent at this time at one of his villas with his concubine, for is it not high summer? Let us give the matter thought and move with circumspection so that he will not suspect us. Callias is stupid as well as cunning. If anything goes wrong we will arrange for him to bear the whole guilt."

They chose the most influential of their members to bring charges of peculation against Pheidias, who was now the closest friend of Pericles since the flight and death of his beloved Anaxagoras. Added to this was his blasphemy in depicting himself and Pericles on the shield of the sacred Athene Parthenos. They well knew that Pericles had insisted that the image of Pheidias be carved on the shield, and they knew that the shy sculptor had refused—unless Pericles, "for are you not greater than I?"—also permitted his profile on the shield. So Pericles, with a jest, had allowed it for all his reluctance.

The matter of the alleged peculations of Pheidias was somewhat more difficult. Then two of the aristocrats went to the head-keeper of the public records of the treasury and under duress and a large bribe—from Callias—he agreed to forge several of the records so that they would reveal that Pheidias had not only received enormous stipends for his work on the acropolis, and the work of his students—stipends that were unbelievable—but had frequently, and arrogantly, demanded even more, saying that the Head of State, himself, had approved of this, and had presented proof in various letters.

"Can we not also prove that Pericles has enriched himself through similar peculations?" asked Callias.

Though the aristocrats and Thucydides had more than hinted of this to the rabble they knew that an open accusation of criminality against Pericles would only rebound on themselves and lay themselves open to punishment. They were well acquainted with the cold and relentless wrath of Pericles. They knew he was ruthless in pursuit of those who had unpardonably offended him. So they persuaded Callias that this would be impolitic, at least at this time. Attacks on Pericles' friends were one thing; attacks on him personally were quite a dangerous other. "As yet," they told Callias, who was disappointed.

They consulted among themselves. The stipends paid to Pheidias and his students had been very small, on his own gentle insistence. How, apart from the forged records, could it be proved that he had literally stolen the people's gold? Where had he hidden it? That was a great problem, for all knew how humbly the sculptor lived.

Callias had another suggestion, which made them catch their breath. They pondered on it, and finally agreed that it had more than a small merit.

So, while the weary Pericles rested in the happy company of his Aspasia and their son, and Paralus, on one of his more remote farms, Pheidias was arrested for peculation and thrown into prison, after the forged records had been presented to the King Archon, who was a cousin to Daedalus, and so a relative of Pericles, himself, the nephew of Daedalus. An intelligent if a gloomy and rigid and proud man, he had never forgotten Pericles' "attack on my house, and even on his own." Worse still, he had tried to induce Dejanira to marry him, for she was very rich, and she had rejected him through her kyrios, crying that none could replace Pericles in her affections.

Pheidias had been openly arrested in the very midst of his students and assistants, while he had been planning the marble pediments for the statues he was designing. He had gazed silently and incredulously at the police, and then, still stunned, he gave the architectural plans to one of his students and had gone away with the police without uttering a single word, his bald and rosy head suddenly sallow, his face slack with shock, his broad old shoulders sagging. His sandaled feet had been dusted, as with flour, with the dust of marble, and his rough clothing also, and crowds stood aside, wondering, and staring at each other questioningly. Theft? Peculations? Never had anyone possessed less of the aspect of a thief.

One of the students, who was a young man with considerable money of his own, selected a horse from his fine stable and rode away at once to Pericles' farm, though it was sunset and the hot night was approaching without a moon. It was almost the first dawn when he reached the farm, but he awoke the slaves and insisted on seeing Pericles at once, and even the soldiers who guarded the villa were impressed by his despair and his urgent pleas.

Pericles, awakened and pale, his face lined with chronic worry, threw on a tunic, rose from Aspasia's bed where she was sleeping peacefully, and went into the small atrium of the house. The student, overcome, fell on his knees before Pericles, whom he adored, and burst into tears and could hardly speak. It was some moments before Pericles could understand, and when he did, he was disbelieving.

"I was standing beside my master, Pheidias, when they arrested him," cried the young man, seizing the hem of Pericles' tunic. "Before God, I tell you the truth!"

Pericles turned aside, his pallid face twitching. Who could be guilty of this enormity? He rubbed his eyes, still incapable of accepting this dire news. Anaxagoras' case had been bad enough. This was much worse, for Pheidias had not thrown any doubt privately or publicly on any dogma. In truth, he was the most pious and devoted of men, the least controversial, the least apt to provoke hostility. He was most shy and retiring, and never had been known to utter an impatient word. All his ways were gentle, and compassionate. He could not pass even the most scurvy of beggars without giving him a coin from his little purse. The beggars had known it and he had only to appear to have them crowd about him, whining, thrusting out their hands. That such a man, such a stupendous genius, could be accused of blasphemy and theft was not to be believed. It was accepted widely that he was the glory of Athens, above all others, and multitudes openly reverenced him and foreign and distinguished visitors insisted on meeting him and speaking with him. All had been impressed by his modesty, his tenderness of character, his shining and gleaming eyes in which there was no malevolence but only charity.

I am a calamity to those I love, thought Pericles. He said to Iphis, who almost always accompanied him these days, "If blasphemy has indeed been committed, it has been committed by those who have accused Pheidias. I will go to him at once, and arrange to defend him." He added, with a grimness even Iphis had never seen before, "This time the vile accusers will be dealt with, and I swear this, before God, and I will never rest until they are brought to justice."

He rode away with Iphis and two of his soldiers and the student, just as the dawn was throwing pale purple shadows on the quiet countryside. He had a premonition of disaster beyond anything he had ever felt before, and so he uttered not a word, not even when the company entered Athens. He went to his house and bathed, for he was silvery with dust, and he was sweating, and dressed himself in his official robes, forced himself to eat a small breakfast and then went at once to his offices.

There he summoned his cousin, the King Archon, Polybius, to him. His head was throbbing under the heated helmet; it seemed to him that his heart would burst from his chest. He had no doubt that he could save Pheidias and have him exonerated; all but the rabble and a few aristocrats loved him for the virtue not only of his genius but for his kindness and lack of ostentation.

The crime, to Pericles, was in the accusations and the calumnies and not in the actual imprisonment of his friend. Pheidias was in no danger. Tomorrow his accusers would be the laughter of Athens. They would also suffer the vengeance of the Head of State for the insult to Pheidias.

The old King Archon had been over ninety-five years old when he had died. The present King Archon, Polybius, was less than sixty, a small slight man with a parched pale face, small dull eyes, a large nose and a tight wide mouth and thin gray hair. His hands were dry and cold, his manner precise and formal and unbending. He shook hands with Pericles who courteously invited him to sit down and asked him if he desired wine and refreshments. "No," said the King Archon shortly. "You summoned me, Pericles, son of Xanthippus. What is your wish?"

Pericles recalled him in his own youth; they had never liked each other. Pericles' handsomeness had offended Polybius. Too, his father had desired to marry Pericles' mother, Agariste, after the death of Xanthippus, and she had refused firmly. Both he and his father, then, had been repudiated by the women of their family and for some obscure reason, totally irrational, Polybius felt that Pericles was guilty.

Pericles said, "I have been informed that my friend, the glorious artist, Pheidias, has been arrested on charges so absurd that the very dogs on the streets laugh in wonderment."

Polybius drew a rasping breath and he fixed Pericles with a granite stare. "The charges, lord, are not absurd. They are based on evidence."

Pericles leaned back in his chair with a negligent smile while he raged inwardly. "What evidence, Polybius?"

The older man shook his head. "You, of a certainty, know the law, Pericles. Evidence is not shown or revealed until the criminal appears before the judge and jury. So, I cannot tell you. I can tell you this, however, I am convinced of the truth of the charges. I have seen the evidence myself."

Polybius might be unlovable as a person, at least to Pericles, but he was known for his integrity, and if his judgment was severe it was at least just. Pericles' incredulity was not pretended.

"You truly believe that Pheidias is guilty of peculation and blasphemy?"

"I do, lord."

Pericles said, "I know exactly how ridiculously modest were the fees Pheidias received. He set them, himself, though I urged him to accept more. Many of his students and associates accepted nothing at all. It was enough for them to be helping the master." He tried to control his wrath.

"I have seen the evidence, myself," Polybius insisted.

"Then it was forged evidence, and the scoundrels who did it will be discovered and punished. I can promise you that."

Even the King Archon was intimidated by the daunting blind look directed at him, and he moved uneasily in his chair. "Are you threatening me, Pericles?"

"No, not you. I know your character too well. But, you have been appallingly deceived by fraudulent evidence, presented by men of no scruples. This, I shall prove, and let them beware for nothing will halt me in bringing them to justice."

"If you can prove it I shall give the matter my closest attention."

"I have no doubt of that, Polybius. The only amazing thing to me is that you could believe, on forged evidence, that Pheidias is guilty of anything but possessing the sweetest of natures. You are an intelligent and educated man; you are not a fool who can be persuaded by inconceivable lies. Hence my amazement."

Polybius carefully examined his gray hands, and did not speak for a moment or two. Then he said, with obvious reluctance, "If I had not seen the evidence for myself, and listened to the oath of the man who best knew that the evidence was true, I should not have believed it myself. I confess I was aghast until finally convinced. I have no love for your Pheidias, I confess, but the evidence is against him and I was forced to order his imprisonment. There is also the matter of his blasphemy."

"Of what does that consist?"

Polybius regarded Pericles with open animosity. "He put his face, and yours, on the shield of Athene Parthenos."

Pericles smiled. "At my insistence." He paused. "Are you accusing me of blasphemy also, Polybius?"

"I am not sitting in judgment on you, lord."

"Ah, you are evasive. Judges are famous for that so I will not reproach you. But does not such an artist as Pheidias deserve to have his face or name in an inconspicuous place on the shield? It is there for future ages to reverence."

"Your face is also there."

Now, in spite of his emotions, Pericles laughed. "Pheidias insisted. If you think it best I will have it obliterated, for future ages will not remember me but they will remember Pheidias and give him honor."

When Polybius did not speak, Pericles continued: "You must admit that the statue is the most exalted and prodigious creation."

"It was very expensive." The older man's tone was obstinate.

Pericles remembered that Polybius was as penurious, if not more, than had been his cousin, Daedalus. He said, in a soft voice, "My dear Polybius, is not our patron goddess worthy of any cost?"

The desiccated face of Polybius flushed. "She would not wish Athens to bankrupt herself."

"The cost of the statue was like a mean copper in comparison with what we have spent, and are spending, on these dreary little wars and skirmishes with Sparta and her allies."

The King Archon had heard much of the rumor that Pericles had created diversions with those wars, in order to direct attention of the market rabble and others from his own derelictions. This, the King Archon did not believe, though he would have liked to do so. Moreover, there was the honor of their mutual house to consider. "Still," he said, "in these dolorous and costly times it was folly to spend so much on the statue—even if it is in honor of our patron goddess. The gods do not like extravagance in men."

"If Athene is aware of the statue raised to her, which," said Pericles very soberly, "no doubt she is, she will be so gratified that we have sacrificed so much for her that she will bring us peace, or at least chastise Sparta."

"That is a sophistry to excuse extravagance, of which you, yourself, Pericles, are guilty." Now the small dull eyes glittered under their lids.

"Oh, I am a very reckless man!" said Pericles. "I desire only the best and the most beautiful for our goddess! So, indeed, I plead guilty to too much piety."

"If so, I have not heard of that piety," said the King Archon, with a tight little smile, and Pericles smiled also.

The King Archon said, "There is no love between us, Pericles, but I can assure you that Pheidias will be given a just trial before me."

"You need not have said that, Polybius. I know it without any declaration from you. I do not fear the jury. My anger is not based on anxiety or apprehension for Pheidias. It is based on the cruel absurdity of the charges against him, the monstrous calumnies."

The King Archon was silent. Pericles refilled his own goblet.

"You will not tell me who brought the charges?"

"No. That will be revealed at the trial."

Pericles studied him thoughtfully. "You know who the men are?"

The King Archon did not reply. Pericles' eyes narrowed. "Can you tell me, at least, if they are honorable men?"

"Of that I can assure you."

For the first time Pericles felt a thrill of alarm. The men, then, were his powerful enemies and they would stop at nothing to injure him through his friends. He ran their names through his mind. Then, all at once, for no reason he could discern, his thoughts stopped at the name of Callias, the despicable, the swinelike, the brutish. He told himself that Callias, though malign, did not possess the intelligence to deceive such as Polybius, whom Polybius disdained, himself. Whatever else Polybius was, and Pericles disliked him intensely, he could never have been suborned, though he would not flinch at causing Pericles pain under unimpeachable circumstances. Therefore, he had been, without his knowledge, completely deceived, not only by the men who had brought charges against Pheidias but by their lofty station, which, in the mind of Polybius, would render them incapable of lies and perjury.

Pericles did not know what made him say, "Is Dejanira's son, Callias, part of the plot against Pheidias?"

"I have not seen Callias since his return from exile."

"You have not answered my question, Polybius," said Pericles with much sternness.

"Do you think honorable men would associate with Callias?" asked the King Archon, and his voice was indignant. "Do you believe that I, though his kinsman, would believe a word that rascal said?" His indignation increased and he pushed himself to his feet and his face was as angry as Pericles' own. It was as if he had been mortally insulted.

Pericles said, "No, you would never believe him. But still, there is something nebulous that flutters in my mind about him, in this matter."

"No man of integrity or family would receive Callias."

"With that, I agree. But a man will pick up even the dirtiest stone to hurl, if it serves his purpose."

The King Archon bowed stiffly. "If you will permit me, lord, I shall leave, for there are three cases waiting to be tried before me this morning, and I am late."

Pericles dismissed him. Then he called for his guard and rode with them to the prison, where he found Pheidias in a reasonably clean cell. The sculptor received him with affection but said, "You have endangered yourself in coming here, my best of friends."

"Nonsense. I am going to defend you, and make your enemies, and mine, the hilarity of all of Greece."

Pheidias was not afraid. He only wrinkled his brow and mused, "There are moments when I laugh, myself, but better men than I have been murdered by lies, Pericles. How have I offended the people of Athens?" His look was ingenuous and bewildered, and Pericles was much moved and again powerfully angered.

"You have done nothing but devote your life to Athens. So do not fear, Pheidias."

"I do not fear." Pheidias sat down on his bench and bent his head. "I do not understand. There is some error."

"Which I will rectify."

Pheidias looked up and smiled. "Of that I have no doubt. But I am wounded in my heart that anyone should suspect me of evil."

Pericles touched him on the shoulder. "To ease that wound I have brought you two bottles of my very best wine and some of my more distinguished cheeses and a çold but delectable roasted fowl. I will order that you be tried tomorrow, at the very latest—when I will defend you—so that you may return to your work on the acropolis, to the applause of all of Athens."

The face of Pheidias became radiant. "Ah, yes. We must order the marble for the pediments. I was engaged in consultations for their exact dimensions when I was arrested."

The prison guards looked inquisitively through the bars of the cell while Pericles laid the excellent provisions on Pheidias' bare table. He had also brought fine cutlery and linen from his own house. Pheidias looked with that candid child-likeness of his at the array. "It comes to me," he said in surprise, "that I have not eaten this day, and now my appetite is aroused."

Pericles, pressed by other business, left him to enjoy the meal, after embracing him.

Pericles was less cheerful than he had shown Pheidias, not that he truly feared for the life or safety of his friend but because of his wrath against those who had accused the sculptor. But I will know their names tomorrow, he told himself, and I will confront them, those "honorable" men! They will learn, to their sorrow, what justice really is!

He returned at twilight, full of care and weariness, to his house, empty now of the beauteous presence of Aspasia and his gay young son, and Paralus, who was now espoused to the daughter of a very notable house. He had become a young and acknowledged philosopher himself, under the tutelage of Socrates. He was writing a thesis on his studies, which even his skeptical father had acknowledged as original and full of clarity. The young man's presence was so charming that few noticed the shrunken lids over his blind eye, and Pericles loved him dearly and was proud of him.

Xanthippus was now a captain in the army, and was endlessly engaged in the skirmishes in Attica against the Spartans. He wrote to his father that though the Spartans were ridiculous they were also valorous.

Pericles dreaded the return to his house and its loneliness. He hoped that at least there would be a letter from Xanthippus. But in the atrium he was greeted by the joyous shouts of young Pericles, and the smiles and embraces of the luminous Aspasia, still lovely though there were strands of gray in her wonderful hair, and the faintest of wrinkles about her topaz eyes. Paralus was also there, smiling widely; he came to embrace his father when Pericles could disentangle himself from the vehement arms of his youngest son.

"Did you think we would not be here with you, beloved?" asked Aspasia. She studied Pericles' face with some anxiety. "We were almost on your heels, after the slaves had informed us that you had returned to Athens."

"But you are tired," said Pericles, kissing her warmly, as was his custom on entering or leaving his house, much to the disapproval of the Athenians who had heard of this.

"No. We had a pleasant journey."

"But, it is very hot and fetid in the city now."

"What is that to us, when we cannot endure being separated from you?"

Later Pericles told her of Pheidias. Like himself, she was incredulous and the brilliant color left her cheeks and lips. Paralus said, "It is unbelievable! Pheidias, and peculation and blasphemy!"

"I did not believe it, myself, at first, Paralus. But these are incredible days. We call ourselves a free democracy, but long ago I discovered that there is no freedom in a democracy, for all it is called the rule of a state by free men, with their own elected officials. Subornation and treachery are the marks of democracies; their suicide is inevitable."

That night he spent a long hour in his library, thinking, and preparing his case to defend Pheidias. At intervals he rose and paced the floor, shaking his head. Now he was truly afraid, not for Pheidias, but for his city, for if such things could happen to a man like the sculptor then no man was safe, and there was no real justice, but only chaotic emotions and falsehoods, and the worst of venalities.

CHAPTER 14

Pericles arrived at his offices very early the next morning, so early that the first rays of the still invisible sun were just striking the vast golden face of Athene Parthenos on her pediment. Her calm and noble eyes stared to the east, her helmet illuminated, her hand grasping her spear. Its tip appeared ignited with flame. But her gilded and ivory body was still only shadowy. The stupendousness of the work of Pheidias never failed to amaze and awe Pericles. It was immortal. Even if the goddess disintegrated with time, which was inevitable, future ages would remember that she had existed, and had been brought into existence by an unassuming man. Who, then, was the god, Pheidias or Athene?

Athens lay below that majesty, still dark and amorphous in the arms of her hills, and the great golden face so far above her, fired by the first fierce rays of the sun, challenged the very sun, itself.

The Agora, never empty at any time, had only a few men hurrying along the street, carrying lanterns which they had not as yet extinguished. The clatter of the hoofs of Pericles' horse and the horses of his soldiers on stone startled them. A few raised a shout of acclamation. He saluted them absently. He entered his offices and began at once to search his dossiers. But the King Archon had intimated that Pheidias would be tried only before him and the jury, so grave were his alleged crimes. For, if proved guilty, he would be sentenced to death, and not to mere exile.

If only I knew the names of his accusers, thought Pericles. He fumed, sitting at his table. But he would soon know. He studied many of the dossiers, slowly drinking wine and eating brined olives and cheese. He had slept little; his mind had been in a turmoil whipped to the utmost intensity by his anger. He had informed Aspasia the night before that he would bring Pheidias to his house for dinner, and that she should send slaves to invite others of their friends also, to rejoice with Pheidias and to laugh with him over his trial and his exoneration.

The scribes and bureaucrats were beginning to arrive. Pericles could hear their sleepy voices and their footsteps. The darkness was already gray and diffused. The sun would soon climb the top of the eastern hills. The slight fresh coolness of the night was fast disappearing and pulses of heat came through the windows and the city was throbbing again. Now a ray of sunlight flashed into the offices, like an arrow of light.

The case of Pheidias, because it was so important, would be brought before the King Archon and the jury just before noon, when it would be the hottest. Minor cases would be heard first. In the meantime there were many scrolls and papers on Pericles' table, tedious but necessary, written meticulously by bureaucrats, and Pericles must attend to them. He was already sweating. He took off his helmet and laid it near his hand, for rarely was he seen without it outside his house, and after all these years he was still sensitive about the towering height of his brow and skull. His thick tawny hair was gray at the temples and there was a furrow of gray rising above his forehead, sharp and defined, so that he appeared more leonine than in his youth and young manhood, and more formidable. This was accented by his face, which had become haggard and lined in recent years and grimmer, and had lost all its smoothness.

Less than two hours before noon one of the bureaucrats came in to announce that the King Archon was without and prayed an immediate audience with Pericles. Ah, he thought in exultation, he has come to tell me that Pheidias will not be tried at all, that all charges against him had been withdrawn, and that he was free! Smiling, he rose to greet Polybius, who was ceremoniously ushered in, and took a step towards him. Then he saw the older man's face, and stopped short and a great plunging ran through his heart.

For the face of the King Archon was grayer than ever, and he seemed much agitated, and his lips moved soundlessly. For one of the few times in his life Pericles began to tremble. He seized the Archon by the arm and forced him into a chair, and exclaimed, "What is it? Why have you come?"

Polybius sagged in the chair. He put his hands over his face and rubbed all his features, while Pericles loomed over him, crying, "Tell me! You must tell me!"

Polybius panted. He rubbed his eyes with the ends of his fingers. Then he dropped his hands and Pericles saw that his eyelids were scarlet and dry, as if burned. He had suddenly become very old, and weak.

"Wine, in the name of the gods," he croaked. With hands that shook violently Pericles poured him wine and held it to his lips, racked with a terrible impatience and foreboding. The King Archon drank, coughed, almost strangled, then let the still half-filled goblet drop nervelessly to the table, where it rolled and poured out its contents in an acrid stream. It then fell to the floor with a crash. The wine filled the office with a pungent odor.

"Speak," commanded Pericles. His dread had become unbearable.

"Pheidias," said Polybius in so faint a voice that Pericles could hardly hear him and had to bend forward. "He is dead."

"Dead," repeated Pericles, and the word had no meaning for him, for he was stricken with an icy coldness in all that heat, and his chilled sweat rolled down his face and body and legs and arms.

"Poisoned," said Polybius.

Now Pericles could not stand any longer. He fell into his chair and stared numbly at his kinsman. "Poisoned," he repeated. "When? By whom?"

He was taken by a total incredulity. It was not possible. He was uttering mad words, words given to him by an elderly madman. Pheidias, the glory of Athens, could not be dead. He could not have been—murdered. No, it was not possible. It was all insanity.

Pericles, losing all his control, reached across the table and seized the brittle wrist of Polybius and shook the wrist and the hand so ferociously that Polybius' entire arm was flailed like the arm of a puppet. The ferocity even caused his body to move limply, so that he slid on the seat of his chair. Only Pericles' iron grasp kept him from falling to the floor. Polybius saw Pericles' face as in a nightmare, and he shrank from its aspect.

Polybius' voice, as frail as the crackling of a fallen leaf underfoot, issued from his lips. "He was found dead just after dawn, by the special guards. There was some wine before him, and remnants of food." Polybius paused and regarded Pericles with appalled eyes. "The guards said that you, Pericles, had given them to him. The food was set before—a dog —and he died of it. It contained hemlock."

The room darkened and swayed about Pericles. Whirling within it he said over and over to himself, No, I am dreaming, or dying. As from an enormous distance he heard Polybius say, "I was brought the news but an hour ago, and when I could order myself I came to you."

Murdered, thought Pericles. There was a frightful ache between his temples, rushing over his forehead in intolerable waves of anguish. He did not know that he had closed his eyes and was shuddering.

"I am a just man," Polybius said. "I know that you did not do this thing, for did you not love Pheidias and had you not come to his rescue? You are incapable of such an act. You are also—my kinsman. But who placed the poison in that unfortunate man's food? I have questioned the guards."

Pericles opened eyes so weighted that he could scarce lift his eyelids. His face was the face of a man near death. His throat was so arid that he had to swallow over and over to moisten it with viscid spittle. He said, "I ate of that food, myself, in my own house, and my old cook filled a basket with it. It was not poisoned, either the wine or the cheese or the fowl." The anguish in his head was in his throat now and stabbing down into his heart. The face of Polybius advanced and retreated before him in a mist.

He felt rather than saw Polybius start. "Wine? Cheese? Fowl? But what of the broiled fish and pastries you also sent him just before dawn, today, for his breakfast?" The older man's voice was bewildered yet stronger.

"I sent nothing," Pericles whispered. "I did not send those. I brought him, yesterday, but wine and cheese and fowl, for his supper. With my own hands, I brought them."

Polybius stared. He thought Pericles had become calmer. "But one of your slaves brought the fish and pastries, saying to the guards that you had commanded that he do so! That you wished the illustrious Pheidias to be refreshed and strong for his ordeal!"

Pericles began to shake his head, helplessly, and could not stop. "I sent no one. My slaves have been in my house for many years, and I trust them all. None would have reason to murder Pheidias."

Then he struck the table with a loud crack of his palm upon it, and when a scribe rushed in Pericles commanded that his soldiers be brought into the office. The scribe bowed, after first gazing at Pericles with astonishment. Then he ran off. The two men sat in silence, and Pericles' great shuddering did not cease.

The soldiers entered in haste, and Pericles said to them, "Did anyone leave my house at any time in the night or the morning?"

Iphis said to him, "No, lord, none left the house. I myself, patrolled long before dawn, and my men reported that no one had even approached your house, and none had departed. Not even a mouse could have come or gone without our knowledge."

The other soldiers nodded emphatically, and saluted. Iphis looked at Pericles and was alarmed at his color and expression. "You must believe me, lord. Has there been some calamity?"

Polybius spoke, for Pericles seemed beyond speaking now. "Do you trust the slaves in the house of Pericles, Captain?"

"Yes, of a certainty. I know them all; I have known them many years. There is no newcomer among them, male or female."

"There is no young man of a pleasing aspect, and of a good height with an engaging voice and an agreeable manner, as if he had had considerable education?"

"No, lord. The youngest man is over thirty years of age, and he is partly crippled. The master wished to set him free, with a lifelong stipend, but the slave pleaded not to be sent from the house and refused his freedom."

Pericles could now speak, with short gasps. "Pheidias, Iphis, was found poisoned this morning, by food someone brought him, saying it was at my command and from my house. The stranger declared he was my slave, of my household."

Iphis uttered a strangled word that was a hardly disguised oath. "That is impossible!" he cried in a raised voice. His brown eyes bulged upon Pericles. "I do not believe it."

"It is true," said Polybius. "The guards described him, to me, when I sent for them. They were as aghast as myself. They are not regular guards of the prison, Captain. They are soldiers of your own company. I have no reason to believe they are lying. They were sent to me by your superior officer, at my orders, for I had come to believe"—he paused and glanced at Pericles—"I had come to believe that Pheidias was innocent of the charges brought against him, and I wished him well protected."

Pericles roused himself. "Why did you fear, Polybius, that someone might desire him to die before his trial, so that you ordered those soldiers?"

Polybius hesitated. "Call it an old man's intuition, an old man's doubt, after I talked with you yesterday, Pericles. I have never done this before, for any prisoner. I told myself it was folly, and I am not a foolish man as a rule. But still, there was uneasiness within me and I have no name for it."

"But why should Pheidias be murdered, lord?" asked Iphis, and he moved closer, protectingly, to Pericles. "The charges against him were grave. I have heard it in the city, and from Pericles, himself. He might have been condemned to death, or exiled. Therefore, why was he murdered?"

Again Polybius hesitated. "I have no proof. But I say this: Someone was afraid he would be exonerated and freed. Or someone hated Pericles enough to strike at him in this manner, so he made certain that Pheidias would die. Or—"

"Or what, lord?"

Polybius averted his face. "Or, someone wished to spread the rumor that Pericles, himself, wished Pheidias dead."

"But why?" cried Iphis. "It is known that they were the closest of friends, closer than brothers!" His strong soldier's face was astounded.

"Yes," said Polybius. He thought for a moment, passing his hand over his face. "They killed, as Aesop would say, two birds with one stone. They deprived Pericles of his best friend, and so wounded him almost to the death. They may also have prepared a rumor that Pericles had poisoned Pheidias, so as to make him accursed in the eyes of all Athens."

Iphis himself shuddered. His thoughts were now only for his general, Pericles, so that he almost forgot Pheidias. "But it will be easy to prove that no such slave is in Pericles' house, such as came to the prison."

"They will then say the stranger, the murderer, was a hired assassin. If they can convince Athens of that, then the disaster of what happened to Pheidias will be less than the diaster they will be able to inflict on Pericles."

"Gods," Iphis whispered. He poured some wine for Pericles and forced him to swallow it. He put down the goblet and clenched his fists. His eyes glowed with fire. "I would I had them before me, now!"

"I have another thought," said Polybius. "It is possible that now many will believe that had Pheidias been brought to trial he would have implicated Pericles in peculation and heresy."

"But the people will not believe any of these things!"

Polybius sighed. "I am an old man and I have never confessed this before: There is nothing the people will not believe of one such as Pericles."

Pericles now roused himself. He fixed Polybius with a deadly look.

"Tell me now, Polybius, my kinsman. Who were the men who brought charges against Pheidias?"

Polybius threw up his hands. "As Pheidias is dead, there is no harm in telling you, for the evidence is useless. Thucydides, the money-lender, came to me with Polycrates, the head-keeper of the treasury in Athens, saying that Polycrates had come to him, as an old friend, to show him records that Pheidias had received enormous sums for his work on the acropolis, sums of unbelievable amounts, and that on several occasions Pheidias had said this was your command. Pheidias had shown him letters purported to be from you, letters which he took away with him. I made Polycrates swear the most solemn of oaths that this was so, and he repeated his charges and expressed his distress, for was he not a friend of yours and had you not appointed him keeper of the treasury? He implored me not to speak of this to you, for fear of your grief, but his conscience had been tormenting him, he declared. He had come to believe that you gave no such letters to Pheidias. Yet, if the sums became public property he would have to speak, in defense of himself."

Polybius paused. "Again, he repeated to me that he did not believe that you, Pericles, knew of this robbery, this peculation, and once more implored me not to tell you. I, alas, had no doubt of his sincerity. His distress, it appeared to me, was genuine."

He added, almost piteously, "Is not Polycrates of a great and noble family? Why should I have doubted his word?"

"Or the word, Polybius, of the old usurer, Thucydides?"

Polybius spread out his old hands. "Yes, I know he has always hated you and complained of your extravagance, among many other things. But he is a friend of Polycrates."

Pericles stood up suddenly, and then to keep himself from falling grasped the back of his chair. He went to his cabinet and then brought out a scroll. He sat down and began to read it to himself, and his face, white as death, burst into fresh sweat. Then he said, "Polycrates, son of Arrian. Yes, of a great and noble family. But they have become impoverished, through unwise investments and certain fires which destroyed much of their property, fires lit by the Persians. They have never recovered from that calamity, for they are proud. It was to assist Polycrates that I appointed him to the treasury, so that he would have a considerable income. No doubt but that made him hate me."

He looked at Polybius. "He has been bribed, and bribed well. Moreover, his wife is not of Athenian birth, though only I knew that. In some manner, years ago, the record-keepers were induced to inscribe her name, though a humble one, in the archives of our city as an Athenian. She was very beautiful. How I came upon the knowledge is not pertinent. I have kept my silence out of compassion." He flung the scroll from him. "Apparently my own silence was not enough. Others learned of the forgery, and used it against Polycrates."

Polybius, whose hetaira was an Ionian, and whom he loved passionately for all his age, felt one of the first impulses of pity he had ever known. "Alas," he said, "Polycrates was under great duress. His wife—and money. Love—and greed. They are not to be underestimated. It is not that I exonerate him. I can only understand why he did this."

Pericles said to Iphis, "Take some of your men and bring Polycrates to me at once. And Thucydides."

CHAPTER 15

Polycrates, a man near Pericles' own age, was tall and athletic and patrician of appearance, with a long pale face and large brown eyes and an esthetic expression. He dressed soberly, as befitted the position he held, which once had made Pericles remark, "The sanctity of money is held greater by the people than the sanctity of God. Let the philosophers say, in their innocence, that money is of no importance. The people know better, and those who engage in money do so with the reverence of priests." As the keeper of the treasury, and as the man who had insisted that Athens coin her own gold instead of allowing Persia to do that, Polycrates never permitted a jest in his presence which might belittle either money or his calling. To him that was sacrilege.

Thucydides, not to be confused with the historian of the same name, was, in the eyes of Polycrates a man to be respected, for all he was a money-lender and therefore pernicious in his dealings. He was rich, and despite his own aristocratic lineage Polycrates held some deference for the old man, though the latter had no ancestors of which he could boast. He was short of stature, broad of shoulders and thin of body, with a mane of white hair and a thick white beard, which was like gleaming silk. It was his only physical asset, for he had little sharp eyes and a nose like a vulture, to which many of those who owed him money likened him.

The two men had been kept separated by the soldiers, so that neither could speak to the other, though this did not prevent them from exchanging glances of fear and dread while they were being conducted to the presence of Pericles. Neither had yet heard of the death of Pheidias, for neither had been in the plot to kill him, for their companions in conspiracy to arrest and try Pheidias had thought it wise not to mention that part of the scheme to them. First of all, they thought their fellow aristocrat, Polycrates, had become too prudent since he had been master of the treasury, and though he hated Pericles for what he called the "despoiling of the people's money," and because Pericles had befriended him when he was in dire need, he was too circumspect to be a murderer, and too self-protective. Thucydides might be shrill and hate Pericles for certain personal reasons, such as Pericles' prosecution of him for outrageous usury, and he might desire that Pericles be ousted from office and that his friends be imprisoned or exiled. But he was too cautious by nature, and too cowardly, to sanction bold killing. As a youth he had been expelled from the army after the first month, for those two traits of character which the officers hardly considered soldierly, even the urbane Athenian officers who were not of too strong a military mind.

Both Polycrates and Thucydides believed they were to be brought to Pericles because in some fashion Pericles had heard of the plot to imprison Pheidias, and to bring him to trial and eventual exile, or, in the last extremity, to be condemned to death by the proper and legal authorities. But to engage privately in murder, or sanction it illegally and in cold

503

blood, was beyond their temperaments. They had both persuaded themselves, when uneasy thoughts came to them, that they had acted virtuously, even Polycrates who had forged the records against the innocent man. Polycrates had actually begun to believe that Pericles had swindled the treasury for his grandiose plans for Athens, and had given some of the booty to Pheidias, for was not his extravagance bankrupting the city? Therefore, the forging of the records against Pheidias was justified, if false. There were many ways to catch a felon, including criminality, itself, if the law were impotent.

Polycrates, being more intelligent than Thucydides, had brought himself to the thought, just before entering the presence of Pericles: Of a surety Pheidias has blasphemed Athene Parthenos, and doubtless was given large sums from the treasury by Pericles, and this will be proved at the trial; Pericles intends to intimidate me—but I have friends almost as powerful as he, and they will not desert me. Thucydides was less trusting in his terrified thoughts, and he said to himself, If our friends betray us then I shall embroil them to the utmost. So they composed themselves as well as they could and when conducted into the offices of Pericles they had lost some of their terror.

They were astonished to see the King Archon there, for was he not to preside at the trial of Pheidias, which would be held despite the delay in the appearance of the chief witness, Polycrates? Even Pericles, himself, could not stop the trial and would be forced to release Polycrates, despite any of his accusations, which he could not prove. One has only to be valiant, said the most unvaliant of men, Polycrates. But could it be that the King Archon, before the trial, wished to hear his testimony to ascertain if it were valid? Polycrates, at this, gave the King Archon a faint smile, and was dismayed when Polybius averted his head. As for Thucydides, he could only gape, for his mind was not as agile as that of Polycrates, and he was an old man.

The two culprits then dared to look at Pericles who was sitting tall and stiffly in his chair, and they shrank when they saw his face and again began to tremble with terror. He studied their countenances. He knew both well, particularly Polycrates, whom he had assisted so generously. As he was a most perceptive and astute man, and understood human nature in all its varieties and venalities, he had his first doubts. Polycrates was quite capable of bending under harsh pressure, but he was not a violent man. Thucydides was an avaricious usurer and swindler and a vulgarian on his mother's side.

Therefore, he was also a coward. He might be party to libel and slander and covert attacks, and he was notoriously malicious. He loved money as a man loves his mistress; he would not endanger that money—however he might jeopardize his life in the pursuit of it—by engaging in murder. It was not in the character of either man, and Pericles wondered if they knew that murder had been plotted by their fellow conspirators. He doubted it. It was more likely that they had never been informed by their more malignant companions.

Nevertheless, he said to them in a quiet and frightening voice, "What have you two murderers to say for yourselves?"

He saw that both of them were instantly stunned. He had spoken to them while they were bowing to him, and they stood paralysed, half-bent, and their faces were grotesque with shock, their mouths dropping open, their eyes bulging. They stared at him, unblinking, as at a basilisk. Thucydides' ophidian eyes did not waver; those of Polycrates were dazed.

"Why did you murder Pheidias, that great artist?" he asked, for they were unable to speak, and seemed not to breathe.

Polycrates, the man more likely by breeding to find his voice first, gasped, " 'Murder' lord? Surely you are jesting!"

"Jesting," repeated Thucydides, wavering on his feet.

Pericles said in that dreadfully quiet voice, "I am not jesting. He was poisoned early this morning, in his cell." Now he raised his voice so that it cracked in the room, "What had he done to you that you plotted against him and killed him?"

"Gods," groaned Polycrates, and he turned feebly to the King Archon and held out his hands as if for succor. But the King Archon's countenance was as pitiless as Pericles'. Polycrates then turned to Pericles and cried out in anguish, "If he was murdered I knew it not, and had no part in it! Before the gods, lord, I swear it!"

"Before the gods, I swear it also!" Thucydides quavered, and his eyelids fluttered as if he were about to faint. He began half to retch, half to sob. He looked at Polycrates, then he caught the younger man's arm to keep from falling. His white hair rose like a mane in the worst fright he had ever felt in his life. "Why should anyone—" He could not continue for a moment. "Why should anyone murder Pheidias?"

"I do not know," said Pericles, in the most terrible voice anyone had ever heard him use. "But as you two were part of the plot to destroy him you are also capable of murder, if that will serve your purpose."

He had accomplished what he had desired: He had shaken them to their very marrow and rendered them feeble and petrified and helpless. Perjury and bribery were one thing; assassination was another. Before they could recover their sense of self-protection and seek to lie to him, he said, "You see my captain and my soldiers. It is lawful to execute murderers on the spot, if they confess. Why do you then not confess and die easily, and not face trial, public ignominy and public death? You, Polycrates, are a man of a noble house. You would prefer private execution to exposure to the eyes of the populace when you die. Iphis!"

Iphis stepped forward. Polycrates regarded him with ghastly terror, and retreated a step. Pericles lifted his hand as if to restrain his captain.

"And before you die, Polycrates, it will be revealed openly that you had your wife's name forged on the public records as an Athenian. Therefore, she is not your wife; she is your concubine, and your sons are illegitimate. They will inherit nothing from you, and your family will shun them forever afterwards."

Then all Polycrates' last resistance disappeared, and he fell to his knees before Pericles and clasped his hands beseechingly and wept and said, "Lord, have mercy on the helpless, if not on me—who am innocent of murder and knew nothing of it! I will die gladly to spare those I love from infamy and shame—"

"You did not spare Pheidias, whom I loved. Why, then, should I spare you, who killed Pheidias?"

Polycrates groaned over and over. He bent, still on his knees, and beat his head on the stone floor until it suddenly bled. Pericles gave a signal to Iphis, and the soldier seized Polycrates by the neck and dragged him to his feet. Tears and his blood ran down his face. He repeated, "I am innocent of murder! Do with me what you will, but spare my wife and children! I am not afraid to die; I fear only the destiny of my family. You have sons, lord, and so you are not insensible to their fate—"

Thucydides stood shaking and whimpering and wringing his hands. Pericles gave him a glance of awful loathing, but he spoke only to Polycrates.

"It may be that you did not murder Pheidias, or give orders for him to die and that you did not know that his death was plotted. I will accept that for a moment. But you did forge the public records of the treasury that Pheidias was a thief, that he had received boundless sums for the glorious work he has done. You did accept a bribe for that evil work. You were threatened with exposure concerning your wife and sons."

Polycrates wiped the blood and sweat and tears from his face with the back of a palsied hand.

He said in a despairing tone, "Yes, that is true. I would have resisted the bribe, however I lusted for the money. I confess that in the end I even convinced myself that it was indeed true, that Pheidias had looted the treasury with your consent, lord. Yes, I confess that, for were the sums not enormous which were poured out on the acropolis? I had my conscience to overcome first, before I could accede to pressure. The bribe alone—yes, I might have resisted that. But I was threatened by exposure of my illegal marriage to my beloved wife, and that I could not resist."

Pericles' pale lips tightened. The man's obvious agony was beginning to affect him. So he turned to Thucydides.

"What part did you play in this most monstrous plot, you senile old wretch?"

Thucydides whimpered, "I never knew. Mercy, lord. I was maddened by your extravagance. I confess that. I hated you, I confess that. So I joined in the conspiracy against you, to strike at you through Pheidias. But, murder! Gods, not murder!"

Pericles leaned back in his chair and considered him with intense hatred.

"Had Pheidias been found guilty, through the force of Polycrates' forgery, and your accusations and conspiracy, he would have been executed. And that would have been murder, would it not?"

Thucydides wagged his head and whimpered louder. "No. I would not have thought it murder. It would have been execution. But, I was assured that almost the most that would happen to Pheidias would be exile, or imprisonment, and public disgrace. I had nothing against Pheidias as a man or an artist. There was only your extravagance. Again, yes, I hated you. You had me prosecuted as a usurer—" He had become incoherent and now he could only utter whining and incoherent sounds.

"I, then, of a surety, was intended to be your victim. That is so?"

The silence of the two men was more of a confession than words.

The King Archon spoke for the first time to the culprits. "You, Polycrates, of an aristocratic family, would have sworn most solemnly before me today that Pheidias was guilty of peculations. You, Thucydides, would have declared that Pheidias was also guilty of sacrilege, though even the market rabble has not yet reached that conclusion. Neither of you dared to attempt the assassination of your Head of State openly, or to defame his character openly. But you plotted to do that through Pheidias. This, in my opinion, is worse than murder. Alas, that there is no adequate punishment for both of you!"

Now he rose in the full dignity of his official robes and said to them with bitter sternness: "I am your judge, before the gods. Before me, Polycrates, you would have committed perjury against an innocent man, for his destruction. You are more guilty than your companion, Thucydides, who is very old and considers money sacred, and is of a lowly house through his mother. Therefore, I now put you both under arrest and confine you to prison to await a public trial, where all will be exposed and nothing hidden."

"A moment," said Pericles. "I need the names of your fellow conspirators, for they shall not escape my own judgment. Speak, Polycrates. You have nothing to lose now."

But Polycrates hesitated, for he was of an aristocratic house. It was Thucydides who took a trembling step towards Pericles and cried out, "I will name them, lord, if you will have mercy on me! I am an old man, white of hair and beard, and I would die in prison. Have mercy!"

Pericles said, "I will promise you nothing, but I will take into consideration that you have made a full confession of your guilt, and that you have not withheld the names of your guilty companions."

He lifted his pen and drew parchment towards him. "Well?" he said. Thucydides glanced swiftly at Polycrates, who could only stand, the blood trickling down his face.

So Thucydides named them. The King Archon listened in silent horror, for several were his friends and one was married to his niece. Once or twice he made a gesture of despair and sickness. Pericles wrote down each name as Thucydides mumbled it, still wringing his hands. When Thucydides stopped speaking, Pericles contemplated the names he had written and his eyes had the blank look of a statue staring at the sun.

He said, most quietly, "Polycrates, I thought that I, and I alone, knew of your illicit marriage. I never told you I knew. I had pity, as you did not have pity, or gratitude for my appointing you keeper of the treasury. If you remain alive and are tried, that marriage will become public knowledge. I assure you of that. If you are not tried, your companions will keep their own silence, for they are of your class. They will also believe that you never betrayed them, and so will not speak."

He then turned to Thucydides. "I do not wish you tried, ei-

508

ther, for you might blurt out the pathetic concealment of Polycrates. Yes, I call it pathetic, for do I not, myself, love a foreign woman? You are not to be trusted in open court, Thucydides. So, you must leave Athens at once, for self-appointed exile, for life. And," again his voice rose dauntingly, "if you speak of Polycrates, and his family, then even in exile you will be sought out and you will die."

Thucydides, overcome with feverish joy, clasped his hands and beat them against his bearded chin. "Lord, may the gods bless you for your mercy! I will leave, today, today, with no word to anyone, not even my kindred!" Tears of both exhaustion and relief spurted from his eyes.

Pericles made a mouth of total disgust. He said, "You have not told me which man it was who bribed Polycrates."

Now Thucydides himself hesitated, for he had withheld the name of Callias out of fear of Pericles, himself, for was not Callias the son of Pericles' rejected wife? Callias might hate Pericles, and Pericles detest Callias, but he was the brother of Pericles' sons. He was in a dilemma, and again he darted a glance at Polycrates. But Polycrates had bent his head and appeared to be meditating.

"Was it you, Thucydides?" said Pericles.

Terrified again, fearful that the mercy offered him would be withdrawn if Pericles believed him guilty, the old man exclaimed, "Lord, you must not be angry, for have I not confessed and given you the names of the others? Lord, the man who bribed Polycrates and threatened him was—was—Callias, brother to your sons."

There was a prolonged silence in the room, while all stood as statues, even Iphis and the soldiers. Then Pericles said, without any emotion apparent at all, "I should have guessed it. Yes, I should have known."

He laid the pen down on the table with a steady hand. He began to roll the parchment as if he was not aware of those about him.

Finally he looked at Polycrates and now Polycrates looked at him steadfastly. The blood was clotting on his forehead.

"You are a brave man, for all your venality, Polycrates, and all your crimes against a good and innocent and illustrious man. Yes, you might have resisted bribery, but not the shame of your family. You see that I am merciful, after all."

Polycrates bowed in silence, and his face was the face of a dead man.

"You understand entirely, Polycrates?"

"Yes, lord," Polycrates replied. His smile was heart-broken

but unshaken. Thucydides stared. Polycrates was more guilty than himself, yet Pericles had spared him and he gaped and frowned. Polycrates was not even condemned to exile!

"You may both leave now," said Pericles and turned in his chair away from them. Then he said to Polycrates, "Go in peace. Embrace your family."

When they had left the King Archon said in a wondering and tremulous voice, "I have deeply wronged you, myself, Pericles, and I beg your forgiveness, for you are a noble man." He stopped and smiled a little. "For all you are also recklessly extravagant!"

But Pericles said nothing, and after a compassionate glance at him the King Archon departed also.

Polycrates did indeed embrace his beloved family that night, then retired to his chamber, alone. Then with a firm hand he plunged his dagger into his heart and quietly died. His suicide was never explained.

Callias was followed a few nights later when he went to one of his disreputable haunts near the sea, wrapped as always in a cloak and hood. He was murdered in an alley. His murderers were never found, but it was said that he had been slain by robbers, who had taken his purse.

The other conspirators were deluded that Polycrates had died rather than implicate them, so in gratitude they did not betray him in his death. As for Thucydides—where was that old vulgarian? No one ever saw him again. He had fled, they concluded, when he had heard of Polycrates' suicide. Therefore, the only two witnesses who could have brought them to trial had vanished. But when Callias was murdered, ostensibly by thieves, they guessed a little of the truth, if only a little. As for the stranger who had poisoned Pheidias, he was to remain undiscovered.

One by one they silently left Athens for prolonged absences, and a number of them did not return. But the rumor they had begun, that Pericles had had Pheidias poisoned, was believed by the market rabble.

CHAPTER 16

Paralus requested permission, through a slave, to speak to his father in Pericles' library. When the permission was given Paralus entered the library where Pericles, his face like gray marble, was studying some war maps and plans of strategy.

His heavy and white-streaked mane gave him an implacable look as it fell over his brow and ears, and he was no longer Head of State in his appearance but again an indomitable soldier, for the war with Sparta and her sister city-states had suddenly broken out in tragic thunder and fire. Athens had never been so ominously threatened since the Persian wars.

He looked up at Paralus almost as if he did not see him, then motioned to a chair. He returned to his maps. He wore a thick robe of crimson wool and a brazier burned warmly near him, for it was winter, and snow already lay heavily on the far Macedonian mountains and the air in Athens was as sharp as a sword to the flesh and a dull sky overlay her blasted hills. Pericles' feet were encased in fur-lined high boots, and his hands were chill and he rubbed them for a moment, absently, not taking his pale eyes from the maps.

Paralus did not sit down. He merely waited, gazing at his father, his face strangely resembling Pericles' own, for all his dark remaining eye. Pericles continued to study the maps, frowning. However, he was well aware that his son stood near him in silence. He was thinking. He heard the clang of iron-shod shoes outside on stone, as his soldiers guarded the house. The lamplight flickered in a draft; the woollen curtains were not quite drawn over the windows and the moon stared in, pure white ice drifting on a black sea.

Since last summer, when Pheidias and Callias had both been murdered, something had changed in Paralus. He had never been garrulous like his antic brother, now in command of a huge garrison of soldiers guarding the approach to Athens. Paralus was not subject to abrupt changes of moods, as was Xanthippus, and his humor was more ponderous, for all it was telling. He was steadfast and somewhat slow, in comparison with Xanthippus' volatile and witty nature. He was never noisy and he spoke only when he had something to say. Still, he had become more and more quiet since last summer, and his natural gravity had increased and often he appeared abstracted. Pericles, despite his awful problems, had finally become aware of this, though he had not remarked on it. Like Paralus, he never invaded the secret thoughts of others, except Aspasia's, for to him she was a second heart, a second mind, a second spirit. Even his loved sons never approached him as closely as she did; she was, to him, his own flesh.

Now he looked up at Paralus and said, "You asked to see me, my son. I must beg of you that what you have to say will be short, for it is very late and I have more maps to study."

Paralus said in the voice of Pericles' youth, firm and resonant, "I should like your permission to visit my mother for a time, until her grief subsides. She is all alone, except for her very aged mother, who cannot leave her bed any longer."

Pericles looked at him intently. Then he said, "You are not a child, or even a youth, Paralus. You are a young man. It is for you to decide."

Paralus bowed a little. Then their eyes fused together for several long moments. Finally Pericles sighed, and said, "I know there is something troubling you. I do not ask you to tell me, for you are a man and have the problems of a man, and it would be wrong for me to intrude on your thoughts. I have the fate of Athens in my hands; even my family must not supersede my duty there, or my strength."

"I understand," said Paralus. "I am not a petulant woman, demanding attention when weightier matters must be considered. I am the son of a soldier, the brother of a soldier. I would I were a soldier, myself. No matter. I thought, in all courtesy, that I should ask your permission to visit my lonely mother for a time, for I am still under your roof."

Pericles regarded him even more intently. He leaned back in his chair, and his light eyes were curiously shadowed though they glistened in the lamplight. It was as if he gazed through clear ice at his son, and not membrane. His hand tapped the maps slowly. Still holding Paralus' eye he said, and his voice had changed and become hard and slow:

"My son, Athens will never recover the glory she had in my dear friend, Pheidias, so heinously murdered. Part of the soul of Athens died when he died. He was of a stature of a god. When men die their families and friends mourn them. When a god dies the very heavens are shattered."

A small spasm passed over the face of Paralus, but he remained silent. For a moment his eye shifted; then it returned to the countenance of his father.

"Pheidias," said Pericles, "was, as you know, murdered not because he was hated—for who could have hated such a soul as was Pheidias? He was murdered in order to render me desolate. There was also a plot against me, your father, to despose or exile me."

Paralus said very quietly, "Yes. I know. I have heard rumors in the city. Athens is the very well of gossip."

Suddenly Pericles became almost wildly impatient. "Enough! I am glad that you have shown filial devotion to your mother, who indeed is alone. Return if and when you wish." He thought to himself, What father ever knows his son, or can break through the barrier of selfsame flesh to the profound spirit of complete understanding? We do not give our children their souls; we give them only their material bodies. We are not one with our children, as we are one with a beloved woman, and there is something mysterious in that, something arcanely ordained. The fruit of our loins are strangers, after all, and can sometimes be our deadliest enemies.

Then he softened somewhat towards Paralus, and held out his hand to him. "Is it farewell, my son?"

Paralus took his father's hand; his own fingers were very cold. He said, "No, it is not farewell, my father, but it may be for a long time."

Pericles tried to smile. He held his son's hand and said, "There are many things you do not understand, Paralus, which must remain a secret to me. There are others who need my silence, and their needs are greater than your own, or even mine. Go, then. Console your mother, who grieves for her dead son. She has, in you and Xanthippus, deeper consolations than she knows, unfortunate woman."

Paralus bowed again to his father, then left the room with Pericles' own stateliness, and Pericles watched him go and his heart was heavy. He returned to his maps and scrolls and pen. Suddenly he felt exhausted and sorrowful. Pheidias' death never left his mind; all at once his pain was as acute and as unbearable as if Pheidias had just been murdered, and his old incredulity returned that Pheidias was dead. Savagely, he flung a scroll from him and it dropped to the marble floor, which was so cold that even the thick Persian rug and his boots could feel the penetration of it. He shivered. He blinked his tired eyes, for a film had formed over them, which dimmed his vision. For the first time he felt a bitter anger against Paralus, who was obdurate and who had, in spite of his admirable self-control, a streak of softness in him and emotion. He would never have made an excellent soldier, thought Pericles. There is little ruthlessness in him, and not enough iron, and I am disappointed as well as saddened that his youth prevents him from understanding that what a man must do he must do. He does not think things through to their conclusion and accept them. Strange that I never knew that before, and I am chagrined.

Xanthippus, for all his seeming frivolity at times, and despite his easy laughter and mercurial temperament and gleefully ascerbic jests, and all his high grace and extreme elegance, was a stronger man than his brother, and, above all, a soldier. He had written of Callias, "I rejoice that such a monster has met his just fate, for he strewed disaster as careless children strew crumbs, or birds their droppings. The world is a cleaner place in that some unknown assassins sent him to Hades. I would that Chilon had drowned him in the Styx! Or Cerberus devoured him. If I knew his assassins I would send them my greetings and my congratulations."

Pericles' embittered heart warmed. He forgot that Xanthippus had disagreed with his father's latest strategy and had written him very recently to that effect, in colorful and eloquent protest. Xanthippus could not be outwardly calm, as could Paralus. He was either joyous or furious, depressed or elated. But always he was a soldier. When his wife had given birth to his son he had expressed his pleasure and gratification to her in vehement language in a letter which she cherished. Yet under his vivid froth there was the essential iron of a soldier and a man dedicated to his country, though often he had laughed at too-fervent patriotism. Despite his surface appearance of animated lightheartedness, and his mockery of those who were too serious and pompous, he was, in his inmost being, as inexorable as his father when it came to truly trenchant matters, and as immovable. Pericles considered his elder son with something like gratitude.

He blew out the lamp and went to his large chamber. Aspasia was not yet asleep, though it was very late. She seemed to know when he was disturbed and ill at ease, even if she never spoke of it. She held out her arms to him and he dropped on his knees beside the bed and rested his head on her breast, and she held him close to her. Her flesh was warm and sweet and fragrant; her hair fell over her shoulders and far down her back. Her touch was one of comfort and tenderness. Her eyes quivered with many sparkling lights, like brown wine in the sun.

He said, revelling in the clasp of her arms, "Paralus asked me for permission to leave my house and visit his mother—for a long time."

"I thought he would do that. I have thought he would for several months."

Pericles was astonished. "But you never told me."

"No. Were you not anxious enough, and distressed enough, at the outbreak of this great war which has been smoldering for many years? Until the hour came when Paralus had finally come to a decision was time, alas, for you to know. Before that, the added burden would have been too much."

He clung to her. He said, "Did I ever tell you that I love you, my darling?"

She rested her cheek on the top of his head, and laughed so that she would not weep. "No! Never did you tell me!"

His body was cold, and he shivered again, and he threw aside his robe and went under the blankets to her, and they made love as if this were their wedding night and they were young and ardent lovers, exultant and cleaving together, one flesh, one soul, consumed with passion and rejoicing in it, and it was a reprieve.

Among the associates of Xanthippus was a dissolute and very rich young man of considerable brilliance of mind, and a general in the army. He was also a relative of the family of Pericles, for he was of the house of the Alcmaeonidae. He was notable for his extreme handsomeness and his love for fine horses, and was infamous for his dissipation. His name was Alcibiades, and he was considerably younger than Xanthippus. When he chose to display it—which was not very often—his intelligence was extraordinary. He was somewhat of the character of Xanthippus and a great favorite among his men and the populace, for unlike Xanthippus in this regard he had a suave tongue and rarely offended anyone by a joke touched with the urbane cruelty Xanthippus could smilingly display. His men jested with him, but they knew they could not go too far in this respect, and loved him as they did not love Xanthippus, who, on occasion, could reveal a sudden flash of his father's cold hauteur and ruthless command. Alcibiades and Xanthippus were not friends, even if courteous to each other as fellow officers, for they were too close in character to be congenial.

Xanthippus held some resentment against Pericles, his father, because Pericles was fond of his young relative and esteemed his qualities as a soldier and as an incipient and potent politician, who could charm, Pericles often said, the marble peplos off a Vestal Virgin statue, and cause her immediately to lie supine, warm flesh and blood. At all times, even in the field, he was immaculate in appearance and even perfumed, and languid of manner and effeminate in gesture, though he was completely masculine of personality. It vexed Xanthippus that Pericles admired the young exquisite, for Xanthippus held a secret jealousy of his father and often had been annoyed when Pericles showed too overt an affection even for Paralus, whom Xanthippus himself loved dearly. So Xanthippus often surprised his father with complaints of Alcibiades in his letters, complaints not always justified.

This puzzled Pericles, and added to his woes, for he was

ever susceptible to the members of his family and too sensitive concerning them. Callias' father had been married to another woman before he had married Dejanira and she had borne him a daughter, and before Callias had been murdered he had given his sister in marriage to Alcibiades. Xanthippus now began to refer to this fact in his goading letters to Pericles, and he would show those letters to Aspasia. She said to him, "Xanthippus is jealous of you, my love, and would have you love no other so strongly as you love him. He was, at times, even jealous of your affection for me."

"Nonsense," Pericles would reply in irritation. "That is a womanish interpretation." So his perplexity was not assuaged. Aspasia would tell him, "When writing to Xanthippus, do not refer to Alcibiades very often," sage advice which he ignored. So Xanthippus' complaints of his kinsman, who was already a general, took on a bitter edge, though the complaints were not entirely explicit. Once he wrote, "No doubt your affection, my father, for Alcibiades rises from the fact that at one time he saved the life of your friend, Socrates, on the field of war. But Socrates," he added, "returned the favor, if you will remember."

It was at that point that unknown to Pericles Aspasia wrote to Xanthippus: "Your father feels grateful to Alcibiades in that he saved the life of Socrates. Alcibiades is also very amusing, and your father needs all the amusement he can encounter in these direful days." To which Xanthippus replied, "I am subtle enough, my dearest friend, Aspasia, to understand that you wish to soothe my natural resentment against Alcibiades, who is corrupting the morale of our men. He often drinks with them, and gets drunk with them, and their bawdy laughter and shouts are not in the military tradition." Aspasia smiled at the last, for Xanthippus could be very bawdy indeed, even when speaking to her and his wife. She answered him, "Your father speaks of you constantly, for though a long time has passed Paralus has not returned home and rarely visits your father's house. You are Pericles' surrogate in the field, and his pride in you is overwhelming."

For a time Xanthippus was placated and did not mention his kinsman, but as Pericles inquired of him more and more Xanthippus' dangerous temper grew stronger, and his resentment. His letters became fewer and more formal, and again Pericles was distressed. Aspasia could only sigh. It was bad enough that the great war was raging and Athens endangered, and Athenians, long ago wearied by skirmishes and small battles that were incessant, regarded the rising conflict not only with alarm but with increasing anger. The treasury had been drained by the intermittent wars and was now being impoverished to a huge extent in the larger struggle, and young Athenians were dying in enormous numbers. The Peloponnesian War had reached a perilous climax, and many said that even the Persian wars had not been so frightful and so devastating. Moreover, Athens' ally, Aegina, reluctant member of the Athenian empire, protested that Athens was taxing her too heavily for this war, and that Pericles had refused to grant her the Home rule established by treaty. It was no secret that her revolt both against the government of Athens and the war itself was very probable and soon. She had not too secretly been engaged, lately, with overtures to the enemy, Sparta, and her allies. Sparta, though a city-state of warriors, had preferred in the past to let her allies skirmish with Athens, and had contented herself with raids into Attica. Now she was only too eager to fight Athens to a finish and break up the Athenian empire and its maritime supremacy and its formidable navies. Moreover, Potidaea, another ally of Athens, or rather a subject ally, was showing alarming signs of betraying Athens, and some of her people had taken up the war-cry of Sparta, "Liberate the Hellenes from the rule of the despot, Pericles!" "Liberty or death!" cried young men in the streets of Potidaea, and often they fled rather than fight Sparta.

All this, darkened by the disaffection of many Athenians, notably the young, was a heavy burden to Pericles. "Do they not understand, our people, and our allies, that we are fighting for our very existence?" he would exclaim. "Sparta, if victorious, will not only make us a subject state but will enslave our people and impose on them her gloomy and barbarian philosophy, and make of Athens one vast prison camp, where all will labor and no song ever be sung again."

"The lion is at bay at last," Pericles' enemies said. They exulted in this, though their own lives would be forfeit if Athens were conquered. Many of the rich aristocrats scoffed at Pericles' alarm and his grim determination to save his city no matter the cost. These particular aristocrats had had no part in the old plot against Pericles, and had been honestly horrified at the murder of Pheidias, preferring their ease and feast and the Great Games and the theatre to controversy. But now that their own fortunes were being diminished in taxes in the war they wanted only peace with Sparta, forgetting that Pericles for many years had sought such a peace in vain, for Sparta had never given up her determination to rule all of Greece, and force it to adopt her own way of life. "Do they not understand, these idle sybarites, these effetes, that if Sparta wins they will be the first to be eliminated?" Pericles would ask his friends. "Barbarians detest such as these. Yet, our lazy covert traitors would even have us surrender to Sparta, or grant her incredible concessions for what they call 'peace and amity.'" He would add with icy rage, "If my city would be able to throw off the rule of Sparta, in the future, I would delight in watching what Sparta would do to these elegant dissidents."

"They have deluded themselves that Sparta would give the governing of Athens, with all despotism, to them," Aspasia suggested, and eventually Pericles had to agree with her. "They not only want to keep their money but they desire power, too. Power," said Pericles, "is the final and deepest lust of those who have too much money and too much amusement and too much leisure. They are jaded; they would have absolute authority over our industrious middle class and abolish it, and have a nation of docile and voiceless slaves."

Now once more the old allegations that Aspasia had urged this war upon Pericles, and that the gods were in a vengeful mood, and that Aspasia was angering them with her impiety, her corruption of the young girls of Athens, and that her house was only a house for courtesans and assignations, began to be heard louder than ever and publicly. The rabble milled and seethed with hatred, inspired by the aristocratic enemies of Pericles and their money. They told each other that Aspasia, as an alien, had no love for Athens and wished to see her downfall.

One day, when Pericles was absent, visiting the garrison of Athens in the company of his son, Xanthippus, Aspasia was arrested "for her many crimes, this foreign woman, against Athens, including treason."

CHAPTER 17

On the pretext that he needed the advice of an excellent physician, Polybius granted Helena permission to visit him at his house. He took to his bed, and even his beloved hetaira was not admitted. He was a widower. Helena entered, and he marvelled that time had so little changed her, for though she openly admitted that her once auburn hair was now dyed to its original color, and though the years had fattened her so that she appeared even more robust and rosy and hearty than ever, her big blue eyes had lost none of their vital hue and she still exuded the enthusiastic and expectant air of youth, and that abounding animal exuberance which men found fascinating.

Once Polybius, the King Archon, had been one of her lovers, and when she fondly dismissed him he had wept for many nights. Out of her kindness for her rejected lovers she inevitably found younger and more complaisant hetairai for them, and the King Archon was no exception. His hetaira was young, gentle, intelligent and attentive to all his needs, and for this he owed Helena deep gratitude.

He was eating a light meal of anchovies, sardines, wheaten bread, goat's cheese, fruit, roasted onions with garlic, cold roasted pig, broiled fish, olives and wine in his chamber when Helena arrived with her two female attendants, whom she left outside. She regarded the meal on the table and said, "I see we are eating very sparingly these days, dear Polybius!"

"Spare me your sarcasm, which I well remember, dear Helena," said the very slender Polybius. "After all, I am not really ill; this was your own suggestion. Join me, will you not?"

"And deprive you of your meagre sustenance?" exclaimed Helena, with pretended astonishment. She picked up an anchovy in her fingers and said, "Too much salt. I have warned you about this, my cherub, but you will not listen. Hippocrates taught that salt is harmful in middle age, and should be used in only slight measure. Do you desire to die suddenly in the arms of Daphne?"

Polybius' friends would have been astounded at his grin and to hear him say with rare humor, "Would that not be the death best to be desired?"

Helena shrugged as she sat at the table with him and accepted a goblet of excellent wine, Polybius' only real extravagance in the matter of niceties. Though an austere man of prudent conversation, who preferred to listen and not comment, he loved gossip of the city, and Helena obliged him until his laughter was so loud that his distant slaves heard him and were amazed.

At last Polybius became sober and he looked at Helena with his piercing and knowledgeable eyes. "Now that we have had our hilarity, dear Helena, I must say that I know why you entreated this visit. Aspasia." His face became very somber.

"Of a certainty," said Helena, sipping at her refreshed goblet. Her pink cheeks had turned quite red with the wine. "Who else? You know the charges against her are ridiculous, Polybius."

He considered her thoughtfully for a long moment or two. Then he said, "I have no love for Pericles, as he is extravagant and I do not approve of his war strategy, which is costing too much money and too many Athenian lives. No matter. However, I respect him deeply, and I know him for a just man, who, therefore, attracted enemies. I have never seen a rascal who did not have a legion of devoted friends. A good man, no. As Pericles' enemies struck at him through Pheidias they now strike at him through Aspasia. They thought they could put him to flight through Pheidias, but he was stronger than that. They know Aspasia is his most vulnerable Achilles' heel. To save her, they believe, he will agree to be deposed, or banished."

"You think he will agree to that?"

"You know he will not, Helena. It would not even occur to him. Athens is dearer to him than all else, Aspasia, his sons, his friends, his life."

When Helena was considering this, which she knew to be true, the King Archon said, "This is a grave matter. Charges have been brought against Aspasia through not only the Eponymous Archon, who tries civil suits, the Polemarchos Archon, who presides over metics (foreigners), but through the Thesmothetai Archon, who protects the city's material interests. Also, alas, through me, on the charge of impiety." He added dryly, "But not through me, on the charge of murder! That would have been absurd."

"You know she is not guilty of any of these things, Polybius."

Prudence came once more to the King Archon. He pursed his lips.

"What you and I or any other may believe, Helena, is not pertinent. The charges have been brought before me. They must be resolved in open court, before a jury also. I have no other choice."

"You cannot give me the names of those who have brought these comically monstrous charges against Aspasia?"

He looked at her rebukingly. "Helena, you know I cannot, not before the trial." He hesitated. "Have you sent for Pericles—I know his own government would not inform him, alas."

"Instantly, on learning of Aspasia's arrest."

The King Archon turned the goblet around in his fingers and stared at the wine. "It is the desire of his enemies that

Aspasia be tried, and convicted, and disposed of, before Pericles has the opportunity to be here in time. Sad for them, is it not, that the King Archon, the chief magistrate, is so stricken at this time that he cannot preside, as he alone must? I am an old man; I have such palpitations of the heart, and such indigestion, that I am completely indisposed, and no one can take my place—for mine is not a mortal illness."

Helena stood then, threw her arms about his neck, and, with tears in her eyes, she kissed him soundly over and over. He deftly slipped his hand under her peplos and she leaned against him. "I know it is not for your magnanimity that you dare to caress me, lord, and that I permit it. It is your justice, and so my pulses bound towards you."

She then slid the bolt on the door and blew out the lamp and they repaired to his bed. He would remember that night for the rest of his life, for Helena had given him once more the passion of youth, which he had thought he had lost forever. Even his young hetaira had been clumsy and inexperienced compared with this delightful wise woman, whom he had never forgotten.

Helena, as she did daily, visited Aspasia, carrying with her a basket of dainties and fine wine. She had already noticed, before, that special military guards were in attendance and not the usual prison police, and that the guards compelled her to eat the food she brought for Aspasia before releasing it for Aspasia's consumption. They had told Helena, "It is the orders of the King Archon, Lady." At each admonition Helena felt her heart swell with tenderness for Polybius and she promised herself that she would occasionally give him her favors whenever he desired. She almost loved him. A just man, she would reflect, is a rare jewel among politicians, or even among other men, and he should be cherished as the adornment of his country. However, he is more frequently despised, rejected and murdered, or, at the least, defamed. Mankind, at the last, cannot endure justice and honor and integrity.

Aspasia's cell was really a comfortable chamber; at whose instigation Helena could only guess. She had with her her favorite furniture and books and ornaments, and there was a large window which admitted light and air, though it was barred. Moreover, one of her slave women was permitted to attend her, a woman she could trust.

Helena laid down the basket, which also contained plates, a

521

jeweled goblet, silver cutlery and linen napkins, and she prepared the table for Aspasia. She said, robustly, "You must eat every morsel of this. Do you think Pericles, on his return, will be disposed to rescue a hag?"

Aspasia had been confined but a week; her face was already white and thin. Her wonderful hair was now more deeply mixed with silver so that light alternately picked out golden gleams or pallid ones. "I have, here, my favorite cosmetic," said Helena, "a mixture of pounded almonds and honey, which you must use several times a day around those despicable wrinkles which you have insisted on acquiring. There is also here a jar of milk of almonds and lemons, perfumed with oils, which you must daily rub on your arms and body and hands. There is, too, a pot of attar of roses, Pericles' favorite scent. How dared you neglect yourself, you darling fool? Do you think a man loves a woman only for her mind and her solicitude for him? No, being a man, he desires physical assets also. Have you forgotten?"

"Alas," said Aspasia, "I have ruined him."

Helena was disgusted. "So, then, did Pheidias and Anaxagoras and Socrates and a multitude other of his friends. So did I. So did the old King Archon; so did the middle class Pericles is desperately trying to save. So did Zeno of Elea. Shall we, still on earth, and the others in the Blessed Isles—I hope—then cover our heads with ashes and moan our guilt?"

Aspasia, despite her terror and despair and anguish over Pericles, laughed involuntarily. She said, with pretended meekness, "Physician, I shall obey your orders." She forced herself to eat of the repast. She said, "How is my son, Pericles?"

"As you know, he is in my house, and has an imperative disposition like his father. He commands my slaves, in a regal manner, for which I must occasionally slap him. I must remind him, ever, that he is a guest in my house, and a youth, and that he must defer to me. He has taken, mockingly, to calling me 'Mama,' I, who never bore a child, thank the gods. Children are no blessing, as the farmers once believed. They can become your most mortal enemies, worse than any other foe."

Aspasia, eating of the repast Helena had brought, considered. "I have heard, from eastern philosophers, that when the Unknown God is born to us His most terrible enemies will be of His own house."

"Of a certainty," said Helena, chewing on a citron. "Who else can be so malign as a brother or a child or even a parent, if a man attains eminence? 'Who is he,' they will say, 'who dares to be above us, our kinsman? Is he not of my blood? Therefore, he is not superior to me.' "

Aspasia said, "The gods choose among men, for their holy purposes, and their kindred have no part in it."

Helena said, with cynicism, "That is a matter which should be brought to the attention of envious relatives."

"Helena, dearest friend, I do not wish Pericles to jeopardize his position in defending me."

Helena threw up her hands. "Dear fool! I must say again that you are but one little shaft in the hands of his enemies! Why do you persist in your belief that if you die they will stop their attacks on him? Their goal is despotism. They use the mindless rabble to that end. In defending you, sweet idiot, he will be defending the dignity of men, the workers, the middle class, the artists and scientists, freedom of speech, the laws of Solon, civilization itself, the glory of Greece, law and order, national security—all of which the rich and powerful and lusters for authority hate. They are, in their souls, tyrants, and have nothing but loathing for those who toil and love their country."

Aspasia never forgot the words of her friend. She was never to see Helena again. For, on the way to her house in her litter, the ebullient physician was killed by an unknown congregation of the whimpering rabble and those overpowered by opium, which had been distributed to them by the plotting aristocrats, who knew that drugs were the best way of controlling potential rebels and rendering them impotent among impossible dreams. Her litter was attacked, her slave women slaughtered. Helena, who had loved life, for all the monsters who claimed to be men, was done to death because she was a compassionate woman who regarded humanity, despite its terrible errors, worthy of living. She, who had cherished the world, and who had believed in the dignity of men, was disproved at last, at least to the satisfaction of those who craved despotism, and had ordered her murder.

The King Archon, on hearing of the murder of his loved Helena, clenched his fists, wept alone, and said to himself, "At the end, my lustrous pomegranate, you have been the victor. For, if the gods are just, they will honor those who have died in the defense of freedom. But only God can give them complete honor."

He, being a prudent man, made up his mind and grimly resolved that, for once, justice must prevail, despite the rabble.

He did not deceive himself that he was exceptional. History

today, and history tomorrow, would prove that he was right. But, alas, not until all the ~~eroes~~ were slain, and the whole world brought to disaster and the eager fat multitude was enslaved, as they deserved to be enslaved.

Truth, he remembered, was always on trial, always murdered, always defamed and ridiculed. Those who lived for truth were endlessly in bondage and endlessly crushed. Was it, at last, worthy of pursuit? Only God knew.

When Aspasia and Pericles met in her cell they were both stunned at the appearance of the other, for, in the short time of their separation, they had aged. Pericles was aghast at Aspasia's emaciation, the lost brilliance of her complexion, her sunken eyes, and she, in turn, was stricken by his air of utter exhaustion and despondency and pallor. Deep clefts were in his cheeks, on his brow. There was much more white in his hair, and his lips were purplish.

She wept in his arms and said, "I have brought you nothing but calamity," to which he replied, smoothing her hair, "You have brought me my life. If I had never known you I would still be in my present situation. Only you have given me comfort."

He did not speak of the estrangement of his sons, nor of the mysterious plague which was beginning to seep through Athens from the east, and was already decimating his soldiers in the field. He sat with Aspasia on her bed and held her hands tightly and tried to smile in her devastated face, while she searched his own despairingly.

"Helena has been murdered," she said, sobbing, "and only because she was my friend."

"I know of her murder," said Pericles. "I have posted an enormous reward for the apprehension of her assassins. No, it was not because of you, sweet. Do not be so egotistic," and he attempted to laugh. "Helena has long been hated in the city because of her philanthropy, her enlightenment, her lack of sentimentality and mawkish speech, her courage, her refusal to lie charmingly, her open support of liberty and her friendship for me. She was hated and derided before you came to Athens. Her ultimate fate was certain. None of the multitude she has saved and delivered from suffering has uttered a single word of reproach for her murder, nor has cried out against it." The bitterness in his voice was lethal and full of hate.

"I would that I were dead, too," said Aspasia miserably.

"Nonsense. Would you leave me alone among my enemies, with none to console me? That is selfish of you."

524

"You must not defend me," she pleaded, clinging to him.

"You would ask me not to defend my very life?"

They spoke of their future together when all this was over, and they spoke of their son, Pericles, who was now in his father's house. "He declared to me today, the impudent lad, that his name will be greater than his father's," said Pericles and his face became affectionate and even a little humorous. "I told him he need not strive. I would not be famous in history." They spoke of Aspasia's school, which was under the stern guidance of her well-trained and loyal teachers. Then Pericles' face changed subtly and became darker. "What would this world of savages be without teachers? And how do we repay them? With miserable stipends, if any, with contempt. Yet, they hold the future of men in their selfless hands." He paused. "Do you recall, my treasure, one of your young ladies, named Iona, daughter of Glaucus, who is a minor magistrate?"

Aspasia, wondering why he should speak of trivialities in the midst of their sorrows and anxieties, said, "I know the girl. Her mother was a woman of mind, and before she died of the flux she forced her husband to promise to send Iona to my school. Unfortunately, the girl did not possess her mother's intelligence and self-control. I dismissed her. That was a year ago. Why do you ask?"

But Pericles said, "Tell me of the girl's character, not her lack of intelligence."

More and more wondering, Aspasia replied, "She was, in addition to being remarkably sly and malicious, a trouble-maker. Discovering that she could not compete with her companions, and resentful of her teachers' reproaches, she concocted scandals concerning both her teachers and companions. Strange to say, they were clever scandals, elaborately conceived, so that even I once believed one of her tales, so detailed were they and spoken with the utmost sincerity. She has the face of a nymph, the soul of a demon, and is soft-spoken, gentle in manner, apparently meek and earnest, and has a demure way of licking her lips. She deceived many for a considerable time. That is the high art of the wicked."

"When you dismissed her, what did you say to her, Aspasia?"

She stared at him, gently puzzled. "Why do you speak of the little wretch at all? I said to her, 'You are unfit to be among my maidens, about many of whom you have spread calumnies. Moreover, your mind is not extraordinary, except in the manner of evil. Therefore, you must leave us and return to your father's house.' " She thought for a moment, then frowned. "Her father, Glaucus, whom she resembles, came to me in a great anger and demanded the reason for her dismissal. As I had been a friend of the girl's dead mother I wished to spare her memory. I told Glaucus that I did not believe his daughter to possess the gifts necessary for her to become distinguished. Still angered, he left me." Aspasia concentrated her gaze on Pericles. "I do not understand. What is this girl to you, or her father?"

Pericles glanced away from her, evasively. "I have heard that Glaucus is seeking higher office. I wished to know if he were worthy to be presented to the voters."

"Oh," said Aspasia, "he has integrity enough—for a bureaucrat—if they have any integrity at all. He is very careful of himself and has a not inconsiderable intelligence."

"A bad man with intelligence is only a little less dangerous than a bad man who is stupid," said Pericles. He continued with an artless manner, "I think I will oppose his nomination."

One of the military guards entered the cell with Aspasia's dinner, which was well prepared and appetizing, for Pericles had brought it and it had been in an oven to keep it warm. The guard saluted Pericles respectfully, hesitated, then said, "It is the command of the King Archon, lord, that whosoever brings the Lady Aspasia food must first partake of some of it before she dines."

Pericles smiled with gratitude at this care of his mistress, and said, "I cannot thank the King Archon enough." He took a morsel of each of the dishes and the guard watched him with a sheepish expression of apology. Pericles winked at Aspasia who smiled for the first time since he had come to her. "Would it not be of interest to the great poets, Aspasia, if we died together of poison?"

She did not consider this amusing, nor did the guard. To please Pericles she forced herself to eat and to drink. Though it was now advanced spring, and the air outside was hot, the cell was pleasantly cool. At least, thought Pericles, my darling is safe in this guarded place, thanks to the King Archon. She is in no danger of being murdered as was Helena.

Aspasia asked of the war between Athens and her allies and Sparta and her allies. Again, to spare her worry, he was evasive. "We are doing well enough," he said. "Xanthippus is optimistic, but when was he ever not? I wish, however, he was not so hostile towards our kinsman, that beautiful reprobate, Alcibiades, who, himself, is a notable soldier. Paralus?" Pericles hesitated. "He believes his mother's grief has not yet diminished enough so that he can leave her."

He did not tell Aspasia that his military guard had been more than trebled, for the market rabble was becoming perilously inimical, and unusually vocal when seeing him in the Agora or on the streets. While he detested them he knew that they were not to blame. They were being incited by his enemies to the point of violence against his person.

When he left Aspasia, after sternly admonishing her that he would defend her despite her protests and tears, he found his soldiers perturbed. Iphis said, "General and lord, the rabble seems very restive today, since your return this morning. I have reports that many of them are armed, and threatening."

Pericles was not a man to take threats lightly, even from rabble. So he pulled his hood over his face and kept his sword in his hand while his guard rode tightly about him. He had removed his helmet, the harder for his appearance to be recognized. But he was indeed recognized, for all the shade over his features, for a vast crowd was awaiting him near the prison, and bloodthirsty shouts roared to his ears from hundreds of voices.

"Tyrant! Despot! War-bringer! Robber of the treasury! Malefactor! Poisoner! Deceiver! Liar! Thief! Pervert! Defamer of the gods! Heretic! Shame of Athens! Traitor! Resign!"

And higher voices, "Impeach him! Exile him!"

"Aye!" screamed the crowd.

Iphis said, "Give the word, my general, and we will charge them."

"No," said Pericles. "It is not they who shout. It is the soft safe others who hide in their luxurious houses and meet in secret, and plot against Athens. Who dares accuse them, touch them? They are too rich, too powerful."

But he wondered silently how long he could endure this infamy, the estrangement of his sons, his labor to save his country, the ingratitude of his people, and all the burdens which leadership had imposed on him and which had made him the loneliest of men, isolated, with few friends.

But now, above all, was his terror for Aspasia and he could think of nothing else.

He felt a momentary refreshment when he raised his eyes to the acropolis, that forest of statues and columns, of temples and gardens and fountains, and to the Parthenon where the enormous gold and ivory image of Athene Parthenos glittered in the sun. Her great face seemed to glow down on him, and he said to himself, "Above all things, protect my city and my people." It seemed to him that she had the face of Helena, and his eyes moistened.

CHAPTER 18

The King Archon had miraculously recovered. It was true that when he appeared in court, before the whole Assembly and the Archons, they noted that he seemed somewhat distraught and absent, and that the rims of his eyes were sore and reddened, as if he had been weeping in the night. Otherwise, he was composed and compact as always and, for all he was a small man, he had immense dignity. It had been rumored for a few days that he had been stricken by the plague, which had already reached Athens, though it had not as yet been of considerable alarm to the physicians, who kept it from the people that their military had been widely afflicted.

The day was hot, the hall steaming, and every face was avid except the faces of Pericles' friends. They had lined themselves against the wall and they gazed at him with deep distress. But he walked confidently in his robes of office, carrying his ivory wand of authority, his helmeted head higher than the heads of any of the others, his ravaged face noble and restrained, his eyes unmoved. He had refused the presence of a single guard, except those at the doors which were not his. However, he wore his sword under his cloak.

"Once let them see that I am afraid and they will be gleefully at my throat," he had told the anxious Iphis. "One never flinches before mad dogs. It is too inciting."

He now stood before the King Archon, whose gray face twitched involuntarily, but whose eyes met his with a steadfast gaze. They greeted each other formally. The King Archon said to the guards, "Bring in the prisoner, Aspasia of Miletus."

Before Aspasia arrived Pericles studied the faces of the Archons who had brought charges against her of treason, vice, corruption, impiety and various minor crimes against Athens and her people. They stared at him, impassively. None were his friends. He did not believe that any of them was essentially corrupt or had been bribed; they had been compelled, by law, to have Aspasia arrested "on information." He then studied the jury, that large body of men. They would do their duty, one way or another, after receiving dispassionate instruction from the King Archon.

Everyone was sweating in the smoldering heat except Pericles. He was cold with fear and dread. The charges against Aspasia were formidable, far more grave than the charges brought against Anaxagoras and Pheidias, for she was a foreign woman, and the metics were always suspect.

Pericles had warned Aspasia before he had left her on his last visit that she must appear tranquil and serene before this assemblage, that she must attend to her neglected appearance, that she must assume pride and fearlessness. He turned towards the door through which she would enter, and when she did enter he felt a weak surge of relief. For she seemed as a queen, tall and slender, clad gracefully but discreetly in a lilac tunic and a robe of white linen, her face calm and pure, her hair raised and bound in the Athenian fashion with white ribbons, her feet in light leather slippers, her manner distant. She had not reddened her cheeks or her lips, and they were as smooth and still as marble, and she had not used kohl on her eyes. She wore no jewels, at Pericles' behest. "There is nothing so maddening to anyone, who cannot afford it, as jewelry on another." Envy, he knew, was the most powerful emotion of men, and the most deadly.

When Aspasia was beside him it was as if she were merely an acquaintance of his, and she looked at him as if he were only her appointed defender. She bowed to him in silence, then folded her hands before her, and waited. All watched this encounter, the majority with enmity, the few with compassion and anger.

Pericles said to the King Archon, "Let the accusers of this woman speak, lord."

The Eponymous Archon, who tried civil suits, stood up portentously, and addressed the King Archon. "The woman is accused of the corruption of young women in her house which she alleges is a school, of procuring them for unspeakable purposes for gain. The witness, the father of one girl who resisted pollution and so was dismissed from the house of Aspasia of Miletus, is here to testify. It was to me that he pressed charges. He desires redress, three thousand gold talents, for his daughter had been forcibly taken by three men in the house of Aspasia of Miletus, and has been ill in her father's house ever since, overcome by shame."

A subdued roar of anger came from the assemblage, and the King Archon raised his neutral voice and said, "There will be no demonstrations before me. This is a court of justice." He turned to the Archon and said, "Produce your witness, the father of the girl, one Glaucus, a magistrate of the city."

The Archon beckoned to one among the crowd and he stood up and shambled towards the King Archon's seat. But he stood at a distance from both Pericles and Aspasia, and his face was malign. He was a lean and nervous man with a countenance too mobile even for an Athenian, and his features were narrow and restless, his head bald.

The King Archon looked at him with no expression at all. "Repeat to me the words of your daughter, under oath."

Glaucus was duly sworn. He never took his malignant eyes from Aspasia, except to give a flickering glance at Pericles, who was faintly smiling. As for Aspasia she seemed to be stunned. But only her hands visibly trembled.

Glaucus said, "My daughter was dismissed from the school of the foreign woman. She had been sent there at the request of my beloved dying wife. I could not deny my wife, though I objected. My daughter returned to my house in tears, obviously suffering. She took to her bed without speaking at that time, for she was too ashamed at what she had endured in that infamous house. Puzzled, I visited the foreign woman who stands before you this day, lord, and she gazed at me with contempt and informed me that my daughter had been dismissed because she was not suited to her studies and the school. Though I was glad that my daughter was returned to my house—for I do not approve of the education of women —I observed that Iona's illness became more obvious, and then I questioned her more closely." He shut his eyes as if he could not bear the disgrace of his daughter. After a moment he said in a weaker voice, "She then informed me that she had been taken by force, by unknown men, in the house of Aspasia of Miletus, and that now she wished to die. I have warned her slave women never to leave her for a moment; I fear her suicide. She is a virtuous girl. In her smirched name, I demand redress, not only in money—I am not a rich man— but in the punishment of this depraved woman."

It was rare that a woman was permitted to speak in her own defense before an assemblage of men, but Pericles broke precedent. He said to Aspasia in a cool voice, "Speak, Aspasia of Miletus, and tell us of this matter of which you are accused." His eyes admonished her to compose herself.

But for a moment she could not speak. Then she could do so, in her clear sweet voice, which only faintly shook. "The accusation, lord, is false and malicious and untrue. I had doubts about admitting Iona to my school, for I already knew

530

that she was not suited to it. However, her mother had been my friend, and she had been a kind and gracious soul and a woman of intelligence. So, I admitted Iona."

Aspasia drew a deep and audible breath, but she gazed at the King Archon and he saw the vivid brown of her eyes, like jewels. "Iona was not only mentally incapable of absorbing her studies, she lied, she slandered, she caused great trouble in my school and among my teachers and pupils. She had an innocent appearance, which deceived many for nearly a year, among them, I must confess, myself. I investigated her calumnies thoroughly and was finally convinced she was a liar. I then dismissed her. I did not tell her father of her crimes against her companions and teachers, for I respected the dear memory of her mother."

Again there was a faint roar of indignation against Aspasia in the hall and the King Archon protested. He said to Aspasia, "There is no truth to the accusation that you procured men to rape this girl?"

"None, lord." She hesitated, then added, "If the girl is not a virgin she did not suffer the loss of her virginity in my house."

Glaucus cried, "She lies against my child! I demand——"

But Pericles interposed. "Iona is not a child. She is fourteen years old and of an age to marry. Tell me, Glaucus. Have you had your daughter examined by a competent physician, who can discern her lack of virginity or her possession of it?"

"No!" he almost screamed. "Has my child not suffered enough that she must endure the harsh examination of a physician? She is modest, also."

The King Archon pursed his lips.

Aspasia said, "Iona was not too modest to attribute the vilest of perversions and other unspeakable acts to her companions and teachers. Where she learned of these I do not know, unless it was from the female slaves in the women's quarters of her father's house."

The King Archon frowned at Aspasia, for it was unseemly of a woman to speak without being first addressed by a man. He looked at Glaucus. "It is my command that a physician be sent immediately to your house to examine your daughter. I will choose the physician, so he will not be suborned. You do not consent, Glaucus? Well, then, your charges against Aspasia of Miletus will be summarily dismissed."

Glaucus said at once, "I agree to your edict, lord. Choose the physician and let him be sent at once to my house."

531

So, thought Pericles, the father has also been deceived by his wretched daughter, and in spite of everything Pericles felt some pity for him. The King Archon summoned a guard and whispered in his ear and the guard departed at a trot. Pericles then had another thought: What if the vicious wench had indeed been deprived of her virginity by someone unknown? Yet, she had been sedulously guarded in the school of Aspasia, and no doubt in her father's house also. However, it was well known that lust had a thousand entries, even to a prison.

"The next witness against Aspasia of Miletus," said the King Archon, and the Thesmothetai Archon, who protected the city's interests, rose and said, "Aspasia of Miletus has been accused of treason, that she has been giving aid and comfort to our enemies, to the danger of our existence."

"Produce the accuser," said the King Archon. The Thesmothetai Archon beckoned and the accuser came forward, a fat little old man with an eager face. Aspasia started at the sight of him, for he had been a teacher of history in her school. She had been compelled to dismiss him, for he had made obscene advances to several of her pupils.

"What have you to say before the King Archon?" asked the Thesmothetai Archon.

For a fat man he had an unusually thin and insistent voice.

"I taught in the supposed school of this woman," and he pointed at Aspasia, "until a year ago. I am a teacher of history, and am a patriot. One day she entered my school-room—it was her want to do this with other teachers, also, on occasion—and she heard my fervid eulogies about our history. She listened, with a contemptuous smirk on her face, and then interrupted. She said, 'It is not enough to utter eulogies. It is also necessary to utter the truth.' I then asked her what was truth and she shrugged and said, 'Only God knows. Certainly not historians.'

"And that is not all," he continued rapidly. "I confess that I was shocked, but she was always enigmatic. Then one day I was passing through a colonnade and heard her speaking in a low voice to an evident stranger, of a foreign appearance. She put a large purse in his hand and said, 'Give my kinsman, the Spartan, this purse from me and tell him I wish him victory.' That was just before I was dismissed."

The King Archon looked down at Aspasia, whose stunned appearance made her seem unconscious though she did not waver on her feet. He waited a moment or two then said, almost gently, "What have you to say to this, Aspasia of Miletus?"

She spoke, just audibly: "I did dismiss this man, for he had made lewd overtures to some of my serious innocent girls, and they complained to me. I did say to him once, 'It is also necessary to utter the truth.' I am not charging that this man lies in entirety. But too many historians have colored history with personal prejudices, and I wished my pupils to know facts and not fables. Of what use is learning if it is based on mere opinion, lord, and not verity? It is not truth at all."

Now she turned the restored brilliance of her eyes upon her accuser. "He lies, and deliberately so, when he says that I gave a purse of gold to any stranger, and that I said the words he alleges to that non-existent stranger. I am an Ionian, and have no love for the Spartans. I was born in Miletus, lived in Persia and then in Athens. I have no relatives in Sparta; I have never met a Spartan and I devoutly wish never to meet one!"

At this a dim surge of amusement ran through the hall, and even the King Archon smiled. He said, "Lady, I also wish never to meet one." He paused then looked at the teacher. "There is but your word against this woman's, though she is only a woman and you are a man. She has accused you of lewdness against innocent girls, and for that she dismissed you. If you still insist she lies then it will be my most distasteful duty to summon the girls who brought the accusations against you, to Aspasia of Miletus. Here, before you, I will ask them the truth. Lewdness against the young and defenseless is a very grave crime, as you know."

The teacher's face quivered. Then he threw out his hands and bowed to the King Archon. "Lord," he said, "it is not my desire to subject those young things to public gaze and public questions. I revere the young; they have my tenderest regard. Therefore, though it is true, I withdraw my charges against this woman."

"You withdraw your charges of treason?"

The teacher bowed meekly. "Yes, lord. I must protect the young females, at whatever cost to myself and my honor."

"You are a liar!" exclaimed the King Archon with a rare display of emotion. "You have been caught in a trap. You have lied under the most solemn of oaths. You have accused this woman of treason, and then when the iron jaws of the trap threatened you you dexterously attempted to escape them. I, therefore, exonerate Aspasia of Miletus of treason, but I do not exonerate you for lying to me under oath. I sentence you to a year in prison."

The little fat man, stricken with terror, turned as if to flee but guards seized him and bore him away, yelling incoherently, his legs kicking the air. It was then that the physician appointed by the King Archon appeared in the hall and the King Archon beckoned to him. He bent his head and the physician whispered in his ear. The face of the King Archon became tight. He summoned Glaucus who came to him, shambling rapidly, his face expectant.

The King Archon leaned over his bench and said to Glaucus in so low a tone that only Pericles and Aspasia could hear: "The physician declares that your daughter has never known a man, but he did find evidences of perverted activity. He questioned your daughter very closely on this matter and she confessed that she had not only submitted to the sexual advances of her female slaves but that she instigated them, herself. As this physician is not your physician, nor your daughter's, but was appointed by me to inquire into the truth, he has not violated any confidence, and he is famous for his skill and his probity."

Glaucus' face turned yellow both with shame and fear, and there was a flicker of rage in his eyes.

The King Archon continued in his low voice, "If it is your desire I will put this physician under oath, and demand his testimony."

Glaucus covered his face for a moment with trembling hands. When he dropped them his eyes were now filled with tears. "It is not my desire, lord."

The King Archon, who also felt some pity for this deceived father, said in a louder voice, "We will proceed with this matter. Glaucus, do you still wish to press for alleged redress in money and punishment against Aspasia of Miletus?"

Glaucus gulped. He stared at Aspasia, still with hatred, as if she had brought him to this pass. But he said loudly enough, "I withdraw my charges, in the interests of my daughter's modesty."

It was not enough, however, for the King Archon. He said, "Answer me: Do you completely withdraw your charges that your daughter had been forced to engage in lewd actions with three men in the house of Aspasia of Miletus?"

Glaucus struggled with himself. The hall was totally silent. He clenched and unclenched his hands at his sides; he looked at Aspasia as if he desired to strangle her.

Then he said, "I completely withdraw my charges." He gasped. "As my daughter is an innocent child she has most probably used her imagination, as do all the women in the women's quarters, for want of better employment."

The King Archon inclined his head. "It is well known that salacity flourishes in the women's quarters."

He looked at the jury. "Aspasia of Miletus is exonerated of the charges brought by Glaucus in behalf of his daughter." Then he became stern. "However, there is another matter, Aspasia. You did not report your teacher of history for obscene overtures to the young ladies in your care. Your silence is reprehensible. Therefore, I hereby fine you six talents in gold."

She bowed her head and said nothing, and the King Archon stared down at her in genuine rebuke. In the meantime the unfortunate Glaucus left the hall, his head bent. So he escaped the scornful glances of Pericles' friends.

Now a heavy silence fell on the hall for the gravest charge of all was to be brought against Aspasia. Polybius regarded her with intensity, and Pericles moved closer to her as if in protection. The King Archon's face lost all expression except for his eyes which studied Aspasia as if to read her soul. Socrates, near the wall, leaned forward, holding his breath, his radiant eyes fixed on the eyes of Polybius, as though he felt a foreboding about his own future. The heat of the hall increased. The sun which came through the high windows was an intense flaming light, too hurtful for any gaze, and many blinked in it and averted their heads.

"Aspasia of Miletus," said the King Archon at last, "you have been exonerated of the charges brought to you heretofore in this court and before this jury and Assembly. However, there is the most horrible of all—that you are guilty of impiety and I must judge you, for I am the King Archon, and in my hands lies the power of life or death for heresy, the greatest crime against the gods and the people of Athens."

Aspasia lifted her head and she stood very tall and straight and her eyes were open and serious and the shifting lights in them were like liquid mercury.

The King Archon looked down at her now in silence, and he thought, This woman is not only beautiful but she is brave and proud, like my rosy Helena whom I shall never forget. For an instant he squeezed his eyes together in pain and sorrow. When he opened them he pretended to be studying a document before him, for he could not continue until a moment or two had passed. Then he looked at Aspasia again and she wondered that his eyelids were moist and tremulous. Pericles saw this also, and his dread lifted without a reason.

"You must answer me truly, Aspasia of Miletus," said the King Archon, and his voice was not as loud and steady as it had been before. "It has been told me that you are a heretic, a mocker of the gods, that you have denied their existence. I need not bring forth witnesses to this, for I, myself, have heard the accusations many times before. Pause before speaking; collect yourself; compose yourself, for on your word lies your life."

Again the heavy silence descended on the hall so that it seemed to be empty of tenants, and everyone craned forward, staring at Aspasia. A few bees and wasps had blown through the windows and their buzzing was harsh in the silence, as if they were filled with anger. Pericles drew even closer to Aspasia and under his cloak he grasped his sword convulsively.

But Aspasia did not turn to him. All her regard was only for the King Archon. She felt no enmity in him, no hostile contempt, no menace. He was the judge, and he would judge her in what she said in the next moments. If her heart beat a little faster no one else was aware of it. She lifted her head even higher. Her eyes were without fear or evasion.

"Lord," she said, "I do not know what you have heard, what calumnies, what falsehoods. You have asked me concerning my heresy. I can only answer that from my earliest youth I have felt the Presence of the Godhead in all things, that my soul has been shaken as a lily in the field at the thought of Him, that I have gazed on all He has created with wonder and awe and delight and reverence, and that, to the measure of my poor power, I have served Him. His Law has been sweeter to my spirit than honey; His graciousness has caused me to weep with joy. I see His shadow on the mountains, His reflection in the water, His heralds in the skies, His majesty in the smallest flower in a crevice. Because He is in everything that lives there is no ugliness except in the perverted eyes of men. The very stones proclaim Him; the stars sing of His might; the rains whisper of His mercy. What is seemingly dead breaks into blossoms at His gaze; the winds shout of Him at midnight. Before Him there is no despair, there is only bliss and hope. I hear His voice, I see His grandeur in the morning, at noon, in the evening. When I am sad He comforts me. When I laugh I hear His laughter also. When I see a lamb leaping in the spring, my heart leaps also, for the lamb in his dance celebrates God and I celebrate with him. The world teems with the effulgence of God, and only men see darkness.

"Lord, if someone with all authority convinced me that there is no God then I should die, for what is life without Him, and pleasure without His grace? There is only death, and in this death I could not live. He is all, and there is none else."

She paused, then said with simplicity, "If that is heresy, lord, condemn me. God, alone then, shall be my Judge."

Someone among Pericles' and Aspasia's friends raised a cry of exultation in the silence, a cry of reverent praise, and many eyes were suddenly wet. The King Archon's old face was inscrutable and still. Now his regard on Aspasia was earnest. He said, "I have been told that you have a small temple in your garden, Aspasia of Miletus, with a bare altar and no statues. To whom has that temple been erected, and why is the altar bare?"

Aspasia smiled like a loving child. "The temple was built to Him, Whom our priests reverence without knowing why they reverence, but their spirits know if their minds do not. The temple was built to One Whom we feel in our hearts, Who has yet no name that we have heard. Yet Greeks erect temples to Him with waiting altars, and inscribe on them: 'To the Unknown God.' The altar is bare because we are still waiting for Him, He Who has been promised through the ages to all nations and all men."

The King Archon bent his head as if meditating, and all waited for his next words. After a long minute or two he raised his head and said to the jury, "This woman is not guilty of heresy. If you believe she is, after hearing her words, speak now or never speak again."

The silence that followed his speech was even more ponderous and weighty than before. The men of the jury looked at each other furtively, peering over each other's shoulders. Some nodded; some shook their heads; some were gloomy; some were threatening in their glances, some sullen, some moved, some angry, some resentful, some impatient, some with tears on their cheeks. Pericles watched them closely. He had begun to tremble. The life of Aspasia lay with them for all of the King Archon's grave remarks.

Now he could not restrain himself. He swung about and faced the jury and his face changed and became passionate, as none had ever seen it before.

"My countrymen!" he cried. "I am Pericles, son of Xanthippus, the great warrior whose name is honored among you! I am your Head of State, because it was the will of our people, despite the efforts of my enemies, and yours. It is not Aspasia of Miletus who stands waiting your judgment. It is I. For, I have been condemned by the vile and the envious and the lusters of power, those who desire to enslave you. Because of the strength of you, my fellow countrymen, they dared not attack me directly, or kill me.

"But they have attacked, killed or exiled those I have loved. They sought to kill my son, Paralus, because he is my son. They slew Helena, the physician. They murdered Pheidias, though he was the glory of Greece. They drove a mighty scientist, a gentle man, Anaxagoras, into flight with their persecutions. My son, Xanthippus, is fighting to save our beloved city, and is prepared to give his life. He is fighting as I fought, and as my fathers fought, not for money, not for elevation, not for power, not for shouts of honor. We fight and we have fought, for the love we hold in our souls for our country. If a man does not love his country then he is not a man. He is not even a traitor, for to be a traitor a man must first have loved, then turned aside. He is a beast who does not know that he is a beast. One trough anywhere is only a trough to him, for his feeding. One master, to him, is no different from another. He asks only to live in his animal living.

"For what does a true man live? He lives for his God, his country, his family, or he does not live at all. He lives for truth, for the liberty which God has bestowed on him on his birth. But our enemies, yours and mine, hate all these blessed things, for so long as you adhere to them they cannot reduce you to slavery, or force you to your knees, or compel you to bow before them as your lords, nor strangle you with chains, nor take from you your holy manhood, nor make you less than the beasts of the field.

"God has put a price on your liberty. The price is your vigilance, your sleepless guard, lest it be taken from you. Prizes will be, and are, offered to you in this, your city, for your obedience, for your subservience, for your acceptance of a life that is really a death. If you accept, for a momentary flattery, for a few drachmas in your hands, for a shameful peace, you will be accursed before God Who detests the coward— the true traitor to his humanity, the man without dignity and pride in his being before the God Who made him. He has committed the absolute treason against all that lives, all that has endurance and magnificence and truth.

"Many of you here know their abominable names, but they are not present! They lie among their sleek women, and dine in luxury and count their money and bejewel themselves and breed fine horses for the Games, and build palaces for their pleasure. They tell you that their hearts bleed for you, that they would have you kings among men, that with their help you will ride in chariots and walk on marble and never know hunger or pain again. They lie! A man is born to labor and to rejoice in his labor, for he who does not serve is condemned

538

to death, not by men, but by God and nature. To serve God and country, in whatever fashion God ordains, is the highest servitude and the highest freedom.

"Men of Athens! Sons of the laws of Solon! We Greeks, for the first time in known history, have brought a dream to mankind, the dream of liberty, of law which all men, rulers and ruled, must obey, of just rewards for just service, of freedom of speech and freedom to write, of judges and juries, of punishments to fit the crime, of order not imposed but self-imposed, of the power to vote and the power to seek redress under a dispassionate government, even against that very government, of equal taxation instead of the tribute other rulers exact of their helpless people, of the right to protest and dissent, of the right to demand justice if oppressed or reviled or harmed or defamed, and, above all, to be free in your persons, your property, your houses, your opinions.

"Of all these your enemies would deprive you and me. They would silence our voices. They would drive justice from her altars. They would make of our country but a vast prison camp where all would labor and none would be rewarded and none, ever again, be men!"

No one shifted or stirred and now only a few revealed malignant and cunning faces. Before that countenance turned upon them, before that eloquence, the majority were deeply moved.

Then Pericles took the hand of Aspasia and looked at her, and suddenly he was weeping and the tears ran down his face, and never had they seen this before and a great sigh rose from the assemblage.

Pericles drew Aspasia to his side and put his arm about her.

"Behold this woman, whom I love, as you know I love her. She is a symbol to you, in the vicious accusations brought against her, of what awaits us if our enemies prevail. They sought her death, not because she has done any wrong, but because she is innocent and fearless and will not bend before tyranny and lies. But more than that, they would kill her because I love her. They would take from me—as they would take from you—all that we hold dear, out of their hatred for us. They would set the rabble on us, the avaricious rabble who would seize the fruits of our labors, who would stain the glory of our fathers with their envious spittle, the envious rabble which has no honor and no soul and no manhood but only greed and spite and malice and bottomless bellies. They would do this in order to crush you and silence you and overcome you with terror, for a rabble armed is more frightful than an army with banners and bloody spears. They would give the rabble arms for your destruction, to subjugate you.

"It is your choice: to stand on your feet as men, or crouch on your knees as slaves. The dream of Solon can endure, or it can die. It is your choice, for now you appear at the bar of history and God is your Judge."

The silence remained, even though the white walls seemed still to vibrate with the power of Pericles' voice. Every man looked at him, and looked at Aspasia at his side, and saw his tears and the resolute set of his mouth and the force of his eyes, which challenged them, not with rage or contempt, but with their mutual brotherhood.

At last the King Archon spoke. "Before this jury of equal men, I exonerate Aspasia of Miletus of all the accusations brought against her. Speak then, if any man wishes to speak."

But the jury did not speak and the King Archon appeared to examine each face and though a number were still malignant their tongues were silent. The King Archon then said to Aspasia, "Go, then, in peace, absolved of any charges."

Pericles bowed to the King Archon and Aspasia bent her head. Pericles took Aspasia's hand and walked through the voiceless assemblage with her and the guards opened the bronze door wide so that the sun burst in and covered the two with light.

PROLOGUE

"The past is only prologue." SOCRATES

The Great Plague came to Athens and overwhelmed the already demoralized citizens. It struck down in particular the women of child-bearing age and the young, and equally decimated the middle-aged and old. A multitude of voices rose that the gods were avenging the insult to their dignity imposed on them by Pericles and his friends, and "that infamous harlot, Aspasia of Miletus." Few paid heed to the fact that Pericles' two sons, Paralus and Xanthippus, died of it, without being fully reconciled to their father, that his friends were well one day and conversing with him, and dead the next.

The clamor against him rose even higher when, from the walls of Athens, the Athenians could see their enemies pillaging their countryside. The best of the navy had been destroyed. It did no good for Pericles to recall to the government that they had permitted Sparta to grow so strong that she had been able to attack, with her allies, and gain tremendous victories. "Did I not warn you that we must increase our armaments?" he demanded of the Assembly. "But you talked of 'peace' and a more benevolent attitude towards Sparta, who has always hated us. Can you come to terms with a nation which is determined to destroy you and rule the whole of Greece? We were a prosperous people, we of Athens, and became fat and complacent and scorned those who warned us of the approaching conflict. There is no substitute for the military and the navy in this dangerous world filled with ambitious men. There is no substitute for liberty, which so many of you have ridiculed. Human nature never changes. Therefore, those who desire peace must resolutely prepare for war, horrifying though war is. Only a strong man can resist his enemy. Placating that enemy, assuring him that your intentions are peaceful and that you desire only trade, is a signal to him to attack.

"But when I warned you, endlessly, you shouted to me that I wished to be a king, have absolute power over you, that I was a dictator and a tyrant and a despot. I did not want a

541

strong army and navy, you said, because I feared for Athens. No, you said, I wished to have a powerful military so I could turn it on you!"

"We want peace!" the people cried. "Our sons are dying in the prison camps and the quarries of Syracuse!"

Pericles was himself stricken by the plague, but recovered under the devoted care of Aspasia. But despite his recovery his spirit seemed to have been overcome by somberness and his physical condition never became stalwart again. It was as if something had died in him, as it had died in Athens: the will to resist. Athens' great navies were almost totally destroyed, her armies put to flight, while the Spartans, a disciplined and gloomy and warlike people, proclaimed that they had driven Athens from the sea and from the land. It was no matter to Sparta that she had, herself, suffered huge losses of men and arms and ships. Only victory had been her dream, and power, whereas Athens had desired only prosperity and trade and commerce. Now Persia, never forgetting her defeat by Athens, allied herself with Sparta. The internal enemies of Pericles suddenly rose triumphantly in Athens and betrayed her, saying that "the experiment in general freedom has failed," and that it was now time for an oligarchy to seize power. They opened negotiations with Sparta, particularly the rich haters of liberty, Antiphon, Peisander and Phrynichus. That they were defeated later and crushed by Alcibiades and Theramenes, who established the Constitution of Five Thousand, and continued the struggle with Sparta, meant nothing to Pericles then.

For he had died of exhaustion and the debility brought on him by the plague, and of, said his devoted kinsman Alcibiades with bitterness, a broken heart "inflicted on him by an ungrateful people."

Alcibiades said, "The glory of Greece was not the glory of the whole city-state. It was the glory of a handful of great men, though their fellows were sleeplessly at war with those heroes and murdered or exiled them. Athens heaped infamy upon Pericles, and only at the very last was he permitted to inscribe the name of his son, Pericles, in the public records of fraternity. If the name of Athens survives the ages it will not be because all Athenians were men of grandeur, patriotic men, artists and scientists and philosophers, and men of extraordinary stature. Only a few labored and loved, and were hated for these qualities. They were not of us. They were visitations of the gods. And we did them to death."

An immense numbness came to Aspasia, mercifully, when Pericles had died, sighing, in her arms, one hot midnight. It did not lift. She gave up her school and immured herself in her house, with her son, Pericles, until he was called to active service in the war. Then she was alone, seeing few if any of her friends.

It is only the foolish who say that one can live on happy memories, she would mourn to herself, dry-eyed because she could not weep and had not wept even when Pericles had died. Her grief was too deep, too immutable.

It is better to have lived a life of sadness and pain, unalleviated by joy or peace or happiness, she would think. For then one approaches death with relief and gratitude. But joyful memories of a love that has gone, of arms once filled, of gardens which no longer bloom, is a torment worse than any torments in Hades. Ah, if I could have the memory of my love blotted from my mind it might be possible for me to endure with some measure of equanimity, and think of tomorrow. But now I am desolate and memory is the curse of Hecate. Would that I had never lived!

Her only dim consolation—and it did not always console her—was when she looked up at the white and gold glory of the acropolis at sunset or dawn and could contemplate the ineffable majesty of temples and terraces and friezes and columns and colonnades. It was the crown of Athens and it seemed to her that it was deathless and that men would always remember what stood there and bow their heads in wonder and reverence.

Pericles had been entombed near the Academia. But to Aspasia he walked under sun and moon with his friends in the colonnades, Pheidias, Anaxagoras, and all the others who had made Athens glorious, and they were eternally young and their faces eternally illuminated, and, as they walked and conversed they would sometimes pause to look down upon their city and bless her and love her again.

"Ah, my beloved, my dearest one, my love and my god," she would murmur aloud, lifting her arms to the glory above her. "Wait for me. Forget me not."

There were occasions when she felt a gentle comfort, and promise.

GREAT ROMANTIC NOVELS

SISTERS AND STRANGERS   PB 04445 $2.50
by Helen Van Slyke

Three women—three sisters each grown into an independent lifestyle—now are three strangers who reunite to find that their intimate feelings and perilous fates are entwined.

THE SUMMER OF THE SPANISH WOMAN
                    CB 23809 $2.50

by Catherine Gaskin

A young, fervent Irish beauty is alone. The only man she ever loved is lost as is the ancient family estate. She flees to Spain. There she unexpectedly discovers the simmering secrets of her wretched past . . . meets the Spanish Woman . . . and plots revenge.

THE CURSE OF THE KINGS   CB 23284 $1.95
by Victoria Holt

This is Victoria Holt's most exotic novel! It is a story of romance when Judith marries Tybalt, the young archeologist, and they set out to explore the Pharaohs' tombs on their honeymoon. But the tombs are cursed . . . two archeologists have already died mysteriously.

8000